Peter F. Hamilton

SALVATION

THE SALVATION SEQUENCE

MACMILLAN

First published 2018 by Macmillan
an imprint of Pan Macmillan
20 New Wharf Road, London N1 9RR
Associated companies throughout the world
www.panmacmillan.com

ISBN 978-1-4472-8132-0

9 8 7 6 5 4 3 2 1

A CIP catalogue record for this book is available from the British Library.

Typeset by Palimpsest Book Production Ltd, Falkirk, Stirlingshire
Printed and bound by CPI Group (UK) Ltd, Croydon, CR0 4YY

SALVATION

Peter F. Hamilton was born in Rutland in 1960 and now lives in Somerset. He began writing in 1987, and sold his first short story to *Fear* magazine in 1988. He has written many bestselling novels, including the Greg Mandel series, the Night's Dawn trilogy, the Commonwealth Saga, the Void trilogy, the Chronicle of the Fallers, short story collections and several standalone novels.

Find out more about Peter F. Hamilton at

www.facebook.com/PeterFHamilton

or discover more Pan Macmillan and Tor UK books at

www.torbooks.co.uk

By Peter F. Hamilton

The Greg Mandel series
Mindstar Rising
A Quantum Murder
The Nano Flower

The Night's Dawn trilogy
The Reality Dysfunction
The Neutronium Alchemist
The Naked God

The Commonwealth Saga
Pandora's Star
Judas Unchained

The Void trilogy
The Dreaming Void
The Temporal Void
The Evolutionary Void

Chronicle of the Fallers
The Abyss Beyond Dreams
Night Without Stars

The Salvation Sequence
Salvation

Standalone novels
Fallen Dragon
Misspent Youth
Great North Road
The Confederation Handbook
(a vital guide to the Night's Dawn trilogy)

The Queen of Dreams trilogy
The Secret Throne
The Hunting of the Princes
A Voyage Through Air

Short story collections
A Second Chance at Eden
Manhattan in Reverse

Music as background for reading *Salvation* has been created by film and TV composer Steve Buick. His long, evocative musical piece works as the perfect atmospheric accompaniment to any part of the book. Search 'Peter F. Hamilton's *Salvation*: Atmospheres and Soundscapes' on Amazon, iTunes or Google Play. You can find out more at www.stevebuick.com.

List of Major Characters

Sol System and Human Terraformed Worlds

Akkar *Ecowarrior*

Yuri Alster *Connexion Corporation security chief*

Javid-Lee Boshburg *NY gang boss*

Cancer *Dark-ops mercenary*

Savi Chaudhri *Connexion Security undercover agent*

Eldlund *Callum's advisor*

Rayner Grogan *NY gang boss*

Gwendoline *Ainsley's (unacknowledged) granddaughter*

Callum Hepburn *Emergency Detoxification team leader*

Raina Jacek *Detoxification team, IT (ex-hacktivist)*

Emilja Jurich *Utopial movement founder*

Feriton Kayne *Connexion, exosolar security division*

Alana Keates *Detoxification team*

Kruse *Akitha Home Security Bureau*

Poi Li *Connexion head of security*

Loi *Yuri's assistant and technology advisor*

Kravis Lorenzo *NY lawyer*

Rose Lorenzo *NY socialite*

Moshi Lyane *Team deputy*

Kandara Martinez *Dark-ops mercenary*

Alik Monday *FBI, Senior Special Detective*

Jessika Mye *Yuri's assistant*

Nahuel *Buddhist monk, 2199 ecumenical delegation*

Jaru Niyom *Utopial movement founder*

Oistad *Home Security Bureau*

Henry Orme *Detoxification team*

Salovitz *Detective, NYPD*

Horatio Seymore *Gwendoline's boyfriend*

Lucius Soćko *Connexion security squad captain*

Dokal 'Dok' Torres *Connexion lawyer*

Tyle *Home Security Bureau*

Colin Walters *Detoxification team*

Ainsley Baldunio Zangari *Connexion founder & CEO*

Juloss

Immerle Estate Boys

Colian

Dellian

Orellt

Falar

Hable

Janc

Mallot

Rello

Uret

Xante

Immerle Estate Girls

Yirella

Tilliana

Ellici

Immerle Estate Adults

Alexandre *Year tutor*

Jenner *Principal*

Uranti *Munc-tech*

Kenelm *Captain of the* Morgan

See the end of the novel for the Salvation timeline.

Earth Calling

Drifting through interstellar space, three lightyears out from the star 31 Aquilae, the Neána abode cluster picked up a series of short, faint electromagnetic pulses that lasted intermittently for eighteen years. The early signatures were familiar to the Neána, and faintly worrying: nuclear fission detonations, followed seven years later by fusion explosions. The technological progress of whoever was detonating them was exceptionally swift by the usual metric of emerging civilizations.

Metaviral spawn chewed into the cometry chunks which anchored the vast cluster, spinning out a string of flimsy receiver webs twenty kilometres across. They aligned themselves on the G-class star fifty lightyears away where the savage weapons were being deployed.

Sure enough, a torrent of weak electromagnetic signals were pouring out from the star's third planet. A sentient species was entering its early scientific industrial state.

The Neána were concerned that so many nuclear weapons were being used. Clearly, the new species was disturbingly aggressive. Some of the cluster's minds welcomed that.

Analysis of the radio signals, now becoming analogue audio-visual broadcasts, revealed a bipedal race organized along geo-tribal lines, and constantly in conflict. Their specific biochemical composition was one which, from the Neána perspective, gave them sadly short lives. That was posited as the probable reason behind their faster than usual technological progression.

That there would be an expedition was never in doubt; the Neána saw that as their duty no matter what kind of life evolved on distant worlds. The only question now concerned the level of assistance to be offered. Those who welcomed the new species' aggressive qualities wanted to make the full spectrum of Neána technology available. They almost prevailed.

The spherical insertion ship which left the cluster – it didn't know if it was one of many being dispatched, or alone – measured a hundred metres in diameter, a mass comprising active molecule blocks. It spent three months accelerating up to thirty per cent of lightspeed along a course to Altair, a trip that took just over a hundred years. During the lonely voyage the ship's controlling sentience continued to monitor the electromagnetic signals coming from the young civilization that was its ultimate goal. It built up an impressive knowledge base of human biology, as well as a comprehensive understanding of their constantly evolving tribal political and economic structures.

When the ship reached Altair, it performed a complex flyby manoeuvre that aligned it perfectly on Sol. After that, the physical section of the sentience's memory which contained all the astrogration data of the flight from the cluster to Altair was jettisoned, and the constituent blocks deactivated. Its weakened atomic structure broke apart into an expanding cloud of dust which was quickly dispersed by Altair's solar wind. Now, if it was ever intercepted, the insertion ship could never betray the position of the Neána abode cluster – for it no longer knew where it was.

The last fifty years of the voyage were spent formatting an emplacement strategy. By now, human ingenuity had produced starships which were flying past the insertion ship in the other direction, in quest of new worlds out among the stars. The information blasting out from Earth and the solar system's asteroid habitats had become increasingly sophisticated, yet conversely there was a lot less of it. Radio signals had been in decline since the internet began to carry the bulk of human data traffic. For the final twenty years of the insertion ship's approach it received little apart from entertainment broadcasts, and even those were shrinking year by year. But it had enough.

It flew in south of the ecliptic, shedding cold mass in irregular bursts like a black comet – a deceleration manoeuvre which took three years. This was always the riskiest part of the voyage. The humans' solar system was scattered with a great many astronomical sensors scanning the universe for cosmological abnormalities. By the time it passed the Kuiper belt, the insertion ship was down to twenty-five metres in diameter. It emitted no magnetic or gravitational fields. The outer shell was fully radiation absorbent, so there was no albedo, making it invisible to any telescopes. Thermal emission was zero.

No one perceived its arrival.

Inside, four biologics began to grow within molecular initiators, attaining physical patterns that the ship's sentience had designed, based on the information it had acquired during the long voyage.

They were human in size and shape; skeletons and organs carried the mimicry down to a biochemical level. Their DNA was equally authentic. You would have to go a lot deeper into the cells to find any abnormality; only a detailed audit of the organelles would reveal alien molecular structures.

It was the minds of the biologics which gave the insertion ship the greatest difficulty. Human mental processes were complex, verging on paradoxical. Worse, it suspected the performances in all the fictional dramas it received were over-emphasizing emotional responses. So it constructed a stable primary architecture of thought routines while including a fast learning and adaptive integration procedure.

As it closed to within a million kilometres of Earth, the insertion ship discarded the last of its reaction mass as it performed a final deceleration manoeuvre. Now it was basically just falling towards the southernmost tip of South America. Tiny course correction ejecta refined the descent vector, steering it towards Tierra del Fuego, which was still thirty minutes from greeting the dawn.

Even if it was detected now, it would simply appear to be a small chunk of natural space debris.

It hit the upper atmosphere and began to peel apart into four pear-shaped segments. The remaining matter broke away in fizzing sparks that produced a short-lived but beautiful starburst display streaking through the mesosphere. Below it, sheltered under their blanket of thick winter cloud, the residents of Ushuaia, the southernmost city on Earth, remained oblivious to their interstellar visitor.

Each segment carried on down, aerobraking with increasing severity as the atmosphere thickened around it. They slowed to subsonic velocity three kilometres above the surface, plunging through the clouds, still unobserved by anyone on the planet.

The segments were aimed at a small inlet a few kilometres west of the city, where, even in AD 2162, the rugged land lay unclaimed by developers. Two hundred metres from the shore, four tall splash plumes shot up into the air like thick geysers, crowning and splattering down on the slushy ice that bobbed along the waters of the Beagle Channel.

The Neána metahumans floated to the surface. All that now remained of the insertion ship landing segments was a thick layer of active molecule blocks covering their skin like a pelt of translucent gel, insulating them from the dangerously cold water. They began to swim ashore.

The beach was a narrow strip of grey stones cluttered with dead branches. A dense woodland occupied the slope above it. The aliens scrambled a short way up the incline as the pale dawn light began to seep through the murky clouds. Their protective layer liquidized, draining down into the stones, where it would be flushed away by the next high tide. For the first time, they drew air down into their lungs.

'Oh, that is cold!' one exclaimed.

'Good classification,' another agreed through chattering teeth. 'I'll go with it.'

They looked at each other in the grey light. Two were crying from the emotional impact of arrival, one was smiling in wonder, while the fourth appeared singularly unimpressed by the bleak landscape. Each carried a small pack of outdoor clothing copied from a winterwear advert broadcast eighteen months earlier. They hurried to put it on.

When they were fully dressed, they set off along an ancient track up through the trees until they came to the remnants of National Route Three, which led to Ushuaia.

The Assessment Team

Feriton Kayne *New York, 23rd June 2204*

I was never really that impressed with New York. The natives always banged on about how it was the city that never slept, how it had elevated itself to the centre of the human universe. Self-justifying their choice of living in cramped, over-priced apartments – even today, when they could live anywhere on the planet and commute in through a dozen different Connexion hubs. They claimed it still had the buzz, the vibe, the kick. Bohemians came to dose up on *the experience, maaan*, which helped them create their art, while corporate drones sweated through their junior management years to prove *commitment*. But for service staff proximity was simply convenient, while the truly poor couldn't afford to leave. And yes: guilty, I lived in SoHo. Not that I'm junior management. Right there on my desk the nameplate says: Feriton Kayne, Deputy Director, Connexion Exosolar Security Division. And if you can work out what I actually do from that, you're smarter than most.

My office is on the seventy-seventh floor of the Connexion Corp tower. Ainsley Zangari wanted his global headquarters in Manhattan, and did he ever want everyone to know about it. There are few other people alive who could get a site on West 59th Street just along from Columbus Circle. He had to keep the facade of the old hotel as the base of his hundred-and-twenty-storey glass and carbon monstrosity – why, I don't know, it had no architectural value as far as I can make out, but City Hall listed it as a landmark structure. So there you have it. Not even Ainsley Zangari, the richest man there's ever been, can argue City Hall out of *heritage*.

I'm not complaining. My office gives me the greatest conceivable view out over the city and Central Park – one which the mere super-rich along Park Avenue can't afford. I've actually had to position my desk so I work with my back to the floor-to-ceiling window. I'd be too distracted otherwise. Mind, it is a swivel chair.

That cloudless June afternoon I was standing looking out at the view, mesmerized as always; the vista resembled one of those seventeenth-century oil paintings where everything glows with heavenly radiance.

Kandara Martinez was shown in by a receptionist. The corporate mercenary wore a plain black singlet under a jacket from some mid-range fashion house. The way she carried herself made it look like a military uniform. That part of her life just never left her, I guess.

Sandjay, my altme, splashed the data at me, which the tarsus lenses I wore over my eyeballs presented as a grid of green and purple text. The file didn't tell me much I didn't already know. She had enrolled in Mexico City's Heroico Colegio Militar when she was nineteen. After graduation she saw several active deployments in the Urban Rapid Suppression Force. Then her parents were killed by a drone bomb some bunch of anti-imperialist anarchist whackjobs launched at the sneering symbol of their evil foreign economic oppressors – or, in English, the Italian remote drone systems factory where her father worked. After that her escalating kill rate in action started to 'concern' her superiors. She received an honourable discharge in 2187. Freelance corporate security ever since – the real dark jobs.

In the flesh she was a hundred and seventy centimetres tall, with chestnut hair cut short, and grey eyes. I wasn't sure if they were real or gened-up; they didn't quite seem to belong with the rest of her Mexican ancestry. There'd certainly been some bodywork.

She kept herself trim – in her line of work that was survival 101 – but that couldn't account for the thickness of her limbs; her legs and arms were heavily muscled. Gened-up or Kcells; the file didn't say. Ms Martinez left a very small dataprint on solnet.

'Thank you for accepting the contract,' I said. 'I'm a lot happier knowing you're coming with us.' Which was only partially true. Her presence made me uncomfortable, but then I know who she's eliminated during her career.

'I was curious,' she said, 'because we all know Connexion has so few people in its own security division.'

'Yeah, about that. We might need something that goes beyond our guys' paygrade.'

'Sounds interesting, Feriton.'

'My boss wants protection, serious protection. We're dealing with the unknown here. This expedition . . . it's different. The artefact we've found is alien.'

'So you said. Is it Olyix?'

'I don't see how it could be.'

A small smile lifted her lips. 'Not going to hide from you, I'm very interested. And flattered. Why me?'

'Reputation,' I lied. 'You're the best.'

'Bullshit.'

'Seriously. We have to keep this small; the three other people coming with us represent some serious political interests. So I wanted someone with a genuine track record.'

'You're worried that rivals will find out about where we're headed? What sort of artefact have you found?'

'Can't tell you that until we're en route.'

'Are you retro engineering its tech? Is that why you're worried about rivals?'

'This isn't about new technology and market impact. We have a bigger problem than that.'

'Oh?' She lifted her eyebrows in query.

'You'll get a full briefing when we're underway. Everybody does.'

'Okay, that's a reasonable containment strategy. But I do need to know: is it hostile?'

'No. Or at least, not yet. Which is where you come in. We need to pack a large punch in a small place. Just in case.'

'Even more flattered.'

'One last thing, which is why you and I are having this meeting before I introduce you to the rest of the team.'

'This doesn't sound good.'

'There are some first-contact protocols involved, severe ones. Alpha Defence insisted. We're going to be very isolated for the duration of this mission – something none of us are familiar with. Today, no matter what disaster hits you, everybody can shout for help wherever they are. Everyone functions under the assumption that an emergency team is two minutes away. It's all we know. I consider that to be a weakness, especially in this situation. If things go wrong – badly wrong – that's when the Alpha Defence first-contact protocol applies.'

She caught on fast. I could see the slight change in body posture, humour retreating, muscles tightening.

'If they're hostile, they can't know about us,' she said.

'No prisoners. No data downloads.'

'Really?' Her humour swept back in. 'You're worried about an alien invasion? That's very quaint. What does Ainsley Zangari think they're going to plunder, our gold and our women?'

'We don't know what they are, so until we do . . .'

'The Olyix turned out okay. And they had a shitload of antimatter on board the *Salvation of Life*. There isn't another conventional power source powerful enough to accelerate a vessel that size up to a decent fraction of lightspeed.'

'We were fortunate with them,' I said carefully. 'Their religion gives them a whole different set of priorities to us. All they want to do is travel across space in their arkship to the End of Time, where they believe their God will be waiting for them. They don't want to expand into new star systems and bioform planets to live on; it's a whole different imperative to ours. I guess we didn't really understand what *alien* meant until they arrived in the Sol system. But,

Kandara, do you really want to gamble our species' survival on every race being as benign as the Olyix? It's been sixty years since they arrived, and we've both benefited from trade. Great, but we have a duty to consider that at some time we're going to encounter a species which isn't so benign.'

'Interstellar war is a fantasy. It makes no sense. Economically, for resources, for territory . . . it's all crap. Hong Kong doesn't even make drama games about it any more.'

'Nonetheless, we must respect the possibility, however remote. My department has developed scenarios we don't ever reveal to the public,' I confided. 'Some of them are . . . disturbing.'

'I bet they are. But at the end, it's all human paranoia.'

'Maybe. However, the non-exposure protocol must be enacted if the contact species turns out to be hostile. Will you accept that responsibility? I need to know I can rely on you if I'm incapacitated.'

'Incapacitated!' She took a moment, breathing in deep as she finally realized what I was asking.

Getting her assigned to the mission on that basis – that thanks to her quirks she was genuinely dedicated and fearless enough to initiate the self-destruct sequence – had been an easy sell to Yuri. He had never questioned my choice.

'All right,' she said. 'If it comes to that, I'm prepared to press the big red button.'

'Thank you. Oh, and the other three, they might not appreciate—'

'Yeah. We'll keep that part to ourselves.'

'Good. Let's go meet them, then.'

Exosolar Security occupies seven consecutive floors. The departmental conference room is on the seventy-sixth floor. I took Kandara down the big spiral stairwell in the middle of the tower.

Naturally, the conference room occupies a corner of the tower, giving it two glass walls. The oval teak table stretching along the middle of the floor probably cost more than my salary. That day it had fifteen chairs spaced round it. More chairs lined the non-glass walls for flunkies to sit in. Pure psychology, emphasizing the importance of those invited to sit at the table with the grown-ups.

There were seven people waiting, none of them using a wall chair. As far as I was concerned, only three of them were relevant, the representatives of true power: Yuri Alster, Callum Hepburn and Alik Monday.

Yuri was sitting at the far end, with his executive assistant and tech adviser Loi next to him. He's one of the real old-timers, born back in St Petersburg in 2030; all broody and sullen like only Russians who emigrate from the Motherland can be. Couple that with his age, and I doubt his mouth was even capable of smiling any more. He'd got his first telomere extension therapy about a century ago and then progressed to gene-up to keep himself alive. If you call that living; most people call all the myriad extension therapies *the undying*, stretching out their existence at any price. I've seen people who never got rich until their eighties then go for treatments. It's not pretty.

All those treatments and procedures had left Yuri's appearance suspended in his late fifties, with his round face slightly bloated and his thin sandy hair shading lighter as it was infiltrated by grey strands that'd resisted the gene-up. Hooded grey-green eyes completed the image of a man who was suspicious about the whole universe.

But for Yuri an eternal fifty wasn't so bad. As well as his deferred face there had to be replacement organs, too. For a start, no original liver could survive immersion in that much vodka. His replacement parts would all be high-end bioprinted clone cells. He was too xenophobic (and maybe snobbish) to use Kcells. The alien biotechnology was the main trade item between the Olyix and humans, cells with a biochemistry compatible with a human body, which could be assembled into organs and muscles at a significantly lower cost than gene-up treatments and printed stem cells. They had a reputation (unfounded, in my opinion) of being slightly inferior to human medical technology. But, in making advanced medical treatment available to millions of people who had been too poor to receive it before, it had become the biggest boon to social improvement since Connexion Corp started providing universal egalitarian transport through its portal hub network.

I nodded respectfully at him. After all, he was my boss, and the author of this whole expedition. Me, I'd seen it for the terrific opportunity it was.

As usual, Loi was wearing an absurdly expensive suit, as if he'd strayed in from Wall Street. Not too far from the truth, given he's Ainsley's great-grandson (one of many). Twenty-eight years old, and always keen to tell you about his shiny new quantum physics degree from Harvard – earned, not bought, as he'll explain. Right now he was desperately validating himself by working his way up through Connexion Corp the way everyone does. Because everyone aged twenty-eight pulls an assistant's job with a department head as soon as they join. Just a regular guy, all smiles, after-work drinks with colleagues, and bitching about the boss.

Interestingly, Callum Hepburn had chosen to sit next to Yuri. He'd arrived twenty minutes ago from the Delta Pavonis system, where the Utopial culture was based. These days he was one of their senior troubleshooters, possessing a craggy face that gene-up had failed to soften with age. His thick crop of hair was the bold silver-white that all redheads turn, rather than the insipid grey that lies in wait for most humans.

I could sense a great deal of unhappiness behind those blue-grey eyes of his. From my briefing with Ainsley, I gathered Callum hadn't exactly volunteered for the expedition. Allegedly, the Utopials with their perfect democracy can't be ordered to do anything, no matter what level of citizenship you've attained (and he's grade two). So that must be one hell of a favour domino Ainsley Zangari knocked into Emilja Jurich – given Emilja was the closest thing the Utopials had to a leader, and therefore the only one who could pressure Callum into coming back to Earth.

And I don't suppose having Yuri along on the expedition was helping his temperament. The two of them hadn't talked since Callum left Connexion in what I can only describe as intriguing circumstances a century ago, after he officially died.

Actually, it was a hundred and twelve years ago. Whatever. That's an impressive amount of time to hold a grudge. But then he's Scottish, and in my experience they're just as stubborn and dour as

Russians. It says something about the alien artefact we'd found that those two were prepared to put personal issues aside and cooperate – however nominally. Having them together in the bus was really going to make this a full-out funtime trip.

Callum had brought two assistants with him from Delta Pavonis. Eldlund was obviously from Akitha – the Utopials' main world, orbiting Delta Pavonis. Like all people born into the Utopial movement today, sie was omnia; genetically modified to be both male and female, spending hir adult life in a thousand-day cycle between genders. That baseline genome alteration to every person born into the Utopial culture – enabling and enhancing their core philosophy of equality at a fundamental level – had been hugely controversial when it first began, back in 2119, condemned as extremist by some religions and old-school moralists. There had been plenty of discrimination and even violence against the omnias to begin with, by the usual suspects – the ignorant and prejudiced and fearful. But, as always, what was once exceptional decayed to mundane over time. Today, Eldlund could probably walk down most streets on Earth without any trouble. Sie would be noticed, mind you, but that was down to hir height; all the omnias were tall. And Eldlund was an easy fifteen centimetres taller than anyone else in the room, and also marathon-runner thin with it. Normally I'd call that willowy, but there was nothing fragile-looking about hir – although sie had a very pretty face with sharp cheekbones highlighted by an artfully trimmed beard.

And I could tell just how much confrontational attitude was coiled up in that rigid pose. Utopials from Akitha are always the most evangelical about their way of life; I hoped that wasn't going to be a problem. Sandjay's data splash listed hir as a Turing specialist.

Callum's other companion was Jessika Mye, the greatest political flip-flopper of us all. A Hong Kong native who at twenty went all radical and aligned herself with the Utopial ethic so she could train as an exobiologist on Akitha, only to flip back politically, enabling her to earn those dirty capitalist big bucks available in the Universal culture. I knew she was seventy-four; my altme was spraying the data up as my glance swept across her. She didn't look it. Interesting fact: she worked for Connexion Security back in the day, which is where she got the money for telomere therapy in her early thirties. Then, after one volatile case, she upped and moved back to Akitha, where her experience dropped her right into their Olyix Alien Observation Bureau. Five years ago she was promoted to Callum's senior assistant – an appointment which clearly gave her plenty of time off to work out in the gym. If I was the cynical sort, I'd say Callum appreciates that.

And finally we had Alik Monday. Access 'corrupt' in the dictionary, and it'll likely give you his name. A genuine made-in-America bastard. Occupation: FBI senior special detective, operating out of D.C. Believe it or not, when I tried a data mine, his age was classified. He's a walking talking Federal secret, all personal data restricted. Connexion's Security G8Turing could have hacked his profile easily enough, but cracking an FBI core would be a huge deal, and not just for the Feds. I'd have pattern sniffers all over my ass, and Yuri would be asking questions I could do without. I needed him to keep thinking this was his mission. Some things you just have to let go.

Anyway, I guessed Alik at about a hundred and ten; he wasn't so much an undying as a reanimated corpse. Easy tells. That plastic smooth skin came from so many therapies you'd have to use electric shocks to get his facial muscles to express an emotion. And I suspected the colour was gened-up, too. Most African Americans are a light brown, but Alik was black as if he'd been sunbathing on the equator for a decade; you can't get any darker. Full bodywork, too. Take his shirt off, and you'll see the physique of a twenty-year-old Olympian, with every replacement muscle designed and bioprinted in a top San Francisco clinic. I'd give good odds there were some aggressive peripherals lurking in amongst all those perfect tendons and muscle bands, too.

But . . . all that time and money, wasted. Anyone looking at him knew he was old, and terribly calculating.

He was connected to the globalPACs operating out of D.C., the rich old men who really run Earth, who make sure Universalism,

14

the established democratic-capitalist society, stays in place and doesn't get seduced away from its oh-so-holy guiding principles by shiny new concepts like Utopialism. Just like everyone, the PACs wanted to get a jump on the implications from the artefact. And Alik was their eyes on the prize, with a loyalty that only serious quantities of dollars can buy.

I sat with my back to Central Park and smiled graciously. 'Thank you all for coming, and the people you represent for agreeing to this.'

Alik frowned at me. 'You're in charge? I thought I was requested because Alpha Defence was running this.'

'Technically they are,' I said. 'We're running this investigation under their authority. But it is Mr Alster's expedition. I'm basically just admin.'

'Keep 'em in their place, huh, Yuri?' Alik grinned.

Yuri's impassive gaze looked down on Alik from some immeasurable height. 'Every time.'

I caught Alik mouthing 'smartass'.

'What's the schedule?' Callum asked.

'We'll go from here directly to Nkya in the Beta Eridani system. Our transport is ready. Journey time from the base camp to the artefact should take about forty-eight hours, maybe a bit longer.'

'Fuck's sake,' Alik grunted. 'Why so long?'

'Quarantine,' Yuri said tersely. 'We need to keep it completely isolated. Physically and digitally. So that there's no portal opening to it; we're going the old-fashioned way, by ground vehicle.'

'Digitally isolated?' Alik's stiff face registered nothing. It didn't have to; his tone revealed all. 'Please tell me you have access to solnet on site?'

'No access,' Yuri said. 'It's the Alpha Defence contact protocol. We can't take the risk. I'm sure D.C. appreciates that.'

Callum smirked.

'There's a science team already on site,' I told them and gestured at the three assistants. 'And we welcome the additions you're bringing.'

'The additions,' Jessika said. 'Makes us sound like a band.' She and Eldlund shared a smile. Loi ignored them, staring directly at me.

'You'll be given total access to the science team's data,' I continued. 'And if there are any further aspects of the artefact you want to examine, we'll prioritize them for you. In effect, you'll be determining the direction of the investigation.'

'How long will we be there for?' Callum asked. I could still hear an Aberdeen burr in his voice, even though the file said he hadn't been back there for over a century.

'Our investigation has two priorities,' Yuri pronounced. 'First priority is to assess the artefact's threat potential. Is it hostile, and if so to what extent? Secondly, based on that, we're required to formulate a response recommendation. That's going to take as long as it takes. Good enough?'

Alik wasn't happy, but he nodded.

'If there's nothing else?' I queried. Nobody seemed to have a question. 'Excellent. Please follow me.'

The seventy-sixth floor had a portal door direct to Connexion's Exosolar Division in Houston. Alik Monday was a hundred and eighty-eight centimetres tall, so he walked straight through after me, but Eldlund had to duck slightly. Connexion Corp portal doors are a standard two metres fifteen centimetres high. Maybe sie didn't really need to duck, but no denying it, sie was tall.

We came out into a circular hub with fourteen other portal doors around the edge. Bright morning sunlight shone in through the glass cupola above. Air conditioning thrummed loudly as it battled Texan heat and humidity. Our trollez were all waiting for us in a cluster at the centre of the hub: metre-high pearl-white cylinders with very flexible wheels, carrying all our personal luggage. Sandjay pinged mine, and it locked on. Of course, Loi had two trollez. All those designer shirts need careful packing.

I walked clockwise round the wall, trying not to peer through the portal doors. Some led into neat department lobbies while a couple opened directly into big assembly halls that looked empty.

The door to Connexion's Exoscience & Exploration Department

was the fifth one along. I stopped in front of it and waited until all the trollez had caught up with us before going through.

Given that interstellar travel is *the* most glamorous activity the human race has ever undertaken, the building housing E&E is surprisingly ordinary. Concrete, carbon and glass, just like the thousand other corporate blocks scattered across Houston's technology zone. The entrance lobby had four portal doors opening into it, all of them with a picket of security barriers – slim silver bars spaced close enough to prevent physical access. That was the visible obstacle. There were other more discreet, and lethal, security measures (the company got quite jumpy after the *incident* a hundred and twelve years ago that caused Callum to switch from being a good and loyal Connexion Corp employee to a full-on Utopial). The G8Turing that managed building security interrogated Sandjay and scanned us all. Then the bars slid down into the floor.

Geovanni, the Beta Eridani mission director, was waiting for us just beyond. He bobbed about uneasily as so many alpha visitors stepped into his domain. Introduced himself, shook hands tentatively. And finally said: 'This way please.'

He led us down a long corridor, with pictures of various starfields and cheerless exoplanet landscapes on the walls. Our trollez trundled along quietly behind us. The few Connexion personnel we passed gave us curious glances; most of them recognized Yuri. Amazing how many people suddenly look guilty when they're face to face with that level of authority.

'What's the planet like?' Kandara asked.

'Nkya? Fairly typical, if you can say that about exoplanets,' Geovanni said. 'Let's see: ten thousand three hundred kilometres in diameter, which gives us a gravity of point nine, Earth. Thirty-seven-hour days; so not good for our diurnal rhythms. Atmospheric pressure is two thousand pascals, which makes it two per cent Earth sea level pressure; that's made up mainly of carbon dioxide, with traces of argon, nitrogen and sulphur dioxide. It's orbiting five and a half AUs out from the Beta Eridani, so cold cold cold. Minimal tectonic activity, meaning no volcanoes. No moons, either. Nobody's going to be terraforming this baby.'

'So no indigenous life?'

Geovanni turned round and grinned at her. 'Not a chance.'

'Does Beta Eridani have any other planets, save Nkya?'

'Three. Two small solids, both in close orbits to Beta Eridani, as hot as Mercury and tidal-locked so you could melt bricks on their lightside. One gas mini, fifteen AUs out; makes Nkya look tropical.'

At the end of the corridor, a pair of solid doors swung open for us, taking us through into a nondescript anteroom. Then Geovanni practically rushed through an identical set of doors on the opposite wall. The Nkya egress chamber looked remarkably like an industrial warehouse. Smooth polished concrete floor, high blue-grey composite panel walls, black composite roof obscured by bright lighting strips hanging down over the aisles. Metal racks ran almost the length of the chamber, three times Eldlund's height, stacked with white plastic pods and bulky metal cases. Commercial cargo trollez rolled along, either collecting supplies from a couple of portal doors that led away to distribution centres and slotting them into the correct place on the racks, or picking equipment from the racks and taking it down to the portal at the far end.

One wall was inset with long windows that looked into a series of labs where samples were analysed. Technical personnel wandered round their benches loaded with expensive equipment, dressed in double-sealed white environment suits, peering through bubble helmets.

'Sure there's no indigenous life there?' Kandara asked, staring into the labs. 'Looks to me like you're taking contamination protocols very seriously.'

'Standard procedure,' Geovanni replied. 'It takes seven to twelve years to receive preliminary Sol Senate Exolife Agency clearance, confirming there's no autochthonous microbiology. Personally, I think that ought to be increased to fifty years, with a quadrupled sample range, before you can formally announce an all-clear with any form of authority. But that's just me. Over the years we've found some interesting microbes on some otherwise inhospitable planets.'

Kandara stared round as if she was trying to memorize the facility. 'Any chance you missed something on Nkya?'

'No. Beta Eridani was a classic by-the-book arrival procedure. *Kavli* spent a couple of months decelerating down from point eight C. She arrived in-system this February. We sent a squadron of astronomy satellites through her portal. So far all standard and good; my people know what they're doing.' He waved a hand at the semicircular room at the end of the labs, nearest the portal to Nkya. It was a control centre, with two lines of big high-resolution holographic windows all along the curving wall. Several desks had smaller screen stacks, with senior researchers and their gaggle of graduate astronomers drooling over images of strange, dark planetary crescents, orbital paths, fluctuating data tables, starmaps and rainbow graphics that to me resembled bad abstract art. 'We picked up the signal straight away. Hard not to. It was multispectral, low-power but constant.'

'Signal?' Alik barked in surprise. 'Nobody said this was an active artefact. What the fuck are you sending us to?'

Geovanni gave Yuri a quick, resentful glance. 'I don't know. I don't have clearance.'

'Go on, please,' I told him. 'What happened after you detected the signal?'

'It was just a beacon signal, coming from the fourth planet, Nkya. So we followed protocol, and informed Alpha Defence. A robot lander was flown down from orbit, keeping a minimum designated quarantine distance from the source. Once the lander put a portal on the surface, we started sending equipment through.' He pointed at the big circular portal at the end of the egress chamber. 'I've never set up a base camp so fast. Just about the first thing we sent through was a twelve-person science ranger vehicle. Connexion Security drove it and two Alpha Defence officers out to the artefact and came straight back. That was ten days ago. Next thing I know, Alpha Defence has ruled the whole expedition ultra-classified, and I get orders to send a secondary base through. That's a joke, because it's actually better than base camp; it even includes its own hospital, for crap's sake. Some trucks hauled it out to the

19

artefact, and an engineering crew set it up. They only got back yesterday. The preliminary science team left seven days ago, with another convoy of trucks packed with research equipment. Now you guys are here, and I've been ordered to give you total priority.'

'Sorry about that,' Loi said.

'Why?' I asked him. 'Everyone is doing their job.'

The kid blushed, but had the smarts enough to shut up.

Geovanni took us right up to the five-metre-diameter portal. They don't come much bigger; it was circular with an elevated metal ramp bridging the rim at the bottom so the cargo trollez could drive over unimpeded. Bundles of thick cables and hoses snaked through to Nkya underneath the ramp. Three sentinel pillars stood on either side, blank ash-grey surfaces concealing the formidable weaponry they contained. God help any alien that tried to come through without Ainsley's approval.

Not that it would ever come to that. The G8Turings would cut power to the portal in a millisecond if any bug-eyed tentacled monster even approached the other side.

I stared through the broad circle. It opened directly into a thirty-metre-wide geodesic dome, also stuffed full of supply racks. Two multisensor globes on chest-high posts were positioned on either side, letting the G8Turing scan anything that approached.

'This is it,' Geovanni said proudly, sweeping an arm towards the portal. 'This is what we do. Welcome to another world.'

'Thanks.' I went up the ramp's shallow slope after him. I couldn't help a little flash of unease as I drew level with the portal's rim. The Nkya base camp was less than a metre away from me now – *a single step*, as Connexion's famous first advert said. A step which would span eighty-nine lightyears.

Using ordinary Connexion Corp portal doors to walk between the company's Earth-spanning network of hubs never bothered me. The most distance one of those doors covered was transoceanic, maybe six thousand kilometres. But . . . eighty-nine lightyears? You couldn't not be aware of the time and effort it'd taken to cover that awesome gulf.

Long before Kellan Rindstrom demonstrated quantum spacial

entanglement at CERN back in 2062, human dreamers had been coming up with semi-realistic plans for starships. There were proposals to mine Jupiter's atmosphere for helium3 that could power a town-sized pulse-fusion ship which would scout nearby stars. Country-sized sails a molecule thick that would ride the solar wind out to the constellations. Skyscraper-sized laser cannon that would accelerate smaller lightsails. Antimatter rockets. The Alcubierre drive. Quantum vacuum plasma thrusters . . .

Kellan Rindstrom's discovery consigned them all to the history folder marked quirky-inventions-that-never-made-it-past-the-concept-study. When you can connect two separate physical locations via a quantum entanglement portal, so many problems cease to exist.

Even so, starships require a phenomenal amount of thrust to accelerate up to a decent percentage of lightspeed, and Connexion Corp's modern designs achieve in excess of eighty per cent. Before Rindstrom, that would have required carrying vast amounts of energy and reaction mass on board. Now, all you do is drop a perfectly spherical portal into the sun. Meta-hot plasma slams into that hole at near-relativistic speed. At the same time, the portal's exit is fixed at the apex of a magnetic cone, which channels the plasma into a rocket exhaust. There is no limit how much plasma from the sun you can send through, and the starship masses very little – just the portal and its nozzle, guidance units and a smaller portal communication link to mission control. It can accelerate *fast*.

When it reaches a star, it decelerates into orbit, delivering a portal link back to Earth's solar system. That means you can start sending through entire pre-assembled asteroid industrial complexes straight away. Within a day you're ready to start crunching minerals and begin manufacture. The pioneer crews build habitats which house the workforce, which builds the next generation of starships, which fly off to new stars. It's almost an exponential process. And in their wake the newly discovered exoplanets are ripe for terraforming.

Connexion Corp has been one of the major players when it comes to sending starships out from Earth, building and flying them for over a hundred years. Every new Universal settled star system is another huge income source for the company. Beta Eridani is the furthest star humans have reached. Eighty-nine lightyears from Earth.

One step.

I felt the slight drop in gravity as soon as I was through the portal. Not quite enough to mess with my balance, but I took the down-ramp carefully just in case.

The dome was a smaller version of the egress chamber back on Earth, piled high with pods and equipment cases. A quarter of it was given over to life-support equipment: big spherical tanks, air filters, pumps, ducts, quantum batteries, thermal exchanges; everything to keep humans alive in a hostile environment. If the main portal, and the redundant emergency portals, were closed for whatever reason, those chunks of machinery could sustain the base personnel for years if necessary.

Sandjay coupled to the base camp's network and splashed local schematics across my tarsus lens. Connexion Corp's foothold on Nkya was laid out in a simple triangular array, with passageways leading out radially from the main dome to a trio of slightly smaller domes.

'Ordinarily, this would be full of geologists and exobiologists,' Geovanni said as he headed for one of the three big airlocks at the edge of the dome. 'But right now we're keeping base staff to an absolute minimum. We've taken local samples, but further field trips are on hold. The only people here today are engineering support and your security teams.'

He took us through the airlock, which was large enough to hold all of us and our trollez while it cycled. The passageway on the other side was a plain metal tube with lightstrips and cable conduits running overhead. Even with all the insulation layers built into base camp's structures, the surface had a faint mist of condensation – proof of just how cold Nkya was.

The air in the garage dome held a throat-tickling sulphur tang. It was cool, too. But I didn't pay that much attention; I was too busy staring at the waiting machine. The Trail Ranger occupied the floor like a possessive dragon come to cosy down in its lair. Like every-body in this day and age, I'm completely unfamiliar with ground vehicles. This brute was wildly impressive. It came in three sections. A cab and engineering section were at the front, with a smooth fluorescent-green egg-shaped body. Lights resembling insect eyes clustered round the blunt nose, just below a curving windscreen; smaller sensor wands protruded like thick black stubble hairs on the underside. The heat radiators were four slim mirror-silver strips running perpendicular down both sides, as if the designers had added missile fins just for the hell of it.

Behind the cab, linked by an articulated pressure coupling, were the two cylindrical passenger sections. They were made of the same smooth metalloceramic, with slit windows on both sides.

Each section rode on six fat tyres, individually powered by an electric axle motor. The damn things were as high as me, with tread patterns deep enough that I could put my hand in them.

Everybody was smiling in appreciation; even Alik managed to twitch his lips with interest. I joined them. I wanted to drive the beast; it was an impulse I guessed most of the team were experien-cing. No such luck. Geovanni introduced us to Sutton Castro and Bee Jain, the Trail Ranger drivers.

The interior convinced me Yuri had ordered the Trail Ranger printed specifically for us. I don't believe Connexion's exoscience staff would generally be bussed about a new planet in such comfort. The rear section contained sleeping pods with a locker for every-one's trollez. Forward of those, I peeped into one of the four small washroom cubicles, finding a miracle of convertible units and com-pact storage cabinets to cater for every need, from a toilet to a shower. There was also a tiny galley with packets of gourmet meals that a servez was still loading into the fridges.

Our lounge dominated the middle section, fitted with luxurious reclining chairs. Everyone settled down in there as the drivers went forward to the cab. A couple of stewards came in and asked us if we wanted any food or drink. It was all slightly surreal. I've seen old videos that included plane flights and travelling on the Orient Express. For a moment I could believe the portal to Nkya had actually transported us into the twentieth century. This was travelling in history.

I have to admit, there was a degree of elegance to it. If it wasn't so ridiculously time consuming, I could probably get used to it.

'We're sealing up in two minutes,' Sutton Castro announced over the PA.

Sandjay splashed the garage airlock schematic, showing me both doors closing and undergoing pre-start pressure tests. I didn't ask for it, but Sandjay was an adaptive altme, about as smart as an old G6Turing, so it can pretty much anticipate what I want and need to know. The biometrics my medical peripheries were reading would've revealed rising heart rate, a small adrenalin flush and raised skin temperature. All its core algorithms would interpret that as one thing: *anxiety rising*. So Sandjay did what it could to reassure me and showed me lots of systems working smoothly.

The garage dome pumped its atmosphere away. 'Access the vehicle net,' I whispered soundlessly. The peripheral fibres riding alongside my vocal cord nerves picked up the impulses, and Sandjay coupled to the Trail Ranger's net. 'Give me an external camera feed.'

I closed my eyes and watched the image splash. In front of the Trail Ranger, the big garage door was opening, slowly hinging up.

It was dark outside. Grey sky lidded a rust-brown rock plain. A fine dust suspended in the super-thin atmosphere gave everything a hazy quality. Yet I could see tiny zephyrs twirling along across the metamorphic mesa, sucking up spirals of sand. Spectacularly sharp mountains shredded the eastern horizon. The sight was entrancing. Virgin land, desolate and alien.

The Trail Ranger rolled forwards. I could feel the movement, the slight rise and fall of the suspension pistons as if we were a yacht sailing over mildly choppy waters. Then the tyres were biting into the loose regolith, churning up big fantails.

I opened my eyes and Sandjay cancelled the camera feed. Yuri, Callum and Alik were all doing the same thing as me, watching the images coming from the Trail Ranger's net, while Kandara and the three aides had chosen to stand, pressed up against the long windows, seeing the landscape for real. I guess that's a comment on age.

It wasn't long before the base camp domes were white splinters on the horizon. The Trail Ranger was purring along at fifty kilometres an hour, with the occasional lurch as we rolled over a ridge. Sutton and Bee were following a line of marker posts that the original science rover had dropped every four kilometres to mark the route, their scarlet strobes flashing bright against the sullen rock.

The stewards came round again, taking drinks orders. I asked for a hot chocolate. Most of the others had something alcoholic.

'Right,' Alik said. 'We're out of range from base camp, and I can't access solnet. What the fuck is out there?'

I glanced at Yuri, who nodded. 'I can give you the initial team's report,' I said, ordering Sandjay to release the files for them.

Everyone sat down, closing their eyes to survey the data.

'A spaceship?' Callum blurted in astonishment. 'You're taking the piss.'

'I wish we were,' Yuri said. 'It's a spaceship all right.'

'How long has it been here?' Alik asked.

'Preliminary estimate: thirty-two years.'

'And it's intact?'

'Reasonably. It didn't crash, though there is some hard-landing damage.'

'I'm surprised by the size,' Eldlund said. 'I'd expect a starship to be bigger.'

'The drive – if that's what it is – doesn't use reaction mass. We believe it has exotic matter components.'

'A wormhole generator?' Callum asked sharply.

'Currently unknown. Hopefully the science team will have some results for us when we arrive. They've had a week's lead on us.'

'And there's no sign of whoever built it?' Kandara asked thoughtfully.

Yuri and I exchanged a glance.

'No,' I said. 'However, some of the . . . cargo is intact. Well, preserved, anyway.'

'Cargo?' She frowned. 'What's the file number?'

'There's no file on the cargo,' Yuri said. 'Alpha Defence ruled that we absolutely cannot afford a security breach on that one.'

'Something worse than an alien starship?' Callum said. 'This should be good.'

'So . . .?' Kandara narrowed her eyes.

I took a breath. 'There are several biomechanical units on board which can only be classed as hibernation chambers, or modules that . . . ah, fuck it, you'll see. Whatever: they contained humans.'

'You are shitting me,' Alik growled.

'Again no,' Yuri said. 'Somebody took humans from Earth thirty-two years ago and flew them out here. The implications are not good.'

I smiled at Kandara. 'Still think we're paranoid?'

She glared back at me.

'How many humans?' Eldlund asked; sie sounded badly shaken.

'Seventeen,' I told hir.

'Are they alive?' Jessika asked quickly.

'The hibernation chamber machinery appears to be functional,' I said diplomatically. 'Half of the science team we sent out are medical personnel. We'll be given a more definitive answer when we arrive.'

'Fuck me,' Alik said, and took a big drink of bourbon from his cut-crystal tumbler. 'We're eighty-nine lightyears from Earth, and they flew here thirty years ago? Is the ship FTL capable?'

'Unknown. But possible.'

I watched them, Callum, Yuri, Kandara and Alik, as they stared round at each other, trying to read their expressions, to see any forgeries amid the shock and surprise. They gave nothing away. And I still didn't know which one of them was the alien.

Juloss

Year 583 AA (After Arrival)

'They've gone,' Dellian declared with a mixture of excitement and resentment as he raced out of the changing pavilion and onto the short grass of the games fields. His head was tipped back to gaze up at the bright blue sky. For all of his twelve years, there had been a great many sharp points of silver light orbiting far above Juloss, like stars that could be seen in daytime. Now several of those familiar specks (the larger ones) had vanished, leaving the remaining sky-forts to their lonely vigil, constantly alert for any sign of the enemy's warships approaching their homeworld.

'Yeah, the last traveller generation ships portalled out last night,' Yirella said wistfully as she tied back some of her hair.

Dellian was fond of Yirella. She was nothing like as solemn as the other girls in the Immerle clan, who were uniformly quiet and smiled so very little. And, unlike her, none of them ever joined the boys in the pitches and arenas as they played their team competitions. But Yirella had never been content to take her place in the arena's command pens, observing and advising.

As he stared up into the empty sky he could feel the sweat starting to bead on his skin. Immerle's estate was in the planet's semi-tropical zone, and this close to the coast the air was permanently hot and humid. With his red hair and pale skin, Dellian always used to slather himself in sunblock for the five afternoons a week when the kids played games on the estate's sports fields. But since he and his yearmates had reached their tenth birthday, they'd moved on to more combative games in the orbital arena.

'I wonder where they've gone?' he asked.

Yirella pushed her shaggy ebony hair aside and smiled down at him. Dellian liked that smile; her rich black skin always made a flash of white teeth seem quite dazzling – especially when it was directed at him.

'We'll never know now,' she said. 'That's the point of dispersal, Del. The enemy will find Juloss eventually, and when they do they'll burn its continents down to the magma. But when that day comes, the generation ships will be hundreds of lightyears away. Safe.'

Dellian answered with a grin of his own, acting as if it didn't matter to him, and looked round at his muncs to check they were paying attention. All the clan's children were assigned a group of six homunculi on their third birthday to act as permanent companions and playmates. It was Alexandre who had told the breathless and excited children that the stocky human-shaped creatures were 'homunculi' – a word that Dellian and his clanmates shortened to muncs within a minute, and it had stuck ever since.

The muncs were genderless, a hundred and forty centimetres tall, with thick arms and legs that were slightly bowed, alluding to a terrestrial ape heritage somewhere in their DNA. Their skin had a glossy grey and chestnut pelt, with a thicker, darker fur on their scalp. They were also extremely affectionate, and always anxious to please. Their creators hadn't given them many words, but they had instilled a strong sense of loyalty and empathy.

Around his ninth birthday Dellian had finally grown taller than his cohort. It had been a thrilling moment when he realized he'd gained that advantage, after which their play-tumbling took on a different aspect, becoming more serious somehow as they all squirmed round on the dormitory floor, laughing and shouting. He still adored them – a feeling now mingling with pride as they read his intent, providing an instinct-driven extension of his body during games. The years spent with him during childhood allowed them to learn his moods and identify his body language perfectly, which would pay dividends later in his life when he began his military service. The best integration in his yeargroup, Alexandre had acknowledged approvingly. And Alexandre's approval meant a great deal to Dellian.

Dellian and Yirella shuddered in unison as they heard the distinctive drawn-out ululation of a lokak's menacing hunting cry coming from beyond the estate's perimeter fence. Thankfully they rarely saw the agile, serpentine beasts slipping through the snarled-up forest outside. The animals had learned not to stray too close to the estate; but the fence and the sentry remotes that patrolled in endless circles were a constant reminder of how hostile Juloss could be to anyone who let their guard down.

The arena's portal was on the edge of the sports field, sheltering under a small Hellenic roof. Dellian shook off his chill as he walked through. He and Yirella stepped directly into the arena, a simple cylinder seventy metres long, with a diameter of a hundred metres, with every surface padded. He breathed in happily, feeling his heartbeat rise. This was what he lived for, to show off his prowess in the tournaments and matches, for with that came the prospect of beating the opposing team, of *winning*. And nothing on Juloss was more important than winning.

The arena was in neutral mode, which was spinning about its axis to produce a twenty per cent Coriolis gravity around the curving floor. Dellian always wished there was a window – the arena was attached to a skyfort's assembly grid, orbiting a hundred and fifty thousand kilometres above Juloss, and the view would have been fabulous.

Instead, he did what he always did when he came in, and studied the arena's interior to see if the stewards had made any changes. Floating above him were thirty bright hazard-orange hurdles: polyhedrons of various sizes, also padded.

'They've bigged them up, look,' Dellian said enthusiastically, as he took in the hurdles, committing the positioning to memory. Alexandre had promised the senior yeargroup they would receive their databuds in another couple of months, uniting them directly with personal processors and memory cores that would handle all the mundane mental chores Dellian had to labour away at right now. He considered it monumentally unfair that all the clan's adults had them.

'You mean they have enlarged the hurdles,' Yirella said primly.

'Saints, you've gone and joined the grammar police,' he moaned. At the same time he saw how intently she was studying the new layout, and smiled to himself. They started to walk along the floor, necks craning up, his cohort studying the hurdle layout as attentively as him.

The rest of Dellian's yearmates started to show up. He saw the boys grinning at the larger hurdles suspended above them, relishing the extra bounce the wider pentagonal and hexagonal surfaces would give them – if they landed true, of course.

'Saints, we'll reach the axis like lightning,' Janc said.

'Going to ace this,' Uret agreed.

'Is it going to be a capture the flag, do you think?' Orellt asked.

'I want to play straight takedown,' Rello said wistfully. 'Just hit them and knock them out of the arena.'

'Inter-clan matches are flag captures,' Tilliana said loftily. 'They allow a greater range of strategy options and cooperative manoeuvres. That's what we train for, after all.'

Dellian and Falar exchanged martyred grins behind Tilliana's back; the girl was always dismissive of any enthusiasm the boys showed to expand the tournament. Even so, she and her pair of muncs were reviewing the new arrangement keenly.

'Where are they?' Xante exclaimed impatiently.

They didn't have long to wait. The visiting team from the Ansaru clan, whose estate was on the other side of the eastern mountains, came jogging into the arena in a single regimented line, their munc cohorts forming columns on either side. Dellian scowled at that: the Ansaru boys had discipline. With his own yearmates spread halfway round the curving floor, joking around, their cohorts scattered and jostling spiritedly, it already put the Ansaru team ahead on style. *We should organize like that.*

Alexandre and the Ansaru referee came in, talking together cheerfully. Dellian was grateful he had Alexandre as his year mentor; some of the other adults who looked after the clan children didn't have hir empathy. He could still remember the day, six years ago, when he and his yearmates had it gently explained to them that they weren't omnia like the adults, that their gender was binary, fixed – like people on Earth millennia ago.

'Why?' they'd all asked.

'Because you need to be what you are,' Alexandre had explained kindly. 'It is you who will be going out to face the enemy in combat, and what you are will give you the greatest advantage in battle.'

Dellian still didn't quite believe that. After all Alexandre, like most of the adults, was nearly two metres tall. Surely soldiers needed that size and strength, and sie'd also told the boys they were unlikely to reach that height.

'But you will be strong,' sie'd promised. Only that was a poor consolation for Dellian.

He always felt mildly guilty whenever he studied their mentor too closely nowadays, drawing comparisons in his head. Despite Alexandre's considerable height, Dellian could never consider hir as strong as a body that size could (or should) be. Of course age played a part in that.

Out in the middle of the zone floor, Alexandre remained reasonably robust-looking; though Dellian did wonder if the black V-neck referee's shirt sie wore revealed maybe too much cleavage for someone with so many years behind hir (dorm rumour put hir at a hundred and eighty). But Alexandre's cinnamon-shaded skin was practically wrinkle-free, contrasting nicely with hir thick honey-blonde hair, which was always cut in a severe bob ending level with hir chin. Wide grey eyes could express a great deal of sympathy, yet as Dellian had found on the many occasions his misbehaviour had been discovered, they could also be stern. And this year Alexandre had decided to grow a thin beard. 'Because it's stylish,' sie told the kids, slightly defensively, when they asked and snickered. Dellian still wasn't sure about that.

Alexandre caught his eye and gestured: *Get into position.*

The teams started to line up along the centre of the floor, spacing themselves evenly, each taking a half, with the referees between them. Dellian and his cohort claimed his customary place in the middle of the Immerle team's semicircle. Yirella was at his side, her two muncs flanking her. Girls only had two muncs each – why would they need more? Dellian craned his neck, giving the visiting team a fast appraisal, seeing which player's cohort seemed tightest and most responsive.

'Their number eight,' Yirella said. 'I remember him from last year. He's good. Watch him.'

'Yeah,' Dellian muttered absently. He remembered number eight as well – remembered spinning tackles which sent him cartwheeling away from the hurdles, cursing as his opponent streaked away with the flagball.

Number eight was a thickset boy with brown hair oiled back over his skull. From a quarter of the way round the arena floor he gave Dellian a fast dismissive look, calculated to insult; his munc cohort copied it perfectly.

Dellian's fists closed in reflex.

'Mistake,' Yirella chided. 'He's goading you.'

A quick flush rose to Dellian's cheeks. She was right and he knew it. Too late to try and return an insult; number eight was no longer looking in his direction.

The Ansaru team's three girls took their place in the command pens around the rim, walking across the floor with a grace Dellian envied; his own gait resembled a boulder leading an avalanche – no style but it did get him places. However, he enjoyed their obvious disapproval as they registered Yirella remaining in the arena, wearing her protective bodysuit and an easy forty-five centimetres higher than the tallest boy. Teams were restricted to thirteen members, including tacticians, but there was nothing in the rules about one of the tacticians actually taking part. Yirella had won that argument a long time ago.

With a theatrical flourish, Alexandre and the Ansaru referee produced two flagballs each, holding them up high; the Immerle pair started flashing with a red light, Ansaru's were yellow.

Both teams grinned as they saw them.

'Two,' Dellian breathed in delight. *Now that's more like it.* Until now, they'd always played one flagball. This was going to be a real test of skill and teamwork. He and the rest of the team put on their helmets, giving each other slightly nervous looks.

This was both the pain and joy of being the first generation of binary humans to be birthed on Juloss. There wasn't an older year to pass down the wisdom, like warning them that the arena game rules would change. Dellian and his yearmates were always dropping hints to the younger years about how to handle themselves in games and tournaments. But they were the pioneers, everything they underwent in the estate's training programme was fresh and new. Sometimes it felt an unfair burden – not that he'd ever admit that to Alexandre.

'A point will only be given when both flagballs are put through the goal,' Alexandre announced. 'Winner is first to fifteen points.'

'Janc, and Uret, play defence on one flagball,' Ellici's voice announced in Dellian's helmet comms. 'Rello, you take the second.'

'Gotcha,' Rello announced greedily.

'Hable and Colian, go midblock on Rello's flagball,' Tilliana said. 'Let's lure them in. Only intercept when they're on final snatch flight.'

Dellian breathed out in relief. He'd been fearful the girls would assign him defence – *again*. He knew he was so much better at intercept.

'Ready one,' Alexandre said loudly.

Everyone tensed up. Dellian's munc cohort clustered round him, holding hands to form a ring.

'Ready two?' the Ansaru referee asked.

Ansaru's boys yelled: 'Yeah!' Dellian and his team let loose their signature call – a hooted warble they'd developed over the last couple of years, which to their ears sounded magnificently savage.

Alexandre smiled tolerantly. The lightstrips ribbing the arena walls turned gold. Dellian felt the gravity start to reduce further as the arena's spin slowed. All the boys swayed about like seaweed in a current. As always, falling gravity made him feel bizarrely lightheaded. The referees both threw the flagballs upwards. All four of the flashing globes soared up towards the axis.

Gravity reached about five per cent. Alexandre blew the whistle.

Dellian's muncs crouched down fast, thrusting their clenched hands into the centre of the ring they were forming. Dellian hopped onto the platform of stumpy hands, squatting down. The cohort read his every muscle movement perfectly; he jumped as if he was trying to power himself all the way to the planet below. The muncs flung their arms up in perfect synchronization, slim flower petals bursting open.

He rocketed upwards, body turning a half-somersault as he headed for the first polyhedron – and a hexagonal surface that was angled *just so*. Drawing his knees up almost to his chin. And hit-kick. The power bounce. Soaring towards the polyhedron two up. The air around him full of flying boys. Tracking them and the flag-balls, trying to project where they were all going. Then the muncs were rising, from above looking like an impossibly hefty bird flock startled into the air.

Dellian saw which of the Ansaru boys was going defensive on one of their flagballs. 'Intercepting a D,' he yelled.

As he thumped down onto the next polyhedron, he altered his angle and bounced on a good interception course.

'Mallot, take Dellian's D-2,' Tilliana called. 'Yi, snatch it.'

The Ansaru defender saw him coming, and curled up. Dellian rotated round his centre of gravity, drawing his legs up, ready for the kick.

They collided hard. The defender tried to grab Dellian's feet (technically illegal, you could only bump opponents, not grapple), but Dellian only used one foot, which gave him an unexpected slant. The defender's hands swung through empty air. He made good contact on the boy's hip, sending him spinning away to thud into a polyhedron, which whirled him off along a horizontal trajectory.

Yirella zipped past him as Mallot struck the second defender. She bounced accurately off a polyhedron and streaked straight towards the yellow flagball. Dellian's cohort caught up with him and formed up in a globe cage of tense limbs with him in the centre. Together they bounced off a hurdle, four munc legs kicking to give extra velocity. He rose towards Yirella, providing cover.

The arena lightstrips flashed violet for three seconds. Dellian grunted in dismay. The cohort bundle read his micro-flexing and twisted, legs rigid, arms extended so they spun slowly – ready.

The gyroscopic shells which contained the arena shifted round and spun faster. The centrifugal gravity direction altered sharply. The hurdles suddenly appeared to be moving through the air, like solid clouds in a stormfront. A couple of cohort bundles were swatted, flailing away chaotically. Tilliana and Ellici were both yelling instructions, redirecting the team. Dellian saw a hurdle approaching fast, and his cohort bundle shifted their dynamic slightly. Hit and bounce-kicked in roughly the right direction. Not that he'd ever been at sea, but Dellian thought the arena's irregular shifts must be like being in a ship as it was tossed about by a hurricane.

Yirella had stayed on course. She grabbed the Ansaru flagball, and shot through the axis. Her muncs clung to her hips, producing a X shape. They twisted gymnastically, flipping her as they went through the axis – and even Dellian was impressed by the smoothness of the manoeuvre. Yirella bounced off a hurdle to dive headfirst towards the floor that now had an apparent tilt of forty-five degrees.

'Yi, incoming three o'clock Z,' Ellici called. 'Now! Now now!'

Dellian bit back his own comments; the girls always got over excited in the games, he felt. They were supposed to be the calm analytical ones. He saw the Ansaru defender (number eight shirt) at the centre of a cohort star formation, pinwheeling towards Yirella.

'Got him,' he yelled. A hurdle on his right. His awareness and posture had two munc arms shooting out, slapping, which gave the whole bundle a fast roll – putting them on course for the next hurdle. Bounce – and he crashed into the number eight's bundle a couple of seconds before he took Yirella out. The impact was strong enough to break the bundles, and muncs and boys twirled apart like explosion debris riding a blastwave.

Yirella made one more bounce and landed hard on the angled

floor, rolling gracefully to absorb the impact. She raced to the Immerle goal hoop and dropped the ball into it.

Dellian smacked painfully into a hurdle and flailed about, trying to stabilize himself. Two of his muncs scrambled over a hurdle and jumped towards him. Lightstrips started flashing violet.

'Oh, Saints,' he groaned as the arena shifted again. A hurdle came sweeping through the air at him. A munc caught his ankle. They spun end over end, and he just had time to crouch and bounce.

'Zero on Rello,' Tilliana commanded. 'Quick quick!'

Dellian searched round frantically. Saw Rello cartwheeling next to their flashing flagball. Three Ansaru bundles were heading for him. Instinctively, Dellian bounced another hurdle and flew, arms outstretched in summoning. In five seconds his cohort had coalesced around him again and together they flashed across the arena to help Rello.

The Ansaru team managed to capture an Immerle flagball and dunk it into their goal hoop, then fifty seconds later Xante snatched the second Ansaru flagball. The arena stabilized, and both teams bounced gently down to the floor.

'Two minutes,' Alexandre announced.

Dellian and the rest of the team went into a delighted huddle. Getting first point was always a good sign, and it demoralized the opposing team. Tilliana and Ellici started telling them everything they'd done wrong. They barely had time to snatch a gulp of juice before the referees called them back to play.

The four flagballs went zipping high into the arena. Alexandre's whistle blew.

Immerle was 11–7 up and playing the next point when things changed. The arena was producing centrifugal gravity at right angles to the axis – which Dellian always hated – when the hurdles themselves started tumbling.

'What the Saints?' Xante exclaimed in panic as he bounced off a moving surface in a completely unexpected direction.

Dellian just laughed in delight. The lights flashed violet, and the arena shifted again; it had been barely thirty seconds since the last shift.

'Concentrate, for Saints' sake!' Tilliana yelled furiously, as a flailing Janc missed the Ansaru flagball he'd been aiming to snatch. He careered into a hurdle, whose rotation flung him away towards the arena's centrepoint.

Dellian glided towards a hurdle, manipulating his limbs carefully. His cohort bundle flexed responsively, and he could tell which surface they were going to land on, how it would be angled. He altered fractionally, and munc legs bent accordingly. The bounce propelled him straight up towards the Ansaru flagball. Four munc hands reached out as if they were lifting a trophy in victory.

Yirella sailed across his trajectory and snatched the flagball. Curling round to land square on a hurdle.

'Too slow,' she chided, laughing – and bounced.

Admiration for her agility mingled with the annoyance at being beaten to the flagball. Dellian studied the tumbling hurdle he was now heading for and judged the rotation almost right. Bounced to follow Yirella down, ready to provide support against any Ansaru intercept.

Two Ansaru players tried. But the moving hurdles were an unexpected complication for them, too. Both missed, swishing ineffectually behind Yirella as she flew true towards the goal hoop below.

Violet light flashed again.

'Oh *come on*,' Dellian groaned. If the arena kept this up, it would take them hours to get the final points. And he was already tired.

He could see from the course Yirella was on that she only had one more hurdle bounce planned out, which would put her directly on the floor. Then he caught sight of Ansaru's number eight going for a last-minute intercept. The boy was good, he admitted grudgingly as he watched his munc bundle smack into a hurdle and break apart in a complex slingshot-spin that transferred a lot of kinetic energy to him. Number eight soared out of his collapsing cohort, alone and at a speed that startled Dellian.

Things came together in his mind as he examined number eight's trajectory: that the boy would have to slow down, because to strike anything at that speed would hurt, maybe even break some bones; that he couldn't slow because there was no hurdle close by to bounce off and transfer momentum. The way he flew, with arms thrust out above his head and hands clenched into fists – that was deliberate, calculated to injure Yirella. Then there was the sullen resentment number eight had shown throughout the game when Yirella scored a point, and she'd got six of Immerle's total. That was back with a vengeance.

It's not the flagball he's going for, Dellian knew. His arms jerked round, hands in a grasping motion. The muncs reacted instantly, elongating the bundle shape. One of the muncs hit the side of a hurdle, managing to grab an edge for a brief moment. It was enough. The hurdle's rotational velocity was transferred through the cohort, and they slung Dellian away.

Now he was the one going far too fast.

'What . . . ?' Tilliana gasped. 'No! Yi, Yi, look out!'

Dellian's elbow punched into number eight's side, and the two of them rebounded, veering sharply away from Yirella. The force of the impact dazed him as something like fire engulfed his arm. Somewhere close by he heard his target cry out in pain and fury. They were both twirling round each other like twin stars bound in a single orbit. The arena's lights strobed scarlet as a siren went off.

Dellian hit a surface hard enough to knock the breath out of him. It must have been the wall, because he was immediately slithering down to thud into the floor. Number eight landed on top of him.

A fist struck Dellian's leg. He shoved back. Both of them were yelling wordlessly. Hands scrabbled at each other. Then Dellian made a fist and drove it into number eight's stomach. The boy let out a howl of anger and pain, and immediately headbutted Dellian. Their helmets made it pretty ineffectual, but the adrenalin was pumping now. Dellian tried to chop his opponent's neck.

'Stop it!' Tilliana and Ellici were both shrieking in his ears.

Then both cohorts of muncs arrived and jumped on the

wrestling boys. Yirella was shouting. Small fingers clawed at the boys; high-pitched squeals of distress rose. Little pointed teeth snapped viciously. Dellian hit out twice more as they writhed round, only to receive a punch which dislodged his helmet, squashing it into his nose. Blood started to flow out of a nostril. No pain, just rage. He brought a knee up with all his force, feeling it sink deep into his enemy's abdomen.

That was when Alexandre and the other referee arrived. Hands closed round the snarling kicking boys, prising them apart. The scrum of muncs were going berserk, both cohorts tearing into each other. It took another couple of minutes for them to break apart and cluster anxiously round their beloved masters. By then Dellian was sitting heavily on the arena floor as it spun up to full gravity, gripping his nose to try and staunch the unsettling quantity of blood pouring out. Number eight was curled up, hugging his stomach, his dark complexion now sickly pale as he drew juddering breaths. The two teams had grouped together on opposite sides of the antagonists, staring belligerently at each other. Even the girls had joined them.

'I think the match is now officially over,' Alexandre said firmly. 'Boys, back to the pavilion, please.'

The Ansaru referee was also ordering hir boys out of the arena. Alexandre consulted with hir for a moment, the two of them nodding together and keeping their voices low, as adults always did when a serious infraction had been committed. 'And no team tea,' they both announced.

Dellian walked slowly through the portal, emerging blinking into the bright afternoon sunlight searing over the estate's pitches. Boys from the younger yeargroups were playing football, oblivious of the drama that'd just transpired in the arena. The normality of the scene somehow made Dellian feel sheepish.

The Ansaru referee was walking with hir team, keeping them in line as they marched off towards the guest team changing pavilion. Several of the boys glowered at Dellian. He stiffened, wondering how far he should take it . . .

An arm came down on his shoulder. 'To Zagreus with them,' Orellt said. He raised his voice: 'We won! 12–7.'

The Ansaru team switched their glares to Orellt.

'Enough,' Alexandre snapped behind them.

Orellt grinned unrepentantly. 'Saints, but you got him good,' he confided to Dellian.

Dellian managed a weak grin of his own. 'I did, didn't I?'

'No you didn't,' Ellici said.

Both boys looked round and up at the girl looming over them, their expressions locked into guilt. 'You put no thought into it,' she continued. 'That's tactically stupid. You should have planned how to strike. People can be incapacitated with a single blow. All you had to decide on was the severity of the damage you wanted to inflict.'

'I didn't have time, it was too fast,' Dellian protested. 'He was deliberately going to hurt Yirella.'

'It was nice that you thought to protect her, I suppose, but the Saints know the way you did it was stupid,' Ellici said. 'Next time, either shout her a warning, or be more forceful when you attack.'

'More forceful,' Orellt said softly in wonder as Ellici dropped back to talk to Tilliana.

'Not a bad idea,' Dellian admitted.

'I think you were forceful enough with him. Alexandre is going to chuck you into the world's deepest hole. And then Principal Jenner will fill it in – probably with poo.'

'Maybe.' Dellian shrugged. He looked round at his cohort. They all had bruises and scratches, and two were limping. 'I'm proud of you guys.'

The muncs nuzzled up against him, each wanting the reassurance of touch. He stroked the glossy fur on their heads, smiling fondly. Dellian glanced round for Yirella, the one person who hadn't thanked him or even said anything. She was walking behind Tilliana and Ellici, her face devoid of expression.

As if nothing's happened, he thought, *or too much.*

In the home team changing pavilion the boys took their muncs away to clean up first. Sports kit was thrown into the laundry hopper, then the cohorts showered, soaping then sluicing their pelts before standing on the air-dryer, where they larked about under the warm jets. Finally they put on their everyday tunics – simple sleeveless one-pieces which went over the head. Dellian had chosen a fabric of orange and green stripes for his cohort, which stood out from the blander choices of his yearmates.

Once the muncs were done, he showered himself. Standing under the hot water, he suddenly felt profoundly tired. His nose was swelling badly now, and it was aching. His arm felt horribly stiff, and a little numb. Bruises were making themselves known. The brief flight replayed in his mind, and strangely he began to appreciate Ellici's comments. It was all dumb instinct, no thought, no strategy. Hit and be hit. 'Stupid,' he told himself.

Uranti, the munc-tech, was waiting in hir clinic. Arena matches always produced a variety of injuries and bruises among the cohorts that sie patched up. This time Uranti's head shook in bemusement as Dellian brought his cohort in.

'My, my, what have we got here?' sie said with acid sarcasm. 'Am I tending your cohort or you?'

Dellian stared at the floor. Uranti was female cycling, which Dellian always found more intimidating than when sie was in a male cycle. He didn't know why; he just did. When the grown-ups were female it somehow managed to make any guilt bite deeper. With a groan, he remembered Principal Jenner was also in hir female cycle now.

*

The clan's dormitory domes were all clustered together in the middle of the Immerle estate – grand white marble buildings with tall arches around the base, and inset with slender dark windows. After he finished in the clinic, Dellian started off towards them through the lush gardens, but when he was still a hundred metres away he caught sight of the figures racing round the thick base columns, heard the chatter and laughter of his clanmates – all so perfectly normal. He promptly turned off the path and wandered through the tall old trees (great for climbing), winding up in one of the sunken lawns surrounded by high hedges of pink sweet-scented flowers. There was a stone-lined pond in the centre, with two fountains playing in the middle. He sat on the edge and watched the long gold and white koi carp slide about below the surface, hiding from the curious muncs under big lily pads.

Right now he just didn't feel like company. He knew his year-mates would be gathering in the lounge, gossiping about the match. By now the news of the fight in the arena would have spread to every yeargroup. The clan would be talking about it for days; all the younger kids would ask him a thousand questions.

But I did the right thing, he told himself. *He was going to hurt Yirella.*

It wasn't long before he heard someone coming down the stone steps behind him. His muncs all turned round, but he kept staring at the fish; he was pretty sure who it was. All the clan kids reckoned the adults who looked after them could mainline the genten which managed the estate; it was how they kept track of where everyone was the whole time. Because, sure as Zagreus, this wasn't a random encounter.

'Something on your mind?' Alexandre asked.

Dellian supressed a grin at being right. 'I'm sorry.'

'Why?'

'Huh?' Dellian twisted round to find a surprisingly lively smile on hir lips. 'But . . . we were fighting.'

'Ah, but why were you fighting?'

'If he'd hit Yirella at that speed he would have hurt her. It was deliberate, I was sure of it.'

'Okay, that's good enough for me.'

'Really?'

Alexandre's arm swept round. 'Why do we have a fence round the estate?'

'To keep the beasts out,' Dellian replied automatically.

'Right. If you haven't learned just how unsafe Juloss is by now, you never will. The enemy is out there, Dellian; they search for humans constantly. And because we have to be silent, we never know how successful they are. We live in a dangerous galaxy, and it may be that Juloss is home to the last free humans. You have to look out for each other to survive. That's the real lesson you're learning here. And you practised it today. I'm pleased about that.'

'So . . . does that mean I'm not in detention?'

'Very calculating, Dellian. No, you're not in detention. But you don't get a reward either. Not yet.'

'Yet?'

Hir smile grew wider. 'We'll leave that for when you get to the real battle games in your senior years. For now, you need to learn about strategy and teamwork, which is what the arena tournaments are all about. So let's concentrate on getting that right first, shall we?'

'Okay!' He grinned, and his cohort began reflecting his relief, smiling and flapping their hands in contentment. 'Good good,' they cooed.

'Now get yourself back to the dormitory. You need to eat something before afternoon class. And the longer you put off talking to your clanmates, the longer they will want to talk.'

✳

The afternoon class for Dellian's year was held in the Five Saints Hall, which sat at the western end of the estate, a good five-minute walk from the dormitory domes. He always enjoyed the stories they heard in the Five Saints Hall, because they were always about the Five Saints, who one day would defeat the enemy.

'How's the nose?' Janc asked as they sauntered along the palm-lined path. The fronds were just stirring above their heads, a sign of the evening breeze starting its daily journey along the massive valley from the sea.

Dellian just managed not to touch it in reflex. 'Okay, I guess.'

'Saints, I still can't believe you didn't get detention!'

'Yeah, me too.' He saw the three girls up ahead, keeping together as they always did. 'Catch you later.'

The girls turned as one when he called out. Tilliana and Ellici gave Yirella knowing looks. For a moment Dellian thought she might not stop – or worse, the others would wait with her. Thankfully, they walked on.

'Sorry,' he said as he caught up.

'For what?'

He looked up into her heart-shaped face, troubled that she was treating him like this. They normally got on so well. Girls were all destined to be smart – a lot smarter than boys, Alexandre had explained; it was how their genes were sequenced. But he just knew Yirella was going to be the smartest of them all. Having her as a special friend was something he didn't want to lose. 'Are you angry with me?'

She sighed. 'No. I know why you did it, and I am grateful. Really. It's just . . . it was very violent. Saints, Dellian, you were both going so fast when you hit! Then there was fighting. Your nose was bleeding. I didn't . . . it was awful.'

'Ellici said I should be more forceful next time.'

'Ellici is right. You can debilitate with a single strike, you know. Then it would all be settled quickly.'

An image of the boy's expression inside his helmet at the moment of impact flashed through Dellian's mind. 'I know. Maybe I should learn how.'

'In three years, we'll get combat tutorials for the battle games.'

'I bet you could hack the data now.'

Her lips twitched. 'Of course I could.'

'Seems funny to be talking about it. Hurting people.'

'It's a dangerous universe out there.' She indicated the four-metre-high fence they were approaching. There was only silence outside in the valley's tangled vegetation, which somehow managed to be even more threatening than when the creatures were on the prowl.

'So everyone tells us.' He stared through the fence. Twenty-five kilometres away, across the flat expanse of the valley floor, the crystal and silver towers of Afrata rose up amid the lower slopes of the mountains. Even now the old city was impressive, which Dellian found quite sad. No humans had lived in it for forty years. It seemed that every day the verdant vines and creepers had twined their way several more metres up the skyscrapers. The streets had long since been engulfed by wild greenery. And all those fancy apartments were now home to the various predatory animals of Juloss who stalked each other along Afrata's broken boulevards.

'Doesn't make it right,' Dellian said. 'Saints, I know we're all okay and safe living here in the estate. It's just . . . I want to be out there!'

'We'll get there,' she said sympathetically. 'One day.'

'Ugh, you sound like Principal Jenner. Everything good's going to happen *tomorrow*.'

She smiled. 'It is.'

'I want to walk outside the fence. I want to climb one of those towers. I want to go to the beach and swim in the sea. I want to be on board one of the warships they're building up there, and fight the enemy.'

'We're going to do all those things. You. Me. All of us. The clans are what's left, we're the pinnacle of Juloss, the best and greatest of all.'

Dellian sighed. 'I thought the Five Saints were the greatest?'

'Their sacrifice was the greatest. We have to live up to that.'

'I'm never going to make it.'

Yirella laughed. 'You will. Out of all of us, you will. Me? I just dream the Sanctuary star is real.'

'You think it is? Marok is always saying that Sanctuary is just a legend, a fable that the generation ships carry with them between worlds.'

'All myths start from a truth,' she said. 'There must be so many humans spread across the galaxy now; it isn't hard to think they found one star that's safe from the enemy.'

'If it is real, we'll find it together,' he promised solemnly.

'Thanks, Del. Now come on, I want to hear what Marok has to tell us about the Saints.'

*

Five Saints Hall was the most ornate building in the estate – a long entrance hall with glossy black and gold walls leading to five big chambers. Hot sunlight was diffused to a pervasive glow as it shone through the gold-tinted crystal roof.

The fifteen boys and three girls of Dellian's yeargroup filed into chamber three. It contained plump sprawling chairs of faux-leather that they could flop into, the cushions undulating to take their weight like sluggish liquid. Up above them, the crystal roof was etched with monochrome images of the Saints themselves, while softboards around the walls had dozens of pictures pinned to them, drawn by the younger clan kids, the phosphorescent parchments glowing gently. This wasn't a classroom in the usual sense. They didn't make notes, there would never be an exam. The tutors wanted them relaxed, eager to take in the stories of the Five Saints. This was to be something they wanted to know, to learn.

Marok, the estate's Sol historian, came in and smiled. Sie was in female cycle, so sie'd grown hir chestnut hair to down to hir waist. Hir face was composed of long thin bones, giving hir a very attractive if somewhat delicate appearance. Dellian always thought that, if he'd been lucky enough to have a parental group like the people who'd left on the generation ships had, he'd want Marok to be part of it.

'Settle down,' sie told the kids. 'So then, has everyone recovered from the arena?'

There was some giggling, and plenty of glances thrown in Dellian's direction. He bore it stoically.

'I ask because violence isn't something we've really talked about concerning the Saints,' sie continued. 'Up until now we've only dealt in generalities. Today, I'm going to start filling in formative events. To put the Five Saints in context and to appreciate what they did, we need to examine their activities in greater detail. Just what motivated them? How did they come together? Did they really get on so perfectly as the tales you've heard said? And, most importantly, what was going on around them? All these things need to be looked at properly.'

Xante stuck his hand up. 'Weren't they friends, then?'

'Not necessarily, no. Certainly not at the start. Remember how Callum and Yuri had parted a hundred years earlier? It wasn't on the best of terms, was it? So who can tell me the two reasons they were brought back together?'

'Politics and treachery,' everyone chorused.

'Well done.' Marok smiled softly. 'And where did that happen?'

'New York!'

'Quite right. Now, New York in 2204 was a very different city from anything you know, even from Afrata. And Nkya was even stranger . . .'

The Assessment Team

Feriton Kayne *Nkya, 23rd June 2204*

When the Trail Ranger was an hour out from Nkya's base camp, the stewards started serving dinner. The gourmet food packets were microwaved, but they still tasted pretty good to me. I chose seared scallops on mint-pea risotto for a starter, followed by minute steak and fries with red wine sauce. The wine was a three-year-old Chablis. Not bad. I finished with lemon crème brûlée drizzled in raspberry sauce. I ate mostly in silence; everyone else was running through the files, consuming every piece of data we had on the alien ship. It wasn't enough to draw any definitive conclusions. I knew. I'd been trying to work out what had happened for ten days.

'Have you identified any of the humans on board?' Callum finally asked as he finished off his salted almond truffle tart.

'No,' Yuri told him tersely. 'We can't do that.'

'Can't, or won't? An identity check is one of the easiest search requests to load into solnet. Nobody can hide in our society, right, Alik?'

The FBI agent gave him a soft smile. 'It's difficult,' he conceded. 'Government keeps an eye on people.'

'For their own good,' Callum sneered.

'How many terrorist attacks have there been in the last fifty years? The last seventy-five, even?'

'Not many,' Callum agreed grudgingly.

'Your infamous pre-emptive rendition,' Eldlund said sharply. 'Arrest people because a G8Turing thinks they might do something based on behaviour and interests. What sort of justice is that?'

Alik shrugged. 'What can I say? Pattern recognition works. And FYI, every National Security removal warrant has to be signed off by three independent judges. Nobody gets exiled without a fair hearing.'

'That must make your citizens feel so much safer. What is it every authoritarian government says? If you've done nothing wrong, you have nothing to fear.'

'Hey, you want them to be free to emigrate to Akitha or one of the Delta Pavonis habitats, pal?'

'That's not a justification, that's a threat.'

Alik's stiff mouth managed to crank out a self-righteous smile, and he poured himself a shot from the bottle of vintage bourbon he'd brought in his luggage.

'Why haven't you tried to identify them?' Callum asked. His gaze had never left Yuri.

'The same reason there is no solnet out here, and that Alpha Defence insisted we keep a very secure separation distance between portal and ship. Security.'

'Man! You're still fucking doing it, aren't you? Still claiming everything you do is the *right way*, the only way. Anyone who says or thinks different isn't just wrong, they're evil with it.'

'Because this happens to *be* the right way. Try thinking about this – because that's what you're actually supposed to be here for, to produce an impartial informed opinion. Though fuck knows why Emilja and Jaru sent you.'

'Because I'm actually capable of having a rational thought, not just paranoid ones.'

'You'll give it away,' Kandara said in a weary voice. She'd taken her jacket off, exposing heavily muscled arms as she sat in the recliner, picking at the vegetarian meal on her fold-out tray.

Yuri and Callum both turned to stare at her.

'What?' Callum asked.

'Sorry, but Yuri is quite right,' she said. 'The aliens, whoever they are, are going to know who those people in their ship are. So if we start loading their image or DNA sequence into solnet, they'll know we found the ship. And as keeping this discovery secret is our one advantage . . .' She shrugged.

'Thank you.' Yuri grinned. 'What she said. Which is what I was trying to explain.'

Callum growled and held up his empty tumbler. A steward came over to pour him a shot of malt whisky.

Alik sat back, swirling his bourbon round the glass. He looked at Yuri, then Callum. Came to a decision. 'Okay, I gotta ask. What did happen with you two? Even the Bureau doesn't have files on it, but I heard rumours. And now here you are, both of you trying to make nice – and screwing that up.'

'This is bigger than us,' Yuri said sourly – a tone that would have made anyone else stop as if they'd run smack into a stone cliff.

'Showing some humanity now, are we?' Callum said.

'Fuck you,' Yuri spat back.

Jessika, Loi and Eldlund watched the scene, intrigued, and maybe a little nervous. Understandable – you don't often see two powers of this magnitude go head to head.

'You're a corporate robot,' Callum said. 'You were back then, and nothing's changed. You're not just employed by Connexion, you're its high priest, leading the worship.'

'You're alive, aren't you?'

'Am I supposed to be grateful?'

'It wouldn't hurt!'

'Really?' Callum sneered. 'You want me to tell them? Let them judge? Because it's not just my story, is it?'

'Go ahead,' Yuri said belligerently. He reached for the bottle of iced vodka.

Callum looked round at the rest of us in turn. Uncertain.

'Do it,' Kandara said with a small smile, daring him.

'It was a long time ago.'

'Ha!' Yuri snorted. He downed his vodka shot in one. 'Was it a dark and stormy night, too?'

'You didn't know where it started. That was a huge part of the problem. And you didn't know because you don't fucking care about people!'

'Fuck you! I cared – about her. Not you. Nobody cared about you. Asshole.'

'The real beginning was in the Caribbean,' Callum said, his expression softening at whatever ancient memory he was reliving. 'That's where Savi and I got married.'

'Illegally,' Yuri countered. 'If you'd told us like you were supposed to, it would never have happened.'

'It wasn't illegal. For all its size, Connexion is a company, not a government, and we didn't need your fucking permission! Just because Ainsley paid our salary didn't mean he owned us. So screw your fucked-up corporate policy! And it did happen.'

'We have those policies for a reason. If you'd told us you were in a relationship, if you'd been honest, everything would have been different. You created the problem. Don't try and make me out as the bad guy.'

I couldn't have planned it better. I wanted their stories, especially Yuri's. It had taken me a while to convince him he should come along on the mission in person, rather than just rely on my reports.

And now here they were, angry but uncensored, with something to prove. All they could use against each other now was the truth, because it was truth that could inflict damage more accurately than any smart missile strike, and their animosity hadn't even begun to heal over, not after a hundred and twelve years. It always amazes me how long humans can hold on to grudges.

I glanced round as unobtrusively as I could. Saw Kandara and Alik holding back smiles, enjoying the show they'd provoked. Yuri and Callum reheating their old war, ready to say anything, spill any secret.

'So it wasn't a dark and stormy night,' Callum began. 'Quite the opposite.'

Callum and Yuri

Head to head *AD 2092*

The beach was perfect. That was a major part of Barbuda's appeal. The tiny Caribbean island had a single Connexion portal door, which led to its larger and more prosperous neighbour, Antigua. In 2092, a solitary portal serving an entire population made it almost unique on Earth, where quantum spacial entanglement had brought everywhere *one step away* – as Connexion's tag line ran.

The resorts spaced along Barbuda's southern coastline depended on that exclusivity. The prices they charged for a week of privacy and seclusion were phenomenal. Callum Hepburn considered it entirely worthwhile. The Diana Klub just north of Coco Point was a sprawl of thirty boutique cabins set a few metres back from the top of the pristine white sands. By day it was gorgeous, a tropical sun searing down out of a cloudless azure sky to enhance the verdancy of the palm trees that ran along the top of the beach, turning the sand into a dazzling slope that by midday was too hot for bare feet to walk on. The turquoise water with its languid waves was clear enough to reveal the colourful shoals of fish that flittered playfully through the shallows.

At midnight it was equally lovely. The silver light of a crescent moon poised above the horizon bathed the warm sands in a spectral radiance, while deepening the lapping water to a dark and mysterious expanse. Atop the beach, the crowded border of trees cast a ragged ebony silhouette along the base of a starry sky.

Two figures in white towelling robes held hands and giggled as they scampered along the path from the cabins and down onto the sands.

Callum let out a gasp as his feet touched the hot surface.

'What's the matter?' Savi asked in concern.

'Hotter than I was expecting,' Callum admitted.

'This?' Her feet slid through the sand then flicked some up. 'This is nothing. You're a wimp.'

'I'm from Aberdeen,' he protested. 'You put your bare foot on the beach there, and it'll freeze to the pebbles. That's just in summer.'

'Wimp!' She let go, and ran on. 'Wimp wimp.'

Laughing, he sprinted after her. Caught her and swung her round with a loud happy howl.

'Shush! Callum. They'll hear.'

He glanced back at the tall trees with their long palms swaying in the gentle night breeze. The shadows amid the smooth trunks were an impenetrable black, deeper than the gulf between stars. Anything could be hiding in there; he'd never know. 'Who'll hear?'

'Them,' she said with a snicker. 'Our fellow vacationers. The staff. All the peeping toms.'

He put his arms round her, pulling them together, and kissed her. 'Would that be naughty for you?' he asked, nuzzling her throat. 'Being watched?'

'No.'

But there was that familiar edge to her voice that made him smirk. Savi had no inhibitions when it came to exploring her sexuality. 'No need to worry about them telling anybody,' he said. 'They'd die of envy before we finish.'

Savi licked her lips. 'Promises, promises,' she murmured hotly. 'Now take your robe off.'

'Yes, wife.'

She smiled broadly. 'You're the one that wanted to have sex on the beach. So: get on with it, husband.'

Callum shrugged out of his robe and spread it out on the sand. The very same sand they'd stood on that afternoon, him in a T-shirt and swim trunks (plus trainers with soles thick enough to stop his feet catching fire); her in a white bikini and a scarlet sarong. The ceremony had barely lasted five minutes. Only four other people were there: the padre from the local town, who performed the ceremony, the resort's assistant manager and two of their fellow guests, somewhat bemused to be serving as witnesses.

Savi giggled again, eyeing the treeline defiantly. 'Lie down,' she told him. 'I get to go on top.'

Callum heard the rising excitement in her voice and did as he was told. Savi stood above him, her feet planted outside his hips. She made a show of slowly undoing her belt, then let the robe fall open.

He gazed up in wonder at his wife, her lithe body gleaming in the pastel moonlight. *My wife!* 'You're a goddess,' he said hoarsely.

She slipped the robe from her shoulders, and tossed her long ebony hair. 'Which one?' she taunted.

'Parvati, the goddess of love and feminine energy.'

'Clever boy.' She grinned down hungrily.

Thank you, internet, I will never curse you again, Callum promised.

'Did you know she bestows a woman's skill and power to the whole universe?' Savi murmured as she sank to her knees.

Callum whimpered helplessly.

'And prowess.' Her eyes flashed wickedly.

In the sky above Savi's head, a shooting star scorched a silent scintillating tail across the heavens. Callum made a wish.

It was granted.

*

Callum woke to find strong morning sunlight filtering through the cabin bedroom's wooden shutters. The air conditioning was humming softly, but the temperature in the bedroom was already warmer than midsummer in Scotland. He turned his head to see Savi lying naked on the mattress beside him.

'Morning, husband,' she said drowsily.

He gently brushed thick strands of tangled black hair from her face. All he could do was smile at how lovely she was.

'What?' she asked.

'I thought I'd had the best dream of my life,' he said softly. 'Turns out it's actually a memory.'

'Oh, Cal!' She reached for him, and they began kissing ardently.

'I'm a married man,' he said, and there was no way to keep the incredulity out of his voice. 'I can't believe you said yes!'

'I can't believe you asked!'

'I was always going to ask.'

'Were you?'

'Yeah. From the moment I saw you. But I knew I'd have to wait. You know – actually say hello first, maybe find out your name.'

'Silly man.'

'I thought I'd blown it yesterday.'

She stroked his cheek. 'You didn't.'

'We're married!' Callum started laughing.

'Yes. Now we just have to work out how to tell everyone.'

'Oh. Crap. Yeah.' He frowned; just the thought of it was a real passion killer.

Savi gave him an interested look. 'You're not worried about that, are you?'

'No. No, it's fine.'

'You're scared of telling my father,' she decided shrewdly.

'Am not.'

'You are! Fine husband you make; you're supposed to fight demons and dragons for me.'

'I'm not scared of your father. Your mother, on the other hand . . .'

'Mummy likes you.'

'She's very good at hiding it.'

'You know what they say: if you want to know what the girl's going to grow into, look at the mother.'

Callum had a brief, if frightening, memory flash of his own father, standing in the Pittodrie stadium, cheering on the Dons, a beer can in each hand. 'I would be delighted if you turned out like your mother.'

Savi's mouth parted to a wide O, which she covered with her hand as she laughed. 'Oh no, I married a horrific liar!'

'Well, you have to admit, they are a bit conservative. And I am white.'

She ran her hand through his short ginger hair. 'White and red. Proper Scottish. I could get snow-blind staring at your skin.'

'Hey, you said my freckles were cute.'

'Freckles are cute on a ten-year-old, Cal; when you're thirty-one they're just funny.'

'Oh, thanks.' Callum kissed her. *Best way to shut that conversation down.* 'Anyway,' he said, shrugging, 'it's not family we really have to worry about.'

'Ah, our bloody Connexion Corp lords and masters. I hate them!'

'Company policy. Human Resources gets right tight-assed about personal relationships. They're paranoid about sexual harassment lawsuits.'

'I never had to harass you for sex.'

'True.'

'Actually,' she said, 'it's not HR that's the problem.'

'What?'

'Anyone employed by the Security Division has to have their friends vetted.'

'Vetted? You mean, they get to say who you can date? That's outrageous! They can't do that.'

She grimaced. 'Ah. You see, in fact, there's this clause in my contract about who I can associate with outside work. It's very clear.'

'Wait . . . you didn't sign it, did you?'

'It's the Security Division, Cal; it's the way it is. If you work in Security you have to know who you're seeing. *Exactly* who. If another company is trying to launch an infiltration mission, we can't afford to be vulnerable.'

'Bloody hell, that's depressing.'

'I know. But realistic. The world is a bad place filled with bad people.'

'Okay, so . . . what was my report like?'

'Ah.' She flinched. 'I haven't actually told them.'

'This doesn't sound good.'

'I . . . It's . . . Cal, that day when we met, it was so much fun, remember? I thought it was . . . you know.'

'What?'

She sucked her lower lip in faux remorse. 'I thought you were just going to be a one-night stand.'

'Shit!' He slumped back, and stared up at the ceiling, feeling quite petulant. 'It wasn't actually one night,' he said, acting the martyr.

'Oh, the male ego! Yes, all right: a one-weekend stand. And when it turned out you wanted more than that, I was so happy. But, the point is, I didn't report it at first because I thought I wouldn't see you again, and you were Connexion, too. So it wasn't a huge security risk, and a girl doesn't want a big file of these things following her round. We still get judged, you know. It's unfair. Men don't.'

'I get it,' he said.

'Then, when we started seeing each other properly, I was in an awkward position.'

'Is this going to cost you your job?' he asked, suddenly anxious.

'No. Look, it's still only been six weeks. Yuri will understand if the notification goes in a little late. He's an okay guy.'

'Yuri?'

'Yuri Alster. My boss.'

'All right. So we both come clean together, then, as soon as we get back. Good plan, actually. You go fess up to Yuri, and I'll notify Brixton HR. We'll say it was a spontaneous thing. Right; this is it, okay? We met here on Barbuda, we fell in love, we got married. It's not really a lie. If people are going to be that reckless about love, it's going to be on an island like this one.'

Savi grimaced again. 'Um, we might just have to wait.'

'What? Why?'

'It's my current assignment.'

'What about it? Actually, what is it, this assignment?'

'Hey, no fair. You promised you would not ask about my under-cover assignments.'

'Sorry.'

'There will always be aspects of what I do that I can't tell you. You know that, don't you?'

'Yeah, yeah, I get it.'

'You have no idea how hard it is for an Indian girl to make a decent career for herself in this business. I worked bloody hard to get into covert ops, and I love what I do. I can't risk crashing it now.'

It's exciting too, which is what you really like, but he wasn't going to say that to her face. 'Sorry, sorry. You know I just get concerned for you.'

'I know. It's very sweet. But your work is physically dangerous, too; one slip up, and you've got a disaster area on your hands. And I know how dedicated you are. So just think how you'd feel if I asked you not to take the worst assignment.'

'Emergency detoxification isn't quite as extreme as the media plays it up to be. And I'm not asking you to give Security up. I was just showing an interest in my wife's work, like a good husband.'

'Nice try,' she mocked.

'Er, it's not really unsafe, is it?'

'You judge: there's this evil billionaire with a fiendish plan for world domination – no: solar system domination. My assignment is to use all my feminine assets to seduce him and steal the plans from his bedroom safe.'

Callum grinned lecherously. 'That should work, 'cause those are amazing assets.'

She laughed and kissed him again. 'In fact, this one is really boring. I go around university campuses pretending to be a student and showing up at anti-corporate rallies and meetings – with par-ticular attention to anti-Connexion gatherings – seeing who's there, who's the angriest of them all, who's the silent smouldering type, who's all talk . . . We're monitoring potential future troublemakers.'

'That sounds quite sinister, the company keeping profiles on a bunch of twenty-year-olds. Is it legal?'

'They're kids, Cal. Ninety-nine per cent are just rebelling against their parents now they've finally left home. But they're susceptible to radicalization. Somebody's got to stop them being exploited by the real zealot shits; the university deans don't do a damn thing.'

'Also true.'

'It's important work. Work I'm proud of. Urban violence is in decline for the first time in decades, Cal.'

'I wasn't arguing. So, how exactly does this prevent you from telling Yuri about me?'

'I'm in the middle of an assignment. It was a miracle I managed to swing this four-day break. If I tell him about us on Tuesday when we get back, he'll lift me from the job until you've been vetted. And if I'm away for too long, it might make the group I've been hanging out with suspicious. The whole assignment collapses.'

He frowned in confusion. 'It can't take more than a couple of hours for them to read through my file, surely?'

'That's not how you vet someone, Cal. Internal Assessment will put a couple of case officers on reviewing you, and now that we're married you'll have to come in for an interview. If you're clean, it'll only take a week; but if there are any question marks, you're looking at months for verification.'

'Bloody hell! If I'm that questionable, how come they let me do what I'm doing? Look at how potentially dangerous my job can be; I could cause Connexion more grief than any street mob. Just one hesitation or wrong action, and tonnes of toxic crap leak out, into the water, across a city . . .'

'You're not getting it. Intelligence-gathering is about acquiring information and analysing it. What we do is try to find the people who are looking to subvert you. Yes, if you'd been turned you could probably cause two or even three bad toxic spills before Security realized you'd become a militant. Our job is to halt that subversion before it happens.'

'Are you telling me that if one of my clean-up operations does go pear-shaped, Security will come looking for links with fanatics?'

'Depends on how big the damage is, but basically: yes. And if there are suspicious patterns in behaviour or your data footprint, our division's G5Turings will find them.'

'Shit on a stick! I didn't know that. It's not even a whisper in the department.'

'Which, as you've now got an undercover security agent lying about her relationship with you, is going to be really bad if they do stick a pattern analysis on you. So we're both on the line here. Don't screw up your next job.'

'Hell! I'll do my best.'

Savi kissed him, resting her face against his. 'I love you, husband.'

'Not as much as I love you, wife. So how long before we can shock everyone with the announcement?'

'Couple of weeks. No more, I promise.'

'You're not going to be away all that time, are you?' he asked in dismay.

'I'll try and finish as quickly as I can. But be prepared, contact's going to be difficult while I'm active.'

'Come on, you can sneak a minute to call me. Just an email will do. Let me know you're okay.'

'If I can, I will, but I can't risk blowing my cover, Cal.'

Which he found frustrating, as if she wasn't willing to make the effort. Which wasn't fair. Like she said, to get where she was at just twenty-six must have been tough. That resolve of hers, pursuing what she wanted without hesitation every time, was intoxicatingly attractive.

'I understand,' he told her.

'Thank you.' Savi rolled onto her back, and stretched sensuously. 'This is the first day of our honeymoon now, isn't it?'

'Yes.'

'That means I'm entitled to sex with my husband all day long.'

'It certainly does.'

'So what are you waiting for?'

*

The alarm woke Cal. A vile insistent buzz coming from the antique digital clock with numbers that glowed scarlet in the gloomy bedroom. He reached for it. But of course it sat on a neat stack of plastic storage boxes half a metre from where his fingers stretched to. 'Bastard!' He had to scramble to the edge of the mattress and swing his legs out from under the heavy duvet before he could reach the cube of black plastic.

In the silence that followed he shook his head, trying to wake up properly. An ex had set up the beyond-reach trick. Savi had thought it was a great idea, so he claimed it was all his own. Wives – so touchy about old girlfriends.

He looked round at the empty bed and sighed. Five days without her now. There'd been no call, not even an email. *How is some bunch of dickhead students going to notice anything wrong with a two-minute call? Do they all live together in a cult compound, or something?* That wasn't a thought he wanted to explore.

The alarm started off again. He'd only hit the snooze button before. Cursing, he switched it off properly and headed for the shower.

His flat was on the top floor of a grand old Georgian terrace house in Moray Place, one of the best addresses in Edinburgh, so the estate agent swore. A small beautiful park of ancient trees, circled by the New Town stone architecture for which the city was renowned. That was why the flat was only four rooms and, even on his salary, paying the rent was a stretch. But as a bachelor pad it was a classic.

Maybe too much of a classic, he thought as he went back into the bedroom with a towel wrapped round his waist and hair still damp. He'd spent serious money on the king-sized bed. But that was where the extravagance had to end. His clothes were all supposed to be put away in the three towers of plastic boxes along one wall, but mostly they were dumped on the washing pile in the corner. The Barbuda break had messed up his laundry service routine. It also seemed to have messed up his shopping program.

'House,' he yelled.

The wallscreen lit up with the G3Turing's house utilities menu – two years since he'd installed it, and he still hadn't got round to customizing the cheap, obsolete, unit. 'Good morning, Callum,' it said in a sharp female voice. He hadn't changed that from the factory setting, either.

'Why are we out of shampoo? I had to use the shower glass cleaner on my hair. It smells weird.'

'Your household items replacement order has been placed on hold.'

'What? Why?'

'You are now over your pre-approved monthly credit limit by three and a half thousand pounds. The credit company has suspended all future account payments until this is resolved.'

'Shit! How did that happen?'

'The last large payment was to the Drexon International Leisure Group for five thousand eight hundred and ninety pounds, which put you over the specified limit. Your credit company suspended the account at midnight and is now charging you double interest on the excess amount.'

'Bloody hell.' He hadn't realized Barbuda had been quite that expensive. *Worth it, though. She married me!* He gave the empty mattress a forlorn look. *Five days, and it's already unbearable without her.*

He started going through what was supposed to be the underwear box. There was only one clean pair of boxer shorts left. 'House, why didn't you warn me I was maxed out?'

'You have told me to be silent six times in the last four days when I asked your permission to review your current financial status.'

'Oh yeah, right. You should have told me it was about the current account.'

'I did. The credit company has issued five statutory warnings.'

'Okay. Uh, next time just throw the debt figure up on all the wallscreens in red. I'll catch it properly, then.'

'Very well.'

Callum could've sworn the G3Turing's voice sounded disapproving.

He found a fresh shirt and started putting it on. 'Is there any breakfast in the kitchen?'

'There is some printed bacon available. Eight containers of natural food currently need to be removed from the fridge for recycling. All have passed their use-by date. A new food and beer delivery is pending resumption of credit.'

'Yes, mother,' he grumbled under his breath. 'So resume it.'

'You will first have to agree to a new overpayment charge with the credit company.'

'Right. Look, just sort the thing out, okay? I get paid in a couple of days, anyway.'

'Your next salary payment is in six days.'

'Whatever. Get my credit flowing again.'

'The new extension terms they are offering are not favourable.'

'Hey, stop being such a bloody lawyer! You're supposed to be adaptive software, right? Well pay attention and learn. I don't like being distracted with this kind of crap while I'm working. This is why I buy programs like you, so, just . . . make my life easier, okay?'

'Very well, Callum.'

He held back on a bad-tempered reply. That easier life could've been real if he'd bought a fifth-generation Turing. They were so much smarter; one of them would have picked up on all his nuances and understood what he wanted, sparing him this grief of having to spell everything out. But a G5 was beyond his current budget.

Next time I get promoted . . .

Callum pulled on his trousers. There were no clean socks. 'Fuck's sake!' He tugged a reasonable-ish pair out of the washing pile. His trainers still had beach sand in them; he grinned fondly at that as he strapped them up. Next to the alarm clock was the tube with his e-contacts, and next to that was a pair of basic screen glasses. He chose the glasses. Somehow this morning he was in no mood to faff about with contact lenses. *Damn, I miss her.*

Finally he put his smartCuff on, a simple band three centimetres wide that could have passed as black glass if it hadn't been so flexible. Once he'd slipped it over his knuckles it shrank to a perfect fit around his wrist. It ran a biometric to check his identity and immediately linked to his dermal grains through mInet. A neat column of sapphire data slid down the left-hand side of his screen lens.

He didn't bother reading it. Just having it there, up and active, was reassuring. The mInet made him part of the world again.

'Hey there, Apollo, are we running smooth?'

'Good morning, Cal,' the mInet's electronic identity replied through the audio grain embedded in his ear. Everybody gave their mInet a tag, and Callum had been obsessed with the Apollo moon-shot when he was in his teens, to the extent of building flying models of Saturn Vs.

'You've got full mInet connectivity with your peripherals,' Apollo said. 'Your blood-sugar levels aren't good.'

'Yeah, it's morning, pal. Keep a watch on House, I want to know when my credit's back up.'

'You're already solvent again.'

He would have said 'thank you' to House, but some deep Luddite part of his mind refused to recognize the G3Turing as a genuine personality.

Like all meat these days, the bacon was printed, with a use-by date eighteen months away. He dropped a couple of rashers in the frying pan. Didn't need to check the bread's use-by, it was mouldy, so no bacon sandwich. There was one egg left, a natural one. Couldn't scramble it because the buttermilk was ripe enough to make his eyes water when he sniffed it; his grandmother had drilled into him, that was the only true way to make scrambled eggs. Black coffee, then. He shoved a capsule into the outsized chrome-plated Italian barista machine, and waited while it ran through its usual tune of choking steam noises.

'Stream the overnights for me,' he asked Apollo as he cracked the egg on the side of the frying pan. By some miracle the yolk didn't break.

The kitchen wallscreen produced a grid of news streams determined by adaptive preference filters. He sipped the coffee with growing satisfaction as five of the ten news channels focused on disasters across Europe. He scanned them quickly to see if any of them threatened to contaminate the surrounding area; those he might well wind up dealing with during his shift. The major one that had developed while he slept was a blaze in a Frankfurt theatre. Seven fire tenders were dealing with it, sending long white arcs of foam playing over the inferno. 'No,' Callum said. Apollo tracked his gaze slipping to the second grid, and pulled that one to the front. A landslide in Italy brought on by excessive rains, three houses in a mountain village washed away. He glanced at the next grid. A sinking yacht in the sea off the coast of Malta, surrounded by coastguard ships and news drones. 'Sorry, my friend, can't help you.' He flipped the bacon. Fourth, a radioactive-waste disposal facility just outside Gylgen, Sweden, which had undergone an evacuation during the night. Unconfirmed reports that the waste storage containers had cracked. 'Crap.' A live feed gave him a company spokesman standing outside the gates, assuring reporters that evacuation was 'just a precaution' and there was absolutely no spillage.

Callum stared at the uneasy spokesman, not believing a word of his clichés. 'Call Moshi,' he said.

His deputy's comms icon came up in the screen lens. 'Are you monitoring the Gylgen facility?'

'Way ahead of you boss,' Moshi Lyane replied cheerfully. 'The G5Turing caught it within a minute. There's been a lot of executive chatter with the Environment Enforcement Agency.'

'Spillage?'

'Satellite's not showing anything. Yet. But the containers are below ground level. If there's a leak, it's not vapour.'

'What does Dok say?'

'She's talking to Boynak executives. And we're on an open channel to the EEA in case they order intervention.'

Callum's screen lens showed him the Boynak file. The owner of the Gylgen plant, in turn owned by a tangle of interlocked holding companies, was registered in a scattering of independent asteroids. He grunted in contempt. 'Fucking typical.'

'Boss?'

'Can their in-house team handle it?'

'Best guess: no. They're shouting "nobody panic" quite loud.

And we're not seeing any clean-up equipment on its way through the hubs.'

'All right, I'll be with you in ten.'

'I welcome that.'

Callum grinned, then looked down at the frying pan. The rashers were overcooked, and the yolk had turned solid. 'Aww, bastard.'

*

The huge old trees in Moray Place were all budding early, thanks to the unseasonal winds that had been blowing in from the south-west for most of February. With the low morning sun striking them, it looked as if an emerald frost had materialized overnight to coat the circular park. What had been the cobbled road surrounding the verdant urban isle was now broken up by two lines of raised circular troughs with cherry trees planted in the centre of each one. Callum smiled up at the cherry blossom glowing a luminous pink in the bright sunlight. Savi had enjoyed the blossoms on her last visit.

He walked round the troughs, keeping a wary eye out for cyclists. Ever since Connexion had started establishing its hubs across the globe, civic authorities had been pedestrianizing cities and towns, starting with the centres and gradually expanding out as the hub network coverage increased. There was still room for taxez, delivery bugez, and emergency vehicles to manoeuvre along Moray Place and the neighbouring streets, but even the taxez were few and far between these days. The only time Callum really saw them was during one of Edinburgh's not-infrequent rainstorms. Cyclists, though – cyclists were very intense about their right of way, which seemed to include every flat surface in existence.

Callum turned down Forres Street. 'Any emails from Savi last night?' He didn't know why he asked. The inbox was on his screen lens and had nearly two dozen emails pending, most of them work related, with one from his mother.

'No,' Apollo replied.

'What about everything you sent to the junk archive? She might be using a one-time address. Check them for a personal message.'

'There are none.'

'Calls? Ordinary phone calls or a sightyou?'

'No.'

'Calls made but no answervoice recorded?'

'No.'

'Has she made any social posts?'

'Not since she posted her Barbuda videos the night before you left. Her parents and sister have both left messages on her MyLife site in the last thirty hours, asking her to call them.'

'How about . . . have I been tracker pinged?'

'None since you lost your smartCuff last November. You left it at Fitz's apartment after his party.'

'Yeah, yeah. Can you ping Savi's mInet?'

'Yes.'

'Do it.'

'Her mInet is not responding.'

'Ping it again.'

'No response.'

'Fuck.' *She's super-smart, so why isn't she doing something to let me know she's all right? Anything?*

*

Like every city, Edinburgh's Connexion hubs were arranged in a spiderweb pattern. On a map, it registered as concentric loops intersected at right angles by radial spurs. Commuters could walk in both directions around the loops, clockwise or anticlockwise, and inbound or outbound along the radial spurs. A simple mInet app called Hubnav told everyone the quickest route to their destination. Callum never bothered with it in the morning; his route to work was so familiar it'd become simple muscle memory.

He walked into the metrohub on the junction with Young Street. It was a loop hub, with five pay barriers across the entrance leading to a drab grey and green tiled lobby. Apollo gave the barrier his Connexion code and he went straight through. Like every hub lobby, portal doors faced each other on opposite sides. Standing between them was like staring at the infinity image when you stand

67

between two mirrors, except it wasn't himself he could see in all the identical lobbies stretching out ahead. Looking through the portal doors he could see his fellow commuters walking between a few lobbies then turn off.

He automatically turned right to go through the clockwise circuit portal door which led to the Thistle Street hub, which in turn opened into the St Andrew's Square hub, which was an intersection hub, so turn right and through the inbound portal door of the radial spur directly to Waverley hub.

Waverley was the centre of Connexion's Edinburgh metro network, standing on the site of the old train station. The twelve radial spurs that led into it emerged onto the floor of a plain circular building with a glass dome roof overlooked by the severe old castle perched on its stone cliff high above. At the centre of the hub were two wide portal doors for the National City network – one in, one out. Even this early in the morning, it was busy. Callum took the portal door out.

The British National City hub was the Waverley hub built on an industrial scale, constructed twenty-five years ago on a cheap derelict industrial zone in Leicester; because its physical location was irrelevant, the accountants just wanted the lowest local tax rate on offer in the country. It was an annular concourse a hundred metres wide with high polished black granite walls and a black and white marbled floor. Huge lighting galleries hung from an arched ceiling, bringing an intense noonday glare to the dense throng of 24/7 commuters.

It was built to operate a hundred and thirty portal doors. Sixty-five on the inner wall, all exiting their respective cities to deposit people into the concourse; and a matching sixty-five on the outer wall, the outbounds, each one with its city name glowing in bright turquoise neon above. There were no neat channels along the concourse designated for people to walk between them, no convenient moving floor strips, no smiling staff to help. The concourse was a purely Darwinian melee. Travellers used their Hubnav app to find where their city door was, then they just put their heads down and went for it, resulting in a permanent rush hour of intolerance and mid-level aggression, of people running urgently only to clash with the slow movers, people cursing each other, parents checking children were keeping up, luggage and shopping bugez being booted as they strove to follow their owners. All of them kicking up a noise to rival a football stadium crowd.

Callum slipped through them all as if he were Teflon coated. The door to London was six to the left of the Edinburgh exit. He made it in forty seconds. Through that and he was in the Trafalgar Square hub, with its twenty-five radial doors to take you out across the huge capital city plus one door in a recess, guarded by a security barrier. It opened for Callum, allowing him directly into Connexion Corp's internal hub network.

Three portals later he was in Emergency Detoxification, a big purpose-built facility in Brixton where for once no expense had been spared to give it eight specialist handling garages full of support machinery, wrapped around a core of offices and maintenance depots.

ED operated seven active response crews, ensuring two would always be on standby at all times to cover most of Europe. The division's mission was to prevent any emerging contamination situation from getting anywhere close to the point where leakage occurred. That meant getting the first-response teams in fast and early, and dealing with the problem directly, with the resources that only a company like Connexion could deliver. That required a full backup for the on-site teams, from full technical support in the Brixton office to fast civil evacuation procedures and emergency medical crews that could be brought in from right across the globe in worst-case scenarios.

Everything depended on the first-response teams to manage things professionally and dispose of the problem in minimal time (and at a minimal cost). The practical, political and financial expectations focused on the team leader were huge.

Callum's first-response crew used an office that had a window wall overlooking the facility's Monitoring and Coordination Centre, whose architects had clearly modelled it on Connexion's starflight mission control. Callum greeted his crew and stood beside the tall glass, watching the activity in the M&C Centre. He could see the long lines of consoles below and noted that a full support crew was already in place, bolstering the normal monitoring staff. A sure sign of a building situation. They were studying fast-changing data displays under the supervision of five separate operation directors. The wall they faced was covered in a dozen screens. Most of the secondary screens showed the same news streams of minor disasters he'd seen in the flat. One of the two main screens was showing the clean-up at an ageing chemical plant on the banks of the Wista just outside Gdańsk. The ED crews had been working that one since before his Barbuda trip. The land around the plant had been used as a chemical drum burial ground for decades, and none of the contents or locations had been logged. The Environmental Enforcement Agency only discovered the site when the drums started leaking into the Wista. ED was having to excavate the whole area down to fifty metres to clear it.

The second big screen relayed the gates of the Gylgen disposal plant, with snow falling as if to soften the problem. There wasn't much activity going on outside the long dark buildings behind the double chain-link fence. That was when Callum knew for sure Brixton would be sending a crew in.

He watched Dokal Torres, their corporate liaison counsellor, standing beside Fitz Adamova – in Callum's opinion the best of ED's operations directors. The two were having a very intense conversation.

'That looks serious,' he decided.

'There's money in play on this,' Moshi Lyane said cheerfully. 'Corporate always gets serious when money's in the room.' At twenty-eight, Moshi was keen to prove himself; he had a puppyish eagerness combined with fierce intelligence. Callum was convinced that back in the rocket age, his deputy would have been a right stuff astronaut for NASA. But now Connexion had changed the world, so Moshi was at the new cutting edge of risk-taking, and helping to make the world a better place at the same time. It was like an addiction; all the crew had it. 'Update?' he asked.

'We're going to get the call,' Moshi said. 'Boynak still haven't moved anything that can help through their hubs.'

'Nothing?' Callum asked in surprise. 'Are we even sure there's an emergency?'

'They might not be moving equipment,' Alana Keates said, 'but Dok just confirmed four of their top engineers arrived on site an hour ago.' She glanced through the window at the counsellor.

'Evaluating,' Callum said. 'That must be it.'

'Dok thinks so,' Alana agreed. 'By the way, what happened to your hair?'

'My hair is fine.' Callum ran his hand over his hair. It seemed a bit stiffer than usual, and he could still smell the glass-cleaner fluid. 'Okay. Do we have plans of the plant?'

'Way ahead of you,' Raina Jacek said. She was the crew's data expert, and privately Callum would trade any two of the others for her. She knew her way around network systems better than anyone with a standard degree out of university. Most of her teens had been spent as a hacktivist, mainly for political and environmental causes. She'd been arrested several times and even served three months in a Norwegian junior offenders' camp. Normally that would red flag her as far as Connexion was concerned, but her file said she switched sides after rehabilitation.

One night at a party when they were both mildly stoned, Raina had told Callum that she had actually had a near-death experience after her friends were sold a bad batch of crystal Nsim. Her boyfriend had died, but the paramedics were good enough to revive her. It made her realize just how dark the underworld could go. So it wasn't a switch of allegiance exactly, but Emergency Detoxification was making a visible difference, even if she didn't like the profit motive . . .

They sat around the office table, and Raina threw schematics of the Gylgen plant on the wallscreen.

'Standard disposal set up,' said Henry Orme, their radioactive materials expert. 'Boynak have a contract with a whole bunch of European companies to get rid of their radioactive waste.'

'What sort of waste are we taking about?' Callum asked.

'Standard items: medical tracers, research lab material. Nothing too bad, until you start to lump it all together.'

'Which is what they do?' Colin Walters said knowingly.

'Yep. There's a portal between the Gylgen plant and one of the ventchambers on our Haumea asteroid station. Boynak gather the waste into batches at the Gylgen plant, and send it through to Haumea, which vents it away into deep space along with all the other crud Earth's desperate to dispose of. Forty AUs being what everyone agrees is a safe distance. It's a simple and easy system.'

'What could possibly go wrong?' Raina said happily.

Callum ignored the snark. 'Show me.'

Colin used a pointer to highlight a section of the plans. The centre of the main building had five large cylinders, four metres in diameter and fifteen long, arranged in a vertical cluster. Each of them funnelled down to a metre-wide pipe at the bottom, and they all connected to the one-metre portal below via a series of valves. 'These tanks are pressure chambers,' Colin said. 'You collect the waste from clients in small sealed canisters and drop them into the tank through an airlock at the top. When the tank is full, you pressurize it to five atmospheres.' His pointer dot reached the bottom of a tank. 'Then you open the valve. Gravity and pressure send the waste straight down to the portal, along with the vacuum suck from Haumea. Whoosh, out it all goes.'

Callum nodded. He'd seen variants on the system dozens of times. It was deliberately simple, keeping the process safe and reliable. Tens of thousands of tonnes of toxic waste were sent harmlessly into space from Haumea every year; it was all the asteroid did.

'Unfortunately it's not going whoosh in this case,' Dokal Torres said. The counsellor was walking in from the M&C Centre. Unlike the rest of the crew, she was wearing a light grey suit with dark claret blouse – that way she stood apart and emphasized how far up the management chain she'd risen. For all her insistence on following protocol and routine, Callum liked her. She was smart enough to know when to give him the leeway to deal with problems. It was a good professional relationship. On rare occasions she'd even been known to join the rest of the crew for a beer after work.

'What's happening?' Moshi asked.

'Blockage at the base of the tank. It's been pressurized and Boynak are worried about some of the seals holding for a prolonged period. We're creeping outside the design specs.'

Callum tried to keep the excitement from his voice. 'Do we go in?'

Dokal took a breath. 'Yes.'

The crew whooped and gave each other high fives.

'Boynak and their insurers have authorized a full breach and vent. Whatever it takes.'

'What's the blockage?' Callum asked.

'The valve won't open,' Dokal said.

'Uh huh.' Callum nodded shortly, instinct warning him something was wrong; the way she gave a lawyer's answer only confirmed it. 'We can tack a blister to the base of the tank, and blow through the wall.'

'Your call,' she said.

'Okay.' He clapped his hands. 'Let's get moving. Moshi, Alana, Colin, with me. Load our bugez with a couple of blisters and a pack of fifty-centimetre shaped charges. Raina, you're in the facility's control room – I want to know the real state of that cylinder and its seals. I'm also going to need every spec on the tank, especially what it's made of.'

'On it, boss,' she said happily.

'Henry, take Haumea station. Thread us.'

'Oh, come on . . .' Henry complained.

'You're at Haumea,' Callum said in a level tone. Henry's partner was seven and a half months pregnant. It made Callum feel strangely protective, especially as a newly-wed himself. Having Henry away from the dangerous material at Gylgen made him feel a lot better.

Henry held up his hands. 'You're the boss.'

'I want to be through the hubs in ten minutes. And it's max hazmats, people; this is radiation we're dealing with.'

The crew hurried out. Just as he reached the door to the handling garage, Dokal said: 'A word, Cal.'

Instinct made his skin crawl, but he just said, 'Sure,' as if it was routine, some stupid paperwork to clear first.

'What's with the hair this morning?' she asked as they hurried up the stairs.

'It's . . . nothing.'

She raised an eyebrow, but didn't push it.

Dokal's office was on the ED core's second floor, which gave her a rare outside window. The white blinds were shut, preventing anyone from seeing out – or more relevantly, Callum thought, in. Two people were waiting for them. He recognized one: Poi Li, Connexion's security director, who had been with Ainsley Zangari since the very beginning. Company rumour had it she supplied him with pirated firewalls the day he rented his first office in Manhattan, because he didn't have the money to buy legit copies. Just the sight of the old woman made him feel guilty. She couldn't be here about Savi. *Could she?*

Poi Li gave him a quick appraisal. 'You look worried, Mr Hepburn,' her deceptively light voice challenged.

Bastard! 'My expenses are all legitimate.' He made it light, office banter.

The second visitor stood up.

'This is Major David Johnston,' Dokal said. 'From the Ministry of Defence. Nuclear Division.'

The Major was a heavy man in his early fifties, moving with some difficulty and wincing every time he bent his knees. Callum imagined he had been injured during some kind of dark ops mission. A thin monk's band of white hair circled his scalp, and he wore wire-rimmed screen glasses, which gave him the air of a classics professor. His presence worried Callum a great deal more than Poi Li's ever could. 'Really?'

'Pleased to meet you, Callum. Counsellor Torres here has been singing your praises.'

Callum gave Dokal an ironic glance. 'Nice to know.'

'We have a delicate problem,' the Major said. 'And by we, I mean the British government. So we're asking for your help and discretion.'

74

'Which Connexion guarantees,' Poi Li said. 'Correct, Callum?'

He spread his arms wide, trying not to let the dismay show. 'Sure. So what's the problem?'

'The '68 Global Disarmament Treaty,' Major Johnston said. 'Terrific breakthrough event for global politics. Lots of voter happiness all round.'

'I've heard of it,' Callum said cautiously, not that he could remember details; politics and history weren't exactly his strongest subjects.

'It was inevitable, given the development of atomic bonding generators. Every major city in the world has an air shield now. Missiles and drones can't get through, and if you bond enough air together, it can withstand a nuclear blast. Whole national arsenals were rendered obsolete overnight – well, five years plus. That just leaves us with low-level threats now: terrorists building their own nukes, rogue nations, extreme political groups, etc., etc. Everyone understood that the only way to prevent that menace being realized was to get rid of the world's stockpile of weapons-grade fissionable material.'

'After the '68 Treaty, everybody abandoned their warheads and their material stockpile,' Dokal said. 'It's one of the reasons Haumea was so profitable for Connexion right from the start; everyone made a show of shoving their nasties through.'

Callum watched her closely. He really didn't like where this was heading now. And the vivisectionist gaze that Poi Li was using to study him didn't help.

'So we did,' said Major Johnston. 'Everybody minimized. Britain was left with five functioning warheads for deterrence purposes alone, and no ability to build more. However, I'm afraid we had a . . . uh, inventory issue.'

'Oh fuck,' Callum groaned.

'The trouble is, back in the twentieth century and a fair bit of the twenty-first, the government was somewhat paranoid. It didn't declare the true amount of plutonium it had created.'

'Jesus fucking wept! Are you telling me there's plutonium in that malfunctioning tank?'

'We were trying to dispose of it quietly,' Major Johnston said. 'To avoid an incident with the Transnational Inspectorate.'

'You didn't tell them?' Callum said, aghast. 'You didn't tell Boynak what you were sending through their disposal system?'

'Our senior management was aware,' Poi Li said.

Callum turned to her, frowning. '*Our* management?'

'Connexion has a share in Boynak. However, the Gylgen facility staff were not informed. There was no need.'

'So we're helping the British government to dump its illegal plutonium?'

'The plutonium was a mistake made by a previous generation,' Major Johnston said emphatically. 'We were trying to do the honourable thing and correct it.'

'Is that what you call it?'

'Actually, yes.'

'We need you, as crew chief, to be aware of what you're actually facing in Gylgen,' Dokal said.

'Big thanks, pal.' Callum rubbed his forehead with the tips of his fingers, trying to think. 'I don't get this. Is the malfunction a terrorist group sabotage?'

'I don't believe so,' Major Johnston said. 'We have sent several batches through previously without any problem. Our canisters of plutonium are listed as medical waste from various London hospitals. The plutonium itself is broken down into small pellets, each of which is encased in a ceramic to prevent it oxidizing, then sealed in a standard canister. What I believe may have happened is plain bad luck. One canister dropped from the top of the tank landed badly. The ceramic might have cracked, or even shattered.'

'You didn't test the ceramic for impact,' Callum said in realization.

'It's a quiet project,' Poi Li said. 'Failure to fall test that particular ceramic was an oversight.'

Callum closed his eyes, trying to remember his physics. 'If you expose plutonium to moist air, it oxidizes and hydrides, then it expands by . . .'

'Up to seventy per cent,' Johnston completed. 'The canister itself may have ruptured from that expansion pressure. It is only a standard commercial plastic, printed in the Gylgen plant and shipped out to customers.'

'Never designed to contain accidental plutonium expansion,' Callum said wearily. 'I'm guessing the residue trickled to the bottom of the tank and blocked the valve. Unlikely, but . . .'

'Our scenario is worse than that.'

'Oh bloody hell!'

'The powder which plutonium oxidization and hydration produces has been known to flake off and ignite spontaneously.'

'*Ignite?*'

'Yes. If there was a fire resulting from that initial fracture, it would probably breach further canisters. And each one would multiply the problem.'

'How many plutonium canisters are in this tank?'

'Twenty-five. That's a kilogram of plutonium in total.'

'Fuck me! Well, let's hope I can vent the whole mess before that fire starts.'

'Cal,' Dokal said quietly. 'The Gylgen facility engineers didn't pressurize the tank.'

'But you said . . . Oh.'

'Yeah, there was a fire inside the tank,' Major Johnston said. 'That's what caused the pressure increase. There's only a limited amount of oxygen in there, so that'll be consumed by now. But we suspect that while it was burning, it turned a lot of the other canisters molten, releasing more plutonium along with all the other residue. That is probably what's broken the valve. There are no sensors left inside; the fire took them out. We don't know what state the waste is currently in. The canister plastic may be liquid, or it may have re-congealed. If you blow a hole in the bottom of the tank, the waste might not vent.'

'We can't take the risk the fire restarting, Cal,' Dokal said. 'Some of those canisters contained radioactive water. If we get any more oxidization on the plutonium, it could combust and rupture. Time is becoming critical. You've got to send the whole tank through.'

'It's fifteen metres long and weighs sixty tonnes!'

'But it's only four metres wide. Whatever you need, Cal. There is no budget here today. You can thread up to six metres, our largest portal. I checked, and we have a pair available.'

'All right, I accept the risk,' Callum said calmly. 'But my crew needs to be told.'

'Not Raina Jacek,' Poi Li said immediately. 'Not with her political background.'

Almost, he argued. Almost. But a very bad part of his brain was thinking about being vetted by security. The problem simply wouldn't exist if he had Poi Li's trust on this one.

'Okay, Raina will be in the Gylgen control room. I'm talking about Alana, Colin and Moshi; they're the ones who'll be physically tackling the tank with me.'

'They can be told,' Poi Li agreed.

'Let's go, then.'

*

When Callum got to handling garage five, the crew was almost ready to go. Moshi, Colin and Alana were in their green and yellow hazmat suits, running tests on the life-support packs. Raina was sitting on a bench, with a thick hi-rez wraparound screen band on her face, muttering away to her mInet, hands raised mid-air as she deftly moved virtual icons around. Henry was with two support staff, already wearing his thermal regulator suit, which resembled a body stocking knitted out of slim tubes. The staff walked him over to the Govnex Mark VI spacesuit, a rigid torso with a hinged back-pack that was already open for him. He had to wriggle through the small rectangular opening. Legs went in first, then he had to bend almost double, shoving his arms into the sleeves as he pushed his head through the neck ring. Callum winced in sympathy as he started to pull on his hazmat suit.

'We're going for full disposal,' he told them. 'I want to drop the whole tank out through Haumea.'

'What? Why?'

'You're kidding, chief.'

'That's crazy!'

'It's not crazy,' Callum said levelly. 'Something in those containers has leaked and blocked the valve. We don't know what, and we don't know how much. I cannot risk a partial clearance; that'd leave us a worse problem than we have now. So the whole thing goes, quick and clean. Dok has already cleared it with corporate.'

Raina had pulled her wraparound down to give him a sceptical stare. The others were all exchanging glances.

'It's four metres in diameter, chief,' Colin protested.

Callum's lips twitched a grin. 'So we thread up to six. There's a portal pair waiting for us on Haumea.'

'You're shitting us!' Henry exclaimed in delight. 'Nobody gets to use a six-metre portal.'

'We do.'

'Okay, then.' Alana pursed her lips in approval. 'Now you're talking!'

'So. Henry, we'll be taking two portals. One to depressurize the tank, we blow a hole in the side and put it into vacuum. That way we don't have the problem of seals getting overstressed and failing; and without oxygen the fire can't restart – that'll buy us some time. The second portal will thread up for complete disposal. That's going to take some serious cutting. Moshi, electron beams for all of us. Colin, we're going to need at least two cases of shaped charges. Raina, how's your timing? We're going to need some serious precision on this.'

'I'm insulted you asked.' But she was smiling. Like the rest of them, she had her eyes on the big prize. This operation was going to look great on their CVs, and the bragging rights they'd have over the other crews were incalculable. There was also the prospect of a bonus, always index-linked to the scale of the hazard you averted.

They used Connexion's internal European hub network to get them to Stockholm, then there was a private portal to the Boynak offices, which put the Gylgen facility one step away. As soon as they got there, Raina went straight for the operations control room. A technician in a hazmat suit led Callum and his crew to the disposal building.

It was a standard industrial structure of metal girders covered in composite panels. Inside was a three-dimensional lattice of pipes and loader rails interlaced with stairs and suspended walkways. At the far end was the reception bay, with cargo portals linked to various collection stations across the continent. Right at the centre, suspended over a deep pit, were the five tanks.

Callum took one look at the imposing matrix of metal – a brutal edifice made worse by the red emergency lights flashing across it. The sirens had been switched off hours ago. Apollo threw up a swathe of schematics, identifying components. 'Leave the bugez,' Callum said. 'They'll take too long to scale this. We'll carry the cases from here.'

They didn't say anything, just did as they were told and plucked their equipment cases from the bugez. Callum guessed they were still in shock. He'd explained about the plutonium on the way over, cutting Raina out of the comms circuit.

It was two flights of stairs up to the walkway which led to the top of the tanks. He was sweating by the time he got up there. The cases were heavy, and he had an electron cutter slung over his back.

Loader rails ran parallel to the walkway, silent and still since the pressure warning started. He glanced at the blue plastic canisters frozen in position, stretching all the way back to the loading bay. Each one had a prominent radiation warning emblem. Ordinarily that might bother him; today he just didn't care. *Like they're going to make a difference if we screw up.*

Dokal had shown him the confidential file Johnston had provided. It had estimates of the potential damage should the tank rupture. Likely quantity of plutonium particles to spew out, wind patterns, ground dispersal . . . Emergency evacuation procedures to enact for anyone within two hundred kilometres, contamination effects on local wildlife and vegetation. Cost of a clear-up – shocking in both financial and environmental terms.

'Mini Chernobyl,' she said grimly.

Apollo had shown him that file. It banished his usual level of confidence, which he fought hard to hide from his crew.

They arrived at the cluster of tanks. Each one had a couple of airlocks on top, the size of oil drums, with a feeder mechanism above them to channel the canisters off the loader rails.

'Alana, clear the insulation off the top of our tank, enough for a blister. Moshi, get me a temperature reading, then prep a puncture charge. Colin, the blister, please. And guys—'

They turned to look at him, caught by the unaccustomed gravity in his voice.

'Calm and careful, okay? We cannot afford screw-ups.'

'You got it, chief.'

While the others got organized, he took a minute to study the tank and the network of steel girders which held it in place, working out where the supports would have to be cut. The schematic his mInet threw up across the hazmat helmet visor confirmed the load points. *Twenty of the bastards.*

Alana used a power plane to slice the insulation foam off the tank, cutting a circle over a metre across.

'Thirty-eight Celsius,' Moshi said. 'That's well inside tolerance.'

'Good,' Callum said. 'Let's keep it that way. Place the charge.'

Colin put the puncture charge in the middle of the area – a black plastic circle like a fat coin, three centimetres across.

Callum opened the first of his cases. The portal it contained was a disc thirty centimetres in diameter. On one side it was a hole that opened into a metallic chamber in Haumea station, while the other side was a twenty-centimetre stratum of molecular circuitry, stabilizing the entanglement. When Callum looked through, the portal was facing a wide airlock hatch, with amber caution lights strobing around it. As always, he had to resist sticking his hand through and wiggling it round.

'Henry? How are we doing?'

'I'm in the ventchamber. Portal is locked in position. Ready to open outer door.' Henry's spacesuited hand came into view through the portal, giving a thumbs-up.

'Stand by.'

Colin held up the blister – a hemisphere of incredibly tough metalloceramic, with a meld-bonding rim. Callum twisted the portal disc into its locking slots in the apex of the blister and they both lowered it onto the patch Alana had prepared.

'Seal it,' Callum said. 'Henry, open the ventchamber hatch, please.'

'Confirmed, chief. Opening now.'

Callum watched the data Apollo was throwing onto his visor display, seeing the pressure inside the blister wind down to zero. 'Fitz, status, please.'

'Haumea systems all stable,' the Operations Director said. 'Portal power supply confirmed and buffered. You're go, Cal.'

'Raina, update?'

'Blister seal melded to the tank. It's secure, Cal. Good to go.'

'Thank you. Moshi, blow the puncture charge.'

There was a dull *crump* from the blister. Callum heard a loud whistling sound. Apollo showed him the pressure in the blister rising sharply.

'It's venting, chief,' Henry reported. 'Good plume. Mostly gas. Some particles.'

It took three minutes for the tank to empty. Callum, Moshi, Alana, and Colin all kept watch on the casing, but although it trembled as the gas was expelled, nothing else happened; the whistling noise reduced to nothing after a couple of minutes. 'Right, then. Let's get it prepped for dumping,' Callum said. 'Henry, I'm looking to start threading up in about an hour.'

'I'll be ready at this end, chief.'

Moshi had the job of blowing the horizontal support struts which fastened the tank to the surrounding lattice. He clambered along the metal girders, fixing a double charge to each strut. Alana and Colin used their electron-beam cutters and severed the disposal pipe at the bottom of the tank below the jammed valve, then went on to slice out a two-metre section. When they were finished there was a clear space below the valve.

While his crew were working on readying the tank, Callum started clearing an area to work in, level with the gap Alana and Colin were preparing. He cut into the girders, creating a cave to bring the portals through unencumbered. It was tough work, sending long lengths of metal tumbling down into the pit below, where they bounced and spun off the thick pipes leading in from the other tanks, clattering away to the very bottom of the pit. Several struck the side of the portal chamber five metres below him.

To hold the six-metre portal, they'd brought three support rails with them – telescoping composite tubes that Callum and Alana set up underneath the tank's severed pipe. Bonding pads at each end secured them to the remaining steel girders.

The whole procedure took nearly seventy minutes. Callum was sweating profusely when they finished and Raina confirmed the rails had bonded correctly to the molecules of the lattice girders. Standing on the precarious walkway, he opened the second case, which contained another thirty-centimetre portal, and placed it base-down on the mesh.

'Henry, we're ready. Start threading.'

*

As soon as the tank's gas evacuation was complete, Henry had cycled out of the ventchamber airlock and headed back to the ED ready-one compartment. Haumea station's broad passageways were simple metal tubes with nearly a metre of insulation foam sprayed on the outside to help combat the cold imbued by the asteroid's lonely trans-Neptune orbit. The station didn't warrant the investment of its own manufacturing module; all its sections and components were shipped out directly from Earth. They were laid out across Haumea's ice-crusted rock surface in a series of basic geodesic spheres with radial spokes leading out to cylindrical ventchambers of varying size. There were over eighty ventchambers already, most of them with their outer door permanently open, allowing plumes of misty vapour to fountain up out of their portal as toxic chemicals or radioactive gases were shunted far away from Earth. The remainder would intermittently produce bursts of canisters, which streaked out across interplanetary space like a blast of giant shotgun pellets. New spheres and ventchambers were still being added as Earth methodically disposed of its historical pollution.

Technicians were already assembling the threader when Henry

arrived in ED ready-one. The inside of the dome was the same triple-level layout as a freefall space station; with Haumea's minimal gravity it made manoeuvring large machinery a lot easier. The central deck was the assembly area for threaders. Henry smiled inside his helmet as he saw the six-metre one being prepared; the big machines always delighted him.

The core of this one was the pair of six-metre portals, currently pressed together so tightly they formed a single disc of molecular circuitry a metre and a half thick. Nine robot arms were carefully integrating an elegant egg-shaped frame of brushed aluminium ovals around them, containing a multitude of mechanical components and actuators, wound with power cables and data fibres.

Henry clicked his spacesuit boots into the floor grid, holding himself in place while the technicians glided round the growing threader like curious fish investigating a shining reef. He watched the process advance while the voices of the crew back in Gylgen babbled away in his ears.

Once the first part of the threader was complete, a similar, smaller version was attached to its front end, then finally an even smaller edition was attached to the end of that. The three together resembled a bizarre Russian doll mechanism caught in mid-separation.

'Henry, we're ready for you,' the lead technician said.

Henry picked up the second of the two suitcases he'd brought with him from Brixton. He kicked off the floor and floated easily through the air to the threader. To stop he grabbed one of the ceiling handholds and manoeuvred himself back to a vertical relative to the decking. Working in zero-gee, constantly having to manipulate your whole bodymass with a single arm, built muscle bulk like no gym exercise ever could. All space-workers developed upper bodies like pro-swimmers. And because portal doors meant everyone went back home to Earth at the end of shift, nobody suffered the kind of calcium loss and muscle wastage early astronauts had been plagued with on long-duration flights.

He opened the suitcase and took out the circular thirty-centimetre portal. It locked into place on the front of the threader. 'Integration complete,' he reported.

'Reading it,' Fitz said. 'Running threader procedure checks. You are go to egress the ventlock.'

The magnetic monorail grip on the bottom of the threader powered up, propelling it along one of several rails on the deck. Henry waited until it went past, then grasped one of the curving aluminium ribs at the back, and let it tow him along. The rail led down a passageway to the largest ventchamber on Haumea.

As soon as it was inside the cylindrical metal cave, the inner door slid shut and sealed with a fast succession of metallic *clunks*. The threader extended ten legs which engaged with loading pins on the chamber floor.

'In position,' Henry said. He looked up, checking the outer door above the threader. A ring of amber caution lights were flashing around the heavy-duty hydraulic actuators.

'Callum's almost ready,' Fitz told him. 'Stand by.'

Henry drifted over to the airlock at the side of the big egress door he'd just come though, and opened it in readiness. Once everything was in place he was going to have to leave the ventchamber fast. His mInet was throwing up several data columns on the spacesuit visor, showing him the threader status.

He'd been listening to his friends back in Gylgen for several minutes before Callum said: 'Henry, we're ready. Start threading.'

Henry gave the instruction to his mInet. The smallest of the threader's three mechanisms started up. At its centre was a paired portal, like a particularly thick dark-grey paving slab, twenty-five centimetres wide and one and a half metres long.

'Initiating spacial entanglement on unit alpha,' Fitz said, as the data on his displays showed him the system's progress. 'Okay . . . we have zero-gap. Power stable to both sides. Uncoupling now.'

The actuators inside the threader mechanism split the slab apart into identical rectangles, whose quantum spacial entanglement transformed them into linked doors. No matter how great the physical distance between the twinned segments, the entanglement provided an open gap that was no length at all: the portal.

Henry grinned in delight as the threader supports holding the portal pair lifted the two identical rectangles away from each other. Actuators moved with the fluidity of metal muscles, sliding one of the twins – short edge first – through the waiting thirty-centimetre portal, its edges just clearing to emerge directly into the Gylgen facility.

'Got it,' Callum said.

In front of Henry, the threader mechanism rotated the remaining portal slab by ninety degrees, so its longer opening was ready to receive the shorter side of the next stage.

'Initiating spacial entanglement on unit beta,' Fritz said.

Unit two was another rectangular portal, larger this time, one and a half metres by six and a half. The support arms pulled its twin segments apart, and immediately slipped the short end of the upper segment into the waiting unit alpha portal, with a clearance of less than a centimetre. Inside the threader, the remaining unit beta portal was rotated to present its wider side to unit gamma, the six-metre portal.

'Here we go,' Henry muttered. 'Unit gamma ready for you, chief.'

*

Callum caught the unit alpha slab as it threaded through from Haumea, and placed it on the floor in the section he'd marked out. Unit beta quickly emerged out of it, and the legs on its back deployed, lifting it up, and flipping the open side ninety degrees so it finished up horizontal. He checked it was aligned with the rails bridging the gulf under the tank. Apollo adjusted its height until he was satisfied. Alana fixed its legs to the walkway's grid.

'Let's have it,' he told Henry.

The six-metre portal came through, sliding out across the rails. Callum glanced into the opening, seeing the ventchamber's outer door dead ahead. He watched the data column showing him the state of the rails and their bonding points. Everything was well inside tolerance. 'Looks good from here. Let's go.'

Along with Moshi, Alana and Colin, he clambered back up the

metal stairs to the top of the lattice. Moshi had prepared straps and harnesses for all of them, fastened to the thickest girders. Callum eyed the top of the tank as he clipped himself in.

'Everyone secure?'

'Good to go, chief.'

'Raina, I need you to keep watch on the building sensors.'

'I'm on it, chief.'

'Henry, open the ventchamber door,' Callum said. 'Moshi, get ready.'

It began with a faint hissing sound. A breeze started up, plucking at the thick fabric of his hazmat suit. The hissing deepened, quickening his heartbeat. Peripheral vision showed things moving on the walkways that criss-crossed the lattice. Old abandoned plastic cups, paper, scraps of wiring, plastic slivers, all wiggling and rolling along.

'Door at fifty per cent,' Henry reported.

The hissing had become a storm-roar now. Its force was buffeting him more than he'd anticipated. Instinct made him check the harness clasps. Colin and Alana were already on their knees, gripping the walkway rail for extra security.

'Seventy-five per cent,' Henry said.

Callum could hear the whole building protesting now. Metal was creaking overhead. When he glanced up, he could see the lights swinging wildly. Above them, the ceiling panels were buckling, starting to peel from the frame.

'Hundred per cent!'

The snarl of air venting into interplanetary space became a hurricane howl. Vapour was streaking across the lattice at incredible speed. Two roof panels ripped free, and slammed down onto the tank, vibrating furiously as they were sucked away down the sides.

'Blow it,' Callum shouted.

The charges on the tank support struts detonated simultaneously. He couldn't even hear them above the gale that was clawing at him. Snowflakes transformed to dangerous ice bullets, strafing down from widening cracks in the roof. The top of the tank vanished, dropping so fast he barely caught the motion. More lethal panels were scything through the air, following it into the cyclone funnel which had formed in the gulf the tank's departure had created.

'It's clear,' Raina yelled across their comms.

'Close it, Henry!' Callum shouted.

The gale took an age to subside as the ventchamber's outer door laboured against the incredible pressure. Twice as long as it took to form, Callum was sure.

Silence, when it came, was like a physical force slapping him. Callum took a shaky breath and stood up, tensed against the eerily still air. 'Everyone okay?'

They called it in, voices unsteady with relief. Callum slowly unclipped the harness. Snow was falling through wide fractures in the broken roof. The inside of the building resembled a bomb site. He checked his radiation sensor, which showed him background levels only.

'Bloody hell, we did it!' he said. Then started laughing at the surprise in his own voice.

*

The alarm clock's buzzing woke Callum. Someone had turned the volume up to stadium-rock level and added earthquake-shake to it. Callum moaned weakly and opened his eyes – actions which were hideously painful. Hand groped round for the alarm clock. Some-where in his aching brain he cursed the smartarse out-of-reach trick.

That was when he realized he wasn't even in the bedroom, let alone his bed. He was sprawled on the settee in the living room with a cricked neck and one arm wedged under his torso. And the alarm was still buzzing away. His vision was blurry, but he could see through the open door into the bedroom where the red glowing digits taunted him.

'House,' he croaked.

'Good morning, Callum.'

'Switch the alarm off.'

'That is not possible. Your alarm clock has no interface. It is very old. I believe it was manufactured in the nineteen-nineties.'

'Bastard.' He staggered upright, groaning at the wave of pain the motion caused at the very centre of his brain. The living room lurched nauseatingly around him. Somehow he managed to coordinate his limbs and tottered into the bedroom. He didn't bother with the snooze or cancel buttons on the clock, just switched the fucker off at the mains.

Relief lasted about five seconds. 'Oh shit,' he gasped, and sprinted for the bathroom.

He didn't know what he'd had to eat last night, but he certainly managed to throw up most of it into the toilet bowl. He pressed the flush, then slumped on the floor with his back to the washbasin, breathing heavily as his body abruptly turned to ice and his clearly lethal bastard of a headache hammered at the inside of his skull in an attempt to break free.

They'd spent another hour at the Gylgen disposal facility yesterday, after dumping the tank. First helping the staff check to make sure no waste canisters had split or leaked during the chaos; then threading the portal doors back to Haumea station. Media drones had caught the roof buckling and the snowy air screaming into fissures as the panels were sucked down into the massive emergency vent. Everyone assumed the tanks had imploded. It took Connexion's PR team a while to calm fears and reassure everyone that ED had worked their usual miracle, preventing a radiation leakage from contaminating the surrounding area. Under Dokal's forceful guidance, the PR team underplayed the potential damage level, emphasizing that the debris would have only been mildly radioactive medical waste.

The news streams ignored that modesty and started playing old Chernobyl videos. By that time, Callum and the crew were all back in Brixton, kicking back in their office, cheering and jeering at the deluge of alarmist reports. *If only you knew*, he thought smugly. After that, they all went out for a quiet celebratory drink.

The shower helped a little. But he took four ibuprofen as soon as he got out. Washed down with half a carton of fresh orange juice he found in the fridge. A fully stocked fridge. 'Oh, thank Christ for that.' He slapped bacon rashers into the pan. Plenty of bread today, so two bacon sandwiches. Two mugs of extra strong coffee to go with them.

Found some clean clothes. Shoved the entire dirty laundry pile into the housekeeping service's bags – they could sort everything out, and screw the extra cost – and left them outside his door for pick-up.

Then he sat back down at the breakfast bar and took a couple of paracetamol, because a paramedic ex had told him it was okay to mix them with ibuprofen. Wasn't quite up to the walk to the Young Street hub yet. Couldn't be arsed to watch the overnight news streams. If there was anything bad, ED would have called him in.

He slipped on his screen sunglasses. 'Hey, Apollo, any calls or emails from Savi?

'No.'

'Ping her mInet for me, pal.'

'No response.'

'Bastard.'

Callum didn't get it. *Six bloody days and not a single minute away from dumb student radical eyes?* Maybe it'd all been some kind of con. She'd married him for his money, and the whole Diana Klub staff were in on it. They jacked a couple of romance-bewitched tourists every month, laughing as they cashed in his . . . his what? All he had was good prospects. *Can't take that to the bank.*

He shook his head wearily. 'Grow up, you moron,' he grunted angrily.

It was clear what his brain was doing – trying to deny the obvious conclusion. *Something's happened. Something bad.*

'Apollo?'

'Yes, Cal.'

'Set up a new news filter. Find any female students fitting Savi's description, but not her name, reported missing from campus in the last six days.'

'Which campus, Cal?'

He shrugged. 'All of them.'

'On the planet?'

I'm paranoid. But am I paranoid enough? 'Yes,' he sighed. 'Everything on Earth.'

'That might take a while. May I purchase additional processor time?'

'Do it.'

*

When he walked into the crew's office, he might have laughed at the state of Alana and Colin – except he didn't exactly occupy the moral high ground. Besides, he suspected he looked even worse than they did. Their sunglasses weren't as dark as his. Raina looked as lively and peppy as she always did. And he was sure he had a memory of her matching his vodka shots. There was even a vague recollection of a cocktail glass alight with blue flame.

Raina gave him a weary, sympathetic smile. 'How's it going, chief?'

'Still alive. Why aren't you hungover?'

'Younger, smarter, know where to score better drugs.'

'Bastard,' he grumbled.

Moshi was at the small kitchen bar in the corner, washing down pills with a big mug of tea. He hadn't shaved, and Callum was pretty sure he was wearing the same shirt as yesterday. 'Morning,' Moshi said, and slumped back into one of the settees, before closing his eyes.

For Henry it was just another morning, and all was well with the world. But then Henry had been a responsible adult last night, and gone home before midnight to be with his expectant partner.

Callum looked through the glass wall into the M&C Centre. Fitz grinned and gave him a mocking two-finger salute. Callum responded with one finger.

'Okay.' Callum tried to focus on the news streams running across the wallscreens. One of the central pair was still showing the Gylgen facility; there'd been a heavy snowfall overnight, covering some of the more blatant damage to the building. 'What have we got?'

'Why do we care?' Moshi asked, his eyes still closed.

'Nothing even close to interesting,' Raina said. 'Especially no plutonium scares today.'

Callum gave her an irritated glance. He knew she'd find out eventually. But she needed to be smarter about it, particularly inside their own office. *Does Security bug us?*

Dokal walked in, and took a disapproving look round the human wreckage. 'Jesus Christ, guys. You're supposed to be professionals. Couldn't you even wait till the weekend?'

'We'll probably have saved the world twice more by then,' Moshi said.

'Not in this state, you won't. Are you actually active-ready?'

'Alternatively,' Raina said, 'well done for yesterday, everyone; Connexion is delighted, so I come bringing news of your enormous thank-you bonus.'

'There are two other crews on shift,' Callum said. 'If we get called after them, we'll be ready.'

Dokal gathered herself up for a rebuke. Relented. 'Actually, Corporate's appreciation will manifest in your next salary payment.'

There was some feeble cheering from around the office. Only Henry looked genuinely grateful. But then recently he'd been telling Callum horrific stories of how much new baby gear cost.

'Cal, a word.'

'Yes, ma'am.' He followed her out of the office.

Dokal gave him a closer inspection. 'Damn. The state of you.'

'Hey, it's mild hangover, okay? I'm entitled.'

'Yes, but you're not as young as you were.'

'Bloody hell, don't you start.'

'At least your hair is normal today.' She gave his clothes a final inspection, and sighed in disappointment. 'Come on, someone wants to meet you.'

'Who?' Callum asked.

'You'll see. But let me tell you, your upcoming bonus is going to reflect the company's sincere appreciation of how you handled yesterday. There were some very senior people watching the feeds from the M&C.'

'You didn't tell me.'

'Would it have helped improve your operation?'

'No,' he admitted.

Four portal doors in Connexion's internal hub network, and Cal found himself stepping out into a huge construction site. He knew it was London's Greenwich Peninsula before Apollo threw the Hubnav data onto his screen glasses. The old arena dome had been demolished two years ago, to colossal news stream coverage. Now he was standing about ten metres below ground level, a circular pit with metal retaining walls and a floor of frosty mud. Big construction vehicles rumbled around him, some of them manually operated, the drivers sitting in high cabs, using small joysticks to control their machinery. In the cold morning light, it was a slice of a post-apocalypse world ruled by steampunk dinosaurs.

'He's over here,' Dokal said, and set off across the mud.

Callum followed, realizing that this was probably the first time he'd seen her out of heels. She led him over to a group of suits who looked even more out of place in the pit than he did. Then he caught sight of who was standing in the centre of them.

'You might have warned me,' he grumbled.

'What? The man who saves the world before lunch every day, scared?'

'Fuck you.'

'Remember, don't smile too wide for the photographer, you'll look insincere. But do smile. Oh, and be respectful.'

'I'm always—'

The praetorian guard of lawyers, accountants, architects and PAs parted. Ainsley Baldunio Zangari looked round in interest. The side of his mouth lifted in wry acknowledgement. 'Callum!' His voice was like a shout as he put his hand out in greeting.

Just like the news streams.

'Good to meet you, son,' Ainsley said, shaking hands effusively. 'People, this is Callum, who saved our collective asses yesterday.'

The entourage finally mustered smiles of approval.

'Let's him and me get a picture here, for history's sake.'

The entourage spread out as if they'd been threatened by a cattle prod. Callum saw one of them, in a slightly cheaper suit than the rest, stand directly in front of him, adjusting his screen glasses. To one side, Dokal mouthed 'smile' with a furious expression.

Callum slowly produced a lopsided grin and said: 'Honour to meet you, sir.'

'Good man.' Ainsley's smile got even wider and his other hand clamped down on Callum's shoulder.

Callum felt ridiculous. Ainsley was sixty-one, with thick silver fox hair and a large frame that wasn't entirely apparent beneath a suit that was superbly cut to de-emphasize his bulk. Cal couldn't tell if it was fat or muscle; could have gone either way. And here he was in what media trolls would caption as a wrestling lock – or worse – with his boss, the richest man there'd ever been.

'Give us a moment,' Ainsley said. And the entourage melted away faster than an ice cube dropped on lava. 'Good job yesterday, Callum. I appreciate it.'

His hand and shoulder were released. 'Just doing my job, sir.'

'Shit.' The jovial patriarch persona vanished. 'You ain't a kiss-ass, are you, son?'

Callum took a moment and glanced at the nearest group of the entourage, which included Dokal, all clustered together and care-fully not looking in his direction. 'No. I live for this shit. I fucking saved Sweden from a nuclear catastrophe – well, me and my crew. You don't know what that is. But it's my life, and it's the best.'

Ainsley grinned. 'And you, son, have no idea how envious I am. These dicks that can only say yes –' his hand waved round the pit – 'this is my life. Don't worry, I'm not going to come ride-along with you. Insurance for one thing, and the board would go apeshit.'

'Each to his own.'

'Yeah, but seriously: thanks for yesterday. Fucking Brits, can you believe that? Don't they get plutonium is a century past its sell-by date?'

'They were trying to get rid of it.'

'Ha! Fucking Johnston; you shake hands with him, son, you count your fingers afterwards. Nations are dissolving; Connexion's made sure of that. Everyone's a neighbour now. It's not a race to kill each other any more. We're off to the stars instead. How about that? You going to emigrate when the starships reach a proto-Earth exoworld?'

'Dunno. Depends how long it takes to terraform one.'

'Yeah. I just got back from Australia yesterday, you know. Icefall was impressive, even by my standards.'

Callum hoped he wasn't looking too blank and stupid right now. He vaguely recalled seeing something about Icefall on a pub's news stream late last night as a fickle media finally moved on from Gylgen.

Apollo threw up details – a Connexion media briefing. It was one of Ainsley's pet projects, irrigating the central Australian desert. 'I heard it started well,' Callum said uncertainly.

'Certainly did, apart from some dickhead protestors trying to spoil progress like they always do.'

'Right.'

'The beauty of it is: we can spin Icefall as a grand humanitarian project, but actually it's planetary engineering one-oh-one. That's why I'm really backing it. Get some experience in. This way we'll be ready to make the truly big decisions when the time comes. And it will.'

'I guess it's reassuring to know someone's planning for the genuine long term.'

'That's why I'll never make it as a politician; I want to actually achieve something in life.'

Callum put his hands on his hips and regarded the cluster of hulking machinery that was seeding piles deep into the pit floor. 'I'd call this achievement.'

'Bullshit, son. This is a just a building. Egyptians and Incas were building big shit three thousand years ago. Sure, it's gonna be impressive – Connexion's European grand hub and headquarters, never going to be anything else. But it's already three years behind schedule and we ain't properly started. Fucking bureaucrats here . . . Jeez, I thought they were bad in the US. You been to New York, son? The tower I'm putting up next to Central Park is going to be a real statement, like this one. But at the end of the day: just a pile of concrete and glass.'

'Are you going to put Emergency Detox in here?'

'Fuck knows. I leave the small shit to assholes in the office ten floors under mine. Let them worry about it. I'm the concepts and deals guy.'

Callum laughed. 'Now I'm starting to envy you.'

'Yeah, it's a long way from New Jersey to here. Not that I was ever New Jersey trash. Did you know that?'

'Your father was a hedge fund manager.'

'And I followed him to Wall Street and made the right investment, huh?'

'No, your Harvard degree was in machine intelligence. You liquidated your inheritance to set up Connexion.'

Ainsley nodded in satisfaction, as if Callum had just passed a test. 'Not just a college jock on a rodeo ride at my expense.'

'Sir?'

'You're smart, son, and I don't mean your degree. How many of your crew know about the big boss without their mInet throwing it up?'

'Some.'

'But you did, and that counts. We're expanding, Callum, the human race. And Connexion is going to make it possible. The asteroid habitats were just the start. How did you feel when *Orion* reached the Centauri system?'

'Happy and disappointed: I was hoping for a decent exoplanet in orbit.'

'Likewise, son. Zagreus was well named; that is one crappy little loser of an exoplanet. But we didn't let that stop us, no, not this time. We went into that goddamn useless star system hard and built us another wave of starships. That's what our society is these days. We've got the balls to look outward and dream like JFK again. Fuck, that makes me proud to be human. One of those new starships will find us somewhere worth terraforming, and if it doesn't, then the following wave will, or the twentieth wave. It doesn't matter. We are going to build new worlds out there, son, and Connexion is going to take you out to the stars – you and a billion others desperate for a fresh start on a new planet. Twenty years' time, you'll be standing on this very same spot, and you'll be able to walk into our interstellar hub and step onto one of a dozen planets that we've tamed. Connexion is going to be huge. It's going to span the whole fucking galaxy one day.'

'It's pretty big now, sir.'

'Sure. But this one solar system is just the start. And if the company is going to grow the way I know it can, I'm going to need me some real smart tough bastards to wrestle it into shape for me. What do you say to that?'

It was probably the hangover damping his emotions down, but Callum was pleased with himself for not overreacting. He just kept his cool, and said, 'You offering me a job, Mr Zangari?'

Ainsley chortled. 'Oh, I like you, son, sure enough. But no. No fancy job offer. Not today. What I'm saying is enjoy your macho time in ED these next few years, and watch out for the next generation who'll rise up like fucking crocodiles to snap at your heels. Then, when the time comes you're tired of the sound of those teeth getting closer and you apply to go on senior management courses or maybe do an MBA, you'll find Connexion is supportive. You're what I'm looking for, son. Don't get headswell, now; I talk to a hundred like you a week. But you got yourself noticed and approved yesterday. No small thing in an organization this size.'

'Duly noted, sir, and thank you.'

Ainsley put his hand out again. 'Okay. Now I need people to say yes to me again.'

Callum's smile stayed in place as he walked back through all four portal doors to the ED office where the crew was waiting.

'Ainsley fucking Zangari?' Alana yelled. 'Himself?'

'Yeah.'

'What did you say? Wait! What did he say?' Moshi demanded.

'He said: Well done. Said to thank you guys, too. Christ knows why.'

'What's he like?' Raina asked.

'Same as on the news streams. Loud.'

'Holy shit. Did he know our names, too?'

'I don't know. Probably. You'll be in the report file – under mine.'

'Fuck off!'

Callum laughed and went to make himself some tea. The pills had squashed his hangover now, and he'd had too much coffee already. His crew chatted away happily behind him. The richest man who'd ever been, their boss, knew they existed, and was pleased with their work. *So how big is the bonus, do you think?*

He sank back into a settee facing the glass wall into the M&C, giving the news streams a proper look this time and getting Apollo to summarize potential problems. It seemed the world of toxicity problems wasn't too dangerous today.

When he thought back to the meeting, it still seemed slightly surreal. *I could have mentioned Savi, told Ainsley we'd got married. He would have congratulated me. That way there'd have been no way Security could have kicked up about it, not with him approving. Except . . . he'd see me as a troublemaker. Probably blow my chances of getting fast-tracked to the top.*

Why doesn't she just fucking call?

Dokal sat down beside him. 'Congratulations.'

'Cheers.'

'I mean it. Ainsley does that to about three people a year.'

'Huh? He said he sees a hundred a week just like me.'

'Who'd have thought it?' She smiled softly. 'Someone like that not telling the whole truth.'

'Wow!'

'Well don't forget us when you're lording it over Connexion's whole northern hemisphere operations in twenty years' time.'

Callum turned to look at her, wondering just how far her corporate loyalty went. They'd always got on well, but . . . she was ambitious. And now she knew he was a favourite, she might be agreeable to some mutual backscratching. *I only need some advice.* 'We're at Donington this weekend. Come along if you've got a spare hour. Be good to see you there again.'

Her smile was endearing; he didn't get to see it very often. 'Thanks, Cal. Is Savi going? I liked her.'

'Hands off, she's my girlfriend.'

'Well, try and use your brain for once. She's a keeper.'

He knew he was blushing, and didn't care. 'Yeah, I figured that.'

*

Callum made it past the Craner Curves and throttled back into Old Hairpin. He leant into it, and the Ducati 999 followed the track like it was a rail. *You beautiful machine, you.* Through Starkeys Bridge, and he opened the throttle again. The twin cylinder engine roared like a small rocket. The instrument panel blurred as the bike accelerated hard. He wasn't wearing screen lenses. This was all about authenticity. Didn't need precise readings; he *felt* the bike.

Slowing to take the bastard sharp McLeans turn, he was slicing close to the patch of crumbling tarmac and slowed another fraction, weaving wide. A Kawasaki ZX-17B shot past him, followed by an Aprilia RSV4 1000. 'Shit!' he screamed into his helmet mic. Throttled up hard – too much for the turn – and had to brake. Losing even more ground.

'Shit! Shit! Shit!'

'What's up, Cal?' Alana asked in his headphones.

'Overtaken,' he called out in frustration.

Gunned the throttle again and charged at Coppice for the turn into the long Dunlop Straight. Opened the Ducati full, and revelled in the sheer power as the landscape stretched out into streaks of colour on both sides. Focus spot was the track and the screaming bikes ahead. But they were throttled up full, and just as fast. He wasn't going to catch them.

Four laps left. He did okay. Didn't slip any further down the field. But his edge was gone, and he knew it.

Nine days now, and nothing. Something's happened to her. This is serious. How bad is student radicalism these days? How violent do they get?

Chequered flag waving on the gantry overhead. Ninth place; there were only fifteen bikes in the race. He took the slow lap round to the exit, and drove through the paddock. The support vehicles parked in long lines down the tarmac lanes were even more antique than the Ducati. Spectators enjoyed them almost as much as they did the bikes. People were wandering along, wrapped against the cold February air, gawping at the old camper buses and engineering caravans, parents pointing out shapes and company badges to semi-interested children.

Callum's team had an old Mercedes Sprinter van converted to a mobile workshop for the Ducati. It was parked down at the far end of the paddock, opposite the Redgate turn. Colin and Henry had set up an awning beside it, covering their collapsible chairs. A barbecue stood just outside, where Henry was turning the sausages.

Callum tried not to grin at Henry's expectant-father routine. After all, it had been an excited Henry who originally found the bike on a specialist auction site eighteen months ago, just as Callum was appointed crew leader. They'd formed a syndicate, all of them chipping in for the privilege of riding the superb old machine at rallies and club meetings. Between them they could afford it. As they'd soon found out, though, it wasn't the initial cost that was the problem, but the maintenance upkeep. And, as for the price of specially synthesized petrol . . .

Callum parked the Ducati and took off his helmet.

'So was that a good result?' Dokal asked with apparent innocence. She was sitting under the awning next to her girlfriend, Emillie, both of them with a can of beer.

'We need to have a handicap scheme for these club meetings,' Callum said gruffly. 'Some of those bikes are more powerful than the Ducati. They're a lot younger, too.'

'That's the spirit, chief,' Raina said. She came out of the back of the Sprinter, zipping up her leathers. 'I'm going to have a couple of practice laps before my race, okay?'

'All yours.' Callum dismounted, trying not to make old-man grunts as his legs protested. 'Watch out for the tarmac at McLeans and Redgate. There's a patch starting on Craner, too.'

'Thanks.' She swung her leg over the saddle and started the engine.

'Should you be racing on broken tarmac?' Emillie asked in a light French accent.

Callum shifted his gaze from a fabulous scarlet and black Yamaha YZF-10R on the other side of the paddock lane. 'Huh? Oh, the track owners do their best. There's only so much they can charge to hire Donington for a day. We're just enthusiasts, that's all. It took three clubs combined to fund today.'

'Owners have a legal responsibility. They can get into all kinds of trouble with negligence, all the way up to corporate man-slaughter.'

'Drivers sign a waiver before we go out.'

'I'm not sure that's good enough.'

'Excuse my friend,' Dokal said. 'You can take the girl out of the risk assessment department . . .'

'Just saying,' Emillie replied with a pout.

'Test of skill,' Callum told her. 'I'm going to get these leathers off. Henry, how are we doing?'

'Fifteen minutes, and we're eating.'

'Roger that. Where's Katya?'

'Too tired,' Henry said. 'But she sent her salmon quiche.' He pointed at the foil-wrapped flan on the camping table.

'Now you're talking.' Callum went into the dark Sprinter and struggled out of his leathers, trying not to jab elbows into the racks of tools along one side.

'Not like you,' Dokal said. 'Ninth place?'

He glanced over at her as she stood in the van's open doorway. 'I wasn't concentrating,' he admitted.

'I can see that. Have you and Savi broken up?'

'No.' Callum shook his head. 'Quite the opposite.' He started to explain.

Dokal's hand covered her wide-open mouth. 'Married?' she squeaked, when he'd finished. 'Seriously?'

'Deadly so.'

'That's wonderful.' She came over and gave him a hug, smiling widely. 'You old romantic. How long have you been going out? Two months?'

'When you know, you know.'

'Callum Hepburn, a married man. Who'd have thought it?'

'Thanks.'

'Are you going to have a proper reception? Oh. please say yes. I love weddings! Her parents are quite old-style, aren't they? What did they say?'

'There's a few . . . formal issues we have to settle first. I wanted to talk them over with you.'

'Of course.'

'Human Resources, for a start.'

She closed her eyes for a long moment, dropping right back into her corporate lawyer mode. 'They'll grumble, but don't worry about them. They only have that notification procedure in case an injured party goes all hypersensitive and fires off a workplace sexual harassment suit. You two didn't – quite the opposite: happy-ever-after ending.'

'Yeah.' He scratched the back of his neck, pulling an awkward face. 'But she's in Security. They take it all a lot more seriously.'

Dokal grinned evilly. 'My oh my. You should have been vetted. What will they find?'

'I'm not bothered about being vetted. It's the not telling them earlier when we should have bit that's the problem. I don't want a black mark on her file.'

'That's easy. Companies aren't allowed to do that any more.'

'What?'

'It's discriminatory. As an employee, you have the right to see your full file, including disciplinary entries – which you can challenge in tribunal if you think said remarks are having an undue negative impact on your career prospects. If the tribunal agrees they're disproportionate, they can be wiped. And they can't be handed on to a subsequent employer, either.'

'Really?'

'Yes. That's why HR chiefs are always networking so hard with recruitment agency account managers. And why Corporate treads but softly on their entertainment expenses. A lot of shitlists get passed over in bars.'

'Bloody hell! I didn't know that.'

'You have a long way to go before you're ready to sit behind a desk, don't you?'

'So it would seem.'

'I know some people in HR who deal with Security personnel issues. I can have a quiet word. Best to get this kind of bollocks smoothed out before it even happens.'

'Would you?'

She smiled. 'You have to pick up my bar tab.'

'Deal. And thanks.'

'I'm just looking after number one. Ainsley thinks the sun shines out of your arse, remember?' She winked. 'Leave it with me.'

*

Savi walked through the international hub and straight into Rome's Municipio III metro network. Five hubs later and she was out on Via Monte Massico, a sloping road in the Tufell area, lined by high trees which partially obscured the five-storey apartment blocks on both sides. Sunlight was only just beginning to filter through the boughs which interlaced above the pavement, forming a verdant tunnel.

She loved Rome, but at this time of year and this early in the morning, it was almost as damp and cold as Edinburgh. The only difference was the trees here were all evergreens, though even those in the sheltered yard at the front of her apartment block seemed lacklustre right now, waiting for the warmer spring air to pep them up.

Her apartment was on the second floor, so she ignored the creaky old lift and climbed the stairs, her bugez lumbering along after her. She'd chosen the one-bedroom place for its compact size. Nice for one person to live in by herself, especially after twenty-three years crammed into a comfortable Mumbai house with a large family. Here there was quiet and solitude. Family was welcome to visit, but wouldn't be able to stay.

The house G4Turing had used its flock of drudgez to vacuum the carpets and clean the surfaces while she was away on her

Caribbean break, even polishing the centrepiece rosewood table properly. When she got to the galley kitchen, the fridge was properly stocked. She took out the pot of organic yogurt and fresh milk, then measured out a cafetiere with natural ground beans from the delicatessen two streets away.

After a quick shower to wash away the last of Barbuda's insidious sand she put on a robe and went back into the tiny kitchen. The yogurt had lost its chill, the way she liked it, and the coffee had brewed properly. She sprinkled granola into a bowl and poured the yogurt on top.

After four days of indulgent, large, and highly Westernized breakfasts delivered to the Diana Klub villa's balcony, it was quite a relief to come home to this. The memory made her hold up her hand and admire the single gold ring she was now wearing.

I'm married!

While she ate breakfast, she told Nelson, her mInet, to run the Icefall news streams. Preparations were well underway for the first fall day. Connexion's giant airships were buzzing along a kilometre above Australia's Gibson Desert in a careful holding pattern. Further south, in Antarctic waters, the harvester boats were circling Iceberg V-71, which had broken off the Ross Ice Shelf three months ago. It was a colossus, with a surface area of almost three thousand kilometres, making it larger than Luxembourg. Nelson refined the filter for any mention of opposition groups, political or active. There were a few global and Australia-based ecological groups posting about the sacrilege on social media, but not much of that was relayed by the mainstream. The Walungurru People's Review was more strident, but wasn't saying anything new.

As always, the prospect of jobs and fresh money pouring into the outback *now* was winning the day. Deserts didn't have many committed friends in 2092.

Savi checked the time and went back into the bedroom. The bugez was standing obediently at the foot of the bed. She opened the luggage panniers and carefully placed all her dirty linen into the laundry basket ready for the concierge service to collect. Her lips twitched – *not that I wore much.*

She gazed at the gold ring again, and very reluctantly took it off. It went into her jewellery box in the bedside cabinet. Cal had promised an engagement ring as soon as her assignment finished. 'I know we did it backwards, but you still deserve the set.'

I miss him already. It shouldn't have happened, but I'm so glad it did. Maybe it is true: opposites attract. Except we're not really that different. He's smart, and funny, which is more than most men. And considerate, and over-sensitive in that way Western men can be. She sighed. *And behaves like a sixteen-year-old half the time. Which is quite fun.*

Her gaze was drawn to the bed. Cal had stayed over several times, which left her with some memories . . .

Stop it!

She dressed in neutral clothes. Blue denim jeans and a thick purple roll-top sweater. Flat-soled pumps and a simple leather bag. Long hair plaited with practised efficiency. To finish, she slipped into a pair of wire-rimmed screen glasses. Inspected herself in the mirror and nodded in satisfaction. Nothing special, nothing that would draw attention in a crowd. One of hundreds of thousands of identical young women thronging through Rome's metrohubs, on their way to their corporate office to fend off another day's over-familiarity from male managers.

Outside, the sun was making progress up the sky. Sharp bright beams were slicing through the canopy of leaves as she walked back to the hub on the junction with Via Monte Eporneo. Five hubs took her to the centre, where she switched to the national network. The Naples hub had a portal door into Connexion's internal network. Eight hubs later she emerged onto the ground floor of a skyscraper in Sydney's central business district.

The glass walls of the big lobby looked out onto a night-time city, with pedestrian roads long since cleared of clubbers. Even with the air conditioning thrumming away, she could feel the heat radiating in from the concrete pavements outside. A night watchman glanced up from his desk and gave her a quick wave.

She got into the lift, and sensors performed a deep scan. Only then did the lift take her up to the fifteenth floor; the Security offices.

Here, Australia's time zone didn't apply. The fifteenth floor was wrapped in one-way glass that stopped anyone looking in, day or night, so nobody could see a department that kept the same operational level 24/7. Its layout of corridors and offices was similar to any of the commercial departments in the building, but instead of the usual conference rooms there were armouries and special equipment centres. Right at the centre, through another two sets of safe checks, was the active ops centre.

Australia's head of station's office was next to it. The door slid open to allow Savi in.

Yuri Alster looked up from the semicircle of screens on his desk. 'You're late,' he said.

'No, I'm not.' Savi didn't much like Yuri. Thankfully, that wasn't a requirement of the job, but she certainly respected his toughness. His infiltration operations brought impressive results. She'd been on two of them so far and seen first-hand how his field agents were deployed to maximum effect. It didn't matter what a new operative's file said, or how well they'd done in training and simulations. Yuri was only interested how they performed in the field. If anyone showed emotional weakness they were out, and he made sure your first mission would slam you straight up against cutting moral dilemmas.

For her first operation, he'd given Savi a case involving two brothers who were trying to sting a Connexion manager to pay for their mother's medical treatment. The woman had a brain tumour that needed some very expensive drugs. Savi always suspected he'd known her own mother had been treated for cancer, even though it wasn't on her file. She hadn't wavered. The brothers had got seven years for attempted extortion. Their mother had died eight months later.

'I hope you enjoyed yourself,' he said. 'We have the plastic explosive ready for you. Technical Support tweaked the formula, so it's only ten per cent as powerful as the real stuff. Even so, be careful around it.'

'That's good. Should prevent too much damage. Thank Tech Support for me.'

'You got a cover story?'

'Yes, sir.' She half-expected him to ask for it. But this wasn't high school, and she wasn't sitting an exam. A cover story was required, so a cover story for her short absence had been fabricated to tie in with her fake identity. It hadn't taken her long.

'All right.' He tilted back in his chair. Savi just knew she was being judged. He treated everyone like that – with suspicion. Rumour around the department said he was ex-Russian Federal Security. He'd been in the border security department of the Russian National Portal Transport Company when it merged with Connexion; plenty of his colleagues had been made redundant, but he'd made it through the reorganization and come out in a strong position. Connexion Security approved of his methods and the efficient way he ran his intelligence-gathering agents, infiltrating them into anti-Connexion groups. 'When are you going back in?' he asked her.

'Right away. Akkar wanted the charges by tomorrow, so I'm guessing their attack will be timed for first fall. Maximize the publicity.'

'Okay. So you know, Ainsley himself will be at Kintore, for the starting ceremony.'

'Shit.'

'Which means Poi Li will be there.' His finger pointed at the wall between him and the active ops centre. 'Making very sure no one gets near Ainsley, especially anyone hauling plastic explosives around. So this needs to go right, or we'll both be hunting new jobs.'

'Got it.'

'If the charges are for a suicide vest, we need to know right away.'

'I don't think that's what Akkar is planning. But I'll update you via micropulse. Tech Support seeded Kintore with relays, so I can shout from anywhere in the town. Akkar's group don't have the tech to spot that.'

'Let's hope.'

'I know them. They're dedicated politicals and greens, several hotheads busting for a fight, even some good technos and hacktivists, but they're not at this level.'

'Yes, I read your report.'

Of course you did, she thought. In a way, it was reassuring. She was almost tempted to blurt out that she was married – *Just get it over with*. But she couldn't risk him pulling her off the case until Cal was vetted. Procedure was Yuri's bible.

'Sir.' She got up to leave.

'What did you do?'

'Excuse me?'

'Your long weekend off. What did you do?'

'I went to the Caribbean. With a girlfriend; she thinks I'm a company economics analyst. We stayed at a spa, had a lot of treatments and drank cocktails in the beach bar. It was relaxing. Just what I needed.'

'Uh huh.' He returned to the semicircle of screens. 'Well, make sure you don't smell nice when you get back to Kintore. Poverty-line cause-committed politics students don't go on middle-class spa breaks. Remember, it's the simplest things that can derail an op.'

'Yes, sir. Thank you.' Savi couldn't even summon up a mental sneer. He was quite right.

She went down to the prep facility. In the changing room she deactivated Nelson and put her gold smartCuff (a present from her father when she got the Connexion job) on her locker's top shelf, along with her screen glasses. Poor Cal would go slowly crazy when she didn't call, but she'd make it up to him. Next she stripped down to nothing, hanging up her jeans and sweater; pumps went on the floor of the locker. She shut the door, keying it to her fingerprint, leaving Savi Chaudhri hanging in limbo alongside her clothes.

Time for Osha Kulkarni, disaffected politics student, to return to the cause and fight capitalist imperialism with the only tools the corporate fat cats ever took seriously. Osha's clothes were in the next locker, exactly where she'd left them, unwashed. Heavily used olive-green jeans, a brown sleeveless T-shirt. Trainers with soles almost worn through. Kangaroo-skin outback hat – though no corks dangling round the rim; she drew the line at that cliché. Cheap screen sunglasses with audio facility. A decades-old watch which seemed to be running a three-year-old mInet program tagged Misra, which bloated the strap's ancient processor. Finally, a backpack that'd been bleached several shades lighter by the sunlight of three continents.

Sometimes she worried that Osha fitted the angry young woman profile a little too well.

Tech Support after the changing room, and there was Tarli waiting for her, yawning heavily. He held up a pair of resealable plastic food boxes.

'Your explosives. Please be careful with this stuff.'

Smiling, she took the boxes from them and started putting them in her backpack, under her spare clothes. 'I thought it was only TNT which blows up when you drop it.'

'I'm sure it is. But just don't make any sudden moves while you're next to me.'

'You take such good care of me, Tarli.'

'I do, don't I? Okay, let's run your super-spy kit.'

She held her arm out. Tarli swept a scanner over her hand, his eyes dream-staring as he watched the data thrown up in his contact screen lenses.

'All right, your tracker grain is good. We can trigger a ping anytime if we need to. We'll always be able to find you, Savi. So you're safe.'

'Fine. And Osha's mInet?'

'Old crappy and slow if anyone takes a keen interest. But level two is running in parallel underneath. You can use it to compose a message and squirt it out in a micropulse. Your *antique* watch is the primary. But if they're properly paranoid, you'll be told not to wear it on the mission, so the tracker grain will take over. Give active ops a test call, please.'

'Misra?' she asked, subvocalizing for her audio grain. 'Give ops a location ping.'

'Confirmed,' Misra replied.

'Got you, Savi,' the level voice of active ops replied. 'Full reception.'

She nodded at Tarli, trying to rein in her nerves. 'Thank you.' It was always bad just before she hit the street, heart pumping away, anxiety making her jumpy. Once she was out there and the assignment was underway she'd smooth out fine.

'Hey, I'm going to be in the active ops centre myself when this one hits the fan,' Tarli said. 'Don't worry, I've got your back.'

'Good to know.'

'Come on, I'll walk you through to Brisbane.'

They went through four hubs to a Connexion subsidiary building in Brisbane. Outside, the sun was starting to rise. The Brisbane Security office was a locked room that had a single portal inside.

'Good luck,' Tarli said. 'You're on truck Eight-Five-One. Pete's driving it.'

'Got it.'

'Go get 'em.'

The portal came out in a toilet cubical. She unbolted the door and looked round. It was inside a metal cargo container, one of six identical cubicles. Nobody about. When she closed it, the bolt slid back, locking it. There was an Out of Order sign pinned to the door.

She went outside into a swirl of warm dusty air. The old portable toilet container had been dropped next to a high chain fence that enclosed an area almost eight kilometres across: the North Brisbane Commercial and Government Services Transport hub (C&GST). She thought it looked like a protective pen for endangered vehicles. There was hardly any greenery, just an expanse of tracks worn into rust-red earth that had spent a decade being compacted beneath big pounding tyres until it reached the consistency of concrete. Various civil engineering companies had their own compounds staked out in the area, where big earth movers and civil construction machinery were parked. Container stacks were laid out in grids like small towns, with G4Turing-managed gantries lifting them on and off flatbed trucks.

Right in the middle of the transport hub was a broad ring of tarmac, as if a land reclamation team had forgotten to break up a chunk of old highway. Around the outside of the ring, its off ramps were just tongues of concrete leading to the tangle of dirt tracks snaking across the C&GST. The inner rim, however, hosted a circle of six-metre portals laid out like some modern homage to Neolithic standing stones. Even this early in the morning, trucks were rumbling round the tarmac, their powerful electric motors whining loud in the still dawn air as they drove in and out of the portals. Only a few had human drivers in their cabs, the rest were truckez.

Savi left the toilet container behind, walking across the hard rutted ground to the nearest container zone. She only saw a couple of other people wandering about, both in hi-viz jackets stained with the ruddy dust. If they saw her, they didn't pay any attention.

Misra threw a nav guide across her screen sunglasses, and she wound up at the end of a container row where a truck was parked on the loading pad. It had Eight-Five-One painted on the side of its cab. Someone (presumably Pete) sat inside, not looking down at her. She stood in the shade of the containers as the gantry slid along the row and carefully lowered a battered blue container onto the truck. Once the gantry moved away, Savi clambered up the couplings and found herself a ledge in the board gap between cab and trailer. She jammed her feet against some cable, bracing herself; the axle motors began buzzing, and Eight-Five-One moved off.

They drove along one of the tracks, heading for the big loop of tarmac. She breathed in the grubby air, relishing the role she was now immersing herself in.

If Callum could see me now.

He'd be having kittens, she knew. Maybe one day she'd tell him. When they were home and cosy. In twenty years' time. After he'd had a lot of beer.

She daydreamed about what they were going to do next. No way did she want to leave fabulous Rome, certainly not for freezing Edinburgh. The Scottish capital was pretty enough but even in summer it was bloody cold. And she certainly wasn't going to move into Cal's slob-out bachelor pad. He was going to need some serious house-training once they got a place together.

Savi nearly asked Misra for the *agenzie immobiliari* who'd found the Tufell flat for her, before she realized Misra wasn't the mInet storing that file, and Osha certainly wouldn't have had any reason to access it. The mistake chilled her mood. Yuri was right; it was the simple things that betrayed you.

Truckez adjusted their speed, allowing Eight-Five-One to slot into the stream of traffic going round the tarmac ring. A minute later they drove through the portal to Kintore. The town was half a continent away from Brisbane, so it was still the middle of the night there. Darkness closed around her and the temperature took a big leap upwards. Even growing up in India didn't acclimatize Savi for the scorching desert air. It was the lack of humidity, she'd realized the first time she came to Kintore. Desert air was dead air.

Originally Kintore had been a remote Northern Territory town, founded in the early 1980s by the Pintupi people, who resented the white Western culture that was slowly constricting them. After that it kept going in its quiet way for a century until the newly formed Water Desert consortium signed its deal with the investment-hungry Australian government.

Once again, the Pintupi suffered a massively disruptive invasion. For the last five years Kintore had expanded exponentially as Connexion set up the C&GST portal linking it to Brisbane, turning the town's abandoned airstrip into a huge cargo and civil engineering facility. Along with the heavy-duty earth-moving equipment pouring through the C&GST portal, truckez brought prefab cabins for the hardy site workers who didn't commute in every day from the coastal areas. Bars and clubs and stores followed the money trail, along with other services – some legitimate, some otherwise, all bringing in their own prefabs. With such a population bump, the government had started to expand its own infrastructure. And if Icefall was successful in transforming the desert, Kintore would double in size again within two years.

Eight-Five-One slowed down near the edge of the old airfield and Savi jumped down. The walk into town wasn't far, for which she was grateful. Kintore even had a tiny portal network of its own, but she didn't want to use it. Everyone knew Connexion had sensors around each of its hubs, scanning for illegal substances such as drugs and weapons. The plastic explosives would have brought a whole platoon of Urban Suppression forces down on her, probably with drone support. Most of Kintore's illegal drugs were brought in through the C&GST route by truck drivers. If she'd come through any other way, Akkar would have been suspicious.

She reached her digs – a new boarding house of silvered composite panels that'd been dropped down on the west side of town, identical to every other building on the street. There were still several hours until dawn, so she flopped down on her bed and turned the air con up. Five minutes later she was asleep.

*

Breakfast was a croissant in the Granite Shelf, one of the new cafes on what was now a long Main Street. A limp oblong of pastry that'd been microwaved for too long. The little cube of butter which came with it was as cold as ice. But the orange juice wasn't too bad. The waitress put it down with a semi-apologetic expression and hurried off to take an order from a group of digger drivers who'd just come off shift.

Savi gazed out of the window. The desert soil surrounding Kintore was rust red, broken only by wispy tufts of petrified grass, bleached to a cream-white by the relentless sun. Today, like every day for the last two years, the air was stained with dust. Somewhere out across the desert, massive irrigation canals were being dug. Hundreds of kilometres long, they were destined to channel water across the parched lands, allowing the desert to bloom again. If Icefall worked, it would ultimately become an oasis over a thousand kilometres across. Theoretically that would create its own new microclimate, changing wind patterns and luring in rainclouds from the coast.

But in the meantime, the powerful diggers working 24/7 were kicking up dust which lingered for days in the tranquil air. A lot of people had taken to wearing plastic surgical masks when they were outside. What with the empty canals, the locals had started to call the whole enterprise Barsoom. The Mars reference wasn't pleasantly ironic.

After she'd finished eating, Savi put on her own mask and tramped down Main Street for a kilometre before turning off onto Rosewalk. Akkar had a tiny store repairing air-conditioning units – possibly the greatest boom business in Kintore. The dust was forever clogging motors and filters across town, giving Akkar as much work as he chose to accept.

She knocked on the bugez garage door at the back, giving the camera on the frame above a mildly narked look. It opened, and she walked through into the gloomy composite cave. First glance revealed a typical printer store operation with metal shelving holding cartons of liquid crudes, plastics and metals, ready to feed the printers. One cabinet down the far end held phials of the more expensive crudes, those used to produce electronics or pharma. Medium-sized printers were lined up along the back wall, their central glass hatches making them look for all the world like a line of washing machines. Eye-twisting violet light shone out through the glass as they chittered away, building up components molecule by molecule in their extrusion cores. A couple of long benches held broken-down air conditioners and impressive racks of electronics.

Akkar was sitting at a battered office chair, using a small vacuum nozzle to clear a filter grid. He was a tall North African in his late thirties, with a shaved scalp and plenty of tattoos chasing up his neck from a muscular torso that was always wearing vintage T-shirts with the logos of long-departed gamer companies. The tails of those tattoos snaked out of his sleeves to coil round his arms. When he spoke, light would sparkle on the rubies embedded in his teeth. He was one of the few people who could make Savi nervous just by him looking at her. Like Yuri, he was perpetually judging everyone.

'Welcome back,' he said. 'I heard you got in early this morning.'

Savi glanced at the two other people in the garage. Dimon was a lot larger and even more menacing than Akkar, filling the role of lieutenant and enforcer. He never spoke much, and when he did it was in a whisper that emphasized his words more than any shout. Unlike most of Kintore's residents, he always wore a smart suit, which made him look like a former sports star.

Julisa sat in a chair next to Akkar, a twenty-two year old from

Cairns whose family used to run a crocodile farm just outside the town. Its bankruptcy and subsequent sale by the banks to developers hungry for such a prime chunk of land kicked her environmentalism into something approaching religious devotion, drawing her deeper into the movement until she reached the status of Akkar's cyber queen. She was painfully thin, surviving on caffeine and nose candy as far as Savi could tell. Bleached blonde hair was cut to an all-over centimetre bristle, giving her the face of an angry, strung-out pixie.

'I didn't tell anyone that,' Savi said. She was impressed as always by Akkar's intel. Given he refused to use the internet or any kind of mobile network to communicate with his radical friends, he had to have a pack of real people watching Kintore's barren streets. *At four o'clock in the morning?*

'I know.' He smiled. Violet printer light twinkled off his teeth jewels. 'Did you get it?'

Savi nodded, giving herself a long moment of satisfaction, showing them how pleased she was with herself, how committed. 'Sure.' She unslung her backpack and brought out the two plastic food boxes. 'Don't drop it,' she warned, as Julisa picked one up eagerly.

'You have interesting friends,' Dimon said.

'Who said they were friends?' she shot back.

Akkar held up a hand. 'You've done well, Osha. Thank you for bringing us this.'

'Does this get me in on the action?' she asked.

'Do you want to get into the action?'

'I want to do something, make people take notice of what's really going on here. Posting rants on MyLife don't do shit.'

He glanced over at Julisa, who had carefully opened one of the food boxes. She stuck a small sensor on it and glanced at the readout on a screen.

'Real,' she said.

'Okay,' Akkar said slowly. 'Three days' time.'

'First fall,' she said approvingly.

'Yes.'

'What do you want me to do?'

'Turn up here at eight. We'll give you something to do.'

'Okay.'

'Aren't you curious?'

She returned his gaze steadily. 'Yes, but I get how security works. If you don't know, you can't tell.'

'Smart girl. But I'll be asking you to plant some of this fine explosive you've brought us. Do you have a problem with that?'

'Just tell me, will I have to put it near people?'

'No. People are not the target. Life is sacred.'

'Okay.' She slung her backpack on again. 'Be seeing you.'

Savi walked home slowly and used Misra to message active ops.

I've been told the operation will happen on first fall. 90% certain that's for real. They're being cautious. I will be taking part. Details as soon as I find out what they're doing.

Misra sent it in a microsecond pulse while she was still on Main Street. Savi wouldn't have put it past Julisa to put e-surveillance round her digs.

An answering pulse came thirty seconds later.

Stay safe.

Yuri.

*

The gigantic earth-moving equipment digging canals across the desert stopped work at midnight before first fall day. Water Desert's PR agency hoped that would at least reduce the quantity of infernal red dust in the air by the time the great event began mid-morning, allowing cameras a decent view. All the big vehicles began driving across the desert to Kintore's airstrip field, where the contractors had scheduled them for maintenance.

A lot of people started arriving through Kintore's portals as dawn began to break, coming in not just from Australia's cities, but from across the globe. Icefall promised to be quite a spectacle.

From Kintore, they went through a newly installed portal to a viewing area that had been prepared ninety kilometres from the town. Long tents serving iced drinks and snacks had been set up, along with air-conditioned medical marquees ready for the inevitable heatstrokes. One of the dry canals ran close by, its three-hundred-metre width giving everyone a sense of the project's scale.

A temporary VIP stadium had been built inside a high-security fence, its overhanging roof protecting the dignitaries from the severe sunlight, but nothing could be done to keep the desert heat at bay. The forecast had it rising to thirty-three degrees Celsius by mid-morning.

Savi had never seen so many people in the desert town before. A month ago, Cal had taken her to a football match in Manchester. The crowds of boisterous supporters pouring into the stadium gates had been easier to push through than this. Everyone was heading along Main Street to the portal that would take them to the viewing area.

She made it to Akkar's store and went into the bugez garage. There were a dozen people inside, most of whom she recognized from the anti-Icefall meetings which Akkar had used to recruit them. These were his senior cell leaders, each of them in charge of around fifteen activists, as far as she'd been able to determine. *So, over a hundred and fifty mobilized for today, then.*

Julisa saw her and came over. 'You ready for this?'

'Sure.'

She was led to the back of the garage, where two young men were waiting beside the silent printers. They were introduced as Ketchell and Larik. 'We're relying on you three,' Julisa said in a low voice. 'You've got the second most critical role today.'

Which Savi didn't believe for a second. She knew she still wasn't fully trusted, that it would take several events like today to prove herself to them. *Events which are never going to happen, thanks to what I'm doing now.*

The lanky girl handed Savi a leather shoulder bag. The men were given small backpacks.

'Your target is the substation at the end of Fountain Street,' Julisa went on. 'That's where the whole town's electricity comes in via portal from the national grid. It's a huge amount of power; the damn thing supplies every piece of equipment Water Desert uses.

So, this is how it happens. There's a three-metre-high fence round the transformers and switching gear, which is topped by razor wire. There's one super-secure gate, which they've rigged with all sorts of scans and codes. We're not going in or over. You're going to blow a hole in the fence. The charge in your bag is armed by a dual-action switch. Look.'

Savi peered into the bag, seeing the neat cube of plastic explosive with a small rectangle of electronics on the end. The only feature was a red hexagonal switch that seemed disproportionally large.

'Turn clockwise one-eighty and press,' Julisa said. 'Okay? Simple: twist and press.'

'Got it.'

'Once it's armed it cannot be disarmed. I've set the timer to detonate at exactly ten fifty-seven local time. So at about ten fifty-five you stroll past the fence, arm the charge and drop the bag beside a post. Then you get away fast.'

'Okay.'

'Once the fence is breached, Ketchell and Larik, you're in there right away. Your targets are the two main transformers. Here.' She showed them a crude map of the substation, with the transformers marked. 'It's easy enough. Arm your backpacks. Drop you backpacks. They will detonate at eleven oh-three. Now, they're bigger charges than Osha's, but we've built in enough time for you to get in and out. Any questions?'

'That's it?' Savi asked.

'That's it. Look, this is all about distraction. The ice starts to fall at ten thirty. We've got a lot of supporters crowded into the viewing area. They'll start a protest demonstration at ten forty-five outside the VIP enclosure. Smoke bombs, netruptors, throw some stones at security – fuck knows there's enough rocks lying round. That's where Water Desert will be looking to protect their precious guests – all the celebrities, corporate fat cats and public pig parasites. So you get in and cut the power to the whole fucking town.'

'What good is that going to do?'

'You don't need to know.'

'Like bollocks! I never asked for details, but we're taking a huge risk here. For what? Cutting power to everyone's air conditioner for a few hours?'

'Problem?' Akkar asked. He was standing right behind her. She hadn't noticed him approach.

'No,' she said. 'I'm happy to help. I asked for this gig, remember? I just need some assurance this isn't a token statement.'

'It's not,' Akkar said softly. 'Trust me, Osha. Today is unique, and not because of Icefall. Today Water Desert has put a lot of its most expensive eggs in one basket. And thanks to Julisa's skills, we're going to crack them open. You will provide us with that window of opportunity.'

Savi gave him a hard glance. 'Okay,' she said. 'That sounds more like it.'

'Good luck,' he said. 'All of you. We'll meet back here in thirty-six hours.'

As she left the garage, she saw Dimon handing out homeprinted semi-automatic rifles to three other men. He saw her watching, and Savi gave him an approving nod. Dimon grinned in return.

Outside, Savi, Ketchell and Larik set off across town, avoiding Main Street and the crush of eager Icefall spectators.

'I've got my team waiting for instructions,' Larik said. 'How do you think we should deploy them?'

'Deploy them?' Savi said. 'We don't. You heard Julisa: this is the three of us.'

'Yeah, we have the primary task, sure,' Larik said. 'But what happens if there's a security patrol heading our way five minutes before we blast the fence? We need coverage. So whoever you think you are, you shut the fuck up and leave me to get on with my fucking job – of which you know fuck all. Clear?'

'The hell with you, dickbrain,' Savi pressed back on a smile, enjoying the way she'd been designated a necessary pain. He didn't realize it, but he now included her as part of the team. The only thing he'd suspect now was that she'd screw up. Posting lookouts might be a problem, though.

She composed a message for Misra to send.

Large group activity starting. Distraction protest planned for observation zone 10.45. I am on team assigned to blow the sub-station on Fountain Street. Explosives pre-set for 10.57 to take out fence. Transformers targeted for 11.03. Location of main target unknown. I've seen homeprinted semi-automatics handed out to group members.

Good work, came the answering micropulse. Do you know nature of main target?

Savi thought back. Exact target unknown, but it's a software attack, assembled by Julisa. The power cut will allow them access. Akkar said Water Desert has all its eggs in one basket. May be up to forty people involved.

Thanks. Analysing now. Watching you. Tarli.

Savi kept her gaze level as they tramped through Kintore's back-streets. But it was so tempting to look up at the sky and wave at whatever satellite or drone active ops was using to observe her.

They met up with several of Larik's team as they made their indirect way to the substation. Larik and Ketchell studied a street map of Kintore on their screen sunglasses and assigned people to various road junctions around Fountain Street. Savi immediately sent their locations to active ops.

By ten twenty, Kintore itself was practically deserted. Everyone who'd arrived to witness first fall was out at the observation zone, along with every local who was off duty. A news stream playing across Savi's screen sunglasses showed her the guests, including Ainsley Zangari himself, take their places in the VIP stand.

Down in the Antarctic, the five Connexion harvester boats closed on V-71. Ex-navy frigates, their prows had undergone a drastic profile alteration during the refit. Instead of a sleek wedge shape they were now bulging hemispheres ten metres wide, pre-senting the open maw of a portal to the frozen sea, like the mouth of a giant whale. Below the hull, two extra sets of newly installed propellers turned slowly, their huge electric motors powered from the global power grid via portal. They weren't designed to give the harvesters extra speed. Rather, their phenomenal torque allowed them to push the vessel forwards relentlessly.

At just after ten thirty, the first harvester reached the sheer cliff of blue ice, its captain curving round so the portal rim grazed the surface at a thin angle, but then immediately sliced deeper inwards. The propellers spun up, maintaining the ship's speed and momentum as fractured ice began to fall into the portal. For a brief moment, desert sunlight shone out of the gaping hemisphere, then the front of the harvester was almost completely buried in the cliff. Yet it continued to churn along parallel to the ice, gouging out a nine-metre-wide gash. Behind it, the second harvester struck the cliff at a similar angle, its portal biting deep.

In the desert observation zone, people squinted up into the glaring sapphire sky. The long dark ovals of the airships maintained their positions a kilometre above the dessert's desiccated white grass and Mars-red soil, five klicks from the front of the VIP stadium. It was close enough to see everything.

Gasps came from the crowd as a slim stream of glittering white splinters began to fall from the belly of an airship. It quickly grew wider, so that by the time the first few boulders of Antarctic ice smashed onto the desert, the flow was nine metres wide as it emerged from the portal slung below the airship. By that time, the second cascade of ice had begun from the neighbouring airship.

Cheering and enthusiastic applause filled the dry air. By ten forty, all five airships had solid white cataracts pouring out, catching the sunlight in a dazzling refraction blaze as they tumbled downwards. On the ground below, the five ice cones began to grow upwards and outwards with remarkable speed, their surface a constant avalanche of shattered ice. Sub-zero vapour churned up out of them, flowing with the viscosity of oil. The wavefront of fog obscured the land, billowing upwards to thin out and disperse as the heat of the sun finally began to impact.

The entranced crowd waited for the final aspect of the promised miracle: to be enveloped by freezing mist in the middle of a desert. As the brilliant cloud rolled towards them, angry shouts began to rise above the background buzz of chanting and laughter. Placards were raised. Firework rockets zoomed unnervingly low over heads.

Smoke bombs were thrown. Cheers turned to screams. Lines of riot shield-equipped police and corporate security officers snaked through the throng. Stones began to rise in short arcs. The screams grew louder. Images playing across the big screens set up across the zone to show everyone dramatic close-up shots of the harvesters and airships broke up into a mash of static.

The crowd surged in random directions as people struggled to get away from the protestors. Police strove to get past them. Just as the chaos on the ground reached its peak, a colossal wall of fog rolled across the observation zone, blotting out the sun in a blast of cold so profound it seemed to suck oxygen from the very air. Then the panic frenzy really struck.

*

Whoever named it Fountain Street clearly had a very misplaced sense of irony. Savi looked along the depressing track, with drab single-storey prefab cabins on both sides, that led away from the intersection ahead of her. The compacted soil here probably hadn't seen any free-flowing water this side of Earth's last ice age. A double irony, she thought, considering what was visiting the desert today.

It was definitely the poorer side of town, home to the labourers who sweated through the endless changeless desert days performing Water Desert's dirty low-paid jobs. Their kids were left behind to find what fun they could amid the tired silvered boxes where they lived. One gang was playing basketball in an open area that passed for a park, trying to slam-dunk their ball into hoops on poles that were now leaning badly.

Savi had her white surgical mask on again, like Ketchell and Larik who walked along with her. Nobody could see their faces. But that didn't matter; all the kids and the few adults sitting outside their homes knew they didn't belong. Not that they cared.

What do you want me to do? Savi asked active ops. **When are you going to intercept?**

We are working on isolating the main target group. Continue with your mission.

Confirmed, she sent back. Her apprehension was growing, and with it the thrill. What she was doing was going to take a lot of these people out of circulation. It was all that mattered to her. Talish would be proud. It was eight years now since her little cousin had been caught in the crossfire between the police and a radical group called Path of Light, as the militants stormed a government building in Noida. He had his cyber legs now, and an artificial kidney, but for three months the whole family had been immersed in an agony of waiting and praying around his hospital bed. Now Savi was playing her part in making sure no other innocents got hurt by psychotic ideologues who believed they had an absolute right to use force to achieve their goal.

Arrest team moving into your area, active ops sent.

They're going to have to hurry. Only six minutes left.

These are our own real special forces. You're getting the red-carpet treatment. Told you I've got your back.

She smiled beneath her mask.

They reached the end of Fountain Street. The substation was twenty metres ahead of them: a small square compound with a high grey metal fence around it, the base clotted with fast-food wrappers and loose clumps of desert grass. She could hear the hum of the transformers as they fed power across the town and out to the airfield, keeping the air con going and the civil engineering machines moving. Kintore's consumption was phenomenal.

It was twenty-three years since the China National Sunpower Corporation had dropped the first solarwell into the sun. A simple spherical portal that plasma poured into, whose twin was sitting at the bottom of a giant MHD chamber on a trans-Neptune asteroid. The solar plasma flared out of the chamber like a rocket exhaust, its powerful magnetic field generating a phenomenal current in the chamber's induction coils. In one masterful stroke of ingenuity, the Chinese had solved Earth's energy drought. Now the entire planet's power came from a multitude of solarwells, producing vast amounts of cheap energy at zero environmental cost.

Ten fifty-two. Five minutes left to go, and they started loitering round the last houses. Three other roads ended in the same area.

There was nothing on the other side of the substation other than the desert. Kids laughed and shouted behind them.

Savi turned to Ketchell. 'Have your people seen anything?' As he swung round she caught a glimpse of the shoulder holster he was wearing under his white cotton jacket, weighed down by a large automatic pistol. *Oh shit.*

'No. We're clear. Let's do this.'

Some of the group with me are armed. Warn the arrest team. Will do.

They began sauntering along the stony road. Savi put her hand into the bag and found the hexagonal switch. There was only a moment's hesitation before she turned it. *I hope to hell Julisa built this right.* She pressed down, hearing the button click.

Ketchell and Larik both glanced at her when she exhaled loudly. 'It's armed,' she said.

Ten fifty-three.

They reached the fence. Savi kept walking but unslung the bag. Dropped it at the base of a post.

Without saying anything, the three of them picked up their pace. Thirty seconds later they reached the top of Rennison Road. They crouched down behind a flimsy fence marking out a prefab's yard. Savi worried the thin composite might fragment in the blast, producing a blizzard of shrapnel. 'Did anyone see us?' she asked urgently.

'All quiet,' Larik said. He started putting in a pair of foam ear-plugs.

'Damn,' Savi grunted. 'You got any spare?'

He gave her another of his contemptuous glances and handed her a couple. She squeezed the first plug and started to worm it in. Something moved across the stony ground behind her. She stared in disbelief. A football was rolling out of Fountain Street heading straight for the substation. 'No,' she whispered.

Ketchell looked at her, then he saw the ball and his eyes widened in shock. 'Shit.'

The ball was only a few metres from the fence, and a boy was trotting along behind it; he was maybe eight or nine years old.

'No,' Savi stood up. 'No, get back.'

'Stay down,' Ketchell growled at her.

'Get away,' Savi yelled. 'Away!'

The boy looked round, seeing a woman wearing a white plastic mask waving frantically. He cocked his head and carried on following his ball.

'Fuck!' Savi screeched. All she saw now was Talish, lying in his hospital bed, with so many tubes and organ-support machines inserted into his flesh that he'd ceased to become purely human. She started running.

'No!' Larik bellowed behind her.

The boy had almost reached the ball, which was rolling to a halt a couple of metres from the fence, level with the abandoned shoulder bag. He turned again, his expression growing uncertain as Savi sprinted hard towards him. 'Get away, get away,' she yelled frantically.

He didn't know what to do. Took an uncertain step back, away from the wild eyes of the crazy woman. Then realized she wasn't going to stop, that she was going to run right into him. Turned and started to run.

She flung her arms around him, picking him up despite his frightened wail and thrashing limbs. Kept running, desperate to build distance between her and the bag.

Savi saw a flash, then nothing—

*

The waiting room for the surgical wards was neutral in every respect. Pale grey carpet, white walls with twin floor-to-ceiling windows looking out over night-time Brisbane. Two rows of back-to-back settees were lined up down the centre, their cushions thick and comfortable enough for worried families to spend the night curled up on them. High-quality vending machines and a big wallscreen silently running news streams completed the decor.

Yuri Alster had been waiting in it for over an hour, but refused to sit. It meant his deputy, Kohei Yamada, couldn't sit either, which clearly pissed him off no end. They were the only two in the waiting room.

Finally, long after midnight, the Reardon family came out of Ward Two. Ben Reardon was a short bulky man in his early forties, with a bald head and a face that looked as if it had been squashed flat. He seemed angry, which Yuri suspected was a permanent expression. Ben was employed running the machines that dug out the Icefall canals – tough work that he was well suited to. Dani, the current girlfriend, was barely twenty. A cliché relationship, Yuri decided, endorsed by her short denim skirt showing off heavily tanned thighs, and a cheap green sports shirt which had the Alcides cafe logo on both sleeves.

They walked down the corridor on either side of nine-year-old Toby Reardon's wheelchair as the boy was pushed along by a ward nurse. Ben scowled as Yuri stood in front of them.

'What do you want?' he asked, exhaustion and fear giving him a raspy voice.

'Just a couple of questions for Toby,' Yuri said as pleasantly as he could. He winked at the boy, whose cheeks and right arm were covered in patches of medskin. There was a cast holding one leg rigid, too.

'No way,' Ben snapped. 'We've answered every question a dozen times.'

'I'm not police,' Yuri said. 'I'm from Connexion Security.'

'Clear off, mate. Come back in a week. My boy got blown up. You understand that? He's nine years old, and the bastards blew him up!'

'I know. And Connexion's medical plan covers your family, even for this. That's worth a minute, surely?'

Ben took a step forwards, his fists bunching. 'Are you threatening me?'

'I'm asking you to do the right thing.'

'I don't mind, Dad,' Toby said.

'We're going home!'

'A few questions and you won't see me again, okay? I can arrange for an extra week's paid leave, which you can spend here in the city, or maybe in a Gold Coast resort – next to the sea. Be nice, that. Big change from Kintore. You can be with Toby while he recovers. That's something we all want, isn't it?'

Ben hesitated, clearly hating himself for being tempted.

'It'd be good,' Dani said tentatively.

Ben ignored her. 'How about it, big fella?' he asked Toby. 'Only if you're up to it.'

'Game on, Dad.'

Ben glared at Yuri. 'Be quick.'

'Sure.' Yuri knelt down so his face was level with Toby's. 'Did the doctors fix you up okay?'

'Yeah. I guess.'

'So, you were playing football, right?'

'Yeah, with some of me mates. It's my ball, see. Dad gave it me. I think it's gone now. I didn't see it after.'

'I'll get you another one,' Ben said.

'Was all this happening at the end of Fountain Road?'

'Yeah.'

'And what happened?'

'Jaze kicked it. Hard, like. I went to bring it back.'

'From the electric station?'

'Yeah, it didn't go in or nothing. Honest. Dad's told me it's dangerous in there.'

'Your dad's quite right. So you got the ball?'

'No. This woman was shouting, stuff like No and Go Away. She ran at me.'

Yuri held up a small tablet, which was showing Savi's picture. 'Is this her?'

'Yeah,' Toby nodded solemnly. 'That's her.'

'She ran at you – then what?'

'Picked me up. She was really strong. Then it happened, the bomb. It went off.'

Yuri could see the moisture glinting in the boy's eyes; he was starting to withdraw. It was too vivid, too terrifying. 'Now this is important, Toby. I need to know about what happened after. What happened to the woman?'

'They took her,' Toby said simply. 'She was hurt bad. There was . . . was blood. It was all over her.'

'The police took her?'

Toby nodded, silent as he relived the memory.

'What did they take her away in?'

'Big car. Bigger than a normal police car. Same colour, though. They carried her into the back, along with the other bloke.'

'Another man? Was he injured, too?'

'I guess.'

'Did they say anything to you?'

'Just that I'd be okay. He said they'd called the paramedics.'

'The policeman that talked to you, what did he look like?'

'I don't know.'

'Okay. Was he black, white, Indian, Chinese? Short guy, tall guy?'

'I don't know. He never took his mask off.'

'What sort of mask, Toby?'

'They were all in armour. It was black. You know the dull kind of black.'

'I do, Toby. Thank you.' Yuri stood up.

'You finished?' Ben asked.

'Sure. Hey, Toby, you did okay. You're lucky to have a dad like this.' He watched as the Reardons went into the lift.

'Threw them into the back of a car?' Kohei said sceptically.

'Savi told us she was with Ketchell and Larik. But there were more activists scouting round for them.'

'So it was likely Ketchell or Larik who was caught in the blast with her. Everyone else would have got lost fast.'

'They were both badly injured. Let's start with admissions to hospital emergency departments.' Yuri let out a reluctant breath. 'And morgues.'

*

Yuri's office had full access to all the information from over a dozen primary medical networks across Australia. Their reports covering the last week were open, swamping a pair of his desk screens. The

Security Department G5Turing was even running a real-time scan through hospital emergency department files for a Jane Doe matching Savi's description. So far it had turned up precisely zero. Savi had effectively vanished from the digital world the moment the bomb went off.

He was more concerned by Connexion Security's own logs. Kintore's files of first fall day had been deleted from the Sydney office's servers, transferred to New York under Poi Li's authority. Yuri's repeated requests to review the drone videos of Fountain Street had been blocked. There was going to have to be a showdown with Poi Li, and soon. Savi had taken the worst of the blast, protecting Toby Reardon. She needed treatment – if she wasn't already dead.

And the Sydney department was running another eight current operations, which all required his complete attention, all as important as the infiltration of Akkar's group. Those agents were depending on him as well. He dropped his head into his hands and massaged his temples. The text of the screens was out of focus no matter how many times he blinked.

The three empty coffee mugs lined up underneath the desk screens made him sigh. According to Boris, his mInet, he'd been in the office for eighteen hours straight. Yuri *did not* lose his own operatives. It weighed heavily on him. His people had to trust him, they had to know he had them covered. Everyone in Connexion regarded him as a real hardarse, which he strove to be, but with asking people to undertake dangerous missions came responsibility. And Yuri took that very seriously indeed.

There was a swift rap of knuckles on his door, and Kohei Yamada came right in without waiting. 'Sorry, chief, we have an incident outside. It's odd.'

Yuri frowned and glanced over at the window, slightly surprised to see bright morning sunlight pouring down the skyscraper canyon of Sydney's central business district. 'What's happening?' Boris hadn't alerted him to any crowds gathering on the street below.

'Callum Hepburn is in reception. He's refusing to leave until he sees you.'

'Why do I know that name? Is he one of our targets?'

Kohei grinned. 'No, chief.' His mInet threw Callum's picture on the wallscreen.

Yuri peered at a young red-haired man with a mildly bewildered smile on his face as he shook hands with Ainsley Zangari himself. Boris backed it up with a biography file. 'Riiight . . . he cleared up Gylgen. I remember.' Connexion's Emergency Detoxification team had been headlining the news streams after the potential disaster at Gylgen had been averted . . . until Icefall took over media interest. 'What's he doing here?'

'No idea. But he's started shouting quite loudly at our people when they asked him to leave – most impolite.' Kohei pointed at the screen. 'Given who he knows, I thought it best we shouldn't just sling him out on the street. He's angry about something.'

'But—'

'Publicity, chief. We don't want it.'

'Fuck it. Bring him up here.'

'Yes, sir.'

'And, Kohei, I want two uniform staff outside my door.'

'Way ahead of you, chief.'

Yuri spent the intervening minutes reviewing Callum Hepburn's file. It was ordinary enough. Except for one entry concerning Gylgen, which was classified higher than Yuri's rating could access. He raised an eyebrow at that.

Callum stomped into the office. On his pale skin, the red flush of anger was very pronounced.

'Mr Hepburn, please, have a seat—'

Callum marched over to the desk and put his hands down on it hard so his face was thrust over the screens, glaring down at Yuri. 'Where is she?'

Yuri glanced over at Kohei, who was standing in the doorway, curious and amused. 'I don't respond well to people shouting at me, Hepburn. So you need to back off, calm down and tell me what this is about.'

Callum paused for a moment, then took his hands off the desk, straightening up. 'Savi Chaudhri. She's missing. Where is she?'

Training allowed Yuri to keep his face expressionless, but only just.

'I'm sorry. I've never heard of that person.'

'Bollocks. She's one of your covert agents. She went undercover for you. She didn't come back.'

'What makes you say that?'

Callum breathed in deeply, his nostrils flaring. 'She's my fiancée. She went undercover after our holiday. It was supposed to be for five days. It's double that now. No way does anyone stay out of contact for that long.'

'Your fiancée?'

'Yes. And yes, I know she's supposed to inform you lot so I can be vetted. But it was a whirlwind thing. So . . . What's happened and where is she? Just tell me she's safe and I'll piss off and leave you alone.'

Yuri could read the anxiety burning away behind the man's anger. 'Okay, it's like this. If one of our agents is undercover, they have specific contact protocols. That includes several emergency methods of alerting us if they get into difficulty. If we had received one of those alerts, then we would extract them at once.' He spread his hands: the reasonable man. 'It's been quiet round here.'

'Like bollocks has it. There was a riot out at Kintore when the Icefall started. Were her students there? It's the kind of stupid stunt those morons live for.'

Once again, Yuri was startled by how close the man was to the truth. He was furious with Savi for compromising herself so badly – and for what? An impetuous fling? When he tracked her down, her career with Security was over. 'What students?'

'She was . . . monitoring student groups for you, playing spot the radical. Are they the ones who protested Icefall?'

'No. No student groups Security watches were there. And you have my word on that.'

'So where is she?'

'Look, I appreciate your concern. This is your fiancée, you've every right to be worried. But all of my personnel are accounted for. So I'm sure she'll be calling you as soon as she surfaces.'

Callum stood still for a long moment, processing what he'd heard. 'All right then.' He nodded as if he was generously letting Yuri off a felony charge. 'I'll give it a couple of days.'

Yuri watched him walk out of the office. 'You're welcome,' he told the empty doorway.

Kohei came in. 'Did I hear that right? They're engaged?'

'So it would seem. And someone like Hepburn isn't going to lie about that. He's a fool; he sees the world in black and white.'

'What do we do?'

'Only one option left now.'

Yuri knew he should wait until he'd had a sleep, at the very least. His rumpled shirt, stubble, tired eyes, all spoke of someone not making the best decisions. But this couldn't wait any longer.

*

Poi Li's Manhattan office was in one of Connexion's downtown buildings, a temporary location until the new American headquarters was built overlooking Central Park. Like Yuri, she didn't put a lot of weight on expensive fittings as symbols of status.

Somehow he wasn't surprised that she was in there, working away in the middle of the East Coast's night. Very few senior management worked their physical office time zone's standard hours.

'You look like crap,' she said as he came in.

'Thanks.'

'Tea?'

'No. I've had enough caffeine today.'

'I recommend camomile. Very gentle.'

He shook his head, trying to ignore the irritation. 'We have a problem.'

'You and I would be out of a job if there were no problems in the world.'

'Very Zen. It's Savi Chaudhri.'

'Your infiltration agent?'

'Yes. You've got her, haven't you?'

'No. Why do you say that?'

'I went back over our detention records,' Yuri said. 'I was surprised.'

'In what way?'

'Akkar's idea was a good one. Using the power drop-out while the super-truckez were recharging would've created a reboot window for Julisa's rogue control program. They would've taken over the ancient G3Turing drivers and had themselves the world's greatest demolition battle smashing those brutes into each other and every other piece of equipment out there. Some of those things weigh over fifty tonnes. Everything would've been wrecked.'

'I know,' Poi Li said. 'I was in active ops when Tarli worked out their methodology.'

'Yes. And that was when we all realized how many activists they would be sending to the old airfield. That's also when you stood down the original arrest squads and the Arizona Search & Engage team was brought in. Your decision, your authorization.'

'You originally tasked the Australian Internal Suppression force with the arrests. I judged they weren't large enough, nor capable, for a hundred and twenty-odd fanatics. Quite rightly as it turns out. S&E handled containment and detention very well.'

'They were a bit too efficient; they scooped up Savi as well. They didn't know she was our asset. I'd like her back, please.'

'We don't have her.'

'Have you even checked?'

'As a matter of fact, yes. Arizona S&E were given the code for her tracker. We don't have her.'

Yuri sat back in the chair and gave her a careful look. 'Is this a dark rendition operation? Is that it? Have we got them stashed away at some Guantanamo in North Korea, or something?'

'That would only multiply our problem, wouldn't it? You can't hide that many people and not have anyone ask where they are. We'd have to let them go or bring them to trial eventually.'

'I personally interviewed the only witness of the substation explosion. He told me the Arizona paramilitaries you sent threw her into the back of their vehicle. You have her.'

'A nine-year-old boy suffering an explosion trauma is not the most reliable witness.'

'You *know* I saw Toby Reardon? You're keeping tabs on me?'

'There was only one survivor of the Fountain Street attack according to our files. Are they incorrect?'

'No,' Yuri said, hating the way he was being put on the defensive. 'Look, I get that screw-ups happen, especially on a day as intense and confusing as last week's. Just let me access the Arizona S&E records. I'd like to see who they processed.'

'You don't have clearance for Arizona S&E documentation. They're an internal outfit we deploy during extreme security events.'

'I'm a divisional commander, for fuck's sake!'

'And that level does not give you clearance do go digging through Arizona S&E files. I'm sorry.'

'Oh, come on, Poi, you've got to give me something. Let me walk down to the holding cells and quietly take her out of there. She's Security, one of us. She's not going running to some piece of shit libertarian civil rights lawyer.'

'Can't be done.'

'You do it, then.'

'Again, we do not have her.'

'She's dead, isn't she? That's what's being covered up here.'

'I'll pretend you didn't say that.'

'It's not going to go away, you know.'

'The file is closed, Yuri. Drop this. That's a direct order.'

'It's not me that's your problem,' he said softly. 'Have you heard of Callum Hepburn?'

'How is he the problem?'

'Wait – do you know him?'

'I know of him. I can't tell you why. But I can assure you he is a solid Connexion employee.'

'Not for much longer. He's going to be trouble.'

'Really? Has he joined a radical group?'

'Turns out he's Chaudhri's fiancé.'

Poi Li sat up, all humour leaving her compact frame. 'He's what?'

'All I know is they went on some kind of screw-fest holiday together in the Caribbean. And a nice diamond ring was the result. They didn't bother telling the department.'

'This is unfortunate,' she said. 'He carries media weight right now.'

'Exactly. So let me have Savi. I'll reunite the star-crossed lover idiots and everything goes away.'

'I do not have her.'

'Why are you doing this?' His voice was raised, which was never a good idea with Poi Li. But somehow, Yuri no longer cared.

'Yuri. Please. We genuinely don't have her. You have my word on that. I did check. And please don't call me a liar to my face. That would be bad for both of us. This is closed. Accept it and move on.'

Yuri took a moment, but in the end he just nodded and said: 'Okay.' He simply couldn't afford to challenge Poi Li. Not directly.

*

'How did it go?' Kohei asked when Yuri got back to his Sydney office.

Yuri slumped into the chair behind his desk. Boris switched all the darkened screens back on, which showed the same mass of data as before – and still told him nothing.

'Question for you,' he said to his deputy. 'You're a criminal, in the middle of a serious criminal act, and someone assaults you. Who do you complain to? And what do you say? "*While I was trying to sabotage a hundred million wattdollars' worth of equipment, someone beat the crap out of me, then threatened me so badly I'm terrified for my life.*"'

'You cut a deal,' Kohei said immediately. 'You get into the witness protection programme in exchange for testifying.'

'Nice theory. In practice, witness protection is for organized crime informants who can bring down whole cartels. Somehow I doubt some radical hothead smashing up our equipment is going to be given that same deal.'

'You mean Akkar's eco-radicals who tried to bust up our super-trucks?'

'I do indeed. They were rounded up by a Connexion Security sub-division called Arizona S&E. It's a paramilitary group we use for crowd control in bad urban disturbances.'

'Do they have the authority to operate in Australia?'

'Yes. They've got an office registered here in the building, actually, and a private police licence issued by the government. That allows them to detain persons found committing a criminal act. They then hand them over to the local justice department along with evidence of the alleged felony.'

'Neat,' Kohei said approvingly. 'And if the suspects are held incommunicado?'

'Then who's going to notice them missing?' Yuri concluded. He massaged his temples again, which made no difference to the fatigue draining the energy from his muscles and thoughts. 'There were over a hundred and twenty of them.'

'Including Savi?'

'Given the way I was warned off, yes. But . . . a hundred and twenty people, maybe more. One of them has to have a family or friends kicking up a fuss. Poi can't vanish them with impunity. Can she?'

'Were there actually any witnesses?' Kohei asked. 'It all happened out at the old airfield. That's ours.'

'And New York has all the logs.'

'Shit, Poi Li's thorough.'

'Akkar's people will be well-chosen activists, totally dedicated. The last thing they'll do before going on a raid like this is tell anyone. So it's going to be days before anyone even asks where they are. Weeks before there's any concern raised. And even if you can get some friendly official to start investigating on your behalf, there's no evidence linking them. No one apart from us knows the size of the group. As self-generating cover-ups go, it's impressive.'

'You can't rendition that many people in this day and age,'

Kohei said. 'The holding location would leak. Some smartass would fly a drone over it.'

'I can't believe Poi Li would cut us out without reason,' Yuri replied. 'We know Arizona S&E picked Savi up right after the explosion. And Poi Li swears the Arizona guys haven't screwed up. She claims she checked personally.'

'So she's running scared of the media getting hold of this? Christ, chief, what do they do to these people? Are we working for psychopaths?'

'I don't know – and that's bad, whatever way you look at it. If Savi died because they didn't give her medical treatment quickly enough, why not just give us her body back? Why leave it like this? It doesn't make any sense!'

'So do we pack it in?'

'Savi is one of mine.' Yuri closed his eyes, fighting the exhaustion that was stopping him thinking straight. 'I'm going home to catch some sleep. I need a clear head to figure out what to do next.'

*

Callum stepped out of the Kintore portal hub onto Main Street. It was mid-afternoon, and the town had been roasting under the desert sun for over ten hours. He wasn't prepared for the heat, nor the dry scratchy dust he inhaled with every breath. Sweat emerged from every pore, and he was only wearing shorts and a purple T-shirt – along with factor fifty sunblock. He fumbled in his shoulder bag for his new surgical-style mask and slipped it on.

Apollo threw a navmap up on his screen sunglasses, and he began to walk down the street, following the direction graphics. There were very few of the dust-tarnished buildings with a second storey. Why would you bother? Single-storey prefabs were cheaper, and land more so; if you wanted a big house here, you just spread outwards. Or at least land had been cheap until a week ago, when the ice started to fall across the desert.

Now when he looked to the west, he could see a thick, oddly stable bank of cloud rising from the stratum of ice that lay over the red sand. The chunks already covered an area more than two kilometres across, and that was with only five of the big airships on station. Another three were scheduled to join the squadron before the end of the month, with a further fifteen planned within a year. Meltwater was now trickling along the waiting canals, soaking into the arid sand, but creeping a little further every day. While, in the air above, the freezing vapour was creating a microclimate alteration to the desert's ancient, lethargic wind patterns. Regular breezes had started to blow down Kintore's streets as the cold-sink drew in air from the coast to the north. For now all they brought was more dust, but within six months, Water Desert's climatologists were predicting, clouds would be lured inwards across the continent, accelerating change. Within a couple of years, Kintore would become the newest, most exciting, oasis on the planet. Money would flow in with the new rains, and speculators were already buying up plots along the canals.

But for now, Kintore retained its frontier atmosphere – a convenient home for its tough workforce, and scattered with the commercial establishments that supplied them with whatever they needed. Callum eyed the neon and hologram signs above the plethora of thriving small enterprises. He stopped outside the Granite Shelf, seeing just another prefab with long windows and three big air-con cabinets barnacled to the wall at one end. The glowing blue sign was younger than the prefab which it crowned.

Raina had found it for him, of course. After Yuri Alster had stonewalled him, he'd confided in his crew that he'd actually gone and made a commitment to a woman. That she was Security. Undercover. That she was missing, and he suspected the company was busy pulling together some kind of whitewash.

'Fucking typical,' Raina had grunted.

They were all on board, all wanting to help. 'Whatever it takes, chief. Whatever you need.'

He'd nearly got emotional at that. But so far it was only Raina's expertise he'd needed.

Savi's mInet, Nelson, might have been taken offline, but that didn't leave her totally isolated, Raina explained. If she was undercover, she was going to be using a different mInet identity. They didn't have its universal address code; however, Savi's dermal grains would be networked with it. They all had a unique interface code, which would be incorporated into the mInet metadata. It took Raina less than an hour to track down the codes, extracting the data from the Mumbai clinic which had implanted them five years ago. It was the kind of webhead skill which both impressed and troubled Callum, that so much of a life could be accessed so easily.

If Savi had used a mInet connection to call anyone or access the internet, it would be logged in the local server, Raina told him. All she needed was a probable location, then she could hack into the servers. A search engine would be able to find the data.

Callum's only suggestion for a location was Kintore. It made sense to him when he confronted her boss, Yuri. Icefall had been the centre of the biggest anti-Connexion protests for over a year – just the kind of thing student wannabe radicals would join (or be manipulated into joining). Which was what Savi was investigating.

Perhaps Parvati had chosen to smile on his quest. Whatever. He'd been right about Kintore. It'd taken Raina just ninety-seven minutes to track down Savi's grains; they were interfaced with a mInet tagged Misra, which had authorized payment for meals at the Granite Shelf. The last had been a croissant and orange juice the morning Icefall started, a few hours before the protests. After that, there was nothing.

Callum walked into the cafe and sat down. He asked the waitress for orange juice and a croissant. When she brought it, he showed her the picture of Savi, and asked if she recognized her.

No.

There were three other waitresses on that shift. He asked each of them. Two said no, one hesitated and said maybe. The Granite Shelf was a busy place, she said, we get a couple of hundred people every day. Your girl, she might have been in a few times, not dressed as smart as the photo, but it was a while ago now.

The rush of relief was so strong Callum had to go and sit down for a while. Apollo called Raina for him.

'One of the waitresses thinks she recognizes her,' he said.

'So she should,' Raina replied. 'I've hacked the cafe's main server. It's got the internal surveillance video files. I accessed them at the time she made her last payment. Downloading it to you now.'

Callum watched the image playing on his screen sunglasses, not knowing the Savi he was seeing, the shabby clothes, sun hat and backpack. *She's good at undercover*, he thought admiringly. The clothes and hairstyle dropped her age back several years. Typical student type, maybe on a gap year.

When she walked out of the Granite Shelf that morning, she turned left and walked along Main Street.

'I'll see if I can get some more video files,' Raina said. 'But a lot of the surveillance cameras in Kintore are cloud stored, especially the civic ones covering the streets. Hacking them is going to be a little more difficult.'

'Do what you can,' he told her.

He left the Granite Shelf and turned left, just like Savi. The next cafe along was Alcides, serving Portuguese food. He sat at a table and showed Savi's picture to the waiter. A clothes printing store next. Then a food printer. Bugez mart. A bar. Didn't bother with the finance house. Another cafe.

The sky was shading down to a rosy dusk when he left the cafe. Streetlights were coming on, blue-green cones of light revealed in the dusty air. More people were walking about now, not that the temperature had dropped. He could feel the ground radiating its daytime heat at him.

'I think I've got her turning into Rosewalk,' Raina said. 'That's about a klick from where you are. It's not the best image.'

'You're doing better than me,' he said. 'The food store owner says she may have been a customer. Couldn't say when.'

'There's not much camera coverage down Rosewalk. It's more residential down there.'

'I'll take a look.' Apollo threw up the navmap, and he started walking.

Three men came out of a bar just ahead of him. He moved to avoid them.

'Internet connection is dropping out,' Apollo said.

'What?'

'Network signal lost. Unable to reconnect. My reception is being subject to access overload.'

'How's that—?'

The three men from the bar shifted to stand directly in front of him.

'Oh shit,' Callum grunted. Spun round fast. Two men right behind him. One dressed in a smart suit, holding up a taser baton and grinning in anticipation.

'Wanna make a break for it?' the suited man taunted.

Callum had only ever been in a couple of bar fights, and that'd been with people his own age at university – boozy shoving matches with added swearing. The bouncers had stepped in fast and closed it down. These five men looked as if they could chop those bouncers apart as a warm-up routine.

'I've not got much cash on me,' Callum said, wishing his voice wasn't shaking so much. *This is Main Street. Why isn't anyone calling the cops?*

'Down here, pal,' one of the group from the pub said.

Callum saw the narrow street he was indicating, and started to panic. 'Look, I've got a smartCuff. I can wipe the universal code and the trackme app. It's top of the range, worth plenty.'

'If only we wanted you for your money.'

'Or your body,' another sneered.

'Move.'

It was his last chance to attempt a run. He was too frightened of the pounding they'd probably give him. Being put into hospital wasn't going to help Savi. But then, being forced into a dark alley wasn't exactly promising . . .

A hand shoved him between his shoulder blades. He tensed. If he ran to the right he'd be going directly down Main Street. *They won't chase me there . . . will they?*

The taser baton poked him in the back of his knee. It must have been a reduced charge. He yelped at the fast burst of pain, but didn't quite fall as his leg jerked about.

'Don't run,' the voice warned.

Humiliated and fearful, he went with them.

Raina will know the link was deliberately broken. She'll hack the cameras and see them taking me. She'll call the police, or our local Security officers. She'll help. She'll get me out of this. Come on, Raina. Come on!

They turned down another street, then made regular turns after that. Apollo's navmap tracked every turn, plotting their route. He could trace each footstep he was being forced to make.

Fat lot of fucking use that is.

After seven minutes thirty-eight seconds they finished up at a roller door in a sleep-pod hotel that was being refurbished. It slid up, and he was shoved into the dark cavern beyond. The door rattled as it rolled down again. Then the lights came on.

It was a storeroom, with empty metal racks on the walls, and plenty of dust on the rough concrete floor. The air was hot and stale. Right in the middle was a sturdy wooden chair with four handcuffs, two hanging off the arms, two on the front legs.

Callum took one look at it and—

The taser baton hit him. Full power this time. The only muscles he could make work were in his throat, so he screamed as he tumbled over. The baton struck again, and the universe dissolved into terrible pain. His body jerked about and he howled, all sense leaving him.

His limbs were on fire, which slowly subsided, leaving him with painful cramps. Vision returned – or at least he could see light streaks amid the darkness. Tried to blink into focus. The shaking was bad. And he couldn't move his hands.

He was cuffed into the chair, wrists and ankles.

'Oh shit. Shit shit.'

His screen sunglasses had either fallen off, or been taken. Whatever. He didn't have them any more. When he looked at his wrist, the smartCuff had been removed.

'Apollo?' he whispered.

A hand smacked him on the side of the head. Hard. 'Don't do that again. Your mInet is dead. You are alone.'

The red stars slowly faded. There was a man standing in front of him. Tall, African, with a bald head beaded by sweat, and tattoos running sinuously along his arms. He wore a black T-shirt with a picture of a crystal prism splitting a beam of light into a rainbow.

Callum's chuckle was almost hysterical. 'I have that album too.'

'What?'

'Pink Floyd, *Dark Side of the Moon*. Classic, but not as good as *Wish You Were Here*.'

'Smartarse,' the man grunted. His hand lashed out again, striking the other side of Callum's head.

Pain spiked through his ear, and there was the taste of blood in his mouth. 'Fucking hell, what is this?'

'Where are they? Where have you taken them?'

'What? Who?'

'My people.'

'What the fuck?' Callum eyed the hand as it rose threateningly again. 'Which people? Wait, who do you think I am?'

'I know exactly who you are, Callum Hepburn.' The African held up a piece of paper, printed with the publicity shot of him with Ainsley at the Greenwich Peninsula site. 'Connexion's newest golden boy. Saved Northern Europe from a radiation plume. The world is so grateful.'

'Why am I here? And who the fuck are you?'

The man raised his hand again and Callum flinched.

'Where are they?'

'Who?' Callum bellowed back, more frightened than ever now, not just for himself but mainly for Savi. If these were the student radicals she'd been shadowing . . .

'You are either a fool or a very good actor.'

'I'm not fucking acting. I don't know who you are or who you're talking about!'

The man walked round the chair. Callum tried to turn and watch him, worried that he'd be hit from behind. But he re-emerged on the other side, carrying a tall glass of water.

'Tell me what you want to know,' Callum said desperately. 'Exactly what. If I know, I'll tell you. Fuck's sake.' He had to tip his head back then; the man was standing directly in front of the chair.

'My name is Akkar, but I think you know that already, company boy.'

'No. I don't fucking care, either.'

Slowly Akkar tipped the glass, pouring the water down over Callum's crotch.

'What?' Callum stared down at his soaking shorts, then back up at his captor. 'What the fuck?'

'To encourage the telling of truth,' Akkar said. 'Took us years and years of research, but we've found water improves conductivity to skin.' He smiled mockingly. 'Who knew?'

The suited man came round the chair to stand grinning down at Callum; he held up the taser baton.

Akkar's smile turned mirthless. 'Dimon, how big a charge does it take to fry a man's balls?'

Dimon patted the taser baton. 'Don't worry, boss, we have more than enough.'

'No!' Callum yelled. 'Fucking no! I'll tell you what you want to know, but I don't know what it is. Tell me! Fucking explain! What is going on?'

'First fall,' Akkar said. 'My people went into Water Desert's maintenance compound. Is that clear enough for you?'

'I know there was a riot out at the observation area that day,' Callum said desperately. 'Is this the same thing?'

'No, it is not the same thing, Callum Hepburn. One hundred and twenty-seven activists went into that compound. They were going to strike the greatest possible blow against the corporate criminals who are here to rape the desert. A blow that took me over a year to plan.' His hand shot out, gripping Callum's chin. 'One hundred and twenty-seven, company boy. None of them came home. Where are they?'

'I don't know,' Callum said. 'I wasn't here. I work in fucking Emergency Detox, for Christ's sake! I don't give a flying shit about your stupid fucking desert. Nobody does, only freaks like you.'

144

'First they came for the rocks in space and took them away from us saying they now owned them,' Akkar said in a low, dangerous tone. 'And we did nothing, because they were just rocks. Then they came for the desert . . . You understand? You know how it goes? But this time, company boy, this time we will not let them ruin what nature has given to every human, the beautiful land which belongs to all of us. There are many with my belief, and our numbers grow, accepting the truth of our cause.'

Callum gave his captor the most contemptuous look he could manage. 'I've only seen six of you. That's not an oppressed minority with a cause, that's a mental health issue.'

The baton jabbed down into Callum's shorts. He screamed, then realized there was no electric shock.

Both men were laughing at him.

'Fuck you!' he shouted. 'I hope Connexion fucking drowns you in melting ice. I want the last thing you see to be green plants conquering every fucking useless rock in your worthless hell. I hope the water rots your corpse and turns you into fertilizer to help more plants. That's the only way dumbarse shits like you will ever help any ecology.'

'I think he means it.'

'I think you're right.'

Callum glared up at them. 'You're fucking morons! A hundred and twenty-seven people don't just disappear. That's . . . That's . . . crazy. You're being fucked up the arse by your own cracked conspiracy theories.'

'You're quite right, Callum Hepburn. People don't just disappear. It is madness.' Akkar produced the picture of Savi and thrust it into Callum's face. 'So where is she?'

'I . . . I . . .' Callum knew guilt would be lighting him up like a solar flare. 'She's not . . .'

'Not what?'

'Not one of you.' He knew he was blowing it, and didn't care. They knew Savi, and she'd vanished along with their fellow maniacs. Callum couldn't imagine a worse possible lead, but at least it was real. He was one step closer to her.

'Who is she?' Akkar asked in a deadly whisper.

'She's my fucking *wife*, you piece of shit! And if you've touched one hair on her head, I will fucking kill you!'

Akkar snatched the taser baton from Dimon, and jabbed it into Callum's chest. The pain was abysmal. Callum writhed helplessly, unable to think, transformed to nothing but a lump of screeching agonized flesh.

Dimon pulled Akkar's hand, moving the baton away. 'This is not you, my friend. We need him talking, not screaming.'

Akkar nodded reluctantly, but beneath his anger he was giving Callum a puzzled look. 'Speak to me. Your wife?'

Callum coughed pitifully, his body still shaking. 'Yes, she's my wife. What do you think I'm doing coming here to shit-city central asking where she is? I want her back.'

Akkar and Dimon exchanged a glance again, which Callum guessed was bad.

'What's her name?'

'Savi Hepburn.' He knew he shouldn't tell them but it was just a name. And appearing to help, to cooperate, might kick something loose. Where she was . . .

'A Connexion undercover agent,' Akkar said in quiet fury. 'She led us into a trap. Your bitch did this to us!'

Callum glared at him. 'Yeah, so? She outsmarted you. It couldn't have been difficult. Where did you see her last?'

Akkar glared at him. 'She betrayed us. I should make her watch while I cut your throat in front of her.'

'You've got to find her first. When did you see her last? Come on! When?'

'I ask the questions, company boy.'

'Yes, you do. So try asking this. How do you – you who's hiding in a crappy prefab cesspit in Kintore – how do you get into Connexion to find your precious people? How do you recruit someone on the inside? Someone they'll never suspect? Someone who's a lot more desperate than you are to find out what the fuck happened? Got any ideas on that, pal, huh? Got a name, maybe?'

Akkar gave an incredulous snort. 'You want to work with us?'

'I would sooner chew my fucking leg off. But what choice has either of us got?'

'No way,' Dimon growled.

'Really? Go on, then,' Callum challenged recklessly. 'Explain your alternative. Savi is with Security. She was watching you, recording you, gathering every detail of your pathetic little eco-cause lives. Connexion Security know it all. A multi-trillion-dollar company with a security division budget bigger than the sodding CIA. The only thing – *only* thing – that they don't know about is your current location. But you can't get out of Kintore now, can you? Not through a portal, and drones or satellites will spot any vehicle driving away. You're in a jail just as secure as your missing comrades. Nicer food, maybe, and invisible walls. But this is where you'll stay for the rest of your life. Which, with drone surveillance and G5Turings searching the internet, probably isn't going to be more than another week. So go on, tell me your super-smart master plan to bust out and save everyone, wherever they are. Got an address on that, have you?'

'How can Osha be missing as well?' Akkar asked.

'Who?'

'Your wife; that was the name we knew her by. If she's Connexion Security, why is she missing?'

'I don't know. I can't even get the bastards to admit she was working for them.' He jerked his wrists against the cuffs. 'Unlock me. Come on. We need to work out what to do next.'

'A hundred and twenty-seven people vanished, Callum. Including one of their own, if we believe you. The only thing we're going to find now is their grave.'

'No,' Callum shouted. He tugged hard, as if that alone would break the handcuffs. 'She's alive. I know you're paranoid enough to believe Connexion can murder that many people; it's all part of your sad little echo chamber conspiracy bollocks. But they don't. And I've met Ainsley. He's a ruthlessly clever businessman, sure, but he's not fucking Hitler.'

'There won't be a grave to uncover,' Dimon said. 'Haumea station gets rid of all Connexion's problems, all the evidence.'

'*Bzzzt!* Wrong! Have you ever been to Haumea station? I have. I go every week. I know every ventchamber. I've watched our grandparents' toxic crap sail off into space. There aren't any corpses going through.'

'If not Haumea, then another invisible asteroid out beyond Neptune. It's a big company, as you said. With infinite resources.'

'She's alive!' Callum cried. 'Now fucking let me go. I'm going to find her, with or without you. Do you want to know where your friends went or not? Because I'm your only chance to find out.'

After a long moment, Akkar nodded. Dimon sighed in disapproval but bent down and unlocked Callum's handcuffs.

'Okay, company boy,' Akkar said. 'What do we do now?'

Callum rubbed at the red marks on his wrists. 'Secret rendition, that's what's happened here, right? They're all sitting in some deep hole somewhere: disused mine, hollowed-out volcano, North Korea. We're agreed on that, yes?'

'Yes.'

'Then there's only one thing we can do now. They vanished down the rabbit hole. We have to dive in after them.'

*

The sun had set two hours before, leaving the Sydney skyline ablaze in neon and office lights. As always, Yuri hadn't noticed.

'We've got movement, chief,' Kohei Yamada said breathlessly.

Yuri looked up from the screens on his desk to see his deputy leaning on the doorframe, grinning excitedly.

'Movement?'

'Dimon just broke surface. Active ops is tracking him.'

'Now?'

'Yeah. We're live!'

'Shit.'

The two of them hurried along the corridor to the active ops centre. Omri Toth was duty operations manager. He gave Yuri a thumbs-up. 'Facial recognition got him outside the Kintore hub five minutes ago.'

'Where did he go?' Yuri asked.

'He didn't.'

'Show me.'

Omri gestured at Tarli, who was on one of the desks. Yuri peered at the main screen at the front of the room. It had a camera view of the Kintore hub: a hexagonal green and white tiled lobby with four portal doors, two for the town's tiny loop, the other pair leading to the Northern Territory central hub.

'Seven minutes ago,' Tarli said.

Yuri watched Dimon linger just outside the entrance barriers, looking round slowly. The big man spent a couple of minutes observing pedestrians come and go, then left.

'Current location, hanging round outside twenty metres away,' Omri said in a bemused tone.

The screen switched to one of the hub building's external cameras. Sure enough, Dimon was standing further down Main Street.

'Kohei, get me the duty captain at the Northern Territory central hub,' Yuri said. 'And put our armed response team on active alert.'

'Yes, chief!'

'And no national police. Let's keep this in house.'

He watched Dimon, who was still standing in Main Street. The man was wearing one of his charcoal grey suits, which must have been disturbingly hot in Kintore's evening heat.

'Is his mInet using the internet?' Yuri asked.

'Difficult,' Tarli said. 'I'll put our G5Turing into the local servers, see if we can identify his digital signature.'

Boris threw a communication icon across Yuri's screen lenses.

'Captain Dalager, Northern Territory hub network security chief.'

'Okay, captain,' Yuri said. 'We have some activity at the Kintore hub. A suspect on our critical wanted list may try to get through central hub. I need you to start shutting it down.'

'Sir?'

'You heard me. Let everyone currently in the hub go through, but close the barriers and every portal door to new traffic apart from Kintore. My authority.'

'That's going to cause chaos!'

'I don't care. Once the hub is empty, deploy the tactical response team to pick him up. I want him to walk straight into this, eyes open.'

'Yes, sir.'

Omri was chuckling. 'Oh man, regional control is going to dump on you from a great height. You shut central, and you're closing down the whole Northern Australian Territory.'

'The Hubnav app will throw everyone a route through the secondary networks; that's why we have multiple overlaps. It'll take people thirty seconds longer.'

'As long as I don't get hauled in to Corporate to explain this.'

'You won't be. Now, get all our Kintore spy drones into the air. Do not lose Dimon. I don't care about stealth. This needs to be wrapped.'

'Already launched.'

'Tarli,' Yuri said quietly. 'Open a secondary cache and copy all this operation's files into it. My access only, not New York.'

'Got it, chief.'

'Boris, notify Poi Li we have a situation developing—'

'It's him,' Tarli exclaimed.

'Who?' Yuri stared at the screen.

'Akkar. That uniform isn't fooling anyone.'

Yuri felt his excitement building as he saw the tall eco-warrior walking along Main Street towards Dimon. 'He wouldn't dare,' he breathed. Akkar was wearing the brown and green jacket of Step-Smart couriers, along with matching shorts. The company's standard-issue canvas satchel was slung over his shoulder. His cap had a long peak which he'd pulled down until it almost touched his broad wraparound sunglasses. That, along with several days' stubble, was possibly enough to confuse a low-level facial recognition program, but not anyone in active ops.

'Ten dollars he's going to try,' Kohei said.

'Bloody hell,' Omri said. 'Dimon was scouting it out for him in person. These blokes never use the internet for anything. They're religiously old-school.'

'Keep on them,' Yuri yelled. 'Kohei, with me. Dalager, empty the hub, now! Our suspect is coming through.'

He ran out of active ops. There was a portal door twenty metres away. Boris threw a route to the Northern Territory central hub on his screen lenses. The portal door led into Connexion's internal network. Left turn, through two more doors, right turn at the ten-portal junction hub. Three straight—

Poi Li's icon sprang up. 'What's happening?' she demanded.

'Akkar's surfaced. We're about to take him down.'

'All right, I've got the feed. I see him. What's in his courier bag?'

'We don't know. The portal sensors will pick up anything dangerous.'

'I don't want him in a central hub.'

'If I send the tactical team through to Kintore now, he'll run.'

'They can catch him,' she said.

'There isn't time. Let him through, and he's contained on our territory.'

'I need a decision,' Omri said. 'Akkar is ten metres from the Kintore hub.'

'If the bag's a bomb, if he's going to suicide, we can't let him do it on Kintore's Main Street,' Yuri yelled. 'Too many people.'

'Central hub is almost empty of pedestrians,' Dalager confirmed. 'Team assuming interception positions.'

'Very well,' Poi Li said. 'Let him through.'

'Dimon is walking away,' Omri said.

'Keep the drones on him,' Yuri said.

'Yes,' Poi Li said. 'And route their feed to me. I'm sending a team through the C&GST portal; they'll intercept before he can vanish on us again.'

Yuri almost smiled at the déjà vu moment. It was exactly like first fall, when Poi Li had jumped in, putting her own people into the operation – but now she didn't have exclusivity on the operation's data. 'Tell them to be careful,' he said. 'Akkar is the brains, but Dimon is the muscle. He'll likely be armed.'

'I can access a file, thank you, Yuri,' Poi Li said.

Yuri sprinted through the last portal. He was in a windowless corridor. At the far end a locked double door closed off the hub. Boris sent it his access code, and the bolts clicked open.

'He's in the Kintore hub,' Omri said. 'Using a cash code. Through the barriers now.'

'Scanners picked up some kind of flask in the bag,' Tarli shouted.

'Is it a weapon?'

'The flask's metal. Can't scan the interior. No residual molecular traces. He's going through to central—'

'Dalager, intercept!' Yuri said. He burst through the double doors, with Kohei right behind him. They shot out onto the central hub floor, quarter of the way round the big circle from the Kintore portal. Shouts rang out, echoing along the eerily empty space.

'Down!'

'On your knees!'

'Hands where we can see them!'

'Down down!'

'Do not move!'

Up ahead, Yuri saw the Kintore portal door. Akkar was in front of it. On his knees, his hands raised. Five figures in light armour were closing on him, their carbines raised, ruby target lasers slicing the air to form a neat grouping of dots over Akkar's heart.

Yuri skidded to a halt behind them. 'What's in the bag, Akkar?'

Akkar smiled grimly. 'Open it and find out.'

'Put it down slowly,' the tactical team's leader instructed. 'There is too much firepower in here to risk making people nervous.'

Akkar lifted the StepSmart satchel from his shoulder, holding it by its strap, a grin spreading across his face. Yuri didn't like that grin at all, but they had every angle covered. *Unless he's going to suicide. But he's not the type, according to Savi.*

'You mean this bag?'

'It's over, Akkar,' Yuri said. 'Put it down.'

Akkar stared at him for a long moment, then the defiance collapsed and he put the bag on shiny tiled floor and raised his hands.

Moments later the tactical response team had his wrists zip-locked and hauled him away. Yuri and Kohei stared at the satchel nervously.

'Bomb squad on the way,' Omri said. 'Ninety seconds.'

'I don't feel the need to stand this close,' Kohei said. 'We can't contribute at this point.'

'Yeah,' Yuri growled. They both walked back, around the curve of the concourse.

The three members of the bomb squad jogged out of the double door Yuri had just used, their bulky protective armour parodying a sumo-suit. A safetez followed them, its tracks a blur. The spider-leg array of manipulator arms locked around its stubby central cylinder.

'Omri,' Yuri asked. 'How are we doing with Dimon?'

Boris immediately threw a drone camera image across the screen lens. It was the green and black monotone of light amplification circuitry, looking down on a street in Kintore's industrial zone. Dimon was running into a big warehouse, with a Warbi Crude Metal Corp sign on the gable end.

'Bugger!' Tarli exclaimed.

'What is it?' Yuri asked as the drone's camera image flickered.

'He's got electronic countermeasures operating down there. It's nearly military grade. I can't send the drones in any closer, or we'll lose them.'

'Use the drones to surround the warehouse. Make sure he doesn't leave.'

'That's kinda Rule One-Oh-One, chief, you know?'

Yuri nearly smiled at the man's hurt tone.

'My team will be there in two minutes,' Poi Li said. 'They've cleared Kintore C&GST.'

Yuri's heart rate was calming. By unspoken agreement, he and Kohei walked a little further around the central hub.

'Well, look at that,' Kohei said wryly as the drones showed them two big 4x4 vehicles pull up outside the Warbi Crude Metal Corp warehouse, one at each end. 'Like police responder cars, but bigger.'

Yuri watched impassively as seven or eight men deployed from each 4x4, all wearing dark head-to-toe armour. 'Packing them in,' he murmured.

Boris gave him a private channel to Poi Li. 'I want to interrogate Akkar myself.'

'He will be questioned by professionals,' she replied.

'At least let me sit in.'

'Yuri, we have this. You run an excellent department. Believe me, I am aware of that. Just trust our procedures. They exist for a reason, understood?'

'Yes, ma'am,' he said resentfully.

Five minutes later the bomb squad chief announced: 'Clear and safe.'

Yuri and Kohei walked back to the StepSmart satchel, which was now being held aloft by one of the safetez's arms. The squad chief had his helmet visor hinged up. He was holding the flask and a several sheets of paper.

'Two kilos of plastique,' the chief said cheerfully, shaking the flask. 'And plans.'

'Plans of what?' Yuri asked.

The squad chief thrust the sheets towards Yuri. 'Connexion's Sydney headquarters. Looks like he was coming to pay you blokes a visit.'

'Holy shit,' Kohei grunted.

Yuri watched the chief seal up the plans and flask in evidence bags, and record their barcode.

'We have Dimon,' Poi Li announced. 'Well done, everyone. Yuri, looks like you can close down the Akkar file now.'

*

The screens on Yuri's desk were showing three pictures: Savi, Akkar and Dimon. He sat there motionless in his black leather executive office chair, staring at them.

Kohei walked in, carrying two empty shot glasses and smiling brightly. 'Chief! If you fancy sharing some of that god-awful vodka of yours, I thought we might toast our success. And the team's heading out to a club. Everyone invited.'

Yuri looked up. Kohei's smile faded.

'Too easy,' Yuri declared.

'Which part, the bit where we nearly got blown up? Come on, chief. We won.'

'Savi didn't.'

'Chief, Poi Li will fire your arse.'

'Why would Akkar walk into one of our hubs? He knew our facial recognition systems would send up red rockets.'

'He was disguised.'

'Yes. Superficially. And this is a man who is so paranoid about our digital security systems he doesn't allow any internet-connected technology within a hundred metres of himself. So what does he do? Sends his lieutenant – in his customary suit – to scout the hub out. It was a shout. He wanted us to know he was coming.'

'That's ridiculous. If he knew there was a chance we'd grab him, he wouldn't be carrying a satchel full of explosives.'

'Right, and not forgetting a map with a big red cross on it, because what does that make him?'

'I don't get it.'

Yuri grinned without humour. 'Guilty. Without question, without the slightest ambiguity. He was going to blow up Connexion's headquarters. Us! He was coming for us. Guilty.'

'I'm not arguing.'

'And what do we do with guilty psycho eco-terrorists?'

'Rendition, by the looks of it.'

'Yeah. He's gone to join his friends. That's what this was all about. He was never going to blow anything up.'

'Okay, so he's joined them. Or he's dead, if it turns out we really are on the side of the fascist psychos.'

'But how did he know they're all missing?'

'There's been nothing about his people raiding the Kintore maintenance depot in the news streams, no Connexion managers bragging about arrests, no prosecutors grandstanding that charges are pending. He had to know we've disappeared them.'

'True. But you'd have to know, really fucking *know*, if you're going to pull a stunt like this. Akkar isn't stupid. He's not going to gamble his life on some piece of hyped-up underground propaganda. He must have been completely certain.'

'How? Nobody knows.'

'We know – because of her.' Yuri stared at the picture of Savi. And in his mind the puzzle silently resolved itself, every factor slipping neatly together.

Boris obediently changed the picture of Savi at his command.

'And so does he,' Yuri said, pointing at Callum Hepburn. 'He knows his fiancée is missing. What happens when you put those two facts together? A member of Connexion's undercover security team and the company's fanatical opponents, both vanishing in the same incident. You'd know there is a huge dark operation in play.'

'But how would Akkar ever know Savi is one of ours?'

'Boris,' Yuri said calmly. 'Access Callum Hepburn's Connexion travel account.'

'Online,' Boris replied.

'How many times has Hepburn visited Kintore?'

'Five times in the last three days.'

'Oh shit,' Kohei whispered.

'And when was the last time he arrived in Kintore?' Yuri asked.

'Seven hours ago.'

'Has he left yet?'

'No.'

*

'Why here?' Kohei asked as they approached the Warbi Crude Metal Corp warehouse.

'The other piece of this that makes absolutely no sense,' Yuri said. 'Dimon knew we'd identified him. Why run here?'

'It's where they've been hiding out.'

'Most likely, but he led the drones here. And he'd got it screened with electronic warfare protection. Nobody could see what was going on inside. All communications were down.'

'That didn't stop the Arizona S&E team.'

'Didn't it?' Yuri had been reviewing the copied drone files as they walked through Kintore. The video images showed him sixteen armoured figures enter the warehouse. Then the minutes ticked away, with the drones carefully holding station above the warehouse, until the electronic jamming was switched off. The drone's secondary data table reported all sixteen of the team linking to Connexion Security with secure encryption, sending in personal video feeds and basic telemetry.

'Confirm target detention,' the Arizona S&E team reported. 'No casualties.'

They emerged triumphant. Two of them were escorting Dimon. Three more were carrying the modules of electronic countermeasure systems. The remaining eleven completed a sweep of the warehouse, confirming there were no further hostiles.

Dimon was put into one of the big 4x4s, and the team departed.

'I bet those vehicles are fitted out with a portal door in the back,' Kohei said. 'That way, you can send prisoners directly to North Korea, or wherever they're being stashed. Be useful if there's more trouble than you're expecting, too. Just bump the S&E team numbers up directly from their barracks.'

'I think you're right,' Yuri said.

They reached the warehouse door. The Arizona team had broken it down when they went in after Dimon, then re-secured it with a padlock and chain when they left. Yuri produced a power knife from his pocket and sliced through a link in the chain. He and Kohei took out their pistols and slipped inside.

There were no windows. Apart from maintenance crew inspections, people didn't work in the warehouse. It was all automated by an old G2Turing. Floor-to-ceiling shelving racks ran the length of the building, holding big drums of liquid metal crude of every type. They were held ready for the large-scale printers out at the airfield maintenance depot which could fabricate any of the moving components in the civil engineering machines that were abraded by the desert's infernal dust. A metre-diameter portal door was installed at one end of the building, with a conveyor belt leading through it back to Warbi Crude Metal Corp's main refinery in Japan. A couple of forklift truckez slid silently along the long aisles, placing newly arrived drums on the shelves, their bright amber safety strobes the only light in the warehouse.

Yuri glanced round the eerie building where strobes sent sharp-edged shadows leaping across every surface. His screen contact lenses were trying to compensate for the darkness with an amplified image, but the strobes were disrupting the program. 'Boris, can you interface with the warehouse Turing, get some lights on in here?'

'The warehouse light circuits have been physically disabled,' his mInet reported. 'The fault has been logged with the company maintenance office, and a repair crew is scheduled to arrive in ten hours' time.'

'Damn,' Yuri grunted – though it did confirm his suspicions.

They started edging forwards, pistols held ready. Illumination beams mounted on the barrels sent out slim fans of white light.

'Why this place?' Kohei asked. 'These racks channel you. There's nowhere to hide.'

'Yeah, but Dimon rigged it with a jammer. He knew this was going to be his last stand.'

'What are you thinking, chief?'

'I'm thinking he deliberately lured our people here.'

'But we got him.'

Yuri glanced round at the drums towering over him. 'The Arizona S&E team were out of contact with each other. All they had were helmet-mounted infra-red beams and light amplification goggles.'

'He could see them coming?'

'Not just him.' Yuri looked up and down the aisle, then lowered his pistol. 'Hey!' he shouted. 'Anyone here? We're from Connexion Security. Can you hear us?'

Kohei was giving him a puzzled look. 'Who are you expecting? Some more of Akkar's group?'

'No.' Yuri shook his head. 'Hey, are you in here? If you can't shout, make some kind of noise.'

'What—?'

Yuri put a finger to his lips. 'Shush. Listen.'

It was faint, but definite – a soft thudding sound.

'What is that?' Kohei murmured.

'Okay,' Yuri called. 'We hear you. Keep making the noise. We'll find you.'

They carried on down the aisle, then went back up the next one. The noise was originating somewhere just along the third aisle. Both of them knelt down, shining their pistol beams through the slim gaps between the drums of crude.

'There's space behind here,' Kohei exclaimed. 'Something's moving in there. I can't see what.'

They had to shift three barrels aside before there was a space wide enough for Yuri to crawl through. The back of the rack was covered in a thin metal mesh that had been fixed to the struts with gaffer tape. *Faraday cage*, Yuri realized with reluctant admiration. *It'll block any grain signals, but passively; doesn't show up on a sensor scan.* His power knife sliced through it, and he peered into the narrow gulf between the racks. A man in a T-shirt and shorts was lying on the concrete, looking as if he'd been cocooned in gaffer tape. As well as binding his limbs, a big strip was across his mouth. More tape secured his shoulders to the rack's struts. The only part of his body he could move were his legs; he'd been pounding his ankles on the concrete.

Yuri wormed his way in. 'This is going to hurt,' he warned, and pulled the tape from the man's mouth in a fast jerk.

'Motherfucker!'

'Who are you?' Yuri asked.

'Phil. Phil Murray.'

'You're from the team we sent in after Dimon, aren't you?'

'Yeah,' Phil said furiously. 'Arizona S&E squad seven. Our comms were out. Bastards must've jumped me. I think I got tasered. What's happened?'

'Where's your armour?'

'I don't know. I woke up like this. Fuck, I've been here for hours, man. It's . . . not good. Get me out of here.'

Yuri checked his screen lens display. There was no signal. 'One minute.' He pushed his way back out through the rack.

'Hey, don't fucking leave me! Get your ass back in here.'

The internet icon came back on as soon as Yuri was back in the aisle. He gave his knife to Kohei. 'Cut him loose.'

'You got it, chief.'

'Boris, call Poi Li, emergency priority.'

'Confirmed.'

'What is it?' Poi Li asked straight away.

'They stung us.'

'What?'

'Callum Hepburn and Akkar. We didn't catch Akkar and Dimon, they caught us. The warehouse was a trap. They snatched Phil Murray when the Arizona team's comms were down. We've just found him, without his armour. I'm guessing Callum is wearing it, escorting Dimon to whatever rendition site you bury our opponents away in.'

'Holy fuck!'

It was the only time Yuri had ever heard his ice queen boss swear, which he found strangely satisfying. 'You going to tell me what the hell is going on now?'

*

Wherever the facility was, it seemed to be deep underground. The corridor's walls, floor and ceiling were all concrete, with ribs of more concrete reinforcing it every ten metres. Utilitarian ducts ran along the ceiling, carrying thick bundles of cable. Air grilles gusted dry stale air down constantly.

Akkar and Dimon had been dressed in quilted black and green jumpsuits and calf-high boots, their wrists cuffed in high-security steel restraints. They were marched along past identical metal doors. Six Arizona S&E guards wearing full body armour with helmets and carrying snub-nose carbines were escorting them.

The group stopped outside a blank door no different from any of the others. It slid open, and the guards nudged them in.

The room awaiting them was about twenty metres long, and seven wide. There was a broad window in one wall, revealing a small control room with three consoles, all occupied by technicians. A thick conveyor belt ran down the centre of the room, leading directly to a portal door set against the wall at the far end. It was dark, with small purple scintillations erupting across the surface, indicating it was active but not open. Four yellow plastic cylinders, one and a half metres high, sat on the conveyor belt.

In the control room, the lead technician peered through the glass. 'Stand by,' he said, his voice booming out of the speakers. 'Get the flotation jackets on them.'

'The what?' Akkar said in alarm.

Two carbines swung round to point directly at his chest. One of the escorts picked up a pair of orange flotation jackets that were lying on the end of the conveyor belt.

'Opening the portal,' the technician announced.

'I can't swim,' Akkar said.

'You go through with or without the jacket,' a guard said. 'Your choice, but you are going through. We've done this a hundred times already.'

The scintillations in the portal door faded away. The darkness became a misty grey, revealing nothing. Air from the room started to flow through it. The ceiling grilles hissed loudly as more air was pumped in to compensate.

One of the guards walked over to the portal door and peered through.

'Careful, Phil,' another said. 'Not so close. Ain't no way back.'

'Lowering the exit,' the technician said.

'What is this?' Akkar demanded, his voice rising as his cuffs were unlocked. 'Where are you sending us?'

'Shut up, and put the fucking lifejacket on, tough guy.'

'Watch the belt,' the technician said. 'I'm starting it up. The survival pods will go through first.'

The metal door opened. Poi Li stepped into the room, five armed security personnel fanning out around her, pistols held ready. 'This operation is cancelled,' she snapped. 'Close the portal. Do it.'

All three technicians in the control room stared at her in surprise. The conveyor belt started to move, carrying the four cylinders along.

'Escort guards, stand down,' she ordered. 'Remove your helmets. Now. You, by the portal, step away.'

The guard who'd been staring into the emptiness beyond the portal door stood perfectly still in front of it.

'Take your helmet off,' Poi Li ordered.

His hand went up slowly, gripping the helmet rim, and slowly lifted it off. Callum smiled at Poi Li, then flipped backwards through the portal.

'No!' Poi Li yelled.

The grey mist on the other side of the portal door swallowed him immediately, leaving no trace.

*

The call came in to Brixton seventy minutes after Moshi Lyane had started his shift. 'We need an on-the-ground assessment at the Berat plant,' Fitz said. 'The fire's starting to spread.'

'Where the hell is Callum?' Dokal asked. 'He should have been here an hour ago.'

The crew exchanged glances across the office. Didn't say anything.

'We can handle this,' Moshi said. 'It's just an assessment.'

Dokal glanced though the glass into the Monitoring and Co-ordination Centre. Fitz was standing up at his console, hands on hips, giving her an impatient stare.

'Corporate has authorized our presence,' she said. 'All right. Moshi, take it.'

He grinned reassuringly. 'We're on it'

'Somebody tell me where Berat is,' Colin complained.

Raina slapped him on the shoulder as they headed for the door. 'Albania.'

'Want to know where that is?' Henry asked.

He was shown two vigorous fingers.

They quickly dressed in their hazmat suits and strode through Connexion's portal door network. Plans of the old chemical plant were thrown up across Moshi's screen lenses. They showed him the fire approaching a cluster of storage tanks. Lists of the compounds they used to hold appeared.

'They'll be trouble to vent,' Alana said. 'It's just residuals, sticking to the casing.'

'Let's find out,' Moshi said and stepped through the last portal. 'Going in now, Fitz.'

He found himself in a long courtyard formed by tall dilapidated buildings that had been abandoned years before. The portal door was surrounded by ten paramilitaries wearing full body armour. Each of them was levelling a carbine on the crew as they stepped out. Moshi's mInet reported a loss of connection with the Brixton M&C Centre. 'Oh crap.'

Colin, Alana, Henry and Raina pressed together around him.

Behind the ring of paramilitaries, a big grey 4x4 was parked in the shade. Yuri Alster stood beside it. 'You can all take your helmets off,' he said. 'There is no fire.'

Moshi pushed his visor up. 'What's going on?'

Yuri walked right up to him. 'Please don't be insulting. You know why you're here.'

'Fuck you,' Raina snarled.

'Ms Jacek,' Yuri said. 'Fashionable rebel to the end.'

She spat on the ground.

'You were all in Kintore six hours ago,' Yuri continued levelly. 'You'll be glad to know your plan worked. Callum is with his fiancée.'

'Wife,' Moshi said.

'Excuse me?'

'Savi is his wife.'

'Ah, that explains a lot. Well, it doesn't matter now. I know you all helped him. Your travel logs showed us you were all in Kintore ten hours ago.'

'Proves nothing,' Alana said.

'We're not in court,' Yuri said. 'And, sadly, you're already dead in this terrible fire.' His hand waved expansively at the empty, sun-soaked courtyard.

'Bastard!' Raina screamed. 'I'm not some eco-warrior that you can disappear. I have friends, family.'

'Yeah, it was all very fucking tragic,' Yuri said. 'The fire at the chemical plant reached some chemical drums that exploded. You were all killed. The coffins will be sealed, to spare your families.'

'You can't do this.'

'It's already done. It happened the moment you chose to help Hepburn.'

'What are you going to do to us? Just execute us in cold blood? We didn't do anything wrong! You took his wife from him.'

'Nobody is being executed.'

'What then?'

'You will be joining Callum and Savi.' Yuri turned to the paramilitaries. 'Take them away.'

*

Yuri had been awake so long he'd lost track of time zones. So he wasn't surprised that dawn light was shining through the windows of Poi Li's New York office. He didn't even wait to be invited to sit, just slumped into a chair in front of her desk.

'It's over, then?' she said.

'Yeah. Your Arizona team took them out of Albania. The deaths have been announced. We included Callum.'

'Well done. That was a good catch, Yuri. Connexion appreciates it.'

'So will I get to shake hands with Ainsley?'

'Gunning for my job?' she asked archly.

'No.'

'Yes you are. No need to be coy. We're both realists. You'll get here eventually. This operation showed me you have what it takes.'

'Okay. But I will need to know that Arizona S&E isn't Connexion's secret death squad.'

'It's not. I would never agree to run such a thing for Ainsley Zangari and his associates.'

'Associates? You mean it's not just Connexion doing this?'

'There is a covenant between several of the globalPACs,' Poi said. 'Ainsley is allied with some of them, naturally. They carry huge influence; some would say they are Earth's true supra-government. And as a realist, I looked around at the world we live in and agreed with their proposal.'

'Which is?'

'Society has been under siege from malicious elements for too long now. Law and order must be paramount for any civilization worthy of the name to flourish, especially now we are all neighbours, *one step away* from each other. Those who do not accept due process, who refuse to acknowledge the democratic mandate, are a cancer on society. And it is a terrible irony that our very liberalism allows such danger to flourish. There has to be a time when we say: No more. And thanks to Connexion, that time has now come. As Edmund Burke said—'

'The only thing necessary for the triumph of evil is for good men to do nothing,' Yuri quoted.

'Indeed,' Poi Li acknowledged. 'The globalPACs knew they had to do something if our children were ever to live in a society free from the fear of maniacs blowing things up and killing people in the name of their cause. For there are so many causes. But we cannot descend to their level, where violence and death are the solution to anything that denies them their goal. We do not kill or maim, or even imprison; that is what sets us apart from them. This new trans-galactic society we are about to embark on affords us the opportunity to deal with such unreasoning fanatics humanely. We will simply part company with their kind and allow them to live their life by their own ideals.'

'So what happens to them?'

'Exile.'

*

Callum fell. He knew that was going to happen as soon as he lurched through the portal door. What he wasn't expecting was to keep on falling.

Whatever gloomy mist he was falling through seemed to be

sucking the air from his lungs. When he did manage to inhale, it was as if he was gulping down frigid Arctic vapour.

Is that it? A polar gulag?

He landed in water, creating a huge plume which closed over his head as he plummeted down. He was expecting it to be cold, but it was so hot it was almost scalding. The shock of its heat knifing into his flesh made him yell – big mistake. His mouth and nose filled with disgustingly briny water as his arms and legs flailed round. There was no light, so he couldn't tell which way was up.

Don't panic. Panic will kill you.

He felt round for the torch clipped to his belt. In seconds his lungs had gone from freezing to burning as his body demanded he draw a breath. Water was slowly creeping further along his nostrils.

The torch came on. And he could see through the murky water which was now stinging his eyes. Bubbles swirled round him, and finally he could see which way they were going. Up.

He kicked urgently. Arms scrabbling in a pathetic stroke. The bulk of his saturated clothes and everything he was carrying combined to weigh him down. Progress was achingly slow. The pain in his lungs was growing intolerable. Instinct was trying to prise his mouth open so he could suck down blessed air.

He kicked harder. Arms pumping.

His head broke through a thin surface layer of yellow scum, and he sucked down a fraught breath. Immediately he was coughing and spluttering. The air was dangerously thin, yet heavy with brimstone. He concentrated on staying afloat, getting his breathing under control.

After a few breaths he realized the heat was going to prove lethal in a very short time. Already his skin was on fire. Apollo was throwing up all sorts of medical warning symbols on his screen lenses. Movement was difficult.

He shone the torch round, trying to see anything solid he could swim towards.

'Hey there!' a call came.

'Here! Here!' Callum cried out.

'This way, man.'

A powerful beam of white light swept over the filthy layer of froth. Callum shone his own torch in the direction it originated. The beam found him, dazzling.

'We see you,' the voice yelled. 'Make your way towards us. Fast as you can. This water's gonna screw you up.'

Every movement was difficult now. The heat was stabbing through his flesh to grip his bones, slowly paralysing him. He felt he was being boiled alive, but he kept sweeping his arms around, wriggling his feet rather than kicking strongly. Long flecks of foam streaked across his face. The torch beam moved off to shine just in front of him, presenting a moving target.

'Come on, you can do it,' the voice urged. 'Just a few metres more.'

He wondered why, if he was this close to the shore, his feet hadn't touched anything solid yet.

'There you go. We got you.'

The beam wavered. In the shadows behind it, shapes were moving.

'Catch this.'

A rope dropped out of the dark air to land in the frothy surface. He stretched out a hand, unsure if his burning fingers could even manage to grip it.

'Wind it round your arm.'

He did his best, but even his arm had become sluggish. Suddenly he was moving fast as the rope pulled him along. Then hands were gripping him, hauling him over a rock shelf that sparkled with a dusting of hoar frost. He was dragged out of the water, trailing ripples of rank sludge behind him. Strands of mist threaded through the still air all around.

'Congratulations. You made it. Welcome to hell.'

Callum swayed about on all fours, dripping steaming water and blobs of scum onto the rock. The intense heat permeating him made every movement painful, yet each breath of frigid air was a torment. He was desperate to get out of his broiling guard's uniform. Torchlight fell on him and held steady.

'Hey, what the fuck?' his male saviour exclaimed.

'What is it?' a second voice asked. Female.

'That's a guard's uniform. The bastard's Connexion Security.'

'What?'

'No,' Callum said, or tried to. The glacial air just came out of his mouth as a loud wheeze.

A hand gripped the hair on the back of his head, forcing him to look up. 'You a guard, dickhead? You fall through by mistake, huh?'

'No.'

'I'm going to make you wish this was hell!'

The kick caught Callum in the side of his torso, shunting him across the rock. He flopped onto his back. The torch beam was still on him, blotting out the people behind. He could hear a footfall. Then another kick slammed into his ribs. Pain stars flashed across his vision. He wanted to scream in fury, but didn't have the strength or breath.

'Throw him back in,' the female voice demanded.

'Yeah – eventually.'

Callum reached down to his belt, hoping his memory was good, that his hand was in the right place. Fingers protested every nerve impulse, but slowly closed round the device's grip.

'Gonna make you bleed,' the man growled. 'Gonna make you scream. You'll beg me to kill you before I'm done slicing you. I know how to make that happen. Oh man, do I ever.' There was a flash in the gloom as the torchlight shone off a blade.

It gave Callum a target. He fired the pistol.

There was a furious screech that twisted off into agonized grunting. The man dropped to the ground. Callum could hear limbs thrashing about as the dart pumped electricity into his erstwhile tormentor.

'Shit!' the woman shouted.

Callum shifted round on the ground. The torch was a huge clue to where she was. It was a massive effort to make his fingers respond, but he managed to fire again. Missed. The torch beam swung around, which gave him an indication of which hand she was holding it in, where her body must be. Then it was wobbling from side to side as she started running.

He fired again. She wailed as the dart struck, then fell. The torch tumbled away and rolled across the rock, ending up pointing out across the simmering water.

Callum rolled onto his back and squeezed his eyes shut for a long moment. 'Holy fuck.'

The heat was abating – fractionally. He knew he had to get out of his sodden clothes. The armoured jacket was easy to shrug out of. Vapour billowed off his shirt and trousers, fluorescing a vivid white in the torchlight. He stripped them off quickly but left the slim backpack in place. The sight of his skin, now a nasty shade of salmon pink, made him grimace. But the cold was cutting into him now, almost as bad as the heat from a minute ago. He could feel himself starting to go numb.

'Where the fuck is this place?' he muttered as he bent over the man he'd darted. His victim was in his late thirties with a thick beard, wearing a heavy quilted coat and equally thick trousers, similar to the ones they'd put on Akkar and Dimon.

Callum claimed the coat for himself, but let the man keep his sweater. Next prize was the boots and trousers.

Once he was dressed properly he made himself sit for a few minutes, spending the time sorting through the equipment that was attached to Phil Murray's stolen uniform. His abused skin was one giant itch, and he could feel his blood singing round his body as the adrenalin high gradually dissipated. As his heart calmed, he began to take in what had happened. The air was sub-zero and so thin he was clearly at considerable altitude, yet the lake he'd fallen into had to be a geothermal vent. *Iceland?* But his smartCuff couldn't get a lock on any navigation satellites, which was troubling.

He stood up and walked over to retrieve the big torch. When he shone it on the woman, he saw an elderly lady with ebony skin and a mass of frizzy grey hair flaring out from under a dark wool hat. Her quilted coat was similar to the man's, as were her trousers and boots.

He swung the torch beam back to the man. He'd left him his

sweater, but his bare legs were turning blue, and frost was forming on them. 'Ah, bollocks.'

Callum turned a slow circle, scanning the beam about. If the reception party were on some kind of watch to help the people Connexion dropped into the water, then they'd be ready with dry clothes. Sure enough, three of the yellow plastic drums were standing ten metres from the shore. He went over to them and rummaged through the blankets and coats he found inside. There was also a flask of tea, which tasted bitter – as if he cared.

One of the pouches on the stolen uniform contained zip-lock strips. Callum spent a couple of minutes binding the man and woman together, and wrapping blankets round the man's bare legs so he didn't get frostbite or hypothermia.

Then he pulled up the coat's hood and settled down to wait.

The woman recovered consciousness first. She groaned a lot, and winced, and tried to move.

'Crap,' she grunted when she found how securely she was fastened to her companion.

'Hello,' Callum said.

She scowled at him. 'You shot me, you piece of shit!'

'Just before you two started to cut chunks off me. Yeah, I'm mean that way. And the name's Callum.'

'Start running, Connexion fascist. If you thought Donbul was pissed at you before, wait until he wakes up. The hunt will be fun.'

'I'm not Connexion . . . Well, I do work for them, but not in Security.'

'Liar.'

He shrugged and sipped some more of the odd tea. Sure enough, the woman managed to stay silent for about a minute.

'What are you doing?' she asked, genuinely bewildered.

'Waiting for my friends. Connexion is going to go apeshit that they helped me, so they should be shipping them out here in a day or so. By the way, where is here? I thought Iceland at first, but I'm not so sure now. Antarctic?'

'Like you don't know.'

''Fraid not.'

170

She sniffed in contempt and turned her head away. When she looked back he saw real anger in her expression. 'We'll kill you!'

He grinned, specifically to annoy her. 'No, you won't.'

'What friends?'

'Who am I talking to?'

'I'm not telling you my name.'

'But if you're going to torture me to death anyway, what difference will it make?'

She stared at him for a moment. 'Foluwakemi.'

'Where are you from, Foluwakemi; Nigeria, probably, right?'

'And you know this how, spy? I'm in your files, aren't I?'

'Ah, a promotion: dumb guard to spy in five fast minutes. How flattering. No, I'm not a spy. My mInet suggested Nigeria.' He held up his arm so she could see the jet-black smartCuff.

'My God, you have working electronics?'

'Yep.'

'Then you are a spy.'

'Crap, but you're paranoid.' He waved his hand at the surrounding darkness. 'Mind, I suppose you have that right. Dumped here, wherever here is. Incidentally, my mInet can't lock onto any satnav signals. So that makes this place *extremely* remote. I'm guessing the Antarctic's Ellsworth Mountains. Quite high up them, too, with air this thin.'

Her grin made him uneasy; it betrayed the fact she thought she still had some advantage. 'Wrong. Who are you?'

'I told you: Callum.'

Donbul groaned. His head came up, and his gaze fixed on Callum.

'Untie me,' he demanded.

'So you can start stabbing me?' Callum said archly. 'I don't think so.'

'You are going to hurt so bad.'

'Real tough guy, huh? You need to dial it down there, pal.'

'You think you can outrun us?'

'Do I look like I'm trying to run somewhere?'

That brought a puzzled frown. 'What the fuck is this? Who are you?'

Callum sighed. 'Callum. I'm a team chief in Connexion's Emergency Detoxification division.'

'All I see is a dead man walking.'

'You need to be nicer to me,' Callum said. 'Really.'

'Go fuck yourself, dead man.'

'Why? You know someone else who's going to get you out of here?'

That made them both gawp. Callum grinned. 'Oh, do I have your attention now?'

'Nobody can get us out of here,' Foluwakemi said.

'We'll see.'

'Why are you here?'

'I've come to find my wife. I think Connexion renditioned her.'

'Why would they do that?'

'She was caught up in the protest against the Australian desert being seeded with ice. Did those people get sent here?'

'Yes,' Foluwakemi nodded. 'Over a hundred of them.'

'Christ almighty! How many people are here?'

'There are thousands of us.'

'Thousands?'

'Yes.'

'But . . . Is this a camp?'

'No, there's nobody here but us. Connexion dumped us here to fend for ourselves.'

Callum gave an involuntary shiver. 'Pretty tough, huh?'

'Worse than you think. The crop seeds they provided aren't much good. The biologists among us think there's too much iron in the soil.'

'Crops? In Antarctica? There's no such thing.'

Foluwakemi gave him a pitying smile. 'Look up, detoxification man.'

Callum did as he was told. He hadn't noticed dawn arriving above the glare of the torch. That was reasonable enough, as it hadn't come to the horizon. Instead, directly overhead, a wide strip of the sky was tinged with an insipid grey light. He frowned at the anomaly, scanning round in a full circle. As the light grew he realized he was in the bottom of a canyon, but the poor light was making it difficult to judge the scale of the rock walls on either side. That and his mind was refusing to accept what he saw. He was constantly trying to adjust the perspective.

His jaw slowly hinged open as reality soaked his brain in parallel to the weak sunlight. The sheer cliffs were at least seven kilometres high, probably more, with a floor maybe five kilometres across. He'd been to the Grand Canyon a few years ago, done the whole tourist routine – some rafting, climbed an easy face of rock. This was an order of magnitude larger, which was ridiculous.

'Where the hell are we?' he blurted.

'You just called it, arsehole,' Donbul mocked. 'Hell. Otherwise known as Zagreus.'

'No,' Callum said. 'No no. That's not possible.' He didn't have to consult Apollo's files for that; Zagreus was an exoplanet slightly larger than Earth, but with an atmosphere as thin as Mars and no surface water. It orbited three AUs out from Alpha Centauri A. When the *Orion* starship decelerated into the Centauri system, there had been quite a clamour to begin terraforming it. But it was so much cheaper to build a second wave of starships and send them further out to stars with more suitable exoplanets.

'Still think you can get us out of here?' Foluwakemi sneered.

*

Yuri looked round the domestic disaster zone that was Callum's flat and wrinkled his nose. Partly from the sight, but there was also a weird smell coming from the galley kitchen.

'Don't we pay him enough for a housekeeping service?' Kohei asked.

Yuri grunted. 'Apparently not.'

Two technical officers came in and went over to the small white block in the corner of the room, which was the G3Turing house manager.

'I want a complete memory download,' Yuri told them. 'Unlocked files available to my desk in two hours.'

'Yes, sir.'

He walked across the living area, frowning in disapproval at the large number of empty pizza boxes scattered around. 'Plenty of people were here,' he said. 'He knew he was planning a one-way trip, so what's the point of clearing up?'

'You think they planned it here?' Kohei said.

'Probably. It doesn't matter now.'

'So why are we here?'

Yuri pulled a face, unable to explain fully his sense that somehow they'd lost, that Callum was laughing at them. After so many years in the job you got a feel for things, for people in all their crazy glory. His old training back in Russia concentrated on individuals, where everyone was considered suspect, untruthful, corrupt. Now his corporate staff were all strictly procedure-focused, utilizing data trawls and analysis matrices. If they wanted someone they didn't go out of the office and hunt them, they just waited until facial recognition algorithms pulled them out of a public street camera. There were no real chases, only drones auto-tracking their targets. It was one of the reasons he enjoyed running the undercover ops division; intelligence-gathering was as close as he got to old-school these days. Until Callum Hepburn had come along.

Callum didn't fit any profile they were used to. He wasn't motivated by greed or ideology or religion, wasn't mentally ill or drug addled. Didn't want to rule the world. Callum was a man in love, and desperate. Best of all, he was smart and tough, unafraid to take chances.

'Do you not think something's wrong with all this?' Yuri asked.

Kohei let out a small groan. 'We got them all. What could be wrong?'

'Yes. We were always going to get them.'

'Not necessarily. It was only because you're smart enough to work out what was going down that we found Phil Murray.'

'They stuck tape across his mouth. He'd have chewed through eventually.'

'In a disused warehouse.'

'Due a maintenance visit for the lights. And anyway, when Callum took a dive through the portal into exile, we'd have known Murray had been substituted.'

'They're gone, chief. You need to close the file.'

Yuri stared at a large framed picture on the wall with an August 2091 date along the base. It was Callum and his team gathered round their Ducati 999, all of them with their arms round each other's shoulders, smiling exuberantly. A tight crew.

'Would you do that for me?' Yuri asked his deputy.

'Chief?'

'If my fiancée had been renditioned, and I was planning to go after her, would you help me, knowing that help would be discovered, and the outcome would mean exile? Permanent exile in the most remote hellhole Connexion could find?'

'Well . . . I don't know.'

'No, don't flatter me; you wouldn't do it.' Yuri's forefinger tapped the picture. 'Henry Orme's partner is about to give birth, for God's sake! Callum didn't even let him go to the Gylgen plant; he sent him to supervise the Haumea end of the operation where he'd be safe. And the rest, they all care about each other. They're friends, they face danger together on a weekly basis, they party together, they share the bike. But this . . .' He stared at the sunlit happy faces, trying to absorb the camaraderie. 'To willingly go into an unknown exile together. To make that sacrifice, give up your whole life. Unanimously. I don't believe it.'

'But . . . they did do it. They knew we'd send them after Callum, it's the only way we could be sure this whole rendition thing didn't leak to the media.'

Yuri moved his finger over to Callum's head. 'Yes. Why, though?'

'They owe him, maybe?'

'No, not owe. Trust. They *trust* him. Every time they face a disaster, they trust him with their lives. He plans every operation. We think they take risks, but actually they don't. Callum's too clever for that. He's got backups and fresh angles and cut-offs all worked out in his head long before they actually take that one step into a danger zone. And that's what we're dealing with here.'

'Sorry,' Kohei said. 'I just don't see it.'

Yuri smiled at the picture. 'That's it! We're not seeing it.'

'Chief?'

His knuckles rapped the frame. 'What's missing? They're all there. Callum, Moshi, Henry, Alana, Raina. The whole team.'

'Yes? So?'

'So who took the picture?'

*

It took half an hour, and a lot of shouted insults, but by then Donbul was simply going through the motions. Callum could see doubts troubling the man, that just because he'd come through wearing a guard's uniform didn't actually make him a guard. That and hope. *A way out.*

Callum strapped the guard uniform belt round his coat, checked the weapons and cut the pair of them loose. He stood back, one hand very close to the pistol holster. 'Just so we understand each other, I don't trust you. So keep your distance and no fast moves. I've sacrificed everything to come here. Shooting you won't even register.'

Foluwakemi stretched and rubbed her wrists. Donbul simply glared at him and went over to the drums to find himself new trousers and boots.

Now the daylight had strengthened, Callum could see the lake was actually a rough circle a couple of hundred metres in diameter. Sitting on the rock shelf just out of the water was a raft made entirely of the yellow drums lashed together.

'It's a volcanic caldera,' Foluwakemi said, watching him. 'There's a group of them in this section of the canyon. Without them, we'd be dead. They supply all our heat and water.'

Callum glanced up at the phenomenal walls of rock. 'And the air? Do they vent that as well?'

'Only sulphur gas. We're seven kilometres below the planet's average ground level. That's why we have air. It's a tiny pocket, the last on Zagreus. It must have had a full terrestrial atmosphere at one time, maybe a million years ago. But now it's as thin as Mars, that's why no one bothered to try and terraform it. You'd have to import a whole new atmosphere. Too expensive, especially when exoworld astronomy has found so many worlds with a nitrogen-based atmosphere close by.'

'How long's the canyon?'

'Three hundred kilometres, we think. A few of us remember the *Orion* survey images and news reports. But less than twenty per cent is habitable, and this is the only cluster of geothermal vents.'

Callum squinted up into the sky. It had brightened to an astonishingly deep sapphire blue. 'Where's the portal?'

'It's on some kind of drone blimp, we think,' Donbul said. 'They lower it when they're sending a batch of people through – which only happens at night so we can't ever see it. That way we can't jump on board and go back through the portal. The rest of the time it stays up there somewhere, all nice and safe from us badboys.'

'Makes sense,' Callum muttered. 'So it won't come down again until tonight?'

'Never has,' Foluwakemi said. 'But then we've never had anyone like you come through before, either.'

'It'll take Security a while to work out what's happened. As soon as they do, they'll round my crew up and send them through along with Dimon and Akkar.'

'Akkar?' she asked sharply, and crossed herself. 'They caught Akkar? Well, shit.'

'They didn't catch him. He went visible so I could position myself for this. Very visible, actually.'

'You are joking, detoxification man.'

'No joke.'

'Akkar's coming?'

'Yes. And when he does, we're all out of here. Everyone goes home.'

'I'll take you to the longhouses,' Foluwakemi said. 'You can see if your wife is there.'

'Thank you.'

'If she's not . . .'

Callum grinned weakly. 'Don't worry, I'll still get you all out.'

*

It wasn't far to the collection of buildings that the exiles had built for themselves. Callum ordered Apollo to record everything his screen lenses were capturing. They would all be relying on the images for leverage when he got back to Earth. He didn't know what to look for at first, so it took him a while to recognize what he was walking towards. In his mind he'd pictured a medieval-style village of circular huts with thatched roofs. Stupid, because Zagreus didn't have any vegetation; there were no trees for wood or palms. Instead the outcasts had built themselves stone walls three metres high, forming long rectangles. They were roofed with sheets of transparent polythene.

'It comes in big rolls,' Foluwakemi explained. 'They send it inside the survival barrels, like everything else. It's thin, but really tough, thankfully.'

'What else do they give you?'

'Clothes,' she patted her coat. 'Seeds, eggs, some tools, a few utensils, basic medicine. Food, of course – to start with. You get enough to last a few months, by which time you should be growing your own.' She shrugged. 'At least, that's the theory some desk-expert worked out. In practice, its bloody hard. Poor nutrition causes a lot of health problems. And this air's none too good for us, either. Then there are . . . disputes.'

There were plenty of people milling round outside. Five new longhouses were under construction. Callum stared at the wheel-barrows that stones were being carried about in, marvelling at the ingenuity. Each was made of a barrel cut lengthways, with a barrel rim as its wheel, strips of barrel formed the handles.

'They're damn useful,' Foluwakemi admitted reluctantly as she caught him watching.

She went over to one of the crews building a wall. Callum's hand stayed very close to his pistol as she talked to them. A group started to gather, inspecting him from a distance, their voices a low grumble on the verge of menacing. It was the weapons on his belt that made him stand out, he knew; everyone here would be up-close familiar with the types and who carried that particular combination. He kept his nerve and stared back levelly, as if they were of no consequence.

Then, as he dreaded it would happen, someone was striding across the ground towards him. A big man with a dark beard that hung a good twenty centimetres down the front of his coat. He was carrying an axe, its handle made from thick strips of yellow barrel plastic, bound to a stone blade. His supporters in the watcher group started to flow after him.

Foluwakemi turned round. 'Oh shit,' she grunted.

'You,' the big man shouted. 'Shithead. Who the fuck are you?'

Callum knew that being reasonable was never going to be an option. He drew the short carbine, switched it to single shot, and fired just in front of the man's feet – not bothering to take good aim, just showing how nonchalant he was, how he was The Man now. The noise of the shot was astonishingly loud in the thin air. Everyone recoiled.

'I've got about seventy rounds,' Callum said clearly, 'so I can probably kill about fifty of you before you reach me. Alternatively –' he raised the carbine and flicked on the laser targeting beam, slapping the red dot squarely on the man's face – 'I can take you all back to Earth. Your call.'

The man kept jerking his head about, trying to dodge the beam. Callum kept it aligned pretty well given the circumstances.

'Listen to him, Nafor,' Foluwakemi said. 'He came through alone. They didn't drop any survival barrels with him. That's never happened before. He wasn't renditioned. He came here because he wanted to; he's searching for someone.'

'No way,' Nafor barked. He must have realized how much face he was losing in front of his followers.

'There's a portal door in my backpack,' Callum said, raising his voice so everyone could hear.

That drew a universal gasp of surprise.

'Oh yeah,' Callum said contentedly. 'You heard that right.' He stopped and made an effort to dial down the arrogance. 'I'm the only one who has the access code, so listen good. We are waiting until Connexion exiles my friends here; then – and only then – will I start the thread-up procedure. After that, if you want to come through after me, you're welcome.' He saw Nafor draw a breath, his mouth opening to speak.

'No!' Callum bellowed. He raised the target dot slightly and fired another shot, into the air this time. 'No discussion! No arguing! That's the way it happens. Now either accept that, or fuck off.'

Very carefully, Nafor raised his arms. 'You got it, buddy. Anyone who can get me out of here is my friend for life.'

Callum scowled, covering up just how shit-scared he actually was.

Foluwakemi cleared her throat.

'What?' Callum snapped.

'I think I know which longhouse your wife's in. If you can calm down and not shoot me, I'll take you there.'

She led him along the tracks between the longhouses, most of which seemed to have gullies of steaming water running alongside them. The gullies branched frequently, taking the water through low arches into individual longhouses. They'd only just started off when he realized that Nafor was following him, along with everybody else, all of them keeping a respectful distance. 'I am not the messiah,' he grumbled under his breath.

Foluwakemi opened a door (made from sections of yellow barrel) and they walked into a longhouse. The air inside was thick with strong scents, and hot. The humidity was almost tropical. Hot water flowed down a shallow stone channel running the length of the building.

Callum checked that Apollo was still recording everything he was seeing. Sandy soil was banked up between the water and the walls, with densely planted crops growing out of it. The majority of vegetation was maize, but he recognized tomato plants and avocados, aubergines, breadfruit, dwarf bananas, as well as several varieties he couldn't place. None of them looked particularly vigorous, as if they were suffering from a universal blight. When he looked up, he saw the polythene was coated in condensation which dribbled steadily towards the walls.

'How long is a day here?' he asked, looking at the sickly leaves.

'Nineteen hours thirty-two minutes,' Foluwakemi said. 'It messes with us and the plants, along with the minerals we can't filter out of the water. Nafor putting his stone-age axe through your skull can lower your life expectancy, as well.'

'Is he in charge?'

'He'll tell you he is. This month, anyway. Someone as big and stupid will go for him soon, if we're still here. It's the worst kind of primitive. Frankly, I'm surprised we've lasted this long. Each new group that arrives brings their own set of opinions – with a capital O.'

Pens of close-spaced yellow plastic poles marked the end of the vegetation. Scrawny chickens pecked at the rough ground inside; Callum held his breath against the smell. Beyond the pens was a curtain of polythene. Foluwakemi pushed it aside.

Inside was a sickbay with a row of ten cots, all of them occupied. The smell of vomit and faeces and diseased breath was a miasma worse than anything the chickens produced. Callum nearly gagged as he scanned along the figures wrapped in blankets. Apollo sent out a ping for her grains, but there was no answer.

There. Halfway along the row. Thick, filthy, black hair hung limply over the side of a cot. He let out a sob and sank to his knees beside her.

Savi's face was wrapped in crude gauze bandages, heavily stained with old blood and yellow suppurations. More bandages covered her arms. A leg was splinted. Her breathing was shallow.

The sight of her in this state was terrifying. 'Wife?' he whispered.

She inhaled, coughing. 'Cal?'

'Yes.' He smiled through his tears. 'Yes, it's me.'

Her head turned, and through the apertures in the bandage mask he saw her eyes open. One of them was a milky white orb. 'How can you be here?' she asked.

'Better or worse, remember? I said I will follow you to the ends of the Earth – and beyond. I would never break that promise. Not to you.'

*

Kohei stood inside the Brixton facility's M&C Centre, staring round at the wallscreens with their high-resolution images of potential ecological doom. He'd never really paid attention to the ancient industrial sites that human companies had abandoned all across the planet. Threats of mid-level disaster were a constant background buzz in his life, like taxes and online crime; you just lived with it. But now he was actually watching an unending parade of dilapidated tanks and pipes and storage bunkers flowing across the screens, with associated symbology highlighting impending problems.

'How much crap is out there?' he asked in dismay.

Fitz Adamova gave him a knowing grin. 'Haumea station dumps about a quarter of a million tons a week. That's mostly low-level contaminates and their secure containers.' He pointed to an Iraqi nuclear store. 'And then there's the containment vessels themselves, along with the buildings and local soil. It adds up, volume-wise.'

'Jesus, why do we do it?'

'War and profit, mainly.'

Kohei shook his head, focusing on the job. 'Okay, I need you to run an equipment audit.'

Fitz's eyebrows shot up. 'You are kidding? Our teams burn through equipment faster than a solar flare. We're lucky if we get half of it back from an operation.'

'I'm not particularly bothered about the engineering junk. I want to know if all your portal doors are accounted for.'

'Well, that's easy enough: yes.'

'No,' Kohei said firmly. 'It's not easy. We suspect someone with inside access has manipulated your network. I need you to check. Go down to the storage bays and physically confirm they're all there if you have to.'

Fitz blew out his cheeks. 'Seriously?'

'Yes. And I need to know quickly. This has priority over

everything. We believe someone is currently using one of this department's portal doors, and they really shouldn't be.'

'Okay. Well, actually, that can be checked quite simply.' He went over to his station, looking back at Kohei with a quizzical expression. 'You sure it's in use?'

'Reasonably sure, yes.'

Fitz started calling up data on his screens. 'Do you know how portal doors are powered?'

'Not got a clue,' Kohei said, amused by the way technical types always tried to establish some level of superiority over everyone else. *My knowledge is bigger than yours.*

'Portals.'

'What?'

'Portals power portals.' Fritz smiled and tapped a ridiculously complex graphic on his central screen. 'The solarwells send electricity back to Earth's central grid via portal, and Connexion is the single biggest market for that power. Portals use up a hell of a lot of energy to maintain their entanglement. The greater the distance they bridge, the more power they consume. It's not governed by an inverse square law, thankfully, but this department consumes a pretty hefty number of megawatt hours.'

'Okay, I get it. You can monitor that power consumption.'

'Yes. Every Connexion portal door has a one-centimetre portal built in, which supplies it with power direct from the central grid. And we . . . Oh, wait, that's wrong.' He leant forwards, studying the screen.

'What is?'

'Our power usage monitor is offline, but its display function has frozen in a loop. How the hell did that happen?'

'Can you restore it?'

'Sure. Hang on.' Fitz typed quickly, muttering at his mInet. The graphics on the screen changed. Several red icons appeared. 'Holy shit,' he exclaimed. 'What is doing that? Not even our six-metre portals eat this much power.'

*

Callum sat beside Savi's cot all day long. She slid in and out of consciousness in front of him. Some of the times when she woke, she seemed puzzled by his presence.

The doctor, a middle-aged South African man, ran through her injuries for him. Her clothes had protected most of her skin from the direct blast, he said, but her head and arms and hands had been exposed, and she was close to the bag when it detonated. Callum guessed her grains had been ruined by the explosion, or ripped away when the blastwave tore her flesh off; which was why Connexion Security didn't know who she was when they dropped her through the portal. The surface wounds and burns were slowly turning septic, which, if unchecked, was going to produce severe blood poisoning. Connexion didn't send metabiotics to Zagreus to counter that. And even if she somehow got through that, she would need modern medskin applied under controlled conditions to restore her natural skin. Her eye was damaged beyond repair, although the doctor thought the optic nerve was still intact, so an artificial retina implant might return her vision. His biggest worry was head trauma. Her responses were deteriorating at a rate the other injuries didn't quite account for.

'Just a few hours more,' Callum told her in one of her better lucid periods. 'I have to wait for my crew. They exposed themselves to get me here.' Though he was beginning to wonder if he dared wait that long. The sight of her, so weak and damaged, was an agony. Delaying her admission to hospital was a violation of every feeling he had for her. Time itself became intolerable.

All day long he heard the voices outside, growing in volume. Not with anger, just the sheer number of people who were gathering outside the longhouse. Foluwakemi kept coming in to give him updates. Every human on Zagreus had arrived for the vigil. So far they were being patient, but expectation was growing. With that, tempers were shortening.

'Could you just come out and talk to them?' she pleaded.

'They wait,' he said forcefully, gripping Savi's hand tighter so she moaned. 'If Savi can do it, they bloody well can. When my friends arrive, then this is over. You have my word.'

An hour before sunset, when the sheltered canyon was already reduced to a gloomy half-light, over two hundred people marched down to the arrival lake. Foluwakemi said they were making very sure there were no screw-ups when Connexion dropped his friends in the geothermal vent pool.

Solar-charged lamps were switched on around the sickbay as darkness finally fell, making it appear even more macabre. Callum didn't know when he'd eaten last. Sleep was also a distant recollection, something he used to do in his previous existence. Apollo had to keep sending alert signals to his auditory grains as well as purple flashes to his screen lenses, as he kept drifting off.

His time display told him it was two and a half hours after sunset when the cheering started outside. He frowned puzzled by the sound. Then Foluwakemi rushed in. 'They're here,' she shouted excitedly. Moisture was glinting in her eyes. 'You're telling the truth, aren't you, detoxification man? You can take us home now?'

'I can take you home,' he promised. Somehow his voice had become hoarse.

Then they were there: Moshi, Alana, Colin, Raina and Henry. All wearing thick Zagreus-survival coats, their skin flushed from immersion in the scalding water. Smiling, calling out wild greetings. Akkar and Dimon followed them in, looking dazed.

Callum was pulled to his feet and hugged exuberantly.

'We did it, we fucking did it,' Raina was shouting.

'This really is Zagreus, isn't it?' Moshi said, an astounded smile on his face. 'We've gone interstellar?'

'Oh, yeah.'

'I had money on it being the Antarctic.'

Nafor appeared, and the reunion damped down fast.

'It is time,' he declared, his gaze never leaving Callum.

'We'll set up outside,' Callum told him.

Colin and Dimon carried Savi out on her cot, using it like a stretcher. An area was cleared at the end of the stone longhouse, with one of the hot streams bubbling away along the side. People formed a broad circle round them, more perched on the walls of the longhouse. Over two hundred torch beams shone down.

Callum took off his coat and unfastened his backpack. He pulled the half-metre portal out, and a massive cry went up behind the multifaceted wall of beams.

Alana held it steady on the ground, while Moshi stood in front, ready.

Callum studied the status display on his screen lens. The amount of power the portal was pulling out of the grid to maintain entanglement with its twin back on Earth was spiking close to its internal circuitry safety limits. But it was functional. They had a link. 'Activate it,' Callum instructed Apollo.

*

Yuri walked along the tarmac lane that ran the length of the Donington paddock. He was intrigued by all the old vehicles parked there, surrounded by their enthusiastic crews as they prepped the sleek bikes for racing. The noise of the engines was primal, bringing fond smiles to the older faces among the crowds who ambled along, admiring the mechanical history on show.

He gazed at each of the big vans and trucks carefully, making sure his screen glasses got a clear view. Boris ran pattern recognition, throwing up the model and manufacturer of each one.

The white Mercedes Sprinter van stood out anyway. A small canvas marquee had been erected at the rear end, its side panels zipped up. There was a Ducati bike standing beside it, but no crew or riders, as if the whole area had been abandoned. No genuine race team would leave their precious machine untended.

Sloppy, he thought. *It's always the little things.*

He went into the marquee and banged hard on the rear doors of the van. There was no response.

'Oh, come on,' he said in a voice tired with the chase. 'It's not as if I brought a tactical team. I'm by myself.'

There was a *clunk* as the van's handle turned. Then the rear door swung open.

'Yuri,' Dokal Torres said nervously. 'What can I do for you?'

'You can stop being a lawyer for today.'

'Really? Have you stopped being a security chief?'

'Let's just say I'm on my lunch break. Can I come in?'

She let out a heavy sigh. 'Sure. It's a bit cramped.'

'I'll live.' He clambered into the Sprinter; Dokal checked the marquee was zipped up tight and shut the door behind him.

The threader mechanism almost filled the inside of the van.

'I genuinely wasn't expecting *you*,' he admitted.

Her lips squeezed into a small moue. 'I think that was the point.'

'Callum's good. I should have him on my staff.'

'So what now?'

He regarded the intricate mechanics of the threader with interest. 'I've never been this close to one of these before, and I've been with the company a long time. I think I'd like to see one in operation. So we'll just wait, if that's okay with you?'

'Why?' she asked.

'Professional pride. Savi is one of my agents. I never leave one of mine behind.'

'What does Poi Li think about that?'

'I expect we'll find out soon enough. When will they use it?'

'I don't know. Callum was going to wait until the crew arrived at wherever it is they're renditioned to.'

'Ah. Well they were scheduled to go through ten minutes ago. Apparently it has to be night at the other end.'

They waited in awkward silence for another fifty minutes, then Dokal jumped. 'Bloody hell. The core portal is activating. He did it!' She hurriedly opened both of the van's rear doors. Yuri watched the half-metre portal in the middle of the threader turn a midnight black, then its surface twisted inwards, falling away to leave a gap. Air started to gush through. 'Threading now,' she told him.

The rectangular solid state slab in the first section of the threader split neatly along its narrow length, producing a set of entangled portals. Actuators separated the twinned segments and pushed one through the core portal Callum had opened. A different set of actuators flipped its remaining twin vertical. The airflow through it increased noticeably, making the marquee sides flap about excitedly.

'Help me,' Dokal said, and jumped out of the van.

187

Yuri joined her as the threader's largest portal, a metre-wide circle, divided. One went through to Zagreus. Yuri helped Dokal as the threader turned its twin vertical. Air charged through the opening so fast Yuri had to brace himself to avoid being pulled in. He caught a glimpse of a dull rocky ground surrounded by a weird curving wall of torches. There was a lot of elated cheering going on.

A surprisingly strong impulse gripped him. *If I slip through I'll be standing on an exoplanet. It's centimetres away, that's all. An alien star!* It was difficult to resist. Then the chance vanished.

Callum was crawling through on all fours. He flinched badly when he saw Yuri, and glanced at Dokal, who shrugged.

'Get on with it,' Yuri said impassively.

Callum turned round and started pulling at something heavy on the other side. Yuri's jaw tightened as he saw the state Savi was in.

'Contact the emergency services,' Yuri told Boris as his lost agent was manhandled through the portal. 'I need a paramedic team here immediately.'

Moshi followed Savi, then Raina, who gave Yuri a savage scowl when she saw him standing above her.

'Call Kohei,' Yuri told Boris.

Henry came through the circular portal. Then it was Alana blocking the blaze of torchlight. Colin made up the rear.

Yuri squatted down and looked through at Zagreus. Akkar was on his hands and knees, centimetres from the portal.

'Kohei, kill the power,' Yuri ordered. 'Now.'

Akkar screamed in fury, flinging himself forwards. His hand reaching towards Earth.

The spacial entanglement between Earth and Zagreus ended. Akkar's fist landed on the paddock tarmac, splattering blood as it rolled to a halt.

'You bastard!' Raina shouted, staring at the severed hand in revulsion.

'Why?' Yuri asked levelly. 'Did you want two thousand terrorists living here again, and madder than ever before? Maybe some of them could move into the flat next to yours; I read in your file it's available to rent. This you would welcome?'

'I promised them,' Callum said, aghast. 'I gave them my word they could come back.'

'I didn't,' Yuri said.

'They'll kill us if you send us back,' Alana said in a shaky voice.

'So you need to behave, then, don't you? Because Poi Li is pissed with you at a level even I find scary.'

'You can't do this,' Callum said. He was still on his knees, holding Savi's hand. He looked up at Yuri, beseeching. 'They're people. You can't treat them like this; it's inhuman!'

'No,' Yuri said, suddenly angry. 'What they do – what they have done – goes way beyond simple criminal acts. They seek to destroy anything they dislike, no matter that it is enacted legally, or how many people are dependent on it. They smash and ruin others' endeavours freely, and feel nothing. That cannot stand, not any more. For once I agree with Ainsley and his ultra-rich political collaborators. Your friend Akkar and his allies *have* been judged, and found guilty. Tough, that judgment didn't come after million-wattdollar fee lawyers defended them in public courts, followed by ten years of taxpayer-funded appeals; tough, that we don't spend hundreds of thousands a year keeping them in prison. But judged they have been, and far more leniently than they judge you or I. And even now, we give them a second chance.'

Alana's hand shot out, pointing at the inert threader. 'That planet is not a second chance. That is a death sentence.'

'Because of what they are,' Yuri sneered. 'They have been given an entire world of their own. We provide the means to survive, even to thrive if they learn the basic lessons of society and cooperate rather than fight each other like savages. So I'm really really sorry if Zagreus isn't a five-star hotel with room service, but we can't afford the luxury of tolerating them any more. This *is* the humane solution.'

'Zagreus has one canyon where humans can breathe, a toxic shithole that's poisoning them,' she shouted. 'That's not a world, it's a freak site. Even if you send us back, we've got the recording of their conditions to blow this whole obscenity out of the water. It's already downloaded into a cache vault. Right, Callum?'

'That's your threat?' Yuri said contemptuously. 'Okay, send it. Go right ahead. Send it to every news service in the solar system, every political commentator, every justice department. What do you think is going to happen?'

She glared at him, her facial muscles flexing.

'There'll be referendums in the democracies demanding we bring them back?' he asked in a pitying tone. 'Is that it? There'll be international campaigns, million-person protest marches? Is that what you're counting on? That. Will. Not. Happen. What court are you going to take this to? You think it's just one country that exiles these people? One company? One continent? Some of those psychotic bastards are actually lucky they get sent there. Ten years ago, their own government would have simply executed them.'

'That's not an excuse,' she cried. 'Escaping state-sponsored murder doesn't make this right.'

'By your standards. Sadly, the rest of us can't afford them. Not any more.'

Raina looked down at Callum. 'Chief? We have to go public. Please.'

'This is only the beginning,' Yuri said to Callum. 'You're smart enough to get that, right? That one settlement is an experiment, to see if the most belligerent, dumb, ideological assholes the human race has ever misbegotten can survive on an alien world. And – hallelujah – it worked. They'll go public with it eventually, the unknown, unaccountable people who made this happen, whether you force them to or not. And when they do, that's when the real political pressure will kick in. A planet of no-return, a wonderfully safe four lightyears away, where every vicious criminal can be sent, and has to work all day long to grow their own food. We wipe our hands of them forever: public conscience clean, crime rates down. How do you think that vote will go, huh?'

'You bastard,' Raina said.

'Why aren't we already on our way back there?' Callum asked. 'What's actually happening here?'

'Ms Keates was right. For all of you, Zagreus is now a death sentence. They're not going to wait and listen while you explain nicely that I'm the bad guy. They'll rip you to pieces the instant you drop through – probably eat you, too, given some of the ones we exiled there, I've seen the files.'

'So what's the deal?'

'Very simple. You're all through as far as Connexion is concerned – besides which, you're officially dead, anyway. So you shut the fuck up and go away to live your lives wherever you want. I'm *authorized* to say that if you leave us alone, we leave you alone. Our screw-up got Savi dumped on Zagreus; the explosion must have wrecked her grains so we couldn't track her digitally. But that's it. I got you this one concession, authorized by Ainsley Zangari himself, because of who the two of you are. And now you're right out of credit. This is a one-time, take-it-or-leave-it offer.'

'Hey,' a shout came from outside the marquee. 'Paramedics here. We got an emergency call.'

Yuri cocked his head to one side, regarding Callum carefully. 'So?'

Callum gave his wife a desperate, loving look. 'Take it,' he said wretchedly.

'Shit!' Raina kicked the dead portal door.

'In here,' Moshi shouted. He unzipped the marquee's side panel. 'She needs help – badly.'

Three paramedics ran in.

Juloss

Year 587 AA

Dellian lay back on the warm sands, tired but happy with it, as he waited for the flyer to land. Even after ten days, he was still impressed by the beach – the whole island, actually. The resort was one of the very few which hadn't been allowed to decay naturally after most of the humans living on Juloss had flown off into the galaxy. Its management genten had been left with full control of all its original service and maintenance remotes, to preserve the water bungalows and communal buildings at the same high standard as it had for the previous two centuries.

That standard was one Dellian had swiftly come to appreciate after sixteen years spent in the confines of the Immerle estate and its communal dormitory. If nothing else, he could actually have solitude if he wished. Everyone in his yeargroup had been assigned their own water bungalow – a neat little construction of curving glass walls framed by ancient hardwood beams, topped off with a thatched roof. They stood several metres out from the shore, resting on living coral pillars. The glass floor gave him a fantastic view of the superbly clear water a metre below, and the amazing variety of colourful fish that came sporting through the shallows.

Of course, that solitude had been the last thing on anyone's mind, especially at night. Principal Jenner had announced the ten-day break as a surprise reward for passing their senior year assessments. No adults or muncs would be with them. For the first time in their lives they would be alone, without any external authority to impose order, devoid of responsibility except to themselves.

'So just relax and enjoy yourselves,' sie said. 'And keep it together. This is as much a test of maturity as anything else. We trust you. Don't let us or yourselves down.'

The island had a broad circular lagoon on one side, where the water was barely two metres deep, and as warm as a bath. Perfect for learning how to windsurf. The other side was the wide sun-saturated beach open to the ocean, with long jetties where the resort's boats and power skis waited for anyone who fancied faster, more adventurous, activities. Food was available all day long in the open-walled central pavilion, cooked to perfection by the genten's remotes.

Dellian had swum, powerskiied, learned the rudimentaries of windsurfing, canoed, played tennis and beach volleyball, lazed around drinking by the pool, or sat in the open-air amphitheatre watching old dramas. Then as night fell all the boys would pair up, or form larger groups, and head back to the water bungalows for hours of energetic sex. The sea air and the freedom had reacted with their hormonal bodies to fire their libidos up to a relentless height. In those ten days Dellian had been to bed with over half of the boys, including Xante, of course. Xante, who had everyone queuing up to find out how big his cock really was, and who fucked like an angel.

Some of the boys had even been bedded by Tilliana and Ellici. And that had been a major disappointment for Dellian – which for some reason he couldn't let go of. He'd been extremely eager to find out what sex with a girl was like, but Yirella hadn't shared his enthusiasm. He told himself he could wait until she was ready for that level of intimacy, that their friendship was more important to him. Even so, lost in ecstatic congress with his friends every night, it was her face he'd pictured over theirs.

As he waited on the beach, the skin on his bare torso started to tingle in the sunlight. Every morning he'd put on the highest-rated sunblock, which the bungalow's dispenser assured would last all day, only for him to have to apply it again at midday – or, more often, for someone else to slather it licentiously all over his skin for him. He sat up and started pulling on his T-shirt. As he did, Yirella came off the wooden walkway that led to a cluster of the water bungalows. Dellian waved hopefully. She smiled and walked over.

Now she and the other girls had moulted, Dellian considered her bare skull to be quite erotic. He'd been fantasizing about rubbing sunscreen on for her; after all, who didn't like a scalp massage?

'The genten said our ride would be here in ten minutes,' he said in greeting.

'And you don't think that's odd?'

Dellian frowned, not quite sure what she was talking about. 'Odd how?'

She knelt on the sand beside him, looking down quizzically at his thickset form. Dellian had grown a lot over the last three years, but while he'd increased in shoulder-breadth and weight, mainly due to muscle mass, Yirella had continued her upward climb, leaving her and the other two girls increasingly spindly compared to the boys. When they stood up together now, his eyes were level with her boobs, which he considered a size match about as perfect as you could get.

'Why not just portal back to the estate?' she asked distantly.

'Uh . . . because there is no portal, would be my best guess,' he retorted.

'But why is there no portal, Del?'

He frowned, wondering as always how her brain functioned. Her head was in direct proportion to the rest of her, which he reckoned made her skull a good twenty per cent larger than his – or any boy's. The geneticists who'd designed the clan's binary children had given her a cute flat nose, wide enough to hold additional blood vessels which fed into a carotid rete at the base of her cranium, a configuration of arteries and veins which basically served as nature's heat exchanger. Yirella and the girls needed it to help cool their larger brains, along with the absence of hair, which would've otherwise acted as insulation over their skulls, preventing the heat from escaping.

All that extra grey matter generated more and smarter thoughts than Dellian could ever manage, just as the geneticists intended. But it meant keeping up with her and the other girls was hard sometimes. 'Because now everyone's gone, most of the portals have shut down, especially to somewhere as remote as this.' He gave her an expectant look, pleased that he'd come up with a logical and rational answer.

'The resort is maintained to give people a holiday. Therefore, regular transport is an obvious requirement. So why shut it down?'

'I liked the sense of isolation we had here. It made me feel . . . I don't know, different, like seeing what being an adult is going to be like.'

She grinned. 'Me too. It felt like we were being trusted for the first time ever. That was nice.'

His eyes tracked along her amazingly long legs, wondering how they'd feel straddling his hips. Perfection, he decided. 'Could've been better,' he said wistfully.

Yirella laughed and flicked some sand at him. 'Oh, Del, you're not still cross that we didn't have sex, are you?'

'Saints, no. I wasn't cross. I was disappointed, that's all.'

'It's just, I don't think this was the right place and time for you and me, that's all. The island was purely about everyone partying and having lots of fun sex. We deserve it after all those battle games we've been playing for the last couple of years; they've been tough. Now we're all as relaxed and happy as we've ever been.'

'Yes, but . . . No, sorry, I still don't get it.'

She gave him a genuinely caring smile. 'Look, we both know we are going to have sex, and it'll be great sex, too. But we have feelings for each other, strong feelings – you know this. So being together could mean a lot more for us. I don't want to risk that by making it the same as a simple holiday fuck. That's why.'

'Okay.' Dellian's throat had suddenly become very dry. *We are going to have sex.* She actually said that. *Great sex!* He was frantic to ask: *Saints, tell me when?* 'Shame you didn't have any ordinary holiday fun sex.'

Her smile quickly turned wicked. 'Oh, don't worry about me. I had plenty of sex. I mean, have you seen how long Xante's cock is?'

Hearing that was the same as being taken out early in one of the combat tactics games Dellian had spent so much of the senior year playing. It didn't physically hurt, but it was hugely upsetting. 'I'm glad,' he lied.

The flyer appeared – a matt grey cylinder with rear stub wings, skimming in over the water. It slowed as it approached the beach and trim landing legs unfolded from its fuselage.

Yirella shook her head at the machine as it touched down. 'Doesn't make sense,' she complained.

He laughed. 'You really do want to solve every problem in the universe, don't you?'

'Give me time, and I will.' Her dazzling smiled returned, making Dellian's world a better place again.

They got to their feet together. Then Yirella bent fast, and kissed him. 'You're special to me,' she said seriously. 'You're not like the other boys. I don't want our friendship to end.'

'It won't,' he promised solemnly.

As he joined the queue for the flyer he glanced round the other boys, seeing blissful expressions and hearing all the cheerful chatter. He tried his best to keep sullen resentment off his face when he saw Xante, whose arms were around Ellici's waist and Janc's shoulders, the three of them laughing away merrily.

Compared to the sun shining down on the island, it was so dark inside the fuselage Dellian's eyes took a moment to adjust. He found a seat midway along and settled into it. Yirella sat next to him.

He let his head rest deep in the cushioning and half closed his eyes. 'Advanced development year,' he said, as if surprised by what waited for them when they got back to the clan estate. 'I didn't think it would ever come.'

'What do you think they'll do to us?' she mused.

'Alexandre said not to worry. The implants will help us boost up; we'll be able to merge with any weapons tech the design teams can produce. The surgery's routine, it doesn't hurt or anything.'

'I can't see that I'll be any use fighting the enemy,' she said. 'You and the other boys, yes: you're all tough. But I'm not.'

'You'll command,' he said. 'You have the tactics and the smarts. All we'll ever do is what you say.'

'Suppose I get it wrong?'

'You won't. I trust you.'

'Oh, great Saints.' She shuddered. 'I don't need that.'

The flyer lifted from the beach and headed back out across the sea.

'Flight duration is one hundred and seven minutes,' the genten pilot announced. 'Immerle estate has been notified of your arrival time. Your year mentor, Alexandre, says sie hopes you all had a good time, and is looking forward to seeing you all again.'

A statement that was greeted with boos and cheers in equal measure. Dellian stared out of the window as they went supersonic. The sea was strangely uniform as it slid past twenty kilometres underneath them. He picked out several island groups but couldn't work out their size. Then they were over land again.

Old cities and settlements were easy to see, grey wounds in the verdant blanket of vegetation. Two or three times he saw columns of smoke winding up from bushfires. His view began to shift as the flyer banked slightly.

'Why are we changing course?' Yirella asked.

'Are we?'

'Yes!' She was looking round, as if seeking confirmation. 'Pilot, what is happening?'

The boys in nearby seats glanced curiously at her.

'Stand by for systems confirmation,' the genten said.

'What?'

Dellian pressed his face to the window. The land below was becoming rumpled as they started to pass over some low foothills. The green was diminishing, draining away to more rugged browns and ochres, beset with tiny dark specks.

'Systems undergoing irregularities,' the genten said. 'Please

197

remain seated. Safety restraints will activate in ten seconds. Do not be alarmed, this is a precautionary measure only.'

'Oh, precious Saints,' Dellian moaned. The flyer's nose-down angle was getting steeper. He couldn't be sure, but he thought their speed was increasing. They certainly seemed to be losing altitude.

He held still as the cushions started to swell, extending a series of rib-like restraints around his torso and limbs.

'What is the nature of the problem?' Yirella demanded.

'Propulsion irregularities. Enabling compensation.'

'Del, my databud can't reach the net.'

'What?' he grunted.

'I'm cut off. Are you online?'

'Connection check,' he ordered his databud.

'Global communication net offline,' its voice whispered into his ear.

'Saints! No, it's down,' he told her.

'Pilot, why are we offline?' she asked, her voice rising.

'Attempting to re-establish connection with global communication net.'

'What do you mean, attempting?'

'Temporary connection loss.'

'How can that happen? The network is orbital. Everywhere is in range.'

'Attempting to reconnect. Operating on reserve power.'

'Oh, great Saints!'

'What's our altitude?' Dellian asked.

'Fourteen kilometres. Descending.'

'Saints! Are we going to crash?'

'Negative. Reserve power sufficient to enact zero-velocity touch-down.'

He was proud of himself for not panicking. In fact he was proud of all his clanmates for remaining equally cool, even though it was obvious they were all scared shitless.

The flyer's descent angle slowly became more pronounced as it dropped into a terrifying dive. The foothills expanded fast. Dellian tried to memorize what he was seeing. *Understand your terrain* – one of the golden commandments of tactical training.

The genten levelled them out. Then deceleration kicked in. G-force shoved Dellian down hard into his seat. His vision began to tunnel out, swirls of red closing like a misty iris. He managed to catch sight of ground that was becoming very rocky, and steep.

'Touchdown in four, three, two—'

The impact immediately reversed the flyer's acceleration impetus, flinging Dellian and the others about wildly, shaking them. Deafening tearing sounds filled the cabin as the fuselage skidded along. He saw a wingtip spinning chaotically through the air, overtaking them. Then the whole cabin buckled. A split opened up in the front of the fuselage. Dust blasted in. Everyone screamed. There was a final *crunch*, and all movement ended abruptly.

Dellian fought to get his breathing back under control. His heart was thudding as if he'd just finished a marathon. Dust filled his mouth and nostrils, bringing a strange sulphurous smell. The cabin was lying at a perturbing angle, with the floor tilted a good twenty degrees, and nose down. A jagged sheet of sunlight shone through the forward split, fluorescing the ochre sand that saturated the air.

'Are you okay?' he asked Yirella urgently.

'Yes. I think so.'

'Everyone okay? Any injuries?'

Rello and Tilliana had been sitting close to the split. They were badly shaken. The dust blast had left their exposed skin burned and abraded. Tilliana's face was bloody; Ellici was already at her side, worrying about the damage to her eye.

'The clan medics can fix that easily,' Xante assured her.

'What clan medics?' Ellici snapped back.

'Let's get outside,' Dellian told them, keeping his voice level.

Everyone was keen about that; the flyer now represented chaos and danger. But the doorway didn't open, not even when Janc slapped the emergency release button repeatedly. So they eased themselves out through the gash and stood on the sandy ground.

Dellian looked round. There were hills in every direction, with larger slopes blocking the eastern skyline. Soil was thin and dry, supporting a few straggly bushes with shrivelled leaves. Odd black sleeper trees poked up at random. Boulders were scattered everywhere, most balancing precariously given the angle of the slope. It was colder than it ought to be with such a bright sun and no clouds.

'Now what?' Xante said.

'Rescue will be here soon,' Orellt said positively.

'No, actually,' Yirella said, wriggling through the fuselage gap. 'There's no power in the flyer, and I can't get the genten to respond. It's dead, along with the rest of the systems.'

'The emergency beacon will be broadcasting our position,' Ellici exclaimed.

Yirella shrugged. 'Maybe. Let's hope so.'

'It's self-contained!'

'And the flyer is failure proof. But here we are.'

'What do we do?' Xante asked.

'Just stay calm and stay put,' Dellian said. 'Is anyone connected to the global net?'

The question was greeted with sour and nervous expressions as they all consulted their databuds. Nobody had any connection.

Dellian couldn't think how that was possible. But he knew he mustn't allow them to get spooked by the situation. 'The second the flyer doesn't show up, they'll be searching for us,' he told them confidently.

'We drifted a long way off course,' Janc said anxiously.

'Every skyfort will be scanning for us,' Dellian replied, trying to quash his own concern. 'It won't take long.'

'We need to gather branches and bushes,' Yirella said. 'Build a fire.'

'A fire?' Orellt said sceptically. 'What use is that?'

'First, it's a strong infra-red signature, especially at night.'

'Night? It's only just past midday. We're not going to be here that long.'

'You hope. Face it, nobody's searched for a crashed flyer in our lifetime. We need to be ready for any eventuality. That includes protection.'

'Protection from what?'

'Yirella's right,' Dellian said. 'We have no idea what beasts live in these mountains.'

'After sunset, our best tactic is to retreat back into the fuselage and have a fire burning in front of the gap,' she said.

'Oh, for Saints' sake,' Orellt protested. 'We're not going to be here at sunset! The rescue crews will arrive in an hour.'

'I don't mind you betting your life on that wish,' she retorted. 'But my life isn't yours to risk. We need a fire.'

'We do,' Ellici agreed. 'This is an exceptional situation. We have to adapt to it.'

'There must be an axe in the emergency kit,' Dellian said quickly; he could see Orellt gathering himself to argue. 'Janc, Uret, Xante, you're with me. We'll fell some of those sleeper trees. The rest of you, start gathering the bigger bushes. I'm going to check and see what else we've been left with, especially water.'

They started moving – reluctantly; nobody wanted to consider that they would be here for any length of time – but they did it.

Dellian found two emergency cases in the rear of the fuselage. One was a medical kit, which he handed to Ellici to treat Tilliana's eye. The second contained basic survival equipment. It was mainly thermal blankets and ropes, a couple of knives, torches, and ten flasks filled with a litre of distilled water, along with a hand-pumped filter. He was disappointed that was the total, but the case did have a small axe.

'Not much water,' he said quietly to Yirella as he walked away from the flyer.

'No rainfall here – check the ground,' she replied, equally sub-dued. 'And the flyer is totally dead. I don't see how that could happen; everything is supposed to have multiple redundancy.'

He glanced up at the empty cobalt sky. Far overhead, the bright specks of the skyforts shone with reassuring familiarity. Even Cathar, the system's gas giant, was a sharp spark just above the horizon. 'Do you think . . .'

'The enemy? No. If Juloss was under attack we'd see the skyfort weapons firing. They'll be as bright as the sun – at least. It's not that.

We're living in the last days of this world's human civilization; things are bound to go wrong. I just never thought it would be this bad. I guess we've lived very sheltered lives.'

Dellian scanned round to assess the sleeper trees. There weren't many on the bleak hillside, but at least they stood out.

'I don't want anyone to go more than a couple of hundred metres,' he told his friends as they walked towards the closest tree. 'Once we chop them down we've got to break them apart to drag them back.'

The sleeper trees were never more than four metres high, rising up to form twisted hemispheres of densely tangled twigs that bulged up out of five radial boughs. Dellian remembered from interminable boring botany lessons that they were desert plants native to a planet hundreds of lightyears distant, with huge tuber roots that could hold precious water for years if necessary, while the branches and thick finger-leaves slumbered through the long hot days of baking sunlight between the rains. Given the scarcity of water they received, their trunks were surprisingly hard. It took the boys a good thirty minutes to chop through, and they had to take turns. It was tough work in the cool, thin air.

They'd just felled the first one when they heard it – a high-pitched braying sound coming from further up the mountain.

'What amid the Saints was that?' Janc asked nervously, scouring the ragged slope above them.

An answering cry came from the west.

'You mean them?' a badly perturbed Xante said. 'Saints, how many are there?'

Dellian silently noted how easily Xante was spooked. A petty satisfaction, but the Saints would understand and forgive.

'A whole planet's worth,' Uret replied grimly. 'This is why the estate is fenced in.'

'They sound like morox. I thought they only came out at night.'

'We're too exposed here,' Dellian said. 'Let's get this tree back to the flyer. Come on, we can do it if we all drag it together.'

They each took hold of the trunk and started pulling. Around them, they could see the other clan boys towing bushes through the boulders.

'We need a weapons inventory,' Yirella said when everyone had gathered next to the fuselage.

'Axe,' Dellian said, holding it up.

'Two knives,' Falar announced. 'They're not the best for throwing.'

'Bind them to the end of poles,' Ellici said. 'That'll give you the advantage of reach if those beasts come close.'

'Where the Saints are the rescue crews?' Janc shouted.

Dellian lined an accusing finger on him. 'Stop that. Panic just makes things worse. Help get the fire ready.'

'Wasn't panicking,' Janc grumbled, his gaze downcast.

The boys set about preparing the fire, building a core of the driest bush twigs, then fencing it in with some of the smaller branches of the sleeper tree to work as kindling. The rest was broken apart and piled up ready to throw on once the flames were established.

Rello and Tilliana were helped back into the fuselage, where Ellici and Orellt did what they could with the small medical kit.

Dellian watched Yirella scramble onto the top of the largest boulder, and slowly scan round. Once he'd finished chopping one of the sleeper tree boughs, he handed the axe to Hable and went to join her. 'Keeping watch?' he asked.

'Yes. I can't see anything moving.'

'The morox won't come close until dark, and even then the fire will keep them at bay.'

'We've heard several now.'

'Yes. Don't worry, they'll never get into the fuselage. Even I have trouble squeezing through that gap.'

'What do they eat?'

'Well not our clanmates tonight, that's for sure.' He smiled, hoping it would help ease her.

'I don't mean tonight. I mean every other night.'

'They're predators. So whatever they can catch. Rabbits, wild dogs, birds . . . I dunno. Whatever else lives up here.'

'Exactly. That's my point.'

'What is?'

'We've heard probably four already, right? Yet do you see anything else living up here? The bushes are all dead, and there's no grass. What do their prey live on?'

'Well . . .' Dellian scratched his head, swivelling round to search the forlorn hillside.

'This entire hill can't support one morox, let alone four.'

'They're passing through? Could be a seasonal thing, heading for a fresh hunting ground.'

'Seasonal?' she scoffed. 'This is the tropics.'

'All right! I don't know. Happy?'

'Very much not.' She gave him a nervous smile. 'I wasn't getting at you. I just find all of this weird. The odds of each event that's hit us today are pretty near improbable, but together they're impossible.'

'What are you saying?'

'I'm not sure, but this really doesn't feel good.'

'Yeah, I figured that for myself. Come on, let's get back to the flyer.' He held out his hand. After a moment, she took it, and together they slipped down the boulder.

'No water, either,' she said. 'That may be worse for us than moroxes.'

'Let's get through the night before we start worrying about that. Besides, if the water situation doesn't improve, we can drain the sleeper tree roots. I'm sure I saw that being done in a text or a video or something.'

'No, that's a myth. The tubers are all too deep. You'd expend too much energy digging down to them.'

'There's no water up here.'

'I know. It means that we have to leave first thing tomorrow and get to the bottom of the hill. There should be water there, even if we have to dig for it.'

'Okay. For a bad minute there I thought you were going to rig up something that'd filter our own pee.'

'That's not a bad idea, actually. Usually in this kind of climate, survivalists evaporate it and catch the condensed vapour. But maybe there's no need. The filter pump should be able to handle urine. We should all pee into a container, and save it in case.'

Dellian groaned in dismay.

'It's not funny, Dellian. Dehydration is dangerous.'

'All right. But I can't see anyone doing *that*.'

'They will if you and I carry on doing what we have been doing.'

'What's that?'

'Combined authority.'

'Huh?'

'My knowledge and your leadership. Together it makes the rest do what we want.'

He opened his mouth to protest, then realized what she said was right.

'What?' she asked with a sly grin. 'You hadn't noticed?'

'Uh, no, actually.'

'Classically, a good leader has the ability to issue orders that people don't argue with. I don't quite know what category a good-leader-doesn't-notice-he's-giving-orders falls into, but it certainly seems to be successful.'

'I'm not the only leader. Janc and Orellt, they're good captains, too.'

Yirella lowered her voice as they approached the flyer. 'In the tactical games, you've been team captain for thirty-two per cent of this year's total. Janc was second with sixteen. You're the clear leader in our year, Dellian. So be a proper Saint, and don't let us down. We're going to need your skills to get through this disaster.'

'Great Saints,' he muttered.

He made a show of examining the filter from the survival case and asking for Ellici's opinion. She agreed with Yirella that it would filter urine.

'Just in case, then,' Dellian said, and peed into a collapsible plastic carton, much to everyone's amusement. He played along with the joshing, then passed the carton to Janc, fixing him a level stare. Janc took a moment then undid his fly.

They lit the fire as the sun fell below the horizon. The general mood was subdued. In their hearts, everyone had expected rescue within the first couple of hours.

'We have to keep the fire burning as long as possible,' Yirella said. 'That'll give the skyforts their best chance to spot the thermal signature.'

'Three of us on one-hour duty outside to keep feeding the fire,' Dellian said quickly. 'Each with a weapon, that way we can watch each other's backs. No one else is to leave the flyer. I'll take the first watch with the axe. Falar, Orellt, fancy taking it with me?'

Both boys nodded without noticeable reluctance. The mountain air was a lot colder now the sun had gone. Even with the modest fire burning three metres from the fuselage, the boys wrapped thermal blankets round their shoulders.

The moroxes began calling to each other. Dellian was convinced there were now at least six of them out there in the darkness beyond the firelight. *Yirella's right. What do they eat?*

Dellian flung some more logs on the fire. Sparks skittered up into the night, swirling like orange galaxies. Boulders glimmered yellow, transforming to dusty moons in a frozen orbit around them. The moroxes were closer now, the cries lower, more intense. Something moved in the gloom between boulders, a deeper shadow eclipsing empty air.

'Come back in,' Yirella said from the fuselage split. 'Pile some more logs on, and get safe.'

Dellian was inclined to agree. Looking at Falar and Orellt, he couldn't see any argument. He bent over to pick up a couple of logs.

'Look out,' Falar yelled.

The morox came hurtling out of the dark, skipping onto a boulder and leaping. The beast had pale grey skin like wet leather, mottled with green webs. The forelegs had huge paws, with seven knife-like talons fully extended. Its head was slim and streamlined, almost aquatic somehow, with wide white eyes and fangs longer than a human hand.

Some deep xenophobic instinct told Dellian this rapacious creature had never been born on Earth, adding to his fright. It was the fear of the *other*. He dropped to one knee, swivelling as he did so to bring the axe round in a powerful arc. On either side of him, Falar and Orellt were assuming a lunge pose, their knife poles stabbing forwards. The three of them acted in unison as they'd done so many times in battle games, coordinating as fluidly as any munc cohort.

Too late, the morox tried to turn from the trio of deadly blades. Dellian's axe caught its flank, ripping open a huge cut. Dark purple blood squirted out. The morox howled and landed badly, legs scrabbling for purchase.

'Fall back,' Dellian shouted. 'Falar in first.' He could see another two black spectral shapes circling the fire's radiance, biding their time.

'I'm in,' Falar called. Then: 'Danger left!'

Dellian and Orellt faced the new morox as it sprinted towards them. This time Orellt dropped to his knees. Dellian instinctively knew what he was doing – thrusting the knife blade ahead and low, forcing the morox to leap. Orellt began his swipe. Sure enough, the creature saw the blade solid and unmoving at its own head-height, and sprang—

The axe hit it directly on the side of its short neck, penetrating so deep Dellian could barely wrench it out. Only the inertia of the creature's falling corpse helped free it.

Orellt was squirming backwards through the gap. Dellian took two fast paces and saw the next morox appear on the top of the fuselage. No time. He flung the axe, sending it spinning through the air as the morox leapt at him. It hit the side of the beast's forelimb and bounced away, clattering off the rocks. And Orellt was standing in the gap, the knife pole ready to throw like a spear.

The creature smashed into Dellian, its forelimbs lashing out. He felt talon tips slash down his left arm, then it juddered, a knife pole sticking out of the back of its neck. Its weight was on top of him, carrying him to the ground. The fall dazed him, and all he knew was the mass of the dead carcass pressed unmoving against him, pinning him down. Then boys were yelling all around. Hands dragged the dead creature off him. He glimpsed Orellt and Falar back in the open, their knife poles jabbing into the darkness. Hable retrieved the axe. Xante, Janc and Colian were holding burning branches, scything them about furiously. Uret picked him up and manhandled him through the gap, where Yirella half-carried half-dragged him to a seat. She and Ellici were immediately busy with antiseptic sprays and long strips of a-skin while behind them the boys performed an orderly withdrawal back into the flyer's cabin.

'You'll be fine,' Yirella was saying loudly as torch beams wobbled about, shining on his arm. There was plenty of blood. 'The cuts aren't deep at all.'

Orellt's face loomed up in front of him, grinning wildly. 'We got another one! And we reset the fire. It'll burn for another hour at least.'

'Terrific,' Dellian gasped, and winced as Ellici applied a strip of a-skin to his bicep. It stung as it adhered.

'Drink this,' Yirella ordered, shoving a flask at him. 'You need fluid.'

'It's not piss, is it?'

'No.' She grinned. 'I'm saving that for breakfast.'

*

The surviving moroxes howled to each other for the rest of the night. One even ventured up towards the gap in the fuselage again, only to have Xante and Colian ward it off with the knife poles.

Dellian dozed for most of the time, falling into a deeper sleep some time well past midnight, only to be dragged from slumber by a fresh morox howl. He saw Colian in the gap, holding a knife pole ready, but not jabbing or shouting for help.

The next thing he knew, it was dawn and the cabin was full of his yawning friends. A wan grey light was shining in through the small windows, and the smell of smoke was heavy in the air.

'Decision time,' Yirella said as she inspected the strips of a-skin on his arm. 'We can't hang around here if we're going to make it to the foot of the mountain before nightfall. We either set off now, or we don't do it at all. If the satellites didn't see the fire last night, then they never will. And if we leave it another day, we'll be a lot weaker.'

'And an easier target for the moroxes' Dellian said. 'We won't have the fuselage to shelter us, either.'

Her face crumpled into a puzzled frown. 'That's another thing wrong. They should never have ventured so close to the fire.'

'But they did,' Xante said. 'Wishing they did what they're supposed to isn't going to help us.'

Yirella gave him a long, disappointed look, and shrugged. 'So what do you think we should do?' she asked.

'You tell me,' Dellian said urgently. 'I'll back you up.'

'I don't know. In situations like this, you're normally supposed to stay at the crash site and wait for the rescue teams. But this isn't normal, is it?'

'Let's take a look outside,' Dellian said reluctantly.

The fire had died down to a mound of embers that was barely warmer than the sand. Thick rose-gold sunlight was pouring over the tops of the hills, casting long sharp shadows from the boulders.

Dellian carried the axe, scanning round cautiously. 'I can't hear the moroxes.'

'It's daytime,' Xante said. 'They'll be back in their lair.'

Dellian saw Yirella shaking her head, but she didn't say anything. He looked at the three dead moroxes. The first one, which he'd caught with the axe, had crawled fifty metres away before collapsing from blood loss. The other two were closer.

'We could eat them,' Ellici said.

'Can we?' Dellian asked. 'They're alien. Doesn't that make them enati – enty – enamo—'

'Enantimorphic? No. We can eat them if we have to. Their biochemistry is different, but not by much. Their flesh contains nutrients we can use. I'm not so sure about the taste, though.'

'We'll hold off for now,' Dellian said with as much authority as he could summon. 'First we need to build a bigger fire. Maybe burn a whole tree and then add more. Yeah,' he nodded, staring at the biggest sleeper tree, standing a hundred metres away. 'We'll light that one, and chop down others, add them to it. We can do it, all of us. A fire that's going to overload the skyfort sensors it's so big.'

He had them. He knew that. They were all gathering courage and hope from his determination. Even Yirella agreed.

'No walk down the hill then,' she mumbled as he divided them up into three teams, each with a weapon.

'It makes no sense, exposing ourselves to more unknowns. The clan know we've been alone overnight now. Alexandre will bring back the Saints themselves to help find us. Sie will. We all know that.'

'I suppose so.' She stared at the closest morox corpse. 'I need to know something,' she said, and picked up a rock half the size of her own head.

'What?' he asked, then recoiled as she brought the sharp edge of the rock smashing down on the morox's head. Two more blows and she'd cracked the skull open. She shoved the edge of the rock through the fissure and began to prise it further apart.

'Yirella!'

He had to fight back nausea as she began examining the segments of gore that was its brain.

'Why didn't it get eaten?' she asked.

'Huh?'

'They were so ravenously hungry they ignored a fire to try and kill us. Yet here they have three fresh corpses of their own kind, and they ignored them to carry on attacking us.'

'Do they eat their own?' he asked, trying not to look at the way her carrion-slicked fingers were probing the brain tissue so enthusiastically. Yet there was something horribly fascinating about the scene.

'I don't know. I don't suppose we should judge them like they're terrestrial animals. Although you'd think basic instincts would be almost identical.'

'I guess,' he said. 'So what are you hoping to find?'

'Don't know till I find it,' she answered grimly.

'Okay.' He knew that tone; she wasn't going to be stopped by anything he could say.

Cheering broke out around the sleeper tree. His clanmates had piled scrub bushes up around the trunk, which were now burning hot and fierce, their smokeless flames shooting vertically into the tree's boughs above, which were starting to smoulder.

Dellian was glad of the excuse to look away from Yirella's gory task. Despite the fresh air gusting across the slope, he was feeling sluggish. Lack of sleep and his throbbing arm seemed to be making his body intolerably heavy. Which was strange, given he was very aware of his empty stomach. With growing dismay, he knew it wouldn't be long before they'd have to start using the hand-pump filter . . .

Falar and Uret were taking it in turns to attack another sleeper tree with the axe, the thuds reverberating through the crisp air. More boys were dragging bushes back to the rapidly expanding blaze. Dellian looked up at the invitingly empty sky with its flotilla of artificial stars. 'Why can't the skyforts see us?' he murmured.

'Why fill Juloss with alien predators?' Yirella said. She'd risen to her feet, wiping jelly-strings of clotted morox blood from her hands. 'I mean, seriously! Sure, keep some in orbital xeno-habitats, and store their genetic molecule for study. But release them into the wild? That makes no sense at all. Our ancestors put in a century's effort just terraforming this world up to habitable status so a whole civilization of humans could flourish and expand. Now we can't even set foot outside our clan compound it's so dangerous.'

'Dangerous to the enemy, too.'

'Like they're ever going to set foot here. The only landing they'll ever perform is with a dozen apocalypse-event asteroids.'

'So what, then?'

'So I don't know!' she shouted bitterly.

Dellian was surprised. It hurt him to see her like this, so wound up and frustrated. Close to tears, too, if he was any judge. Yirella was always the cool rational one. But then this situation was extreme. Without thinking, he put his arms round her. Her whole body was held as rigid as steel. 'I remember someone telling me there are always answers; you just have to know where to find them.'

She nodded, slowly and very reluctant. 'I know.'

'Did you find anything in the morox's brain?'

'No.'

'What were you looking for?'

'Not sure. Something that would make it act the way it did.'

'They all behaved the same.'

'I know. And that worries me. I'm scared, Dellian.'

'Me too,' he said softly. 'But we'll get through this.' He kept hold of one of her hands as he turned to face the sleeper tree, which was now a giant column of flame, burning with the aggression of a rocket exhaust. The boys who'd lit it were having to stand well back, the heat was so strong. 'The skyfort sensors will think we're zapping them with a laser when they pass over, the infra-red emission is so strong.'

'Yes.' Yirella bent down and kissed him again. 'You know what I'm thinking?'

'What?'

'This place is our Zagreus. So you know what that makes us?'

'Up shit creek without a paddle?'

'No! You and me. Look at us. You with your red hair, you're Saint Callum.'

'And you're my Savi.' He laughed. 'Yes!'

'They escaped, didn't they? They got back home.'

Dellian heard the urgency in her voice, the desperation. 'Yes. They did. They even lived happily ever after for a couple of decades on Nebesa.'

'If they can do it, so can we.'

'Callum was always my favourite Saint,' he confessed.

'Really. Yuri's mine.'

'How come? I'd have you rooting for Kandara.'

'Oh no. She used violence to solve everything. Not as bad as Alik, though. But Yuri used to think through his problems. Remember the missing boyfriend story? He investigated properly and made decisions based on facts, and he never stopped until he finished the case. That's what I aspire to.'

'He could be pretty ruthless, too. A lot of people died when he was hunting for Horatio.'

'That wasn't his fault – well, apart from the matcher. And people like that deserved to be sent to Zagreus.'

'Yeah . . .' He frowned at the latest outbreak of shouting, glancing round to see the boys yelling his name and pointing wildly. Xante had brought up the knife pole he was carrying, pointing it towards Dellian and Yirella. But the expression on his face . . . Dellian slowly turned round, fear turning his skin to ice.

Standing on top of the flyer's fuselage was a cougar. It shook its head, staring down at them. A small growl emerged from the back of its throat. The forelegs bent, taking it down into a pre-pounce crouch.

'Move back towards the flames,' Dellian said, barely moving his lips, shifting slightly so his body was between the cougar and Yirella.

'Del—'

'Now!' He began his own slow backwards creep, pushing her along, eyes frantically scanning the ground for a loose stone like the one Yirella had used, anything he could strike the lethal beast with. He knew it was hopeless, but he wasn't going down without a fight.

The cougar leapt, powerful muscles flinging it vigorously through the air towards them. Then it exploded. One instant a perfectly evolved killing machine . . . the next a cloud of flame and tatters of meat. Stinking steam belched out. The charred mess splattered down two metres from a paralysed Dellian.

He dropped to his knees and vomited hard. Yirella was screaming. Clanmates ran towards them en masse, yelling and shouting.

A shadow fell across all of them. A shivering Dellian raised his head, watching in total incomprehension as the big flyer descended silently out of the clean morning sky.

The Assessment Team

Feriton Kayne *Nkya, 24th June 2204*

I was fascinated by the way Yuri and Callum resurrected their ancient conflict, shouting over each other, bickering with barrages of obscenities about trivial points and who was responsible for what, with neither giving ground. When the whole uncensored account was finally aired, I'd learned very little that I hadn't already accessed in Connexion's secure files.

From my tactical standpoint, Callum had always been a good suspect for an alien agent. I'd wondered about the whole: *died in an Albanian chemical plant explosion* 2092 death certificate, along with the rest of his Emergency Detoxification crew. The Berat 'disaster' was on the British government's official births and deaths registry for all of them. Then he and Savi officially popped up again in 2108, in the Delta Pavonis system, with their kids in tow, as if nothing untoward had happened and his death had been an unfortunate bureaucratic misunderstanding. He was listed as being a senior technical manager for the Nebesa habitat construction project.

That discontinuity was precisely the kind of record-keeping mistake I was looking for. Undercover agents assuming the identity of the recently deceased had been standard practice within the intelligence community, dating all the way back to the twentieth century. And Callum was well placed. Ainsley recognized his drive and ability a century ago; since then he'd worked his way up the Utopial ladder to personal technology adviser to Emilja Jurich herself, one of the original Utopial movement founders. It put him in a perfect position to feed their Senior Council's growing xenophobia towards the Olyix, had he been an alien agent.

The hostile policies of the human elite towards the Olyix have been growing steadily, ever since the *Salvation of Life* arrived at Sol in 2144 – fifty-two years after Callum's supposed death. Suspicion of an alien species is part of the human condition, and relatively understandable. What cannot be explained by logic is the rising paranoia people like Emilja Jurich and Ainsley Zangari have exhibited over the last couple of decades. Somebody, somewhere, *has* to be feeding that paranoia with a whole load of damaging bullshit.

The conclusion we have come to is that a very different alien species – an ancient enemy of the Olyix? no one knows for sure – arrived undetected at Sol (time uncertain) and has been busy insinuating their way into positions of influence. My real task in the Connexion Exosolar Security Division is to expose their possible agents.

And now, with his 'death' explained and even confirmed by my boss, Yuri, it's likely not Callum. Obviously, no Earth company or Sol system habitat would employ him after 2092. But the emergent Utopials with their ideological goal of a pure and decent post-scarcity society, with a correspondingly technology-heavy infrastructure, were an ideal choice. Delta Pavonis welcomed everyone who rejected the Universal culture that dominated Earth and their terraformed planets. Which, actually, made the Utopial society his only choice.

'Did Savi recover?' Loi asked. He was sitting at a table with Jessika and Eldlund, where the three of them had remained silent the whole time.

Callum stirred from his sojourn into the bitter past, and it took his heavy grey-green eyes a moment to focus on his old adversary's assistant. 'Yes, thank you. Savi recovered. We were together for over a quarter of a century, even had a couple of children. So, yes, it was worth it.'

Yuri merely grunted and downed another shot of arctic-cold Tovaritch vodka. The stewards had been providing him with a steady supply of the tiny frosted glasses all evening. I was beginning to think my boss had a special peripheral to filter out alcohol toxicity. He certainly didn't betray any signs of being drunk, apart from his ever-shortening temper.

Alik seemed to have the same resilience – or peripheral. He was sitting back in his chair, on his third glass of bourbon. His eyes were almost closed, but that didn't fool me; he'd been deeply absorbed by the confrontation.

Kandara, by contrast, was sitting straight-backed, fearsomely attentive from start to finish. 'I had no idea Zagreus was a dark rendition site to begin with,' she said.

'History,' Yuri grunted. 'The Conestoga asteroid went public with the penal colony's existence three years later. Exactly as the project's instigators always intended. And as a registered independent government, Conestoga couldn't be penalized in any international court the way corporations could.'

'Government, my arse!' Callum said gruffly. 'Conestoga was a chunk of valueless rock a hundred metres in diameter, in a trans-Jupiter orbit, with an automated industrial base that had a dormitory module bumped on. Total population: fifty.' I watched him eyeing the three assistants in the lounge, anxious for them to understand, to take his side. 'Every one of them was a corporate lawyer.'

'Conestoga offered other Sol governments an exile destination for undesirables,' Yuri said. 'Everyone agreed on an improved standard for the survival packages and, *bam*, the queue of convicts was suddenly six months long. It's a tough life on Zagreus, but it works. The surveillance satellites show an expanding civilization. They're even venturing beyond the canyon now, building pressurized domes out on the surface. We tamed the bastards.'

'Hoo-bloody-rah,' Callum said. 'Do the satellites tell you how many people died in the process?'

'If it bothers you, offer them a new terraformed world. Or maybe open up one of your precious Utopial planets to the poor misunderstood princesses. No? There's a surprise.'

Callum stood up. 'Zagreus is not the way we should judge civilized progress. It's a bloody disgraceful throwback. Education and a dignified standard of living is the true solution to elevate the poor and disenfranchised. Utopial society produces so few of what you class as exile-level criminals we don't even exile them. They are removed from the general population, given a comfortable residence, and supported. That is our society's triumph.' His glance swept round the Trail Ranger. 'I don't know what time zone you're all from, but I'm off to bed.'

Yuri waited until he'd disappeared into the rear compartment. 'Our judges don't have to hand out so many exile sentences because the threat of Zagreus keeps people in line. Actually!'

Loi nodded, making sure his boss saw his approval.

'No, actually, it's despicable,' Eldlund said, and stalked off back into the rear compartment. I wandered how sie was going to fit into a sleeping pod. They were all standard size, so . . . Slight oversight on our part there. Maybe sie'd stick hir legs out into the aisle for the night, and no doubt complain about bias and anti-omnia discrimination tomorrow.

'I think that's it for me, too,' Kandara said.

'Not a bad idea,' Yuri conceded.

The others all made their way back to the sleeping pods. Sandjay connected me to the drivers. Bee Jain assured me we were making good time, and the Trail Ranger was running smoothly towards the alien ship. With that, I went to bed.

*

Loi, Eldlund and Jessika were all awake and sharing a table for breakfast when I got up. At least they seemed to be bridging the deep ideological chasm between Yuri and Callum, but that's youth for you.

Alik came in, his hair still damp from the shower. He sat down opposite me. 'No gym,' he complained.

'Yeah. Really sorry about that.'

He laughed and ordered coffee and toast from the steward. 'Quite a showdown your boss had last night. I felt like I had a front-row seat into some real history.'

'I knew the basic facts, but, yeah, some of the details they spilled were something else.'

'Surprised they're both on this trip.'

'It's important.'

'Sure, I get that. But do they maybe have a little extra data to go on?'

I raised an eyebrow, scanning that handsome face with its immobile flesh. Alik Monday would make the perfect poker player; he lacked the ability to produce a single tell. The voice, though – that could convey a lot of emotion. I'm guessing he must practise that. 'Connexion didn't play favourites here, Alik,' I chided. 'The Utopials were extremely keen for representation on the assessment team.'

'And Callum is their prime troubleshooter.'

'He's a grade-two citizen.'

'If you think he's here to produce a technical assessment, you're fooling yourself. He might have been technical back in the day, but he's got his young acolytes for that now.' Alix's hand waved discreetly at Eldlund and Jessika.

'What are you saying?'

'He reports directly to the Utopial Senior Council, and maybe not even that. I expect it's going to be Jaru and Emilja themselves who'll have first access to his opinion. And that opinion will be entirely political.'

'I concur,' I told him. 'As does Ainsley. That's one of the reasons he had me include representatives for all the truly important interested parties.'

'Really?' It came out a challenge – old interrogation technique. *Back up what you just said.*

'There's an interesting parallel in history,' I explained.

'Go on.'

'When the original Space Age was underway back in the

nineteen-fifties and -sixties, part of the ideological struggle was the hypothesis surrounding first contact. The Soviet Union postulated that any civilization advanced enough to travel between the stars would logically be socialist, and would therefore choose to deal only with Moscow. The battle for ideological supremacy would be over, the world would undergo conversion to enlightenment, and the age of capitalism would be at an end.'

'Aliens are all communists? Bunch of bull. The Olyix are savvy traders.'

'Maybe. But today, instead of the Soviet Union, we have the Utopial culture –' I glanced over at Eldlund and Jessika, still chatting happily with Loi – 'who will explain, at great and boring length, how their post-scarcity equality is not socialism, but a technology-driven evolution of egalitarian humanist society.'

'Jeez, you mean Callum's here to confirm starfaring aliens will all be—'

'Good little Utopials? Yes. Beware, my son, the end days of capitalism are nigh.'

'He'll swing contact their way?'

'Utopial society is very benign and nurturing. The thinking goes that aliens will instinctively favour that.'

'Benign, my ass. Tranquil verging on stagnant, more like.'

'Indeed.'

'Oh, come on, you work for Connexion, for fuck's sake. The Universal market economy worlds and habitats are goddamn dynamic. The Olyix don't do much business with Utopials.'

'The Olyix are a single arkship colony who care only about continuing their voyage to the end of the universe, where they will meet their God at the End of Time. Anything else is secondary to that doctrine, so by necessity they adapt to local conditions. In the Sol system, trade with Earth and the habitats is the method by which they can acquire the energy to build up their supply of antimatter and continue that voyage. Therefore, they trade. The argument being, had they arrived at Delta Pavonis instead, they would now be following Utopial doctrine in their contact with Akitha.'

'Doesn't that kind of blow the shit out of the pan-galactic Utopial theory, that every species will embrace post-scarcity benevolence?'

'In the case of the Olyix, yes. Which is why Callum is hoping for a more favourable outcome this time.'

'So what's the deal with Yuri, then?'

I leant in a little closer, lowering my voice. 'I didn't say this, but Yuri is a xenophobic son of a bitch. He's got a real bug up his ass about the Olyix.'

'Why?'

'He doesn't like Kcells, apparently.'

'That's crazy. They've turned out to be a medical miracle. Goddamn cheap one, too. Everybody wins.'

I shrugged. 'It's just the way he is.' I smiled and sat back to watch if that particular seed of doubt would grow into anything I could use on my mission.

*

Outside the Trail Rover, Nkya's landscape was turning darker. The long screes of sandy regolith we traversed were now as black as volcanic dust. And maybe that's what the stuff actually was; I'm no geologist.

Callum appeared mid-morning and gave the coffee machine a thorough work-out. He and Yuri exchanged a curt nod. Their war wasn't yet over and probably never would be, but the truce was holding.

Alik went and sat next to Yuri. For a moment they both looked out of the window as we passed the scarlet strobe of a beacon post. The intrusive light caught their faces, shading them both a strange blood red, its time-lapse flashes pulling the shadows out of hooded eyes like dramatic tears.

'So if after considered analysis we declare the alien ship hostile, what happens?' Alik asked. 'Are we carrying a nuclear capability?'

'Our security drones can handle a high level of aggression,' Yuri told him. 'If the spaceship becomes actively belligerent they will contain it while we retreat.'

'Retreat in what?'

Yuri frowned, as if he'd misheard. 'In this, of course.'

'Jeez, you call this a getaway car?'

'The alien ship is isolated. It doesn't pose a threat to anything except the immediate vicinity. If that happens, we can return in a more forceful mode.'

'Unless it wipes us out. Then the guys sent to find us get taken out, and the guys who get sent in after that . . . What's the cut off? Team twenty?'

'There is no link with solnet, but the satellites are keeping watch. If the mission's G8Turing spots any trouble, then the appropriate protocols will be followed.'

'Great,' Alik grunted. 'And we're still racing away at walking pace.'

'You were aware of the risk before we started.'

'Risk, yeah. Your paranoia, not so much.'

'We have to guarantee the safety of our entire species. That is no small obligation.'

'Come on. If you can travel between stars, you aren't doing it for the glory of the empire. There's no such thing.'

'Our own history and rationale cannot be used as a template for analysing the motives of an extra-terrestrial species,' Yuri said levelly. 'The alien ship was probably on some kind of scout mission – an exploration and assessment maybe, the equivalent of this very assessment mission. Whatever the exact classification, they *stole* humans to examine them. Already that puts them into an antagonistic classification.'

'Do we know they were stolen?' Alik challenged. 'Hell, they could have been fleeing some catastrophe or war, and the aliens were doing these people a favour. We're eighty-nine lightyears from Earth, right? So if this ship was flying below lightspeed, it could have left Earth at any time in the last five hundred years. There was some pretty bad shit going on then; not our finest era.'

'Fleeing what?'

'Second World War, for starters. Think on it. You're stuck in the Blitz in London, and some strange dude offers you a way out. The

221

chance for you and a few others to start a new life on a new world. The only price is that you can't ever come back. You know you'd take that offer. We've got close to twenty terraformed planets now, every one of which cost us the biggest financial and political effort our species has ever known. If we'd spent half that much fixing Earth, we'd have us a genuine paradise. But no, getting a second chance is the greatest human dream and delusion we have. It even outranks religion.'

'Benign aliens intervening to save us?' Yuri sneered. 'What's that, second on the wish list?'

Alik spread his hands wide. 'Then why are humans on board?'

'We don't have nearly enough information yet to confirm the intent.'

'Hell, man, I know that. I'm offering up possibilities, that's all. Thinking wide. That's why we're all here, aren't we? Everything is up for consideration.'

'So which do you think it is?' Kandara challenged. 'You put up a good case for them being benign. Are they saving worthy people from Earth's brutality, or are they hostile imperialists, capturing specimens for the all-time rectal probing record in their laboratory?'

Alik gave her a quick salute. 'I'm prepared for it to be the hostile, but intellectually I'm kinda thinking it's unlikely.'

'Why?' Yuri said, his voice sharpening.

'Every reason given. You don't cross interstellar space for conquest. You do it for politics and wanderlust, like we have; and you do it for science, like we also have. But most interesting motive of all: as art. Because you can.'

'You are a fool if you think that. You are assigning human behavioural traits to aliens – the worst form of anthropomorphism and intellectual dishonesty. They have taken these people, most likely against their will. Whoever they are, they're not our friends.'

'You've pre-judged, then?'

'My judgement comes from the – admittedly small – amount of information we've uncovered so far. It is what we don't know that bothers me even more. The potential for conflict here is enormous.

Aliens can affect us in the most subtle ways. Our encounters with them show that we are always changed.'

'Them?' Eldlund queried. 'How many do you think we've encountered? As far as I'm aware, this is only the second.'

'It is,' Yuri said. 'But look at what the Olyix have done to us.'

'They brought knowledge.'

'No they didn't: a few clever chunks of biotechnology, that's all. Not real knowledge, no revelations. They're the greatest example of passive aggressive we've ever known. But what else do you expect from a bunch of religious fanatics?'

I'd heard this speech many times. It was one of the reasons I'd urged my boss to come on the expedition in person. My hope was that he'd open up to his peers in a way he never would to me and provide some kind of insight into his xenophobia. As Callum was to Emilja, so Yuri was to Ainsley – and a more paranoid son of a bitch you cannot find.

Kandara regarded Yuri with some surprise. 'I don't see the aggressive side of them. They seem more full-on passive to me.'

'That's all part of the act. They adapt to circumstances. I don't blame them; it's an excellent survival trait, which is exactly what you need if you're on a voyage to the end of time. Even the Olyix don't know what they're going to encounter next, so they have to be ready for anything.'

'Are you saying we're not seeing the real them?'

'No, quite the opposite. They see us, and adapt themselves to the systems we live by. That is the real them, even though for us it's looking into a mirror.'

'You, the Sol system, turned them into traders,' Callum said.

'Of course we did,' Yuri said. 'They came, they looked round, they saw what they had to do to get the energy they needed to rebuild their antimatter fuel supply – and they did it. No hesitation, no regrets. And to hell with the consequences.'

'And there are consequences to them trading Kcells with us?' Eldlund asked in surprise. 'I don't see how. Kcell treatments have saved the lives of millions of people in the Universal star systems.

People who are too poor to afford stem-cell printing and cloned organs. That's the only outrage here.'

'I'm not saying Kcells have been bad for us,' Yuri said. 'But the nature of the Olyix, this adaptability, is detrimental when they encounter a species with politics as complex as ours. They lack discrimination. Because they are driven so relentlessly to achieve their own goal, it doesn't matter to them how they achieve it. They need our money to buy our electricity, so they will adopt our own methodology to obtain it. Any methodology we have, they see an opportunity. Anything else is probably a sin to them.'

'You object to them because they've become capitalists!' Eldlund exclaimed.

'No,' Callum taunted. 'It's because they're better capitalists.'

'You don't get it,' Yuri said calmly. 'They don't have our moral filter. It doesn't matter to them what they do to get money, nor the consequences. And there is an awful lot of money involved with supplying the *Salvation of Life* with energy. That's why we have to watch them very closely.'

'Money is always going to distort everything,' Alik said. 'Nothing new in that. Greed is a constant. That just makes them more human, if you ask me.'

'You're wrong,' Yuri said flatly. 'You, with your job, should know the levels to which people will sink when there's real money involved. And because we race to the bottom, so do the Olyix. We are the architects of their current behaviour. And I've seen the consequences first-hand. They're not good.'

I watched with immense interest as Alik finally made his facial muscles contract, an expression approximating scepticism. 'Such as?'

Yuri's Race Against Time

London, AD 2167

The summer of 2167 was exceptionally warm, even by Europe's new standards. In Yuri's London office, the whining air con was making no difference to the wretched late-August temperature. By quarter past ten on Thursday morning he wanted to open the window – not that he could; his office was on the sixty-third floor. Connexion's extraordinary European central office rose out of the Greenwich Peninsula, a neo-Gothic helix-twist skyscraper of glass and black stone that topped out at ninety storeys, like the watchtower of some fallen pagan archangel charged with guarding the city against invaders sailing up the Thames. From his office Yuri had a perfectly framed view of the huge old Dartford Bridge curving up out of the distant horizon. But that same panorama was one which poured sunlight through the glass all morning long.

Earth had been using solarwells to supply its power since 2069, with the last coal and gas power stations shutting down in 2082. That had given the biosphere eighty-five years to reabsorb the excess carbon monoxide and dioxide produced in the twentieth and twenty-first centuries. Climatologists kept saying that was long enough for the atmosphere to stabilize at pre-industrial revolution levels, the idealized norm. Unfortunately, their elegant computer predictions never matched reality, and they all agreed 2167 was a fluke spike on the obstinately shallow cooling curve. One which the neogreen movement, whose ideology trumped science, was quick to blame on unusual solar activity, created by solarwells abusing the corona.

Yuri didn't care why it was ridiculously hot; he just wanted the god-awful heatwave to end.

'Executive priority call,' Boris announced. 'Poi Li for you.'

'Crap.' Yuri resisted the impulse to pull up his tie and fasten his top button. He couldn't think of any event that would warrant a personal call from Poi Li. She'd retired nineteen years ago, then immediately become an independent security adviser to the board – much to her successor's dismay. 'Give her access.'

'Yuri,' Poi Li said.

'Poi, been a while.'

'Anything of interest to report?'

'Not really. Any interesting reason you're calling this office?' He'd been appointed head of Connexion's small but elite Olyix Monitoring Office two years ago. At the time, Yuri hadn't been sure whether or not it was a promotion from director of the Sol Habitat Security Office which he'd held before, but it had been created by Ainsley himself ten years after the Olyix arkship *Salvation of Life* had decelerated into the solar system in 2144 and had provided Yuri with almost unlimited authority. Despite being completely office-bound, it was interesting work, plotting the political and financial influence of the Olyix across Earth and the habitats. It also gave him personal access to some very influential people. He'd come to regard it as an essential rung on his way up to Connexion's security chief, proving he had the executive skills to match his operational ability.

'There is a matter which we would like you to investigate personally,' Poi Li said.

'We?'

'Ainsley and me.'

Reflex made Yuri sit up fast. 'I see.'

'It is somewhat urgent.'

*

He took the Security Department's portal door into the company's general London network, from there he could walk straight into the London metrohub inner loop. Took a radial out to the Sloane Square hub. A short walk down King's Road, where there were a lot of silver-blue two-person cabez breezing about, and he was at the address Poi Li had sent. An elegant brick Regency-style building that contained phenomenally expensive pieds-à-terre for the wealthy, overlooking a small square with tall plane trees. He counted five security guards positioned around the square, dressed like normal people, hanging casually, and wondered how many more he was missing.

Boris gave his code to the entrance, which scanned him. The glossy black door – it looked like wood but wasn't – opened smoothly. Two guards in expensive suits were standing in the hallway. They gestured him in.

Yuri just had to admire the ancient lift with its iron grid doors and manual brass operating handle. He was the sole occupant as it rattled and groaned its way up to the fourth floor.

Poi Li was waiting on the landing for him. She looked the same as she had when he first started working for Connexion almost a century earlier, but somehow more delicate now. The telomere treatments seemed to be gnawing away at her core, leaving only the shell of a woman.

'Thank you for coming,' she said and led him into the penthouse apartment.

The decor was classical: marble floors and high ceilings, gold-plated chandeliers illuminating Old Master oil paintings and baroque modern canvases with equal intensity. The furniture style was unremittingly Louis XVI, heavy handcrafted pieces that looked hugely uncomfortable to sit on.

Ainsley Zangari was waiting in the lounge. Yuri was impressed. At 136, the richest man there'd ever been had clearly spent something approaching a medium-sized country's arms budget on genetic therapy; his anti-ageing treatments went far beyond the simple telomere extensions on which Yuri had spent decades of his generous bonuses. Anyone who didn't know him would think he was a normal forty year old who ate sensibly and exercised properly. Even his hair had turned from silver back to a youthful brown, as if follicle hues were merely seasonal and now spring had come once more.

'Yuri, good to see you.' A handshake, with a strong grip, underscoring easy vigour.

'Sir. Poi said this was urgent.'

'Yes, let me introduce you. This is Gwendoline.' Ainsley gestured at a teenage girl sitting awkwardly on one of the antique settees.

'Pleased to meet you,' Yuri said automatically. Boris was running facial recognition on her, but there was nothing in Connexion's database. That didn't bode well. Connexion had files on everyone remotely important. He told Boris to find out who owned the penthouse. Answer: a firm registered on Archimedes, a post-Jupiter-orbit habitat whose major industry was as a zero-tax enclave.

'Sorry to be so much trouble,' Gwendoline said. Her voice was high and hesitant. Yuri stopped analysing her, and actually looked. She was pretty, of course, but not just in that way all teenage girls were. Gwendoline was groomed to perfection. Casually, of course, but not cheaply. Personal stylists and the right schooling had created an effortless ingénue elegance. He decided she was maybe seventeen or eighteen, with a thin face and strong jaw, giving her glass-cutter cheeks. A button nose was heavily freckled, and her long strawberry blonde hair possessed a healthy gloss that rivalled the gold ornaments glittering around the lounge. Her dress was also deceptively simple: white and scarlet cotton with a square-cut neck and a hemline high above the knee. Yuri just knew it had never been printed in any fabricator; this was Rome or Paris couture with an eye-watering price tag. Gwendoline was a true golden-child heartbreaker. So then: spoilt brat, or wallet-busting mistress?

'I'm sure you won't be,' Yuri said with as much sincerity he could assemble.

'Gwendoline is my granddaughter,' Ainsley said, letting the pride seep into his tone.

Yuri was suddenly much more alert. That fact wasn't listed in any Connexion Security network, which was extremely odd. Ainsley already had nine marriages under his belt, producing thirty-two acknowledged children, most of whom worked in Connexion management. In turn they had numerous grandchildren and great-grandchildren, forming a large dynasty covering the full spectrum from dedicated workaholics to high-maintenance airhead princesses, every one of whom was guarded with a vigilance that was once the province of Earth's nuclear codes.

'I know,' Ainsley said contritely. 'You can't find a record of her. But her grandmother Nataskia and I only had a brief fling; Evette was the result. Nataskia didn't want Evette involved with Connexion, or the rest of the family. I couldn't blame her for that – fuck knows we're not exactly a convention of saints and introverts – so I respected her wishes. There was a discreet trust fund set up, which was increased when Gwendoline came along. The three of them have lived outside of media attention and corporate politics, and done well for themselves. I kept minimal contact, which hurt, but I sucked it up and everyone was happy ever after.'

'I see,' Yuri said diplomatically. 'So what's happened?'

'Horatio Seymore,' Gwendoline said, tears welling up.

'Who is he?'

'My boyfriend. He's vanished.' It was a classic summer romance, she explained. Her first true love. She'd just started an internship with a London finance software firm – obtained entirely on her own merit, Ainsley chipped in proudly. Horatio was a waiter in one of the HazBeanz franchises in the City, frequented by her office. He was nineteen, and Bristol University had offered him a place studying social sciences, which was why he was signed up as a trainee barista for the summer, to earn some money towards the fees. He wanted a career working with underprivileged children in the ribbon towns, helping them get their lives in order.

Yuri did his best not to groan and roll his eyes. Classic wasn't the word, he thought; it was *Lady Chatterley* rewritten for the twenty-second century. She was comfortably off, leading a sheltered socialite life amid her own class, while he was poor and modest, dedicating his life to a worthy cause. The attraction was enacted at an atomic level. When Gwendoline's altme sent Boris a file loaded with images, Yuri found it hard to decide which of the two kids was the prettiest. Even given the summer's anomalous heat, there were an excessive number of pictures of Horatio with his shirt off – playing football with pals, at the beach, lazing in the park. As well as being adorably noble, given the whole social-worker gig, he was quite a sports hunk, with Caribbean heritage giving his nicely muscled body a dark-honey sheen and dusting his brown eyes with a vivacious sparkle. His heavily curled hair was long and unkempt, adding to his desirability.

'Okay,' Yuri said slowly when the story of the world's newest, greatest ever love affair had been recited. 'So when you say vanished, what exactly makes you think that?' He could well imagine how besotted and loyally devoted the lovely Gwendoline was to her new beau, but boys Horatio's age . . . The lad would be a magnet for babes and cougars alike; he could quite easily be staying in some lingerie model's luxurious bedroom, fucking himself senseless night and day. *Lucky little bastard.* Yuri tried to focus on the girl again.

'I spent Tuesday night in his flat with him,' Gwendoline said. 'I left early Wednesday morning to come back here and get changed for work. We had tickets to see SungSolar play at the J-Mac club that night. He never showed up.'

'So that's a day and a half?'

'I know what you're thinking,' she said with sulky resentment, 'but we liveline each other all day long. I visit his HazBeanz once or twice a day. After I left here on Wednesday morning, his altme was offline. He didn't respond to any type of call, not even a straight phone ping. He wasn't in HazBeanz when I went to check at lunch, and the manager said he never came in that morning. My altme ran a check through London's A&E registries, and he wasn't admitted to hospital. When he didn't show for the concert, I even called his parents. They didn't know where he was, and now they're worried. I went back to his flat but he never came home last night.'

'You stayed there all night?' Yuri queried. 'By yourself?'

'Yes. I accessed the London police network this morning, but their Turing said I can't file a missing person report until Horatio's been gone for forty-eight hours.' She hung her head, long hair falling like a ragged curtain across her face. 'I know you must think I'm really stupid for calling you, Grandfather, but I didn't know what else to do. Horatio wouldn't just vanish without telling me, I know he wouldn't. We know everything about each other. We've never kept secrets.'

'Does he know who you are?' Yuri asked.

'He knows Mummy and Grandma are well off, but that's all.'

'So he doesn't know you're actually a Zangari, that you are Ainsley's granddaughter?'

'No,' she said in a tiny voice. 'Please, I just want to know he's okay.'

Ainsley patted her shoulder. 'It's all right, sweetheart, you did the right thing letting me know. We'll find him for you. Can you give us a moment, please?'

Gwendoline nodded meekly and left the lounge.

'I ran a check through the London police network,' Poi Li said. 'Horatio wasn't involved in any incident yesterday morning, and there's no arrest record. The police don't have him in custody.'

Yuri pulled a face. 'He's young. That opens up a few options, especially if he's not the entirely faithful type.'

'Ha!' Ainsley grunted. 'If you were a horny nineteen-year-old and you had Gwendoline in your bed every night, would you go wolfing round the block?'

'It's been known,' Yuri replied, as tactfully as he could.

'This whole thing: it's unusual,' Ainsley said. 'I don't fucking like unusual, not when there's family involved. Especially exposed family.'

'We need to bring the women in,' Poi Li said. 'Give them proper security.'

'Yeah,' Ainsley agreed. 'Shit, Nataskia will bust my balls. This is everything she didn't want. And fuck knows how Neva will react.'

'Who's Neva?' Yuri asked.

'My second-to-last ex. I was married to her when Nataskia had Evette. She doesn't know about that.'

'Oh.' Yuri's gaze locked on Poi Li as he tried to remain expressionless.

'So what do you think?' Ainsley asked.

'Okay,' Yuri said, and took a breath. 'We have a few scenarios to consider here. Horatio has run off with another girl or boy, and he's too guilty right now to call Gwendoline and tell her it's over. Second: he's had an accident and the hospital hasn't identified him – unlikely in this day and age, but possible. Third: he's dead. We'll need to check the morgues, but again he should have been identified already. Last option, and the most likely: he's in trouble with people you really should not be in trouble with.'

'It's not blackmail?' Ainsley asked, he sounded surprised.

'I'm going to take Gwendoline at her word when she said that she never told him she's related to you. If this is blackmail, that would mean someone found out.'

'How?' Ainsley snapped.

'Some junior in the legal division got the wrong file by mistake; same thing but with an employee in the finance company handling the trust fund; her mother or grandmother let something slip by accident.' He paused, extrapolating the possibilities. 'But if a professional gang did find out, they'd snatch her, not him. Unless . . .'

'What?'

Yuri glanced at the door Gwendoline had closed behind her. 'She's scamming you.'

'No fucking way!'

'Sir, she has no real bond with you, and she's excluded from the dynasty with all the wealth, privilege and prestige that brings.'

'Okay, I've only seen her a few times in her life, I admit that, but she knows there's a place for her in Connexion any time she wants. She chose to be independent, she worked hard at her exams – and got herself good grades, too. And she's only seventeen, for Christ's sake! Girls like that, brought up the way she's been, they don't come up with criminal master plans. If she wants money, she can have it. I'm not broke. She just has to ask.'

'All right, acknowledged. So that scenario would be doubtful.'

'We need to find out what's happened to Horatio,' Poi Li said.

'But without any fuss. Which is where you come in. This has to be kept quiet.'

'Poi Li recommended you,' Ainsley said. 'She said you were the one we needed for a job like this. I know this is a big ask, but fuck it, this is my family!'

'It's a logical ask,' Yuri said, trying to make it sound businesslike – although inside he was flying. *A personal favour for Ainsley fucking Zangari? This is my cast-iron route to head of Security.* 'My office already has executive authority, and uses it. I can request any file or operation we need without anyone wondering why.'

'Thanks,' Ainsley said. 'I appreciate that, Yuri, I mean it.'

Yuri held up a hand. 'This is not a one-person investigation, sir. I understand and appreciate the need for discretion, but I'll be bringing in some of my team to assist. Not many, but people I trust.'

'Of course.'

'If this is ordinary bad, I need to get started right now.'

'What's ordinary bad?' Ainsley asked.

'He's got a dependency problem, or he's placed some bets offline – neither of which he'll tell Gwendoline about, for all their lovey-dovey honesty with each other. If he owes money to those kinds of people, then right now he's in some blacked-out room having the shit kicked out of him. The danger there is that once they break him – and they will – he'll call Gwendoline, begging for money. So, first priority, we install a link diversion on her altme. If he calls, that gets routed straight to me.'

'Whatever you need, whatever it costs. Just get it done.'

'Yes, sir.'

*

Yuri called Jessika Mye while he was still in the rickety old lift on his way back down to the entrance hall. She'd joined the Monitoring Office as one of its first recruits, at age thirty-four – a Hong Kong native who'd emigrated to Akitha, where she'd got her exobiology masters degree. When he asked her why she'd come back to Earth, she'd told him that Akitha was too quiet for her, and she wanted the money to buy full telomere treatments. Yuri could sort of appreciate that; the Utopial principle strove for egalitarianism, but even their society couldn't afford to provide telomere treatments for the entire population from such an early age. Akitha democratically decided that, for a thirty-four year old, it was vanity not necessity. Jessika was attractive, and clearly motivated to remain so. Yuri quite liked that determination, to be able to reject past choices with confidence if they didn't meet her own demanding standards, so he gave her the job there and then.

'What's up, chief?' she asked.

'We have a new investigation. I can't even give you a priority rating it's so high.'

'Sounds cool. What is it?'

'Missing person.'

'Seriously?'

Yuri smiled at the doubt in her tone. The lift reached the ground floor, and he tugged the cage door open. 'Oh, yes.'

'Why the hell are we doing a missing person?'

'Because it's important. And that's why I want you. I'm sending the address over now. Be there in five minutes.'

Yuri walked straight back to the Sloane Square hub and went out along a radial to loop, then around that to the Hackney hub at the end of Graham Road. As he went, Boris started loading instructions into the Olyix Monitoring Office G7Turing. He wanted a record of Horatio Seymore's travels through the Connexion network for the last four days. Bank search for financial status. Facial recognition search through Hackney's public surveillance cameras, going back three days. A request routed through the Connexion Metropolitan Police liaison office for gang activity in Hackney.

Those would do for a start.

Eleanor Road, on the edge of London Fields, was half old brick terrace houses with tall slate roofs that had all undergone conversions to add a loft room for the budget middle classes still inhabiting London's suburbs. The remainder of the buildings were newer, purpose-built tenements, narrow and tall to fit in as many one-bedroom flats as possible, with the rent and management optimized for a fast turn-over of young low-wage workers with service jobs in the City. Exactly like Horatio.

Jessika's heels clattered on the pavement behind Yuri as he approached the front of Horatio's building.

'Good timing.' He smirked as she caught up with him. She was wearing a smart cherry-pink office suit and white blouse, with slim five-centimetre heels; her face flushed even through her perfect make-up. Her normally immaculate jet-black hair was ruffled from hurrying along the street.

'And you blend in so flawlessly.'

'Hey!' she protested. 'I'm strictly an office-meetings-and-cocktails kind of girl.'

'Right.' He told Boris to let them in; Gwendoline had given him the code.

The hallway and stairs were bare concrete, shaped by one-time printed moulds and formed by civic construction bots – cheap and coldly utilitarian. Horatio's flat was two rooms: a slim shower and toilet suite; and the living room equipped with a tiny galley kitchen, a built-in wardrobe and a bed settee. With two stools standing beside the kitchen bar, there wasn't even room for a chair.

'Depressing,' Jessika said as she glanced round.

'No sign of a struggle,' Yuri said. 'So he wasn't taken from here.'

'Outside, then.'

'Boris, what have you got for me on Wednesday morning?'

'Connexion has no record of Horatio Seymour using the hub network since twenty-one seventeen hours on Tuesday night, when he left the Hackney hub on Graham Road. That is a global negative, not just London.'

'Did I ask for a global search?'

'No, but the G7Turing deduced it was relevant.'

'Crap. If it gets any smarter, we'll be out of a job. Okay, what about Gwendoline?'

'Her record is complete and current. She entered the Hackney hub at six fifty-eight on Wednesday morning and went straight to Sloane Square. After a day at work in the City, using her usual hubs, she returned to Hackney on Wednesday evening at twenty-one forty-nine. She left this morning at seven fifty.'

'Right, get me a visual record of Eleanor Road on Wednesday, starting at six thirty that morning. Let's see where Horatio went.'

'Confirmed,' Boris said.

Jessika opened the wardrobe door. 'Not much in here,' she said, eyeing the clothes.

'He doesn't have any money.'

'Then why are we interested?'

Yuri gave her an apologetic shrug. 'Super-classified: he's the boyfriend of one of Ainsley's granddaughters.'

'Ah.'

'There is no visual record of Horatio leaving his home address on Wednesday morning,' Boris reported.

Yuri and Jessika exchanged a glance. He went over to the window at the rear of the flat, which gave him a view of the tiny gardens backing onto the houses of Horton Road, parallel to Eleanor Road. The window was locked from the inside. 'Okay, check Horton Road for me. If he jumped out here, he had to go through a house. Maybe he knows his neighbours well enough.'

Jessika frowned and went back into the narrow shower room, checking the frosted glass cubical. 'Well, he's not here.'

'You're looking in the shower cubicle?' he asked sceptically.

'Check out an old movie called *Psycho*.'

'No visual confirmation of him on Horton Road on Wednesday or today,' Boris said.

'What is this, the case of the vanishing magician?' Jessika asked.

'No,' Yuri said, not liking where his thoughts were going. 'Boris, run a visual recognition for Gwendoline on Eleanor Road Wednesday morning.'

'There is none.'

'How can that be?' Jessika grunted.

'Confirm she entered Hackney hub at six-fifty-eight on Wednesday, please?'

'Our files have visual confirmation of that.'

'Right, use public surveillance files. Backtrack her from entering the hub.'

'There is a discrepancy. The visual record can track her back to the point where she emerged from the end of Eleanor Road onto Wilton Way.'

'So the records for Eleanor Road are corrupted?'

'The Turing is running a diagnostic.'

'What are you thinking?' Jessika asked.

'This snatch was well planned and executed,' Yuri said. 'We're dealing with some serious professionals here. Given Horatio was one very fit, good-looking adolescent, I'd say we need to think absolute worst case.'

'Shit. You're talking a body snatch? For . . .? What? Ransom?'

'A dark market brain transplant. What we've seen so far certainly seems to fit the idea.'

She closed her eyes and shuddered. 'Thanks. I wanted to go on believing that is urban myth. You got any evidence other than you watch too many Hong Kong drama games?'

'A myth has to start somewhere,' he said. 'And it did only start after the Olyix arrived.'

'The Olyix are behind it?' she asked incredulously. 'That's crazy.'

'Not behind it, no; but their Kcells make it possible.' Yuri flinched from her sceptical stare. 'Supposedly.' He sighed, wishing it to be untrue. But the possibility of dark market brain transplants had become an insidious rumour, whispered between law enforcement agencies for several years now. The perfect explanation that case officers offered up to their directors whenever a major-league criminal suspect eluded them: they were walking round in a whole new body.

Hong Kong drama game production houses loved the concept and pushed it eagerly into their mainstream crime series. The alien science of Kcells made it sound deliciously plausible.

Until the Olyix arrived, cloning organs or using stem-cell replacement tissue was expensive. But the Olyix were eager to trade, enabling them to buy the energy they needed for their arkship *Salvation of Life* to continue its pilgrimage voyage to the end of the universe. Their advanced biotechnology produced the poly-function Kcell, which could be assembled in a number of ways from veins to skin, bones to muscle, and even some organs. Like the flesh they replaced, they drew energy from blood, living in perfect symbiosis with the human body, and they were also cheap.

The versatility of Kcells was the root of the whole brain transplant story. Kcells, so the theory went, could be used to form a neural bridge between brain and spine – an ability still far beyond human medical science. And as it involved Kcells, Yuri's office had a dedicated team to investigate and analyse possible cases to see if there was any truth in the claims. So far their conclusion was: we don't know.

'Let's just see where this leads,' Yuri temporized. The idea that this might be the case which proved the dark market for brain transplants existed was thrilling. 'Boris, how are we doing with those surveillance files?'

'The memory files for the public surveillance camera on Eleanor Road were altered,' Boris said. 'The hours between six and nine were replaced by a synthesized image.'

'This is not an amateur operation,' Yuri said. 'Not if they can do that. So we're now time critical.' He closed his eyes and told Boris to spray a map of the area across his tarsus lens. 'We know the Wilton Way camera files are good. Boris, get the G7Turing to run a search on all the surrounding roads, extending out for a kilometre. Tie it in with the local traffic net records. I want to know every vehicle that drove down Eleanor Road between six and nine on Wednesday morning. No, make that five and nine.'

'How long do you think we've got?' Jessika asked.

'They've had Horatio at least twenty-four hours, so not much longer.'

'There were two vehicles using Eleanor Road during the time-frame you designated,' Boris told him. 'A civic contractor cleaning truckez, with six ancillary brush wagons, and a builder's merchant van.'

'What was the builder's merchant?'

'Tarazzi Metropolitan Supplies. They are based in Croydon.'

'Get into their network, find the delivery address.'

'There is no delivery address. Error. That van is not licensed to them.'

'Well, who is it licensed to?'

'Tarazzi Metropolitan Supplies ADL. That is a company registered on the New Hamburg asteroid. The company was formed on Tuesday, twelve o'clock GMT, and dissolved at five o'clock GMT this morning.'

'Smart,' Yuri conceded. 'Any ownership records?'

'There was one share issued, registered to Horton Accounting. That is also a New Hamburg company, a Turing virtual that is now inactive.'

'Horton?' Yuri glanced out of the window again at the backs of the neat row of houses that made up Horton Road. 'Someone's taking the piss. Okay, what time was the van here?'

'It turned into Eleanor Road at six twenty-two. It left, travelling along Wilton Way, at six forty-eight.'

'Where did it go?'

'At six fifty-seven it entered the Hackney Commercial and Government Services transport hub on Amhurst Road.'

'Track it. I want to know the destination. Jessika, we've got to split up. Call a cabez, follow the fake Tarazzi van to its destination, then find out what happened next. I'm going to assign you a tactical team; they'll follow you. Use them for any face-to-face situation. You're investigation only, understand? I don't want you physically exposed to any member of this dark market operation. They haven't eluded the authorities for years by being the forgiving type.'

'Okay.' She gave him a small wild smile. 'What are you going to do?'

'Come at it from a different angle. The more routes into this dark market we can open up, the better chance we have of getting Horatio back.'

A cabez was pulling up outside the building by the time they walked out of the front door. Yuri watched Jessika climb in, then hurried back to the Hackney hub.

*

Seven minutes later he was coming out of the hub at the eastern end of Royal Victoria Docks, buffeted by the humid air gusting off the Thames. If he looked south across the river, the Connexion tower dominated the skyline. Around him, the buildings were a strange mixture of old industrial and new residential; at one time they'd all been hotels and restaurants to serve the vast exhibition centre that stretched out alongside the docks. But with the advent of Connexion making every location on Earth *one step away*, such overnight business hotels had become obsolete. They'd subsequently been refurbished as apartments, though some had remained derelict for decades.

Boris hacked the lobby lock of what had once been the classiest hotel on the block. Yuri walked across the high-ceilinged chamber and past the lifts to the stairwell. The office G7Turing was infiltrating the building's security network – which was top of the range, but hardly a match for a G7. He didn't want to be trapped in a lift, with the doors opening at someone else's convenience.

The third-floor corridor ran the length of the building, but only had half a dozen doors. Two men stood at the end, giving him a hard stare as he walked down the length of it towards them. Yuri ignored them and halted a couple of metres from the double doors they were guarding. He tipped his head to one side in his best condescending manner and looked at where he guessed the camera was hidden.

'Open it,' he said in a tired voice.

'Don't—' one of the guards began.

'Not you,' Yuri said, sounding even more tired.

The door buzzed and slid open. Yuri tipped the guards a silent salute and walked in. The inside had been the hotel penthouse suite a century ago and remained an opulent apartment overlooking the docks.

Karno Larsen looked as if he'd been in residence for most of those hundred years. He was a huge man, whose sixth decade had been stretched out for a punishingly long time by telomere treatments, making him seem more like a mannequin than a flesh-and-blood person. He wore a burgundy silk gown embroidered with mythical creatures that barely covered his dome-like stomach. Thick bare legs waddled him forwards from the outsized chair he'd been sitting in.

One of the high walls was covered in screens, all of them playing cult shows from fifty years ago. Karno prided himself on his encyclopedic knowledge of historical trash culture. Glass-fronted cabinets displayed a huge range of incredibly detailed miniatures and limited edition merchandise from the last hundred and fifty years. It all looked like cheap tat to Yuri, though he knew it was actually priceless.

'Yuri, my friend, what a surprise. I never thought you would visit me here. Welcome, welcome.'

'Really?' Yuri asked. The screens were all playing crap now, but he guessed that a minute earlier they'd been displaying a tangle of finance data. As underground accountants went, Karno Larsen was the preferred go-to for the top men of London's underworld.

Karno performed a humbled shrug. 'A short warning would be appreciated next time.'

'Actual human guards. I'm impressed.'

'One has to cultivate an air of civility. Their peripherals alone cost more than they do.'

'I'm sure.'

'So why are you here, Yuri? You're not good for business, you know.'

'I need a name, and I don't have time for bullshit.'

'In some ways, that is almost flattering.'

'Who's the best matcher in East London?'

Karno's face locked into a rictus smile. 'Matcher?'

'Don't,' Yuri said.

'Yuri, please, I have a reputation to consider.'

'The only reputation I know is of the person who sets up one-time virtual companies to use the Commercial and Government Services hubs. We talked about that misbehaviour before, Karno, and we agreed you have to be useful to me in order to carry on existing. I need the name, and I need it now. I'm asking politely.'

'Yuri, please, I don't move in such circles. I facilitate finance, you know this.'

'Play close attention, Karno, because either I leave with what I want, or you get renditioned to a world that makes Zagreus look like a fucking holiday resort.'

'Jesus, Yuri, there's no need for this!' Karno's agitation was making his flab wobble obscenely. 'We are friends.'

'*Name!*'

'Conrad McGlasson.'

'And where do I find him?'

There was no physical address, only an access code. The G7Turing was running tracers before Yuri reached the lobby.

He called Jessika as he went through the doors back out into the unrestrained heat of the street. 'How's it going?'

'I'm on Althaea; some town called Bronkal. The Tarazzi van drove into the dredger docks. There's no traffic network so I haven't got a final destination yet.'

Yuri didn't have to get Boris to gather data on Althaea. It was a gas giant moon in the Pollux system, which after fifty years of aggressive terraforming was just about capable of supporting terrestrial life. The flip point had almost been reached, when the biosphere would become stable without any more intervention. 'Okay. Call in our local office.'

'Already have. And the tactical team is with me.'

'Good. Those frontier towns can be rough in places.'

'No kidding.'

'I've got a possible lead here. If it checks out I should be with you in half an hour.'

'Can't wait.'

Boris sprayed up a file of Conrad McGlasson's hub travel record. He moved around London at lot, Yuri noted, which fitted the whole matcher profile. The G7Turing pulled up a lot of ancillary data: the flats he used, financial data which was nowhere near complete; that could only mean Conrad had dark accounts.

'What was his last hub use?' Yuri asked.

'He left the QEII South Road hub seventeen minutes ago.'

'Okay, he's probably on the bridge; there's a lot of footfall there. Cancel his hub access. I want to keep him there.'

'Done.'

'Send three hawkeye drone squadrons through to find him. And dispatch a tactical team to both ends of the bridge. They're to remain on standby until I call for them, zero public exposure.'

'Confirmed.'

*

Yuri walked out of the QEII South Road hub two minutes later and looked up the imposing concrete road ramp which rose up to the Dartford Bridge. As part of London's old M25 orbital motorway, the huge old suspension bridge which crossed the Thames used to carry a hundred and thirty thousand vehicles a day over the muddy tidal estuary. Now it was simply a monument to the obsolete past. He couldn't imagine what it had looked like while it was in use.

Since the last cars and lorries drove away into history, new money and real estate opportunities had allowed the bridge to re-invent itself. Big tubs had been fixed to the carriageways and planted with trees, turning the whole edifice into a flying greenway. Lightweight buildings had colonized the edges of the bridge, glass walls giving bar, club and restaurant customers an unrivalled view along the river, both into the city and out across the surrounding countryside. Smaller pop-up specialist fabricator stores shared the ancient tarmac with the verdant trees, completing the transform-ation to a funky concrete rainbow of small-trader commerce.

Yuri began the long walk up the ramp, sticking to the shade offered by the tree canopy. Here above the river, the humidity was reaching a dismal crescendo. He slung his lightweight suit jacket over his shoulder and wished he had some kind of hat. Unseen above him, the hawkeye drones spread out and started searching for Conrad McGlasson.

They found him sitting at an outdoor table, halfway along the southern side. A beer glass was on the table in front of him as he watched the people thronging along the central greenway. Yuri approached at an unhurried pace, keeping his eyes on the target. 'Boris, shut down the local internet nodes in a hundred-metre radius around him.'

'Confirmed.'

The man was in his forties, with short-cut hair as black as his skin. Shorts and an old orange T-shirt gave him an unremarkable air. The only unusual thing was his lack of sunglasses; everyone else on the bridge that day was wearing them as if it was a compulsory dress code. Conrad's eyes were too precious for that. He scanned the people wandering past, studying them.

Conrad saw Yuri while he was still twenty metres away, and immediately tensed up.

He's good, Yuri admitted to himself.

Conrad hunted round for other potential hostiles. When he didn't find any, he returned his gaze to Yuri.

'I'm not going to chase you,' Yuri said as he arrived at the table.

'Nice to know,' Conrad replied, trying to keep it cool. Small beads of sweat on his high forehead were giving away his inner anxiety.

Yuri pulled out a chair and sat down. 'My teams will do that. They're all young and fit, and eager to show me how efficient they are. They're armed, too. Ever been hit with a taser dart? Ours are very good, because we can't be arsed restricting them to the legal maximum charge. Oh, and I've revoked your Connexion account. You'd have to run the whole way home. I imagine that would be quite exhausting in this heat. The teams will probably start a book on how far you'd get. I'd say about a hundred and fifty metres. What do you reckon?'

'What do you want?'

'I want you to tell me about me.'

'Excuse me?'

'You're a matcher. You find specific people, ones who fit a profile. Any profile you're given. So show me how good you are.'

'This is bollocks. You've got nothing on me.'

'I have your name, and I was told you're the best.'

'No proof, pal.'

'Don't need it. You find people – people who are vulnerable without realizing it. I know how it works; my office has to deal with plenty of cases.'

'Your office?'

'Yeah. All those starry-eyed graduate kids who've just grabbed themselves a shit job at the very bottom of a big company and think they're going to make it to CEO one day. You see their weakness, you *know* them. It's a special and rare talent you have there, Conrad. You read something in them that tells you they'll be tempted if they're offered some mild narcotics in the right circumstances, by their new best friend. You see one, out here on the bridge, or in a pub, and you sell his name to groups who specialize in trading information. And in a month's time that kid'll have a serious addiction, his credit will be deep negative, he'll do anything to get his next squirt, including handing over access to the company system. Or a girl, pretty but shy, one who can be corrupted easily. And the next thing she knows she's met a great guy, with a great smile and who's showing her a life she only fantasized about, one that pulls her in deeper and deeper. Bingo! Then after a time he's not just her boyfriend, he's her pimp. Another kid ruined. Are you getting the picture here, *pal*? Do you see I know you? Gotta admire the irony.'

'You know nothing, you piece of shit! You're blind.'

'This isn't personal, so don't make that mistake. You need to do better, a lot better. Am I right? Now tell me about me.'

Conrad McGlasson glared at him. 'You're not police.'

'That was a fifty-fifty guess. Even I could get that one. Come on, live a little, Conrad. Impress me.'

'Russian; the accent's still there. Received plenty of telomere treatments, and good ones. You're over a hundred, but hide it well. You work at that – body posture and clothes. The clothes are important; they indicate status. You don't cling to the old comforts; you make yourself stay fashionable. You have arrogance and surety, and you found me easily, so there's plenty of money behind you. It's corporate, not private wealth. You've done your time in the ranks, but you're now too important to be a tactical team leader, which means that if you're taking point, I'm valuable. I know that because people around us are getting antsy now that their internet feed's mysteriously dropped out. You did that to stop me alerting anyone that you've found me. That takes clout, digital and political. You're a senior officer in Connexion Security.' He picked up his beer and raised it in salute.

'Not bad,' Yuri admitted. 'A proper little Sherlock Holmes.'

'So why am I valuable? What are you doing here?'

Yuri took out a card and told Boris to spray a picture of Horatio on it. When he put it on the table next to the beer, Conrad gave it a cursory glance.

'Did you match him?' Yuri asked.

'No.'

'Okay, I'll accept that for now. But it's a small market, there can't be many of you.'

'Is that a question?'

'No. Actually, I'm quite impressed. A Turing above G5 can do a similar job to you, but it requires access to a thousand databases. But you, you just look. I find that fascinating.' His finger tapped the picture on the card. 'What do you see?

'Him? A nobody, which is something of a paradox considering how desperate you are to find him.'

'Not really. He genuinely is a nobody. Your problem is that he met someone who is most definitely not a nobody. So tell me, what do you see, what do you *match*, when you have a contract?'

'This is hypothetical, right?'

'I don't give a shit about you. Your value is measured solely in the information you provide me today. There is no deal on the table here. So? What do you look for?'

Conrad's hands came up to massage his temple. 'All right, it goes like this. You have a client, someone who wants information on a company, maybe for a share short, some corporate shit, and—'

'No.'

'What?'

'I don't want a company scam. I'm a serial killer, a rich fuck who's more twisted than any politician. The cops are closing in, and I need to escape.'

'What?'

'I need a new body. One I can transplant my brain into.'

'Oh no. No no no! Do not do this. You have no idea who you're fucking with.'

Yuri leant in closer, his skin warming with excitement. Conrad's reaction was the first indication that brain transplants might really be happening.

Conrad, of course, saw his reaction, and winced. 'Walk away, pal. Tell your boss or whoever it is pulling your strings that you got it wrong. These people you're asking about, they won't respect who you are. You'll wind up with someone like Cancer on your arse, or worse'

'I didn't think there was anyone worse than her.' Yuri knew all about Cancer – so-called because she always got her victim in the end; a black ops specialist for the extremely wealthy, but illegitimate, playa. She'd never taken a contract which hadn't been fulfilled, and never a contract from anyone remotely legitimate – presumably to make sure it wasn't an entrapment sting. Feared and respected by everyone in the trade, and the dream arrest of every law enforcement official in the Sol system.

'Don't do this,' Conrad pleaded.

'If it helps, think of me as Cancer's opposite. You are my target. When you give me what I want, then – and only then – will this be over.'

'It's a death sentence for both of us, you understand?'

'Completely. But just so you understand, if these people are not scared of me, then they're exceptionally stupid.'

'Fuck you! Look, this deal, what you're asking for, it's rarer than unicorn shit, okay?'

'What? Snatches for a brain transplant?'

Conrad winced, glancing round nervously. 'Stop saying that. I don't know what the client wants these people for, okay? It's weird, but it pays well.'

'What people?'

'Low-visibility people; that's what they ask for. People so

insignificant no one will ever notice when they go missing. There's not as many as you'd think, actually.'

'So you don't know for sure they're being snatched for a brain transplant?'

'Listen, pal, we don't exactly have contracts, you know.'

'Okay, so why get so twitchy whenever I mention brain transplants? What do you know? Are they real?' Yuri had to work hard at keeping the enthusiasm out of his voice.

'I just think it through, you know,' Conrad said edgily. 'Working out the options. You gotta watch out for yourself in this trade, make sure nothing comes back to bite you. So when I look hard at some of the aspects I have to take into account, that kinda narrows the options, see?'

'All right, how does this work? Exactly? Tell me – all of it.'

'Okay, it plays like this: you've committed a serious crime, something the authorities are never going to quit on – like you said, a serial killer or paedophile, totally bad shit. The only way out for you is a fresh body for your brain, just like on the drama games. That way, not even a DNA sample can show who you really are, because cops only ever sample the body, saliva or blood – semen a lot of the time – but never the brain. So the deal goes down, and I get the word, a request to match, along with the condition that they have to be low visibility. Now what else apart from a brain transplant could it be?'

'Right. What else do they want apart from low visibility?'

'My client gives me a picture. It's not an actual image, a photo file, or anything like that. This picture, it's a description, a data sketch. Height and weight combination, skin colour, hair colour, eye colour. That's the basic parameter.'

'I don't get it. Why would a criminal want to look the same? Why not go for someone who looks different?'

'Rejection. Come on; that part's obvious! This is the mother of all transplants, so I figure you have to have the greatest match possible. Physical traits are a good baseline. I see someone who matches the picture, and I start to assess them. Are they basically healthy, are they overweight? Stuff like that. It's amazing what you get to recognize. Some people are walking beacons for what's happened to them. Accidents make them flinch at the smallest things. Careful around food, they've got allergies. It's all there in the posture, you know? Once I have a potential, then secondary factors kick in, which are even more important. The biggest is: is anyone going to care if they vanish? That rules out the rich, and most of the middle class. So I look for what they wear, where they live, what sort of places they visit, the kind of people they're hanging out with. All these are big indicators of who a person is. So I work it down to maybe ten possibles and get physically close enough to snatch their altme code when they go online – which everybody is, all the time. Once I have that, an e-head friend grabs their digital profile for a real exam. Eighty per cent of the time I'm right and they're nonentities. Dig a little deeper, and they have awkward links – a good job, a big set of friends, things that make vanishing them different. So after you've run those filters, you're left with maybe three or four. Then you step it up a level and go for their medical records. That's when we find out blood type and any congenital conditions. There's normally a genome sequence as well, which gets reviewed by specialist algorithms for biochemical compatibility. If they're optimum I'll pass the file on to my client, and I'm out with a nice fat bonus.'

'Your client always asks for medical data?'

'Yes, of course. That's something else that's telling me what's actually going down. I mean, what else could they need that for, right? And I'll tell you something: crime isn't race specific. All these requests have been really varied.'

'*All*, the requests? I thought you said this kind of snatch was rare.'

Conrad flinched. 'It is. Compared with the other matches I make.'

'So these rare cases – your victim is taken away and killed?'

'The body's still walking round.'

'You know what you are?'

'Yeah yeah: inhuman, a psycho. Call me a bastard to my face, please. This is a tough life, pal. We all do what we have to.'

'No, none of that. I'm beyond insults in your case. You've just described yourself. Who would ever notice or care if you disappeared?'

'Fuck you!'

'Okay, we're almost finished. Who is your client? Who puts in the order for a match?'

'You're kidding, right?'

'Does my face match someone who's kidding right now? Give me the name.'

'I can't do that.'

'Can and will. Don't make me ask again.' Yuri watched with cold amusement as the warring emotions played across Conrad's face. Fear dominated.

'If I do this—'

'When,' Yuri said.

'I'm protected, right?'

'Oh, yeah. Just like doctor–patient confidentiality; I signed the oath and everything. Give me the fucking name, dickhead.'

Boris sprayed the incoming file across his tarsus lens: Baptiste Devroy.

Yuri got up and walked away without another word, heading for the nearest hub out of the six on the bridge.

'Do you want Conrad's Connexion account reactivated?' Boris asked.

'Yes. Let him into the hub network again, but have the tactical team intercept him. He is to be dropped on Zagreus today.'

'Confirmed.'

'Then get me a complete profile on Baptiste Devroy, and run a cross-reference with Althaea; I want to know why the fake Tarazzi van went there. When you get that, send the file straight to Jessika; she can start checking it out. Oh, and put another tactical team on standby for me, a dark one. As soon as we have a location on Devroy, they're to bring him in to the Glastonbury safehouse. I'll talk to him there.'

'Processing now.'

Yuri ducked into the nearest hub and walked round the loop

until he came to a major junction. It had a private access to Connexion's internal network. From there it was five portals until he was walking out of the company's Geneva headquarters. The heatwave seemed to be Europe-wide; it was just as hot and humid walking Geneva's streets as it was in London. It took him three minutes to get to the Olyix European Trade and Exchange embassy on the Quai du Mont Blanc. Baptiste Devroy's file splashed up on his lens within the first twenty seconds. Rumoured to run a crew for the Woodwarde Macros, a south London gang that was rumoured to deal in biosynth narcotics. Also rumoured to have killed a rival gang soldier two years ago.

'Too many rumours,' Yuri told Boris. 'Do we have anything concrete?'

'His criminal activities are coming from the London Metropolitan Police gang intelligence task force files,' Boris replied. 'Legally, they cannot confirm his activities without proof. The information they've gathered on him has come from informers and is not admissible in court.'

'Fucking lawyers,' Yuri muttered under his breath. 'Do you have a location on him?'

'He has a flat in Dulwich Village. According to his Connexion account, he exited the hub on his road at twenty-three forty-seven hours last night. He has not used the account again so far today, which implies he's either at home in the flat or within walking distance. The tactical team are en route to Dulwich. Their G7 Turing is reviewing local civic surveillance, and they will ping his altme before entering the flat to confirm his location before they intercept.'

'Okay, keep me updated.'

The Olyix European Trade and Exchange embassy was a modern nine-storey structure of glass and concrete, facing the Jet d'Eau out in the lake. As well as two armed Swiss Diplomatic Police outside the doorway, there were twin security pillars which scanned Yuri as he walked past them. The police waved him in.

Stéphane Marsan was waiting for him inside – an elegantly

suited Frenchman who served as a technology liaison officer for the aliens.

'Thank you for arranging this at such short notice,' Yuri said as they went through the decontamination suite.

'Happy to oblige,' Stéphane said, pressing his antique black glasses back onto his nose. 'The Olyix are sensitive to any abuse of their technology.'

Decontamination wasn't as intense as Yuri was expecting. A room with big glass doors at both ends was filled with a mist that he had to stand in for two minutes, eliminating the microbes clinging to his clothes – the kind which saturated the city air. Light heavy with UV shone down on him.

On the other side, the temperature was several degrees colder than outside. The embassy had its own life-support mechanism; no alien air was released into Geneva's atmosphere, and vice versa.

A lift took them up to the fifth floor. When the doors opened, a dry spicy air wafted in. Yuri peered round curiously. The fifth floor was different to the rest of the building, which mainly housed human-style offices. In front of him was a wide open space, with a hologram ceiling of an alien sky. Two huge gas giants hung above him, one with a vivid emerald cloudscape, the other more like Saturn but without the rings. Both had a plethora of moons, every one of them different, from planetoids locked under ice oceans to smog-smothered continents studded with sulphur volcanoes, from barren mono-deserts to jungle hellholes.

'Is that . . .?' Yuri began.

'Their original homeworld?' Stéphane finished for him. 'Non. It's an enhanced Jim Burns picture; they bought the rights to the original. Something about it appealed to them.'

Yuri shook his head. Just when you thought you had a handle on the Olyix, the universe twisted ninety degrees and took it away from you again.

There were several of the aliens lumbering about the room. The main bulk of an Olyix was a fat disc two metres in diameter, with a semi-translucent skin that revealed a great many purple organ shapes lurking inside. The thin curving fissures between them were filled with thick fluid which pulsed slowly round the body and always made Yuri slightly queasy. Five stumpy legs emerged from the underside, with the forward limb nearly twice as thick as the other four. Clearly visible within each leg were helixes of muscle bending and flexing around a dark central rod of gristle. The wide hooves lacked the elegance of the legs with their sophisticated flexibility, which for some reason made Yuri think of a donkey clopping along.

He watched carefully as one approached – and yes, each footfall was cumbersome, thudding down loudly on the marble floor. That was to be expected; not one of the weird creatures weighed less than a hundred and fifty kilograms. There was a broad oval head above the body, and a fat ring-neck provided it with limited mobility. The nose extended to the circumference of the body, with a bulging gold-tinted compound apposition eye on the upper surface. At the front of the body's midsection was a flaccid skirt of clear tissue hanging down, which put Yuri unnervingly in mind of a loincloth of jellyfish. The lucid substance formed a shape mimicking a human hand and extended it towards Yuri on the end of a stubby tentacle.

Yuri clenched his jaw against the revulsion he knew he was about to experience and put out his hand. The Olyix flesh flowed round his palm, feeling like oiled velvet that had just come out of a fridge. He smiled as he shook hands. Someone had explained the whole human etiquette routine to the Olyix when their arkship arrived in the Sol system, and the aliens had swiftly incorporated the correct formal procedures into their dealings with people ever since. Privately, Yuri wished a prankster had got there first and shown them *Star Trek*'s Vulcan salute instead.

Boris reported a link being opened. 'Pleased to meet you, Director Alster,' the Olyix's vocalizer unit said in a husky female voice. Another attempt at endearment. If you were male they used a female voice, and vice versa. Yuri wondered why nobody had ever bothered explaining political correctness to them. *Pick a gender and stick with it, guys.* The aliens themselves were indefinable by human standards in both biology and gender. An Olyix defined itself by its mind, which was always distributed between its quint:

five bodies linked via a form of quantum entanglement between the neural structure of its separate brains.

'That's just Yuri, please,' he said, withdrawing his hand as soon as politeness allowed.

'Of course. My quint designation is Hai. I personally am Hai-3.'

'Thank you for agreeing to see me, Hai-3.' Yuri resisted the impulse to look round the room and guess which, if any, of the other Olyix bodies were also Hai. An Olyix quint always kept at least a couple of itself on board the *Salvation of Life*, their arkship.

'I am happy to assist. Your message indicated you proceed with some urgency.'

Yuri glanced at Stéphane. 'That is correct.'

'You need me gone?' Stéphane asked.

'This could be quite sensitive.'

'Officer Marsan has our full confidence,' Hai-3 said.

'Okay. I'm tracking a missing human, which may be a case of an illegal brain transplant. So I need to know if such a thing is theoretically possible, and the critical component behind the theory seems to be Kcells, which would be used to reconnect the nervous system. Is it possible to use them like that?'

A slow ripple made its way along Hai-3's loose flesh, tracking left to right. 'This is most unfortunate,' it said. 'We have heard rumours of our Kcells being misused in this fashion.'

'That's all we have as well, rumours and conspiracy theories. Which is why I'm here. I need to know once and for all if it is real.'

'Have you any proof of this allegation?' Stéphane asked flatly.

'Nobody is making allegations,' Yuri countered quickly. 'Nor levelling charges of illegality. Right now, I have a kid I need to find – and fast. I need to eliminate as many possibilities as I can, so I'm not wasting time. That's all.'

'Once we heard claims of this abuse, our growthmasters looked into the process,' Hai-3 said. 'From a theoretical viewpoint only. We wished to see if it was indeed possible.'

'Of course. And is it?'

'Without actually using a test subject, we cannot give a definitive answer.'

'Best guess will do for me.'

'Our simulation indicated it would ultimately be possible to transplant a human brain from one body to another, given the correct circumstances.'

'What are those circumstances?'

'That the host and donor bodies would have to share a very similar biochemistry, extending far beyond simple blood type matching. The most ideal match would be between humans in the same family.'

Yuri couldn't quite avoid the shudder of revulsion that brought on. He did manage to avoid a small prayer of thanks to the dear Virgin Mary that he'd never had children. He hadn't been inside a church for over a century, but thanks to his mother, the Russian Orthodox Church had been an ever-present influence in his early childhood. 'I see. But if a family member wasn't available?'

'It would still be possible, though the number of candidates would be small. You would have to be very lucky to find one.'

'Or know a man that can,' Yuri murmured. 'Okay. So I've done my research and have a suitable donor body. What do I need from you?'

'Such a procedure would require a great deal more than Kcells profiled to conduct nerve impulses between human neurone junctions.'

'What else do you need?'

'Nerve repair in humans is now relatively successful, if expensive. The use of stem cells to regenerate damaged nerves is approaching an eighty per cent success rate. However, reconnecting severed nerves is extremely difficult. And for a brain transplant, every nerve in the spinal cord would first have to be severed. Before you did that, you would need a micron-level scanner sophisticated enough to identify and tag the individual nerve pathways. It would first be used on the spinal cord of the person whose brain was to be transplanted, then on the victim, in order to know how to match them up.'

'Yeah,' Yuri closed his eyes, trying to visualize the problem. 'I get that. You'd need to join the right pathways up, otherwise you'd think you were moving a leg when you're actually bending your arm.'

'A crude analogy, but essentially correct,' Hai-3 said. 'However, it is not just the nerves that control muscle movement that would be required. You would also have to successfully reconnect the body's entire sensorium, or you would be completely numb and unable to control the muscles which you did command to move. Apparently our human partners have taken to calling it zombie syndrome.'

'Sounds about right,' Yuri conceded.

'I am not aware of any scanner that sophisticated being built,' Hai-3 said. 'Furthermore, as well as this hypothetical scanner, you would require a nanosurgical device to physically connect the severed nerves to both ends of the Kcell bridge. We have been examining this procedure with our human corporate partners.'

'You've experimented on humans?' Yuri did his best to ignore Stéphane's sigh of exasperation.

'Certainly not,' Hai-3 said. 'We have formed development and sales partnerships with several human biogenetic companies; they provide us with their requirements, and we try to profile our Kcells accordingly. There have been attempts to use a Kcell nerve fibre to bridge a missing nerve section in pigs. Some were successful. Some not. Progress is slow, but is being made. I would caution you, the largest number of nerves in a bundle that were reconnected by company research teams was eleven. There are several million nerves at the top of the human spinal cord, so the problem is orders of magnitude more complex than anything currently achieved. If a scanner and surgical device could be built, the procedure would have to be controlled by a G7Turing. Given the number of nerves involved, the subject would probably have to be placed in a coma, and the operation would be conducted over a period of months. I am not certain how much human money would be involved in funding such an enterprise.'

'Right,' Yuri said. 'So basically, what you're telling me is that brain transplants don't exist?'

'Currently, yes, although it may become possible in the future.

Another factor in this equation is the Kcell nerves themselves. As I told you, several million individual fibres would be required for such an operation. In the last seven years, we have provided our research partners with a total of two and a half thousand.'

Yuri felt strangely disappointed by Hai-3's reassurance. At the same time, it did make him wonder exactly what had happened to Horatio. 'That's good to know, thank you.'

'That such a criminal concept has taken root in human culture is most distressing to us,' Hai-3 said. 'This is not why we made our biotechnology available to you. We only wanted to help you before we fly onwards to the God at the End of Time. Death is not something biological entities should suffer any more. I hope you can explain that to people in your media companies who have influence – perhaps upon the successful conclusion of your case?'

'Of course. I'm sorry about the way people have twisted the possibilities of Kcell application. Unfortunately, there are those among us, thankfully a small minority, who live by a different set of rules, which makes such unpleasant stories believable.'

'The Olyix understand. You are new to sentience. Your behaviour is still affected by your animal origin. You seek to advance yourselves at the expense of others.'

'As I said: a minority.'

'We were like you once. Our biotechnology allowed us to modify ourselves, to cast aside such animal-derived impulses. We gave ourselves a higher purpose.'

Yuri maintained a polite expression. He knew what was coming, and out of the corner of his eye he caught Stéphane grin knowingly. The Olyix were unremittingly evangelical. Hai-3's cooperation came with a price – he had to endure the sermon. 'Sadly for now,' he said, 'we are stuck with our more humble bodies and all their flaws.'

'Indeed,' Hai-3 said. 'But consider that if you joined with us, crimes like the one you face today would be a thing of the past.'

'What you ask is interesting, but as a species I don't think we're ready for a voyage to the end of the time. We're not mature enough to face a deity – yours or anyone else's.'

'You can be. That is what we hope to offer you before our ark-ship flies onwards once more. We continue to learn how to adapt our Kcells to function in your bodies. Our growthmasters believe we can one day model clusters to duplicate your neural structure. When that happens, you can become immortal like us.'

'The singularity download. Yes. I think our society has a long way to go before we accept that. If the body is not original, we would not be us.'

'The body, any body – ours, yours – is merely a vessel for the mind. The mind is evolution's pinnacle. Sentience is extraordinarily rare in this universe. It must be cherished and protected at all costs.'

'Good to know we agree on that.'

'Would you consider coming with us, Yuri Alster?'

'I don't know. Anything is possible, I suppose,' he replied diplomatically.

'I will pray for you, Yuri Alster,' Hai-3 said. 'And I urge you to consider what we can offer. Sentient species are the children of this universe, the reason it exists. It is our destiny to travel to the conclusion and join together in bliss and fulfilment with the final God.'

'I see.' He almost said it, almost asked: *what about steady state theory?* Human cosmologists were now almost convinced that the universe was eternal – that the idea of a trillion-year cyclic state, of Big Bang origins and Big Crunch collapses, was no longer valid. *So why do the Olyix think it's going to end?* But he had a job to do. 'You have given me a lot to consider. For that I thank you.'

Another ripple wound its way round Hai-3's midsection. 'You are most welcome. And I consider it an act of friendship on my part to extend our help to you with this unpleasant case you are working on. To devote yourself to the recovery of others less fortunate is an honourable calling.'

Yuri hoped the Olyix couldn't pick up on the flash of guilt he felt. 'I do what I can.' *And what Ainsley Zangari wants.*

'Your dedication is to be commended. I will pray for your success in recovering the unfortunate man who has been abducted.'

Yuri gave the alien a level stare. 'You are most kind. Your help eliminating one line of inquiry has been very beneficial for me.

Thank you.' He steeled himself and shook hands with Hai-3 again. This time he didn't flinch; anger allowed him to keep a tight rein on his reactions.

*

'Baptiste Devroy was not in his flat,' Boris informed Yuri as soon as he was back out on Geneva's streets.

'Shit. Where is he?'

'He deactivated his altme and left the flat at ten fifty-seven this morning. Civic surveillance shows him getting into a cabez, which was requested by Dawn Mongomerie, his current girlfriend. The tactical team are backtracking it.'

'Ten fifty-seven,' Yuri mused. 'Interesting coincidence, that's about when we started looking for Horatio. Where was I then?'

'At Horatio's flat on Eleanor Road.'

'Fuck it, they were watching to see if anyone noticed he'd gone! And then Jessika and I turned up, Connexion Security officers. They must have started shitting themselves.' He called Jessika. 'I hope you've made progress. They know we're coming.'

'How the hell do they know that?' she demanded.

'Best guess, they were watching Horatio's flat. Baptiste Devroy is running; the tactical team is on his arse, but there's no guarantee when they'll catch up with him.'

'Well, you're in luck. I've got a promising lead here.'

'Good. I'll be with you in ten minutes.' He called Poi Li as he entered the Connexion hub.

'What's happening?' she asked. 'I see the tactical team missed Baptiste Devroy.'

'Whoever snatched Horatio knows we're searching for him, which is bad. I'm concerned they'll cut and run.'

'Then you have to find him fast.'

'No shit!'

'Is he on Althaea?'

'I really hope so, because that's my only lead left.'

'All right, do whatever you have to.'

259

'There's a tactical team already there, supporting Jessika. It may get noisy.'

'Althaea's barely been awarded its settlement certificate. It's a world without value. Nobody cares what happens there.'

'You'll cover for me?'

'With our history, I'm insulted you asked.'

Yuri grinned. 'One more thing.'

'What are you, a Columbo wannabe?'

'A what?'

'Old fictional detective. Ask your friend Karno Larsen.'

'Whatever. I need to run something by you, and tell me if I'm being paranoid.'

'Now you're talking.'

'You're a major criminal gang, or one of Ainsley's rivals.'

'Connexion doesn't have rivals.'

'Envious small-timers. You know: the Brazilian SolarWell consortium. Someone who has the resources and patience to run a long con. Humour me, here, please.'

'Have I ever not?'

'Then this is how you operate. You find out Gwendoline is Ainsley's granddaughter and do your research. You create a flawless legend: Horatio and his whole family. Hell, maybe a dozen Horatios, to bump your chances. Then you drop him into place – a place where you know Gwendoline will meet him. And of course she falls for him big time, because they've matched him perfectly. He spends the next two years romancing her, and they marry. He tells her how she maybe should take a job with Connexion after all. She does, and works her way up the family ladder, which is a much shorter route to the executive level than anyone without Zangari blood. Zam-bam-thank-you-ma'am. It's taken fifteen years, but you now have access to the highest level of Connexion – finance, strategy – and the power to influence same. That's got to be a worthwhile investment for people like that.'

'All right, I'm playing. So why pull him away?'

He flinched. 'I'm not sure yet.'

'Because he's a tart with a heart, and really *really* fell for her?'

Yuri hadn't known that venomous level of sarcasm could carry across a solnet link. 'No. I've come across something seriously wrong about this; I need to tell you about it in person.'

'Yuri, a G7Turing would have trouble hacking this encryption.'

'So colour me paranoid.'

There was only a short pause, but with Poi Li that was significant. 'Okay.'

'And in the meantime, run a full check on Horatio. Not just a G7Turing data mine; if he was put into place, his controllers will know we'd do that at some point. Go deeper. Maybe send someone you trust to physically interview his parents, get DNA samples and check them against residuals in his flat, talk to his schoolfriends, his teachers, see if they have any memories of him as a boy. If he was planted, his controllers won't be able to cover everything. I want to know if he's real, Poi.'

'All right, Yuri. Leave it with me.'

'Thank you. I'm stepping into the Althaea hub now. I'll call you as soon as I have something.'

*

The frontier town of Bronkal only warranted twenty-five Connexion hubs and a single commercial transport hub. It was a small town on the edge of the Estroth Plains, a flatland plateau that extended for nearly two thousand kilometres before dropping sharply into the sea. It was that unbroken level ground which swung the decision to terraform in Althaea's favour.

Pollux, as a K0 orange giant star, wasn't the obvious choice for a human world. But it did have a gas supergiant planet, Thestias, which in turn had forty-eight moons. Four of the larger ones, Althaea, Pleuron, Iphicles and Leda, were caught in a rosette orbit in the Lagrange Two point, forever drifting round each other in Thestias's umbra. In most cases, being caged within a supergiant planet's shade would be a gloomy existence, but not when Thestias orbited a mere one point six AUs out from an orange giant. The reduced sunlight striking Althaea's surface was as intense as midday on Earth's tropics. Conjunctions with its L2 co-moons provided a regular variable day–night cycle as it passed between their shadows.

It was midday between Pleuron-conjunction and Leda-conjunction (eighteen hours of light) when Yuri stepped out of the hub on Esola Street in the middle of town. He exhaled sharply. Compared to this humidity, London had been practically Arctic. The monotonous carbon and glass buildings stretched out along the street with geometrical precision. Palm trees provided some shade along the cracked concrete pavements, but not much; they were swaying about from the surprisingly strong gusts of wind sweeping along the street. Few people were walking in the swelter-ing daylight, and even fewer cycled; the road itself was mainly occupied with single-occupant cabez and larger taxez humming along the shimmering asphalt, along with commercial vehicles rumbling between them. It was like a scene from the mid-twenty-first century, Yuri thought.

Boris connected to the local net, and twenty seconds later a three-wheel cabez pulled up in the broad strip of empty concrete to one side of the hub. Yuri climbed in and sat down on the narrow seat, thankful for the air-con vents blasting cool air into the tiny transparent bubble. He always agreed with the saying that you wore a cabez rather than rode one.

It drove forwards, taking him quickly through the town's depressing grid of near-identical buildings, their panel walls mass-fabricated in an industrial estate on the outskirts. There was nothing else to see on the ground, no vista of the vast marshlands stretching out beyond the town's docks. That didn't bother him; on Althaea, the view was all about the sky.

Pleuron's orbit had already dropped it below Althaea's horizon, while Leda was now rising to the zenith – an airless cratered world with its vast silver-grey mares laced with glowing lava-streams. Massive tectonic activity was constantly rearranging its geography, rendering mapping an irrelevance. And beyond that, dominating the apex of the bright azure sky, was the awesome globe of Thestias itself: a circle of darkness crowned by a blazing halo of golden light created by its perpetual eclipse of Pollux. The glowing edges illuminated fast-moving white and carmine clouds, their swirling kinesis producing the bizarre optical illusion that they were somehow spilling over the edge of a hole in space to flow down into its black heart. An optical illusion that made it seem as if Althaea was also falling towards the gas supergiant's eternal nightside. Locals called it the Eye of God.

Yuri shivered, shaking off the giddiness the sight conjured up. The cabez took him to a commercial block on Nightingale Avenue. He walked into the reception, and Boris directed him along one wing to the office suite Jessika had rented forty minutes earlier. The rooms backed onto a small warehouse where the tactical team had parked their farm truck. The team's captain, Lucius Soćko, had brought a thirty-centimetre portal inside a briefcase, which they'd threaded up in the warehouse. The rest of his team was coming through the two-metre portal door, along with equipment and specialist mission support operators.

Lucius was in the main office, standing behind Jessika, who had taken her pink jacket off to sit at a desk with several new electronic modules. Yuri hadn't encountered the captain before, but the file Boris was spraying across his tarsus lens spoke of good work. You didn't get to his level in Connexion Security without being competent. One thing the file hadn't prepared him for was seeing Lucius's arm around Jessika's shoulders.

'What have you got for me?' Yuri asked.

Jessica looked round smiling as Lucius quickly stood up straight. 'I still haven't managed to trace the Tarazzi van in the docks,' Jessika said. 'However, we have no record of it driving away again through the commercial transport hub after it delivered Horatio. It's probably still there.'

'They will have re-registered it,' Yuri said bluntly. 'Probably within ten minutes of it arriving.'

'There have only been seven similar vans departing Bronkal since then,' she countered. 'All of them legitimate.'

'These guys are professional,' Yuri said uncertainly.

'I think we have two options,' Lucius said. 'One: the gang has enough money to scrap the van straight away – break it up, take it to a vapour recycler plant, drive it out of town and dump it in the swamps, whatever. In which case we've lost it permanently.'

'Or?' Yuri queried.

'They're not going to be snatching people every day. The van will be parked up in a shed somewhere, waiting until they get another job. Then it'll be re-registered and given a bodywork make-over.'

'Good call,' Yuri said.

'The dock area's a whole industrial district supporting the bio-reactor site, as well as the barge maintenance companies,' Jessika said. 'Plenty of big buildings. I want to send in a microdrone flock, scan the whole place for the van. Lucius has already brought them through the portal.'

Yuri nodded. 'Do it.'

'Who are these people?' Lucius asked. 'Any idea?'

'I don't know,' Yuri told them. 'I originally thought it might be a dark market brain transplant, but I've been disabused of that notion. Which leaves us with an old-fashioned kidnap and ransom.'

'That's bullshit,' Jessika said. 'Ainsley isn't going to pay squat for the poor kid.'

Yuri shrugged. 'Whoever Devroy works for, they're professional.'

'Are you sure he's working for someone?'

'No, but that's irrelevant at this point. We have to find Horatio, and fast.'

'I'll launch the drones,' Lucius said. 'My people are ready to go.'

'Do that,' Yuri said. 'But I have one other lead. The G7Turing found that Baptiste Devroy has a cousin right here, in Bronkal. Joaquin Beron – he runs some kind of atmospheric sensor company, a one-man shop, has supply and maintenance contracts with the government climate-monitoring board.'

'That can't be a coincidence,' Jessika said with a knowing grin.

'I wouldn't like to work out the odds.'

'You got an address?'

'Yes. Fedress Meadows, block seventeen.'

She paused, reading the information Boris had sent her. 'An

industrial park. Plenty of opportunity to fabricate items and re-route shipping consignments.'

'You have a suspicious mind. I approve.'

*

Ideally, they would have infiltrated slowly, sent some drones to Fedress Meadows. The drones would be followed by tactical team members arriving at neighbouring commercial modules. Then Lucius would have led a three-man detainment group in. Joaquin would have been contained and taken back to the Nightingale Avenue office. If he'd proved reluctant to cooperate immediately, the portal back to Security's more secluded facilities was the first option.

Yuri didn't have time for that. Every minute was putting Horatio deeper into danger.

Boris confirmed that Joaquin Beron's altme was connected to block seventeen's solnet node, and Yuri took the decision to go in hard and fast. The department's G7Turing shut down Fedress Meadows' network. A flock of twenty-five microdrones deployed from Nightingale Avenue, their sensors probing the area in advance of Yuri's arrival. Five big grey 4x4 utility vehicles drove in convoy to Fedress Meadows, which turned out to be a bleak collection of multi-role cubes able to accommodate a variety of small and medium businesses. Yuri stared at the square grey and black walls, inset with silvered glass, the skimped landscaping around them. The industrial park could have been on any of the non-Utopial terraformed worlds, or even the poorer areas of Earth itself. The age of cheap and easy fabrication seemed to have taken away any chance for architectural individuality. Places like Fedress weren't somewhere entrepreneurs went to begin their mega-corporate dream. They were the Darwinist incentive that bestowed deter-mined people with the will to improve their enterprise and get the hell out.

Yuri asked Boris for a secure link to Poi Li as they drove manu-ally along the roads at high speed, causing automated vehicles to break and swerve sharply. 'How's the review of Horatio going?'

'So far he's so perfect and sweet he's like a puppy in human form – I might vomit,' she replied. 'I've got some people en route to his parents. I hope they'll crack any legend, because I can't believe anyone this noble still exists.'

'Ever considered we might be getting too old and cynical for this job?'

'Speak for yourself. However, I am growing concerned that I don't understand the motive here.'

'Money,' Yuri said immediately. 'It's always money in the end. I'm thinking it's a kidnapping; there's nothing else left it could be. Someone found out who Gwendoline is.'

'We haven't had a ransom demand.'

'There won't be one. Not now they know I'm on to them. I'm just praying they haven't already tossed Horatio into the swamp.'

'Damn, that would devastate Gwendoline. Ainsley won't like it.'

'Then Ainsley should keep it in his trousers.'

'I'll pass that on.'

Yuri couldn't help the small grin that played over his lips. 'Look, I've got two possible ways of finding the kid. I'll work them to the end, you know that.'

'I do. Ever considered you missed your vocation? I can recommend to Ainsley you take charge of instructing freshmeat at our training centre.'

'My reply contains some phrase about chewing my leg off.'

'How long until you talk to Joaquin Beron?'

'Couple of minutes.'

'Loop me in, please.'

'You got it.'

The vehicles encircled block seventeen, driving over the surrounding gardens, tyres tearing up the lush grass. Seventeen was one of the smaller blocks, the dark external panelling fading to mud-brown in the relentless assault by Althaea's raw climate.

Lucius led five paramilitaries through the front door, while Yuri and Jessika waited in the vehicle. More paramilitaries deployed around the block. Yuri could see people in the neighbouring blocks pressed up against the glass, watching in amazement. The light outside was dimming as thick black clouds rolled in; big drops of rain began to splatter against the windscreen.

'We got him,' Lucius announced. 'The location is secure.'

Jessika pulled her pink jacket over her head as they scurried from the vehicle to the entrance. The rain was becoming a monsoon deluge, hitting Yuri from every direction as the wind whipped it round, plastering his hair against his scalp.

'So you and Lucius?' he said. 'I didn't know. How long's that been going on?'

Raindrops slithered down the puzzled expression on her face. 'What?'

'He seems like a good guy.'

'Wow, my opinion of your detective superpower just took a massive dive.'

'I know what I saw . . .'

'No you don't.'

'You need to inform HR.'

'*What?*'

'I knew a guy, back in the day; basically a good guy, but a dick with it. He and one of my operatives hooked up. They didn't follow company procedure. It didn't end well.'

'Good pep talk there, boss, thanks.'

'Just saying.'

She shook her head in bemused dismay as they slipped into the block.

'Give Poi Li a visual,' Yuri told Boris. The altme would relay the feed from his tarsus lens.

Joaquin Beron was a small man, a good head shorter than Yuri. His dark hair was styled in braids tight against his skull to try and negate a receding hairline. Tattoos glowed softly on his neck, snaking down below the collar of his green overalls. Yuri got Boris to run a scan on the patterns, but they weren't listed as any gang-type.

Joaquin Beron was in the workshop at the rear of the building, sitting on a chair. The tactical team had followed Yuri's directions perfectly. His ankles had been zip-locked to the chair legs, hands fastened behind his back. Two of the paramilitaries stood on either side, large carbines held ready – not threateningly, but with easy confidence.

Jessika was shaking the water from her jacket as they walked across the concrete floor, surrounded by big fabricator units that were humming away efficiently

'Seems like a legitimate set-up,' Lucius said. 'I can pull some specialists in to go through his network if you want?'

'No need,' Yuri said.

'You guys,' Joaquin challenged, his voice high with bravado. 'You are in shit so deep! I got rights, you know. My lawyer's going to bust your balls for this!'

Yuri smiled down at him. 'For what?'

'You even got a warrant?'

'Why would I have a warrant? I don't work for a government.'

'Huh? Then who the fuck are you?'

'My name is Yuri, and I'm conducting a small experiment.'

Joaquin turned a troubled gaze at the statue-like paramilitaries. 'What fucking experiment?'

'To see how smart you are, Joaquin.'

'What the hell is this?'

'I'm going to talk now. I want you to listen. Understand?'

'Go fuck your whore mother up the ass, you piece of corporate shit!'

Yuri pointed to the paramilitary on Joaquin's left. 'Do you have a knife?'

'Yes, sir.'

'Take it out and stab Joaquin here, just above his knee. Don't puncture a major blood vessel. I don't want him bleeding out before he's told us what we want to know.'

'What the actual *fuck*?'

'Yes, sir.' The paramilitary drew a Bowie knife from his belt scabbard.

'Don't you fucking dare!'

'Why, what's going to stop him?' Yuri asked pleasantly.

'No way. Don't. Okay, I'm listening, all right? I'll listen to you. Just don't—'

Yuri held up a finger to the paramilitary. 'That's good, Joaquin. Now it's important that you realize I'm prepared to cripple you just to get you to shut up before we even start the real session. So I'm thinking, if you annoy me, I'm going to start walking round to see what kind of power tools I can pick up. You'll have plenty I'm sure; you'll need them for your business. Big ones, small ones, very sharp ones, badly blunt ones . . . Am I right? Now try and imagine how I can use them. And on what bits of you.'

Joaquin pushed himself back into the chair, panic making his breathing heavy.

'Now where were we? Oh yes, I was going to say something. Think of this as your starter question for ten points – or in your case, you-get-to-keep-the-toes-on-your-left-foot points. Baptiste Devroy. Who is he?'

'I can speak now?'

'You may speak now. But let's keep it short and focused, shall we?'

'He's my cousin. I don't ever see him, honestly.'

'But you're in contact, aren't you?'

'Some. Maybe a little. Yeah.'

'Not any more you won't be. As of an hour ago, cousin Baptiste will never be talking to you ever again – nor anyone else.'

'Christ, what did you do?'

'I did nothing. Our London division dealt with him.'

'London division . . . Who are you people?'

'People who only a terminally stupid arsehole would piss off.'

'Shit on a stick!'

'You're talking too much, Joaquin.'

'Sorry. I'm sorry.'

'Of course you are. Now you have to decide how far you're going to go to protect your cousin and his friends against how much of yourself you are prepared to lose. Got that?'

'Yes.'

'So. Cousin Baptiste, he sent someone here yesterday, didn't he?'

Joaquin nodded urgently.

'Okay, good boy. So: two questions left. One: why?'

'I don't know, please, I swear on my own fucking mother, I don't know where they go.'

Yuri stiffened. 'They?'

'Yeah. Baptiste, he does this, like, every couple of months. People he's taken get driven here to Bronkal; then they shoot them full of heavy-duty chemicals which put them in this really deep sleep, like a coma. After that they get shipped out again.'

'Why?' Even knowing every second was critical now, Yuri couldn't help the question. 'What for? What are they doing to them?'

'I don't know what the fuck happens to them, man! I'm not crazy stupid enough to ask. I figure it's got to be some weird rich dude who's off-the-scale perverted. I mean, what kind of normal person wants a bunch of unconscious people?'

'That's a very good question, Joaquin.'

'I don't know. Really! Please, I don't. All I do is take care of the vehicles. I arrange new registrations for the vans. That's it!'

'I'll accept that for now. Second question. Baptiste snatched a friend of mine yesterday, a decent boy called Horatio Seymore.'

Joaquin started rocking from side to side. 'No no no. They'll kill me. Please!'

'We know Horatio arrived here in Bronkal –' Yuri clicked his fingers and turned to Jessika. 'When?'

'The van came through the commercial transport hub thirty-one hours ago,' she supplied.

'Thank you. Thirty-one hours ago. The van then drove to the docks. Where in the docks?'

'Please,' Joaquin whimpered.

'Ah, you were making such good progress, too.' Yuri held out his hand, and the paramilitary gave him the Bowie knife.

'Shit. All right. Christ!' Joaquin eyed the blade frantically. 'It's the bioreactor complex.' His shoulders slumped in defeat. 'Okay? That's it. Please, just let me go.'

Yuri slammed the knife down. Joaquin screamed. He looked

down in terror to see the blade sticking into the chair, a centimetre from his crotch.

'Oops, missed,' Yuri said. 'Let me have another go, see if my aim improves, because that reactor complex is huge, and you fucking know that.'

'Building Seven! They've got them in Building Seven!'

*

The docks were the reason Bronkal existed. They sat on the edge of Althaea's lungs – the expansive sprawl of the plateau which was now a marshland that extended all the way to the cliffs. It was riddled with canals that had a flotilla of dredgers keeping them open, allowing the barges access to the entire area. Every day they would dock at the bioreactor next to the moor and load up with freshly grown algaox. Then they'd chug off down the canals, their powerful pumps squirting out long arcs of blue-green sludge to coat the saturated land. For thirty-eight years the genetically engineered algae had been photosynthesizing the oxygen which made Althaea's atmosphere breathable for humans. And the barges were scheduled to keep going for another fifteen years at least, until the Sol Senate's climate-monitoring board awarded Althaea its final clearance certificate.

A good seventy per cent of Bronkal's working population was employed by the reactor complex or the docks, which is why eight of the town's twenty-five hubs were sited in the district. Yuri ordered them to be closed down, along with the commercial transport hub, which was also adjacent to the docks.

As soon as Joaquin had given them the location, Lucius and the paramilitaries got back into their vehicles and drove through the deluge of warm rain to the docks. Yuri had to grip the sides of his seat, the vehicles slid and skidded so much on the wet asphalt. He simply wasn't used to ground transport, and the motion was making him feel queasy.

'The rain is hindering our drones,' Lucius complained. 'Especially the microdrone flocks.'

'But on the bright side, it's covering our approach, too,' Jessika said.

'We need to be certain,' Lucius said. 'If Joaquin gave us the wrong information—'

'He didn't,' Yuri said, recalling the way Joaquin was pleading to be believed at the end.

'Okay,' the tactical squad captain agreed. 'We'll go with it.'

Jessika peered out through the windscreen as the wipers flashed back and forth. 'Must be getting closer,' she said. 'I can see the hangars.'

Yuri looked out over the inundated road. Squatting on the horizon were four massive airship hangars. As well as maintaining the algaox barges, Bronkal's docks supported the airships which circled for months at a time over the ocean beyond the plateau's cliffs. They all had ten-metre portal doors fixed underneath their hulls, which were twinned to portals carried by ice harvesters pushing inexorably across the frozen ocean of Reynolds. At forty-three AU's out, Reynolds was the most distant planet orbiting Pollux – a planet with a Mercury-sized rock core coated in a hundred-kilometre mantle of ice. All of Althaea's water had come from there, arriving in colossal streams of ice shards that poured out of the airships to splash down and melt into the new seas. He stared at the big grey buildings in bemusement, remembering the first time Connexion had trialled icefalls in the Australian outback – now a lush savannah.

'Wonder what Akkar would make of this,' he murmured.

'What?' Jessika asked.

'Nothing.' They were speeding through the outside rank of dock buildings now. Yuri checked the map Boris was spraying over his tarsus lens. The bioreactor complex and the airship hangars were positioned at opposite ends of the docks. A small purple star was shining in one of the reactor complex buildings – number seven, an old three-level warehouse and office block which was registered to an independent maintenance company. Drones were orbiting it, keeping a safe half-kilometre distance. Through the heavy rain, their visual image was very low resolution. Normally they would release a flock of microdrones – biomechanical flies that would swarm through the target area, sending back detailed information via secure comlaser. But Lucius hadn't launched them; this rain would knock them out of the air.

'They'll know something's wrong,' Jessika said. 'Our Turing's taken solnet offline across the complex.'

'She's right,' Lucius said. 'We can't do a stealth insertion. This is entry by the front door, all alarms screaming.'

'Very likely,' Yuri said grimly. 'I'll need some body armour.'

Lucius handed a bag over without comment. It contained a bulky jacket and thick over-trousers along with a lightweight helmet. 'You as well,' Lucius said, holding another bag out to Jessika.

'I'm not going in there,' she said indignantly.

'Of course not; you don't have any combat training for one. But if we do wind up in a firefight, I'd like you to have some protection. We don't know what sort of weapons Baptiste's people are carrying.'

Jessika glanced suspiciously at Yuri, who was doing his best not to smirk. The bodywork of the vehicle they were riding in was practically nothing but kinetic armour.

'Thank you, Lucius,' she said dispassionately. 'That's very considerate.'

The tactical squad deployed in the same fashion as they had at Fedress Meadows, their vehicles encircling the building and coming to a halt. This time, when the paramilitaries climbed out, they were accompanied by a group of combat-support drones; thick dark discs with squat muzzles protruding from their rim, flying nimbly above the squad.

Yuri followed Lucius outside. Warm rain hit him full on, immediately soaking round the edge of his armour jacket. A thick unbroken layer of black cloud had closed off the sky, obscuring Thestias and its halo of golden sunlight.

'I guess God isn't going to be watching over us,' Yuri muttered. He pulled down the enhanced-vision visor. The squad's tactical grid sprayed across it, highlighting the locations of individual team members in green. The interior of the building was laid out for him, with the ground floor divided into three large spaces, and the upper two floors split into a maze of rooms.

'Are you in the network?' he asked Boris as they walked behind eight paramilitaries who closed on the front door.

'The G7Turing has acquired limited access.' A smattering of purple stars appeared, most of them on the first floor. 'These are the heavy processing cores.' Yellow circles materialized. 'And these are the main power drains.'

'Three overlaps,' Yuri said. 'Okay, Lucius, those three are our primary targets. Take them first, lock them down. You are authorized to use appropriate force.'

'You heard the man,' Lucius said. He snapped out orders to individual four-man squads and assigned each a target.

The combat drones shot forwards. A camera on one showed Yuri somebody racing away from the entrance lobby, sprinting deeper into the building.

'Take the doors out,' Lucius ordered.

A drone fired its scattergun at the glass doors, sending crystalline splinters slamming into the lobby. Twelve drones swooped in, followed by the paramilitaries.

'Yuri,' Poi Li said quietly. 'Stay safe.'

'Working on that.'

Yuri had decided on checking the biggest power drain point first. Whatever creepy procedure Baptiste was performing on his snatched victims, it would need power. He pulled out his semi-automatic pistol and headed up the stairs behind Lucius. His visor was showing him an array of images as the rest of the team smashed their way into the building. Drones zoomed along corridors, scanning for gang members.

He'd almost reached the first-floor landing when the shooting started. Gang members armed with machine pistols came crashing out of rooms, raking the corridors with full-magazine discharges, then snapping in reloads to carry on the carnage. Whatever weapons they'd fabricated had an astonishing fire-rate, shredding walls, floors and ceilings in chaotic shrapnel clouds. Drones returned fire, sending out a barrage of thunderburst grenades. They exploded in incandescent blooms, the blastwaves shattering windows and tearing doors off their hinges. The drones advanced, electromagnetic rifles slamming supervelocity rounds towards any hostile their sensors detected. Gang members reeled back, diving for cover. Paramilitaries crept after them, directing the drones' fire, sometimes opening fire themselves.

Yuri hit the ground as soon as the shooting started. Just in time. Half the wall behind him disintegrated into a swirling cloud of fragments and dust as a gang member strafed it. Yuri's two escort drones zipped forwards, blasting away in retaliation.

'Holy shit,' he screeched. His head came up. Lucius was on the ground in front of him, also scanning round urgently.

'Looks like they saw us coming,' Lucius shouted.

'No fucking kidding!'

The first clash ended as gang members either died or retreated deeper into the building. Yuri scrambled up and hurried down the smouldering wreckage of the main corridor. 'How many gang members are there?'

'Four fatalities,' Boris said. 'Estimated seven hostiles remain active on this level.'

Yuri reached the room that was drawing all the power. Its door was gone, wrenched off to leave a slim jagged rim still attached to the hinges. Four drones sailed through the hole ahead of him. Someone opened fire on them. The response was swift. He heard the definitive sound of supervelocity rounds punching through furniture. A man started screaming – a long terrified wail of pain.

'Hold fire and isolate the hostile,' he ordered the drones. The visor graphics showed them surging deeper into the room. One of the paramilitaries went in just ahead of him. 'Careful, sir, there's a floor breach.'

'Got it,' Yuri said. It took him a moment to make sense of the chaos laid out before him. So much of the room had been damaged by grenades and bullets. There were five hospital-style gurnez lined up along one side, most of them lying on their side. Medical equipment towers were shredded, pulsing out fluids from their torn casings. Two of the gurnez had unconscious bodies lying on them, which made Yuri's heart lurch in panic until he realized they were both female. One had taken a bullet to the thigh and was bleeding profusely.

'Shit!' He stared round, searching for a first-aid kit. Couldn't see one.

Another firefight erupted somewhere down the other end of the building. He flinched, ducking down as bullets came slamming through the thin composite walls. 'Jessika?'

'Hell, boss, are you okay?'

'Yeah. I need a combat medic case. Fast!'

'Are you hit?'

'Not me. Found our first victims.'

'On my way.'

'No. Stay in the vehicle. I'm sending someone to collect.' He turned to the paramilitary who'd accompanied him. 'Go!'

As the paramilitary left, Yuri snatched up a sheet from one of the fallen gurnez and jammed it against the woman's bullet wound, tying it on hard with a length of tube from the wrecked medical tower. Then he went over to where a pair of drones were hovering over the wounded gang member. Two laser target dots illuminated his forehead. The man had taken three hits, two in the arm, one in the chest. He was already ashen, gulping down breath. Blood was pooling on the floor. 'Help,' he beseeched.

'Sure thing,' Yuri knelt down and pushed his visor up. 'One of my people is bringing a medic kit. You'll be fine.'

'Yeah?'

'Sure. I've seen worse.'

'Man, it hurts!'

'I need to know, where are the other people that were brought here?'

'Please. I'm sorry. I just drive the vans, you know?'

'Sure.' Yuri held up the card with Horatio's picture. 'Did you see this kid? Is he still here?'

The man had trouble focusing. 'Jeez, it hurts bad. Deep, you know, deep inside. Is that the bullet?'

'Keep it together. The paramedics are almost here. Before they give you a shot for the pain, tell me: the kid?'

Yuri heard more gunfire hammering in the big warehouse directly underneath. Then a series of grenades went off. The whole room shuddered for several seconds.

'Did you see him?' Yuri persisted.

'Yes. He was here. Overnight.'

'Where is he now?'

'They took him downstairs.'

'Downstairs where?'

'Ready—'

'Ready for what?'

The man's limbs started to shake.

'Ready for what?' Yuri shouted.

'Go.' He held an arm up, fingers grasping for Yuri, as if that contact would somehow help. 'Ready to go.'

Yuri stood up, ignoring the clawing hand. 'Our prime target may still be in the building. Ground floor. Proceed with extreme caution.' He snapped the visor down again and studied the tactical display before striding out of the room and hurrying down the stairs. One of his drones flew point, the other took up position behind.

There was a doorway behind the lobby's reception desk. The door itself had been torn off, revealing a black gulf. The point drone flew through first. Yuri followed it into a long windowless locker room with smashed light panels on the ceiling. His visor enhancements kicked in, converting the darkness into a clinical blue and white monochrome image. The drone navigated its way past buckled lockers that leant against each other like a domino knock-down row that hadn't quite worked. It slipped through another open doorway into the first of the ground-floor warehouses. Yuri came out into a huge space, broken up by floor-to-ceiling cargo racks that were mostly vacant. Grenade blasts had pummelled hundreds of empty plastic crates out of their stacks, scattering them across the floor. Ancient heavy-lift trollez were parked round the five loading-bay doors, the warehouse's vast interior making them look like abandoned toys. Two of the tactical team's drones had been brought down, their blackened armour fuselage casings badly crumpled. Yuri didn't like to think what weapon had done that. There were gunshots coming from the far end of the warehouse, obscured from Yuri's view as he crouched down and ran for cover behind a solid-looking workbench.

One of his drones slid along behind a rack, its sensors scanning round. He saw three gurnez behind a cargo rack down in the second loading bay. Two of them had toppled over, and one was upside down. All three had bodies strapped on. The drone's camera zoomed in. The upside-down gurnez had a big pool of blood spreading out from it.

'Holy fuck,' Yuri exclaimed. One of the other slumbering bodies was Horatio.

'Jessika, Lucius, I've found him!'

A huge explosion detonated on the second floor. The entire warehouse ceiling undulated like an agitated storm cloud and cracks began to appear, ripping along its length. Debris showered down. The gang members at the far end began shooting wildly.

'Shit,' Yuri shouted. 'Lay down suppression fire,' he ordered the drones. They fired a fast barrage of grenades.

Explosions filled the big space with incandescent light as Yuri powered forwards. Twice he fell as pressure waves slammed into him, sending him skidding along the filthy floor. Above him the drones opened up with their electromagnetic guns, firing clean through the metal racks.

'Lucius, some backup!' he yelled as he scrambled to his feet for the second time. A bullet caught his chest armour, spinning him and sending him crashing down again. The drones identified the source and sent more supervelocity rounds ripping down the warehouse.

Pain was a hot ball in Yuri's chest. Grimacing against it, he scrambled up into a crouch position and carried on towards Horatio's gurnez. His own semi-automatic was lost somewhere behind him. Flames were roaring up the wall at the far end, ignited by the hellish burn of the grenades. The drones hovered above him, constantly scanning for hostile activity.

'Lucius? We've got to get him out of here.'

'Lucius has dropped out of contact,' Boris said.

'What? Is he hit?'

'Unknown. His altme is no longer transmitting.'

Yuri flinched. Connexion tactical team members were equipped with multiple access links, both implanted and on their armour – a hard lesson the department had learned after it lost track of Savi Hepburn. Today, it was practically impossible to take one of their personnel offline. Yuri didn't want to imagine the level of violence which weapons would have to inflict on Lucius to make that happen – nothing survivable.

He tried to focus on the tactical display. Five of their paramilitaries' icons were amber and red now, showing they were injured, and pulling back. There was no sign of Lucius's icon. 'Fuck!'

He arrived at the gurnez and practically collapsed over it. Horatio's unconscious face was caked in dust, but it was definitely him. Yuri felt unreasonably angry at how peaceful the boy looked. He worked the buckle on the strap. Another firefight broke out somewhere in the building.

'How much fucking ammunition have these bastards got?' he bellowed furiously. 'Okay, everybody get out now! We have what we came for. And I could do with some help down here.'

A low tortuous rumble came from somewhere overhead. Yuri flinched, glancing up. The ruined ceiling was bulging down, the cracks multiplying. Rubble began spilling through the gaps, hurling thick grey dust clouds ahead of it. They churned in a mad tango with the black smoke gushing out of the inferno.

'Oh shit.' He started to wonder just how good the body armour truly was. The tiny piece of rationality left in his mind was hunting down escape routes. They were all a long way off.

The loading-bay door burst apart, and one of the tactical team's 4x4s came screeching through the rent. Wheels locked on full turn, and its back end swung round, tyres howling as they left a U of scorched skid marks on the concrete floor. The front door opened. Jessika was gripping the manual steering wheel with manic strength. 'You called for backup?'

A line of bullets stitched deep craters in the windscreen. The drones hurled grenades and supervelocity bullets in reprisal. Above everyone, the ceiling cracks multiplied like black lightning bolts.

Yuri snatched up Horatio's limp form and lunged into the 4x4. Jessika was already accelerating away before the door closed.

'Out out out!' he screamed. The tactical display showed him the paramilitaries moving fast.

Then they were outside, bucking across the wide parking lot, rain pounding the bodywork. A slender contrail streaked through the monsoon, moving so fast Yuri was still staring at it in bewilderment as it passed barely five metres above the 4x4.

The hellbuster missile slammed into the collapsing building and detonated, obliterating it in a sun-bright plasma cloud. The blast-wave punched the 4x4 with extreme force, sending it tumbling across the asphalt, every impact a hammer blow.

Yuri recovered consciousness amid a cluster of slowly deflating airbags that had completely filled the 4x4's interior. A lot of the flaccid white fabric in front of him was smeared with blood. The roof was below him, and the windows were all a mosaic of cracks, though amazingly they'd retained their integrity.

Horatio Seymore was sprawled on the roof beside him. Yuri watched for a few moments, checking the boy was still breathing. Then he heard Jessika groaning. When he looked round, she was hanging upside down in the front seat safety harness, blood dribbling out of her nose to run down her forehead.

'How are you doing?' he asked.

'Just peachy, thanks.' She dabbed at her nose, and winced. 'What *the fuck* just happened?'

'I have no idea.'

Juloss

Year 587 AA

Muncs didn't normally have names. It wasn't an infraction, but the clan's grown-ups had always discouraged it; the cohort should be uniform, they explained, no favourites. Language was also considered a communication impediment. Muncs should know their master's wishes without having to be designated and instructed; instinctive identification of any requirement or deployment was so much quicker. That also meant the boys had to learn how to communicate those commands at a subliminal level. The process was symbiotic.

Yirella had been five or six when she started mentally assigning her two muncs as Uno and Dos. They'd been studying old-Earth languages at the time, and she'd liked the softness of classical Spanish. By the time she was seven, Uno had become Uma, because even Yirella rather enjoyed the idea of having a goddess as a companion, while Dos had become Doony – for no reason whatsoever except it sounded kind of fun. When she reached eight the names had become an ingrained facet of their association, and even Alexandre had given up asking her not to use them.

Now as Yirella leant on the wall, staring through the big window into the treatment room, Uma and Doony had their arms wrapped round her legs in a loving hug. Her hands stroked their skulls, providing reassurance that she was all right and still cared for them despite leaving them behind for eleven days. When the rescue flyer had landed back at the Immerle estate, everyone's cohorts had come charging out of the dormitory to greet them. They ran into a wave of emotion – the relief and stress her year-mates were radiating in the wake of their ordeal. The poor muncs, expecting a happy reunion, had reacted badly, demanding affection, embracing their masters and mistresses in unbreakable hugs. It had taken a long time to calm things down. Uranti, the munc-tech, was called to deal with Dellian's semi-hysterical cohort, to allow the doctors to treat their injured master without having to constantly bat them away.

Yirella had watched the spray shot that was quickly administered to each of the creatures with interest. She was sure it wasn't a sedative, as they didn't become drowsy. Instead the drug seemed to banish their emotions. Then she realized Alexandre was studying her. For once in her life she didn't bow her head or look away; she returned hir gaze levelly.

'Did we pass?' she asked belligerently.

Surprisingly, Alexandre looked immensely sad and turned away. Yirella had followed the medical party as Dellian was carried into the treatment centre. Now that the casualty team had finished with him, he was lying on a wide clinic bed, his wounds covered with long strips of surgical-grade a-skin, with various tubes emerging from blue blisters stuck to his arms. His munc cohort was snuggled up around him, drawing warmth and comfort from the touch – a scene reminiscent of puppies nestling round their mother. After spending her time on the resort island successfully playing the unattainable ice queen, she rather envied them, and let out a sigh of regret.

Uma and Doony immediately tightened their hold on her legs, sensing her affection was being directed elsewhere. They only came up to her hips now, so they couldn't see through the window. She stroked them again, down the nape of the neck, the way they enjoyed most, and cooed reassurance at them, body posture reinforcing the feeling, *I'm fine, and I'm relieved for my friend too. Everything is going to be good.*

The chief doctor emerged from the treatment room and came over to her. 'You can go in now, if you'd like,' sie said. 'You'll need to be quick. The sedatives are already making him drowsy.'

'Thank you.' For a moment Yirella hesitated, then shook her head at her own reluctance. After everything they'd been through, having to find courage to face Dellian now seemed ridiculous.

She flicked a finger up, indicating that Uma and Doony should wait outside. They pouted and hung their heads, but didn't protest as she went in.

Dellian peered up at her and smiled in recognition amid his chemical-induced serenity. 'Hey, you.'

'Hey yourself. How are you?'

'Doing okay, I think.'

'Your poor arm.'

'S'okay.'

'I hope the a-skin brings your freckles back. I always liked them.'

'We're alone in a bedroom together . . .'

She twitched a smile. 'So we are. Savi and Callum, together again.'

'You kissed me.'

'What?'

'Back there, when we were stranded all alone on the tippity ippity top of the mountain. You kissed me.'

She took his hand and brushed the knuckles to her mouth. 'I did, didn't I?'

'Do I get another?'

'Maybe. If you're good and do as the doctors tell you.'

'How's that going?'

'The moroxes didn't cut you too deep.' She arched her eyebrow. 'How lucky was that? Unbelievable, in fact. I guessed right.'

'So am I boosting?'

'What?'

'This is my boost, right? I'm being implanted with all my super-wooper fighting gadgets?'

'Wow, what are they giving you? I could do with some myself. We don't start boosting until next week. That's to give us time to recover from our test.'

He let out a long sigh, his head sinking deeper into the pillow as his muscles relaxed. 'Are you testing me?'

'No. We never left, you know. Never got signed out of our training. The resort island, the fun we all had there, it was just the half-time break in another combat tactics game. That's all. It's never going to end, Dellian, not ever. Not for us.'

'All righty,' he mumbled as his eyes closed.

She gazed down fondly at the sleeping boy and kissed his forehead. 'Get well. I need you.'

*

Principal Jenner's office was at the top of the tallest building in the clan estate. Nothing as majestic as the skyscrapers in Afrata over the other side of the valley, but the view through the curving transparent walls was nonetheless impressive. The sight of the valley stretching away into hazy distance even roused Yirella from her mood as she stepped out of the portal door.

Alexandre was waiting for her and gave her a gentle embrace as soon as she entered. That was when she realized she was now a few centimetres taller than hir.

'How are you, my dear?' Alexandre asked, gesturing her to a couch.

'Absolutely fine,' Yirella replied stiffly. She gazed at Jenner, sitting behind hir desk. The principal was male cycling, dressed in a suit of some shiny ebony fabric with a slim white collar and scarlet piping, which made hir look more imposing than any head of a simple educational establishment should be.

'But then I was never in any real danger, was I?'

Jenner and Alexandre exchanged a glance.

'No,' Alexandre admitted with deep reluctance. 'If you'll indulge me: when did you work it out?'

'Why? So you can avoid making the same mistake with the next yeargroup?'

'That's not quite as detrimental as you seem to think,' Jenner said. 'We are all of us learning here. We simply wish to know if we should adapt our procedures and tell the girls in advance.'

'But not the boys?'

'No.'

'Why not?'

'They are the point troops. You know this. They have to learn how to act together in a unit.'

'I think even the boys have got that by now,' Yirella growled. 'Eighteen years of indoctrination tends to make that very clear.'

'We are not indoctrinating you,' Jenner said immediately. 'This is a training facility, that's all.'

'Training us to fight for you.'

'Humans are a hunted species, Yirella. Sometime, somewhere in this galaxy, we have to stop running and fight back. You have known that is your destiny, to confront the enemy, from the very beginning. We never withheld that from you. Everything which has followed, everything we have taught you and trained you to do, is designed to give you the greatest chance of success.'

She raised her eyebrows. 'Including the cougar?'

'No,' Alexandre said ruefully. 'The cougar was a mistake. We didn't know one was in the area.'

'But the moroxes, they're not real, are they? They're just genten remotes.'

'They used to be real,' Alexandre said. 'Thousands of years ago in a star system lightyears away. A traveller generation starship found a planet with indigenous biological life not dissimilar to terrestrial evolution, which is always a rare and wonderful surprise. They stopped and studied the xenobiology for a century before moving on. We replicated the basic morox form in molecular initiators. It provided you with a believable threat.'

'It nearly ripped Dellian's arm off!'

'No, it never did that. They were deep scratches, that's all. Plenty of blood, but no real damage.'

'You scared the living crap out of us to give us *motivation*? You bastards!'

Alexandre sat next to her and reached out to put hir arm round her shoulders. She shook hir off angrily. 'Don't. Not you. You were supposed to be the one we trusted, our almost-parent. You betrayed us.' She wiped her eyes, struggling to hold tears in.

'I would die before I would betray you,' Alexandre said. 'I might not be your biological parent, but my love for you is just as strong.'

Yirella shook her head. 'No parent would do this. Doesn't matter what kind.'

'All of us who volunteered to stay behind while our families left for the safety of the generation ships did so willingly, knowing the suffering – *this* suffering – that we would face raising you,' Jenner said quietly. 'We made that sacrifice freely because we not only love you, but we believe in you. You are destined to be our salvation.'

'We're not your salvation. We're your slave soldiers,' Yirella spat. 'Why did you even birth us? Why not just use genten remotes?'

'Because of you, Yirella,' Alexandre said softly. 'You are the reason.'

'What do you mean?'

'A genten is smart, fast, but ultimately has limits – in imagination, in intuition. You don't. You are human.'

'That's . . . stupid. I'm not as clever as a genten. It doesn't matter how physically large my brain is. I could never match one of them.'

'Not in absolute processing power, no. But like all technology, Turings have plateaued. There is no "next level" for them, no eleventh generation.'

'I'm not a next level of evolution,' she cried. 'I'm the opposite. I'm a throwback, a binary human. You wanted us – the boys – for our aggression, for the primitives we are.'

'Yes, we wanted boys for their aggression. We omnias don't possess their level of testosterone bellicosity – not permanently, because we cycle. But a constant male gender . . . that gives them the greatest advantage a human can have in a combat situation. We have to win, Yirella. The enemy will never stop, we know this. They haven't stopped for thousands of years. We cannot send less than our best against them.'

'Then what do you need me for? I'm not the best of anything.'

'Deep down I think you understand perfectly well why. I know acknowledging what you are is difficult, and for that I am so very sorry. But you are what you are, Yirella: smart. Do you really think a genten would have worked out what was happening at the crash? A genten is not suspicious. Simply asking questions is not the same as possessing curiosity. Curiosity is a human trait, derived from emotion. A genten can analyse its situation and environment, but to believe what it experiences is fraudulent without prior knowledge – no. That was you. You worked it out, and not just because you were clever, but because you had feelings. To make the decisions you will be making . . . That is another flaw a genten cannot compensate for. You see, once you are out among the stars, face to face with the enemy, you will confront the final question – the very human question of trust. If you were to order Dellian and his yearmates into action, they will trust you because they know you would never, ever let them down; that whatever attack plan you come up with, it is the very best a plan can be. A genten's plan of action might be equally good – possibly better – but there will always exist a tiny fissure of uncertainty in those required to carry it out. In those circumstances, hesitancy can mean death. Trust is at the core of human nature, one of our greatest curses – and blessings.'

'You think you're the pinnacle of sophistication and human culture, but you're not. You are monsters,' she said coldly. 'You bred us poor backward animals for one purpose. We have no choice; you have taken it away from us. Our life is pre-ordained, controlled by you. We are nothing. You have denied us a soul.'

'You are the salvation of the human race. That is not nothing.'

'I don't want that!' she yelled. 'I want a life! My life. I want to live in a culture where people respect each other, where we have the liberty to follow whatever goals we can find for ourselves. I want to be free!'

'We all do,' Jenner said sharply. 'But we had that freedom taken from us when the enemy found us. Now, all that is left is for humanity to run. To fly between the stars and find a refuge world for a few hundred years where we can breathe for a brief sweet time before running again. I too want to live a life without fear. I want a home to go to. But there is none in this damned galaxy, not for humans. None of us has a choice any more. So now we will join the Five Saints, and fight back. We have to. My part in this campaign is trivial. It is so small that it will never be known. But you, you and the boys – you will gather together with others like you, and you will win. You will liberate this galaxy. And humans will have a home again.'

*

Three days after they were rescued from the crash, the clan's senior year finally moved out of their dormitory dome in the middle of the main campus complex. Genten construction remotes had built them a crescent of neat little bungalows in a fresh section of the clan compound. They all had the same basic layout of five rooms and a cohort den under a curving roof, with broad glass doors opening onto a terrace shaded by palms and vines. In the centre of the crescent was a communal hall, with indoor and outdoor swimming pools and gyms and a dining room if they still wanted to eat as a group, as well as lecture theatres and design studios and all-body combat simulation eggs. There were also portals to various sites for combat exercises with live weapons, and out to a skyfort for more zero-gee training.

After breakfast on the exodus day, muncs and remote wagonettes carried everyone's belongings out of the senior dorm and across the compound to their new homes. Behind them, the new senior year swooped on the vacated dormitories and started heated squabbles over who got which bed.

Dellian had been tempted to leave everything behind. After all, the only things in the boxes on the wagonette were relics of childhood. He considered that to be over now, obliterated by the resort island and subsequent ordeal on the wilderness mountain. But there were blankets the muncs were fond of, and books and old drawings that still managed to tug at a few sentimental strings deep inside. So he brought it all, telling himself he'd chuck most of it into his new home's disposal chute. Somehow, he suspected the long line of his fellow yearmates had come to the same conclusion.

The door opened for him and he stepped over the threshold. *Everything's so blank*, he thought in dismay. The walls were tastefully coloured, of course, in greys and reds and golds. The wooden floors in each room were dark polished hardwood, with simple furniture. Blank. Waiting for him to change it, to mould it into his own.

He didn't have any idea what he wanted. Just . . . not this.

His arms were by his side. He lifted them slightly and wiggled his fingers. The muncs bounced about happily at the freedom he'd just bestowed and rushed round the bungalow to explore. There was an outbreak of happy squeaks and groans as they discovered their den, with its shelf beds, next to his bedroom. They liked that.

Dellian stared down at the boxes they'd abandoned and the remote wagonette waiting patiently for his instruction, and scratched his head in perplexity. *Now what?*

'Hello?'

He turned to see Yirella framed by the open door, her head only just below the lintel. 'Hey, you. Come in. Welcome to my home. Saints, that is so weird saying that!'

'I know.' She walked in, looking round, her expression of dismay as deep as his. 'Nice,' she teased. 'What are you going to do with it?'

'I have absolutely no idea.'

'I can pull up some old files on decor if you'd like. Our ancestors seemed to have a much greater imagination than us, especially when it came to artistic flare. It may give you some ideas.'

'Sounds good. Have you done that already? Looked, I mean?'

'Yeah. These homes all have a good fabricator. They can produce just about any effect you want, and the remotes will fit them for you. I've already been trying some stuff out.'

Dellian realized he hadn't seen her in the line of yearmates walking into the crescent. 'How long have you been here?'

'A couple of days. My bungalow is next door.'

'Really? That's great!'

'It wasn't chance.'

'Yeah? Who made that happen?'

'I did.'

'How did you manage that?'

'We're the brains of the outfit, us girls, remember?'

'I thought this is an equal society?'

'No, Dellian, it isn't. It is very far from that.'

His good humour faded at how serious she'd suddenly become. 'Sorry.'

'Don't be. We didn't choose any of this. It's not our fault.'

'Are you okay?'

'Sure. How about you? What did the doctor say?'

'Oh, that? The a-skin has peeled off. So I'm fine.'

'Dellian, you got attacked by a beast. That's not fine.'

He grinned. 'But I fought it and killed it. We won. That's what matters.'

'I suppose so. Yes.' She came over to stand in front of him, and for the first time Dellian felt strangely resentful that she was so tall. He didn't want to have to tilt his head back just so he could look at her wide enchanting face.

Her hand reached out and stroked his sleeve where the morox claws had sliced his arm. 'Take your shirt off,' she said quietly. 'I want to see.'

Dellian undid the buttons and slipped out of the shirt. He had no idea why, but standing in front of her, bare-chested, he felt strangely vulnerable. His cohort were peering round their den door. He turned his hand, palm outward, banishing them.

Yirella's fingertip stroked down the streaks of pale skin where the medical skin had been. 'No freckles,' she said sadly.

'They'll come back.' He paused, uncertain. 'Did you say . . .?'

'Yes. I like your freckles.'

'I wasn't sure if that was real,' he said. 'Those sedatives they gave me when we got back were quite something.'

'That was real,' she said. 'The second-most real thing about it.'

'Second? What was the first?'

She smiled and tipped her head forwards so their noses touched. Her wild hair tickled his cheeks. 'The cougar.'

'Oh. Right. Saints, that thing frightened me!'

'You put yourself in front of me,' she said huskily. 'To protect me.'

Fingers stroked his chest muscles. Dellian couldn't believe how such a delicate touch could light lines of fire across his skin. 'I had to,' he confessed. 'I couldn't let it hurt you. Not you.'

'That's the second time you've done that.'

The side of his mouth lifted in a fond smile. 'The arena match against the Ansaru team. Yeah! I remember. We were, what? Thirteen?'

'Twelve.'

'Saints, we're old now, aren't we?'

Yirella kissed him. 'Which room is your bedroom?'

*

'About time,' was the most common remark among their year-mates.

They didn't quite move in with each other, not like Orellt and Mallot, and a few of the other boys who were finally pairing up. But they certainly spent each night together. Some meals were taken in the dining room with their friends – after spending their entire lifetime in the company of everyone, no one wanted to be isolated. But they did take breakfast and sometimes dinner with each other in the solitude of a bungalow.

Combat training was kept to a minimum while the booster programme was implemented. No one was surprised when Janc volunteered to be first.

'I hate it,' Yirella exclaimed on their third night. They'd finished dinner and moved outside to sit on the terrace while the sun dropped out of the sky. The bungalow was playing some music recorded on Earth thousands of years ago. Yirella liked having music available. Back in the dorm it hadn't been particularly popular – at least not the quieter, more melodic tracks she always chose.

'Hate what?' Dellian asked in surprise.

'Boosting. They're changing us. We have no control.'

'We do. Alexandre said; we don't have to do this.' He poured the last of the beer into their glasses.

'And if we don't? If we don't go out there and fight, what do we do? Stay on Juloss? Because there's so much opportunity available here, isn't there?'

'Not everyone is going to be part of the war effort.'

'Yeah, I can join the remotes scrubbing the decks on board our battleship.'

He reached out and gripped her hand. 'I hate it when you're this unhappy.'

'This is not me being miserable. This is me being angry.'

'Okay. Angry is scary.'

She grinned weakly and took another sip of the beer. 'I just hate that we can't control our lives, not really. I know we don't have to go to war, but, come on, what is there for us here? Everyone on Juloss is going to leave when the youngest yeargroup finish their training and get boosted. I don't know about you, but I can't see myself staying behind and waiting for the enemy to arrive. And they always do, you know. They go through any star system we settled like a plague, destroying everything.'

'I know.' He stared out at the dark trees at the end of the garden, where colourful birds were settling for the night. 'So you will come with us? The boys need you. *I* need you.'

'Of course I'm coming with you. I'm no martyr, waiting out in the jungle by myself for the enemy to finally find Juloss – if they ever do. And I will not let you down. Remember? But we're not a yeargroup any more, are we? Not just a team playing tournaments against the other clans. You and the boys are becoming a proper military squad.'

'For now. After the war, we can live how we want.'

'If we win.'

Dellian gave her a shocked look, but she seemed very earnest. 'We'll win. We have the Saints on our side.'

For a moment she looked as if she might argue. But in the end she raised her glass to him. 'That we do.'

*

The next morning they went to the medical facility to visit Janc. His cohort were in a special den, with a long window allowing them to look in at their master, helping to keep them calm. But they weren't allowed into the recovery and activation room.

When Dellian and Yirella walked in, Janc was lying in the middle of a wide bed with his limbs covered in thick sleeves of green a-skin, and a broad strip across the top of his skull, running over the crown to the nape of his neck like a particularly flat mohawk. The rubbery membranes sprouted a multitude of fibre optics that were plugged into the clinic's genten, which monitored and modified the boost implants.

Rello was sitting on the side of the bed, holding Janc's hand, the two of them grinning as if they'd just got away with some inane mischief.

'Well, you look okay,' Dellian said cheerfully.

'Feeling good,' Janc said. 'I'm thinking the happy-juice glands might be kicking in already.'

Yirella knew that wouldn't be happening, but kept quiet.

'Timing is everything,' Rello said. 'We were just talking about that, how fine the control is going to be, if you can trigger a gland discharge when you're fucking. Double it up.'

'Going to be doing plenty of experimenting there,' Dellian agreed.

'Oh, yeah.'

Yirella sighed. 'Don't you boys ever think of anything else?'

'No!' the three of them replied.

'I'm not sure any of the glands are amphetamine-based. They won't act as a serotonergic agonist.'

'You had to say that,' Rello complained.

'Whatever the crap it means,' Janc laughed.

Yirella couldn't help her own smile. 'What else did they give you?'

'Apart from the glands? The main arterial valves are in.'

'Always going to be useful when you get a limb ripped off,' Dellian said with mock-enthusiasm.

Yirella knew his humour was slightly forced. Undergoing

boosting had finally made it physical and actual. They really were going to be embarking on a battleship and portalling off into the galaxy. There weren't even statistics about how many of them would survive, if any.

'If there's any limb ripping going on, it'll be me doing it,' Janc said. 'They put the first batch of nerve induction sheaths in, too. For the larger muscles.'

'So six more batches,' Rello said, 'and you'll be fully emittive.'

Janc held a hand up to his face, flexing his fingers one at a time as if testing them. 'Yeah. I didn't realize just how many subliminal gestures we make to the little guys. It's just natural now, you know?'

Yirella glanced over at the window where Janc's munc cohort were looking in on them. 'After all this time, they're a part of us now, like mobile extra limbs. And you're going to need them,' she said solemnly.

'When do they start modifying your cohort?' Dellian asked eagerly.

'Tomorrow,' Janc said.

'Aren't you sad about that?' Yirella asked.

The boys looked at her with such incomprehension she thought she could actually hear the gulf splitting open between them. It was over, she realized; they weren't her family of brothers any more. Difference now outweighed love. It was all she could do not to burst into tears in front of them.

'No,' Janc said, careful not to sound indignant. 'This way they'll still be relevant to me. More than relevant: necessary. Relationships change. We're growing up, Yirella. I don't need a bunch of cuddly pets any more.' He grinned up at Rello, who squeezed his hand fondly.

'Growing up,' she said distantly. 'Yes, we are.'

Dellian put his arm round her, knowing something was badly wrong. 'Nobody's changing that much,' he assured her.

*

The munc centre always used to be a reassuring place for Yirella. If Uma or Doony ever got knocked about, she would come to Uranti, knowing scratches and bruises would be tended to and soothed. If they'd stupidly eaten something bad, they'd get medicine and treatment in a ward. This time when she walked into the broad entrance hall which ran clean through the diameter of the dome, the old sensation of comfort was nowhere to be had. The hygienic white tile floor and light grey walls were too functional for her now, too symbolic of the true nature of muncs: artificial, doomed . . .

Uranti was in a treatment room at the back of the clinic, tending to a munc belonging to a boy in the clan's fifth yeargroup. Sie smiled and waved Yirella to a seat as sie finished wrapping a cut in black a-skin. Boy and munc held hands delightedly as they were dismissed, with Uranti's dire warnings not to exert themselves for twenty-four hours following them out.

'The arena?' Yirella asked.

Uranti stripped the sanitary gloves from hir hands. 'Hockey. I have no idea which genius though it would be a good idea to give muncs hockey sticks that they can wave around on a crowded pitch.' Sie sighed, shaking hir head. 'This whole bonding procedure is one giant malleable experiment.' Sie looked round. 'Where are yours?'

'Back at the house.'

'Really? Don't they mind being apart from you?'

'I guess. A little. I don't have the kind of bond the boys have with their cohorts. I suppose I'm more reserved. It's rubbed off on Uma and Doony.'

Uranti gave her a soft smile. 'And yet, no one else in your yeargroup has given their muncs an actual name.'

'We're not allowed to.'

'Dear me, is that a touch of rebellion I hear in your voice?'

'I was just being practical – and polite. Which seems a bit pointless now.'

'How so?'

'The modification – which is the kind of phrase an old-Earth politician would use – given what you're going to do to our poor muncs.'

'I see. Is that why you're here?'

'Yes.'

'What do you want to know?'

'I want to see them.'

'Them?'

'The combat cores you *modify* them into. I've seen the images, and I've studied the blueprints. But it's not *them*.'

'I understand. The map is not the territory.'

Yirella frowned for a moment. 'Something like that. Yes.'

Uranti led her back into the main corridor, and into a hexagonal hub chamber. The portal sie chose emerged into a section of the building Yirella had never been in before. She was in an observation gallery that ran along a clean assembly facility a hundred and fifty metres long, with seamless pearl-white walls, floor, and ceiling; smaller glass-walled rooms lined the sides. In her T-shirt and shorts, with sandals on her feet, Yirella felt totally out of place. The few people she could see walking amid the industrial-sized fabricators were all wearing hospital-style gowns.

'Those are Neána-style molecular initiators,' Uranti said, a degree of pride in hir voice as sie indicated the row of large cubes on the floor below. 'We think, anyway. The insertion metahumans were never quite sure they had mastered all the principles. Our own biogenetic science plateaued a long way short of this technology's ability.'

'They made the muncs,' Yirella said tonelessly.

'Yes. The muncs are biologics. But, I'm proud to say, a completely human design. We never had access to the creation programs the Neána insertion ship possessed.'

'And the combat cores, what are they?'

'A fusion of biologics and human weapons. This way.'

They walked along the gallery until they were overlooking the construction bays. A cohort of combat cores lay in their cradles, with genten remote arms moving round them, integrating the final layer of components. The living machines were matt grey cylinders three metres long and two wide, with a wasp-waist constriction a third of the way along; both ends curved to form sharp cones. Their skin had rings of silver studs and sockets, ready to linc with external armaments and sensors. Even additional propulsion systems could be linced if they were operating in space or within a gas giant's atmosphere.

'Aren't they amazing?' Uranti said, hir eyes fixed on one with complete admiration. 'The centre section has a life-support nucleus which will house the munc brain after it's removed from the body. Drive units are exotic matter gravatonic manipulation. It's all powered by triplicated aneutronic fusion chambers. Quantum entanglement keeps them connected to their master.'

'From the muscle sheaths,' Yirella said.

'Yes. The muncs can read every single body language posture the boys produce. They understand and respond to it all, big or small, refining the simple verbal orders. It's the closest we'll ever come to telepathy. In combat situations, that will be a monumental advantage. No time wasted shouting orders or interpreting what to do. The combat cohort instinctively knows what their master wants, and deploys accordingly. You've all spent sixteen years refining that empathic bond. The fight response will be instantaneous. And you and the other girls will direct it; you'll be the lords of strategy.'

'You must be so proud,' Yirella said savagely.

Uranti gave her a long, questing look. 'Yes. I am.'

'I wonder if the muncs are.'

'You're anthropomorphizing, Yirella. That's a mistake. The muncs are just biologics, that's all. They're alien machines.'

'That's bollocks. They're alive. Their neurology is modelled on a human brain. They have memory and emotional responses. Just because their cellular biochemistry is slightly different, that doesn't make them a machine. They're sentient. That's why they willingly undergo . . . this.' Her arm jabbed out, taking in the combat cores. 'They want it because the boys want it.'

'Of course they do. It's why we're all here. This is our purpose.'

'To wage war isn't a purpose, it's a threat reflex. We should be trying to think our way out of this mess.'

'We've tried. We cannot flee out of their reach, for the enemy is more widespread than us. The Saints themselves know there is no Sanctuary star to be had, so the legend that a generation ship in our past vowed to look for one is nothing more than that: legend. We cannot call out to the Neána for help, even if they still exist, because to do so would betray our position to the enemy. We are alone, and their hunt is inexorable. Our only hope is to spread our generation ships wide and one day to turn and fight. Look it up; the files are open to you now. All the files. Principal Jenner authorized it. We don't even know how many humans have died or been taken trying to achieve that noble goal. All we have left now is our crusade to defend the human race. To destroy an enemy so relentless that this whole galaxy is unsafe.'

'You can't be certain we'll win.'

'Of course we can't. But we are striving to create the greatest army our science and technology can produce. This is my project. We've worked hard to achieve this level of success. If we fail, it will not be from weakness.'

'Congratulations. And when does my boost begin?'

'Whenever you're ready.'

'You're very confident about our empathy with the muncs, aren't you?'

'Yes. However, your muncs' neurology is slightly different to those in the boys' cohorts. They'll be your filters.'

'Yes, but only when you've ripped their brains out and wired them up to gentens as peripherals.'

'I don't have to.'

'What?'

'The physical aspect . . . Its not strictly necessary. It's what they've learned that is important. The thought routines they're using today are the priceless result of sixteen years of your bonding. Think of it. When you finally go up against the enemy, you'll be receiving hundreds of signals from the squads at the moment of greatest conflict. Even your mind can't absorb that much information, no matter how good the direct neural connection boost we give you. You have to filter and prioritize. That's where the munc routines come in, providing a preliminary analysis and grading requests for your attention. The genten will use that interpretive ability to generate the right assessment for you.'

'If the gentens are that good, then you don't need us.'

'You know why we need you. Principal Jenner explained that. There has to be a human in the loop – not just for trust, but for intuition too. We were all so proud of you at the crash site, the way you questioned your situation. None of us was expecting that.'

'Bravo me.'

'Look, if you are genuinely too fond of Uma and Doony to see this happen, I can download their thought routines and run them in a simulated munc neurology within the genten. Their brains have the facility for that built in.' Sie smiled, searching for approval. 'Would you like that?'

Yirella's shoulders slumped. 'You really have thought of everything.'

'I try. But I know I'm not as good as you.'

'All right. I'll let you know.'

*

Yirella woke up as the dawn chorus of birds began to seep across the estate. She lay in bed for a while, allowing her eyes to adjust to the weak pastel light which seeped through the reed blinds she'd chosen for her bedroom windows. Dellian was lying on the mattress beside her, sprawled on his chest, still sleeping. She looked at his pale body, seemingly so childishly small on her long mattress, trying to hold her emotions back. Today was the day he was going to the medical facility for his first boost.

It was the day she was going to lose him. She knew he would still adore her, and she him, but what he was would be changed. No more of a change than every other day they devoted to training, to exploring a new tactical game, or spent in class learning about another weapon. Every day changed them; she acknowledged that readily enough. But this was a physical change underscoring his outlook. Today he would be claimed by inevitability.

He was definitely going to join the war. It was what he'd always wanted, the noblest cause a human could undertake in these strange times. His life was to be dedicated to salvation for all of them. He dreamed of it. He lived for it. And she would never try to stop him.

But that didn't make his choice any less painful for her.

Last night she'd clung to him with a passion that had surprised him as much as he'd been physically delighted. He'd asked if anything was wrong. And as they strained against each other on the bed, she'd clutched him tighter. 'There could never be anything wrong with this,' she'd promised him lustfully.

She'd been as energetic and enthusiastic as he'd ever known. Fulfilling every sexual craving wasn't just for his benefit. Her final time with her original beautiful Dellian deserved such an intimate celebration, locking the perfect memory for an age to come when she'd need it most. Then, after even his stamina had been exhausted, she'd cried silently while he slept.

This morning, she determined, there would be no tears. That was her change. Her choice.

Once upon a time, her favourite Saint had been Yuri Alster because of his logic and perseverance. Now, though, her allegiance had shifted to Alik Monday, in appreciation for his showing her how ruthless you sometimes had to be, how self-belief kept you strong.

Yirella rose silently, making sure she didn't disturb Dellian. She put on a simple robe and slipped into the den next door, where Uma and Doony were awake. She smiled at them, impressed that Uranti was right. They'd woken with her, even though there was a wall separating them. Maybe the empathy bond wasn't telepathy, but it certainly had a kind of magical quality excluded from the rest of her life.

Her soft motions, the way she held herself, prevented them from making the big burst of noise and movement that was their usual greeting. Smiling in welcome – false, so false, yet it fooled them – she stroked their soft pelts in reassurance. They regarded her expectantly, and she tilted her head in a playful gesture. The three of them slipped out of the bungalow and into the warm early-morning air.

The lake was half a kilometre from the snug crescent of bungalows, surrounded by tall lush trees. Swans sailed calmly on the still waters, twisting their heads to give her curious looks as she appeared through the undergrowth.

Without hesitating, she waded straight into the water, shivering slightly at its cool embrace. She held Uma and Doony's hands, urging them in with her. Her posture was so perfect, so easy, that they walked along beside her eagerly, keen to share whatever adventure she was embarking on.

Feet pressed into the mud and the water rose to her waist. The little forest was serene and lovely. A nice sight for your last.

Her arms curled round the muncs' shoulders. 'My choice,' she told them guilelessly, so they would know this was the right thing, that this was what she wanted. Her knees bent until they too were sinking into the thick mud. Uma and Doony knelt obediently by her side. Her head was well above the surface, but the water closed over their scalps.

Uma struggled a little, as she suspected it might. Doony was completely passive as Yirella held them both under the water. She kept her face completely composed as her little companions died in her tight embrace. There were no tears.

And that was the most frightening aspect of the whole scene for Alexandre and the others who eventually came crashing through the trees, far far too late.

The Assessment Team

Feriton Kayne *Nkya, 25th June 2204*

By the time Yuri finished telling us about finding Horatio, we still had another five hours on the Trail Ranger before we reached the crash site. Outside the long window, I could see Nkya's landscape changing again as we descended onto the dusty plain carpeted with red-grey regolith. The beacon posts stretching away to the sharp horizon were almost twice as high as the oddly smooth rocks littering the ground. Ahead of us, the wheel tracks of the earlier caravans cut across the pristine ground, their dark laser-straight lines a monstrous act of graffiti against a geology untouched since dinosaurs walked the Earth.

'So what did happen on Althaea?' Alik asked.

'We're still not sure,' Jessika said. 'I spent a year on the post-mission analysis. A hellbuster was a good choice. Most of Building Seven was vaporized, so there was very little physical evidence for our forensic labs to analyse. My findings were inconclusive.'

She was being modest; I'd checked her report myself. There were some interesting facts to be had amid all those secure files. Ainsley Zangari had certainly thought so. For a start, it's how Yuri claimed the prize: head of Connexion Security. The boss rewards loyalty.

'But the kid came out of it okay, right?' Kandara asked.

I thought she sounded rather amused, as if Yuri had recounted some traditional fairy tale.

'Yes, my father made a full recovery,' Loi said. 'Thank you for asking.'

Like everyone else in the Trail Ranger, apart from Yuri, I turned to look at Loi in surprise. I only knew he was one of the third generation of Ainsley Zangari's offspring, but I hadn't actually bothered going deep enough into his file to check parentage. I admit, the coincidence was slightly unnerving.

'You?' Jessika asked. Her face was lit up with a smile of pure fascination. 'You're Gwendoline and Horatio's son?'

'Yeah.'

'That is one hell of an impressive how-my-parents-met story,' Eldlund said in admiration.

Loi took a while finishing his espresso. 'Depends on your view-point. But, yeah, I guess.'

'Nice happy-ever-after,' Alik mocked. 'But I'm biting.' He lev-elled a finger at Jessika. 'What were your findings? Bad enough to make you switch allegiance back again?'

She gave a reluctant nod, almost as if she was embarrassed. 'That kind of criminality, snatching helpless low-visibility people for profit, simply doesn't happen in the Utopial society. And I really am an office girl at heart. So I went back, looking for the quiet life. How dumb is that?'

Yuri let out a dismissive grunt, but didn't actually challenge her. 'That whole case certainly justified Ainsley's suspicion about the Olyix,' he said.

'How?' Alik said. 'They helped you.'

'That they did. They gave me all the information I asked for about using Kcells for a brain transplant, and how the whole concept remains pure science fiction. All very diplomatic and cooperative. But Hai-3 also said: man.'

'I don't get it,' Eldlund said.

'The exact words it said to me were: I will pray for your success in recovering the unfortunate man who has been abducted.'

'You didn't say who you were looking for,' Alik said, clicking his fingers. 'Male, female, or omnia.'

'Right,' Yuri confirmed. 'Ainsley never quite believed the Olyix were so saintly. And this proved it. They've taken on the aspects of our greed, and run with it to an extreme because they see that as a normal human trait. Unchecked, it's a bad attitude. And it is unchecked, because they don't really understand us, they just mimic us. No moral filter, remember? They just don't have it. That's why we keep a very special watch on them now.'

He glanced at me, and I nodded confirmation for everyone to see. But I understood now where his prejudice came from; it was quite reasonable given the circumstances. Yuri wasn't an agent for alien disinformation; Hai-3 had been stupid. Its mistake there in the embassy had strengthened Yuri's paranoia, and in turn he'd gone on and convinced Ainsley Zangari to suspect the Olyix of limitless intrigue in the pursuit of money. Subsequently, every crime committed in the Sol system, from jaywalking to political manipulation, Ainsley blamed on the Olyix.

Okay, so eliminating Yuri as a suspect was a step forwards, but I still didn't understand where the whole Kcell-enabled brain transplant myth originally came from. Because that is now embedded so deeply in popular culture it's never going away. I'd been hoping for a clue in Yuri's tale, but he was clearly as puzzled by that as I was.

'You think the Olyix fired the hellbuster missile at you?' Alik asked.

'Not directly,' Jessika said. 'That was Cancer.'

Alik's reaction was interesting. He sat bolt upright. 'You're shitting me!'

'No.'

'Je-zus. Can you back that up?'

'Not in a court of law. But our G7Turings went through a lot of data. We composed a digital simulation of Bronkal for the three days prior to Yuri and I arriving, and extending two days after. She turned up with two associates when we were in the middle of interviewing Joaquin Beron. We backtracked her through the hubs to

Tokyo. Before that, we have no idea. The Japanese criminal intelligence agency was unaware she was in their country.'

'And the hellbuster missile? Don't tell me she came through your hubs carrying it?'

'No,' Yuri said. 'We have deep sensors on every trans-stellar hub. You can't carry weapons between star systems.'

'Because you don't need to,' Jessika said. 'We had a little more luck with the hellbuster. It was a custom fabrication in Yarra, Althaea's capital. Someone called Korrie Chau brought it in through the Bronkal commercial transport hub in a taxez about four minutes before Yuri shut the hub down. The taxez was registered as a public vehicle, but that was false-flag; it belonged to Chau. He used to move a lot of illegal fabrications round in it.'

'You did some good work there, tracing him,' Alik said.

'We lost seven of the tactical team members in that explosion,' Yuri said in a dangerously level voice. 'And Christ knows what Baptiste's people did to poor old Lucius as well. Ainsley made sure we had whatever resources we needed afterwards.'

'The hellbuster part wasn't difficult,' Jessika said. 'We found Korrie Chau and his taxez ten hours later, in a parking lot less than two kilometres from the docks. Cancer had slit his throat.'

'Yeah, she doesn't leave loose ends,' Alik said.

'Forensics tore Chau's place apart. We shipped entire rooms back to our crime labs for analysis. Forensic accounting tracked his payments, but they were all from one-shot finance houses based on independent asteroid settlements. Most of them don't even have a human population; they're just a bunch of G5 and G6 Turing rock squatters.'

'So you don't know who paid him?'

'No.'

'But you think it's the Olyix?'

'Not directly, but their actions, their acceptance of what they see as our normality, were ultimately what started this,' Yuri said. 'I told you, there are consequences to what they have been doing. We know Baptiste Devroy went on the run as soon as Jessika and I turned up at Horatio's flat. So he'd obviously got some kind of monitor there. And Hai-3 knew who I was trying to find when I showed up at their Geneva embassy. Whatever people are getting snatched for, the Olyix are at least aware of it.'

'Why, though?' Kandara asked. 'What's their motive?'

'Our working theory is illegal medical research,' Yuri said. 'Twenty-one per cent of the total medical expenditure in the Sol system involves Kcell replacement treatments. That is serious money, because, let's face it, we are a species of hypochondriacs.'

'But the research and development of new applications is slow,' I explained. 'Human regulatory agencies have pretty strict restrictions and protocols. The simple and easy Kcell applications, like a new heart, were first to gain approval, and still form the bulk of their sales. But the more complex organs and glands take time. The Olyix's human research partners have to proceed cautiously, and they're the ones making the investment. We think they might be aiming to short-cut that process. And if they propose an underground deal, the Olyix will adopt that mindset. After all, it's human.'

'Shit!' Kandara looked shocked. 'Are you saying they're experimenting on live humans?'

'Not the Olyix themselves,' I said. 'It'll be the companies doing the Kcell functionality research who've set up some dark labs to accelerate the work. They only get a small percentage of Kcell sales, but everything is relative. And new Kcell medical treatments hitting the market bring in more legitimate money. Which is the Olyix goal. They're complicit; they have to be. As Yuri says, the amount of money involved is phenomenal. Buying enough energy to recharge an arkship for interstellar flight doesn't come cheap.'

'Are they still doing it? Kandara asked. 'Are people still going missing?'

Yuri's laugh was more a groan of despair. 'People are always going missing. Most cases are suspicious. We simply don't know if this kind of illegal experimentation is still going on.' He shrugged. 'There have been some good Kcell transplant products released over the last thirty-seven years; the spleen, lymph nodes, stomach lining tissue, not to mention the cosmetics.'

'The Universal authorities must have some idea if people are being snatched,' Eldlund said. 'How many people go missing each year in suspicious circumstances?'

'Across fifteen solar systems and a thousand habitats? Who knows?' Yuri said. 'On Earth alone, the figure is tens of millions a year. Most of them are what the agencies class as ordinary missing persons – people who are depressed or want out of their relationships or families, or petty criminals or people with debts, or they're girls and boys who've been groomed and get trafficked. Some turn up again, but plenty don't. There is just no way of knowing which of them are snatched by bastards like Baptiste.'

'That many?' an aghast Eldlund exclaimed. 'It can't be.'

'It is,' I told hir. 'It always has been. The percentage is slightly down from twenty-first-century levels because our economy is so much better now, which reduces the level of disaffection in society. But the numbers are still staggering. Worse, they are too great even for our networks and G7Turings to cope with. People are always claiming we live in over-policed states where authoritarian governments oversee every aspect of life. In truth, governments – Universal ones anyway – really don't care about individuals.'

'Until you don't pay your taxes,' Callum muttered.

'Touché,' I conceded.

'The Utopial governments take more care about citizen welfare,' Jessika said. 'It's fundamental to our constitution.'

'Bravo you,' Kandara said. 'But you still have your drop-outs.'

'The percentage is minimal.'

'We're here to assess an alien spaceship,' I reminded them. 'Not have a political pissing contest.'

Alik snorted. 'So whomever Baptiste was snatching people for hired Cancer to destroy all the evidence?' he asked.

'That's the conclusion we came to,' Jessika said. 'A medical research company, with money, zero ethics, and underground contacts.'

Down the other end of the cabin, Eldlund put down hir cup. 'This Cancer assassin, or dark mercenary, whatever she is – did you ever find her? Are you still looking?'

'We're always looking for her,' Yuri said. 'Just like everyone else.'

'The bitch is good,' Alik grunted. 'Even the Bureau can't find her.'

'You know her, then,' Callum said shrewdly to Alik.

'She cropped up in one of my cases, yeah.'

'Did you catch her?'

I watched Alik's rigid muscles creak into a scowl. 'No. But it was an odd case.'

'Odd how?' Callum asked.

'It wasn't strictly a Bureau matter. I was called in as a favour – friend of a friend kind of deal, someone who knows people connected to a globalPAC.'

The Case of Alik's Favour

America, AD 2172

January fourteen, quarter to midnight, and the snow was blasting across New York City like the devil had left his gates open when he hit the town to party. And, Alik decided, the dark prince had partied hard indeed. He was staring down at the corpse when one of the crime scene cops pulled the coroner's sheet back. That spoilt his interrupted dinner, and didn't leave him too keen on breakfast now, either.

The girl was a genuine blonde, he could tell. The roots always gave it away. And whatever psycho had scalped her had left some roots. At least her head was still on her neck, because there wasn't much left of her limbs. Alik studied the wall behind her, which was now a sick mural of thick blood splatter with gobs of flesh embedded in the blast craters. While the victim was standing, someone had used a bulled-up shotgun to take her down. His educated guess was that they blew her arms off first, then followed up with her lower legs. The scalping was last. She might have been alive for it, but blood loss and shock would have rendered her unconscious by that time. Thankfully.

'Je-zus fuck.' Alik turned back to Detective Salovitz.

The cop's face was the colour of a dead fish, but Alik preferred that to looking at the murdered blonde.

'I warned you,' Salovitz said. 'The others aren't much better.'

'She's the only one in here, right?' Alik had arrived thirty minutes after the NYPD had crashed into the apartment, following all sorts of alarms – neighbouring apartments and home security sensors screaming out that gunfire had been detected. He didn't care about that; he'd been asked to check out a specific digital problem originating in the apartment. However, the multiple homicides gave him a legitimate reason to observe and assist the NYPD. His cover, not that anyone would have the balls to query it, was to provide cross-jurisdiction authority, which was highly credible given the nature of the homeowner's apartment.

'Yeah,' Salovitz agreed. 'The rest are all over the place.'

Alik took a proper look around the room. It was a big space, with a classy art-deco layout; walking into it was a time-step back into the 1920s. The ostentatious, genuine period furniture was all arranged to make you look in one direction. That was understandable; he was on the seventeenth floor of a typical Central Park West block. One wall was floor-to-ceiling glass, providing a billionaire's view out across the park, all snug under its thick fluffy snow blanket. He went over to check it out. The glass was programmable, allowing it to flow open onto the narrow balcony outside.

When he looked through, he could see footprints in the snow. 'Come take a look at this,' he called to Salovitz.

Salovitz pressed his face against the glass, leaving faint mist streamers on the cold surface below his nostrils. 'So?'

'Footprints. Three, maybe four, sets.'

'Yeah. Nobody went over, if that's what you're thinking. We'd have found the body on the street when we came in.'

Alik bit back on a sigh. He liked Salovitz, he really did. The detective had seen enough of life's dark side to know how things worked, the dirty political wiring underneath the city that powered things along so smoothly. Every time Alik turned up on a case, no matter how cruddy the given reason, Salovitz knew not to question it. But there were times when Alik thought Salovitz must have got his badge on the back of some positive discrimination bullshit for terminal dumbasses. 'Look again. Tell me which way those footprints are heading.'

Salovitz glanced back out again. Then, 'Holy crap!'

The footprints which Alik had shown him started at the stone balustrade and came towards the glass. One-way traffic.

'They came in from next door,' Alik said. 'Pulled some pretty fine techno-acrobat shit to zipwire across from the neighbouring balcony.'

'Okay,' Salovitz said. 'I'll get the Precinct G7Turing to run checks on next door, ownership and access.'

'Good. Have Forensics prioritize the balcony. Those prints are filling with snow, and Christ knows how it screws residual traces.'

'Sure.'

He went out to find his partner, Detective Bietzk. Alik turned to Nikolai Kristjánsson, a member of the Forensics team, who was busy directing a line of microdrones that resembled snails. A dozen of them were sliding slowly over the carpet around the corpse, their molecular sensors mapping the particles they encountered.

Alik told his altme, Shango, to open a secure link to Kristjánsson. 'Have you analysed the bust yet?'

The way Kristjánsson's gaze slid away from him reminded Alik of ancient high-school jock/nerd confrontations – all very secret agent tradecraft, which Kristjánsson probably got off on. 'Not yet. They've got me scooping residuals to see who was here.'

'I'm no expert, but maybe someone with a fuck-off shotgun? Get that equipment back to your lab and give me a report.'

'It's not easy—'

'Do it.' Even from an angle, Alik could see Kristjánsson scowl. His official job was with the Manhattan Forensic Agency, but friends of Alik's Washington friends also had him on a retainer, which was why he'd been assigned to the case. Those same people had made it very clear to Alik that the attempted digital mischief was of immense importance. To them, the murders were an irrelevance. Glancing down at the blonde again, as the sheet was drawn back over her, Alik wasn't so sure.

The apartment was a portalhome, owned by Kravis Lorenzo, a named partner in Anaka, Devial, Mortalo & Lorenzo (that original Lorenzo was Kravis's father), a very high-end New York legal firm. So high-end it was cleared for ultra-one Pentagon contracts. Which was what drew Washington's attention. Earlier that night someone had tried using the portalhome's secure link to the legal firm's office to try and bust extremely secure Defence Department files.

Alik went out of the park view room through an ordinary door into the hubhall. It was a long oak-panelled cloister with nine portals, which were actually inside the Central Park West block apartment. Some of the doors simply led into old rooms like the kitchen, games nest and utilities where the servicez were stored, as well as the New York entrance. The rest of the Lorenzo family house was widespread – on a whole solar system scale.

Another pair of forensic agents were working the hubhall with a squadron of sensor-heavy drones, along with three ordinary cops. Salovitz was talking to his partner, Detective Bietzk. He turned back to Alik. 'Okay, the Precinct G7Turing went into City Hall records. The neighbour is Chen-tao Borrego. We called him and he's away in a Saskatchewan clinic undergoing telomere treatment. Been there ten days, due to remain for another fortnight. We're getting confirmation from the clinic, but it seems legit.'

'So his place is unoccupied?' Alik asked.

'Yeah. A team's going in now.'

'Okay. What's next?'

The detective pointed at one of the portals. 'The Moon.'

Alik always found it weird stepping directly into a lower gravity field. His body tensed up the way it did when he screwed up a pass at some babe at the end of a too-long night spent partying. It was the wrong thing to do. That involuntary reflex pushed his toes down hard on the black parquet floor, and forward momentum left him gliding further into the room.

Lorenzo's lunar room was a fifteen-metre dome in the Alphonsus Crater. Off to one side of him was a large luxurious jacuzzi, its bubbles fizzing away with low-gravity leisure. Various ficus plants were growing in Greek-style clay pots, their glossy leaves strangely bloated yet also elongated.

Alik looked up, and there was Earth's crescent directly overhead, shining with blue-white splendour. It was utterly captivating. Crazy too, that it was three hundred and eighty-four thousand kilometres or one footstep away. He always thought some little part of the human brain rebelled against quantum spacial entanglement. People needed to have distance in their lives; two hundred thousand years of evolutionary instinct couldn't be junked overnight.

When he finally lowered his gaze, he saw dozens of identical domes scattered across the crater floor, just far enough apart that the interiors couldn't be made out without magnification lenses. Half the resort facilities on the Moon were supposedly used for sex. Once Connexion started opening up the solar system, people soon found out that the so-called wonders of zero-gee sex, which over-romantic futurology writers used to rave about, was a myth. They didn't call the aircraft that early astronauts used for freefall training flights the vomit comet for nothing. Low-gee, however – that was a different matter.

Lorenzo had certainly installed some very wide couches in his dome. One of them had red laser warning tape round it, glowing bright red. The cop who'd pulled the lunar duty gave Alik a respectful nod and said: 'Stay at least two metres from the body, sir. The hazard disposal team is due in twenty minutes.'

First guess on the corpse gave Alik an Italian American, or at least some kind of Mediterranean family heritage. His face was perfectly intact, as were his legs and hips. The chest was fuzzed by what appeared to be a thin grey mist. Underneath that, his torso was just a pile of so much red pulp. The blood pool on and around the couch was impressively big, and congealing nicely. His arms were interesting; the buzz shot had taken them clean off his torso at the shoulder. One was on the couch, holding a custom-made stub-barrel auto-pump-action shotgun – which, judging from the eight-centimetre barrel diameter, Alik took to be the one used to take out the woman in the Central Park West room. A reasonable assumption, because this victim's second arm was lying on the floor, a scalp still gripped in its fingers, the blonde hair sponging up blood.

'Buzz gun,' Alik said. The gun itself was nothing special, just an electromagnetic barrel to ensure the projectile accelerated smoothly. But the buzz rounds it fired were mildly unstable. They were made from incredibly tightly wound coils of monomolecule filament, which expanded outwards on impact, so the target got to experience what it was like to be sliced apart by ten thousand razor blades, all travelling in different directions.

That indistinct fog lingering on the victim's chest was the cloud of filament. Alik knew that if he'd stuck his hand in it, his flesh would have been diced like gourmet burger meat. He couldn't help glancing round nervously. If there were any breakaway strands drifting through the air – not unknown – inhaling one meant a slow, excruciating and unstoppable death.

He let Shango capture the image through his tarsus lenses and stepped away quickly. Then he gave the dome a proper look as Shango pulled the dome's specs and splashed them for him. The transparent dome itself was made from multiple layers. The two inner shells were artificial sapphire, followed by a metre of carbon-rich glass to absorb radiation, another sapphire layer, then a smaller radiation barrier, two layers of photon filters to make sure raw sunlight was kept at bay during the unremitting two-week-long lunar day, and a thermal layer to keep the heat in during the equally long night. Finally there was the outer abrasion layer of sapphire that took all the hits from sandgrain-sized micrometeorites. If anything bigger came along – say pebble-sized – the inner layers would soak up the kinetic energy. They'd been known to leave a nasty streak that would need repairing, but anyone inside the dome could carry on sitting in the jacuzzi in perfect safety. In fact, he'd seen statistics that put standing on one of Earth's tropical beaches during the day more likely to kill you: sunstroke, long-term melanomas, tsunami, satellite falling on your head . . .

'Only one buzz shot fired,' Salovitz said. 'So the killer was either remarkably cool, or very proficient. Our victim managed to get off two shots.'

314

Alik looked where the corpse was facing. There were two yellow tags glowing on the sapphire shell, which showed a broad spiderweb of impact cracks. 'Je-zus, not even these bulled-up shotguns can puncture the dome?'

'No, the developers like to make sure their clients are safe.'

Alik focused on the victim again. 'Anyone with a buzz gun tends to know what they're doing,' he said thoughtfully. 'So Mr Shotgun here takes down the New York Broad, gets nasty on her head, then runs in here—'

'Chased by Buzz Gun Man,' Salovitz concluded. 'That's how we read it.'

'Okay, what's next?'

'Next is where it gets interesting.'

Next was Mars, the western edge of the Olympus Mons caldera, roughly twenty-two kilometres above the lowland plains, where geology had spent the last hundred million years quietly rusting the world to its barren death. The room was one of hundreds in a fifty-storey structure of identical rooms. Its glass wall was facing north. To the west was the endless gentle slope of the solar system's largest volcano, spread out to the crystal-sharp horizon like an infinity plateau. You couldn't actually see the Martian plains; they were too far away behind the flat pale sky. But Alik knew the kind of status-whores who owned a room here didn't care squat about that. They simply wanted The Summit.

Not that the rest of the view was too shabby. Two hundred metres away, the massive cliffs of the caldera wall gave a heroically vertiginous view out across the crater base – though that view was now partially blocked by the wide splash of solidified metal foam that had been sprayed over the big hole in the diamond-molecule-reinforced glass. Two mechez, like mechanical spider-octopus hybrids, clung to the surface, their nozzles alert for any further outbreak of cracks.

Most of the furniture was missing, sucked through the rent before it was sealed. A tide line of mashed-up debris lay along the base of the window.

Keeping a wary eye on the foam metal, Alik edged up to the

window and looked down. Fifty metres below, the ancient god of war's ginger sands showed a smear-plume of fragments that had once been Lorenzo's elegant antique Chinese ornaments. And a body.

Alik shuddered as best his stiff flesh would allow as his mind ran through the sequence of what had happened. It was all so different to a faller on Earth. If you dropped a body off a fifty-metre-high balcony in standard gravity, all the coroner crew would be left with was mopping up the splat puddle. Impact would shatter every bone and split the skin open, leaving a gush of gore and shit to soak the sidewalk. On Mars, with its one-third Earth-standard gravity, the impact was different. The fall probably didn't kill who-ever had gone through the window. On a pain level, the landing would've been like taking a Saturday-night mob beating, but he would still have been alive. In agony. And up on the summit, atmospheric pressure was seventy pascals, which to a human body was indistinguishable from zero. That had pulled the air right out of his lungs, leaving the exposed capillaries to rupture. The blood that vomited out in a boiling pink spume would also be sucked away, to spray in a slow-motion arc across the ground in front of his face before freezing in the minus fifty-five degrees centigrade climate, along with the rest of the victim's body.

That is truly a bitch of a way to die, Alik thought. Whoever blew a hole in the window clearly had no love for the victim he could see on the ground below him.

He had to give NYPD credit; there were already spacesuited figures down there, recording the scene. They had a trollez with them. He just hoped they didn't drop the corpse when they were loading it. It would shatter like a drunk's beer glass.

'It's never the fall that kills you,' Alik murmured.

'It's always the landing,' Salovitz finished.

Alik touched an uneasy finger on the foam metal, praying it wouldn't give. 'So what the fuck punched through this? Another buzz shot?'

'Armour-piercing round. Probably two or three. This diamond-reinforced glass is a tough mother. You got the dough to buy a

room like this for your portalhome, and you get ball-backed guarantees that nothing can go wrong. Forensics picked up the chemical
residue. Faint, because most of it got sucked out along with our guy
down there, but the trace is positive.'

'And it is a guy?'

'Yeah. These two combatants exchanged a few shots in another
room first, then ran in here. The one with the armour-piercing
rounds must have hung back in the doorway and just aimed at the
window. He didn't need accuracy.'

'Which room was he in?'

'The dining room. It's on Ganymede.'

The Ganymede room was a similar set-up to the lunar one. A
fifteen-metre dome, fully radiation proof, with a sunken stone table
in the middle, and twenty black leather chairs around it, their backs
reclined so you could always see the king of the gods a million
kilometres above you.

Alik stood above the edge of the table pit and stared at Jupiter.
It didn't dominate the sky, it was the sky. There were other moons
and stars out there; they just didn't register in the same way.

He instinctively kissed a knuckle, which immediately made him
angry with himself. *You can take the boy out of Paris, Kentucky, without breaking sweat, but try taking the Southern Baptist out of the boy.*

Salovitz was pointing at the lambent yellow tags sticking to the
chairs and table. 'Ordinary nine-millimetre rounds. The pattern
indicates our guy on Mars was in the doorway, shooting in.' He
turned and pointed to the red marker glowing low on the dome
wall. It was sitting on an oval of foamed metal. The explosive-
tipped round hadn't penetrated all the layers that made up this
dome, but the emergency systems clearly weren't taking any
chances. Three mechez were there on the side of the dome, ready
in case the cracks started to multiply.

'The guy in here must have gotten cautious after that first shot.
He didn't fire any more,' Salovitz said.

'So, Cold Martian guy gets scared when the armour-piercing
round gets fired in here,' Alik said, working the events through.
'And ducks into Mars.'

'Pretty much.'

'Dumb thing to do. Are there internal security sensors?'

'No. Guys like Lorenzo don't like the idea of anyone being able to see what goes on inside their house. Someone hacks in, NYPD gets a warrant – all sorts of ways their privacy winds up as i-fodder. The block's entrance down on Central Park West has more security than the pants on a goomah. Then there's equally heavy security on the front door into the hubhall. It's tough for anyone who ain't on the list to get in. But once you're inside, you're totally private.'

'Okay.' He shifted his feet; the blob of foam metal was making him antsy. 'Next?'

The master bedroom was in San Francisco, somewhere on Presidio Heights, looking down on the Golden Gate bridge in the far distance. San Francisco was three hours behind New York, so the streetlights of that fine town were blazing bright into the night while the citizens headed for the Marina and Mission districts to start their revels. Looking at the bed, Alik started to appreciate Kravis Lorenzo's privacy dogma. It was a broad circle with a black leather base, the gelfoam mattress covered in a sheet of royal-purple silk. The four posts were also leather clad, with several insect-eye cameras clustered round them like crystal tumours erupting through the padding. The ceiling above had a circular screen practically the same size as the mattress – that is, before a shotgun blast had reduced it to a rosette of glass daggers and a snow of shattered crystal across the sheets – and the wall behind the headboard (also black leather) sported a broad screen.

Both the duty cops had opened the nightstand drawers to smirk at the pharmacological and electrical aids the Lorenzos took to their marital bed. When Alik and Salovitz came in, they quickly stood upright and studiously ignored the kinky treasure.

Salovitz gestured, and the coroner's sheet was pulled back. Body number four was another male, African, who had been hacked to death; the coup de grâce was a horizontal blow to the mouth, leaving the jaw hanging by a thin strip of skin. Judging from the size and depth of the wounds, Alik reckoned they were made by an axe rather than machete, like a Viking on the rampage. There was another of the big shotguns beside him, identical to the one on the Moon.

'So Hacked-Off here was in the same crew as Mr Shotgun,' Alik said. 'And the boss is badging his guys with these bulled-up shotguns. Anyone like that operating out of New York?' Even as he asked, Shango was searching the FBI database for gangs who'd adopted the model. Plenty of crews used them, but it wasn't standard issue, more a symbol that you were no longer a foot soldier. The higher up the shitheap you crawled, the bigger your gun.

'No,' Salovitz said.

'But you've got to have a decent fabricator to produce one of these,' Alik continued. 'For a start, the barrel will need forty-one, fifty ordnance steel at least.'

'I know where you're going,' Salovitz said. 'And you can stop right there. New York doesn't have fabrication substance permits outside of hazardous or toxic compounds.'

Alik exhaled a martyred sigh. 'Twenty-Eight?'

'Yeah. It's coming, and we're ready for it like the progressives we truly are.'

Like every FBI agent, Alik hated the twenty-eighth amendment: the right for every US citizen to self-fabricate whatever they wish unless it endangers the life or liberty of others, or seeks to overthrow the government. It hadn't been fully ratified, but that was just a matter of time now. In his opinion, the AFA (American Fabrication Alliance) made the NRA look like a bunch of kindergarten pussies when it came to strong-arming Washington. The outcome of Twenty-Eight was that any upright citizen could buy and use weapons-grade material as long as they did not utilize said material to fabricate a weapon. So Alliance members were free to sell whatever raw materials in whatever quantities they wanted. Individual states were already starting to incorporate Twenty-Eight into their legislation in anticipation. The result being that in New York, you didn't need a permit for pretty much anything outside of uranium or nerve gas. Which made life an order of magnitude tougher for law enforcement. In Alik's opinion, Twenty-Eight was storing up serious trouble for the near future. And all because mid-level politicians were money junkies in it for every wattdollar they could be bribed with.

He regarded the shotgun blast in the ceiling. The impact looked as if it was a vertical shot, fired from the bed when Hacked-Off was on his back, under attack from Viking Berserker. A last desperate act, or maybe reflex? It suggested they were creeping round the bedroom, Viking Berserker stalking Hacked-Off, while the others were duking it out it in the rest of the portalhome.

Alik pulled the sheet back over what was left of Hacked-Off's face. 'So this killer got out?'

'Of the bedroom? Sure?'

'How many rooms left?'

'We're over halfway.'

'Fucking wonderful.'

Beijing was the kids' bedrooms. He hesitated in front of the portal door. Kravis and Rose Lorenzo had two kids: Bailey aged nine, and Suki aged twelve. After everything else, Alik wasn't entirely sure he could face dead children.

'It's clean,' Salovitz said, guessing the source of the hesitation.

The view through the Beijing window was tremendously imposing. Skyscrapers – every shape, every style, every direction as far as the eye could see. And all of them illuminated – some artistically, some nothing more than hundred-and-fifty-storey neon and laser adverts. Even with four of Trappist One's exoplanets terraformed by the Chinese state, and immigration at damburst levels, Beijing's population still topped twenty-five million.

Beijing wasn't quite what Alik would give children as their waking view every morning. But, as his sister always told him on his infrequent visits to his nephew, he was a piss-poor uncle, so he reserved judgement.

'Beds are made,' he said after looking in both rooms. The duvets were newly pressed and straight. 'The kids weren't here.'

'We're accessing Kravis and Rose's diaries,' Salovitz said. 'It's taking more time than it should. They're stored on an independent rock squatter G7Turing. It's not cooperating.'

'Get on it,' Alik ordered Shango.

The Antarctic room was the least impressive Alik saw that evening. It was full night outside, and snow was drifting slowly past the curving window. Two forensic officers were on their knees in front of the glass. Sensor drones were infesting the floor like termites spilling from a kicked-over nest.

'What have you got?' he asked the lead tech.

'There's water here, sir,' she said.

'Water?'

Her gloved finger tapped the glass. 'This was opened. The room's climate control logged a sudden fall in temperature fifty-three minutes ago.'

'Did someone come in, or go out?'

She gestured to a clutter of red tags on the floor. 'Blood drops. Preliminary match with the victim in the San Francisco room.'

'Good work,' Alik said approvingly. 'Our Viking Berserker would have been covered in the victim's blood. So he left San Francisco and escaped through here, dripping a trail as he went.'

'Escaped?' Salovitz protested. 'There's nowhere to go out there. It's the fucking Antarctic.'

'You think he slung another body out there?'

'Why hide a dead body? Nobody cared about us finding the others.'

'Okay, good point. And a blood trail isn't proof Viking Berserker actually went outside, just that he was in here.'

'Chasing someone else?'

Alik contemplated the bleak night-time snowscape outside. 'A survivor? Maybe even Lorenzo making a break for it?'

'Out *there*?' Salovitz sneered.

'Bigger survival chance than Mars, or Ganymede. All they have to do is make it to the next portalhome room. There's got to be some close by; developers build them in batches.'

'Shit. Okay.'

'Your people have coats, don't they?' Alik challenged. 'Send them outside. We have to know who went out.'

'We've got coats for New York, not the fucking Antarctic!'

'Okay.' He turned to the lead tech. 'Send a bunch of drones out.

See what they can find. There have to be other portalhome rooms around here.'

She gave the ice vista a dubious look. 'Conditions aren't good, sir.'

'Like I give a shit! I want some kind of camera looking round, even if you have to carry it yourself. I'm going to get some decent cold-weather gear priority-delivered from my office. When it arrives, we can follow up. Meantime, let's take a look at the last body.'

Paris, dawn over the Seine, Notre Dame silhouetted in the cool rose-gold horizon. Very romantic, just right for a guest bedroom. Too bad the man on the floor at the end of the bed no longer appreciated the sight. The shotgun blast had taken most of his head off, sending brain and skull fragments slopping over the thick cream carpet like a rivulet of cold lava.

'So either Mr Shotgun or Hacked-Off did this,' Alik said.

'Yeah.'

'And this is the last body?'

'That we've found. I ain't promising you anything under oath.'

'Which means we're missing whoever was using the axe and the buzz gun.' Alik took a breath, trying to think. 'One person, or two?'

'Once Forensics has finished mapping DNA residuals, we'll have a better picture.'

'Right. Let's see the last couple of rooms.'

Alik had been expecting another gas giant moon, or maybe a comet station, something exotic. Instead the portal door opened into a cabin on the *Jörmungand Celeste*. The huge ocean liner was the most famous on Earth – not hard, considering it was about the only one left. All it did was sail round the oceans on the most leisurely course possible without ever making landfall, but taking in the coastlines of every continent.

He went outside to stand on the private deck belonging to the Lorenzo cabin, and instantly regretted it as he was ambushed by tropical humidity. 'Sonofabitch.' The ocean was a deep grey-blue nearly twelve metres below, with vivacious whitecaps cresting the larger waves. Alik was dressed for New York winter in a nice real-wool suit. The Bureau still hadn't let go of J. Edgar's dress code, and he stuck with it because of the peripherals that could be discreetly incorporated into suit fabric. But a cooling circuit wasn't one of them. Every centimetre of his skin was immediately layered in sweat. 'Where the hell are we?' he asked Shango.

'Approaching Cape Town from the east,' it said. 'The coast will be visible tonight, local time.'

Salovitz was fanning his face with his hand, looking at the swell with disapproval. Neither of them could feel any motion; the *Jörmungand Celeste* was way too big for the waves to affect it.

'If you were going to dump a body, this is the room I'd use, not the Antarctic,' Salovitz said.

'Good point. What's left?'

The tropical island. Alik rolled his eyes as another gust of heat and humidity sluiced over him. He took his suit jacket off as soon as they went through the portal door. It was against Bureau protocol; as well as peripherals, the fabric was lined with a decent armour weave. It made him a sitting duck to a sniper, but he decided to risk it.

The island was where the Maldives used to be – a beautiful coral archipelago in the Indian Ocean whose only industry was tourism. They were beautiful because they were so low-lying, a few metres at best, giving them broad pristine beaches and secluded lagoons. That didn't go well for the indigenous population in the late twenty-first century when the ocean level started rising. The rest of the world built sea defences and tidal barriers to protect their crumbling shorelines and inundated coastal cities. The Maldives didn't have that kind of money, not even with the microfacture revolution brought about by home fabricators and printers, which had liberated so many from absolute poverty.

The archipelago claimed the crown of Atlantis and slowly sank beneath the waves. A true tragedy for a UN World Heritage site.

Then along came astute developers in massive airships with portals fixed underneath. Torrents of desert sand poured down out of the sky, mixed with genetically modified coral seeds. New islands rose up and stabilized.

It was a bitch of a lawsuit. The ex-Maldives population claimed the artificial islands were squatting on their ancestral seabed and should be given to them. But the World Court declared against them – a decision helped by the Chinese, who had long experience with enforcing ownership claims over artificial island territories.

The contemporary islands weren't as big as the old originals. The new owners divided them up like the slices of an exceptionally rich cake, with ten or so wooden shacks on stilts at the back of the beaches.

Stylish mock-antique patio doors slid open in front of Alik, letting him out onto a raised veranda where steps sank into the oven-hot sands. Thirty metres further on, the clear wavelets of the Indian Ocean lapped against the exquisite coral reefs that were still expanding out into the deeper waters.

'Beats the Hamptons,' he muttered in reluctant approval as he walked across the nautical-themed designer-minimalist lounge. A forensic tech was working on the patio door.

'It was forced,' the tech told Salovitz. 'Alarms disabled, and the lock physically cut out.'

'From the outside?' Alik guessed.

'Yes, sir.'

'Any blood in here?' Salovitz asked.

'The preliminary scan didn't show any.'

'One team comes in via crazy gymnastics seventeen storeys up in a night-time snowfall, the other saunters across a beach,' Alik said. 'No prizes here for which team has the brains.'

He and Salovitz walked down the steps to the beach, where he reluctantly put his jacket back on, which earned several curious looks. But he figured that if this was a route in, the team might have a hot backup waiting to provide cover. So if they'd been waiting with growing anxiety for their buddies to return, and the first out of the boutique shack was a bunch of cops heading towards them . . .

Three of NY's finest were making their way back across the beach. They'd all taken their winter jackets off and sweat was soaking their thick shirts.

'Found the way the intruder team got onto the island,' the

sergeant told Salovitz. 'The shack two down. Its patio door was open. We went in. There's a body in the hubhall.'

'Where is the hubhall?' Alik asked.

The sergeant pushed his cap back, and gave him rueful look. 'My altme said Berlin.'

'Aw crap,' Salovitz groaned, raising his eyes to the bright cloudless sky. 'This just keeps getting better. I fucking hate portalhomes.'

'I'll put an official call through the Bureau to the Berlin police,' Alik reassured him. 'I know a guy in the city. They can run forensics at their end, and I'll send you the results.'

'Okay,' Salovitz said. 'Set up a cordon round the shack, and don't go inside again.'

'You got it, detective,' the sergeant said.

The forensic tech in the Antarctic room called over the police scene link. 'We found something, detective. Another portalhouse room, close to the Lorenzo property, with a broken window. I tried sending a drone through, but something killed it.'

Alik and Salovitz looked at each other and headed back up the beach fast. As they went inside the shack, Shango checked with Alik's office. The Antarctic gear courier was en route, estimated three minutes from Central Park West.

'Run,' Alik ordered them.

The tech in the Antarctic room was standing beside the window; her eyes closed as she controlled the drones through her altme. Snow was melting on the floor round her feet.

'Speak to me,' Salovitz said.

'I sent five drones out,' she said. 'Their flight's not good in the snow, and the visual imagery is poor. I'm relying a lot on the millimetre-wave radar. But they found another portalhome room a hundred and fifty metres away. The window is programmable glass, but it's not open; there's just a hole in it, roughly a metre across. I've tried sending two drones through now, but each one died. It's like an explosion. They fall apart, but there's no heat or energy flash.'

'Buzz shot,' Alik said. 'The hole could be tangled with filament.'

'What use is making a hole in the glass you can't get through?' Salovitz asked.

'If you take a buzz gun on a job, you wear the right protective armour,' Alik told him. 'Those filaments aren't the most reliable when it comes to travelling in the right direction after expansion.'

'So they could have gotten through the hole?'

'Most likely.'

The courier arrived with their Antarctic gear – five suits with FBI printed in bold yellow across the back. They were one-piece units, with boots and a hood that had a sealable visor, fully heated. Practically spacesuits. Alik and Salovitz started putting them on, along with the forensic tech and two cops.

'Try and avoid shooting your pistols,' Alik told them. 'The cold will affect them.'

They gave him uncertain glances, but agreed they'd hold off unless they were taking fire.

Alik took an electron pistol out of his underarm holster and clipped it onto the Antarctic suit's belt. The cold would make it brittle, but he thought the components would still work. Probably.

Shango confirmed the suit's integrity and ordered the glass to open. Snow swirled in.

Alik's feet sank a good ten centimetres into the loose snow as he started to tramp across to the next portalhome. He kept the drone sensor imagery on sharp resolution across his tarsus lens, merging the bright scarlet grid of the millimetre radar with his own eyesight. The lens had a low-light amplification program which kicked in as soon as he got outside. He'd never liked the sparkly green shading the two-tone image always produced. It wasn't much use in the Antarctic, either; a snowfield at night had as much contrast as a franchise coffee shop.

At least the suit worked okay, keeping him decently warm.

They all lined up facing the room. Most of the structure was covered in a layer of snow, making it look like a futurist's igloo, with the curving glass panorama window a jarring black bulge along the front. The three remaining disc-shaped drones hovered outside, constantly swooping about like alcoholic sparrows as they tried to hold position in the sharp squalls of freezing air.

326

Alik studied the hole carefully, but not even his tarsus lens enhancements could see if there was a hash of filaments clinging to it.

'If someone in a protective suit went through, wouldn't it clear the filaments away?' Salovitz asked.

'The bulk of them, yeah,' Alik agreed. 'But there will be plenty of strands left behind. You need a proper hazard disposal team to clear the area before it's rated human-safe again. The worse the environment you fire a buzz shot in, the bigger the dispersal problem. We just need to clear the hole enough to send one of those drones through.'

'Your e-pistol?'

'Let's find out.' He knelt down, knees compacting the snow, and angled the electron pistol up at the hole. That way, the beam would only strike the ceiling beyond. Shango selected a de-focused beam on high power. He fired ten pulses.

Snowflakes inside the electron stream vaporized into steam-puffs, shrouded in their own fizz of St Elmo's fire. The hole itself scintillated with bright elongated sparks as the filaments broke down from the energy barrage.

'Send a drone through now,' he said once the mini-fireworks had finished popping.

One of the drones flashed forwards, passing unharmed through the hole. Its visual images improved immediately in the calmer air of the room. There were two bodies lying on the floor, a man and a woman in late middle age. Both shot through the head. The sensors couldn't pick up any active power circuits, and that included the portal on the back wall.

'The escape route,' Salovitz declared.

'Yeah. So now we just have to work out if Buzz Gun Man is also Viking Berserker, or if two of them go out afterwards. I also want to know where this room's hubhall is situated.'

'The DNA profiles will be in within an hour. We can get a better timeline map from that.'

'Okay, then, let's get back to the precinct.'

*

New York's Twentieth Precinct house was situated on West 82nd Street, only two metrohubs from the apartment block on Central Park West. Even in the snow, it was less than three minutes to walk door to door.

Alik and Salovitz got in just before one in the morning. The precinct commander, Brandy 'The Deacon' Duncan, was in her office on the second floor. She was courteous enough to Alik, but he knew he was about as welcome as a stripper in a cathedral.

Salovitz gave her a decent enough summary of the case. Seven bodies, the Lorenzo family's whereabouts unknown and not responding to any calls, their altmes off grid.

'Why would these crews target Lorenzo? What's he involved in?' The Deacon asked, staring at Alik. She was in her late fifties, streetwise, and with enough clout in City Hall to hang onto the Twentieth for eight years now. Her face was etched with the entropy of a lifetime of prize-fights on both sides of the desk – the ones that had got her where she was. Alik respected that; she was actually quite a good cop.

'I'm only here because of the jurisdiction thing,' he said.

'Bullshit,' she grunted. 'Anaka, Devial, Mortalo & Lorenzo.'

'What about it?'

'They have political contacts. Kiss a lot of important asses.'

'I'm here to help. I can short-cut certain areas for you. I'm already helping with Berlin. If this is a snatch case, then time is critical here. Do you want the media to be showing the world a dead family on your watch?'

She looked at Salovitz. 'Is it a kidnapping?'

'No way. Only one person got out of that goddamn abattoir: a genuine axe murderer.'

Her umpire's gaze came back to Alik.

'Then where are they?' he asked. 'We need to find out.'

'I'll take your help,' the Deacon said grudgingly. 'But this is the Twentieth Precinct's case. Don't try claiming anything else, especially not to your media buddies.'

'I have no buddies in the media, and I'm officially requesting that my name and involvement is kept off record. If it is a kidnapping, we don't want to alert them to any Bureau involvement at this stage.'

'Sure, I believe that. If it's not a kidnapping, what else could it be?'

'There was an attempted bust into Lorenzo's secure company network,' Salovitz said.

'What were they looking for?'

'I don't know yet; Forensics have the systems in their digital lab. You know what it's like getting any sense out of those nerds.'

'So one crew breaks in and starts a digital bust, then another crew shows up and the shit hits the fan,' the Deacon said. 'Any chance crew two were a black countermeasures crew contracted by Anaka, Devial, Mortalo & Lorenzo when they realized what was happening?'

'That's a stretch, chief,' Salovitz said.

Her gaze flicked to Alik like a first-grade teacher's laser pointer highlighting the obvious. 'But possible. Right, Agent Monday?'

'At this stage the Bureau is not ruling out anything. We want the surviving killer detained as swiftly as possible. However—'

'Here we go,' the Deacon muttered in antipathy.

'If crew one was a digital bust operation, crew two got there remarkably quickly for countermeasures. Not impossible, but un- usual. They also don't seem that professional. None of them were in the same clothes, and only two weapons were the same.'

'So how do you read it?'

'The Lorenzos are away, for whatever reason. Somebody knew that, and two high-end burglary crews targeted the portalhome. There was a lot of wealth in there. Naturally one team came armed with an i-head; data is as valuable as jewellery, and more so if you have the right files.'

'Coincidence? Seriously?'

'It doesn't read like one crew was there to defend the Lorenzos. If the family was out for one night only, then it's not quite coinci- dence that we have two teams showing up.'

Alik could see how much she wanted to argue. Instead she reluctantly had to concede. 'Okay. Priority one: find and secure the Lorenzo family. Call his colleagues and her friends; somebody has to know where they were going.'

'Yes, chief,' Salovitz said.

'And let me know if anyone slows you down.' Again the laser-pointer stab between Alik's eyes.

Salovitz grinned as they trooped downstairs to the first floor. 'You're still alive. Impressive.'

'Yeah,' Alik grunted. 'She's secretly got the hots for me; you can tell.'

'You really think it's a coincidence?'

'It's a working theory that works. To get a handle on this, we need to know where the Lorenzos are. That's when we start to understand what the fuck actually happened.'

'Yeah.'

The office which the Deacon had assigned the case team was at the back of the building, with frosted glass windows, ten desks and a hemispherical virtual stage at the far end, three metres in diameter.

Bietzk was already there when Alik arrived, along with a couple of sergeants he recognized from the portalhome. The precinct's senior forensic technician, Rowan El-Alosaimi, had claimed one desk, assembling data coming in from the sensors the Forensic Agency team had deployed.

Alik had barely got through the door when the stage lit up with a 3D layout of the portalhome. They couldn't do it to scale; the rooms beyond the hubhall would've overlapped. The corpses started to materialize.

'Anything on the Lorenzos?' Salovitz asked.

'Not yet,' Bietzk said. 'I'm on to Connexion Security. They're going to send us their metrohub logs. Meanwhile, I'm running a continuing global ping on their altmes. No response yet. They're still off grid.'

'We're getting the DNA results in,' Rowan said. 'There are some matches from the general medisure database and three already in the Justice Department POI list.'

'Splash them,' Alik told her.

Tags flipped up over the corpses. Shango interfaced with the stage, and his tarsus lenses magnified the data.

Scalped New York Broad was Lisha Khan. According to Bureau records she was a mid-level soldier for an NY syndicate run by one Javid-Lee Boshburg, who'd carved himself a territory from South Brooklyn all the way down to Sheepshead Bay, thanks to an income from narcotics fabrication and distribution, along with half a dozen clubs and plenty of protection. He trafficked girls in from across North and South America, with Lisha Khan helping to keep them in order.

Mr Shotgun on the Moon: Otto Samule. A lieutenant for Rayner Grogan, whose territory was a tumour bruising the citizens of West Queens, with ties to technology unions across the city, as well as standard-issue interests in clubs and land development enterprises. According to the NYPD gang task force, he also ran a couple of crash crews who went through high-end apartments like a locust swarm when the owners were out. Alik nodded in satisfaction at how that fitted with what they'd found in the Lorenzo portalhome.

The Cold Martian: Duane Nordon. Another known associate of Javid-Lee.

Hacked-Off: Perigine Lexi. Senior lieutenant for Javid-Lee.

Paris Dawn: Koushick Flaviu, on Rayner Grogan's payroll, an inseparable buddy of Otto Samule; the two of them were known to work together most of the time.

'Now we're getting somewhere,' Alik decided. 'Grogan versus Boshburg. Except . . . Otto Samule and Perigine Lexi are on opposing teams, so why the hell did they have the same type of custom-build shotgun?'

'We don't know the shotgun next to Lexi's body was his,' Salovitz said. 'Maybe he grabbed it off one of Grogan's people?'

'Hmm.' Alik wasn't convinced.

Forensic files started to splash across his lenses. Koushick Flaviu and Otto Samule both had sand on their shoes, matching the Maldives island beach. Equally, Lisha Khan, Duane Nordon and Perigine Lexi all had trace water on their soles, indicating they had invaded the portalhome via the Central Park West balcony.

Salovitz stood with hands on hips, watching the data points rising across the stage as Rowan fed in more and more results. The deaths had all occurred within five minutes of each other, approximately eleven o'clock at night. 'And at least one of the Rayner crew escaped,' Salovitz beefed. He turned to Bietzk. 'We need a full list of associates for both crews.'

A secure file from Nikolai Kristjánsson splashed across Alik's lens. He cleared it for the case office, and it splashed into the stage.

'Koushick was performing the secure network hack,' Bietzk said, reading the new data. 'Her residuals were all over the node we pulled out of the Central Park West utility room.'

Salovitz turned to Alik. 'Do you think that's why Mr Shotgun took his head off?'

'None of this was a warning, it was straight-out slaughter. They all knew there was no way out other than over the other team's bodies.'

'Find out what kind of grudge match Javid-Lee and Rayner have going on,' Salovitz told Bietzk. 'If there's nothing on record, get the gang task force out of bed and see what whispers there are. I need some traction here.'

Shango reported that the Lorenzo diaries had been accessed. 'Got something for you,' Alik said, and sent the files across the police case link. Both Kravis and Rose's diaries had the same entry for the previous day: Palm Beach with Niall and Belvina Kanoto, on their yacht.

Shango called Niall Kanoto.

It took a while to get a response. Niall's altme was set for zero interruption, which Alik's Bureau authority overrode. He eventually answered, audio only.

'Yes?' it was a puzzled voice coming out of the office speakers.

'Niall Kanoto?'

'Who is this?'

'Special Agent Monday, FBI. Please access your altme call data certificate for authentication.'

'Yeah yeah, sure. You're FBI. What the hell do you want? Do you know what time it is?'

'I'm trying to locate Kravis Lorenzo and his family. Are they with you?'

'What is this? Is Krav in trouble?'

'Answer the question please, sir. Where is Kravis Lorenzo?'

'Back home, I guess.'

'They were scheduled to visit you today.'

'Sure, man. We were going to spend the weekend together, both families. But we had to cancel, you know?'

'I do not know, sir. Why was the visit cancelled?'

'The goddamn yacht, *Sea Star III*. My marina service company called me this afternoon. They prep her for me every time before I take her out: food, power charge, general maintenance, that kind of shit. This time the engine diagnostics showed a fault. They had to take the old girl out of the water to fix her. So we cancelled. It's a twenty-four-carat buttpain. Bel and Rose had been planning this for months; we were going to take *Sea Star* all the way down to the Keys.'

'So you spoke to Kravis this afternoon?'

'Sure. He was disappointed. Our kids all get on, you know? It was a big family event.'

'You spoke with him? It wasn't just an altme message?'

'Yeah. He was still in the office, at his desk.'

'Did he say where he would go instead?'

'No. What is this? What's happened to Kravis?'

'We can't locate him. Did he indicate if he would go somewhere else for the weekend?'

'No. He was kind of pissed he'd have to spend the weekend at home, you know? Me too. Why, what's happened?'

'We don't know what's happened.'

'Jesus, is he all right?'

Alik put that particular stupidity down to the time of night. 'I need the name of your marina service company; please send it to my altme. And if any of the Lorenzo family contact you, you're to inform me at once. Understand?'

'Yeah. But come on, man, what's happened to them?'

'We don't know.' Alik ended the call and told Shango to load an observation routine on Niall Kanoto's access codes, then put another on his immediate family as well. If Kravis did attempt to get in touch with his yachting buddy, the Precinct G7Turing would know before him.

'Confirming this,' Bietzk said. 'Connexion logged the Lorenzo family entering the metrohub loop in the Village at nine seventeen in the evening, and coming out at the Central Park West hub next to their block three minutes later. That's their last recorded usage.'

A big wallscreen started showing the Central Park West metrohub's video surveillance log. Everyone in the case office watched as the Lorenzo family came out of the loop portal. The scene was exceptional in how ordinary it was. Alik could so easily believe it was some kind of ideal family advert. Mom: beautiful, young, smiling; dad: older and measured; the kids with smiles and laughter showing off great dentistry as they joked and teased each other.

Shango connected to the National Citizenship Records Agency and ran characteristics recognition. It was them.

Bietzk switched from the Central Park West hub to the street's civic surveillance video log. The Lorenzos left the metrohub behind and walked twenty-five metres down the sidewalk, until they turned into the entrance of their apartment block. Metadata time-stamp: nine twenty-one.

'Get the Precinct Turing to run a sweep on that video file for the rest of the night,' Salovitz said. 'I want to know if they come out again after that. And who else went into the apartment block.'

'Got it,' Bietzk said.

While they were processing that, Alik called the Bureau office in Palm Beach, while Shango rode the Precinct G7Turing into the network of the marina service company Kanoto used. It pulled the file for *Sea Star III*, which to his inexpert eye looked like a slightly smaller version of the *Jörmungand Celeste*.

One of the service company's engineers had been on board that morning, running a final seaworthiness inspection when the yacht's diagnostic had flagged up the engine problem, some kind of contaminant particles in the gear system. If the engine was switched on, there was a high risk the entire gearing mechanism would seize up. The service company had logged a call to Niall Kanoto, informing him the whole thing had to be dismantled and cleaned.

The engineer was called Ali Renzi. An infiltration ping to his altme revealed his location in central Miami. Three agents from the Miami Central office were dispatched to pick him up.

'The Central Park West civic surveillance log has been compromised,' Bietzk said. 'Someone's run a sophisticated non-space edit, cutting human-sized areas out and replacing them with looped background. I'm guessing that's Javid Lee's crew entering the apartment block.'

'Can you track the infiltration?' Salovitz asked.

'Our department can't,' Bietzk glanced at Alik. 'I can contract a major digital audit outfit?'

'Do it,' Salovitz said.

'What about the apartment block's internal security surveillance?' Alik asked.

'Deactivated. They infiltrated and shut it down without triggering any alarms. Whoever their i-head was, they knew what they were doing.'

'All right,' Alik said. 'Let's take a step back here. They won't have come in through the nearest hub. That would give any investigation too much data. But . . . they weren't expecting this to be a major homicide investigation, either. So, have your Turing work all the surveillance around the apartment, see if you can backtrack the Javid Lee crew through their edits. Find out where they came from. Somewhere along the line they'll leave their image on a log.'

Bietzk gave the agent a quick nod and started instructing his altme.

'Connexion hasn't logged the Lorenzos in any hub since they exited Central Park West,' Salovitz said. 'So where the fuck are they?'

Alik stared at the holographic display on the stage, mentally reviewing the number of ways out of that portalhome. 'We're overthinking this,' he decided. 'Let's stop relying on Turings and Forensics, and go back to basics.'

'Like what?' Salovitz asked sceptically.

'We've been looking for a technical solution and I'm not sure it's applicable. Think about this: half a dozen fuckheads break into your apartment armed with some heavy-duty shit. You don't have time to get smart. You have to get yourself and your kids *out*, and fast. So, this apartment block is, what? Twenty storeys high? Three or four apartments on each floor? Have we physically searched it?'

'Not yet,' Salovitz admitted. 'Just the seventeenth floor.'

'You need to get it done.'

'I'll call in some more people,' he said reluctantly.

Alik claimed a desk and sat down. Coffee was brought in. Out of a vending machine, but he didn't complain out loud; he needed the cops on his side. Shango splashed a whole load of data on his lenses. He was examining family and known associates for each of the corpses.

And he was pretty certain he wouldn't be the only one looking at those lists. Word of the police arriving at the apartment would be spreading. The survivor who took the Antarctic plunge would have spoken to Rayner. Javid-Lee would be wanting to know why his people hadn't come back; probably sending someone to take a look along Central Park West, and they would have seen the cops establishing a crime scene perimeter. He knew he didn't have much time. It wasn't as if the gangs still practised *omertà*, but even the dumbest street soldier knew the one thing you didn't do was go shouting your mouth off to the cops – or worse: the Feds.

But Alik was a firm believer in the truism that every chain was only as strong as its weakest link. He just had to make the right choice of link.

Twenty minutes later, two agents from the FBI Miami office escorted Ali Renzi into the Twentieth Precinct. To keep the Deacon sweet, Alik suggested that Salovitz should lead the interview, leaving him and Bietzk to watch it on the stage, with a link open to the detective in case they wanted to put any extra questions to him.

The stage hologram was detailed, showing Renzi as a chilled guy, an attitude fine-tuned to show everyone what an innocent he was, how this must be some big mistake. It was a dick move, Alik thought; the genuinely innocent get very nervous being waltzed into a precinct house at two o'clock in the morning.

Ali Renzi was still in his Miami clubbing clothes: a short-sleeved shirt with a weird fantasy alien lion embroidered on it, and tight black pants. A quick march through a New York January night had left him shivering as he stood under the interview room's air-con vent, trying to get warm.

Bietzk gave Shango access to the body scan. Renzi's heart rate was high, as was his blood toxicology. Neural activity showed his brain was cranked up. Alik supressed a smile at the tell of nervous energy.

Salovitz walked in. 'Sit, please.'

Renzi gave the air-con grille a last look, and reluctantly sat at the table opposite Salovitz.

'Would you like a lawyer present?' Salovitz asked. 'If you don't have one, a public defender will be appointed. If you do not have insurance cover, you will be liable for their costs.'

'Am I under arrest? I didn't get read no rights.'

'No, this isn't an arrest; for now you are a material witness.'

'For what?'

'Tell me about the *Sea Star III*.'

'That's a sweet yacht. I run service on it sometimes.' He smiled broadly, putting on the Latino strut.

'Ali,' Salovitz said the name like he was calling out a fifth-grader.

'What?'

'Let me give you some free advice here. You don't have a criminal record, and I can see you're basically a decent guy, so don't get me pissed. Understand?'

'What's up, man? I service it. I told you.'

'We track you down at two in the morning and bring you all the way up here, where I ask you about a yacht you serviced yesterday morning, and you tell me: sometimes? You need to start pumping up your IQ. Because serious doesn't even begin to cover this.'

'Pump my what?'

'Get smart, Ali. What happened to the *Sea Star*?'

'The gearing, man. The diagnostics redlined. It was towed to drydock. The company's working on it.'

'Shit, you're just not listening, are you? Okay, then, this is how it's going to go now. You talking to me, telling me what I need to know, that results in the precinct giving you breakfast and letting you go. No charges, and our thanks for assisting us in a multiple homicide.'

'Multip— *What*?'

'Shut the fuck up!' Salovitz's fist slammed down on the table. 'I'm talking. Now if you don't cooperate, I will tie you into this, and you'll be facing an accomplice charge – and probably conspiracy, too. For this crime – seven bodies that we've found so far – you'll be straight to Zagreus, and not the good end of the canyon.'

'No fucking way, man! I didn't kill anybody.'

'In law, complicity is the same as participating.'

'I didn't do anything!'

'Good. So now I have a question for you, and you're gonna think hard about this, because I'm laying it out real simple. If I run a search through your accounts, which I haven't done yet because you're being a concerned helpful citizen at this point, but *if* I run one, will I find an unexplained cash payment paid in recently? Take your time, and think. The rest of your life depends on how you answer.'

Renzi seemed to have got over his wintery cold. Sweat was breaking out across his forehead, and his skin was turning pale so fast Alik considered he could've had chameleon genes. 'Yeah,' Renzi said, not making eye contact with Salovitz. 'Friend of a friend, he helped me out. These are bad times, you know. The economy.'

Salovitz put his card down on the table like he was a Vegas pro about to scoop the cash. 'Look at the faces, Ali. Are any of them the friend of a friend?'

Renzi glanced down. 'Jesus!' He slapped a hand over this mouth as his cheeks bulged.

'Keep looking,' Salovitz ordered.

The card was showing him all the bodies in situ. In the cases of Perigine Lexi and Koushick Flaviu, a mugshot from records was shown, to clarify their identity.

'That one,' Renzi said, and turned away.

'Koushick Flaviu?'

'He said his name was Dylan.'

'And what did you do for him?'

'Rigged the diagnostic. He wanted to be sure nobody was going anywhere on the *Sea Star* this weekend. Getting it out of the water was the easy answer.'

'When did you meet him?'

'He turned up at my condo that morning. He knew who I was, what I did, everything. Man, you don't say no to people like that! And it didn't hurt nobody.'

Salovitz's finger casually circled the card. 'Nobody hurt, huh?'

'You know what I mean, man! I didn't do anything. This isn't down to me.'

'Maybe. Now, what else did this guy that called himself Dylan say?'

'He didn't say anything, just to disable the yacht. I swear, man! I swear it; on my mother's grave.'

'Did he say why he wanted it out of the water?'

'No. Nothing.'

'So have you ever done favours like this for people before?'

'No, man, no way.'

'You want to ask him anything?' Salovitz asked Alik through the precinct link.

'No. I'll have the Bureau run a full background review on him. If he's clean, you can bounce him out of here after breakfast.'

*

While Salovitz was tidying up in the interview room, Alik put a call in to Tansan, his Capitol Hill contact. They'd met two decades ago, and formed a mutually beneficial relationship. There were small discreet favours asked for, and since then Alik had enjoyed a smooth ride inside the Bureau, with clearance almost level with the director. And the director wouldn't have wanted anything to do with some of the things he knew.

'It was a well-organized operation,' Alik told Tansan. 'To start with at least. But I'm puzzled why a low-level New York gang is trying to bust its way into Pentagon ultra files.'

'You may have to go and ask them.'

'That could get difficult. I suspect they'll be nervous right about now, what with their brothers in arms being butchered, and all.'

'Do you need backup? I have some dark funds available if you need to hire some experts.'

'I'm going to see where this investigation leads for a while. It's a very odd coincidence, both crews turning up at the same time. And if you do want to bust Pentagon ultra files, you don't hire a bunch of New York punks, because that's what these assholes were. I need to find out who escaped through Antarctica. They might have some answers.'

'Very well. Keep me informed. I need to know who wanted those files, and why.'

*

Alik ran through all the dead gang members again and decided that the weakest link was likely to be Adrea Halfon, Perigine Lexi's squeeze. Some of the girls who attached themselves with connected guys could be tougher than their men. This one? Alik had a hunch she was one of the other kind: brittle and dependent. Perigine had lifted her out of the gutter. He was her world; without him she was nothing. If he and Salovitz could just get to her before Javid-Lee sent anyone round . . .

Alik and Salovitz walked along the south radial out of Manhattan, then took the 32nd loop to the Manhattan Beach Park hub. They almost called a two-seat cabez, but it'd stopped snowing by then, so the pair of them walked west along Oriental Boulevard.

'So you think it was a kidnapping?' Salovitz asked. 'Rayner went to a lot of effort to fuck up the Lorenzos' weekend. That crew wanted them at the portalhome.'

'And Javid-Lee's crew thought they were going to be out on a yacht, so the portalhome would be empty. Which is why they both wound up in Central Park West together. But I don't think it was a kidnapping.'

'What then?'

'Access to the Anaka, Devial, Mortalo & Lorenzo network requires some biometrics. Having Kravis present in the flesh would've been a big help to Lisha Khan. Her gear had biometric readers. Plus, if you're holding his family, that gives you plenty of leverage.'

'So it was all about busting the files?'

'Could be, for the Rayner crew. But that still doesn't tell us where the Lorenzos are now.'

They turned into Dover Street just after three o'clock in the morning. Nothing else was moving, not even street cleanez. The snow was thick under Alik's feet, crunching down under his soles.

It was a decent neighbourhood; the houses all had neat yards, several with boats parked outside. Perigine's was halfway along; the only one with its lights on.

Salovitz took the steps up onto the little porch and pressed the doorbell. The house network asked for identification, which their altmes supplied.

Adrea Halfon opened the door and peered out nervously. She'd been crying. 'Yeah?' her voice was soft, catching in her throat.

'NYPD, ma'am,' Salovitz said. 'May we come in?'

She didn't say anything, just backed in and left the door open. Alik and Salovitz followed her. They looked ahead, then looked at each other, careful to remain expressionless, then looked ahead again. Adrea's house coat was a loose weave of black lace, lined with fluffy purple feathers – a Schrödinger masterpiece in being dressed and undressed at the same time. Perigine had found her in one of Javid-Lee's clubs, and she'd obviously thanked him for getting her out by keeping in the exact same shape that had captured him in the first place. Seeing Adrea in the flesh, Alik was certain he'd made the right choice; the smell of insecurity was as strong as her perfume.

'I have some bad news, ma'am,' Salovitz said when they were in the living room. The place was as brash as Alik had expected. Somebody whose taste came straight out of Hong Kong virtuals had been given too much money and licence to create their dream home. Everything clashed – colours, furniture, ornaments, pictures; he counted styles from at least four different eras.

Adrea nodded, a single sharp jerk of the head. She already knew. 'What's that, officer?'

'Your partner, Perigine Lexi, I'm afraid our officers have found him dead. My sympathies.'

She sank into a heavily cushioned couch and reached for the

tumbler on the marble table beside it. A bottle of cheap bourbon was already open. 'That's terrible,' she said.

'The way he died, yeah,' Alik agreed. 'Terrible.'

She shot him a fearful glance. 'How . . .?'

'He was in the wrong place in the wrong time with the wrong people. But you wouldn't know anything about that, right?'

'I don't know where he was tonight. He said he was meeting some friends in a bar.'

'What does he do for a living?'

'He's a manager at Sidereal Urban Management.'

Alik read the file Shango splashed for him. 'City clean-up company, huh? Sidereal has the contract for Gravesend and Sheepshead Bay?'

'Yeah, that's the one.' Her hand shook as she took another slug of bourbon.

'Strange, we found him in an uptown apartment. He was robbing the place.'

'I don't know nothing about that.'

'One of the people with him, we think it's Duane Nordon. Would you mind identifying him for me, please?' He held up his card.

'Sure.' She glanced at the image of Duane's frozen bloodless face, and screamed. Ran out of the room. Alik and Salovitz stared meaningfully at each other to the soundtrack of violent retching.

A couple of minutes later Adrea reappeared in the doorway, clutching her housecoat tight closed; something it just wasn't built for. 'You son of a bitch!'

'Yes, ma'am. There were two crews hit that apartment, and they ripped each other apart like sharks on acid. Your Perigine, he got lucky: a clean shot. Duane, not so much.'

Her hand went to her mouth as the tears dripped down her cheeks.

'They took out two of the other crew,' Alik continued relentlessly, 'but one of them got away. Any idea who Rayner would use for a job like this?'

'I don't know anything.'

'You think Javid-Lee is your friend? That he'll do right by you?

Right now he's looking to cover his ass. So you tell me what you think is going to happen if we take you along to the Twentieth Precinct and hold you there for a couple of days. I can do that – you'll be a custodial witness, so there's no charge filed. That means you don't get Miranda rights, so no lawyer for twenty-four hours.'

'I haven't done anything,' she protested as she sank back into the couch.

'We might need to check that. But it doesn't matter, because Javid-Lee is going to want to know what you said for two days before we let his lawyer in to see you. He'll want to know pretty bad. And if you keep telling him: *nothing*, is he going to believe you, do you think?'

She was really sobbing now, staring up at Alik with more hatred than a whole KKK chapter. 'Bastard. I hope your balls get cancer and it creeps up your spine!'

'Sure thing, sweetheart. On the other hand, we came down here to inform you of Perigine's death, just like the city requires. We stayed a few minutes and left when it was obvious you weren't giving us squat. Do you think that would play better?'

'What do you want?'

'I want to know what the fuck is going on.'

'Perigine didn't say much. I only heard about it after the fire.'

'What fire?'

'The Blueshift Starlight Lounge. It's one of Javid-Lee's places.'

'Where you worked?' Salovitz asked.

'I don't do that no more,' she said petulantly. 'And I never danced there; it's on the way down, you know? But I knew a couple of girls who wound up there.'

'When was this fire?' I asked.

'A couple of days back. The fire started in the kitchen. Supposed to be an accident, but everyone knew that was bull. Peri said Javid-Lee knew it was Rayner that ordered it along with whacking Riek. That's when Javid told Peri to take care of the Farrons to equalize things with Rayner, you know? He can't afford to show any weakness, not after two strikes against him. You let that go, people think

343

you're weak, and next thing you just vanish. He had to send a message, a loud one.'

'Wait,' Alik said. 'Go back. Who the fuck is Riek?'

'He was small-time, right at the bottom of Javid-Lee's organization. But Peri said he did a shakedown for Javid-Lee a couple of days before. Next thing we know, he's being pulled out of the marina – same day as the Blueshift fire.'

'What did Riek do? Who was the shakedown?'

'I don't know – just that it was one of Rayner's people. Whatever it was, it got Rayner pissed at Riek. That ain't exactly hard.'

'And the Farrons? Who are they?'

'The people Peri was going to take care of to get Javid-Lee back level again.'

'So Javid-Lee and Rayner are at war? How long's this been going on?'

She shrugged. 'This week. Peri's been coming home late; he's been like in this real filthy temper the whole time. It's always respect with the boys. You gotta show respect. If you don't, if you step out of line, you get sent a message. That's how it's always been.'

*

The Dover Street air was cold and rich with the sharp scent of the Atlantic that lurked a few hundred metres away. Alik inhaled deeply, hoping it would be like some kind of cleansing agent. 'These sons of bitches, they still live in the Middle Ages.'

Salovitz chuckled. 'You lowering yourself, coming down here from D.C.?'

'Nah,' Alik admitted. 'It's plenty more savage there. Maybe less blood, but twice as much pain.'

'Amen to that, my friend. What now?'

'This still isn't making a whole load of sense,' Alik complained as they started walking back down the street. Shango splashed the NYPD report on Riek Patterson, who had been pulled out of the Caesar's Bay Marina two days ago. He couldn't swim. Well, Alik admitted, it would be difficult for anyone with fifty kilos of metal chain wrapped round their legs. On the same day, the district fire crew were called out to a kitchen fire in the Blueshift Starlight Lounge. 'Okay,' he said, lining it up in his head. 'Whatever Riek did, Rayner was psycho enough about it to order two hits in retaliation. Javid-Lee counters by sending Perigine's crew to take out the Farrons, whoever the fuck they are. Then Perigine winds up in the Lorenzo portalhome, getting his ass blown off by Rayner's crew, who are also running a file bust there at the same time.'

'Still think it's coincidence?'

'I have no idea what to think.'

'Don't tell me. You need more information.'

'You think you don't?' Alik shot back. Then Shango splashed the weirdest file of the night. 'Holy shit!'

'What?'

He shared the file. 'Delphine Farron is the Lorenzos' housekeeper.'

'You are shitting me?' Salovitz barked.

'Access the fucking file.'

'So who do you want to talk to next?'

'Wait one.' Shango pinged Delphine Farron's code. No reply. Her altme was off grid. 'Uh oh. Get a uniform squad round to their address, right now.'

'Christ. I'm on it.'

'Is that why Perigine was round at the Lorenzos' place?' Alik wondered out loud. 'Hunting the Farron woman?' Then he read further down the file Shango had harvested on Delphine Farron. 'Oh, this just keeps getting better. Look at this shit; Delphine is Rayner's second cousin.'

'This can't be right,' Salovitz said. 'If Perigine had whacked the Farron woman in the portalhome, we'd have found her body.'

'Not if they went for a walk in the Antarctic,' I said. 'We barely found the next portalhouse room.'

'Perigine and his crew weren't wearing polar gear.'

'Yeah,' Alik admitted sourly. 'Good point. Ask the Precinct to get Connexion's log on Delphine Farron. I want to know where she is.'

They reached the Manhattan Beach Park hub as Alik finished reviewing Riek Patterson's file. 'Change of plan,' he announced. 'We're going to West Brooklyn.'

'For what?'

'Pay our respects to the widow Patterson.'

*

Geographically, Stillwell Avenue wasn't that far from away from Dover Street, but status-wise Alik was getting vertigo from the drop. They found the small projects where Riek Patterson rented a few rooms easily enough; nearly half of the building was derelict. The rest of the inhabitants vanished like rats into the cracks as soon as the two of them stepped over the threshold. Alik didn't think they'd be dumb enough to try and tangle with one of the city's finest and a Fed, but you never knew what kind of weird neurochemical shit their twenty-year-old synthesizers squeezed out, or how it affected them.

Colleana Patterson was awake. Ordinarily he'd take that as a sign of guilt – three thirty in the morning is when the baddest of them all come out to play – but the two-month-old cradled in her arm was evidence to the contrary. It looked as if she'd been awake for half a year, and crying for most of that. She was a complete physical and emotional wreck. The tiny apartment was a cluttered mess that smelt of stale food and toxic diapers.

'What now?' she wailed; she didn't even bother checking their credentials.

'Did you know Perigine Lexi and his crew were hit tonight?' Alik asked.

She collapsed back into her one big chair in the scabby living room, sobbing. That set the kid off, howling like a small banshee. Alik waited. Sure enough, a neighbour started banging on the wall.

'I need your help,' he said when her misery reached a peak.

'I don't know anything! How many goddamn times do I have to tell you people?'

'I'm not NYPD, I'm FBI.'

'You're all the same.'

'Not quite. I have a lot more authority than Detective Salovitz here.'

Salovitz cheerfully gave him the finger.

'I don't know anything,' she repeated as if it was her shiny new mantra, the one that would solve everything in life. Alik could tell she was on the verge of curling up into a foetal position tighter than junior could ever manage, one she might never uncurl from.

'I've been looking at Riek's file,' he said. 'He had some insurance. Not much, but it could make a big difference to you and the kid.'

'They won't pay out, the company's legal department already said. Bastards. It wasn't an accident.'

'It could be. I can speak to the coroner; they can officially record it as an accident. Like I said, I have authority.'

She glanced up at Alik, her expression sullen and suspicious. 'What do you want?'

'A name. We know Rayner's people took out Riek because of what he'd just done. It was a retaliation hit.'

'Sure. Whatever.'

'So tell me what it was he did for Javid-Lee? I know you know.'

'Are you serious about the insurance company? You can really do that?'

'I can really do that. But you have to tell me everything.'

'It was some bitch. That's why he took the job; not everyone would. But we needed the money. Javid-Lee rewards his people for loyalty, he's good that way.'

'Sure he is. Who was the girl?'

'Samantha Lehito. Javid-Lee wanted a message delivered to her.'

'What for? What had she done?'

'I don't know. Please, I really don't. Riek never asked. You don't. He was a solid soldier for Javid-Lee. He delivered the message like he'd been told. Put that skank in hospital.'

'She's alive, then?'

'I dunno. She was when he left her. Her altme was screaming for the paramedics.'

'All right.' Shango was already splashing Lehito's file across Alik's lens. She was in the Jamaica Hospital on the Van Wyck Greenway, receiving credit-level-three treatment. That confirmed Rayner took care of his people – good politics on his part. But Alik was now very curious what Samantha Lehito had done that would make Javid-Lee send Riek to kick her ass.

'The insurance?' Colleana said desperately. 'What about the insurance? I told you what you wanted to know.'

The baby was grizzling again, picking up on Mom's distress. Alik didn't give a rat's turd about her, but the kid deserved a chance; it was that damn Southern Baptist conscience of his, which never quit, 'I've loaded it in the Bureau's network,' he told her. 'The coroner will pick it up in the morning.'

She burst into tears again.

Alik scowled. He might be a guardian angel, but he didn't have to put up with that kind of shit.

*

'Nobody at the Farron address,' Salovitz sad as the pair of them walked through the practically deserted hubs.

'Yeah?'

'She has a kid, a boy, Alphonse. Our Precinct officers asked around, neighbours say they were about today, but haven't seen them for a while.'

'Add them to the search list.'

'Way ahead of you.'

The staff at the Jamaica Hospital were quite used to NYPD turning up in the bad hours. Salovitz talked to the receptionist, who directed them to the ninth floor. The strata of the hospital's fifty-year-old brutish carbon and glass structure reflected human status in a way the architect probably never intended. If he did, he had a bad sense of irony.

The Koholek Ward was decent enough, several social steps up from the five floors of MedicFare wards directly underneath it. But then again, quite a few floors down from the kind of treatment Alik would receive if he was ever, god-forbid, admitted.

Samantha Lehito was in a bay off the main ward. There were two beds in there, but she was the only patient. A stack of equipment had been wheeled in, with plenty of tubes connecting it to Samantha. Her face and limbs were sheathed in a blue-tinged membrane that told Alik Kcells were being used to replace chunks of flesh that were missing. In medical terms: superficial flesh. But Riek had really carved a number on her face. Just looking at her, Alik was now regretting giving Colleana help with the insurance.

There was another woman dozing in a chair beside the bed. A short woman in her mid-thirties, with black hair in a pixie cut, framing a face that was creased with worry. She stirred when Alik and Salovitz came in, confusion rapidly becoming a disapproving frown. Shango ran facial recognition: Karoline Kalin. There was a marriage licence for her and Samantha, issued four years ago, registered at City Hall. Her employment record was patchy, but she was currently listed as working in a local store called Karma Energy. Shango couldn't find a connection between that and any of Rayner's enterprises.

'What do you want?' she asked in a voice just as weary as Colleana's.

Alik resisted a sigh. The reaction was so common he'd stopped resenting it years ago. But it was a regular quirk of human nature that anyone who'd been mugged or robbed welcomed the police as if they were a lottery win's delivery committee. While at any other time the boys in blue are as wanted as an IR audit.

'I want to talk to Samantha,' Alik told her.

'She's tired. What he did to her . . .' Karoline reached out a hand and caressed her face. 'She's mending now. That takes so much strength. You leave her be.'

'You know Riek Patterson is dead?'

'Yeah. And I've got an alibi, too. I was in here, watching her. There was even a cop on the ward. Good witness, huh?'

'I know you didn't touch Riek. That was Rayner, right?'

Karoline shrugged, running a hand back through her hair. 'If you say.'

'Which means Javid-Lee is going to be looking for payback.'

'No way. It's over now.'

'Between Rayner and Javid-Lee? No. It is never going to be over until one of them gets taken out of the picture.'

'And who's going to do that? You? I don't think so. Not bastards like that. They don't get arrested, they don't stand trial, they don't do time, they don't need their gorgeous face rebuilt. That's what they have poor fucks like Sam for.'

'True.'

'You know it's painful, cosmetic application, having Kcells attach themselves to real flesh? The whole time they're doing it, adapting to the new host body, it hurts, even with the drugs. And it's going to take months to rebuild Sam's features so you can't tell what he did to her. Some people can't take that much pain. My Sam can; she's strong. And when she's done, when I get her home, she is out of this shit! Away from Rayner and all the other psychos.'

'Nice story,' Alik said. 'Do you know how many times I've heard it before?'

'I'm not letting her go back. I won't.'

'Good. Then let me help you. Tell me what she did. Why did Javid-Lee send Riek to do this to her? What was he warning Rayner to stay away from? Once I understand what's been happening, I can go to town on these guys. We've got seven bodies piled up tonight, and that's not including Riek. The Bureau won't ever quit on this case.'

'Sam wouldn't tell you.'

'Of course not, because they've sucked her into their world so far she'll never be able to leave. All your love and pleading, every argument you have, all those dreams about starting fresh some-place – all that's going to do is make her choose. You or them. Are you certain she'll choose you?' It was an effort to convince her, harder than polishing turds, but Alik thought he could see the doubt creeping into her expression.

'She's my fucking wife! She'll leave. For me.'

'Make certain of that. Tell me what she did. I'll take it from there. Rayner and Javid-Lee will be gone.'

'They never go. Only the names change. Some other son of a bitch will take over the territories.'

'But there'll be a gap, a moment when no one is in charge. That's your moment, that's when you get her out.'

'Sam wouldn't even want me talking to you like this,' she said uncertainly.

'And that's the problem. This life she's in, it's a drug. She can't break it by herself. But you can.'

Karoline let out a long sigh and gripped Samantha's limp hand. 'Rayner wanted a message delivered. A clear one.'

She didn't even have to say that; Alik understood the culture perfectly. Messages. Threats. It was all a variant of the old rackets when the shitty words were peeled away. What it boiled down to was the power the likes of Javid-Lee and Rayner could exert over others, enforced by either money or fear. Nobody ever backed down; they had too much dumb pride. To lose face among the gangs was to lose everything.

'What message?' Salovitz asked.

'To back off,' she replied. 'That's all. This woman, she'd got some kind of dispute going with one of Rayner's relatives. So Sam finds out when she visits her spa, a real fancy uptown one. She goes every couple of days, gets the whole treatment – hair, face, full body skin cleanse. And she always has a massage, too, some fancy one, with warm stones or some shit. Thing is, even with an ordinary massage, you're mostly naked. Did you know just taking your clothes off makes people feel vulnerable, never mind lying there with someone standing over you, someone you suddenly find isn't who you thought they were?'

'Sam gave her the massage,' Alik said.

'Goddamn right. But she never hurt her, never did anything like that fucking animal Riek. She just scared the crap out of her. Exactly what Rayner wanted.'

Alik already knew the answer, but asked the question anyway. 'This woman she warned, what was her name?'

'Rose Lorenzo.'

*

Bietzk called just as Alik stepped out of the hospital. In front of him a long line of pine and oak trees stretched the whole length of the Van Wyck, a sweet stretch of parkland cutting through the slowly depopulating urban wilderness. The progressive idea behind converting the old major routes through the city was to soften the environment, and through that make the lives of the citizens that bit more positive and pleasant. All very admirable and worthy.

He knew at its heart it was all bullshit. There had always been gangsters like Javid-Lee and Rayner, right from when the city was founded, and probably always would be. Poverty attracted a certain type – violent, without a conscience – and where there was poverty was its evil twin: exploitation. For all the money locked away in vaults uptown, the city retained a very old-style notion of equitable distribution. A bunch of long skinny parks wouldn't change the attitude of any New Yorker; the eternal buildings and institutions kept them captive in the same old economic cycle as sure as any jail. The only way people growing up inside the projects and low-rent tenements could break their old ways was to leave and immerse themselves in something else, something new and different, such as an asteroid habitat or a terraformed world, Universal or Utopial. But Alik had seen the statistics, always slipped into the appendix of the innumerable reports on urban crime commissioned by state senators calling for 'action'. Depressingly few kids would leave the world they knew, no matter what opportunity was promised by slick government policy advertising. It wasn't a surprise; nobody in a shiny clean habitat wanted a New York punk to screw up the perfect conformityhood they'd woven to hold their neocorporate lives together. And ever since New Washington was successfully terraformed back in 2134, opening its endless verdant prairies to American settlers, New York's population hadn't reduced by more than ten per cent. Most American cities were down fifteen to twenty per cent of their peak twenty-first-century levels, as people, especially the wealthier young, flooded out for that mythical Fresh Start.

As Alik stood in the biting cold, listening to Bietzk, his gaze tracked along Van Wyck's trees with their mantle of thin prickly ice, as if they'd grown thorns to protect themselves through the winter. A mirror of the citizens who walked among them, bristling with hostility and rooted in the structure of the past.

'You're not going to believe this,' Bietzk said.

Alik and Salovitz exchanged a glance.

'Go on,' he said.

'Connexion sent us the logs for Delphine Farron. She and her boy Alphonse walked out of Central Park West hub fifty-two minutes before the Lorenzo family came home. The civic surveillance video shows them walking into the apartment block.'

'You've gotta be fucking kidding me,' Salovitz exclaimed. 'They were both at the portalhome? Where the fuck did they all go?'

'Bietzk,' Alik said, 'I need you to get on to the developer. Find out if they built a safe room into the portalhome.'

'I'm on it.'

'Come on,' he said.

'Where are we going?' Salovitz asked.

'The Lorenzo place. Where else?'

*

There were still a few bored cops in the portalhome, waiting for their shift to end as they watched the forensic teams finishing up. Alik walked straight along the hubhall and into the cabin on the *Jörmungand Celeste.*

'You think there's a safe room here?' Salovitz asked.

'No.' He took his jacket off, ready for the heat outside as they went onto the private deck. Sure enough, the temperature and humidity had both risen in the couple of hours they'd been away. When Alik peered out over the rail, the water was slipping easily along the side of the hull. That was deceptive, he knew. There would be strong currents created by the sheer speed with which the big ship was moving through the ocean. The wake would be even worse: long cyclonic swirls that would show only as choppy ripples, unless you got caught in one. You'd have to be crazy to jump. Or desperate.

'What are you looking for?' Salovitz asked.

'Something missing. Which is always harder to find.'

Both ends of the deck had big red and white cylinders fixed on the wall, containing life rafts. Alik flipped the clips on one and opened it, finding a fat package of orange fabric, and five buoyancy jackets. The other one was empty.

353

'No fucking way,' Salovitz exclaimed.

'They were desperate,' Alik said slowly. 'The kind of desperate that happens when two armed crews burst into your home.'

'Holy shit.'

'Find this ship's coordinates for eleven o'clock Eastern Standard Time last night,' he told Shango, 'then alert the South African coastguard. Ask them to get a boat out there, or a plane if they still use them.'

*

They both went back to the Twentieth Precinct house to wait. Alik got a call from the Bureau while he and Salovitz sat in the case office drinking vending-machine coffee. Agency Forensics had made some progress on the portalhome with the Antarctic room. It belonged to the Mendozas, an elderly married couple in Manila, with zero links to any kind of crime. The person coming through had wiped and crashed the security system. But that was when luck failed them for the first time. Alik and Salovitz watched the image from Manila's civic surveillance on the case office's stage.

A fair-haired woman emerged from the Mendozas' home on Makait Avenue, opposite the Ayala Park. A cabez pulled up and she got into it. Less than thirty seconds later, the vehicle disappeared from Manila's transport logs. It wasn't the best image Alik had ever seen, but it clearly showed their suspect to be just over average height, and wiry with it – the kind of figure that only came from constant work-outs. She wore a bulky parka-style coat to cover her armour – which must have helped in the Antarctic, but in Manila she would have swiftly roasted in that get-up. The enhancement routines rectified her out-of-focus face, and the Precinct's G7Turing ran facial recognition.

'Nothing,' Salovitz exclaimed in disgust.

'Maybe,' Alik said. 'She's not part of Rayner's organization, that's for certain.'

'You know her?'

'No,' he lied. Admittedly it was only a partial lie, but he was pleased with himself for carrying it off through the deep unease that'd just kicked his ass. No characteristics routine could ever grasp this particular suspect, because she changed her features after every job, which was easy now with the new Kcell cosmetics that had hit the market a few years back. Her height and build, however, remained constant to within five per cent, as – bizarrely – did her hair colour, which was always a sandy blonde no matter what style. Then there was the bloodbath in her wake. Not a visual characteristic, but the multiple murder was her signature, sure as Ainsley Zangari had money. *Cancer*, Alik mouthed silently.

He left Salovitz to crank out the usual alerts and requests for cooperation to various global agencies, providing them with the new picture, and called Tansan.

'It's Cancer.'

'Shit,' Tansan snapped. 'Are you sure?'

'The massacre at the portalhome is typical of her operation. That bitch would've made certain no one survived to tell us what actually happened, especially Koushick Flaviu, who was running the data break. I'm thinking the two teams didn't kill each other quite as smoothly as it was laid out. Not that theory matters, I've just seen surveillance of a woman who fits her profile. But she vanished in Manila hours ago.'

'This is serious. Those files need to stay secure.'

'I'm sure the people she's murdered will agree with you.'

'I'm sorry about them, I really am. But the people I represent have other issues.'

'And money.'

'Money isn't actually part of it, this time. This is political.'

'Yeah. I accessed Nikolai Kristjánsson's preliminary report. Those files she was trying to bust dealt with New York's shields.'

'Which is why this is attracting so much attention here on the Hill.'

'Nikolai said he didn't think they actually cracked the files.'

'Not this time, but the fact someone was trying to bust them out is worrying. There's only one reason you want those files, and that's if you're planning to obliterate New York.'

'I don't get it. There are enough freak-jobs in the solar system who can probably build their own nuke if they wanted to. But then you'd just bring the components in through hubs one chunk at a time and rebuild it on the ground. Shields are practically an anachronism.'

'Not entirely,' Tansan said. 'Pulau Manipa.'

Alik winced. Pulau Manipa used to be an Indonesian island. Then in 2073, a reasonably sized chunk of space rock hit the atmosphere above it. Earth's atmosphere had provided a good level of natural protection against cosmic impacts since the end of the dinosaurs, with just a few little blips in its safety record, such as Tunguska in Siberia and Meteor Crater in Arizona. It even broke up the 2073 rock, which basically put Palua Manipa directly under a cosmic shotgun blast rather than a single shot impact. Astrophysicists and weapons techs were still arguing which kind of strike was worse: air-burst or solid smackdown. Nobody on Pulau Manipa could be asked for their opinion. Between the multiple physical strikes, the overlapping blastwaves and the firestorms, none of them was left alive.

Up until that incident, countries had been fairly half-hearted about building shields. They were the tail end of big military spending, and nobody was enthusiastic. There were plenty of political and religious fanatics still waging insurgency campaigns against governments and society in general, but they were slowly and quietly being dumped on Zagreus. The era of national wars and standing armies with nuclear-tipped missiles was long over.

Shields were an artificially generated field that enhanced atomic bonds – a technology that emerged from molecular fabrication. Although air was a tenuous material even at sea level, if the bonds were enhanced within a thick enough section, it produced what was essentially a force field. Enhance a wall of air twenty metres thick, and it would be able to resist a hellbuster blast. But apply that same enforcement to a couple of kilometres of air, and you could set off a nuke outside a city, and all it would do is provide the residents with a grandiose lightshow.

Had there been a shield over Pulau Manipa, the rock wouldn't have made it through. So governments shifted shield construction contracts to civil authorities, and the old armaments companies got a last gulp of public Big Cash. Most big urban areas on the planet were equipped with fully operational nuke-proof shields. Of course, these days, no wild-orbit asteroid would ever make it to within ten million kilometres of Earth. The astro-engineering companies had so many people and so much ultra-sophisticated hardware up there that any approaching asteroid would be mined down to the last speck of gravel before it got inside lunar orbit. But no politician wanted to be responsible for a budget cut that would strip a layer of defence off their voters. City shields remained intact and alert. In the last ninety-nine years since Pulau Manipa, shields had mainly been used to ward off hurricanes.

'But rocks falling on our heads can't happen any more,' Alik insisted. 'We're not fucking dumbasses like the dinosaurs; we're here to stay. It's Darwin.'

'So why did Cancer try and bust the files out?'

Alik ran his hand back through his hair, but not even an imagination pumped by playing innumerable Hong Kong fantasy drama games could give him a viable suggestion on that. 'We're going to get some answers on the multiple homicide soon; that'll point me in the right direction,' he told Tansan. 'But I might need some of those dark funds to finish the case.'

*

It turned out that the South African coastguard did still have some aircraft, a couple of squadrons of Boeing-TV88s. They weren't drones, though they could deploy swarms of airborne and underwater drone clusters kitted out with all kinds of high-grade sensors. They even had actual humans in the cockpit telling the G6Turing pilot what to do. Two of them had zoomed out to the area where the *Jörmungand Celeste* had been at eleven o'clock New York time. They found the life raft easily enough, even though the beacon had been disabled. That told Alik just how scared the Lorenzo and Farron families were.

The TV88s had a portal door on board, so as soon as the families had been winched up, they were brought into the Twentieth

Precinct – seventy minutes after the South African coastguard had officially been asked to help. Alik was impressed.

The two families arrived like refugees from some disaster area, hunched up, hair and clothes sodden with seawater, a silver blanket round their shoulders, clinging onto water bottles and candy bars. It wasn't rescue workers triumphantly bringing the six of them in, but a trio of pissed-off cops.

Salovitz didn't put them into interrogation; he was saving that for the first wrong answer. They sat in a row of chairs at the back of the case office. For people who'd just had their lives threatened then spent hours in the same lifeboat in the middle of an ocean, they certainly didn't look like best buddies.

Delphine Farron had her arm round Alphonse's shoulders. The boy was only ten, but he'd already perfected a teenager's sulk. He scowled at Salovitz, pouting away like a runway model caught breaking her diet.

The Lorenzos were only slightly more civilized. Alik tried not to stare too hard at Rose; she was a real trophy wife. Shango's splash told him she'd modelled for various brands a decade ago – couture and upmarket lingerie. Now she fitted into the perfect corporate spouse mould. Telomere treatments had preserved early-twenties looks, and surrogates had made sure her body wasn't punished by pregnancy, allowing her to play the chic, sultry babe to perfection. Even dishevelled from the ocean ordeal, she stayed classy. He guessed she was also a tiger mom; her kids were kept by her side as they sat, her arms around them. Kravis Lorenzo was the other half of the stereotype package-deal family: Ivy League, preened almost as much as Rose, sitting stiff-backed and defiant, maintaining the kind of pose that said: My criminal law colleague is on fast-access call.

'Quite a night,' Salovitz said. 'Five people dead.'

Delphine Farron let out a short hiss of breath, but that was the only hint of emotion. Rose Lorenzo pulled her children even tighter.

'Let's be quite clear,' Salovitz continued. 'Any smartass answers, any lies, and we take this way on down to the holding cells. City

Social Division will claim the kids. And you know what they say. The difference between City Social and a Rottweiler is that a Rottweiler will eventually let go.'

'You can't threaten us,' Kravis Lorenzo blustered. 'My God, man, what we've been through!'

'It's not just five, though, is it?' Alik said. 'We can add Riek, whom they pulled out of the marina a couple of days ago. And Samantha – maybe not dead, but still in hospital with a face cut up so bad a gorilla would puke at the sight of it.'

'Who are these people?' Kravis asked.

'Wrong answer,' Salovitz said. 'Let's get you down to holding. We'll charge you and start the formal interviews.' He stood up, beckoned—

'Wait!' Kravis said. 'What do you want?'

'For you to cut the bullshit,' Salovitz bounced back at him. 'What in the fuck have you people gone and done? There's a gang war broken out in my precinct, and you're the heart of it. Why?'

'This is all wrong,' Rose said. 'We didn't want any of this to happen. That's the truth.'

'What did Samantha warn you about?' Alik asked. 'And before you claim memory loss, she's the one that gave you a massage with added extras. I've already talked to her tonight – in her hospital bed.'

Rose gave Delphine an anxious glance. All the housekeeper did was stare at her toes.

'Waiting,' Alik said.

'She assaulted my wife,' Kravis said heatedly. 'A sexual assault.'

'Gonna count to three,' Salovitz said. 'And if I don't get an answer—'

'She told me to back off Delphine,' Rose said wearily.

'I never asked her to do anything to you,' Delphine said quickly. 'I don't even know her.'

'Back off why?' Salovitz asked.

'All I said was to return Bailey's game matrix, and I wouldn't enter a formal complaint with the housekeeping agency,' Rose said.

'You're saying my boy stole from you?' Delphine said in outrage.

'Lying bitch! Alphonse is a good boy, aren't you, honey?' She gave him a reassuring squeeze. The kid's head was bowed.

'He was with you the day it went missing,' Rose countered. 'Who else would take it? And you never asked permission to bring him into my home.'

'It was the goddamn Christmas vacation! What am I supposed to do with him?'

'Ask his father to look after him?' Rose sneered. And Alik suddenly understood why Kravis married her, not just for plenty of hot sex with the finest piece of ass on the block. She belonged in his uptown world just as much as him.

'Fucking bitch!' Delphine spat.

'Cool it, both of you,' Salovitz said. 'So.' He eyed Delphine. 'Rose accuses your boy of stealing, and you go running to Rayner? That's the story here?'

'I didn't do that. What am I, stupid? It's only a goddamn matrix, a couple of hundred bucks. And that brat has dozens of them anyway. He probably just put it in the wrong case.'

'You're blaming Bailey?' Rose shrieked.

'You called Al a thief!'

'Je-zus wept,' Salovitz grunted.

'Alphonse,' Alik said softly. The boy still didn't look up. 'What did you tell your Uncle Rayner?'

All that happened was the kid shook his head.

Delphine suddenly gave her son a suspicious look. 'Hey! Did you go and see Rayner?'

'I don't know,' Alphonse sobbed. 'Maybe.'

'You dumb . . .'

For a moment Alik thought Delphine was going to smack him round the head there and then.

'Did you take that matrix?' she challenged. 'You answer me! You tell me the truth *right now*. Did you?'

The boy's shoulders were shaking now as tears dripped onto the floor. 'I was going to give it back,' he wailed. 'I was. Next time we went back there, honest. It's *Star Revenger Twelve*, it's only just come out. I wanted to see what it was like. That's all.'

The expression of satisfaction on Rose's face was so brutal Alik wanted to give her the smack Alphonse deserved.

'Your mom was all over you about the matrix,' he said to Alphonse. 'Right? So you asked Uncle Rayner, man to man, to get Rose to back off. That way you could sneak it back in.'

'I guess,' Alphonse mumbled.

'Did he laugh? Did he say: Yes? Did he say: Well done for taking it? *I knew you were one of us, kid*, is that what he said?'

Alphonse's sobs got louder.

Alik turned to Kravis. 'And you.'

'What about me?'

'Why did Riek go and kick the shit out of Samantha, after she hijacked your wife's massage?'

'I don't know.'

'Really? Because I have a list of your law firm's clients. My altme ran a cross-check. Longpark Developments mean anything to you?'

'No. I've had no dealings with it.'

'Ha, lawyer's answer. It happens to be owned by Javid-Lee. In fact, that's one of fifteen perfectly legal companies owned by him that pay your firm retainers.'

Kravis glared at Alik in stony silence.

'You went to him, didn't you – after the *massage*?' Alik carried on. 'She's your wife, after all. You didn't want justice, not for what Samantha did. You wanted vengeance.'

'You can't prove that.'

'Don't be so sure. You went to him because you believed he was deniable. Wrong. Sure he won't give you up; you're in too deep with him now. He fucking owns you, which I'll bet hasn't even registered yet. You made a deal with the devil, Kravis. He's got your soul by the balls now. But if we looked hard enough, if we leant on the right people, the little people, there would be witnesses. I could send you down as an accessory to a multiple homicide. How long would you last on Zagreus, do you think, a nice well-bred guy like you? Those cannibal rumours, they had to start for some reason.'

'Javid-Lee is a client,' Kravis said in a shaky voice. 'I discuss many legitimate business details with him. That's all I'm prepared to say.'

'There's one thing I don't get,' Alik said. 'Delphine, why did you go to the Lorenzos' place last night?'

'Koushick called me,' she said grudgingly. 'I knew him back in the day. He said Javid-Lee was looking to hit back against Rayner for some kind of firebomb attack on one of his clubs, and that it was getting out of hand, which meant I could be a target. Said we should go quiet for a few days until it was all settled. I was scared; I know what Rayner's life is like. We're not tight, but to these people, we're all family, all the same. So I knew the Lorenzos were off for the weekend, away with their fancy friends on a boat. It was the last place anyone would look for us.'

'Who was the woman?' I asked.

'What woman?'

'Javid-Lee sent two others with Perigine Lexi that night: Duane Nordon and Lisha Khan. While Rayner used Koushick Flaviu and Otto Samule – the two that didn't make it – along with a third, a woman. She survived the bloodbath. Who was she?'

'I don't know. Really, I don't. I told you, I'm not involved in that part of the family life.'

Alik glanced at Salovitz. 'I'm out of questions.'

'Six people dead,' Salovitz said quietly. 'Another in hospital. You started a gang war that's still going on because a kid steals a fucking virtual game. A *game*. Do you have any idea . . .? Je-zus H Christ!'

'I didn't know—' Kravis began.

'Shut the fuck up!' Salovitz bellowed. 'You don't get to talk, not after what you've done!'

'What happens now?' Rose asked. Her kids were pushing up against her so hard it was as if they were trying to bury their heads in her ribs.

'Darwin,' Alik told them.

Salovitz gave him a filthy look.

'I don't understand what that means,' Rose said.

'Survival used to be down to how fast and strong you were, how good a hunter,' Alik told her. 'That was back when we all lived in caves and got frightened by thunder. Today, it's all about being the smartest.'

'Just tell us,' Delphine said. 'Please, tell us the smart thing to do.'

'Option one: we charge you all with criminal conspiracy. Given what's happened tonight, that's an easy trip to Zagreus, certainly for you and Rose and Kravis. Your kids will be taken into City Services care, or handed over to any remaining family.'

'Or?' Kravis asked.

Alik almost grinned. He should have known. After all, Kravis was Wall Street; he could recognize a deal on the table from a block away.

'I make a report to my boss that you were all in the portalhome when two rival crews broke in, trying to burgle the place. You naturally fled and saved your families. All very dramatic, but you're not involved in any criminal act. But that would be a big favour I'd be doing you. And, as we've all learned tonight, those kind of favours don't come cheap.'

'You want money?' a puzzled Rose asked.

'No. I want the two of you to do me a favour in return. A simple personal call. That's all.'

*

The Black Maria went for Javid-Lee first. He was in the Costado restaurant on Broadway, sitting by himself, with three of his lieutenants at the bar where they could watch the patrons coming in, alert for anyone who might have been sent by Rayner; the war was still nuclear hot. He was by himself because Kravis Lorenzo hadn't yet shown up.

Five guys in FBI jackets came in. The lieutenants sat up. Hands went to their holsters. They looked at the boss, not knowing what to do.

Javid-Lee gave a tiny shake of his head. The agents surrounded his table and activated a solnet restriction on his altme, leaving him dark. Lead agent Marley Gardner asked – politely but firmly – that he accompany them to the downtown Federal building. Javid-Lee consented. In the spirit of reciprocity, Gardner agreed he could call his lawyer after they reached the Federal building, but before he was processed.

He was discreetly cuffed and led out to the Black Maria. The NYPD and the Bureau still used them in preference to escorting suspects more than a couple of hubs through the public metrohub network – way too many tiresome attempts to run. Procedure was to send the Black Maria through the Commercial and Government Services network, with the suspect safely contained. The nearest of those hubs was off the north-east corner of Central Park in Harlem. The Black Maria drove in the opposite direction. Eight minutes later it drew up close to Giorgiano's Pizzeria.

Rayner was sitting in a booth by himself, with seven of his lieutenants divided between the bar and a nearby table, watching the pizzeria patrons coming in, alert for anyone who might have been sent by Javid-Lee. He was by himself because Delphine Farron hadn't yet shown up.

As before, the five guys in FBI jackets got out of the Black Maria and walked confidently into the pizzeria. The lieutenants sat up. Hands went to their holsters. They looked at the boss, not knowing what to do.

Rayner held up a hand – a diminutive gesture preventing them from any unwise action. The agents surrounded Rayner's booth and activated a solnet restriction on his altme, leaving him dark. He invited lead agent Marley Gardner to join him. An invitation that was refused, and a counter invitation given that he accompany them to the Federal building. Rayner agreed. In the spirit of reciprocity, Gardner agreed he could call his lawyer when they reached the Federal building, but before he was processed.

He was discreetly cuffed and led out to the Black Maria. The inside of the ageing van was divided into six cages. Rayner stiffened when he saw the only other occupant sitting on a narrow bench, but allowed himself to be placed into a separate cage opposite. Marley Gardner withdrew, and Alik stepped into the Black Maria.

'What the fuck is this?' Javid-Lee asked when the back door slid shut and locked.

'Rendition,' Alik said as the Black Maria drove away.

'Fuck you, asshole!' Javid-Lee shouted. 'You can't do that.'

'Really? Who are you going to complain to? The Justice Department? Hey, maybe you could call the FBI, complain to my boss? Oh, wait, there is no solnet on Zagreus.'

'I'm gonna make you watch your whore mother die slowly before I kill you! That's a promise.'

'How are you going to do that from Zagreus?' Alik enquired lightly. 'See, I was at the Lorenzo portalhome that night. I gotta tell you, that was impressive. That many people dead because of a motherfucking virtual game matrix? Shit, you two have taken dumbass feuds to a whole new level. So as a thank you, my boss and I have decided not to waste taxpayer money on a trial.'

'What do you want?' Rayner asked quietly.

'Nothing.'

'Yes you do. If this was a straight rendition, you wouldn't be in here with us.'

'Darwin, huh?'

Rayner smiled magnanimously. 'I'm on the wrong side of the bars here, pal. Whatever it takes.'

'Cancer,' Alik said.

'Aww, shit.'

'Why did you choose her?'

'I didn't.'

'I'm listening.'

Rayner jabbed a finger at his rival. 'This asshole doesn't know when he's lost.'

'Fuck you!' Javid-Lee screamed.

'I sent Koushick to deliver a message so loud that someone even this dumb could recognize.'

'You were going to whack the Lorenzos,' Alik said in understanding.

'Fucking-a I was; the whole fucking family. That way it's ended. Clean and over. No more loser paybacks.'

'Like fuck it would have been,' Javid-Lee snarled. 'I can take you down any time I want.'

Rayner gestured round mockingly. 'Sure you could.'

'Get on with it,' a weary Alik told Rayner.

'Okay, so Koushick and his crew are getting ready to take out the Lorenzos. Next thing I know, Cancer comes to *me*. I don't know how she knew; Koushick shouting his dumb mouth off round the clubs, most like.'

'Then what?'

'Hey, I wasn't going to turn down that offer. Cancer! She would make fucking sure there wasn't a Lorenzo left alive in this universe. Koushick, he's good, okay. Loyal. But there were kids . . . That wouldn't mean shit to her. And she lived her rep, you know? The way she manoeuvred people: getting the yacht trip cancelled, putting the Lorenzos exactly where we wanted them to be. Shit, like Koushick could ever pull that off a stunt like that!'

'Did she say why she took this contract?'

'Said it was a good fit, and we'd both come out ahead. Told me there was some files Kravis had at his firm that she'd like to bust. I figured what the hell, you know? She's Cancer, and she's working a job with me. Doesn't hurt to be tight with someone like that.'

'Why did she want those files?'

'Seriously, man? You think I'd ask *her* a question like that? I just told Otto and Koushick she was going with them, and do what she said.' He glowered at Javid-Lee, stabbing a finger through the bars. 'And then that ratfuck ambushed them.'

'We didn't know they were there,' Javid-Lee yelled. 'Your butt-ugly bitch cousin Delphine ran there after you warned her. Perigine was on his way to hit her kid. What? You think I was going to ignore you whacking Riek and firebombing my fucking club? You took it up to this level, you fuck, because you have no respect for me. So your rat-fuck nephew – the little shit that started all this – his ass is mine, and you know that; you know that's the price you gotta pay. Only you're too chickenshit to stand up like a man. Your whole family hides and runs like pussies. That's what you are, gaping fucking pussies.'

Rayner yelled wordlessly, and spat at Javid-Lee through the mesh.

'Enough,' Alik said. His finger lined up on Javid-Lee. 'You were hunting Alphonse?'

'Course we fucking were. Perigine's good. He tracked the kid and Delphine to the Lorenzo place, and that's when it all went to shit.' Javid-Lee glared at Rayner. 'Which is your fault because you're a fucking coward. Now look where you've put us.'

'You!' Rayner smirked back. 'Put *you*, pal! Me, I'm cooperating with the Feds. I'm outta here.'

'Fuck you!'

'Okay, then,' Alik said. 'I believe I got everything I need.' Shango opened the back door for him.

'Hey,' Rayner said. 'Hey, wait! What about me?'

Alik paused. 'You have my personal thanks for your cooperation.'

'No! No, that's not the deal. You get your ass back in here and you unlock this motherfucking cage! You hear me?'

The door closed, and Alik stepped down onto the muddy ground of the Lewis County environmental processing site in upstate New York – a patch of rural ground covering six square kilometres, dominated by an impressive atmospheric cleansing plant. Five massive concrete hyperboloid air tunnels stood together in a line, each one sporting a necklace of molecular extractor filters. Three pulled carbon monoxide out of the air, while the remaining pair collected carbon dioxide. Both gases were stored in big high-pressure tanks, ready for disposal.

As reduction efforts went, the Lewis County site alone wouldn't have much effect on the global greenhouse gas legacy that was still uncomfortably high even after a hundred years of scrubbing the excess out of Earth's atmosphere to compliment the biosphere's natural carbon sink ability. But there were over five hundred similar plants dotted all over the planet, and between them they did make a difference. So much that in another hundred years, the experts claimed, it would be down to pre-twentieth-century levels.

Alik could hear Javid-Lee and Rayner yelling obscenities at each other inside the Black Maria. It was parked in a line with six other equally ancient, identical vehicles.

Marley Gardner and his team were waiting in a 4x4 to one side. Alik climbed in.

'Nice job, thanks,' he told them. Alik liked working with Marley on the occasions he needed to go off-book. Marley ran an efficient team and knew never to ask questions. 'Your money will be in the designated accounts by morning.'

'Always a pleasure,' Marley said. His altme instructed the 4x4, and it started driving towards the portal hub.

Behind them, the line of Black Marias were facing a huge metal cylinder, fifty metres long, fifteen high. Alik watched in the mirror as the big circular door at the end slowly swung open. The first Black Maria's autodrive carefully manoeuvred it inside, followed by the second.

Direct disposal was a part of the Lewis County environmental processing site made possible by modern economics. With energy as the Sol system's currency, everything was costed in wattdollars; and with abundant super-cheap energy delivered from the solar-wells, the value of most services and material was incredibly cheap.

A hundred years previously, people on Earth carefully recycled the last generation's garbage, breaking down matter into its component atoms, refining their cast-offs and sludge into useful compounds, ready to supply manufacturing and microfacturing industries. But now, with so much raw asteroid material streaming in at minimal cost, that energy-intensive processing of recycling old things was no longer economic.

Those financial conditions meant that obsolete items – for example, the Bureau's fifteen-year-old Black Marias – were simply disposed of in the most economic fashion possible.

Just before the 4x4 carrying Alik went through the hub, the last Black Maria drove into the giant cylindrical airlock and the door swung shut. The heavy-duty rim seal engaged. Carbon monoxide and carbon dioxide from the big extractor towers flooded in.

After all the nitrogen and oxygen had been expelled from the airlock, the door at the other end of the big metal cylinder opened, exposing the portal behind it, which twinned to Haumea station. The pressurized toxic gases acted like a shotgun cartridge, blasting the Black Marias out into trans-Neptune space.

Juloss

Year 591 AA

The fifteen boys and five girls who made up the Immerle clan's current senior year were clumped together in a big old plaza, in the shade of a dilapidated seventy-storey skyscraper. They had spent six days exploring the ancient abandoned city as part of their training, investigating and analysing unfamiliar environments. The trip had been scheduled to end nineteen hours ago.

Their flyer hadn't arrived. Their personal databuds had been glitchy for the whole expedition and had now dropped out of the planetary network. They were isolated, hundreds of kilometres away from the clan estate. Their supplies were low. They had no weapons. They were completely alone.

The meeting was generating a lot of nervous chatter and some outbreaks of near-panic shouting as they tried to work out what to do. Suggestions were dismissed or endorsed abruptly. A plan began to emerge: they were to set up camp in a more sheltered spot. Weapons were to be improvised. Signal fires to be lit.

Dellian smiled at that, remembering his own insistence about signal fires on the arid hillside where his yeargroup had been marooned. From his vantage point, perched unseen a hundred metres up the side of a nearby skyscraper, he could make out the worry and uncertainty on several faces, while a few of the boys had started to assume a more determined posture.

Time to stir things up.

His biologic pterodactyl's talons let go, and he fell for thirty metres, building velocity. Then his wings opened wide, producing a leathery rushing sound. The avian beast had undergone a few artistic modifications from the original predator that had roamed Earth's skies millions of years ago, specialist designers accentuating a more dangerous aesthetic. Dellian thought they might have been a little too enthusiastic; the big creature was practically a dragon.

He levelled out and powered between the tall empty buildings. The positioning had been selected with a hunter's instinct, keeping the sun behind him, its glare making him invisible to his prey. Genuine birds took flight, squawking in alarm as the huge marauder raced past, a giant flock flowing in a colourful super-geometry murmuration in the clear air.

On the ancient plaza floor below, the clanmates looked up at the sudden airborne commotion, squinting against the sun. Shouts of alarm burst out. Dellian swooped lower, crying out in a long aggressive ululation. The clanmates began to scatter, sprinting for cover. His huge shadow flashed over them. It was all he could do to prevent himself from turning the ominous cry to laughter.

He pitched left, rolling the big body, swooping round the corner of a pyramid-shaped building, seeing the reflection of his fearsome shape fluctuate as it slid across a thousand silvered windows. Then the plaza was behind him and he banked again, wings slowly pumping to gain altitude, terrorizing yet more birds as he rose up and up. The original pterodactyl had been more glider than hawk, but now muscles had been enhanced to pump the big sail-like wings, adding range and speed to its already formidable abilities.

Finally he circled the Bedial tower on the southern edge of the city and slipped down to a sedate landing on its flat roof, dodging the slender air-con heat-pump panels.

Reluctantly he pulled in his wings with a haphazard shake. His databud gave him visuals from the city's sensors, showing him the dispersal pattern on the plaza floor. The boys hadn't kept together, splitting into three main groups, with a couple of stragglers. The girls had stayed together and remained with one of the boy groups. Tactically advantageous, but he felt it had been a random dispersal. Their combat game training hadn't kicked in yet.

'Great Saints, that was pitiful,' Xante sent.

'Yeah. They haven't adapted to the situation; they're still in soft mode.'

'We should change that.'

Dellian had to smile at the eagerness in Xante's voice. 'We will, but gradually. If we suddenly confront them with a tsunami of threats, they might start wondering how come none of the predators were around while they were carrying out their training mission.'

'I guess. That's the kind of thing which clued Yirella in back when we were stranded, wasn't it?'

Dellian's humour deflated. 'Yeah. Something like that.'

'So what do we do?'

'Give them a couple of hours, see how they react now they know the area isn't as passive as they thought. Then buzz them again. Both of us.'

'Okay.'

Dellian released the big pterodactyl from his command bond, keeping his attention on the databud's display to make sure it settled quiescently. Sub-sentient biologics had been known to get *quirky* when released from human control.

He opened his eyes and stretched on the long couch. Phantom sensations tingled along his limbs as the boost sheaths abandoned the biologic's wing nerves. After riding the pterodactyl's neurology for three hours he felt faintly resentful that his human body couldn't actually soar through the sky. His subconscious was busy convincing him he was made out of lead.

The training mission control room was a wide circle, with two tiered levels surrounding a central hologram stage. The couches were on the topmost level, where operatives commanded the various artificial creatures which would soon be stalking the poor innocent clanmates – a threat scenario designed to trigger the instinctive teamwork they'd trained for all their lives.

The graduation exercise had been refined considerably in the four years since Dellian had crash-landed after his island resort holiday. The introduction phase was more gradual to avoid suspicion; the period the exercise was conducted over had been lengthened, allowing a broad range of talents to be brought out and utilized. And the area itself was given a much greater level of scrutiny beforehand, eliminating unforeseen problems such as cougars suddenly cropping up and wrecking everything.

Dellian sat up and looked over at the next couch, where Xante was lying. His friend was still riding his own pterodactyl, eyes closed, limb muscles twitching at random. Most of the twenty couches were currently unoccupied. The threat action wasn't due to be ramped up until later that evening, when darkness closed over the deserted city.

On the tier below, the training masters were busy monitoring their pupils, listening and watching. Dellian's overflight had certainly stirred things up, bestowing a sense of urgency lacking until now. He watched the observers for a while. Tilliana was a section leader now, although the majority of the instructors were the clan's tutors, evaluating their protégés, with Fareana, this yeargroup's mentor, directing the overall set-up. Over the years since Dellian's graduation, the boys who'd been boosted were gradually taking over the animal rider duties. This was his third graduation exercise, allowing him to put his combat training to practical use.

It was a strange. He felt as if he was looking into the past, seeing Alexandre in Fareana's place, with himself and his yearmates performing on the visual stage, while the training masters made sarcastic and amusing comments among themselves at the antics of the hapless trainees. And now he was one of the puppeteers. It was a sensation he could feel his cohort picking up on and puzzling – mainly because he wasn't entirely sure of his own emotions at the development.

'Taking a break,' Dellian told Fareana, and received a quick nod of permission. He left the control room and went through a portal out into Eastmal's riverside park.

The city was now the capital of Juloss, mainly by default; it was the only inhabited city left on the planet. Located four thousand kilometres north of the Immerle estate, it had a temperate climate Dellian rather enjoyed after growing up exclusively in the tropics. Living there gave him a somewhat melancholy glimpse into what life on the world had been like before the traveller generation ships portalled out, taking everyone else with them. Not that he was resentful, he told himself every day he walked through the busy streets.

As he walked, he zipped up his jacket. Autumn was coming, sending gusts of cooler winds across the broad river. All around him, the park's terrestrial trees were wrapping themselves in the spectacularly rich red and gold tones that signalled winter's approach.

For a while he walked slowly along the stone promenade, relaxing into the park's slower pace of life. Below him, on the dark water, swans glided about with arrogant grace. Almost all of this year's signets had lost their grey plumage now, transforming to a pristine white, except for a couple of black swans he could see further downstream. They were the only ones in sight. He grinned forlornly at them. The ratio was similar to the boy–girl quotient within the clans.

Up ahead, someone in a long blue wool coat was leaning on the rails, dropping bread to the big birds. If he had any, Dellian decided, he would've thrown it to the black swans first in sympathy. Then he realized it was actually Alexandre who was feeding the swans, and back in their hangar the cohort reacted with happiness. He knew it wasn't coincidence.

Since he'd moved to Eastmal, Dellian hadn't seen much of their former mentor. It wasn't deliberate; they'd all been so busy in preparation for their starflight. And partying, he admitted guiltily; that was a really good part of city life.

'You're looking very fine,' Alexandre said as they hugged in greeting.

Dellian kept his welcoming smile in place as hir grey eyes gave him a level appraisal. Inside, he was mildly shaken by his mentor's appearance. Sie was male cycled, as sie had been for the last seven years now. It was an usually long time to remain as one gender, and an uneasy indicator of age. Not only did gender cycles last longer as people grew older, the transition phase was also extended. It wasn't detrimental, simply a sign of an older body slowing down.

Alexandre had been there for him his whole life, and Dellian didn't like to acknowledge sie was getting older. But now he looked closely, hir dark-blond hair was thinner now, and becoming lighter from the rise of grey strands. It wasn't something he wanted to consider, that one day Alexandre wouldn't be there to turn to. Death was something he'd only encountered on rare occasions, except poor Uma and Doony that one wretched morning . . .

'You too,' he replied.

Alexandre's grin widened affectionately. 'You were always a rotten liar. That's why you were always in detention.'

'No more than anyone else!'

'I know. Your whole year – it's a miracle any of us came out of the estate alive.'

'But here we are.'

'Aye, here we are. So, how's the graduation exercise going?'

'Pretty good. They've missed some caches that'll be useful, but I just gave them a scare that should send them back to re-evaluate everything. If not, Xante and I are due back later. That should kick them into gear.'

'Ah, the pterodactyls. I remember the arguments we had about introducing those. Some felt it was taking things a step too far.'

'They're magnificent.'

'Yes, you would think that.' Alexandre's hand squeezed his shoulder fondly.

'This yeargroup seems a little more cautious than we were, or more controlled, maybe. Changing the training routines has helped.'

'Somehow, I don't think they'll ever be a match for your year.'

'You made us.'

'Aye, that we did.'

'It's funny to think there's only three more yeargroups left, then it's over. All of us will be real soldiers, and the fight begins.'

'The search begins,' sie corrected gently. 'Who knows? You may never see the final conflict. It might even have happened already.'

'No. We'll see action. I know it. I will meet the Five Saints, and I don't want to let them down.'

'Ah, the optimism of youth. How is Xante?'

'Fine, thanks.'

'Have the two of you moved in together?'

'Not quite. It's good the way it is. We enjoy each other, we're very similar in some ways, and the differences can be fun, too. We're happy.'

'If it's not broke, don't try and fix it?'

'Something like that.' Dellian gave up. 'How is she?'

'Doing rather well, actually. She's smart enough to know she needs to understand herself. It's an arduous process. She can be quite stubborn, but her progress is exceptional. I never expected anything else.'

'She's getting better?'

'Yirella was never ill, Dellian. Just different to what we expected.'

'Different? She killed Uma and Doony!' Some nights he still woke in a sweat thinking about it. To do that to your own muncs . . .

'She liberated herself,' Alexandre said. 'The only way she could. Our arrogance gave her no choice. What we did, the life we gave her, the training and environment of the clan, was simply wrong for her. We are at fault, not her, and we didn't recognize that until too late. Now we have to give her the space and ability to become what she wants to be.'

'And what's that?'

'I don't know. I'd settle for her being happy.'

'Isn't she?'

'I believe she's in a position where that might be possible now. There was so much she had to unlearn, so much to be forgiven. But there are aspects of her life she is comfortable with now.'

It was almost too painful to ask, but he couldn't not – 'Does she . . .'

'Ask about you?'

He nodded silently.

'Of course she does. You meant a lot to her.'

Meant, he thought, not *mean*. 'Can I see her?'

'Not yet. But soon, I hope. She still hasn't quite separated you from what we were moulding you and your yearmates into. I don't want to introduce the possibility of further conflict until I'm sure she can distinguish between what you are and what you will achieve up there among the stars.' Hir head tipped back, and sie stared calmly into the clear, cool sky. 'You are a strong resonance in her life, Dellian. Perhaps the strongest.'

'I want to help.'

'I know. And she knows that, too. But let me ask you this: would you give up everything you have worked for to be with her?'

'I . . . What would we do? We can't stay here and live a planet-side existence.'

'It's not just the battleships that will portal away. There will be one last traveller generation ship, too, for all us old folks.'

'You're not old.'

Sie raised a chiding eyebrow. 'What was it I said about your inability to lie convincingly?'

'I wouldn't want you to be in harm's way. You deserve to see a fresh planet and have a peaceful life.'

'And you deserve your chance.'

'That's what you made us for.'

'Now you sound like her.'

'You think that's a bad thing?'

'No. I always said it would be a mistake to make you all arrogant; it leads to over-confidence. Better you have doubts. That way you will always question what you see.'

'Like she did. I prefer a simpler life. Give me a gun and point me at the enemy.'

'You can cut the humility routine, too. It doesn't work with me.'

Dellian glanced down at the swans. Without titbits of bread, they'd lost interest and were sliding away. 'Will you tell her I asked about her? Tell her I'll wait until she's ready. That I still care. That I always will.'

'Of course.'

'Good.'

They embraced again. Dellian broke away, smiling. 'Now I have to go scare the living crap out of those kids again.'

'That's my boy.'

*

Alexandre had a wistful expression on hir face as sie watched Dellian walk away. After a minute sie turned hir gaze to the nearby clump of tall maples. The grass around them was smothered under a matting of fallen leaves. Yirella walked out from behind the widest trunk. She put her arms round Alexandre and bent down slightly so she could rest her head on hir shoulder.

'Thank you,' she said.

Sie patted her back. 'I'm still not convinced this was a good idea.'

'I needed to know how he affects me. Seeing him in the flesh was a good indicator. I'm glad he's got Xante. He needs someone.'

'I must be firmer with you. I'm too easily manipulated.'

'It's called integrity, and caring. Without you I'd be sitting in a nice comfy room with lots of happy juice in my veins.'

'So what's the result?'

'I looked at him and saw the false beauty of nostalgia for something that I've idealized. We were friends for eighteen years, then lovers, briefly; nothing will ever again be so important in my life. I've managed to self-edit the bad times.'

'I was there for all those eighteen years. There weren't any bad times.'

Yirella pulled some of her wild hair from her eyes where the breeze from the river kept blowing it. 'That's very sweet.'

'He really does care, you know.'

'I heard.'

'Good. I'm not sure if we shouldn't be filling him up with happy juice in the room next to you.'

'I'm happy enough without the juice, and that's mostly down to you.'

'I didn't want to raise any false hope.'

'He does question things now, doesn't he? I think I may have infected him.'

'That's not a bad thing. We don't want gentens. We want humans.'

'You're projecting a future you cannot possibly know.'

'And as he would say: that's why we made all you wonderful binaries.'

She smiled sadly. 'He is what he is. We all are. Humans adapt to the circumstances of their era. I think it's time I accepted that and grew up. This is not what I wanted for myself, but in a thousand years' time it could be. Imagine what we could accomplish as a species if we weren't under threat, if we weren't constantly running. We almost made it before. We were given a glimpse of how high we can climb if we don't have to huddle in the darkness out of fear. That's probably why I always loved the Sanctuary star story, even though I knew in my heart it was probably just a lure. Every planet like Juloss has the potential to become more than a stopover, an island harbour in the long voyage. Then, just as the opportunity opens, we have to flee once more. Imagine what our knowledge and tools could birth if we were truly free and had the luxury of time. I think I'd like to help bring that opportunity to the galaxy. I'm going to go out there and join the Saints in their battle.'

'I'm very glad to hear that, my dear.'

'I won't be any use in the fighting, but there are other ways I can contribute.'

'There are,' Alexandre said. 'But they must be ones you devote yourself to spontaneously. Not out of guilt.'

Yirella looked back down the promenade, hoping to catch one last glimpse of Dellian, but he'd stepped back through the portal. 'This isn't guilt speaking. It's understanding. My graduation exercise is finally over.'

'Did you pass?'

'Yes. I believe I did.'

The Assessment Team

Feriton Kayne *Nkya, 25th June 2204*

'You killed them both?' Callum asked in shock. 'You killed Javid-Lee and Rayner? Bloody hell, man, why?'

I have to admit, I was somewhat alarmed myself. Rendition I could understand, even almost approve of. But such readiness to kill another person was disturbing. I expected it from someone as damaged as Kandara, but I'd assumed Alik Monday was, frankly, more refined.

Alik shrugged, unruffled by the reaction. 'Think of Rayner and Javid-Lee as contaminants that needed venting. It's an appropriate analogy for those sons of bitches. Ain't no need to thank me, I'm just a public servant doing my job.'

'You executed them. No! It was murder; simple as that.'

'What was I supposed to do?'

'Rendition,' Callum said hotly.

'Oh yeah,' Yuri called out with a vicious glee. '*Now* rendition is acceptable, is it?'

Callum glowered at him.

'Strange as it may seem, I don't have the authority to order a rendition directly,' Alik explained. 'I would have had to go through the National Security procedure, and we'd have needed three tame judges to sign off on it. Sure, I'd probably have gotten it for Rayner and Javid-Lee, but that would have involved a whole bunch of other people. The entire problem was a clusterfuck that Washington wanted to disappear fast. We got the media to write it off as gang warfare. And the two asshole families involved got to keep their frightened mouths shut for life. Actually, it was the best solution. Go me.'

'Bloody hell!' Callum dropped his head into his hands.

There was a long silence in the lounge as everyone tried to come to terms with what we'd just been told. I found it interesting to see how being judged riled Alik. He really was that arrogant. A lot of senior government officials come to have the attitude that nothing they do should ever be questioned, or challenged. But it did explain a lot. He hadn't turned up on this case for any other reason than he'd been told to. It was politics, pure and simple. He was a Washington creature, receiving orders and reporting back to the executive and the dark globalPACs. What he reported no doubt contributed to policy, but he wasn't a policymaker. He wasn't the one I was looking for, but I would be very interested in talking to this Tansan character at some time in the near future.

'What about the New York shield?' Jessika asked. 'Have there been more attempts to bust the files since Cancer tried?'

'Beyond my paygrade, my friend,' Alik said, splaying his hands wide.

Like any of us believed that.

'But I did hear the whole national shield project had some pretty sharp security upgrades after that night,' he conceded.

'Civic shields were taken back under military jurisdiction twenty-two years ago,' Loi said. 'In America, at least. So someone must have taken the attempt seriously.'

'Over half of Earth's nations have placed their urban shields under military control in the last fifteen years,' Kandara said. 'Those that still have a military.'

'Why did Cancer want the shield files?' Jessika asked.

'We don't know.'

'Wrong question,' Callum said. 'What did Cancer's employers want with the files?'

'When I find out who they are, I'll be sure and let you know,' Alik said.

'It'll be money,' Eldlund said in a knowing tone. 'It always is with Universal types.'

I thought Callum looked irked with his assistant for the jibe, but my impression of Eldlund was that sie was a devout Utopial – more so than most omnia, who never left the comfort of the Delta Pavonis system. Sie simply couldn't resist the opportunity to establish cultural superiority. I'd guess that was why immigration to Akitha had levelled out in recent years. There's an old saying in the Sol system: Utopial culture would be a great place to live in, but the problem is that it's full of Utopials. And Eldlund was a perfect example of that unconscious patronizing privilege they all possessed.

'How can it be for money?' Yuri asked.

'Shields have protected cities from severe weather for decades,' Eldlund said in a tone that told us sie clearly felt sie was explaining the utterly obvious. 'People are complacent; they take that protection for granted. So if a shield fails during a storm, there'll be plenty of damage. That will have a big effect on spending patterns and insurance payments. If you knew in advance that was going to happen, you could make a killing on the markets.'

'Wow,' Loi said. 'I hope you never become a criminal mastermind. You'd be terrifying.'

Eldlund gave him a knowing grin. 'If whoever wanted the files could afford Cancer, you know it has to be a big deal, right? That's got to be a Wall Street playa.'

Yuri pursed his lips as if in approval. 'Good point.'

You had to be as familiar as I was with my boss to see just how much he was humouring the poor jerk. I'd seen those tactics played in a dozen meetings. It nearly always ended with someone getting fired, or worse.

'So what happened to Colleana's brat?' Kandara asked. 'You?' Her index finger lined up on Eldlund.

'No!'

Loi laughed out loud; everyone else was grinning.

'Who gives a crap what happened to the kid?' Alik grumbled.

'You haven't been checking back on Colleana after you were so noble with her insurance?' Yuri joined in, parodying disappointment. 'Shame on you.'

'Do I look like a fucking fairy godmother?'

'Stranger things,' Callum proclaimed.

'Fuck you all!'

'What about Cancer?' Loi asked. 'Are you still looking for her?'

'Sure,' Alik said. 'The Manila police lost her cabez, of course; she scrambled the city's logs good and hard. Langley assigned a dark team, but even they couldn't catch the scent. The bitch vanished like she always does. We'll catch her one day. And when we do, I'll be having a long conversation with her before we dump her naked ass on Zagreus.'

'No, you won't,' Kandara said.

Alik bridled at what he took to be a challenge. 'Yeah, how do you figure that?'

'Because she's dead.'

'No fucking way. I'd have heard.'

'You didn't hear.'

Alik gave her a suspicious look. 'How do you know this?'

'Because ten years ago, I watched her die.'

The Death of Cancer

Rio, AD 2194

Early morning on Copacabana beach, before the gold-skinned body gods began strutting their glistening physiques for the tourists and lovelorn to envy, the horizontal rays of the sun were playing across the water to create a dazzling shimmer. Not even Kandara's category-four sunglasses seemed to offer much protection from the glare. She pounded barefoot along the sand, careful to keep out of the long tyre furrows. Every day, the city's heavy-duty sand rake servez came out in the hour before dawn, restoring Copacabana to an implausible level of purity in readiness for the daily crowds. In doing so, the wheels often left sharp ruts behind, which could trip the unwary before fresh tides and ten thousand playful feet trampled them flat again.

Just before reaching the southern end, she turned round and ran back. Zapata, her altme, monitored her heart rate and oxygen consumption, splashing the data across her tarsus lens. She used it to keep her pace steady, the optimal cardio routine she'd followed faithfully since leaving Heroico Colegio Militar twenty-four years earlier. Proper diet, some simple telomere treatments, disciplined exercise, and her body had retained the stamina and speed of that twenty-one-year-old cadet.

Eleven minutes later she was closing on the other end of the beach and more people were venturing out onto the sands. Stalls along the promenade were opening, the time-honoured volleyball nets going up. Kandara slowed and walked over the Avenida Atlantica, her soles slapping the old wave-pattern mosaic as she made her way across to her apartment.

The high-rise hotels bordering Copacabana for close on a century had suffered the same economic fate as all hotels post-quantum spacial entanglement, and had long since been redeveloped into blocks of luxury apartments above the street-level clubs and restaurants. Kandara had bought her own relatively modest apartment seven years ago. It was only on the third floor of the twenty-storey building, but it did have a balcony that looked out over the beach.

When she opened the front door, King Jaspar, her elegant Burmese cat, was in the hallway, protesting loudly, as usual. Before she got him, she'd never heard a cat as loud. Mr Parker-Dawson, her neighbour, wasn't talking to her any more because of the 'infernal racket'; he'd also lodged several complaints with the residents' board.

'All right,' she told King Jaspar. 'Calm down, I'll get your breakfast.'

In response he just mewled even louder.

'Shut up. It's coming.'

Another penetrating cry.

'Shut it!' Her bare foot shoved at the cat's silky fur. Not too hard, but enough that he'd get the message. She received a sulky look for her troubles.

'You little—' A hiss of exasperation escaped from her lips, and she made an effort to calm down. *Mother Mary, it's just a goddamn cat. Get a grip.* 'Come on.' She bent down fast and scooped him up. Her finger tickled him under his jaw as she carried him through into the kitchen's small utility room. There was contented purring as she filled his bowl one-handed. Then as she put him down, an extended claw snagged on her lycra running top. 'Hell!'

Kandara glared at the fraying strands he'd tugged from the tight black fabric, now more annoyed with herself for the anger. The whole incident was like a feedback loop. *Ridiculous!* 'Give me a status update on my neurochemistry and skull peripherals,' she told Zapata.

Standing in the middle of the long living room with its tall houseplants and Mexican rug wall hangings. Hands on hips. Impatient for the scan results. Sweat from the run glinting on legs and torso as the sun began to shine sharp gold rays through the big balcony windows.

'Neurochemistry stable,' Zapata announced. 'Gland functionality one hundred per cent.'

She snarled. It would have been easy to blame the little gland. It was a complex, delicate piece of medical bioware, secreting a carefully regulated dose of dopamine antagonist, helping keep the schizophrenia locked away in the darkness at the bottom of her thoughts like a slumbering beast. So she couldn't blame her frustration on that. Maybe it was the run, pumping her up. Or the lack of work – over two months now. And it was no good calling round her contacts. Work came to her, not the other way round.

She walked down the short hallway and opened Gustavo's door. Gustavo had about the same status in the apartment as King Jaspar; he was certainly equally dependent – her house guest, her charity case, her work in progress, her release. She'd found him in an alley behind a swish club seven weeks ago, beaten badly by a furious husband's security team. He was nineteen and male-model handsome, so he explained, which was why he'd come to Rio in the first place, loaded up with excitement and hope. Except the modelling work had never arrived, despite being on the books of three local agencies. Instead the agency bookers suggested he escort ageing fashionistas to parties, *to be seen, darling, so the right people know your name* – a flesh accessory with far less value than their glittering jewellery and this-week couture. The fashionistas, colder and more calculating than any street pimp, began to pass him round their wealthy clients. He partied with them, smiled at their nonsensical jokes, then fucked them for half the night as only a virile teenager could. And when that stamina began to falter from the excesses, he took the right drugs to carry on regardless.

Gustavo was sprawled on the bed, snoring softly. She'd got him on a programme, and he was staying clean; he'd even snagged a couple of gigs modelling sports gear, and once as an extra in a music viz-u. But as charity cases went, she knew exactly what she was doing, and altruism didn't much enter into it. He was convenient. Nothing more.

Her heel knocked the door shut. The noise woke him, and his head came up, showing him blinking sleep-confusion away. She grinned down at him as she tugged the spoilt lycra top off over her head.

'Holy mother, what time is it?' he croaked.

'It's morning.'

'You haven't slept, again, have you?'

'A few hours.'

'You need to sleep more.'

She wiggled out of her shorts. 'I can sleep when—'

'You're dead. Yes. You keep saying.'

'That's right.' Kandara tugged his sheet away, and climbed onto the mattress beside him.

There was a moment when he might have resisted. But instead he gave a sigh that played at reluctance. That left him soon enough as her hands moved proficiently across his lean body, banishing the last fogs of sleep. After all these weeks she knew exactly how to rouse him, how to keep him hard while she rode him greedily. The sexual gymnastics her gened-up muscles let her perform on his bed never strayed into true intimacy. They were fuck-buddies, not lovers. All she wanted was the physical.

The doctors had cautioned her about her anger management. The glands infiltrating her mesolimbic pathway were not a cure, they said with their wise nodding heads; the neurochemicals would only treat the symptoms. In doing so there might be side effects.

Now she couldn't even remember how she used to think before her parents had been slaughtered. Which behaviour trait was new, artificial, psychological, bioneural, divine . . . Her trio of driving demons had been brought under control: psychopathy, hypersexuality, insomnia. She ruled them with an iron fist now, used them as she needed to, gifting herself the perfect personality for her work. An avenging angel, cleansing the world of unchecked evil.

After she'd finished with him, she watched with mild fondness as Gustavo quickly fell asleep again before she slipped out to shower. Breakfast was a smoothie of her own concoction, half a dozen different berries and yogurt (natural organic; she didn't do printed food if she could avoid it) mixed in her blender. She drank it, sitting beside the open balcony door, wearing a robe, her hair wrapped in a towel.

Gustavo wandered in when she'd already drunk half of the smoothie. He was naked, a beauty which competed with the view of the beach for her attention. 'Sheesh, don't you have any real food?' he moaned.

'Such as?'

'Orange juice? Toast?'

'I'm sure they're out there on the street stalls somewhere.'

'Okay, okay. I get it.'

'I can mix some honey with yogurt for you.'

'Gee, thanks.' He slumped on a stool at the kitchen's small bar.

She grinned as she busied herself with the array of expensive cookery gadgets she'd carefully acquired for her galley kitchen. All organic ingredients, blended carefully, the deep-fill tray heating up to the perfect temperature.

'That's yogurt?' he asked, puzzled as she poured the thick creamy liquid out of the blender and into a measuring jug.

'I'm making you waffles. My thank-you treat for this morning.'

His smile won out against the sun.

'You got anything on for the rest of today?' he asked as he wolfed down the third waffle.

'Meetings,' she said. Which wasn't quite true; she'd booked a couple of hours on the shooting range to keep up her proficiency. Then she was due to meet a dark supplier to review some of the new lethal peripherals coming out of northern Russia. She probably wouldn't have any implanted, but it would be good to know their capabilities.

'Can I come? I won't get in the way or anything. I could be your assistant.'

'I don't think so. Not today.'

He gave her a sullen look. 'Fine. Sure. I get it. You think I'm stupid.'

'No,' she said, proud she wasn't sighing in exasperation. After she'd moved him in, she'd told him she was a freelance design refiner for algae reactor initiators, used extensively during the early stage of terraforming. It was a good holding lie. But she hadn't expected this hiatus to last so long. 'You just need some basic qualifications to work in my sector.'

'Yeah, like I'm ever going to have that.'

'You could have, if you went to university.'

'Sure thing, Mother.'

She gave him a sly lecherous smile and stood up. The uncertain look in his eyes was arousing. Her hand closed on the jar of organic manuka honey. 'Would your mother do this?' she murmured, and opened the front of her robe, ready to pour the luxurious golden goo over her chest.

'You have a call,' Zapata informed her. The identity icon of her European agent splashed on her tarsus lens made her stop.

'Go take a shower first,' she told Gustavo. The dramatic return of the pout made her laugh outright. He stomped back to his bedroom.

'Accept,' she told Zapata.

'Good morning to you, my greatest client,' the agent said. 'How are you today?'

'Restless,' she admitted. 'I thought you were dead, or in jail.'

'Like you haven't got a dozen others the same as me tirelessly hunting the worthy jobs.'

'Maybe. If I do, they're a lot more tireless.'

'I'm hurt.'

'I'm sympathetic. Come on, what have you got for me?'

'The biggest. The job of legend, the one that never happens. This is your pinnacle, my dear. You can retire after this and bore everyone in the bar all night long with tales of your imminent sainthood.'

'Bullshit. You said that about Baja.'

'This time, though. Oh yes, this time.'

'I need a better agent.'

'No, you don't, because no other agent could bring you a contract with Akitha.'

A small cold shiver of excitement ran up Kandara's spine. 'Double bullshit! That's Utopial central. They wouldn't touch me with a bargepole.'

'Desperate times, my dear. Can I tell them you're interested?'

'Is this on the level?'

'I guarantee it. I had to meet their representative in the flesh. That I never do. But for you . . .'

'What's the job?'

'Oh yeah, like they're going to tell me.'

'Mother Mary. All right, when do they want me?'

'Now.'

'Seriously?'

'No offence, but if they want *you*, it has got to be monumentally urgent.'

'Give me an hour.' She looked down at the jar of honey she was still holding. 'Make it two.'

*

It was King Jaspar who was the biggest problem. Kandara wasn't entirely surprised by that. Gustavo was simple. She fucked him until the honey was all used up, then told him he had to go. Did the decent thing and paid a fortnight's rent for an apartment in the respectable hilltop neighbourhood of Santa Teresa.

Rage. Screaming. Threats. Pleading. But in the end he packed his bag and stormed out, yelling impressively obscene curses on both her ancestors and descendants.

Easy. Now try booking a pedigree Burmese into a decent cattery in Rio with half an hour's notice. It cost her more than the Santa Teresa apartment. After that she paid a lawyer to find King Jaspar a suitable new owner if she wasn't back in a month. Rule One-Oh-One: always treat every mission as if it's going to be your last. And in this case, she wasn't under any illusions. If the Utopials were asking for her, it was going to be something very serious indeed.

*

The Rio metro network took her to the international hub, from which it was three hubs to Bangkok. That was where it started to get more interesting. She had to take a civic radial out to Prawet, where the Utopial embassy was situated. As she walked through the interminable portal doors with her bagez trundling along behind, Zapata checked her neurochemical balance, which was perfectly level. She breathed calmly into a Zen state. Ready.

A minute later she was walking up the embassy's broad steps, with fountains playing on either side. A Utopial called Kruse was waiting for her at the top, just in front of the main arched entrance-way. Sie looked about thirty, with a mane of chestnut hair in which rainbow jewels glowed discreetly. Hir fawn tweed suit was very formal, with a skirt that came down over hir knees. Kandara had to tip her head up when they shook hands; Kruse was an easy forty centimetres taller than her. But the omnia's smile seemed genuine enough.

'Investigator Martinez, such a pleasure,' sie said.

'Likewise, and it's just Kandara.' Being called *Investigator* threw her slightly, but if that was the way they were going to deal with her, so be it.

'Of course. This way please, Kandara.'

Kruse showed her through a smaller door at the side of the main entrance. A short hall led to a single portal door. Kandara stepped through. She knew immediately they were on a space habitat; her inner ear could detect the subtle difference of rotation-induced gravity. Zapata confirmed the change, linking to the local net and questing its metadata.

'This is Zabok,' it told her.

Kandara had been expecting that. Zabok was the first large self-sustaining habitat built by Emilja Jurich, one of the founders of the Utopial movement. It was still an important centre for them in the Sol system. There were several portals facing the one she'd just come through.

The ever-formal Kruse gestured to one. 'Please.'

'Nebesa,' Zapata informed her after she'd stepped through. Details splashed across her lens. The Nebesa habitat orbited a hundred thousand kilometres above Akitha, a terraformed planet, itself orbiting Delta Pavonis.

Her inner ear detected another change, a slowing of the balance instability. Understandable. Nebesa was considerably larger than Zabok, making its rotation ponderous by comparison.

They walked along a brightly lit passage which opened out on a broad paved square. Kandara looked up, smiling as she took in the habitat's interior. The massive cylinders always engendered sensations of awe and reverence. Most people considered terraforming to be the greatest technological wonder humans had achieved. Nature had taken a billion years to produce multicellular life on Earth; now the human race could duplicate that process on a barren planet in under a century. But Kandara considered that a cheat; simply spreading microbes and seeds across sterile rock plains was merely carrying nature's banner forwards. The habitats, however . . . Ripping asteroids apart, forcing their raw metal and rock into cylinders the size of some of the old nations on Earth, bringing new air and water to the interior of these defiant islands in space – that was real engineering, combining all of scientific history's knowledge into a victory over the most hostile environment possible: the empty universe itself.

'Magnificent,' Kandara said quietly, breathing down the humid air, cleaner than anything the South Atlantic winds swept across Copacabana.

'Thank you,' Kruse said in genuine appreciation.

Nebesa's interior was sixty kilometres long, and twelve in diameter. What looked like a splinter of captured sunlight burned sharp along the axis, bathing the interior in a tropical glare. That surface was a mixture of long lakes studded with islands, confined by land coated in a lush rainforest. There were even some mountains, with slender waterfalls tumbling down rocky slopes. Clouds beset with odd curlicues twisted slowly through the air.

They'd emerged at the foot of a gently curving endcap. The base of it formed a ziggurat ring of black-glass balconies, extending two hundred metres above the paving where they stood. A vertical city that made her mildly dizzy as she traced its course all the way around the rim until she was looking at the tiny ebony band directly overhead.

'How many people live here?' she asked, trying to do the maths without using Zapata. Even if everyone had an apartment ten times the size of hers, the population could be measured in millions.

'Just over a hundred thousand these days,' Kruse said. 'It was more than twice that when the terraforming was at its peak. But everyone wanted to move down to Akitha when it was cleared for habitation. Now it's just the senior grade industrial staff and administration personnel.'

'Uh huh.'

'You sound like you disapprove.'

'I don't get the Utopial grading system, that's all. I thought the ethos was equality.'

Kruse gave a quick smile. 'Opportunity is equal. People are not. In our society, you can progress as far as your talent and enthusiasm can reach.'

'The same as everywhere.'

'Not quite. Here everyone receives a fair share of society's produce, no matter the level of practical contribution you make. If you choose to do absolutely nothing for your entire life, you will still be fed and clothed and housed, and given access to medical treatment or education without prejudice. But in reality, a life of total leisure, or sloth, is rarely chosen. It is human nature to want to perform some kind of activity. The difference is that we do not require it to be what the old communist and capitalist theories interpret as economically viable. With the introduction of Turings and fabricators, the human race has advanced to a technology level which has given us a self-maintaining industrial base. It can provide consumerist products at practically zero cost. Nobody should be regarded as a parasite or sponger, as your media condemns and shames your underclass. Here, if you wish to devote your life to developing obscure philosophy, or an artistic endeavour that is outside the mainstream, that is to be welcomed and encouraged as much as someone who commits to designing new technology or researching pure science.'

'Some are more equal than others?'

'That is how the rich Universal rulers like to spin the Utopial ethos, yes. It is rather childish, don't you think?' Hir hand gestured proudly at the glorious cylindrical panorama. 'Could a flawed society produce and maintain this?'

'I guess not.'

'One day, everybody will live like this. Free from constraints.'

'Indeed.' All Kandara could think of when she looked at the tall Utopial was the local priest who had governed so much of her childhood. The scriptures, his ethos, could never be wrong; he would have a patient smile as he explained away every question bold young minds could think of to challenge God's implacable word. 'So what now?'

'There is someone who wishes to meet you before you can begin.'

'Sounds interesting.'

*

It was quite a hike, which Kandara hadn't been expecting. She followed Kruse into the trees. They'd only gone a few hundred metres before the overhead canopy merged to a single luxuriant emerald roof. Slim beams of light slithered through the long leaves to dapple the ground. Trunks grew closer together, and the undergrowth shorter. Several times they crossed narrow arched wooden bridges with streams gurgling away below. Birds squawked loudly in the high branches, unseen from the ground. It wasn't long before Kandara took her linen jacket off; the still air was so warm even her trademark black singlet seemed excessive.

Finally they came to a small clearing with a stream running along one side. There was a tent in the middle, all billowing white cloth with scarlet edging and bronze guy ropes. The only thing missing to complete the look of medieval pageantry was a royal pennant fluttering from the apex. The whole structure was ludicrously incongruous in a space habitat orbiting an alien star.

Kandara gave Kruse a sceptical look. 'Really?'

It was the first time Kruse's urbane expression faltered. Sie pulled the opening curtain aside. 'Jaru is expecting you.' Sie hesitated. 'Please be aware of the importance so many Utopials assign to hir, though sie will of course dismiss any such devotion.'

Once again Kandara felt a tingle of unease at Kruse's piety. 'Of course.' She walked into the tent.

It was noticeably cooler inside. The fabric seemed to glow with a rich luminosity lacking in the stark light outside. Somehow the interior didn't surprise Kandara. The cushions, small fountain, and a single stiff-backed wooden chair all sang: humble yet mystic guru.

Jaru Niyom sat in the chair, draped in sea-blue monk-style robes; gaining an immense dignity by looking as old as anyone Kandara had ever seen. *It has to be theatre*, she thought. But then sie had already been old when telomere treatments first became available. Old yet rich.

Jaru was the only child of a wealthy Thai family. Hir father had made a fortune in property development as Thailand's prosperity grew. They had been estranged when the elder Niyom had died from a stress-induced coronary at sixty-one, never quite able to come to terms with his cherished offspring becoming kathoey. Most assumed the more gentle Jaru would let the company dwindle, but the family's entrepreneurial gene wasn't recessive. Hir inheritance came at the same time as Kellan Rindstrom demonstrated quantum spacial entanglement. With a flash of intuition sie would often demonstrate in later life, Jaru immediately saw a way of advancing hir company's fortunes, benefiting the environment, and providing cheaper housing which the world so desperately needed.

Thailand became the first country to construct ribbontowns. Jaru bought (at a bargain price) hundreds of kilometres of the nation's motorways and expressway networks, along with the entire four-thousand-kilometre state railway network – all of which were becoming redundant as Connexion continued its inexorable advance of portal hubs across the globe.

Jaru began building houses along the abandoned train tracks. Big vehicles ripped up the asphalt and concrete of the roads, exposing the raw earth ready for new foundations to be sunk. What sie'd realized was that Ainsley Zangari's notorious slogan was correct – everything truly was *one step away*. In this new age of instantaneous transport, habitation didn't need a civic centre any more. All the facilities such as schools, hospitals and theatres could be accessed no matter where your home was physically located; you just needed a portal door nearby.

It was a model swiftly copied by the rest of the world. With governments desperate for the cash which selling obsolete roads and railways to developers would raise, and solving the global housing crisis at the same time, the resulting construction boom went on to save (or at least salvage) many economies suffering from the collapse of the traditional transport industries.

Multi-billionairedom allowed Jaru to expand hir commercial interest out into the burgeoning space industries, constructing new habitats on Sol's asteroids. Then, in 2078, as a direct result of nine Über-corporate habitats declaring themselves low-tax nations open for business, sie sponsored the First Progressive Conclave, where fifteen more idealistically minded space-based billionaires pledged to birth a true post-scarcity civilization for the human race. Each of them committed their habitat to an economy based on a Turing-managed self-replicating industrial base. It was the start of the whole Utopial movement.

Kandara didn't need any prompting to duck her head in a small bow of acknowledgement. 'It's an honour to meet you.'

'You are kind,' Jaru said with a melodic voice. 'Though I fear at my age I am no longer terribly spectacular.'

'Age is wisdom.'

Sie chuckled. 'Age *can* be wisdom. It depends how you spend those years.'

'True.' Kandara was aware of Kruse coming into the tent behind her, and bowing deeply.

'Are you acquiring wisdom, Kandara?' Jaru asked.

'My life has a purpose. You know that. It's why I am here.'

'Of course. This is why I asked to meet you before we commit to this course of action.'

'So you can judge me?'

'Yes.'

'You are free to ask me whatever you wish. But please bear in mind my former clients have full confidentiality.'

'I don't wish to know the darker commercial details of corporations. I am interested only in you.'

'I'm not a serial killer who's found the perfect cover. Nor am I a sadist. If a client wanted someone to suffer before death, I would turn the job down. I execute people. It's that simple.'

'What about those who can be redeemed?'

'If the person causing you trouble can be redeemed, you don't need me.'

'So you judge us in turn, then?'

'Everybody judges everyone else. I don't deem myself infallible. I hope and believe I haven't made a mistake so far. Everyone I've been called upon to deal with has deserved what happened to them, in my view.'

'Surely, we would be better served by you arresting these criminals and quietly renditioning them to Zagreus?'

'Again, if you can deal with them that way, you don't need me. I'm here for the ones who won't come meekly, or who are so far along their path that a fight to the death is what they want – consciously or otherwise.'

'Is this a quest for revenge, then?'

'I don't want any more children to suffer as I did. If you want to call that revenge, feel free.'

'You sleep at night, then?'

Kandara narrowed her eyes as she studied the ancient wrinkled face for any hint of guile, wondering if the Utopials had cracked her medical files. 'My conscience is clear.'

'I wish I could say the same.'

'I can walk away if you'd like. No offence will be taken. No regrets.'

'I believe we are past that point now,' Jaru said sadly. 'The Senior Council has made its decision based on the level of extremism we appear to be facing. I do not dispute this. If those who are harming us do not surrender to authority, then they must be dealt with. I simply wished to see what kind of person you were.'

'I'm sorry to be the serpent in your Eden.'

'I never deluded myself we could achieve a truly peaceful egalitarian society without suffering misfortunes along the way.'

'I am a last resort. Most of my clients regret having to call me in, but they seldom have any choice.'

'So it would seem. I cannot express how disappointed I am that people are so hostile to us.'

'They fear you,' Kandara said, 'for you are change. And change frightens people, especially those with the most to lose as that change is enacted.'

'You approve of us?' sie asked in charmed surprise.

'Yes. The economics you seek to replace are those which ultimately resulted in my parents' murder. How could I not approve?'

'Yet you have not come to live with us.'

'My skillset has no place in your culture. When the human race comes to accept the Utopial ethos, embraces it even, then I will settle here with you – if you'll have me. Until then, I will always be needed.'

'You may be in for a long wait. We are a small nation. The number seeking to join us is disappointingly few.'

Kandara glanced wearily at Kruse, uncertain how the acolyte would respond to the immutable doctrine being questioned. 'Do you mind if I tell you how I see it?'

'Acceptance of truth is fundamental to our ethos. To determine truth we must first listen to all opinion.'

'Okay: you went too far too quickly.'

'The Turings were nothing new, nor was the level of sophistication in the fabricators that manufacture our technology. The asteroids provide us with unlimited elements. Solarwells supply eternal energy. Synergy between such diverse developments was inevitable.'

'Yes, but they were just the economic factors. You took it a stage further.'

'Ah,' Jaru smiled gently. 'The omnia.'

'Yes. You were asking too much of people. You offer converts to the Utopial ethos all the material goods they could want, practically for free, but first they have to accept the gender change.'

'We prefer the term gender expansion.'

'Whatever. The material benefits of post-scarcity shouldn't be wholly dependent on pimping the DNA of your children.'

'But, dear child, the formation of Utopial society was never just about physical rewards. The Universal culture provides much to its citizens – to a great many of them, in fact. Today there are fewer living in relative poverty than ever before.'

'So why insist on the omnia-only clause?'

'Because I seek more from people. I seek universal equality. And the most basic inequality is that caused by a binary gender. It fuels every disparity and bigotry present in the so-called Universal culture. It condemned our history on Earth to variants of the same mistakes because, before genetic modification, it could not be eradicated. I know this. In my youth I experienced it in ways you should be thankful you will never encounter. It is worse than any of the miseries brought about by the old foes of religion, capitalism, communism and tribal nationalism. Those can all be cured in time with education and love, but genders would remain unless we took action.' Hir hand was extended palm outwards towards Kruse. 'And now . . . Even that problem has been solved. Quite beautifully, too.'

Kruse beamed worshipfully. 'Thank you.'

'Nice theory,' Kandara said. 'But all you've done is set up an admittedly worthwhile society which exists in parallel to the majority society. You're not changing anything.'

'The Universal factions are in constant conflict,' Kruse said darkly. 'They will fall as we will rise.'

'Which is why I'm here,' Kandara concluded. 'Not falling the way you hoped, huh?'

'Their hostility is unremitting,' Jaru acknowledged with a profound sigh. 'And recently they have advanced that enmity to a level it is impossible to brush aside as petulance. They seek to inflict physical harm. Much as I would wish it, I am not Gandhi. My father's pragmatism remains strong in me.'

'Tell me what you need,' she said.

'A group of Universal activists has been sabotaging our design bureaus. Some of the most promising research has been stolen and our results corrupted. They are damaging us, Kandara, quite badly – though that cannot be admitted in public. We don't know where they came from or who sent them. They elude us. Find them. Stop them.'

Kandara nodded solemnly. 'It's what I do.'

*

'We've put a team together for you,' Kruse said as they walked back through the trees.

'Oh really? What kind of team? And who's we?'

'Our Home Security Bureau. We brought in a variety of experts and advisers. It is their task to track down the physical location where the attacks come from.'

'Okay, that's good.' Kandara had been expecting to use some of the specialists she was familiar with, but she was prepared to give Kruse's people a chance.

A portal door in the habitat's endcap took them down to a hub on Akitha. Seven hubs later, they reached the central metrohub of Naima, a city of some seven hundred thousand inhabitants sprawling across the southern side of a large island. From there it was ten hubs round a metro loop to the street where Kruse had assembled the team.

Kandara stepped out of the hub and immediately dabbed at the sweat that was starting to bead on her brow. Naima was part of an archipelago in the equatorial zone, making it considerably hotter and more humid here than it had been back in Nebesa. They'd emerged into a white-stone plaza that was several hundred metres above a calm indigo ocean. Naima occupied the rugged slope on all sides and comprised modest stone and glass buildings that Kandara felt were a little too similar. It put her in mind of the Tuscan villages she'd visited in her childhood, when her parents had spent several weeks in Italy on management courses at their employer's head office. Pretty and peaceful, if bland.

They walked along the broad road with its central sentry-line of tall palm trees, her bagez rattling over the authentically uneven cobbles behind her. A minute later they arrived at the villa. It squatted at the top of a small cliff, with a glass-walled living room offering a magnificent view across the broad curving bay below the city. In the distance, a clutter of small pillar-like rock islands stood proud from the sun-sparkled water. Beyond the open doors, a paved patio stretched out to an infinity pool. When Kandara walked over to it, she realized most of the pool must be supported on pillars; only the house itself was sitting on the terraced cliff.

'Okay, this will do,' Kandara admitted.

'The team is in the kitchen,' Kruse told her.

Naima might have been Italianate, but the kitchen clearly followed a more Nordic tradition – a minimalist spectacle of black and scarlet marble, with a dozen worktop recesses from which various culinary devices could slide out of as required, looking more like sculptures than practical machinery. She tried not to show any envy, but it made her little kitchen seem quite tired in comparison.

Three people were sitting at the long crystal table in the middle of the pale-oak flooring, sipping wine from tall-stemmed glasses.

A rebuke was starting to form in Kandara's head. It was ridiculous; these people were acting as if they were on some kind of delightful weekend break, not setting up a covert op that was likely to end with smoking ruins and dead bodies.

Two of them were clearly Utopial omnias – their height alone evidenced that – while the third was shorter and female. Kandara didn't think she was just female cycled, not that she could explain her conviction. With luck it was solid detective's intuition.

The trio rose to greet her, smiling warmly.

'This is Tyle,' Kruse said, introducing the tallest, who had sandy hair and a slim dark moustache with the tips precisely trimmed in neat curls. 'Our network analyst.'

'Excited to be working with you,' Tyle said. Hir voice was high and eager. Kandara thought sie was genuinely young, maybe in hir late twenties. But then hir sharp features were so disturbingly close to Gustavo's she felt she was being haunted.

'Oistad, a defensive program operator.'

Sie was almost as tall as Kruse, but with thick honey-blond hair that came over hir shoulders in languid waves. The flowing blue summer dress sie wore left Kandara no doubt sie was in full female cycle. As always, age was difficult to pin down these days, but to Kandara the poised manner spoke of someone over half a century.

'And Jessika Mye, a strategic profiler.'

Kandara shook hands cautiously. 'What exactly is that?'

'It means I take a look at the crimes and how they were committed, the motivation behind them, and try to work out what's coming next.' She shrugged. 'I used to work for Connexion Security, so I have some experience.'

'They brought you in, too?' Kandara asked in surprise.

'No, I was already here. I decided I prefer the Utopial life, after all. Long story, but I was Utopial before – lost faith, then regained it.'

'Okay.' Kandara sat at the head of the table, pointedly refusing the glass of wine Tyle offered. 'Not while I'm working.'

Tyle pulled the glass back sheepishly.

'Brief me, please,' Kandara told them.

Akitha's research institutes had been under attack for years, they said. Teams from Sol's dynamic and greedy companies got sent to Akitha, where they cracked files on anything that they believed was going to have commercial value. That data got fed into corporate design offices, improving consumer products that were the economic bedrock of Universal worlds.

'Blatant theft,' Tyle said. 'And it's crazy. We release all the data anyway. That's the Utopial way; we want everyone to benefit.'

'Not quite so crazy,' Jessika said. 'It's a fairly basic market force. If you can get something into production before your rivals, you establish a good sales lead. Also, stealing is a lot cheaper than having a big expensive research team of your own.'

'It is about the assignment of value,' Kruse said disdainfully. 'If something people want or need is limited, if it becomes rare, consequently it acquires value. That's the foundation of old-era economics. Giving a *thing* value is the end of equality and sharing. That is how so-called Universal culture maintains its status quo, by monetary force, controlled by the unelected elites. By taking our ideas from us and using them to enhance their wealth, they are inflicting a double violation upon us.'

'Sure, I get that,' Kandara said with careful neutrality. 'But what we're dealing with here sounds like standard-issue industrial espionage. That's been around as long as industry itself.'

'Data theft is just the first crack in the dam,' Tyle said. 'It has been an annoyance for decades, but what else can you expect from Universal-culture corporations, right? So we didn't put as much effort into preventing it as we should. There always has to be a balance between freedom and restriction; that is fundamental to any society. Without law there is anarchy. But too much law, applied rigorously, becomes oppression. Here on Akitha, of course, we favour as little restriction as possible – something that has been exploited ruthlessly by the corporations. Our mistake.'

'Hindsight is always the clearest vision,' Kandara told hir.

'It means our networks are not as secure as they should be, and they're susceptible to black routing. We're working to rectify that, of course, but fortifying an entire planetary network is no small task.'

'And the activity of these Universal agents has changed,' Kruse said. 'They no longer simply steal our work for their own profit. More recently they have begun launching acts of sabotage.'

'On what?' Kandara asked.

'Industrial facilities,' Oistad said. 'It's relatively subtle. Refineries lose efficiency; component failure in manufacturing facilities increase due to glitched management routines, decreasing productivity.

The rate of these attacks has been gradually increasing. We're upgrading our electronic countermeasures, but we're behind on security development. Even our G8Turings have trouble defending themselves against the more sophisticated intrusion attempts.'

'Your G8Turings are vulnerable?' Kandara asked in surprise. G8Turings had only been coming online in the last six months, almost in accordance with the Robson law of progression, which said the rate of development would double between each generation. Though they'd taken slightly longer than expected to develop, the G8Turings should have been utterly secure.

'They can't be cracked, obviously, but defence absorbs more of their processing capacity than I'd like. The G8Turings produced by commercial companies are more evolved in that regard.'

'And this is why you brought me in?' Kandara asked sceptically. 'A few items in short supply?'

'No,' Jessika said firmly. 'There's been a tipping point. Three weeks ago, the public biolife centre here in Naima was subject to an intense digital assault. The entire production facility was taken offline. Black routing opened a clean channel into the network. They penetrated the management routines so deeply they even overrode safety limiters; the machines suffered actual physical damage from overloads. That all had to be repaired. And sleeper bugs were left behind. The entire network architecture has to be wiped and rebooted. And even that doesn't guarantee the bugs are eliminated; they're highly adaptive.'

'What does the biolife centre produce?' Kandara was very aware of the glances the team exchanged as soon as she came out with the question. For a moment she wondered if it was some kind of weapons research, a nice dirty little secret at the heart of Utopial society. *They have to have some kind of physical deterrent, surely? A way to defend themselves.*

'Naima produces ninety per cent of the planet's telomere treatment vectors,' Oistad said gloomily.

'We've had to implement rationing,' Kruse said. 'Treatment therapies have been delayed. We're now buying in vectors from Universal companies, but even they don't have enough. They use demand-match supply systems; nobody stockpiles anything these days, it's not *economically viable*. We were an unexpected new market.'

'The big nine pharmas were delighted, of course,' Jessika said. 'But they're frustrated, too. By the time they expand their production facilities to meet our requirements, we'll have the Naima biolife facilities back up.'

'So all that's happened is the price of the Universal vectors has risen, making the treatments more limited for everyone. Supply and demand.' Kruse said it as if she was uttering a profane curse.

Kandara suspected that in a way, sie was. 'That's not good,' she admitted.

'Thank you for your empathy,' Kruse snapped.

'If you wanted a therapist, you came to the wrong person.'

'They knew what they were doing,' Jessika said. 'They knew the effect damaging the telomere therapies would have. It's an attack on the fundamental principles of our society. In any decent civilization, healthcare is a right, not a privilege. Even their own, the Universals, suffered from this action.'

'I see why you called me in,' Kandara said. 'Life expectancy is precious. Take a day away from everyone on a planet, and you've killed centuries of human life. It's subtle, but very real.'

'I hoped you'd understand,' Kruse said.

Jessika gave Kandara a sly conspiratorial smile, which quickly vanished. She drained her wine glass. 'So. We've been trying to track down where the black routing originated from.'

'And?' Kandara asked.

'We have absolutely no idea. Their routines are better than ours. They left nothing behind.'

Kandara looked round the table, taking in for the first time just how glum some of them appeared. 'You're not going to find the source, are you? Not now?'

'If you can't backtrack the load point within a day, then no,' Tyle said.

'What do you need to find it?' she asked. 'Better routines? I know some experts we can bring in. Good ones.'

'I'm not that bad. And I have been given the Bureau's G8Turing to work with.'

'Then how do we catch them? Give me a best-case scenario.'

'The dark routines are easiest to detect when they are being infiltrated into the target network. If we could just be monitoring that when it happened, we could backtrack effectively.'

'So you have to upgrade security monitoring routines.'

'We are doing that, but there are hundreds of thousands of individual networks on Akitha. I told you, it will take time.'

'All right,' Kandara said. 'Then we need to narrow it down. Jessika, you're supposed to be analysing the strategic pattern. Is this one team or several?'

'We think there are up to fifteen industrial espionage groups currently operating here on Akitha, but most of them are only involved in theft. Judging by how infrequent these active sabotage attacks are, maybe one every six weeks, it suggests a lone team. They're being cautious, and covering their tracks well.'

'Okay. Do you keep track of all non-Utopial citizens in the Delta Pavonis system?'

'Certainly not,' Kruse said.

'Really? Connexion Corp can find anyone using their hubs – any time, any place.'

'Because Ainsley Zangari's company is an oppressive component of the Universal plutocracy. Our portal transport network is public; we don't spy on our citizens.'

'Yeah, you've got civil liberties busting out of your pants. I get it. How about: can the public network be used to watch for individual people in an emergency?'

'Theoretically, yes,' Tyle said. Sie grinned at the annoyed glance Kruse directed at hir. 'There's a sensor on every portal. Even we need basic police procedures.'

'We'd need an order from the Superior Court,' Kruse said.

'You haven't got one already?'

'We thought we could find these criminals through their digital signature.'

'Right. So talk to whoever you have to, and get a warrant.'

'A warrant for every non-Utopial in the Delta Pavonis system? I'm not sure we'd ever get that.'

'A warrant for every region when this team finally tracks down a possible location,' Kandara said. 'That's the absolute minimum we need here. Without that, we're just wasting our time.'

Kruse nodded. 'I'll call my Bureau chief.' Sie went out onto the patio, leaning on the railing to stare down at the ocean with its distant towering islands.

Kandara looked round the others. 'Seriously, you've got nothing after three weeks?'

'I know,' Tyle said bitterly. 'It's a shit result. We're not used to something of this magnitude.'

'Not just that,' Jessika said. 'It's the nature of the people we're up against. They are very professional, and experienced. I keep telling the Bureau we should run an exchange programme with equivalent Sol agencies; that way our operatives gain experience and under-standing. But . . .'

'Too proud, huh?' Kandara guessed.

Everyone glanced out at the figure silhouetted at the end of the patio.

'Stubborn,' Oistad said. 'Self-righteous. Needlessly independ-ent. It's a big dictionary out there.'

Kandara looked at each of them round the table. 'Have you guys ever worked together before?'

'This collaboration is bright shiny new,' Jessika said, and poured herself some more wine. 'The Bureau brought us together because we're the top of our respective fields. So that's got to work well, right?'

'We do help each other,' Oistad said.

'Some,' Tyle said. Hie glanced out at Kruse. 'We need direction.'

'It's called leadership,' Oistad said, flinching. 'You don't get a lot of that here on consensus-world. I'm not criticizing. I love Akitha and what we've built here. The trouble is we have no familiarity in dealing with something at this level.'

'Yeah, I see that,' Kandara said. She stood up. 'I need to think.'

'You're not quitting, are you?' a worried Tyle asked.

'Don't worry; I don't give up on contracts I've agreed to. Professional pride. You're stuck with me.'

*

Kandara's room had a set of wide glass doors opening onto the overhang patio. She unlocked the clothes section of her bagez and let a house servez put everything away in the closet, except her dolphin-skin swimsuit. Her mind was racing as she slipped it on, running through everything the so-called team had given her. It wasn't good. She was used to working with top-grade corporate security, or deniable spooks with bottomless accounts of dark money.

The infinity pool was barely long enough to take five strokes before she had to flip. Warmer, too, than the one in her Rio gym.

So many first planet problems.

After twenty minutes she took a breather, clinging on to the drop-edge of the pool, so she could look down across Naima. The boulevard lights were coming on as the sun dipped below the horizon, creating a wan blue-green haze over the coastal town. Out on the sea, sailing boats were making their way back to the marinas. All very peaceful and bijou.

'This doesn't make any sense,' she told Zapata.

'In what way?'

'Shutting down factories is an inconvenience, but it's not going to kill off Utopial society. In fact, all it's done is wake them up to how shitty their digital defences are. In another six months Akitha will be immune to sabotage.'

'Sabotage at this level. If digital attacks are thwarted, the perpetrator may step up a level to physical assaults.'

'Sure. So, if you're prepared to attack telomere vector production, why not go straight to inflicting physical damage? And while we're at it, who the hell genuinely wants to smash a whole planet full of people back into the stone age?'

'There are a great many zealots with extreme ideologies, even today.'

'*Even today*. I hate that phrase. It assumes we're constantly improving.'

'Is the human race not improving socially?'

'Don't see it myself. Like I told Jaru, this Utopial society of hirs isn't the answer. The way they've insisted the second generation is always omnia is a dead-end structure. All it's done is create a separate culture – which, incidentally, never stops whining on about its superiority. That always ends well.'

'Then it is not unusual for such a culture to be subject to attack from ideological rivals.'

She pulled a face. 'I don't buy it. This is an odd assault. There's something else going on here.'

'What?'

'Mother Mary!' she said out loud 'I don't know. I don't get hired to figure things out. My bit's the simple part at the end.'

'Talking to yourself?'

Kandara looked round. Jessika was standing on the other side of the pool, a small smile on her lips as she held up a couple of wine glasses.

'Sorry,' Kandara grunted and climbed out of the pool. 'I was trying to work something out. Don't know why I bother. Altmes aren't exactly G8Turings.'

Jessika gave her one of the glasses. 'Something wrong with this crime-fighting set-up? I'm so disappointed you think that.'

Kandara grinned. 'It's fucking amateur hour. If this is how they tackle fanatics, the whole Utopial concept is doomed. You should pack your bow and arrows and head for the hills.'

'Yeah, I've been biting my tongue since I got here.'

'Didn't you tell Kruse we need professionals to work something like this?'

'Actually, Oistad and Tyle are good at what they do. And you and me, we are the professionals.'

'Mother Mary help them.' Kandara raised her glass in salute and sipped some of the wine; it was sweeter than she was expecting, and nicely chilled. Not bad.

Jessika glanced into the kitchen, where Kruse was now back at the table, in earnest conversation with the other two. 'What we lack is leadership. Kruse and her Bureau were assuming that if you bring me and Tyle and Oistad together with a decent G8Turing, we'd have no trouble tracking down the perpetrators. Then all we have to do is stand back while you go in and eliminate them.'

'Yeah. But there's something about this whole sabotage thing that bothers me.'

'I know. They can't see it, but the cost–benefit ratio is all wrong.'

'Excuse me?'

'People like Kruse, they genuinely don't get *old-economy* finance. Too enlightened. Here, if something needs to be done, it is done. Hey presto! With post-scarcity resources, no one thinks about the cost of anything, until you reach macro-projects like terraforming. But those are all political decisions reached democratically, and the manufacturing facilities are incorporated into what passes for this society's budget. If something is truly expensive in terms of resources, you don't borrow money to pay for it, you act rationally and spread the cost out, devoting what you can afford each decade. Timescale isn't so important now that we all live for a couple of centuries. It's all very nice and rational.'

'Living within your means.'

'Exactly. Which is why they don't see the problem. It costs commercial companies a lot to place an industrial espionage team here. Most of them pass themselves off as immigrants, converts to Utopials, looking for a better life and embracing the great new future culture. Immigrating here is easy enough; this is the second time I've done it. The only real requirement is that you agree to have baseline genome editing for any kids you have after you arrive.'

'So that they're omnia. Yeah, ideologically that stinks.'

'To you, yes. And it does kind of reinforce the difference between us and them.'

'Actually, I liked Jaru's equality theory. Fuck knows, I put up with enough shit from misogynistic pricks while I was in the military. I just think . . . there's got to be a different solution. Write me down as an old reactionary, I guess.' Kandara grimaced at the slip, and drank some more wine.

'So this is how a standard industrial espionage goes,' Jessika said. 'You're a professional gang tech that gets hired to steal data. You settle in your new town and go to barbecues with your neighbours, play sports in the local league – basically, blending in. But by night, you're a secret supervillain, you spend your time online black routing malware to try and bust medical research files. You succeed, and your corporate employer earns a billion wattdollars from a revolutionary new headache vector. Like I said earlier, it's cheaper than paying a research team. Cost effective. But *this* ... You get no benefit other than making your ideological enemy better prepared to resist further sabotage. Who can afford it?'

'There are a lot of zealots out there. Trust me, cost never deterred fanatics.'

'Okay, so where did this sabotage team get their money from? Their digital ability is astonishing. Tyle is convinced their routines were formatted by a G8Turing, and there aren't many of them anywhere. So far only governments and the bigger companies have them.'

'I don't know,' Kandara said. 'Maybe we are overlooking the obvious?'

'The Universal governments genuinely feel threatened by Utopials? It's a Cold War for our century?'

'Technically, that fits. But I'm thinking: just one team? Even if you're completely paranoid, that isn't how a government works. They have backups, fall-backs, hungry acolytes in training, whole departments given over to an ideological enemy's downfall.'

'Okay: one rich bigoted billionaire, or a globalPAC. They don't care, and don't think logically. Or there's something else altogether going on.'

'Urrgh.' Kandara tensed up. 'You know you're preaching to the converted, right? It's just that I can't figure out exactly what's wrong about this.'

Jessika shot a glance at Kruse, who was staring glumly at the kitchen table. 'Logically, given a poor cost-return, the sabotage is a diversion.'

'For what?'

'Exactly the question we should be asking. When I raised it, I got shot down.'

Kandara raised her gaze to whatever heavens occupied the sky above Akitha. 'Oh great. You want me to be your patsy.'

'That's: Trojan horse. But I think messenger is more accurate. Sie might listen to you. You are the expert, after all.'

'I fucking hate office politics!'

'Me too.' Jessika drained her glass and sauntered back into the villa. Kandara glared at her back, but knew she was right.

*

'The attacks are a subterfuge?' Kruse said incredulously half an hour later when Kandara had changed back into her singlet and shorts, and rejoined everyone in the kitchen.

'I don't know. But we have to cover all possibilities. Especially this one, as it might offer a route to tracking down the team launching these attacks. You cannot overlook this opportunity.'

'But . . . what are we looking for?'

Kandara was pleased she managed to avoid looking at Jessika. 'I'd suggest you review the networks that have suffered the attacks.'

'We already have,' Tyle said. 'No other secure files were cracked.'

'Even if you could guarantee that, which I don't believe you can, that's not what I want.'

'So what are we looking for?'

'Some kind of pattern. Something common to every attack. Start by finding out what other science projects were using the same network.'

Tyle gave Kruse a questioning look. 'It wouldn't hurt. We haven't got anything else.'

'All right,' Kruse said. 'Do it.'

*

It must have been something about the bed, or maybe planet-lag time difference. Kandara slept for almost three whole hours, waking at four o'clock local time when the town was still buried beneath the clear night sky.

She lay flat on her back, eyes open but unable to see the ceiling behind the dense grids of fluorescent data that Zapata splashed across her tarsus lens. The other four had spent most of the night reviewing the affected networks; there were hundreds of research and development projects sharing each one. The Bureau's G8Turing had sorted them into categories and attempted to match them, but there was no real pattern – not with the types of projects involved. Even the amount of resources they'd been allocated had no relation to where the attacks took place. She grinned at that grid column, suspecting Jessika had been the one insisting they provide a cost analysis. But in the end there was nothing. That was the problem with pattern analysis; you had to define the parameters correctly. *If it was easy everyone would do it.*

She began to feed in her own parameters, sending the columns twisting into new formations.

*

At five o'clock Kandara stalked down the villa's main corridor, banging on the bedroom doors. The team appeared grudgingly, rubbing sleep from their eyes, robes and PJs disarrayed as they ambled into the kitchen. They found Kandara operating the sleek coffee machine; she'd already filled a teapot with English breakfast tea, allowing it to brew.

'What?' Kruse demanded.

'I've found the pattern,' Kandara told hir.

'What is it?' Jessika asked sharply.

Kandara grinned. 'Weapons.'

'We don't have any weapons projects,' Oistad protested.

'Which is why you didn't find the pattern.'

Kruse sat at the big glass table and snagged a cup of coffee. 'All right, show us how smart you are.'

'I'm not smart. I got paranoid.'

'Ah,' Tyle exclaimed. 'Developments that could potentially be adapted for weapons usage.'

'Damn right.'

'Which are . . .?' Kruse asked.

Kandara raised a hand, and started ticking off on her fingers. 'The factory that produces pipe drilling remotes used by your water utility services, attacked nine weeks ago, that one shared a network with three teams researching lincbots. It's been a goal for decades, bots that can mechanically cling to each other to multiply their overall physical size and strength, and simultaneously network their processing power. We have lincbots, but the concept has plateaued; the network connectivity protocols are difficult to establish and glitchy even then. Your people are working on bots from ant-size up to big-dumb mechs. The ant-size are particularly interesting; when they linc up it's called the dry-fluid effect, where these things swarm in units of up to half a million. Picture a nest of army ants in perfect synchronization but with added intelligence – and purpose. I don't want to think of the damage they could inflict on a flesh body, while a clump of linced big-dumbs could take out entire city blocks.'

'Okay, I'll give you that could have aggressive applications,' Kruse said. 'What else?'

'The molecular bond fabricators. That research had spin-off research on shields. Obvious.' Kandara sipped her green tea, putting her thoughts in an order that would make the most compelling argument. 'Then there was last month's attack on the assembly core that puts together relays for the planetary power grid. That network was hosting a university lab working on magnetic confinement systems – also for power applications, mainly MHD chambers which the solarwells use.' She glanced round the blank expressions, enjoying the moment. 'No? These ones are small-scale confinement chambers, with monopolar magnetic field generators – very powerful. Perfect for spaceships with plasma rockets – or maybe missiles.'

'Oh, come on!' Oistad objected.

'Coherent X-ray beam emitter tubes, for micro-medical applications. Scale that up and you have gamma and X-ray beam weapons.'

Tyle and Kruse exchanged a look.

'Damn,' Jessika muttered.

'You said it,' Kandara said. 'The data attacks are irritants. This, on the other hand, takes everything to a whole different level.'

'But why?' Kruse asked, genuinely puzzled.

'One aspect at a time,' Kandara told hir. 'Let's try and confirm there is a pattern first. Tyle, can you check those projects I've just mentioned, see if any of their files have been cracked or copied?'

'Sure.'

'If you find anything, then we can start looking for motive.'

*

Servez brought their breakfast on the patio as the sun rose, shining a sharp bronze glimmer across the bay below. Kandara had eggs Benedict, with freshly squeezed orange juice, followed by croissants and wild-blueberry jam. When she was working, she wasn't as strict with her health food regime, figuring you never knew if you'd need the calories for extra energy.

Jessika ate with her, while the others coordinated their review with the Bureau's G8Turing. 'Nice job,' she told Kandara.

'I'm familiar with the game.'

'I wonder who we're up against.'

'The obvious choice is a weapons company.'

'Not so obvious. Why include the attacks? That's political, or maybe ideological. If you're stealing data you need to be stealthy.'

'Misdirection?' Kandara mused.

'But they knew we'd react to this. We had no choice.'

'Once we have more information, like who it is, the motivation should fall into place.'

'But that's the thing. What motivations can there be? They damaged us, the whole of Akitha. Who does that?'

'Fanatics,' Kandara replied automatically. 'I'm no longer surprised by what they do, by the misery and suffering they inflict on others. Ideology is a sick soul-meme; it gnaws basic decency away until you can self-justify the most extreme acts as worthwhile to further the cause. Any cause.'

Jessika gave her a surprised look, a spoon of fruit salad poised in front of her mouth. 'I didn't have you down as the philosophical type.'

'I'm not philosophizing. I'm simply telling you what I've seen.'

'Hell, I thought I'd seen bad stuff when I worked for Connexion Security.'

Kandara gave her a sympathetic grin and reached for another croissant. That was when the villa doors opened and Kruse came out, followed by Tyle and Oistad.

'They cracked the files, didn't they?' Kandara said. She barely needed to ask.

'I had to go deep into the management routines,' Tyle admitted. 'And even then all we found were ghost traces. The routines they're deploying are extremely sophisticated, and incredibly hard to detect. The Bureau is worried. It's like nothing we've ever seen before.'

'So it is a weapons company running an espionage team,' Jessika said.

'I think it might be worse than that,' Kruse said. 'We've only had an hour, but I asked the research teams to check the files. Some of them appear to have been altered.'

'Altered how?' Kandara asked.

'It's very subtle. The researchers are comparing the active files to deep cache copies. There are discrepancies. Not many, and not in all the files they've checked so far. But data has been tampered.' Sie looked worried. 'Entire projects have been compromised.'

'If hardware was built on the basis of those files, it wouldn't work,' Oistad said. 'The sabotage would have wrecked years of research, and lost us all the industrial resources allocated to fabrication.'

'Then it wasn't a distraction,' Kandara said thoughtfully. 'Not entirely. All of this is aimed at disabling your industrial base.'

'It's going to paralyse us,' Kruse said in a monotone. 'We don't know how widespread this is. We can't start to build anything new until the development data has been reviewed. This is . . . a declaration of war!'

'Interesting analysis,' Kandara said, 'given that this seems to be concentrating on systems that have weapons applications.'

'What are you saying?' Tyle asked.

'Your ability to build weapons that you can use to defend yourself against physical assault is being sabotaged.'

'Nobody's going to invade us!' Oistad said. 'That's insane.'

'Pearl Harbor,' Kandara muttered.

'No,' Kruse declared firmly. 'A couple of teams armed with the most advanced routines a G8Turing's written, and consumed by a hate-agenda – that I can accept. But some kind of physical attack? From whom? Nations don't have standing armies any more. You assemble ten thousand people and start giving them military training, and everybody will know. There's another purpose behind this; there has to be.'

'Glad to hear it,' Kandara said. 'Your intelligence service monitors everything on Zagreus, does it?'

Kruse shot her an exasperated look. 'I'm not dealing in hypotheticals.'

'Is that what I'm doing? We have reached over a hundred star systems. Twenty-three of them have planets that have been or are being terraformed. You have no idea what's going on in half of them. Did you know one criminal gang in the Ukraine is claiming to have an independent portal door to Zagreus? If you're truly rich, and managed to hang on to your money, you can buy your way back after you're renditioned.'

'Really?' a fascinated Tyle asked.

'Like I said: rumour. But I'm completely serious about not knowing what's going on in some of the star systems we're settling. And it doesn't have to be a human army. Soldier drones are cheap and easy to build.'

'I appreciate your insights and feedback,' Kruse said, 'but actually this isn't helping.'

'I understand your position. However, what we've found here tells us the kind of projects that this enemy team is likely to strike next. Tyle can load hir monitors into the appropriate networks.'

'Yes. We'll do that. I need to inform the Bureau.' Sie managed a weak smile of gratitude and went back indoors.

'For a society that prides itself on individual freedom, sie certainly talks to hir boss a lot,' Kandara observed.

*

The team was kept busy for the rest of the day, reviewing the initial discoveries and trying to identify more corrupted files. Most of the afternoon was spent trying to cross-index with current Universal visitors, and then recent immigrants. Finally the Bureau had them refining potential future targets.

It all allowed Kandara time to herself, which she spent jogging down to the beach and back up again before spending an hour in the villa's well-equipped gym. After that she ran test procedures on her weapons peripherals, using images splashed over her tarsus lens for virtual target practice. She much preferred physical range practice, but doubted Naima had one. At least none they'd admit to. She supposed Kruse's mysterious Bureau possessed a training facility for agents.

By late afternoon, Kandara was considering another swim when Kruse came looking for her.

'You need to pack your bagez,' sie said. 'We're transferring up to Onysko.'

'Where?' Even as she asked, Zapata was spraying information across her lens; it was the primary dormitory habitat for the Bremble asteroid. 'Never mind. Why are we going there?'

'It's been identified as a high-probability target. The highest, actually.'

*

Onysko wasn't quite as large as Nebesa, measuring only forty-eight kilometres long. This biosphere was temperate, and edging into its chilly autumn season when the team walked out of the portal hub. Once they were out in the open, Kandara turned round to look up at the endcap. She'd been expecting a ring city around the base, the same as on Nebesa. But here the flat circle was mostly a smooth grey faux-stone with several spectacular waterfalls curving sharply sideways from the Coriolis force. A few sections along the rim, like the one they'd emerged from, were urban zones, with their giveaway balcony stacks.

Zapata splashed up the habitat's population. 'Seven thousand?' Kandara asked in surprise. 'Are you sure?' She eyed the closest deciduous trees, which she guessed at a good fifty to sixty years old. The habitat really should have a larger population by now. Some of the larger habitats back in the Sol system were approaching populations of quarter of a million.

'That is the information supplied by the Onysko G8Turing. It is current.'

'Strange.'

They were assigned quarters in the Gloweth residency, a ten-storey ziggurat embedded in the endcap. Their apartment was on the third floor, larger than the Naima villa, but furnished in the same clinically minimalist style that had Kandara wondering if it was some kind of subtle Utopial conditioning therapy. It seemed to reinforce the feeling of middle-class conformity, which she already considered a little too prevalent in Delta Pavonis. It was as if everyone was reluctant about exposing a sign of individuality.

*

Tyle collected her for the meeting, the pair of them walking along a maze of corridors leading through the endcap. Jessika and Oistad were already waiting in the conference room when they arrived. Kandara's mouth lifted in a gentle smile as she appreciated where they were; one wall was a bulging window curving out from the habitat's external shell. She'd never seen anything like it; habitat shells were usually a solid hundred metres thick. Just thinking of the sleet of cosmic radiation striking the window made her nervous, as the transparent material didn't even look particularly thick. Despite that, she sat at the rock-slab table filling the middle of the room and stared unashamedly. The view made her wonder why she'd ever been impressed by the sight of Nebesa.

The window was facing the Bremble asteroid, which from

Kandara's viewpoint described a tight arc across the starfield outside as Onysko rotated laboriously. She could see the town-sized sprawls of machinery hanging limpet-fashion to its dusty grey-brown surface, sharp light from Delta Pavonis sparking on crinkled gold-foil sheets to make it twinkle hypnotically.

Zapata splashed a visual overlay, tagging the image components with identifiers. Most of the machinery clumps were industrial stations, sending root-like tendrils boring deep into the rock, extracting minerals for the refinery level to process before distributing them in turn to the construction units that formed the upper layer. Any elements that weren't available amid Bremble's complex weave of ore seams were fed in through portals linked to other asteroids and the moons of Lanivet, Delta Pavonis's solitary gas giant.

Over half of the stations were replicating themselves, Zapata said. A fascinated Kandara watched the glittering metallic encrustations that were slowly spreading over the oddly smooth regolith like mechanical bacteria. It would take years, but eventually the entire surface would be covered, converting the huge asteroid into a giant technological bauble.

Tags were flickering across the vast free-flying factory modules drifting around Bremble in a loose cloud, the majority constructing new habitats. The layout of the modules was predicated on the elegance of simplicity: a gantry ring eight kilometres in diameter, its plain geometric struts looking crude in comparison to the segments of enigmatically dark equipment they caged. They contained massive bonding field generators, a variant of those that produced city shields. With the refineries supplying a steady flow of vaporized material, the bonding fields squeezed the atoms back into a solid form again.

She stared in admiration at the energetic starlight glimmering across the smooth obsidian-like outer shells of the prodigious cylinders as they extruded out of the factory rings. As with Bremble's industrial stations, the process had an undeniable affinity with organic life.

And out beyond the collection of factory modules, recently

completed habitats gleamed like first-magnitude stars. A swarm that was slowly dissipating across the Delta Pavonis system, travelling on decade-long trajectories that would bring them to their own asteroid, where the mining/refining/manufacturing process would begin afresh. It made her picture Bremble as a dandelion head, casting its expanding cloud of seed to propagate time and again across the hostility of interplanetary distances.

More organic equivalence.

'Real Utopial von Numan-ism,' Tyle said happily as sie sat next to her. Sie smiled contentedly at the vista. 'Machines building machines, practically without any human intervention. Now that Onysko has G8Turings, they can manage so much more these days.'

Kandara pursed her lips as she gave Bremble a more searching assessment. It was smaller than Vesta, which was Sol's leading space industry asteroid, but she thought the systems on show here were a lot more sophisticated. They weren't constrained by conventional economics any more, she realized. 'Is this exponential?'

'Not yet. Give it another twenty years. The industrial stations will have engulfed Bremble, at which point they won't bother replicating themselves. They'll just consume the remaining rock to build habitats. After another fifty years, there'll be nothing left, and they'll fly to new asteroids and begin again.'

'That seems almost . . . dangerous.'

'Not at all. It's a triumph. We really are aiming for a genuine post-scarcity economy,' Oistad said, earnestly. 'The systems we're developing out here will finally make it possible. Right now, everything is macro, too interdependent. The industrial stations have a multitude of separate specialist fabricators, all of which knit together to make self-replication of the whole possible.'

'Cells in an organism,' she murmured.

'Right. Emilja wants to take us to the next, final stage and achieve an order of magnitude reduction in our current level of mechanical complexity. Ultimately down to a single unit which can replicate itself *ad infinitum*, then go on to produce specialist manufacturing systems like the ones out there building habitats.

The G8Turings should finally make all that possible. Once they do, it's the point at which Universal culture economics collapse.'

'And you smoothly replace it with an age of enlightenment?'

'Something like that,' Tyle said sardonically.

'Which, if someone is wrecking your industrial production capacity and advanced research in an ideological crusade . . .'

'Exactly.' Oistad gestured at the window. 'What you see out there is the true beating heart of Utopialism.'

Tyle chuckled. 'Make sure Kruse doesn't hear you say that.'

'Oh?' Kandara was interested. 'Why's that?'

'There are two components to Utopial society being an unqualified success,' Jessika explained. 'We have the physical aspect. That's the technology being developed here, which will make absolute post-scarcity possible by providing an over-abundance of material items. And then there's the philosophy, which will allow people to live fruitful, meaningful lives within such a physically rich environment. It's something humans are unaccustomed to.'

'I get that,' Kandara said. 'Why is Kruse upset by it?'

'Upset is the wrong word,' Oistad said. 'You see, Jaru promotes the philosophy aspect. It's hir belief that equality and human dignity are important above all else, even the material aspects of our culture.'

'Reasonable,' Kandara mused.

'Kruse is quite devout in hir support of Jaru.'

'Wait. There's a conflict inside the Utopial concept?'

'Conflict is a very strong word. There's a question of assigning priorities and resources. You see, Kruse and hir fellow travellers think omnias are just the first stage of human transformation. That if we truly reach an over-abundant supply state for our physical requirements, ordinary human personalities won't be able to cope and we'll collapse into decadence within a couple of generations.'

'The whole heaven-is-boring thesis,' Kandara ventured.

'Yes. Which our more radical colleagues are saying can only be solved if you gene-up basic human neurology.'

'Really? So if the people won't fit the new perfect society, alter the people? That sounds rather fascistic.'

Oistad nodded wryly. 'And yet, without Jaru's original notions of how to achieve equality, I wouldn't exist. And I am so very happy with what I am.'

'So you're in favour of even more artificial evolution?'

Sie shrugged and glanced over at Tyle for support. 'You have to solve the technological challenges first, and create the abundancy problem for real, or the whole notion dissolves into debating how many angels can dance on a pinhead. And for all the progress the von Neumann teams have made here on Onysko, we haven't got that close to single-unit self-replication yet. Humans still have to problem-solve. Not going out there with a screwdriver –' she pointed at the constellation of half-built habitats – 'but developing and enhancing what we have already. Some of us are concerned that the systems are starting to plateau, even with G8Turing involvement.'

'All human technology is levelling out,' Kandara said. 'But we're a starfaring species now. It's to be expected.'

'But we can go so much further. So many problems will simply vanish if we can build a proper von Neumann unit.'

'It never starts with jackboots and black uniforms,' Kandara said. 'Just good intentions. But that's how it always ends.'

'We're not going to impose our vision of how to live on others. That's not what we are at all.'

Kandara grinned at how earnest sie sounded. Out of the corner of her eye, she caught Jessika quashing her own amusement.

'What vision?' Kruse asked as sie walked into the conference room, followed by two other people.

'We're just talking philosophy,' Kandara said. 'As you do.' Then she paid attention to the woman behind Kruse. It was difficult actually to see anything with Zapata suddenly splashing so much personal data across her vision. 'Emilja Jurich,' she blurted in surprise.

Emilja was looking good for someone a hundred and sixty years old – certainly a lot better than Jaru, Kandara thought. Her hair was thick and dark, arranged in an elaborate nest around her head. Sharp cheekbones were prominent under the kind of healthy wrinkle-free skin that a twenty-five year old would take for granted. Light grey eyes gave the room a swift scan, which left Kandara feeling judged, and not in a good way. The woman had an almost regal presence, allowing her to carry off her formal black and carmine high-collar dress of Indian silk with an easy grace.

Kandara took a malicious guess that the telomere treatments she received were probably from an exclusive Earth clinic rather than a standard Utopial medical facility. Then again, she was a grade one, entitled to the best Akitha could provide. In her case, that was fair enough.

Emilja Jurich's parents had emigrated from Croatia to London back in 2027. Their daughter dutifully studied 3D printer programming at the London Metropolitan University, and was working in the distribution division of a food printing company in 2063 when Connexion opened its first portal link between New York and Los Angeles. What she did next became a classic case study for business schools across the Sol system and beyond.

Connexion had of course produced a map app for its burgeoning hub network, but Emilja could see how basic that was – a situation which was only going to get worse for users as more portals were added. So she founded her Hubnav Company that December, and spent every spare hour developing a mInet app to guide people through Connexion's rapidly expanding network. She started coding it when there was a grand total of three hundred and twenty-two public quantum entanglement portal doors in the Sol system, with Connexion already announcing its ambitious plans for fifty thousand more across the continental United States. She coded it because, growing up in London, she'd always appreciated the elegant modesty of Harry Beck's classic London Underground map, drawn with the simple truth that it didn't matter where the stations were, nor the way the tunnels twisted between them, because Beck instinctively recognized that all you really needed to know was where the stations were in relation to each other. She coded it because she knew people were basically stupid and lazy, and their world was about to become more complicated by an order of magnitude.

As Emilja studied the burgeoning tangle of hubs, she saw a series of interconnecting spider webs spreading across the globe. If you wanted to travel from, say, Oakham, in the heart of England, to Atlanta, Georgia, it was a theoretically simple route. Go through the Oakham hub loop into the county hub network, which links to the national hub network, and takes you to London, where there's a link to the international hub network, which takes you to the America Arrivals Port in North Dakota (that state's senators were impressively fast at digging into the government Fair Deal quantum entanglement infrastructure pork barrel, helped by a Washington backroom pact with Texas senators who snagged the National Commercial Goods Import Station for Houston). From there you walk into the inter-states hub to get to the Georgia hub network, and finally on to the Atlanta metro network, where you step out into the welcome of that sunny city's warm muggy air. A maximum of eight portals. Easy. Except with so many portals linking to other destinations each central hub was hell's own roundabout, especially at local rush hours.

And Emilja was right. People were stupid. After decades of sat-navs and autodrive cars, they just wanted to be held by the hand and guided, hassle-free. They wanted an app to tell them one central hub is jammed up with frustrated people, or a portal door is down for maintenance, so they could take a longer (but quicker) route through three alternative hubs. Where to go, which way to turn as soon as they emerge from a portal door, how many steps to the next, a green halo mInet graphic flashing round it just to be certain you've got the right one.

By 2078 there were twelve billion people living in the Sol system. Apart from toddlers, all of them had a copy of Emilja Jurich's Hubnav app, much to the fury of anti-monopoly legislators. By then, of course, the app provided its users with a rundown on their destination's weather, political status, canny bargains, top restaurants, cleanest beaches, hottest clubs, trendiest art, grooviest music events . . . The whole long, long, list of profiled advertising, each one bringing in revenue. Emilja wasn't quite as rich as Ainsley Zangari, but her wealth was enough to found her own habitats,

Dvor and Zabok, fuelled by the age-old dream of a fresh start fully independent of Earth. She was also rich and philanthropic enough to attend the First Progressive Conclave.

Along with Jaru Niyom, she underwrote the Utopial movement.

Kandara guessed Emilja was the leader of the Utopial's technology development faction. She was the practical one, wrestling equipment into obedience, mirror-twinned to Jaru's philosophic dreams. 'An honour to meet you,' Kandara said.

Emilja gave her a sly grin of acknowledgement and sat at the head of the rock-slab table. The pale, redheaded man who'd accompanied her sat on her left.

'Callum Hepburn,' Emilja said formally. 'Our von Neumann project technology strategist.'

'She means troubleshooter,' Callum said amicably.

'Has there been any trouble?' Kandara asked.

'Not on the scale that hit Naima's telomere production,' he said. 'But there have been more glitches out on the Bremble stations than usual. Of course, defining usual here is difficult in itself. All our industrial systems are under constant development as we evolve them up to the von Neumann mono-machine ideal. Some months everything goes smoothly; others we get overrun by problems. This current batch might be normal, or they might not. We'll need to give our files and routines a thorough audit.'

'I'd like permission to install monitor routines in Onysko's networks, and on the Bremble industrial stations,' Tyle said.

'If that's what you need,' Emilja said. 'Go ahead.'

'What happens if you find evidence of tampering?' Callum asked.

'It depends on when it occurs. If it's historical, then we'll pass it on to you. Hopefully you'll be able to assess and compensate for whatever damage there's been. And if it's current –' Tyle glanced over at Kandara – 'we believe we can track the access point.'

'And I'll deal with that for you,' she said.

Callum gave her an uneasy look. 'I think rendition to Zagreus would be more appropriate.'

'We've had that discussion in Senior Council, Callum,' Emilja said levelly. 'As a result, Investigator Martinez has been hired. I believe she is even more necessary now that we know the full extent of the sabotage against us. If you're going to attack Utopial society, this is where to do it; the severity of the other attacks may be a diversion.'

'It's your conscience at stake, not mine.'

'Thank you,' she said coldly. 'Investigator?'

'Yes?'

'If it is possible to apprehend one or more of this team, I would like you to do so.'

'I understand.'

'But not at risk to yourself.'

'I wouldn't expose myself to unnecessary risk; that has a habit of compromising my mission.'

'Very well. But I am very curious about who is behind this. The level of planning and the commitment to damage our entire culture is one which I find profoundly disturbing. I fear it won't be resolved simply by you eliminating the current threat.'

'I think you're right,' Kandara said. 'Do you have any idea who might have launched this?'

'It believe it highly unlikely to be a globalPAC or even a multistellar corporation. We've had our ideological disagreements with them; we still do. But this . . . No. They would understand that as soon as we uncovered their culpability, I would strike back.'

'Also, generating physical conflict is not on the globalPAC agenda,' Callum said. 'Quite the opposite. Zagreus rendition was their idea in the first place.' He grimaced. 'I know that for a fact. They stamp down heavily against anyone who uses violence, especially political violence. And that's what this is.'

'How long will it take to set up your routines?' Emilja asked Tyle.

'Hopefully within a day,' sie replied. 'There are a lot of networks, especially on Bremble. But the Bureau has allocated me additional G8Turings.'

'Very well,' Emilja said. 'Keep me informed.'

*

The team set up in an office on the ninth floor of the Gloweth residency, looking down the length of the habitat. Their desks had a full range of network access nodes and projectors, and there was a drinks dispenser in the corner which produced a great hot chocolate. It still lacked the kind of professionalism Kandara was accustomed to, but she had to admit it was an improvement on sitting round a kitchen table. They'd also acquired additional support from Onysko's small police force – five officers specializing in network security.

Tyle supervised the review of Onysko's projects, examining networked files for the kind of discrepancies they'd found before. It took fifteen hours.

'I've got something,' sie told Kandara. 'There's a materials science team in one of the astro-engineering offices up here; they're running a development project for spacesuits. It researches active magnetic polymers that will deflect cosmic radiation – a layer of that in a spacesuit will weigh a great deal less than the carbon and metal layers we're using now.'

'Okay, I can see that having some weapons capability,' Kandara said.

'It looks as if some of their key files were altered. We're running a comparison with deep-cached copies to see how many, but it fits the profile.'

'What about the access point?' Kandara asked.

Tyle's smile was confident. 'I've been thinking about that. There have been so few traces, and the G8Turing up here isn't that slouchy. It was like the project networks were being accessed directly, physically – which is contrary to all the illegal file cracks I know; they're always remote. I-heads access from as far away as possible with multiple random routing, so it takes time to trace and intercept. But up here, remote access would be risky; the G8Turing can monitor all the links back to Akitha. There are five portal doors that carry all the habitat's digital traffic.'

'They're doing this from inside the research lab?' Kandara said. 'How did they get in there?'

'They didn't.' Tyle's smile was growing broader. The others in the office had all stopped working to look at hir from inside the cages of glowing hologram icons. 'We don't have a huge amount of security up here, but the critical areas are all covered with restricted systems that the Bureau maintains. Someone cleared the standard coverage around the lab, but they didn't know about the additional Bureau systems.' Sie pointed as a projection formed beside hir desk.

It was a standard digital services crypt, filled with row after row of equipment stacks – geometric galaxies of twinkling electronics encased in dark glass, altars devoid of worship. Except for the man walking along the narrow aisles, his stern features illuminated by diffuse blue lighting, a silver-white insulated coverall providing him with a little protection against the icy air.

Everyone watched him slide a glass panel open, exposing the tight-packed racks inside. He ran a hand down them, eyes shut as if he was communing with the systems. Kandara realized that in a way he was; his fingers must contain scanner peripherals, analysing the racks. He stopped and slid one out, exposing the bundled optical cables along the side. What looked like a barcode label was applied to the top of the electronics, then the rack was pushed back into place. He stood there for a minute, watching whatever graphics were being splashed across his tarsus lens, before closing the glass cover.

Kandara pursed her lips. 'Physical intrusion,' she said, almost admiringly. 'That's real old-school. You need a lot of balls to attempt that.'

'We've all got 'em,' Oistad said, grinning at Tyle, who groaned in dismay.

'Onysko's vulnerable to that kind of operation,' Jessika said. 'It was a smart move.'

'They analysed your systems and found the weak spot,' Kandara said. 'That's a professional team. I don't think they'll be the fanatics; all they're interested in is the money.'

'Here you go,' Jessika said. A projector above her desk was showing the man's face, this time with a lazy smile. 'Baylis Arntsen, a botanist from the University of Phoenix on a two-year research exchange scheme; his specialty is developing the synthetic biology of desert flora. We have two habitats under construction scheduled for arid-climate biospheres.'

'Go back through all the restricted security files,' Kruse demanded. 'Find out what else he's done to our networks.'

'The Bureau's G8Turings are running it now,' Tyle said.

They had to wait another ten minutes before the next sensor recording materialized; another man in a different services crypt. Identified as Nagato Fasan, emigrated to Akitha seventeen months earlier, an enthusiastic convert to the Utopial ethos. Then a woman, Niomi Mårtensson. According to her file she had a physics doctorate from Munich University – knowledge she was applying to build synthesizers to create organosilicon life. She was on secondment from a North African open source research institute.

Jessika took one look at her thin face and nerdy pale hair. 'Son of a bitch!'

'What?' Kruse asked.

'That's Cancer!'

Kandara focused on Niomi Mårtensson's bland image, ignoring the way her skin temperature seemed to have suddenly dropped a couple of degrees. 'Are you sure?'

'Goddamn right I am. I spent a year working on a case when I was with Connexion, trying to track her. She's changed her hair, and the eyes are a different colour, but I know her.'

'Everyone, stop right now,' Kandara said abruptly. 'Nobody is to ask any Turing for a check on Niomi Mårtensson. No file to be accessed, understand? Cancer will have loaded monitors into the network that'll spot any reference to her.' She glanced round the office, half expecting to catch someone in the act of making a warning call.

'So what now?' Oistad asked cautiously.

Kandara turned to Kruse. 'First, shut down all Onysko's portal doors.'

'All?'

'Yes. Not just the pedestrian hubs back to Akitha and the other habitats; I want the cargo portals, too. Everything. We need to isolate her up here.'

'I'll . . . ask.'

'No. That's not good enough. Talk to someone – Jaru, or Emilja. Shit, both of them if you have to; whatever it takes, but get the authority without making a big deal of it. No committees, no standard procedures.'

Kruse gave a determined nod. 'Okay. I'll get it done.'

Kandara turned to Tyle and Oistad. 'When Onysko's isolated, and not before, we need to fix their locations.'

'The Bureau Turings can run a visual search,' Oistad said. 'We'll have them straight away.'

Kandara pulled a face as she studied the projections floating above Tyle's desk. 'As soon as the portals shut down, they'll know they've been blown and we're hunting them.'

'I can find them fast,' Oistad insisted. 'Their altmes will be linked to the network. I can run an interface check; it'll register as a maintenance ping.'

'We can go old-school, too,' Jessika said. 'Just call their colleagues, the ones they're supposed to be working with. Actually ask them to confirm who's in the room.'

'Okay,' Kandara said. 'Go wide. All the methods of confirming their location, trigger them together.'

*

Kruse took seven minutes to obtain the authority to divorce Onysko from the rest of the Delta Pavonis system, using an emergency biohazard quarantine procedure that Emilja provided authorization for. Kandara used the time to summon her bagez and to suit-up in the office washroom. Her armour was a skin-tight one-piece, with five individual protective layers; the innermost being thermal regulation keeping her body temperature constant. Then a self-sealing pressure membrane for biological or toxic weapons, which also allowed her to function in a vacuum or underwater environment. Another thermal layer, this time to resist both high temperature or sub-zero exposure; on top of that was a radiation reflector which could ward off energy beams and EM pulses. And then the external layer – four centimetres of kinetic protection armour, which was flexible enough to give her full motion but would harden when struck by bullets or shrapnel; it was also resistant to monomolecule filament. The helmet was a featureless shark-profile, equipped with active and passive sensors, interfaced with Zapata and providing enhanced vision through her tarsus lens. Her slim segmented backpack provided life support, power for beam weapons and projectile magazine storage, as well as a field medic kit. Microdrones clung to the base like a cluster of black beetles. Wrist bracelets contained gamma-laser emitters and mini-grenade launchers, while her left forearm had a vambrace mount for a small magrail rifle, with a projectile feed from her backpack.

She clumped back into the office, weighing in at over eighty kilos.

'Holy shit,' Jessika exclaimed. 'You look like a seriously badass fallen angel. Does that thing pack a flaming sword, too?'

'Not today. But nice suggestion, thanks.'

'I'm about to order the shutdown,' Kruse said.

'Wait until I get down to the Gloweth hub,' Kandara told hir. 'Then I'll give you the go-ahead. When you have their locations, close Onysko's internal hubs, but leave me a route open to intercept whichever of them is nearest.'

'I'm coming with you,' Kruse said.

'No.'

'But we have to deploy our local police. They'll physically cordon off the area you're operating in. I'm responsible for minimizing any damage and casualties.'

'Fine. You can create a cordon to stop any of your citizens getting near, but make it very plain to the police that if Arntsen, Fasan or Cancer exit the area, they are not to try and stop them. I will take them down.'

'Agreed.'

Kandara sighed, which went unheard outside her helmet. 'The rest of you need to keep a tight watch on events. I'm going to need constant operational intel.'

'You'll get it,' Jessika said. 'I know how to filter for this kind of procedure.'

Kandara left the office and went down two levels to one of the Gloweth hubs.

'The police tactical team is ready for deployment,' Kruse announced.

Kandara wondered if Cancer's monitors would be telling her the same thing. 'Jessika, when we have locations, can you cut network access in each area, please?'

'Sure thing.'

The hub was deserted. Kandara stood in the entrance, running a final check on her medical vitals. Took a breath. Switched her weapons systems to active. 'Okay, Kruse: initiate.'

Zapata's display showed her the portal doors powering down, reducing their twin links to a nul-space entanglement. The three hub portals in front of her maintained their integrity. 'Tyle?'

'Ping is active.'

'Got them,' Jessika cried.

Zapata splashed the results across her vision. Arntsen and Fasan were together inside a lab in the Eóin research block on Onysko's other endcap. Cancer was on Bremble, in a silicon refinery module.

A route to Eóin splashed across her tarsus lens. She moved fast, running through the first portal door, turning sharp left in the next hub, another door. People milling round in confusion as portal doors started to shut down. One remained open. 'Nice job,' Kandara muttered as she sprinted through. Twist left again. Four fast steps. And she was out into Eóin's central oval atrium, lined with a broad ramp that spiralled up from the black and white marble floor, looping round eight storeys of laboratories and offices.

'Eóin network suspended,' Jessika reported. 'All portal hubs closed.'

'Can you seal the laboratory doors?' Kandara grunted as she hit the ramp and started sprinting. Arntsen and Fasan were in Lab Five on the second level.

'I think so.'

She could see several people on the spiral, leaning over the white balustrade, frowning as they looked round to see what the problem with the hubs was. Several doors were opening, more people coming out. 'Do it fast. There are too many people exposed here.'

'The police are on their way,' Kruse said. 'They'll help clear the area.'

'We're way past that point,' Kandara said. Her sensors caught hir, with Zapata's feature-recognition routines confirming. Kruse was walking out onto the black and white tiles of the floor below.

'What are you doing?' Kandara snapped furiously. Sie must have followed her from Gloweth.

'I'm responsible for this operation,' Kruse replied levelly. 'I'll supervise the police and start evacuating civilians.'

'Fuck's sake! Just stay the hell back.'

Two people on the ramp ahead of her, turning to gaze in astonishment at the squat armour-clad figure pounding towards them. Surprise and fear rising on their faces in a near-comic slow motion. Then Kandara had barged past, with only one half-circle of ramp left before she reached Lab Five.

Her helmet sensors picked up a drone descending fast down the centre of the atrium. It was a standard bracelet shape, twenty centimetres wide, with internal contra-rotating fans. She instinctively knew it was *wrong*. 'I thought you'd killed Eóin's network?'

'I have,' Jessika said. 'The only channel in is this secure com.'

'Then why is there a remote drone in here?'

'What drone?'

Kandara reached level two, the door to the lab seventeen metres ahead, and the drone was drawing level. Her right arm came up, and target graphics closed on the little machine. A gamma beam sliced into it.

The explosion turned her armour layer completely rigid and slammed her against the wall. A big chunk of balustrade and ramp vanished in the blast, smouldering debris cascading down onto the tiles two floors below. People who'd been on the spiral ramp were struck by the brutal blastwave, bodies flung into the structure, limbs broken, flesh torn and burned. In the first few seconds' aftermath, the atrium was claimed by a vacuous silence. Then the screaming started.

'What the fuck was that?' Jessika yelled. 'What's going on?'

'Weapons drone,' Kandara grunted. Zapata splashed a fast suit status for her. External damage minimal, all systems functional. She pushed herself away from the wall and powered on towards Lab Five. Its metal door had buckled in the explosion. Kandara shot it with a mini-grenade.

Her armour stiffened up again as the grenade detonated, flinging shards of metal in all directions. She skirted the missing hunk of ramp carefully and launched three microdrones through the gaping hole into Lab Five.

Their images splashed across her tarsus lens as they flew forwards. The laboratory followed a standard layout: big bioreactor cabinets lined up along one wall; benches laden with glassware, tended by robot arms; workstations orbited by complex holographic data grids. A tall cylindrical fish tank stood in one corner. The mini-grenade had reduced the room to chaos: cabinets warped and cracked, glassware shattered into avalanches of shards saturated with sticky chemicals. Arntsen and Fasan were on their knees behind a bench, blood dripping from their eardrums, exposed skin cut by flying glass. Fasan was holding a small black tube that the drone's sensors revealed as a beam weapon, while Arntsen seemed to be dazed and disorientated.

The drones completed their scan of the lab. There was no one else inside.

Kandara flattened herself against the wall to one side of the ruined door and shoved her hand out across the gap. Three more mini-grenades were fired into Lab Five, programmed to detonate close to the back wall so the fugitives wouldn't be shielded by the bench.

The drone sensors showed her the overlapping explosions. She saw the fish tank finally disintegrate, sending water sloshing across the floor, with thrashing fish surfing the churning ripples. Several of them slithered to a halt around Arntsen, who was now facedown, his clothes badly ripped by the blasts. Several of his ribs were visible in the gashes where skin had been flayed and burned from his back.

Fasan, by some miracle, was still relatively undamaged. He was crawling towards the shattered window wall. Kandara selected a projectile for the magrail rifle and spun round the warped door-frame. There were three benches between her and Fasan. Target graphics locked on to his head – a coordinate supplied by the mini-drones. The rifle fired, punching the projectile through the benches as if they were holograms. His head exploded in a cloud of gore-vapour and bone shrapnel.

Kandara walked forwards as slender white rods began to slide up out of the bruised flesh of Arnsten's forearms. 'Shit!' She shot two mini-grenades at him. His body ruptured, spraying gobs of skin and organ across the laboratory.

Two of his projectile peripherals fired on her as they sailed through the air – one embedded in his wrist, another rooted in a long chunk of humerus bone that spun like a baton. Her armour's outer layer locked, deflecting the impacts. Even so, they were powerful enough to shove her back towards the broken door. Helmet sensors revealed his peripherals that had survived the grenades, splashing them like a cloud of gold embers across the lab. Kandara's arms moved as if she was karate-chopping an invisible foe, using her gamma lasers to kill the small devices before they could attack her.

Once they were reduced to smoking cinder points, she went over to Fusan's headless corpse and began a precision strike on his peripherals.

'Kandara, what's your status?' Jessika asked.

'Still active. You can restore Eóin's network now. Arntsen and Fasan have been eliminated. Tell whatever clean-up crew you send to be vigilant. I've disabled their peripherals, but they might have left other hostile systems behind.'

'Understood. Kandara, we're worried about Kruse. Hir altme is offline.'

Kandara walked out of the lab. 'I'm not surprised. Sie was completely exposed to the drone explosion.' She scanned round the ramp, her suit sensors picking up the moaning and cries of pain. 'There are casualties. You can allow the paramedics in.'

'Opening the hubs to Eóin now,' Oistad said. 'Can you get a visual on Kruse?'

'I'm on my way down now. Do not open any portal doors to Bremble. It's imperative that Cancer remains isolated.'

'We've got that. But what about Kruse?'

Kandara looked over the balustrade to see police in dark armour entering the atrium in a tactical formation. Debris from the shattered ramp was piled high on the prim black and white tiles, while the air remained hazed with dust.

'Kruse is dead. I can see hir. Sie was caught by the blast and the rubble. My sensors can't find a pulse.'

'Holy fuck!' Jessika cried. 'No!'

'Are you sure?' Tyle asked.

'Pretty much. Have you found out how the weapons drone was being controlled?'

'What?'

'The weapons drone in Eóin. You shut down the local network, yet it was being controlled. How?'

'Kruse is dead?'

Kandara cursed inside the privacy of her helmet as she arrived at the bottom of the ramp. This was what happened when the ops team weren't true professionals. 'Yes,' she ground out. 'But the operation is still ongoing. Now, where's my route to Bremble, and how does Cancer still have access to the network?'

The police watched warily as she hurried through them on her way back to the hub. In front of her, the first paramedics were arriving, each with a tight cluster of medical bagez rolling along at their heels.

'I have three possible routes to Bremble for you,' Jessika said. 'Coming through now.'

Kandara studied the map that splashed across her lens. Three different portal doors, with one inside the silicon refinery's small pressurized control centre, and two outside the main section. 'How good is that last known position?' According to the intel, Cancer was beside one of the material processing cores, almost at the centre of the refinery.

'She was there as of three minutes ago,' Jessika confirmed.

'Okay. I'm entering the hub now.' Kandara didn't say what her exit point was going to be. Maybe basic training, maybe paranoia, but Cancer had compromised Onysko's data network. She might even be listening in to the secure channel.

'I think she's using the same black routing that they used to get into our networks originally,' Oistad said. 'The Bureau Turings are reviewing traffic packages for encrypted Trojans. I'll try to isolate them.'

'Okay,' Kandara said. 'In the meantime, download me whatever real-time intel you can from inside the refinery. I also want you and the Turings to access every sensor in the area. If she goes external, I need to know.'

'Understood,' Tyle said.

Kandara went through the first hub door and turned right straight away. She could feel her heart rate increasing. So many law enforcement and security teams had confronted Cancer over the years, and there weren't many survivors. Every time, Cancer fought as if she was invincible, and with the ferocity of somebody who had nothing to lose.

Now she was going one on one, with no real backup. The only way to do that was to fight fire with fire.

Four hubs – and twenty-three steps – brought Kandara to a long tubular airlock designed for ten people. The hatch swung shut behind her and she triggered the emergency vent. Air screamed around her, turning to white vapour; she could hear it even through the helmet insulation. The noise barely lasted a couple of seconds as the vanishing atmosphere buffeted her with the ferocity of mountaintop wind. Fifteen seconds later, she was in a hard vacuum. The circular hatch in front of her unlocked and swung open, revealing a starfield above the crinkled gold surface of Bremble's huge industrial station.

'Low-gravity environment ahead,' Zapata warned.

Kandara raised her left arm and fired a wide-pattern fusillade of smart sensor pellets at low-velocity. The image they splashed across her lens showed the different industrial modules arranged like city blocks, with a grid of deep metallic canyons between them. The airlock was on top of a storage sector, with fifteen big spherical tanks bunched together, along with their piping and heating mechanisms. They were crowned by a broad circular platform, used as a landing and parking bay for small engineering pods. Five of the little craft were docked to it, their systems plugged into stumpy umbilical pillars.

'Jessika, disable those engineering pods.'

'Way ahead of you. Three are locked down, and I have secure remote access to two of them if you need it.'

'Thanks.'

Half of the smart pellets had struck the refinery module walls, sticking to the flimsy foil surface. They scanned back across the gulf, seeking the signature of Niomi Mårtensson's spacesuit.

'Looks clean,' Kandara said. 'Moving out.'

'Just . . .' Jessika hesitated.

'What?'

'Be careful,' Tyle said.

'Always am.' Kandara moved to the back of the airlock, then ran at the open hatch – and jumped. The airlock itself was still inside Onysko, while its hatch opened into a portal door that was on the top of the Bremble storage tanks. As soon as she crossed the threshold she was immediately subject to the asteroid's minute gravity field. She grinned savagely at the sensation of flying superhero-style above the platform, and out across the gulf between the tanks and refinery. When she passed over the edge, tiny thrusters on her suit torso flipped her upright, and pushed her course down slightly. She released two mini-grenades from her left bracelet.

The refinery module was built around a cluster of long cylindrical material processor cores and their ancillary equipment, all encased in a thin shell of gold-skinned metalocarbon that was tarnished from over two decades of vacuum exposure. It was almost fifty metres tall, and seventy wide, sitting on top of a squat extractor rig the same size. Struts and odd mechanical protrusions stuck out into the dark canyons surrounding it, illuminated by tiny lights that drove down to a black vanishing point where the asteroid's surface was hiding.

The mini-grenades exploded in silence, violet light flaring in perfect intersecting hemispheres, consuming the fragile shell. A swarm of fizzing shards twirled out from the impact. Then the glare was fading and Kandara's suit sensors revealed the irregular hole seared into the side. Her thrusters fired again, refining her trajectory, and she soared through the narrow gap, wincing as she went past the still-glowing jags.

There was no light inside other than the weak illumination seeping through the grenade rent. Her sensors switched to infrared, revealing a three-dimensional matrix of machinery and cables and pipes rendered in green and black. Directly in front of her was a narrow curving gridwork, approaching *fast*. She grabbed a crosspiece and jerked to a halt, straining her deltoid muscle. The refinery machines were producing a constant vibration which she could feel through the gauntlet. High-voltage cables gleamed sunset orange as the sensors picked up their magnetic field.

'I'm in.'

'We're getting sensor glitches on level seventeen,' Jessika reported. 'That's two below the control centre she was in.'

'Okay, going down.'

Zapata splashed up a schematic of the refinery. Kandara started to haul herself along, using cables or support girders, whatever she could grab. Sometimes the equipment was packed so tight she could barely get through the gaps, then she'd be in empty spaces bigger than her apartment. Finally she found an accessway – a tube made from a composite grid allowing mechez and humans easy transit. There were dozens of the tubes winding their way around the interior of the refinery, as if some piece of rogue cybernetics had dug itself a warren. Looking at it all, she'd never felt more like a field mouse lost in a construction site.

'All the refinery's sensors just failed,' Tyle said, a strong hint of panic in hir voice. 'I'm working to restore them.'

'She's still in here then,' Kandara said, pulling herself along inside the accessway. The size of the refinery was going to give

Cancer a huge advantage, she realized. Without sensors, they could spend a week moving round trying to find each other – and that was assuming Cancer would seek a confrontation. 'She's going to want to escape,' she said. 'If she goes down into the extractor rig below, will she have a better route out?'

'Not particularly,' Jessika said. 'The extractor rig and refinery where you are have a physical gap between other modules. She'll have to cross that gap somehow.'

'We've got active sensors on all sides of you,' Oistad said. 'If she makes a break for it, we'll know.'

'And if she switches them off as well?'

'I'm hardening the network,' Tyle said. 'But if she does disable some, at least that'll give us an indication of where she might be.'

Three minutes later Kandara was at level seventeen. If it hadn't been for Zapata's guidance graphics, she wouldn't even have known which way was down, Bremble's gravity was so slight. She gripped one of the accessway's struts and held herself motionless. Her helmet sensors scanned round on their maximum magnification. Nothing.

'Do the G8Turing have control over the refinery's mechez?' she asked.

'No, I shut them out when I restricted the network. We'd have to open up a lot of bandwidth for that,' Oistad said. 'That'd give Cancer more channels to route a call out.'

'Who's she going to call?' Kandara muttered. 'All right, this is how we play it. Reopen the network as much as you need and move every mechez on the refinery inventory to level fifteen and level nineteen. I want every accessway physically blocked, so no one can get through those levels. Are there enough of them to do that?'

'Yes,' Oistad said.

'Right. Once that's done, start moving them into this level. Get the noose round her, and start contracting it.'

While the team started organizing the remotes, Kandara snaked along the accessway. Every time she reached an intersection, she left a drone, then moved on. The one place she didn't venture into was the control centre. She was worried Cancer might have booby-trapped it. In fact, she was surprised there were no smart mines concealed somewhere in the accessways.

Or perhaps there are, and I just haven't come into trigger range yet.

The thought made slithering along inside the dark winding accessways a nervy experience. She didn't usually suffer from claustrophobia, but this was pushing her close.

'Kandara, we might have a problem,' Jessika said.

She froze, surrounded by misty green thermal outlines, with the power cables forming an irregular glowing web around her – none of it real. The refinery's vibration was still present in the strut she was holding. No sign of a human heat signature. 'What?'

'Something's blocking an extractor rig ice-feed chamber. Eight levels below you.'

'You mean a feed inside the extractor rig?'

'Yes.'

'I thought you said there's no way out down there?'

'Oh shit. The feeds, they bring in ice.'

'Ice?'

'Yes. The refinery process uses a lot of water.'

'Where the hell does ice come fr—? Oh fuck! I said shut down all the portals.'

'One of the harvesters on Verby is malfunctioning,' Oistad said. 'The ice feed has shut down. Sensors are offline. I can't see the damage.'

'The *damage* is her, going through,' Kandara realized. 'Where the hell is Verby?'

'It's one of Lanivet's moons,' Zapata informed her. 'The surface is covered with extensive ice oceans. The water has a low mineral content and is therefore an excellent resource for both industrial systems and habitat biospheres.'

'Mother Mary. Jessika, give me a route down to the ice-feed chamber. Fast!'

'Coming through now.'

Kandara started to haul herself along the accessway, following the glowing purple route line now splashed over her lens. 'Is there anyone on Verby?'

'No, just the G7Turings controlling the ice harvest. The operation is completely automated.'

'Good. You know the drill. Shut down every portal. Properly, this time.'

'Kandara,' Oistad said, 'the ice feeds are essential to half of Bremble's industrial systems; and the habitats need water, too.'

'How many people does she have to kill before you listen to me?' she shouted. 'Shut the fucking ice feeds down!'

'Powering them down now,' Jessika said. 'Listen, that harvester she went through, it has three ice feeds into the extractor rig. I've stopped the other two.'

Kandara smiled to herself. *Clever girl*, she thought. The locations of the other two feed chambers were suddenly splashed across her vision. She changed course and went for one that Cancer hadn't used to reach Verby. Most likely the diabolical woman was waiting on the other side, or worse, a drone would be watching, and she'd blow the power while Kandara was halfway through.

Unless she's bluffing our bluff. She shook her head, angry with herself. *Too paranoid.*

The ice-feed chamber was a broad cylinder that sprouted five branches which then went on to branch again deeper into the extractor rig, like the boughs of some ancient tree that had long been entombed by machinery. As Kandara approached, an access hatch near the base slid aside. She eased herself in.

When Jessika shut down the ice flow, the extractor rig had continued to swallow the chunks of ice already inside the feed chamber. Now the cylinder which minutes ago had been packed with a constant stream of crushed ice was empty apart from a tenuous mist of twinkling particles. Kandara pushed off cautiously, and sent several smart pellets on ahead. They revealed very little, just more curving metal walls, which was the mirror image of the extractor rig end; the harvester supplied the ice through over a dozen smaller pipes. But her sensors couldn't detect any other sensors watching for her.

No more calculating risks. No more doubts.

Go!

She pushed off hard, zipping through the portal. Verby's one-fifth standard gravity abruptly tugged her down. She landed with a shoulder roll, springing up fast, which sent her rising off the floor. At the same time she held her left arm out and moved it in a smooth arc, firing armour-piercing rounds as she went. The munitions blasted through the feed chamber's walls on either side and above her, exploding inside the harvester. Her feet were pushed down by the rifle's impulse. She could feel the harvester juddering beneath her soles as it ground to a halt.

'Do you know how much those cost?' Tyle asked drily.

'I thought you guys didn't lower yourself to talk money?'

'In terms of resources, and time to replace it.'

'You wanted an accountant to do this job? Should've hired one.' The ruined feed chamber began to split asunder; she stood directly under the slowly widening gap, and jumped. In the low gravity, her gened-up muscles pushed her an easy five metres upwards, landing precariously on a warped and splintered section of the upper bodywork towards the rear of the machine. 'Now close down the last portals on Verby. Nothing apart from the data links, and if they're above ten centimetres in diameter, cut them too,'

'Already done,' Jessika said. 'There's no way off that moon.' She paused. 'For either of you.'

'You hear that?' Kandara asked, raising her voice despite how foolish that felt.

No answer. But then she hadn't expected one. She started to pick her way along the twisted bodywork as the broken harvester swayed about, settling ponderously.

It was a huge vehicle. The blade scoop at the front was thirty metres wide, cutting a five-metre deep channel through the frozen ocean as it rolled forwards. Power blades along the lower edge could chop through granite if they ever encountered any – not that this moon had any rock even approaching that level of toughness. The harvester fleet operated on the bottom of a pit the size of a small sea they'd gouged out over the last twenty years. In the distance, she could see vertical cliffs an easy three kilometres high.

443

When she looked up, Lanivet formed a vast crescent that filled a third of the sky. Its seething cloud bands were pale pink, streaked with white, with occasional slashes of cobalt blue squirting up from the unknown depths. Myriad cyclones churned arrogantly through them, though nothing the world-swallowing size of Jupiter's Great Red Spot. The waning gas giant radiated a pastel light which shaded the sparkling ice a gentle damask.

Kandara clambered up the harvester's twisted metal and composite bodywork to the highest point and scanned round. 'She's either got the greatest stealth technology ever built, or she's still here.'

'Can you see any footprint tracks leading away?' Tyle asked. 'There's no stealth that can cover that up.'

She studied the surface a little closer, moderately impressed with Tyle's suggestion. Five kilometres away another harvester was slowly braking, with high fantails of ice grains rising in sluggish arcs from either side of its scoop blade. The constant deluge from all the harvesters had coated the pit's surface of solid ice with several centimetres of ice granules, as neat and uniform as a Zen garden. 'I can't see any tracks,' she reported. 'Jessika, can you get me any images of Cancer coming out to Bremble today? Specifically, what spacesuit she was wearing.'

'I think I see where you're going with this. Hang on.'

Kandara moved down the harvester several metres; being perched on top would make her a splendid target. *But I haven't been shot at. Why?*

The whole situation was making her jittery, gnawing at her resolution. Cancer wouldn't hold back. *Did I get her with those first shots into the harvester? Could I be that lucky?*

'Get me a schematic of the harvester,' she told Zapata. 'She's got to be inside somewhere.'

The translucent image splashed across her tarsus lens highlighted the harvester's internal walkways and small maintenance cubicles. Ninety per cent of the interior was solid machinery. Of course, the explosive projectiles had opened up gashes big enough to shelter a human, but not many.

Kandara scattered a dozen microdrones and watched them scurry through the fissures. They'd be able to find her elusive target quickly enough.

'You were right,' Jessika said. 'I'm looking at video of her going out to Bremble this morning. She was in a standard-issue spacesuit.'

'Did she bring it with her from Sol, or is it one of yours?'

'Ours.'

'Ping the beacon.'

Kandara held her breath, but the transponder didn't respond.

'Sorry,' Jessika said. 'She's wiped the standard routines.'

Or one of my explosive rounds hit her. 'Worth a try. But at least it's not armour.'

'Kandara,' Tyle said. 'Are you shooting at the harvester again?'

'No. Why?'

'I'm reviewing the telemetry – what's left. Systems are going offline in the main power network. It looks like they're being physically damaged.'

'Show me,' Kandara instructed.

The schematic splashed up the harvester's power system. A tiny portal supplied power to the vehicle from Akitha's solarwell electrical grid, but there were several quantum batteries distributed through the big machine as backups, keeping essential equipment active in the case of a power failure. If the harvester cooled below thirty Celsius, it would be a lot tougher for the maintenance teams to restore.

She saw the failures were all in the same section, around a quantum battery that supplied power to the rear caterpillar tracks.

'What systems are being hit?' she asked as she sent three microdrones racing to the location. 'Is there a pattern?'

Zapata mapped a route to the section. She'd need go back into the harvester through a hatchway on the left-hand side. But . . . Inside was the last place she wanted to be. 'Find me a target line the magrail can shoot through,' she told Zapata. From what she could see on the schematic, the section was almost completely surrounded by chunks of dense machinery.

'Er, Kandara,' Tyle said. 'It's the safety systems that are being taken out. Two more have just gone.'

A microdrone crawled into the tiny cubical that provided access to the quantum battery and its cabling. Kandara felt her breath catch. Cancer was there, using a tool to work inside a high-voltage cabinet. The woman turned in a smooth motion, lining her right hand up on the microdrone. The connection vanished, but not before its radiation sensor spiked.

Maser, Kandara realized. Cancer was using a peripheral to shoot through her suit. The narrow beam would wreck any active systems in the fabric it passed through, but wouldn't puncture it. Kandara opened her communications to an open broadcast.

'Cancer, there's no way out. You know that. Every portal is closed to you.'

No answer.

'I'm authorized to offer you a deal. Tell us who hired you, and you'll be renditioned to Zagreus. Refuse, and you'll be terminated.'

'She just took out another voltage regulator,' Tyle said. 'There are only two left to limit the quantum battery's output.'

Kandara looked down at her feet. The crumbled bodywork she was standing on was composite – non-conducting. But the frame underneath was boron fibre reinforced aluminium. *Is she trying to electrocute me? But she's inside; she'll receive a lot more of the charge.*

It didn't make much sense, but Kandara crouched down and jumped anyway. Her muscles were strong enough to propel her in a long arc, taking her over the side of the harvester. She landed hard in the mushy ice granules, but managed to keep upright as her boots slithered about. The ice came up over her ankles.

Mother Mary! 'Tyle, if she rigs a full discharge, how far will the ice conduct the charge?' She looked back up at the broken harvester, ready to jump back. Her armour could ward off an electric shock, ordinarily, but that quantum battery stored a lot of electricity.

'Not far. Remember the ground underneath is ice too. It should just travel straight down. She'd be better off rigging . . . Oh,

Kandara, if she shorts out that quantum battery it'll explode – and trigger the others.'

Kandara stared at the harvester in growing panic. 'How big an explosion?'

'Uh – get away! Kandara, she's just taken out another voltage regulator. There's only one left. Run! Get out of there. Move!'

Kandara brought her arm up, and started firing armour-piercing projectiles. The magrail rifle slammed them through dense machinery. An overlapping series of explosions sent dazzling yellow vapour streaming out through the tears in the bodywork. The whole mass of the harvester shifted slightly, the profile distorting.

She turned and jumped. Soaring above the lustrous ground took an age. Landed, wobbling. Jumped again, a lower trajectory this time, carrying her further.

'Last regulator!' Tyle exclaimed.

Landed—

The quantum battery exploded.

Kandara flung herself flat – a movement she never completed. Zapata instantly hardened her armour's outer layer, locking her limbs in mid-leap. Behind her, a flawless hemisphere of blue-white light erupted from the harvester. It flashed across her, physically nebulous but enriched with energy. Milliseconds behind the incandescent wavefront came the shrapnel cloud.

Amid glitching electronics and mutilated lens displays, her outer armour rang like a bell from the impacts. She tumbled anarchically, punched by the disintegrating splinters. Beneath her the ice flash-evaporated from the energy deluge, forming a secondary blastwave. She hit the seething ground and ploughed through the superheated slush.

Red danger graphics plagued her vision. She rolled along chaotically, banging elbows and legs as the solar-bright light dissipated. Finally the universe stabilized. Eclipsing the passive gas giant above, a scintillating debris cloud formed a spectacular short-lived galaxy of coral-pink embers that curved delicately back towards the ground.

Kandara groaned from the pain. Icons stabilized in her vision. Five red-hot fragments had pierced her hardened armour, stabbing through the suit layers underneath to sear into her flesh. No major blood vessels or organs punctured, Zapata reported. The suit's self-sealing layer was already closing, cutting off the flow of air and blood into space. Inside her backpack, the medical kit injected a coagulant agent, helping staunch the flow of blood from the wounds.

She winced as she attempted to sit up. The parts of her body spared lacerations seemed to be a single giant bruise. Where the harvester had been, a steam-cloaked crater had been blasted into the ice ocean, nearly twenty metres deep. A hazy aurora cavorted over it like a demonic will-o-the-wisp. She watched in astonishment as effervescent geysers pirouetted around the jagged rim, their spume freezing before it even reached the ground. Within a few seconds the phenomena had abated and the aurora's phosphorescence grounded out.

Larger chunks of wreckage started to tumble out of the clearing sky. They were scattered over kilometres, shining brightly in infrared, kicking up sprays of ice as they thudded down into the granules.

After a while, Zapata picked up a signal.

'Kandara? Are you receiving this? Can you hear me? Are you okay?'

'I'm here,' she replied.

A burst of cheering came along the comms channel.

'A harvester is on its way,' Tyle said. 'I've diverted it to you. It's not fast, but we're dispatching a recovery team through an ice-feed portal. They'll be with you in ten minutes. Can you last that long? How bad are you hurt?'

'I can last ten minutes.'

'What the fuck happened?' Jessika asked.

'You were right about shorting the quantum batteries. She didn't want to give us her employer, so she suicided.'

'That's just twisted. You offered her a way out.'

'I'm guessing she didn't like the odds. There are a lot of powerful people who'd like to act out some medieval-level vengeance on her. She'd probably never have made it to Zagreus, no matter how sincere Emilja was about the offer.'

'So we still don't know who was paying her?'

'No. You'll have to wait until next time, and hope you make a better job of apprehending them than I did.'

Juloss

Year 593 AA

The passageway was circular, four metres in diameter, its cyan-shaded walls made from something resembling fluorescent cotton candy. Dellian floated down its empty centre, his armour suit's thrusters firing almost constantly to keep his course steady. Four of his combat cohort clawed their way along in front. As they were in zero-gee, they'd linced additional segments around their core to form a segmented oval shape wrapped in a shell of Energy and Kinetic (E&K) armour which bristled with tri-segment arms. Their gripper talons tore long rents in the corridor's glowing organic fibres. The remaining two from the cohort were tail-end-charlies, bringing up the rear, alert for any enemy soldiers creeping up.

What Dellian assumed to be nutrient fluid squirted out of each wound the cohort's talons inflicted, filling the passageway with clouds of shimmering drops – a glow which slowly faded as they merged into larger globules. He batted them away. Suit sensors ran compositional analysis. It wasn't a bioweapon.

'Another fifty metres, then take the third branch, coord, seven-B-nine,' Tilliana told him.

'Got it.'

'Any sign of hostiles yet?'

'No.'

'There has to be something there to defend the asteroid.'

'I'm looking.' Which was almost true. He'd been relying on the cohort to scan the passageway. *That's complacent.* The cohort picked up on his mild anxiety, the way his eyes changed focus to watch the sensor data splash a little more attentively. The two following him immediately released a swarm of dronebugs. They slid through the thin nitrogen atmosphere, as agile as the terrestrial wasps they were modelled on, dodging the oscillating blobs of fluid, their sensors scanning the weird organic walls for any changes.

'Light level is decreasing behind,' his suit announced. 'Three per cent down.'

Dellian checked his squad display, seeing the platoon locations. They were sticking to formation, all of them snaking their way along the fluffy passageways that wound their erratic way through this section of the asteroid city. Their target was a large central chamber that earlier drone sweeps had discovered, containing a negative energy loop. Command had assigned the squad an infiltration mission to discover the nature of the loop, and destroy it. Tilliana and Ellici had split them up, allowing a greater probability that one of them would make it through.

'Janc. Hey, Janc,' Dellian called. 'What's your light level? I've got a reduction here.'

'I'll check.'

Dellian was mildly pleased he'd been the one who found the drop. *More savvy than the others.* And now the fluffy glowing strands had lost five per cent luminosity just behind the two tail-end cohorts. Sensing his interest, they launched a batch of tik-drones. The size and shape of maggots, they landed on the passageway's soft walls. Tiny bodies, with fangs of artificial diamond dust, chewed down into the delicate material. New displays splashed over his vision, detailing the chemical composition of the alien organic. The cells were arranged in a very loose weave and threaded with a fibre conducting electrochemical impulses.

Nerves!

'Yeah, it's getting darker in here, too,' Janc replied.

'For me, too,' Uret announced.

Colian: 'Same here.'

'What's it doing?' Dellian wondered out loud. In response to his misgiving, the cohort stopped moving and began to scan around. Even on his ordinary visual splash, the light level was noticeably lower. Now down forty per cent, his databud reported.

Dellian fired his suit jets, moving himself towards the cohort. All six of them started to close into a protective formation around him. Then the tik-drones began reporting that the structure of the alien cells was changing, the strands shrinking, growing denser. Through his helmet sensors, Dellian saw the darkening walls were starting to contract. Undulations began, moving slowly towards him. The appearance of a giant gullet swallowing was inescapable.

The cohort quickly surrounded Dellian, their limbs lincing to provide a solid cage with him at the centre. Energy beams fired into the fuzzy mass of alien cells. The outermost layers were fried instantly, shrivelling and steaming. But more of the stuff was advancing towards them like a sluggish tsunami, carrying a tide of dead cells and congealing liquid ahead of the still-living tissue. Even the coherent X-ray beams could only penetrate the dead matter so far. The sticky fluids bleeding from the charred strands were absorbing the energy, forming a hot barrier ahead of the living surface. In less than a minute, the cavity was completely full, engulfing him and the cohort. Pressure began to increase rapidly, as did the temperature. It was proving impossible to dissipate the cohort's energy barrage.

Dellian clenched his hands, and the cohort switched off their beam weapons. Sensors located slim tendrils worming their way through the seething liquid towards the cohort. Power blades slashed at them, cutting through effortlessly. But the fluid was becoming more viscous, hampering movement. And still the tendrils kept coming, multiplying like a burgeoning root system.

The tactical feed connecting him to the rest of the squad cut out. Signal Lost splashed across his lens. *Shit.* That shouldn't have happened; they were using entangled comms. He didn't waste time running diagnostics.

When he tried a swimming motion, the armour's actuators strained against the pressure to move his limbs. Low-level joint-seal warnings splashed up. He fired the suit thrusters, but all that did was send thin streams of phosphorescent bubbles out into the darkness.

The cohort immediately started to move, using their gravatonic drives to tow him along, heading towards the rock wall that lined the passageway. It was tough going. The new tendrils were insidious, coming at them almost like a solid wave. Dellian had given up trying to move his own limbs. Now he was starting to worry about the pressure seals; they'd never been designed for this kind of environment. Being immobilized was also starting to conjure up black phantoms in his mind. Bizarrely, for all the force being exerted on the armour, he was still in zero-gee, which was somehow helping the sense of isolation.

Progress was slowing drastically as the tendrils grew thicker. The forward cohort started firing X-ray lasers to break them up; they'd become too thick for the power blades to cope with. Medical monitors showed Dellian's heart rate increasing. The claustrophobia was getting to him. His plan was to detonate grenades against the rock; that was where the thickest nutrient arteries were supplying the cells. If he could cut those, he might be able to disable more of the passageway and claw his way out of this clot.

One of the cohort stopped moving, every limb overwhelmed by the tendrils, and still they kept coming, wrapping it deeper and deeper in layers of alien cells. And tendrils were gaining on a second cohort.

Deep inside Dellian's neck one of his new glands discharged a mild tranquillizer into his bloodstream. It was odd. He knew he should be panicking, but wasn't. Instead he ordered the cohort to fire a grenade. It barely moved ten centimetres from the launch tube nozzle. Tendrils began to coil round it.

Dellian triggered it. His armour was easily tough enough to withstand the blast, but the pressure waves shook him about violently. 'Saints shitting,' he groaned. Some of the suit-seal warnings were now turning amber. His gland pulsed out another discharge. It didn't seem to make any difference. The explosion had died away, but his limbs were still shaking. Body temperature was up, except his skin now felt like ice.

'Calm!' he ordered himself. 'For fuck's sake, keep calm!' His voice sounded thin and pathetic. *What would Yirella do?* A question which brought about a dangerously wild giggle. *Not get into this shit to start with.*

It was looking bad. The cohort had come to a halt; their gravatonic drives weren't strong enough to push any further through the churning knot of tendrils.

Can't use grenades again.

Energy weapons are heating the fluid.

Power blades beaten.

Come on, think!

The suit sensors showed him tendrils starting to wrap round his legs. He'd be cocooned in minutes, probably less. He didn't have the power to tear the strands free.

Power!

He yelled out the old yeargroup games warcry. Shockingly loud in the helmet, ratcheting up the claustrophobia another couple of degrees, and now there was the very real prospect of drowning in alien gunk if the seals were breached. It took him thirty seconds to issue instructions to the cohort. Re-routing the electrical output of their aneutronic fusion chambers, taking safety systems offline, cranking the output to redline.

'Go,' he commanded.

The combined power of the twenty-seven generators discharged through the cohort's shells. Everything went black. Dellian had no displays, no suit functions. He couldn't even sense the cohort, which spiked his fear.

Black panic really hit then. He began to struggle. The suit held him tight. He screamed.

'Hang on,' Tilliana's smooth voice instructed through the unnerving darkness. 'We're getting you out.'

The high-pitched whine of actuators cut through Dellian's frenzy. He forced himself to stop thrashing about and drew some shaky breaths. A crack of bright light appeared right in front of him as the helmet hinged apart. *Faster! Great Saints, I want this to stop.* Then the spongy contact pads which made up the interior of the suit released their grip on his sweaty skin. The helmet finished opening, and he could see the simulation egg's upper segments rising away from his body on the end of metal tentacles. They withdrew into a service globe in the middle of the simulation chamber, leaving him drifting a few centimetres above the pedestal which formed the rear half of the egg. He reached up and peeled the medic patches from his neck and thighs, then pulled the waste tube cap from his dick.

The cohort returned to haunt the back of his mind, and they didn't seem upset at all. It'd all been just another training session for them.

'You okay?' Tilliana asked.

'Sure. Fine.' Right now Dellian didn't want to think what'd happened, how badly he'd reacted to the exercise. The stress had drained away, to be replaced by shabby embarrassment. He could barely bring himself to glance round the spherical chamber.

All the other simulation eggs were open, leaving his squad floating listlessly above the pedestals. Most of them didn't even have the energy to remove their patches and tubes.

That was bad, he thought – although a part of him was wondering if they didn't deserve it. The last eighteen months had seen them run through some of the toughest simulations the tech strategists could dream up – and they could dream nasty. Eighty-three per cent success level, putting their squad well out in front of anyone else. This, though, this was on a whole other level of crap.

He could guess why it'd been created. The senior staff had decided it wouldn't hurt for the squad to have their confidence beaten down once in a while. He could even agree with the theory. But the actual experience – fearing you were about to be smothered, totally alone, without even your cohort, buried alive in the centre of malignant alien goop – it made him worry just how much it would affect them.

But he was squad leader, which made it his job to rally them. *I don't want to let them down.* He pushed off and glided through the air to Xante. 'Well, fuck, huh?'

Xante gave him a weak smile. Even that clearly took a lot of effort.

'Hey,' Dellian shouted, looking round. 'Anyone make it out intact?'

Some shook their heads. Others couldn't even meet his gaze. The atmosphere in the chamber was worse than they'd known when they'd been stranded in the fake flyer accident all those years ago. The sim had taken them right back down to wrecked little kids again. And he resented that, feeling a spark of anger amid the gloom. 'Tilliana,' he called, 'that was an eleven on my utter bastard meter. Uret, no sex for her tonight. That's an order, clear?'

Uret's lips lifted a fraction. 'Clear.'

A few half-hearted smiles appeared round the chamber.

The chamber door irised open five metres away from where Dellian was floating. Tilliana came sliding up through the gap, an arm reaching out to steady herself on Rello's egg pedestal.

Dellian had assumed she'd have a sly smile on her face, a few teasing phrases ready about how useless they all were. The banter would flow, camaraderie restored. Instead she looked troubled, which resurrected all his own doubts about what'd just happened.

Ellici air-swam into the chamber, also looking upset. But with that came a degree of exasperation. She always lacked Tilliana's patience.

'All right,' Dellian said to the pair of them. 'Tell us that wasn't a suicide mission.'

'Of course not,' Ellici said. 'You barely got through fifteen per cent of the asteroid.'

'You?' Xante challenged dangerously. 'What happened to *us*? To *we*? You're supposed to be our guardian angels. We're too dumb to figure out what's happening, remember? We *rely* on you.'

'Ease off,' Dellian said, making it as casual as he could.

'Fucking felt like a suicide job,' Falar grunted. He was plucking medic patches from his neck, his mood dark.

'So how do we get through the asteroid?' Mallot asked.

'Come on,' Tilliana said. 'They don't give us cheat sheets. These sim missions are only going to get worse from now on. Better get used to it.'

'Thanks,' Xante said. 'Demoralized – best way to go up against the enemy for real.'

Dellian gave him a warning glance. 'Enough. We're a team. We go through this together.'

'I was about to warn you about the passageway organics,' Tilliana said. 'I was slow. Sorry.'

'So you did have a way out?' Uret asked her gently.

'She still doesn't get any tonight,' Rello chided.

At least that brought a few grins, Dellian thought.

'No,' Tilliana said slowly. 'But if the bioluminescence was dimming, it must have meant the cells were diverting their nutrient energy for another function. And they were.'

'Hindsight,' Colian said regretfully. 'Always the clearest.'

'All right,' Dellian said, making an effort to get them all back on track. 'We'll have a full review tomorrow before we go back in. It's a wash for the rest of today. The Saints know we need a break after that. Maybe a drink.'

They agreed, their mood lifting slightly. The last connection pads were pulled off bodies. The squad started to air-dive towards the entrance. Uret drifted alongside Tilliana and gave her a soft kiss as they slid past the rim, both of them laughing at the jeers they received.

Dellian was just about to leave when Xante clamped a hand round his ankle.

'We're not a team,' he said.

'What do you mean?' Dellian asked. He certainly wasn't in the mood for this. He had a pleasant time all lined up, which he knew would ease him over his frustration. Then tomorrow they'd be back up here in the high-orbit station ready to kick the shit out of that bastard asteroid assault sim.

'Ellici and Tilliana are only two-thirds of a team,' Xante said.

'Great Saints, rest this! It's been years.'

'And she's not coming back. I get it. But we need someone to replace her. Yirella wouldn't have let us get caught with our asses hanging out like that. Fucking Saints, I thought I was going to die back then!'

'It's a sim.'

'Yeah, like you were all relaxed and calm. We were a fucking shambles in there, all of us.'

'Over-committed,' Dellian muttered. 'They warned us about that. The sims are so fucking real, you cooperate in suspending disbelief.'

'Well you'd better ask them for training to get over that, or therapy – or something.' He shook his head. 'I'm actually nervous about going back in there tomorrow. And that's ridiculous.'

'I know.'

*

After a shower and a change of clothes, Dellian took a portal over to Kabronski Station, orbiting eighty thousand kilometres above Juloss. The heart of the old skyfort formation was a rectangular grid, twenty kilometres long, with weapons systems arranged in neat rows on the outer side, all powered up and vigilant for the enemy's arrival. In the middle of the side which faced Juloss, a gravity anchor pylon extended for fifty kilometres down towards the planet, keeping the whole structure aligned. The pylon ended at a small metal asteroid, where a two-kilometre toroid housed the military crew and construction managers for the battleships being fitted out in the attendant cluster of industrial stations that floated in the grid's shadow. There were also some other, more specialist, teams resident in the toroid.

Yirella was waiting for him in the garden section, a chunk of toroid three hundred metres long, with a geodesic roof of thick transparent hexagons. The vegetation was tropical, and after two hundred years getting quite overgrown despite the best efforts of the horticultural remotes to trim and prune.

As always, she bent down and greeted him with a platonic kiss. After that unthinking greeting, she stopped and studied his face. 'What happened?'

'Saints! That obvious?'

Her smile grew taunting. 'Ah, the asteroid base with bio-wall tunnels.'

'You know about it?'

'The sim team has been preparing that for weeks. They've been giggling like nine year olds telling fart jokes over how you'd all react.'

'It wasn't funny, Yi.'

'I know.' She put her arm through his and walked with him down a path. 'That contraction thing freaked me out.'

'You've been in it?' he asked in astonishment, not knowing if he should be angry or impressed with her.

'Yeah. They needed volunteers for the test runs. I made a few suggestions to improve the effect. The threat of the suit seals failing and drowning you under pressure, that was me.' She sounded proud.

'You helped make it worse?'

Now her grin was mischievous. 'I know you boys best. The sim crew value my input.'

'Bloody hell!'

'The enemy isn't going to go easy on us.'

'I know, but ... You!' He shook his head in mock-bewilderment. 'Such betrayal.'

'Oi.' She gave him an affectionate slap.

It was moments like that, the ease they had between them, that gave him hope for the future. Over the last year they'd regained so much of what they used to have. Meeting when their schedules matched, talking, sometimes viewing dramas together; several times they'd been to concerts. Not quite like the old times. They hadn't become lovers again. Yet. But the relationship, whatever it was, had been too much for Xante. 'I can't compete with this,' he'd told Dellian as he moved out of their quarters.

'With what?' a depressed Dellian had challenged.

Xante gave him a simple shrug. 'Hope. That you'll get back together with her. That the pair of you will fly on to Sanctuary after the final battle and live happily ever after. Crap like that. You're never here any more.'

'I am!'

'Not in your head, you're not. You spend all your head time thinking of her.'

'I tried an electrical discharge,' Dellian now explained to Yirella. 'But I panicked and put too much power into it. Fried every chunk of technology in there.'

'Okay, well, the idea was sound.'

'Yeah? So . . .?'

'No, I'm not giving you any clues.'

Dellian managed a weak smile and put his arm round her. 'But it is solvable? We can get to the chamber with the negative energy loop inside?'

'Probably.' She laughed.

They wandered along to one of their favourite groves, where the trunks of the older trees grew upwards in an identical shallow curvature as they followed the camber of the toroid's rotational gravity, as if they'd all bowed to the same wind. He always found walking underneath them to be slightly disconcerting. Orchids and trailing moss swamped the boughs above, with bright-plumed birds zipping about. On the edge of the grove was a small waterfall emptying into a pond, filled with ancient gold and black koi fish. A marble table was perched beside it, inside the ribs of a radial pergola draped with sweet-flowering jasmine.

When they sat down, remotes started to unpack their meal and lay it out for them. Dellian sipped some of the wine they poured and scanned the small slice of starfield he could see through the shaggy vegetation. Juloss was always visible just above the lip of the geodesic, while the various free-flying subsidiary stations slipped in and out of view, tracing short arcs.

'Is that the *Morgan*?' he asked, as one of the battleship assembly stations appeared.

She barely glanced up from the plate of seared scallops the remote had put down in front of her. 'No, the *McAuley*. You can't see the *Morgan* from here.'

'It's nearly finished.'

'I know.'

He started eating his own scallops, wishing there were more

than just three. Ship assignments had finally come through last week, and the *Morgan* was going to be carrying Dellian and his squad out into the galaxy. He was desperate to know if Yirella was going to be on board with them, but too terrified to ask. If she wasn't, then that was it; the end. Relativistic time dilation would ensure their parting would be final. Though perhaps one day in a few thousand years, one of them might read of the other in a history file, when the human race was finally reunited.

He opened his mouth to ask, but heard himself say: 'How's the lure coming?'

Yirella's smile was bright and genuine. 'Really good. The enemy won't be able to resist investigating this civilization when they start broadcasting radio signals. We're calling them the Vayan. They'll be quadruped, with a double-section body, like two doughnuts one on top of the other, with legs on the lower section, and arms and mouths on the second, then on the top they'll have a prehensile sensor neck. They can move in any direction without having to turn round.'

Dellian frowned as he tried to picture that. 'Really? I thought animals evolved to go in one direction. There's always a front and back.'

'No,' she said. 'It's not an absolute. Wilant had an animal genus that possessed quintuple directionality.'

'Where's Wilant?'

'It's a cryoplanet, over seven thousand lightyears away. A traveller generation starship found it a long time ago. They stopped there for fifty years to study the indigenous species. There was some interesting biochemistry involved.'

'A cryoplanet?'

'Yes.'

'I thought everything moves slowly on a cryoplanet.'

'Their metabolic energy levels are lower, so generally mobile life there isn't as fast as a standard world. But the species on Wilant had a chemical reserve, so they could move faster if they were threatened. Sort of like us with an adrenalin rush.'

'Okay, and they had – What? Five heads?'

'No, they used sound waves to examine their environment. They could process the echo in every direction at once. They had a unique neurology to give them that ability.'

'So these things were predators, like the morox?'

She shook her head in amusement and sipped some of the wine. 'Not quite. More like starfish. They moved through seas of methane, clogged up with a lot of hydrocarbon slush – hence the sonar.'

'You're kidding? You're dreaming up a sentient species based on blind starfish?'

'It's an extrapolation exercise. The Wilant neurology gives us a logical progression to make sentient Vayans appear realistic. We're already growing full-scale Vayan biologics in molecular initiators. They need refining, but they're valid. It's really interesting work, Dellian; very challenging. I love it.'

He paused as remotes cleared the starter dishes away. 'And that's what you do? Make the actual aliens?'

'The biochemistry is fascinating, but no. I'm on the worldbuilding team. We're creating their entire culture based on the physiology we created, along with their history, language, art. Deciding how territorial and aggressive they are, and why.'

'And are they? Aggressive?'

'Oh yes. Not quite as much as we were pre-spaceflight, but enough to give them a believably fast technological development. That way we can get the radio emissions up and broadcasting as soon as we find a suitable planet.'

'The whole history of a species.' He pursed his lips. 'I'm impressed.'

'Don't be – well *do*. But our job is to design the parameters and plot the overall timeline. Even gentens lack imagination at that level, so it's still down to good old human creative brainpower. Once we've got that framework in place, the gentens will churn out the details, like names and places and micro-politics, scandal and gossip and celebrities. Crap like that.'

He raised his wine glass to her. 'So basically, you've become a goddess, creating a whole world.'

She lifted her own glass and touched it to his. 'Yep. So behave, or I'll start smiting you with thunderbolts.'

'I believe you.' Without any thought, he leant over the table and kissed her. 'Come with us on the *Morgan*. Please, Yirella. I can't bear the idea of doing this without you. No, forget *doing this*. I just don't want to be without you.'

The expression she responded with frightened him. He'd seen it once before: that desperation and loneliness, the night before poor Uma and Doony.

Her arm stretched across the table towards him. He saw the fingers trembling, and instinctively grasped her hand.

'Do you mean that?' she asked. 'Really? After everything?'

'I mean it,' he said. 'I've never been more certain about anything.'

'I'm not sure I deserve you.'

'Wrong way round.'

'I am coming with you, on the *Morgan*. I had them assign me there a month ago.'

Dellian couldn't help it; he started laughing. 'You are so much smarter than me, aren't you?'

'No. I just think things through more quickly, that's all.'

'If that's not a definition of smart, I don't know what is.'

She came over and sat in his lap, grinning as she twined her arms round his neck. 'I want to be honest with you.'

'Same here.'

'Dellian, I'm serious. We can't guarantee a long-term future; it's wrong to try and tell ourselves that can happen. You and I aren't traveller generation humans. We exist to fight a war – a fact that haunts me still, and probably always will. We may win, we may not, or we might die achieving victory. The only inevitable part of this is that the *Morgan* will fight. And the odds are not good.'

'I know. But whatever time we have, we get to spend it together. That's all I need.'

Her nose rubbed gently against his. 'My Dellian. So noble.'

Dellian pushed forwards and kissed her. It was every bit as good as he remembered.

The Assessment Team

Feriton Kayne *Nkya, 25th June 2204*

I hadn't known Jessika was part of the team the Utopials had brought together to deal with Cancer. She was sitting down at the other end of the cabin, next to Loi. The pair of them had been sharing quite a bit of time since the Trail Ranger had left Nkya's base camp. And both of them had pasts I didn't know about. Not covered up, but it would clearly take a lot of digging to provide a full timeline for both of them.

Of course, you could say the same for Yuri, Callum and Alik, too. More so, given how many layers of security their records were buried under. But they were my direct route into the real policy-makers – the ones who mattered. The ones who logically could be the source of human paranoia towards the Olyix, and the phenomenal resources various factions had wasted by spying on them. I had been convinced that one of them was working for an unseen malicious enemy who opposed every benefit the Olyix had brought to the Sol system. Kandara had been an outside chance, as well; it had been an odd decision for the Utopial Senior Council to bring her in to eliminate the sabotage. I thought it might be Callum, but now it seemed he didn't approve of her at all. Still, that much coincidence was unusual; perhaps God was trying to tell me something . . .

Alik nodded ruefully after Kandara had finished telling her story. 'So that's what happened to Cancer. I always wondered.'

'Let me guess,' Yuri said. 'Your precious Bureau never found out who had employed Cancer to sabotage Bremble's industrial stations and Onysko's research teams.'

'We looked,' Callum said. 'For years. But for all she was a complete bitch, Cancer was good. She left very little trace, digital or physical.'

'Plenty took her place,' Alik growled. 'There's still a lot of dark ops teams duking it out with national agencies and corporate security. Her death didn't change anything.'

'No big immediate change,' I said. 'But you'd never be able to crack New York's shield files these days. What about Bremble and Onysko?'

'Secure,' Callum confirmed. 'The incident with Cancer made us realize how exposed we were. We use G8Turings to manage and filter our critical networks now. The Senior Council made the Bureau swallow its pride, and set up some exchanges with Sol agencies to share information on activists and fanatics. We developed our own safeguard routines.'

'So everyone's a winner,' Alik grumbled, 'except the people whose lives she ruined before you caught up with her.'

'She won't ruin any more lives,' Kandara said. 'That's a good result to me.'

'The people who hired her will just carry on,' Alik said. 'Killing her was just a glitch to their plans; it didn't solve anything.'

Kandara gave him a frigid stare. 'I didn't kill her. She committed suicide.'

'You should have made a deal.'

'I offered.'

'Not very well, clearly. Genuine law enforcement is about balance. For all her reputation, Cancer was a small fish. Basically, your mirror image.'

'Go fuck yourself!'

The cabin became very still. A moment that stretched out –

'We're almost there,' I said, as the images from the sensors on the front of the Trail Ranger splashed across my tarsus lens. The last thing I wanted was a fight to break out; it would have soured the atmosphere beyond repair. My suspects were still being open with each other, and I needed that to continue. Somewhere in amongst that paranoia which dominated both sides of the Universal–Utopial divide, had to be a clue where it came from. They remained my best hope of finding the origin, the alien.

Everybody perked up at hearing the trip was coming to an end and started to access the Trail Ranger's sensors.

The crash site base had just appeared on the horizon – a cluster of six silver-white geodesic domes, locked together with stubby pressure tubes. Big as they were, they were dwarfed by the inflatable hangar that had been thrown over the alien ship – a rectangle of green and red silicone fabric large enough to cover a football pitch, looking so tight against the structural containment webbing it might burst at any second.

None of the domes had a garage: that would have been a waste of expensive habitation space. Up in the cab, Sutton Castro and Bee Jain carefully manoeuvred the Trail Ranger to an airlock tube sticking out from the side of a dome.

We all waited while the seal clanked and hissed. Then the Pressure Normal icon splashed up.

*

Lankin Wharrier, the base commander, was waiting for us on the other side. One of Connexion's finest troubleshooters, he had an engaging smile that backed up a dynamic air. When he spoke it was with smooth authority, leaving no one in any doubt he was in charge here, no matter what title any of us had stuck on our desks back home.

'I guess you all want to go straight to see the ship?' he asked.

'Of course,' Yuri said.

Lankin gestured down the tube. Like the first Eridanus base, this one gave the impression of being both a rugged pioneer outpost and incredibly expensive. The brief glimpses we got walking past labs and personnel quarters was of every facility and piece of equipment being top of the range, but sitting in the starkest environment possible. I found that reassuring, after a fashion.

The clean chamber was divided into three sections, which was where corporate techno babble had claimed its fiefdom. We had the Alien Environment Suit (AES) egress room (changing room). Followed by the terra-bio sterilization section (eradicating terrestrial bugs from the surface of the AES before visiting the ship). And finally the xeno-bio decontamination suite, which resembled a bunch of cubicles in a country-club locker room, where you were showered and irradiated after leaving the ship, to make sure no alien pathogens got loose in the base.

My AES wasn't as bulky as some spacesuits I'd worn. For a start, there was no need for a radiation layer, nor particle impact armour. The thermal moderator layer was also pretty thin. Basically it was like putting on an overall with an integral helmet. When I'd slipped in through the long opening up the spine, Sandjay interfaced and the opening sealed up, followed by the collar at the base of the helmet tightening to form an airtight seal round my neck. It took another minute for the rest of the pale blue fabric to contract around my skin, flushing excess air out. With the suit forming a thick second skin, my freedom of movement noticeably increased. The telemetry splash showed me everything was stable. If I read the display right, the power in the quantum batteries could keep the air recycler module operating for a month.

The helmets cut down on casual chatter, and the reflective coating hid faces from sight, but I could tell from body posture alone that everyone was keen to get going. They would have read the same thing in my stance.

We moved into the sterilization section, with three pressure doors closing behind us. Jets of grey-blue gas sprayed down from the ceiling to be sucked away by the grilles in the floor. The procedure took five minutes before Lankin Wharrier led us into the final airlock.

As soon as they arrived to set up camp, the engineering team and their remotes had scraped the regolith away from around the ship, exposing the bedrock underneath. With that clear, they'd fused the rim of the hangar directly onto the rock before inflating the envelope. A pure nitrogen atmosphere was pumped in, which had slowly been raised from ambient temperature up to ten degrees Celsius to assist the science teams.

We trooped down the ramp into a bright glare thrown by lights studding the hangar fabric. The ship they illuminated was a dark botanical red, like a once-vibrant flower losing its bloom. It measured about sixty metres long, and thirty wide. At its highest it rose maybe twenty-five metres above the ground. But those were only the overall dimensions. The fuselage itself was probably fifteen per cent smaller, a basic truncated cone-shape with a flattened belly. The extra dimensions were made up from protrusions – call them small wings or fins – nearly three hundred of them sticking out from every part of the ship. Quite a few were bent or broken off, showing the kind of damage it'd suffered from its hard landing. From what I could see, it had struck the ground along its port side before coming to rest more or less flat on its belly.

A hatch was open near the front, where three of the stumpy fins had twisted out of alignment to clear a route to it. The hatch itself used electromechanical actuators, nothing too different to human technology.

'The ship's atmosphere had bled out,' Lankin said, 'so the techs just allowed it to fill with nitrogen; it's a good neutral, non-reactive gas. So far we haven't monitored any adverse reaction in the structure.'

'Do you know what the original atmosphere was?' Loi asked.

'Preliminary examination of the life support indicates an oxygen–nitrogen mix. The percentages seem to be different to Earth, but not much; slightly heavier on the oxygen percentage.'

'What are all the wing-things?' Callum asked. 'Are they functional?'

'They have a core of material similar to our active-molecular technology. As near as the physics team can figure it, they're negative energy conductors.'

'Negative energy? You mean exotic matter? Wormholes?'

'Yes.'

'So it is an FTL drive?' Eldlund said excitedly.

'Possibly.'

'Possibly?'

'The fins are only conductors,' Lankin said. 'We think they were used to channel a flow of negative energy. So far we haven't found anything on board that can create negative energy.'

'So how did it fly?'

'Best guess, it rode along a wormhole the way trains used to ride along railway tracks.'

'But something went wrong,' Yuri said suddenly. 'It jumped the rails.'

'Most likely. If it fell out of the wormhole somehow and emerged back into spacetime, it might not have been able to get back in. There are fusion chambers in the aft section which would serve as rockets as well as generators.'

'So . . . it dropped out of a wormhole tunnel into interstellar space, then flew here on a fusion drive?'

'That's pretty much the consensus here, yes.'

'Holy shit!'

'And you said there are humans on board,' Loi said. 'Which means there's an alien wormhole terminus open in a human star system.'

'Yes,' Lankin said. 'That's about the size of it.'

'The amount of energy required to create a wormhole is phenomenal,' Loi continued, as if he were voicing thoughts as they formed. 'Even the combined output of Sol's solarwells would probably fall short. It would take a type-two civilization on the Kardashev scale to generate the power levels required.'

'Again, yes.'

'Oh Je-zus wept,' Alik hissed. 'Are you telling me the conspiracy crazies were right all along? We're being fucking spied on by little green men? We have been since the 1950s? And they do shove things up our ass when they abduct us?'

'Oh no,' Lankin said in a darkly amused tone. 'They do much worse than that.'

'What the actual fuck—?'

'Let's go in, shall we?'

We followed him inside. The hatch opened into a simple airlock chamber. Engineers had removed the inner door, allowing a dozen power and data cables to snake through and work their way into the ship, branching at every junction.

Sandjay splashed up a schematic of the ship; ninety per cent of it had been mapped. The missing sections were mainly big chunks of machinery, like the fusion tubes and various tanks. Corridors were wide tubes, illuminated with strings of lights threaded along them, stuck into place by dobs of takhesive. A human ship would have corridors running the length of the fuselage with branches at right angles. This ship had them in overlapping circles, some of which were inclined steeply, with the cylindrical chambers arranged in clusters.

Lankin took us to the central compartment, which ran the full height of the ship. It was divided into three levels by walkway grids, but without any handrails. All the bulkhead walls were made of a smooth dull metal that looked as if it had been extruded as a single unit, with no displays or control panels visible anywhere. The only breaks in its surface were small life-support grilles.

Several science techs were working inside, their instruments stuck to the bulkheads. Optical cables formed a messy spider's web, hanging between them and three G8Turings encased in their protective black metal cases, ribbed by cooling fins.

Lankin climbed a rope ladder up to the middle walkway.

'We're calling this the bridge,' he said, 'because this is what seemed to be in charge.'

There was a two-metre-diameter sphere suspended in the centre of the chamber from ten radial rods as wide as my hand. We crowded round it, feet close to the edge of the walkway. It was as blank as the rest of the structure, giving nothing away. Except now it had about twenty sensor pads stuck to it, and some big 3D screens resting precariously on the rods. The image they were showing was like a deep scan of a big egg.

'Okay,' Yuri said wearily. 'What is it?'

'An organic neural processor unit,' Lankin said. 'Or to put it bluntly, the ship's brain. The on-board network isn't optical, or even digital. It's neurological.' He patted the rods. 'These are a combination of nerve conduits and nutrient feeds; think of them as the spine. The nerve fibres link every piece of machinery, and plenty of them are biomechanical.'

'Is it still alive?' Kandara asked in alarm.

'No. However, two of the smaller fusion tubes are still functioning, so there is power. And as far as we can tell, the nutrient organ system that supports the brain was undamaged before it froze. We're theorizing the brain must have been alive to pilot the ship from when it fell out of the wormhole to Nkya, then died some time after the landing. Cause of death unknown, but we're thinking one of the first systems which failed was the life-support heating.'

'A brain this size couldn't work out how to fix a heating circuit?' Callum said sceptically. 'Bollocks.'

'It depends on what else was damaged by the landing. And this is where our alien's biology starts to get really interesting. We sampled the brain cells, of course. The genetic molecule has a similar functionality to Kcells.'

'Shit, this is an *Olyix* ship?'

'I said similar. My team is telling me this is a lot more sophisticated than Olyix biogenetics. All the traits this alien molecule contains seem to be equally valid. There is no equivalent to the junk chromosome we have in human DNA, which effectively gives every cell the ability to become any type of cell required by the designer. It's like a super-stem cell; any function can be switched on by the correct chemical activant code. As long as you have a valid pattern, you can build yourself whatever you want. In this case they chose to build a brain.'

'Christ almighty!'

'It gets better. Some of the tanks on board are full of these cells in neutral mode. All dead now, of course.'

'Enough,' Alik snapped. 'What about the fucking crew? Where are their bodies?'

'There aren't any,' Lankin said. 'None that we've found, anyway.'

'Hell, man, that makes no sense,' Callum said. 'Okay, I get this isn't how we'd design a spaceship, and I have serious problems with the lack of redundancy. But if the brain didn't need a crew, why are there all these compartments?'

'Our working theory is that the brain simply builds itself whatever crew it needs out of the cells in the tanks, like biological Turing remotes. Our major on-board investigation is now focusing on the equipment which the tanks fed, which we're assuming is some kind of biomechanical womb. When the ship crashed here, something in that mechanism broke down. The brain couldn't build itself anything that could repair the other systems.'

'No,' Alik said bluntly. 'That's wrong. You said the hatch was open when you got here, right?'

'Yes.'

'That implies something left the ship after it arrived. The brain had no reason to open it otherwise. Some kind of mobile thinking alien was on board. Have you searched the surrounding area?'

'Right now there are over fifteen hundred drones outside, looking for any trace of activity that's taken place on the surface. So far they've covered just over a thousand square kilometres. There's nothing, not a dint that looks like a footprint – or hoof print, claw mark, or tentacle squiggle – no line that could be some kind of wheel track, or a blast pit from a rocket exhaust. Nothing! If an alien left this ship, it flew off into the sky without touching the ground.'

'If it'd been rescued, they wouldn't have left the distress beacon on,' Callum said.

'We're dealing with alien psychology,' Eldlund said. 'You can't make assumptions like that.'

'If they were rescued, why leave the cargo behind?' Lankin countered.

'Speaking of which,' Yuri said, 'I want to see them next.'

'Of course.'

The cargo section was the largest aft compartment, another cylinder. This one was divided up into four levels. The walkways were a lot narrower to accommodate the hibernation pods. Several medical technicians were occupied examining the alien apparatus and the sensors that were probing their secrets.

'No atmosphere,' Lankin said. 'But the power has remained on for the hibernation systems.'

'Lucky for them,' Kandara said.

'Depends on your point of view,' Lankin muttered.

The corridor had brought us out onto the compartment's second level. I glanced round at the hibernation pods, which were bulky sarcophagi with a smooth curving transparent front. They were all dark and cold, unoccupied.

'These look like something a human designed,' Loi said.

'They're designed to accommodate humans,' Lankin told him, 'which is providing you with a visual bias. But I can assure you the components are of alien manufacture. Whoever made the ship, produced them. You'll see why on the next level.'

One by one we followed him up the rope ladder that'd been rigged to connect the walkways.

'How did the hypothetical crew get up and down?' Eldlund muttered as he swung about.

'The compartments are all positioned at right angles to the assumed direction of flight,' Lankin said. 'So our conclusion was that there is no acceleration force while it flies along the inside of the wormhole, and that the docks at both ends are in freefall.'

I was last up the rope ladder. It was only when I was halfway up to the third level that I noticed everyone had fallen silent. When I stepped onto the walkway grid, the assessment team was bathed in the pale blue-white light that was shining out of the units. They were all staring in. And I could hear the awkward sounds of people trying to control their gag reflex.

The hibernation units did contain humans – just not complete ones. Their limbs had been removed, leaving the torso and heads almost intact. They were held in place against the rear of the hibernation chamber by a blue-tinted membrane that looked as if it had been shrink-wrapped around them. It was translucent, revealing that the original skin had also been removed. The quadriplegic bodies were like medical anatomy models, with all their sinews, bones, blood vessels, and organs visible. The eye sockets were empty, and the ears had also been detached, along with any genitals. Four alien organics, resembling umbilical cords, were attached to the empty hip and shoulder sockets, their veins and arteries pulsing slowly as blood circulated in and out. They were connected to external organs that rested like flaccid cushions of flesh down the side of each hibernation unit.

'No fucking way,' Alik announced.

I watched, mesmerized by the med-remotes which had invaded the sarcophagi through a tiny sterile airlock tube drilled into the glass casing. The insectile machines crawled across the taut restraining membrane, whisker-like feelers probing its structure down to the cellular level. Larger clusters swarmed around the junctions between umbilicals and body, exploring the fusion.

Vital signs were displayed across screens rigged up on a temporary carbon strut framework – a whole genre of symbology beyond my comprehension.

'Are these actual humans, or is this some kind of replica the ship's brain was building out of alien cells?' Yuri asked.

'They're human,' Lankin said. 'Or at least they used to be. The medical team have taken extensive samples. Their brains are completely intact, along with some of the original organs. However, the rest of their bodies have been replaced by Kcells. Basically, the torso organs have been reduced down to the brain's life-support system, which in turn is sustained by the nutrients supplied by the artificial organs in the hibernation chamber. They're powered by electricity, so as long as the fusion generators are working, these people stay alive.'

'Are they conscious?' a horrified Loi asked.

'No. Brainwave activity is consistent with a coma in all of them. Blood chemistry analysis has revealed the presence of some sophisticated barbiturates, which we assume are sustaining the coma state.'

Yuri was leaning so far forwards his helmet was practically touching the sarcophagi casing. 'Why remove the limbs?'

'We can only assume they're not required. Certainly, maintaining the muscle and bone structure would be a drain on the hibernation support organs. Incidentally, those exterior organs are made completely out of Kcells.'

'It *is* an Olyix ship, then?'

'That's the only indicator we have of their involvement. We don't understand why the cells in the ship's tanks weren't used to fabricate the hibernation chamber mechanisms; they're considerably more sophisticated. Presumably it's because Kcells have been proven to work in combination with human biochemistry. Given this set-up has successfully kept them alive for the thirty years since the ship crashed, it would be a valid explanation.'

'They snatched seventeen humans,' Callum said, 'then did this to them to keep them alive. Why? I mean, what's the bloody point?'

'Is it reversible?' Eldlund asked. 'Can they be given their bodies back?'

'We can clone every part of a human body, or print it with stem cells, or replicate it with Kcells,' Jessika said. 'The technologies are established. But actually doing a Frankenstein and stitching all those parts together is just about impossible. I'd say the only way to do it in this case would be to clone the original body, but somehow prevent the brain from developing. Which –' she sighed – 'would take a lot of research. And even if you did succeed, you'd have the problem of transplanting the old brain into its new body.'

'Ha!' Yuri grunted. 'That again.'

'I thought Hai-3 told you it was theoretically possible?' Eldlund challenged.

'Theoretically, yeah. But that's another huge research project. Even if Alpha Defence approved, it would take decades and billions of wattdollars to get them walking round in a decent body again.'

Eldlund's hand gestured at the sarcophagi. 'I imagine they would think it's worthwhile.'

'But the risk . . .' Callum said.

'You want to know if it's acceptable? Ask one,' Kandara said. 'Put one of these poor bastards into a decent human-built life-support system, flush the barbiturate shit out of their brains, and they might wake up.'

'And they might not,' a shocked Eldlund replied.

'Then you learn enough about the failure to improve the technique for the next one,' she said. 'And keep going until we've perfected it. Because we all know we're going to have to try this at some point. We're not going to leave them like this.'

'The psychological trauma alone would be massive,' Loi said uneasily.

'Tough. For the record: if you ever find me like this, either wake me up or kill me. Don't leave me like this.'

'I'm not—'

'There might be a way round this,' Lankin interrupted. 'The doctors are hopeful they can recover the Odd One.'

'The Odd One?' Kandara queried. 'What the hell is that?

'Yeah, sorry. My team is a bit on the nerdish side and they don't have a lot of imagination. They called him the Odd One because he's different from the rest.'

'Different how?' I asked sharply.

'See for yourself,' he said. 'Next level up.'

I went up the rope ladder after Alik. Three of the hibernation chambers there contained the same kind of membrane-wrapped torso we'd seen before. The fourth . . . He was intact. There was no restraining membrane. A single umbilical cord was fused to his navel, hanging down to a trio of external organs, larger than those in the other chambers. Shock froze me to the spot.

'That's not possible,' an equally stunned Yuri said.

'What do you mean?' Callum asked.

'He can't be here. Not him!'

'Wait! You *know* him?'

'Yes. It's Lucius Soćko. He vanished when we rescued Horatio Seymore on Althaea.'

*

They made the decision after dinner. Everyone who'd come on the Trail Ranger settled in the base's lounge to talk it over. Not that it was much of a democracy. Callum clearly had reservations, but in the end he conceded that attempting to revive Soćko was necessary.

I didn't give an opinion; it would be out of character as the mission's humble administration guy. But Jessika approved, as I thought she would. Kandara didn't contribute much; she'd made her view clear back on the ship. Loi and Eldlund were a lot more cautious – we should investigate longer, bring in more equipment and specialists, make detailed risk assessments. Typical corporate culture kids. They had no concept of taking responsibility, because that meant consequences – and Legal always hated consequences. Not that their views mattered. Ultimately it was down to Yuri, Callum and Alik, and they were unanimous.

Lankin sat with us in the lounge as everyone talked it over, but he didn't say anything. When he was given the verdict, he responded with a gruff: 'Okay then,' and left to organize the operation. It didn't take long; his people had been working balls-out to prepare for this ever since they set eyes on the Odd One.

It took them six hours. Remotes cut Soćko's hibernation chamber out of the ship's cargo compartment and carefully manoeuvred it round the circular passages into the research base. The alien environment laboratory had been converted into an intensive care suite in anticipation.

A small observation room ran alongside, with a broad window looking in. We crowded round it to watch the hibernation chamber arrive. The trollez which delivered it was barely visible, the damn thing was surrounded by so many techs and doctors, all in their protective blue suits.

'What's the atmosphere inside that thing?' Yuri asked.

'Earth-standard gas mix,' Lankin told him. 'All the hibernation chambers are the same. No alien pathogens inside, either – that we've detected.' His knuckles rapped on the window. 'But we're not taking any chances. This lab is quadruple walled, with positive pressure cavities on individual life-support circuits. No bugs are going to get out of there and into my base.'

The revival team slowly sliced round the edge of the hibernation chamber's transparent lid, allowing remote arms to lift it away. Out of the corner of my eye I saw Eldlund brace hirself, but Soćko's body remained inert.

The medics closed in. Monitor patches were bonded onto Soćko's skin, providing a more detailed picture of his vitals. Flesh-meld blisters were applied above his femoral and carotid arteries, ready to supply artificial blood or drugs if and when they were needed. He wasn't breathing. The blood generated in the external Kcell organs and fed through his umbilical was fully oxygenated. So artificial saliva was sprayed into his mouth, and they slid an intubation nozzle down his trachea – ready. With the prep done, they moved him out of the chamber and onto a bed.

A crash team stood by, watching and waiting as the extraction team clamped the umbilical cord – and cut it.

No warning went off. His heart kept on beating uninterrupted. Brainwave function remained flat.

The intubation nozzle started to pump oxygen-rich air into his lungs in a slow rhythm.

I watched his chest inflate, sink back down. Rise again. Soćko gave a slight shudder, then another, stronger shiver ran down his body. The medical team tensed up; crash-revival tools were held up ready. Soćko's shakes continued for a while longer before he went quiescent again.

'He's breathing naturally,' the lead doctor announced. There was a note of surprise in her voice.

On the other side of the glass, the medical techs were high-fiving. Two of the doctors were preparing their surgical remotes to remove the stump of the umbilical from Soćko's navel.

'Now what?' Yuri asked.

'We wait,' Lankin said. 'Make sure he remains stable, and give his body a chance to filter out the barbiturates. If he wakes naturally, fair enough. If not, they'll try stimulants.'

*

We all trooped back to the lounge, with its comfy chairs standing on the bare composite panel floor. Loi and Eldlund went over to the freezer cabinets and started searching through the meal packs for breakfast. Alik got himself a Belgian hot chocolate from the dispenser and settled back in his chair.

'It can't be that easy,' Kandara said when she sat next to me. 'What about muscle atrophy? He's been lying there for thirty-two years, for fuck's sake!'

'Something took care of that,' Loi said as he came over, carrying a plate of scrambled eggs, sausages, and hash browns straight from the microwave. 'Something in the blood they haven't found yet. It all came from the Kcell organs, don't forget; we don't fully know what they're capable of.'

'You're talking magic potions,' Callum said dismissively. 'Not real biochemistry. No chemical treatment will preserve an inactive body in a healthy physical shape like that for thirty years.'

'What, then?'

Eldlund sat down beside him, blowing the steam from hir porridge. 'Maybe Soćko is the success? The others are all being rebuilt by the alien cells, but he was just further along?'

'No,' Yuri said. 'The Kcell organs in his hibernation chamber were different. They supplied blood that's rich with oxygen and nutrients – a real hibernation as opposed to what's happened to the others.'

I kept a very careful watch on the faces around me as I said: 'He might not have been asleep the whole time.'

Yuri gave me a look which invited me to continue. He was my boss, respecting my opinion. No change there. Callum was expectant, wanting to hear some options, clearly eager for answers. Alik continued to sit there, mug of hot chocolate in his hand, waiting like every good interrogator for the suspect to talk too much. Those lifeless face muscles of his were as still as a millpond.

'Exercise,' Kandara said eagerly. She grinned at me. 'That's what you mean, isn't it?'

I gave her an appreciative shrug. 'The simplest solution always applies. And the only real way to maintain muscle tone is through exercise.'

'So Soćko wakes up once a week,' she said. 'Or a month. Whatever. And spends a few days getting in some callisthenics sweat-time. Then goes back into hibernation. He's on a timer.'

'Not a chance,' Loi said.

Kandara shot him a challenging glance. 'Why?'

'Where does he do his callisthenics? The ship has been in a vacuum for over thirty years. There's no spacesuit; he couldn't even step out of the hibernation chamber.'

'So why is he in such good shape?'

'Genetic modification?' Loi said uncertainly.

'The medical team sequenced everyone's DNA,' Lankin said. 'Soćko doesn't have any modifications; we didn't even find vectors for telomere treatment in him.'

'We'll find out soon enough if he wakes up,' Alik said. 'We just ask. Meantime, let's focus on what we do know. We came here to assess if this ship indicates a clear and present threat.'

'It does,' Yuri said. 'Aliens with a significantly more advanced technology base have established a secret beachhead either in Sol or one of our settled systems. They snatch humans for unknown, but fucking dire, reasons.'

'That's not necessarily a threat,' Callum said.

'You're kidding, right?'

'Come on, man, face it: we're scary. We can cross interstellar space, and we're still aggressive, unreasonable, badly behaved and own continents full of weapons. Hell, if I encountered us, I'd want to hold back and watch for a while.'

Alik's hand shot out, pointing at random. 'Did you even see what they did to those poor bastards? They *dissolved* them! They dumped humans into some kind of alien version of acid, or something, and dissolved them! What's left is being taken back home to be torture-experimented on. That is a fucking *threat*, you dumbass hippy! You got kids, right? Suppose you found one of them on board – no arms, no legs, their goddamned eyes ripped out. And that's just the start; fuck knows what else would've happened to them if this ship hadn't fallen out of the wormhole. That could be *you* and your family in there, asshole!'

For once Alik's neck and jaw muscles were flexing. Loi and Eldlund were regarding him in concern.

'Their ethics might not match ours,' Callum said. 'They are

alien after all. But they haven't been overtly aggressive. That has to mean something.'

Alik snorted in contempt and turned to Yuri. 'I need to talk to my people.'

Yuri and I exchanged a slightly guilty look. 'There are no direct comms with solnet,' I said. 'That was a major part of Alpha Defence's quarantine protocols.'

'Oh, come on,' Alik's voice dropped an octave to a bass purr, world-wise and oh-so reasonable. 'There's got to be some emergency line out, right?'

'No,' I told him. 'There really isn't.'

'Jesus H Christ. You are shitting me!'

'That's got to be the AI safeguard,' Callum said. 'Am I right?'

'Yeah,' I conceded.

'The what?' Alik asked angrily.

'The ship we've found is from an alien race which, if not actively hostile, is certainly unsympathetic to humans,' Yuri said. 'Suppose that frozen brain-captain thing had been warm and running active routines, or it had an electronic AI like our Turings? If we had a link back to solnet, it could download itself into our networks; multiply itself a thousand times a second. The potential damage it could inflict is impossible to calculate.'

'Je-zus.' Alik wheezed. 'That is one son of a bitch paranoia you've got going there.'

'No,' Yuri said levelly, 'it's a very sensible precaution. Especially now I've seen what we're dealing with.'

'But the aliens who built that ship are already in Sol, or one of our star systems,' Alik countered. 'They have been for decades, and they're smart enough to hide a fucking wormhole terminus from us. If they wanted to crash solnet, they'd have done it by now.'

'We know that now,' I said. 'But we didn't when we set up the research base and started investigating. Deciding to allow a direct connection to solnet is one of the decisions you are here to assess. And we do still have the question of who or what opened the ship's airlock.'

'Yeah, right,' Alik said grudgingly.

'But I can offer you the Trail Ranger to drive you back to the portal.'

Alik looked from me to Yuri. Clearly not a man used to being told *no*. 'I'll give it a day,' he said. 'See if Soćko comes out of it. But after that, I have to file a report, no matter what.'

'I'll tell Sutton and Bee to have the Trail Ranger ready for you to go,' I assured him.

'Which brings us back to what the bloody hell is going on,' Callum said. 'The aliens are watching us; they're taking us to experiment on. Why?'

'It's obviously an intelligence-gathering mission,' Kandara said. 'They're learning our weaknesses. That can only have one outcome.'

'No way,' I said. 'There's no such thing as interstellar war. There is no conceivable reason for it. Once a species gets off its birth world, it effectively has infinite resources. It wants for nothing. Total war is something that belongs to history for anyone who can reach orbit and beyond.'

'They're alien,' Jessika said. 'Who knows what their motivations are? Like Callum said, we're probably quite frightening to a progressive, peaceful species.'

'Taking people apart,' Alik butted in loudly, the chocolate sloshing perilously close to the rim of his mug. 'That ain't exactly what I'd call progressive, lady!'

'Hitler wasn't short of resources,' Loi said. 'Not to begin with. World War Two was an ideological war at heart, a crusade to impose Nazi imperialism on the rest of the world. Same goes for the Cold War which followed, with its capitalism versus communism.'

Eldlund gave him a taunting smile. 'Well thank heavens those economic theories both lost.'

Loi replied with a contemptuous finger.

'Do you believe the shipbuilders are the ones?' Callum asked. He was staring directly at Yuri.

'It's starting to look that way.'

'The one what?' Jessika quizzed.

'We've all experienced it,' Yuri said. 'That's why we were chosen to interpret this. Though I have to admit, Soćko came as a big surprise to me. Didn't see that coming.'

'Experience?' Alik clicked his fingers. 'Ah, right: we've all had experiences which didn't quite add up, somehow.'

'Yes,' Yuri said. 'And those personal cases of ours are the tip of the iceberg. We've been analysing similar incidents for a while now, especially those with critical defence issues.'

Kandara gave me a shrewd look. 'I thought I was here for my professional expertise.'

'That was a bonus,' I told her. 'You and Callum both encountered Cancer, who had been contracted on a sabotage mission which could have crippled the primary astromanufacturing capability at Delta Pavonis.'

'What's the connection between that and this situation?'

'Defence,' Yuri said flatly. 'If Sol and the settled systems are attacked, Bremble would be essential to build – well, battleships, orbital fortress stations, everything we need to protect ourselves from an invasion.'

'New York's shields,' Alik said quietly. 'She was going for those.'

'And she was there on Bronkal, eliminating any evidence of Baptiste snatching low-visibility people – for no reason we could ever find,' Yuri said. 'Which is an even stronger association to what's going down here now that we know Soćko was shipped directly from there to the ship.'

'Nobody on Akitha could figure out the motivation for what Cancer was doing,' Kandara said thoughtfully. 'We all thought some kind of political fanatic was employing her to sabotage their industrial systems, but this . . . aliens scouting round the human race . . . I hate to say it, but this makes a kind of sense.'

'Who the fuck are they?' Alik snarled. 'And how long have they been watching us?'

'Ask the Olyix,' Loi said. 'They're clearly complicit. Maybe it's them.'

I let out a weary breath. 'Not this again,' I said in exasperation.

Callum gave me a sharp stare. 'They lied to Yuri about Horatio

Seymore. They knew he'd been snatched,' he said. 'They were involved. What more do you need?'

Which was an interesting outburst. Someone – some group – had to be pushing both Ainsley and the grade-one Utopials into believing the Olyix were chasing a hidden agenda, fuelling the insecurities and paranoia of the old and powerful who inevitably see change as danger. And the only people with a reason to do that are the other aliens, trying to deflect attention from themselves. Aliens with influential agents in both Utopial and Universal ruling political classes.

'There was something odd about that,' I agreed. 'Maybe they employ corporate intelligence-gathering companies to keep a closer look on things than we realized. I don't know. But, face it, Ainsley Zangari's exposed granddaughter calling him in a panic is going to be noticed by *someone*. It may be Hai-3 was being a little too helpful and cooperative just to keep Zangari sweet. He is the richest, most powerful individual alive, and it would pay politically to keep him sympathetic. And I'm certain this ship we've found can't be theirs. The *Salvation of Life* is a slower-than-light arkship; the Olyix don't have wormholes. Loi, you said the power level a wormhole needs is beyond anything we produce in the Sol system.'

'Yeah,' he agreed almost grudgingly. 'That's right.'

'So it's not them,' I said.

'You seem very certain,' Kandara said.

I gave Yuri a quick glance. He nodded permission. It didn't go unnoticed. 'It goes like this,' I said. 'Ainsley has been suspicious about the Olyix since before Horatio was snatched. He never quite believed their claim to be peaceful religious fanatics.'

'Now that has truly got to be the universe's biggest oxymoron,' Alik mocked.

'Whatever they are, they're not actively hostile to humans,' I said.

'You can't claim that,' Eldlund said. 'There's a lot of evidence piling up against them.'

'Circumstantial,' I replied. 'Or maybe it's disinformation. Look, after Horatio, Ainsley decided to find out what was really going on.

484

So we've been mounting a discreet surveillance on the *Salvation of Life* ever since.'

'And?' Kandara prompted.

'They aren't being entirely honest with us; they are keeping secrets about themselves. But there's no conspiracy.'

'You can't know that. Not for certain.'

'I do.'

'How?'

'Because five years back I took point on a covert mission that broke into the *Salvation of Life*.'

Feriton Kayne's Spy Mission

Salvation of Life AD 2199

I'd been living in Lancaster, Pennsylvania, for over a year to physic-ally inflate my cover story. Data-based legends are easy to install in solnet; these days you can basically be anyone you want to be, pro-viding you have the money and expertise. Connexion Security had both in abundance. Even a G8Turing's search would only turn up the cover history I'd been given. But if the Vatican or the Grand Ayatollah actually sent someone to Lancaster, they'd be able to verify what a great citizen I was and how my attendance at local Quaker meetings was top rate. Not that anyone in the office expected any cardinals or imams to turn up physically and run a deep check. But, given where I was heading, office policy was to make that cover story as real as possible. So, if some dark ops agent did come checking in person, they'd swiftly get wearied talking to neighbours and colleagues and friends, who would all tell them what a great (if moderately dull) guy I was, complete with the per-sonal anecdotes I'd generated by actually living there.

Ainsley Zangari was very clear about getting the mission abso-lutely right. Funding for his Olyix Monitoring Office was already over three-quarters of a billion wattdollars a year. A portion of that money was spent on G8Turings that scoured solnet for evidence of operatives like Cancer corroding and corrupting corporations and institutions, with emphasis on the defence sector. Deals like that were absurdly easy to set up anonymously through solnet. And so, whenever we did come across an op that had defence connotations, it was virtually impossible to backtrack.

Apart from that, the Olyix Monitoring Office had two main divisions with dedicated tasks. The first ran an operation devoted to watching the Olyix embassies, which we mainly did by planting our own operatives inside among the human staff. To be honest, I don't think there was a single Olyix embassy employee that wasn't reporting back to some intelligence agency or other. Our knowledge of their official trade deals and financial status was absolute.

The second, and most involved, division was the one I wound up working for. We were trying to find out if the Olyix had opened any private portal doors between their arkship and Earth – something that would allow them to collaborate with their Kcell development partners without having to go through the official channels established by the Sol Senate – which would explain how they knew about Horatio's snatch. That was a tough one. It's not like the Olyix themselves could move around Earth unnoticed. They would have to use human agents to mount hostile operations.

But it didn't matter how many renditions we threatened and alt-legal interrogations we performed. There was no verifiable line of sight back to the Olyix. I never got that: people who would betray their own species. But I'd been in law enforcement and corporate security long enough to know every bastard in that field simply took the money and skipped the questions. They wouldn't know and wouldn't want to know who they were working for.

Our other problem was why the Olyix would bother. Their sole purpose of stopping in the Sol system is to buy energy to generate antimatter so they can continue their pilgrimage flight. The original theory was that they wanted to increase revenue for the Kcells by introducing new treatments, and didn't care about their human partners performing illegal experiments to develop those procedures. But then we started to notice the build-up of hostile incidents in Sol's defence sector, like the attempt on the New York shield files.

Nobody could figure out what was happening. Then after we heard what Cancer was doing at Delta Pavonis, Ainsley's paranoia skyrocketed up to whole new levels. The attack against Bremble made absolute sense if it was in preparation for an invasion.

My division was refocused on technology, physically locating quantum spacial entanglements between *Salvation of Life* and Earth. If we could find a portal that led back to Earth, or a habitat, we'd finally have solid proof the Olyix were hostile. But while it is possible to detect a portal's quantum signature, the equipment is short-range, large, and expensive. Over half of the Olyix Monitoring Office budget was spent on refining the sensor technology. First they had to perfect it. Then they had to make it small – really small. Finally, and with wonderful irony, they had to make it undetectable.

After that, smuggling it on board the *Salvation of Life* was almost easy. Which is where I came in.

The 2199 joint ecumenical delegation, of which I was a proud member, assembled in Vatican City. There were four such delegations every year. Somewhat inevitably, the Olyix were keen to welcome emissaries from human religions to the *Salvation of Life*. Equally understandably, our priests and rabbis and imams were eager to explore alien religion. Sorry, but the utterly devout Olyix were literally a heaven-sent opportunity in that respect.

There were seventeen of us smiling for the solnet news streams in St Peter's Square, with the Basilica as our formidable backdrop. Most faiths were represented, so nobody was questioning a Quaker's inclusion. The robes some representatives wore were impressive; I thought they looked brand new and obviously professionally tailored.

The most painful part of the mission was that long year in Lancaster learning about my new religion, which seemed to be about the most non-hierarchical, non-judgemental faith anyone had ever formed. It took a great deal of self-discipline to focus on the tenets and (loose) structure, but I got there in the end. Anyone curious about Quaker history and practices would swiftly be bored into retreating as I recited it all to them.

Interestingly, it was Nahuel, the Buddhist monk, who was keenest to talk to me. He told me all about his acceptance and learning in the temple, in return listening politely to my cover story of how I came to my gentle faith. We chatted amicably as we walked through the Vatican's hub, into Rome's metro network. From the city's international hub it was just a few quick paces to the main Olyix transfer portal in Buenos Aires.

I stepped straight through into a rotational gravity effect. The toroid was small, and spinning faster than I was used to, as my inner ears were quick to let me know. I saw Nahuel pause, instinctively holding his arms out in a novice surfer's pose to regain his balance.

'Have you ever been in a space habitat before?' I asked.

He shook his head, which is always a mistake in fast-spin gravity; his lips puckered up as the combinations of deviant motion assailed his ear canals.

'It's okay,' I assured him. 'This is as bad as it'll get. The *Salvation* rotates very slowly; you won't feel the spin at all.'

'Thank you,' he said with an insincerity that his fellow monks would doubtless frown upon.

'Until then . . .' I proffered an anti-nausea tab.

'No. I wish my mind to remain clear.'

'Of course.'

Officially the station we were in was the Arkship Transfer Buffer Facility – a human-built space station that held position ten kilometres out from the forward end of the *Salvation of Life*. Everyone just called it the Lobby.

It was there because the Olyix had been very clear they didn't want a portal inside the arkship, especially not from Earth. They were concerned about a terrestrial plague devastating their biosphere. Fair enough; even we hadn't classified and analysed all Earth's microbes and germs and viruses, let alone what they'd do if exposed to Olyix biology.

Negotiations via radio had started almost as soon as the *Salvation of Life* began decelerating into the Sol system back in 2144. First on the agenda after the Sol Senate's First Contact Committee started exchanging messages was: *You're not bringing that thing anywhere near Earth.* Simple reason: the forty-five-kilometre-long multi-billion-ton arkship was powered by antimatter. The Olyix had enough of the stuff on board to accelerate it up to twenty per cent of the speed of light. Which meant, should they prove hostile, the incoming aliens carried enough destructive energy to wipe out Earth and every asteroid habitat in the solar system, with plenty left over to wreck Mars and Venus for good measure (not that we'd ever bothered trying to terraform them). So the first agreement was that *Salvation* was to park in Earth's Lagrange Three point, directly opposite Earth on the other side of the sun. Even that left some officials and old generals nervous.

Once *Salvation* reached that orbit, physical contact began. The Lobby was assembled in a couple of months – a kilometre-diameter toroid, rotating at the centre of a hexagonal space dock, that serviced dozens of short-range cargo and passenger craft. All the little vehicles did all day every day was fly between the Lobby and *Salvation*'s zero-gee axis dock.

The ecumenical delegation was led into the decontamination suite – a fine name for what was basically a disinfectant shower. It lasted a compulsory eight minutes, ensuring every follicle and flesh fold on a human body was thoroughly saturated. I think prisoner hose-downs were more dignified. But it did give the contact staff time to irradiate our clothes and shoes and luggage.

We all reconvened in a small waiting room, trying not to show how disconcerting the cleansing experience had been. I wasn't sure my hair would ever recover from the chemical assault; it smelt like a toilet air freshener.

'Do the Olyix undergo an equivalent process to travel to Earth?' Nahuel enquired. He was sitting in a plain plastic chair, holding his sandals up to give them a disapproving look. I'm pretty sure his robes were bleached a shade paler, too.

'I've no idea,' I told him – not true, but I had to play the part of my new legend, and a Quaker accountant from Lancaster wouldn't know a whole lot about biological transference protection clauses in treaties the Sol Senate had negotiated. In fact, the Olyix do undergo a mild decontamination on their way to Earth, but then they never leave their embassies, which have a filtered atmosphere. However, when they come back, they're subjected to the same sanitization as humans before they can return to the *Salvation of Life*.

Our delegation took the elevator up to the toroid's axis, and freefall. When we were halfway up, I offered Nahuel a tab again. This time he took it without a word.

A couple of stewards helped us along the zero-gee corridors in the centre. The crossover chamber was a wide cylinder, with four hatchways on the toroid end, and another four hatches at the dock end. Halfway between them was the seal, allowing the two halves of the cylinder to rotate without losing any air. Plenty of people were crossing between them, casually air-diving in and out of the hatches. It all seemed so crude to me, but then I'd grown up in a world that had come to live Connexion's slogan: Everywhere is one step away.

We pushed, wriggled, and knocked elbows along the corridor to airlock 17B, where our passenger ferry was docked. The cabin was a small cylinder, with thin padding on the walls, and twenty-four simple metal seats in a couple of rows, with a lone seat at the front for our 'pilot', who did nothing but monitor the G7Turing that actually flew us. Apparently that dates back to the days when autopilots were taking over more and more aircraft functions, but people still wanted a human in the control loop. Personally, I'd trust the G7 over a human pilot any day.

I hauled myself along the cabin and claimed a seat beside one of the small windows. The dock grid stretched away out to the stars, its structure cluttered with tanks and cables that were covered in silver-white thermal blankets. Like everything in space, it was either sharply lit by sunlight, or sheltering in the utter darkness of shadows. The contrast between sections was immediate and striking.

We left the dock with a soft motion, and loud knocking sounds that reverberated down the cabin as the vessel's tiny rockets fired in short fast bursts. I saw the dock fall away behind us. The flight was due to take twelve minutes. At three minutes, the reaction control rockets began to fire again, rotating the craft.

The *Salvation of Life* slid into my line of sight. I'd seen enough images and diagrams of it, but even so, looking out at the real thing was a hell of a moment. I stared at it the same way jet pilots used to gaze at airships, with a twinge of envy and false nostalgia for a still-birthed alternate history where those giant serene craft were kings of the world. To travel among the stars in an artificial planetoid would've been an awesome existence.

The Olyix had started with an asteroid drifting in some distant orbit around their home star. Humans, with their molecular bonding technology, would have simply mined the ores and minerals and used the refined mass to construct a habitat-sized arkship. But the Olyix used a cruder method, cutting away the rock's rumpled, crater-scarred outer layers until they were left with a smooth cylinder forty-five kilometres long, and twelve in diameter. Further mining excavated the three main biochambers and a huge honeycomb of compartments that formed the engineering and propulsion section at the rear.

After so many millennia travelling between stars, the arkship's exterior was in remarkably good condition, shimmering like polished coal under the sun's unremitting glare. That unblemished sheen was all thanks to the impact defence screen, of course. When travelling across the interstellar gulf, the *Salvation of Life* generated a massive plasma cloud ahead of it to ablate and absorb any particles it ran into at twenty per cent lightspeed. The arkship's forward section was studded with generators, fashioned like golden barnacles, to create the magnetic field which held the tenuous ionized gas in place.

Halfway through the passenger ferry's turn, we were sideways on to the arkship's counter-rotating axis dock, giving me a panoramic view. The dock was a disc, only slightly wider than the Lobby toroid we'd left behind. But its apparent rotation was actually holding it motionless as the *Salvation* spun round its axis. Strangely, it looked the most human part of the arkship, but then most engineering requirements have a common design solution, no matter what kind of neurons create them. As well as possessing a number of airlocks, the dock was used to connect the power utilities. Free-flying human-built stations containing small portal doors, like geometric footballs a dozen metres across, hovered a few metres away from the dock. Their equators glowed with the intense turquoise shimmer of ion thrusters, holding them in position; while thick superconducting cables flexed in extreme slow motion across the gap between the two.

And they were the whole reason for the trade deals between the Olyix and the Sol Senate. The solar system was just another stop on the Olyix's incredible journey to the end of the universe; they'd visited hundreds of stars already, and would visit thousands – millions – more in the future before finally coming face to face with their God at the End of Time. Each solar system they came across was a replenishment stop between flights. A time when they used (or traded) local resources to refurbish the *Salvation of Life*, and generated enough new antimatter to accelerate them onwards again.

Accelerating something that huge took energy. A lot of energy. All the various processes that human physicists had ever come up with to create antimatter were horrendously inefficient, converting maybe one or two per cent of the energy input into actual antimatter. And as the Olyix openly admitted, their procedures weren't a whole lot better.

Yet they needed enough antimatter to accelerate *Salvation of Life* up to a fifth of the speed of light, then decelerate again as they approached the next star. The arrival of the Olyix was the greatest boon Sol's energy corporations had ever known. Every wattdollar the sale of alien Kcell technology brought in was spent buying electricity from human companies. A fifth of the solarwells dropped into the sun were currently being used to feed energy to the *Salvation of Life*, where deep inside its engineering section, alien machinery was churning out anti-hydrogen atoms one at a time.

The passenger ferry completed its flip, and we backed in towards the *Salvation*'s axis dock. Latching on was a series of metallic clunks. Then the airlock opened. As I was unbuckling my straps, dry, mildly spiced air drifted along the cabin, at a temperature several degrees lower than the cabin air. Not unpleasant, but definitely unusual.

The interior mechanics of the axis dock was similar to the Lobby's layout, but with living branches twined round conduits, sprouting waxy purple leaves. Small birds with ovoid bodies and five fin-like wings flittered along the wide corridors, effortlessly rolling round our delegation as we made our cumbersome way through the rotating seal. The reception chamber on the other side was a big hemisphere cut out of the rock, with a craggy surface carpeted in a dull-topaz moss. There were ten wide elevator doors around the rim, made from what appeared to be a glossy honey-coloured wood. An Olyix waited for us outside one of the doors, its feet sticking to the moss as if it was Velcro.

Sandjay, my altme, told me it was opening a general phone link. 'Welcome,' the Olyix said. 'My designation is Eol, and this body is Eol-2. Please accompany me down to our first biochamber. I am sure you will prefer the increased gravity.'

Most of us muttered a quick thank you. There was an undignified surge to get into the elevator, which had curving walls of the same wood as the doors. It rattled and clanked its way downwards, travelling a lot slower than any human elevator would. And the biochambers were ovoids four kilometres in diameter, so the trip down seemed interminable – especially as Eol-2 insisted on trying to make small talk all the way. It didn't help that the spice scent grew more pungent as we descended.

When the doors finally opened, we were in a long rock tunnel, again covered in moss, and lit by bright green-tinged strips at waist-height. Gravity was about two-thirds Earth-standard, for which Nahuel let out a sigh of relief.

The Olyix had made a considerable effort to make their human visitors feel at home. Our quarters were on a terrace in the first biochamber; from the outside they looked like rather glamorous yurts. Instead of using a heavy fabric over the frame, the Olyix employed their ubiquitous wood in thin planks, laying them over a geodesic frame like tiles on a roof. Furniture, too, was all solid chunks of wood, its smooth contours making the pieces resemble a collection of slightly surrealist sculptures. Orchid-like plants had coiled their rubbery roots along the ceiling struts, dangling clusters of dark-shaded alien flowers above my head. At least their perfume was sweeter than the spice that hung thick in *Salvation*'s atmosphere.

Eol-2 did a perfect host imitation, and left us to 'settle in' before the tour began. I unpacked my washbag and went into the curtained-off bathroom section. A peripheral ran a fast scan for electronic surveillance, drawing a blank. I hadn't expected any. The Olyix favoured biotechnology solutions.

The yurt furniture might have been Olyix wood, but the shower, bath, toilet and basin were all imported from Earth, which was quite a relief. I took my shirt off, washed my torso and sprayed on a hefty dose of cologne. Somehow I carelessly managed to miss myself quite a lot with the spray. Then I killed time for a couple of minutes setting up my toiletries, and filled a couple of glasses with cold water. That gave the chemicals in the cologne spray enough time to numb the neural fibres in the flowering plants on the bathroom ceiling.

Previous agents had taken samples of the yurt environment for study to prepare for my mission. Our labs had found fibres amid little cuts of the plant roots and leaves that had conductive properties. Without removing a whole plant and cutting it up under a microscope, we couldn't say for sure what the fibres did and what kind of receptors they were attached to, but visitors seemed to be under some kind of general observation. Ainsley was pleased with that find; it was another strand of proof that the Olyix weren't quite as trusting as they liked to project. Finding out if that subterfuge came from a simple natural instinct to protect their biological heritage from human exploitation, or they really were up to no good, was the whole reason I was in the delegation.

With a degree of privacy assured, I squatted down and crapped out the biopackage I'd brought along. The human anal cavity has traditionally been a smuggler's favourite for most of our existence on Earth. It made me really proud to carry that fine institution on into the starflight era. Yeah, right.

The biopackage resembled miniature frogspawn, which wasn't a bad analogy. I split it in two, and dropped each half into the glasses I'd prepared. From my little medical kit, I took six indigestion tablets and put three in each glass. They foamed away on the surface, dissolving quickly.

You could have eaten the tablets – not that they would've done anything for your indigestion. However, they turned the water into a perfect nutrient solution; there was also a hormone released which would trigger the eggs into growth.

That phase would take six hours.

I shoved the glasses into the cupboard under the basin, then set the cologne bottle to release a spray every quarter of an hour to keep anaesthetizing the plant fibres. Wearing a new shirt, and smelling like a Bel-Air gigolo, I went out to join the delegation for our tour.

*

All the *Salvation of Life*'s biochambers were ovoids measuring eight kilometres along their axis, with a four kilometre diameter at their midpoint. The first one, where our quarters were, had a globe of light suspended in the exact centre, shining a warm, slightly orange-hued radiance out across the whole chamber. Human space habitats tended to have landscapes across the cylinder floor, leaving the endwalls clear. The Olyix biospheres were completely shrouded in vegetation. Trees with fleshy, purple-tinged leaves never grew to the size you found in terrestrial forests, and there didn't seem to be much variety, either; to my mind they resembled giant bonsai – dumb comparison, but realistic enough. Their branches tangled together deftly, playing host to dozens of smaller plants, like the orchid-equivalents in my yurt, along with vines and ragged strings of trailing moss that hung in huge curtains. The loam was covered in the yellow moss-grass, riddled with patches of differing shades, making the ground look like an intricately stained-mosaic rug. Little streams threaded their way through it all, bubbling down the slopes from the axis to empty into reed-packed ponds that were spread around the equator.

Humans would've deployed fleets of remotes to trim and maintain the plants. The Olyix, with their biological-orientated solutions, allowed the plants to grow as their nature intended. According to Eol-2, the biochambers had reached equilibrium thousands of years ago. Supplied with light, warmth and water, they would continue with minimal intervention indefinitely. Small birds resembling overgrown dragonflies buzzed about, while giant snail-equivalent creatures slid along the ground, eating every fallen leaf and leaving a film of rich mulch in their wake. Larger dead branches and trunks were swiftly reduced to powdery loam by a profusion of fungi.

Our delegation was impressed by the slower, more sedate life on show. I suppose it made sense, given how long the voyage was going to take.

Eol-2 took us into the second biochamber on a car that could've been modelled on pre-quantum spacial entanglement era human vehicles. It drove itself through a broad tunnel that had junctions every few hundred metres, with tunnels curving away out of sight. Despite a plethora of discreet recordings made continuously ever since the arkship arrived, humans had never fully mapped out the maze of passages and caverns that riddled the *Salvation*'s interior.

The second biochamber was identical in shape to the first. The difference was in climate, which was more temperate, housing a different genera of plants. The third was the warmest of the three, but dry, verging on a desert environment. Certainly the plants lacked the jumbled-up density found in the first two.

'Our three biochambers contain a vibrant range of our homeworld biota,' Eol-2 explained to us as we walked about on the short reddish moss of the third biochamber, making polite sounds about yet another tiny dull flower sticking up out from tufts of drab grey-green leaves minutely different to the last. 'Beyond here is the engineering section, which is not open to this delegation.'

I looked round my fellow delegates, seeing their poorly concealed expressions of relief. Everyone was profoundly bored; the last thing they wanted now was to walk along halls of incomprehensible machinery, listening to an unending monotonous commentary on power couplings and confinement chamber integrity.

I kept my own, darker, amusement in check. The engineering and propulsion section of *Salvation of Life* was actually a lot smaller than the Olyix claimed. Because Eol-2, like all the Olyix, had lied to us. *Salvation of Life* contained a fourth biochamber.

*

Back in 2189, Ainsley Zangari's Olyix Monitoring Office positioned five stealthed satellites in a rosette formation two million kilometres out from *Salvation of Life*. They contained small portal doors leading back to Teucer, an asteroid in Jupiter's Trailing Trojans. As far as the rest of the Sol system was concerned, Teucer was just another independent tax haven rock, but it actually contained a stealthed station that handled all our passive sensor flights. Day after day, pea-sized probes would be shot out of the satellite portals, flying along trajectories that would take them close to the *Salvation of Life*. Some would spin out thin strands of magnetically sensitive gossamer, mapping the arkship's flux fields. Others scanned for exotic neutrinos, analysing the propulsion system, which remained highly radioactive from the antimatter reaction – itself a strong neutrino emitter. The majority were solid mass detectors with microtransmitters. They would glide along hyper-accurate trajectories, measuring the minuscule course variance as they tracked round *Salvation*, due to its correspondingly tiny gravity field, which varied according to density. That was what gave us our first clues that the Olyix weren't being entirely honest. The rear quarter had a density which couldn't be accounted for by the cavities that the Olyix said made up their engineering and propulsion section.

It wasn't as big as the trio of biochambers which humans were permitted to visit, but right behind biochamber three, the arid one, was a hollow space approximately five kilometres long. That, we concluded, had to be the heart of their clandestine activities. My goal.

*

The delegation reconvened under a broad, high, pergola draped in violet-flowering vines, close to the equatorial ponds of the first biochamber. It was all very convivial, with a refreshment table and comfy chairs in a loose semicircle. Eol-2 rested its heavy body on a wide stool that curved round its lower abdomen.

'I hope you found the tour informative,' it said over the general phone link.

We sipped our teas and coffees as we nodded reassurance. I'd grabbed an espresso, but somehow the taste was dulled by the ever-present smell of alien spice.

'You have three distinct biochambers,' the cardinal said. 'Are you divided along your original cultural lines?'

'I understand your interest in different cultural factions,' Eol-2 said. 'However, after a voyage so long, we are as one, a monoculture.'

'So were there different cultures on your homeworld?'

I watched a small ripple progress round Eol-2's midsection flesh skirt. Xenopsychologists who'd spent a lifetime studying the Olyix assumed it was either irritation or amusement.

'We no longer know what we left behind,' Eol-2 said. 'For we look to the future, never the past. To us, it is obvious that a sentient species will eventually refine and resolve upon a single life philosophy as it matures. You are diverse because you are physically widespread and can indulge any number of experimental principles and ideas. As you are young, such exploration is good for you. However, despite this current period of extraordinary physical and political expansion you pursue, it is our belief that you will regather yourselves eventually, and live under a unified monoculture. The superior, most liberal, most welcoming of your cultures will spread and adapt and eventually absorb to incorporate all others. Your merging legal systems and binding trans-government treaties are evidence of this, to us at least.'

'You believe our religions will merge?' the cardinal asked, which brought a lot of smiles.

'The God at the End of Time will come to pass when all sentience, all thought, binds together within the great collapse of spacetime. During the growth of entropy which is the past and future history of the universe, the God is many. Humans have already been blessed to witness fragments of the ultimate coalescence, which have formed the base of all your religious beliefs, and interpreted in

499

your many ways. We understand this, for we underwent it ourselves when we were first gifted with sentience. But there will only be one God in the end, which is when Its True Form will be revealed to all who have pilgrimaged successfully. If you are lucky, if you remain open to the Divine, as you seem to be, you may hear a whisper of God's message again. Already you anticipate this, I believe. The Second Coming. End of Days. Revelation. Rapture. Reincarnation, to name but a few. So many of God's concepts are already bestowed upon your thoughts. They link many of your diverse cultures and will flourish into a web upon which you can build your eventual unity.'

Nahuel inclined his head towards me and muttered: 'Is it politically incorrect to mention steady state theory in front of an Olyix?'

I just managed to keep myself from laughing out loud.

'I have a question,' the delegation's imam said, an old man with a full white beard and spotless black robes. To my mind, his stern voice indicated he wasn't going with the Olyix's liberal interpretation of how the Prophet's vision came to be. 'You claim to be on pilgrimage to the End of Time. If so, do you welcome humans who might wish to join with you?'

'Certainly,' Elo-2 said quickly. 'There are practical concerns, of course. We would have to adapt your biology to effectively provide you with immortality. Our Kcells are a good start on that endeavour, but considerable work remains to be done.'

The imam gave Eol-2 a disbelieving stare. 'You mean the Olyix are already immortal?'

'The bodies of a quint are the vessel of the mind, carrying it through time. We continue to reproduce physically, for all biological bodies decay over time, even ours. However, our identity remains steadfast.'

'So there are no new Olyix?' Nahuel said.

'No. Physically and spiritually we have matured as far as possible. As you would put it, we have reached the end of our evolution. This is why we have embarked on our great journey; there is nothing else left for us in this universe.'

'I find that hard to believe,' the cardinal said. 'God's universe is bountiful and limitless.'

'We know all there is to know about this creation. Therefore, we await that which is to come after.'

'After?'

'The God at the End of Time will look back upon the life of the universe, and use what It finds to create a new and better universe from the void into which all will collapse.'

'That promise of immortality sounds suspiciously like a bribe to me,' the imam said.

'It cannot be,' Eol-2 replied. 'Immortality, extending through this life and into the next, is something that only a mature mind can accept. If you are not worthy of it, you would never survive such an existence. And remember, there is no return from the path we would share. You would have to be very sure of yourself to accept such a daunting offer. We do not consider it a bribe. Abandoning all that you are – your belief, your life – is a decision you must come to by yourself.'

'Then tell me why you are alone in the *Salvation of Life*,' the imam said. 'You have been travelling for countless millennia; you have visited thousands of stars. Why has no one else joined you?'

'That is the saddest part of our journey, for we have discovered how terribly rare life is in this galaxy. And sentient life is the rarest of all. So many times we have listened to the faint radio cries of civilizations as they rise and fall. Very few ever succeed in reaching the stage you have achieved. Normally all we find are empty ruins, and creatures who have sunk back into the unthinking abyss as their star grows cold. This is why we love and cherish you so much. You are the most precious of all life; and to coexist in a galaxy so vast in space and time, to actually meet you and offer guidance, is truly a miracle. It will probably only happen a dozen times between now and the end of our flight.'

'Statistics can be a real bitch, it would seem,' the cardinal said in a level tone.

I caught the imam's lips twitch in surreptitious satisfaction.

'Do you have any records of these lost civilizations you encountered?' Nahuel asked. 'I would be most fascinated to see them.'

'I will enquire,' Eol-2 said. 'They would be small indeed, for we place no importance on such encounters. Our gaze is upon the future and the glory that awaits us there.'

*

'What are your thoughts?' Nahuel asked me that evening as we ate supper. Thankfully, we'd been entrusted to manage that by ourselves. Eol-2 had shown us a communal area beside the yurts, with freezers full of pre-packaged human meals and a row of microwaves, along with a small selection of bottles. Before leaving us, Eol-2 imparted our schedule for tomorrow, which was mostly lectures going into greater detail of the pilgrimage, and what their equivalent of philosophers thought they could contribute to the God's deliberations about what universe to usher into existence next. There was also time reserved for us to advance our beliefs to the Olyix, but to me that looked like a polite afterthought.

'I think we need an astrophysicist to start asking some difficult questions about quantum cosmology,' I told him.

'I believe those questions have been asked many times since contact. No substantiated astrophysical proof has ever been provided for their assertion that the universe is cyclic in nature, and each iteration can only exist for a finite time. In that respect, they exceed even our most facile popularist politicians when it comes to delivering on a promise.'

'That's what I'm finding the most difficult about this,' I admitted. 'They reached a technological level that allowed them to build the *Salvation of Life*, and heaven knows how many other arkships. They've devoted their everlasting lives to voyaging to the end of the universe – which, face it, is probably going to be physically impossible – yet they can't provide quantifiable scientific proof that the universe follows the cyclic theory.'

The cardinal turned to face me. 'We have enough evidence in cosmological background radiation to confirm the Big Bang, which in itself argues against steady state.'

'At least the Big Bang allows for a theoretical state which will lead to an ultimate heat death,' Nahuel said. 'Not that the heat death of the universe is the ideal sequence to birth this God at the End of Time. I'm not even sure you can call heat death the end of time.'

'An emergent God would have to reverse the maximum entropy state,' the cardinal mused. 'That's not an act of creation. It's regenerating what already exists.'

'We're getting lost in semantics,' Nahuel countered.

'Forty-two.'

'Excuse me?' I queried.

'Old joke,' the cardinal admitted. 'The number of angels that can actually dance on a pinhead.'

'See?' I told both of them. 'This is why we need an astrophysicist.'

'You are right, my friend,' Nahuel persisted. 'Everything they do is based on the cyclic theory, but they have provided nothing to prove its eventuality. It could even be said they refuse to supply it. Yet paradoxically their belief is so strong, so intrinsic to what they are, that a proof must surely exist. Nobody would travel like this without proof.'

'Ah,' the cardinal held up a whisky tumbler and smiled contentedly at us. 'This is why we are here, is it not? We are the ones who understand: above all, you have to have faith. Cheers.' He downed the shot in one.

*

I got back to my yurt and sniffed cautiously. Sure enough, there was a melange of spice, flower perfume and cologne. I went into the bathroom area and carefully opened the cupboard doors. The eggs had hatched, producing five hundred flies that were crawling sluggishly all over the shelf. Most of the nutrient in the glasses had been consumed.

I told Sandjay to switch on my emitter peripheral. The tiny lens embedded in my left eye began to shine ultraviolet light across the seething mass of insects. These flies had synthetic eight-letter DNA, which as well as accelerating their pupal stage, gave them a neuroprocessor instead of a natural brain. My ultraviolet pulse triggered a full boot-up, which took about a second. In response, they all activated their emitters. The cupboard was doused in ultraviolet light as the linc program connected them into a coherent swarm.

Data splashed down my tarsus lens. Hatching rate had been over ninety per cent successful. Malformation rate was under two per cent. Linc connection was enacted. I had a viable swarm, each one endowed with a biosensor capable of detecting a quantum spacial entanglement, courtesy of their eight-letter DNA. Individually, the detectors worked at extremely short range – just a couple of metres. Collectively, that sense was expanded by two orders of magnitude.

Now all I had to do was get the swarm to the general area where we suspected the portals were situated: biochamber four.

Sections of my bagez unclipped into a series of innocuous rods and rings. But, clipped together in the right sequence, they became basic tools – spanner, screwdriver, pliers . . . I took the panel off the side of the bath and set about opening the hatch cover underneath. Like the rest of the bathroom, it was human built, with locknuts on each corner that had stiffened over time. After plenty of sweaty effort I got them all off and levered the hatch up. No matter what angle I looked at it, that opening was not large. Getting through was going to be tight and most likely painful. But other agents had got through on scouting runs, so . . .

I stripped off and took my jogging kit out of my bagez. Like every good fitness fanatic, I used several layers, from inner skin-tights to more baggy outers, finishing with a waterproof for any inclement weather. I was only interested in the skintights, which gripped as tight as any wetsuit. The top even had a hood, which, combined with my sunglasses, covered every square centimetre of skin. Sandjay interfaced with it, and the fabric surface turned a perfect black. As well as being visually non-reflective, it absorbed a vast section of the electromagnetic spectrum should you try probing it with radar or laser sweeps. And that was just its outer surface. Long ribbons of thermal battery were woven into the arms, legs, spine, neck and skull, which used a web of heat-duct fibres to soak up all my body heat, making me thermally neutral. The ribbons could accumulate ten hours of heat before they needed to pump it out. A gill mask neutered my breath, syphoning out the heat and scrubbing tell-tale biochemical leaks. Wearing that stealth suit, I was like an empty human-shaped hole in the universe.

Sandjay linced to the fly swarm and sent them streaming down through the hatchway. I sucked in my gut and slipped through after them.

There was a cramped utility compartment running under all the yurts. It was filled with human-built sanitation equipment which sterilized all the water and effluent from the baths, showers and toilets above. Chemical and solid waste was separated out and stored in tanks that would ultimately be vented into space, while the clean water was released back into the *Salvation of Life*'s main environmental cycle. *That* was the outlet pipe I was looking for.

The compartment's floor was made from thick carbon slabs, as hard as granite. Agents we'd sent in before had cut the slab which the outlet pipe went through, slicing it into manageable rectangles with angled sides to hold them in place. Pulling them up was a bitch. They were as heavy as stone, and I was crouched over, which is a bad position to be lifting. Eventually I got them clear, and dropped down through the hole into a tunnel carved into the naked rock.

Pipes and cables ran along it, not all rigid and fastened into place as humans would lay them, but twining round like ivy clinging to the tunnel walls. They even looked as if they were alive, or at least had been. I thought maybe a plant with hollow trunks, like terrestrial bamboo, that grew along the tunnel, then died and hardened, producing a natural tube. It made a kind of sense, given the way the Olyix liked to integrate their biological systems with mechanical ones.

Sandjay splashed an enhanced image across my tarsus lens. The suit's thermal sensors showed me that several of the meandering tubes were warm, containing a heated fluid of some type, while the magnetic scan gave power cables a gold-sparkle glow. My inertial navigation took a location fix, and I set off down the tunnel.

Twenty per cent of the fly swarm were behind me as I scrambled over the meandering tubes, covering my ass in case an Olyix came along on an inspection or maintenance job. The rest buzzed on ahead, scouting the way. Just like the tunnel we'd driven through earlier, there were intersections and splits. Some went straight up; others branched down into the unknown depths. There were times when the tunnel sloped so much I had to get down on my hands and knees and crawl along to stop myself from slipping.

Inevitably, it wasn't a straight route towards the rear of the arkship. I had to check the inertial navigation every time the swarm found another junction, working out which was the way forwards. Five times I miscalculated, and had to turn back and try again as the tunnel I chose started to curve away. But then some tunnels were almost devoid of cables and tubes, allowing me to jog along for long stretches. Without those, I would never have made it back before morning.

After the inertial navigation confirmed I'd passed the end of the third biochamber, I started looking for a route into the fourth. There were plenty of junctions which had branched off into the bigger transport tunnels, with vehicles trundling along them. I began splitting the swarm at intersections, sending them out exploring further ahead. Eventually, when I was four hundred metres short of where we'd worked out the fourth biochamber to be, I found a transport tunnel that seemed to be heading in the right direction.

The swarm flew on ahead, but there were no vehicles about. My problem now was the light. The transport tunnel was illuminated by long bright strips halfway up the walls. If the swarm saw anything coming, I'd have to sprint for a junction. There weren't many of them.

Four hundred metres. Most Olympic athletes could cover that distance in forty-five seconds. I was fit, and had some gene-up treatments, but not to that level. Besides, I was in a two-thirds gravity field – also not conducive to speed. Best estimate was over a minute.

The swarm snaked through the air in a long line before starting to spread out. There were three junctions between me and the start of the fourth biochamber. That gave me reasonable odds of reaching cover if anything appeared.

I drew down some deep breaths, then started running.

A minute seventeen, if you're that keen to know. I didn't go balls-out because I might need to keep moving when I reached it – or race back.

The fourth biochamber had a climate similar to the first. Its vegetation seemed more wild and ragged, as if they didn't maintain it to the same standard. There were no Olyix near the tunnel entrance.

I scooted into the cover of the shaggy trees and sent the swarm out in a circular formation, scanning for signs of life. A hundred-metre perception bubble revealed dozens of birds, hundreds of insects, but no large alien bodies moving round. My peripherals swept the electromagnetic spectrum, which was almost silent.

The trees threw a heavy shade on the ground. It was useful cover. I stayed underneath the branches as the swarm reshaped into a row, and began a circumferential sweep – the first of many. Sandjay was already plotting a methodical spiral course that would see them cover the entire interior. Looking up through the gaps in the leaves, I saw a distinct clearing along the equatorial line. The trees had given way to a perfectly circular patch of mustard-yellow moss. At the centre was a five-sided pyramid structure, an easy hundred metres high but only twenty metres across the base. I'd never seen any kind of building in the other three biochambers. When I shifted position to get a better view, I caught sight of another clearing, also on the equator. I moved out into an open area between the trees. There were five identical clearings, each with a tall structure in the middle. I diverted the swarm to the nearest one so they could relay high-resolution scans back to me.

The Assessment Team

Feriton Kayne *Nkya, 26th June 2204*

'Okay, and?' Callum asked in fascination.

'Those structures in the centre of each clearing were like slim Aztec temples, or very tall obelisks,' I told my rapt audience. 'Personally, I prefer the second option. They didn't seem to have any kind of entrance, at least not at ground level. And there weren't any openings higher up, either. But the clincher is the hieroglyphics. The exterior of each one was covered in them.'

'Have you translated it?' Eldlund asked eagerly.

'No,' I admitted, letting a hint of frustration show. 'This isn't like a code, or an ancient human language. There is no possible Rosetta Stone available to us here. The symbols are simple enough, just lines and shapes, but they are completely alien. There's just no way of interpreting them. The only way we'll ever get to find out what they say is to ask the Olyix. And we can't really do that.'

'I don't get it,' Loi said in a petulant tone. 'Why would they keep them secret?'

'The one thing the fly swarm did determine for me was the type of stone they were made out of,' I said.

'What is it?'

'Sedimentary. It had a granular structure. There were no sharp edges left anywhere, and a lot of the symbols had worn down. Which is significant in that placid environment.'

'So?' Kandara demanded.

'The *Salvation of Life* was an asteroid,' Alik explained to her in an tediously patronizing tone. 'You only find sedimentary rock on a planet. Which means those obelisks were brought on board from – where?' He lifted a quizzical eyebrow at me. 'The Olyix home-world?'

'That's our theory,' I said. 'The obelisks are incredibly ancient, which makes them the most sacred relics the Olyix possess. Obviously, they have a deeply religious significance. It may even be that those symbols contain their proof of the cyclic state universe – which, given the level of their orthodoxy, can *never* be challenged, let alone by an upstart species like us.'

'Hence the whole secrecy obsession,' Kandara concluded, her head dipping in understanding.

Callum leant forwards in his chair, keen for details. 'What about the fly swarm? Did they detect any quantum spacial entanglement?'

'No.' I shrugged. 'Obviously there's a great deal of volume inside the *Salvation of Life* we haven't explored, but the fourth biochamber is their biggest, darkest secret. And in strategic terms, it's irrelevant. They just don't want us disbelieving aliens contaminating it with our heresy.'

I could tell from Callum's creased brow that he was about to fire off another query, which is when events became strange. I saw Alik starting to pour himself another bourbon from his precious vintage bottle. His focus shifted to me, his eyes widening, betraying surprise. Then his fingers began to open, allowing the bottle to fall. My attention flowed to Kandara in the chair next to him, who was grabbing a handful of roast pistachios from a dish. Her formidable muscles were stiffening in a classic threat response. I even saw her forearm flesh ripple as buried peripherals activated. Suspicion and alarm triggered a strong sense of threat within me, and I determined something very wrong was occurring behind my chair. My head started to turn as I heard Callum's panicked yell begin and I caught a blur of motion. Jessika was standing behind me, face contorted with effort, her arms gripping a long red pole she was swinging towards me. Instinct forced my own arm up protectively even as I attempted to duck. It was no use at all; she was moving too fast. Then I saw the wickedly sharp head of the fire axe as it expanded into my vision, becoming my whole universe. I even briefly heard the cracking sound of my skull breaking as it struck. Then the blade penetrated my brain—

Juloss

Year 593 AA

Before they left, before every item of human technology in the Juloss star system was reduced to its constituent atoms, they went back to Kabronski Station's garden for a final nostalgic look. Their marble table by the little waterfall was still there, the elegant koi sliding about in the water just as they always had.

'I feel we should take them with us,' Dellian said as he watched the fish glide across the pond and vanish under the sluggish waterfall, only to reappear again a few seconds later.

Yirella slipped her arm round his shoulders. 'You can't think like that. Not any more.'

'I know.'

Together they looked up through the vaulting geodesic glass roof. Juloss was a thick crescent below the station, its terminator line creeping across the Deng ocean.

'It's beautiful,' she said wistfully.

'We can come back. When it's over.'

'That would be nice. I don't think there would be many of us, though.'

'Really? I bet most of the squad would come. Hell, maybe most of the *Morgan*. Where else could we go? This is home.'

She gave him a gentle kiss. 'It's where we were born. It's where we trained. But home? I don't think we have one. Not yet. That's something we have to build for ourselves. Afterwards. Hey, who knows? Perhaps the Sanctuary star legend will turn out to be real after all, and we can go and live there.'

He gazed up at the blue and white crescent, his mind filling in the continental coastlines on the nightside. 'You know, back on Earth they said whole continents were lit up by city lights at night, that they were like miniature galaxies. Can you imagine that? There were so many of us on one world.'

'And look what happened to them. Human worlds can't afford that kind of population again. Not until we win the war. We have to have enough traveller generation ships to lift everyone off a settled planet in an emergency. Nobody must ever be left behind. Not again.'

'But if we could've stayed here . . . What a world we would have built.'

Yirella rested her cheek on the top of his head. 'You really are an old romantic at heart, aren't you?'

'I just believe in us, that's all. I mean, look at it!' Dellian gestured extravagantly at the planet. 'We did that! It was a lump of naked rock when our ancestors arrived. Fifty years to terraform it. Fifty years – that's how long it took us to give life to a whole planet! And it's brilliant.'

'It's tragic.'

'It'll still be here when this is all over. We were careful; no signal ever escaped. They don't know humans were here, and they never will, now.'

'I hope you're right. All the worlds in this system have terrestrial life on them now – bacteria in the comets, lichen on the asteroids, weird frogs on Cathar's moons.' She grinned at the memory.

'Damn right. Even if they pulverize Juloss, they can't eliminate us from this system now. Terrestrial DNA is here to stay. We mutate. We adapt. We evolve every time. In a billion years, this will still belong to our life. Because we rock.' He tilted his head back to kiss her.

Beside them, the waterfall cascade slowly shrank away until only drips were falling from the stony lip. A loud chime sounded across the garden zone.

'Time to go,' Yirella said softly.

They both looked up at Juloss again for a long moment, then made their way along the path to the exit.

*

The *Morgan* was made up of seven principal structures, all contained in spherical grids fifteen hundred metres in diameter, with silver thorn thermo-dumps rising up out of the strut junctions like metallic porcupine spikes to radiate excess heat out into space. The rear globe contained the gravatonic drive, capable of accelerating the battleship up to point nine lightspeed. Next came the main aneutronic fusion generators and their ancillaries, along with tanks of boron11 and hydrogen fuel. Ahead of that, the third globe was basically a warehouse containing asteroid mining equipment, along with refineries and one-stage von Neumann replicators. It was the same payload every human traveller generation ship carried, giving them the ability to start an entire high-level civilization in whatever star system they arrived at. As long as there was solid matter available – in the form of planets, asteroids or comets – human society could build habitats and thrive. Globe four was the main life-support section, housing a pair of counter-rotating toroids that offered a pleasant park-like environment and comfortable apartments for *Morgan*'s five-thousand-strong crew. Ahead of that was the weapons level, packed with a long and frighteningly impressive inventory of munitions that could devastate entire star systems, let alone enemy ships. Then came the hangar, with fifty genten-controlled attack cruisers capable of hundred-gee acceleration, along with fifteen troop carriers designed for both deep space and atmospheric flight. Finally, the forward globe housed the main portal-shield which would open out like an umbrella around the warship to swallow any interstellar dust and gas the *Morgan* encountered at its incredible velocity, shunting it harmlessly away through twinned portals trailing a light second behind the ship.

Dellian and Yirella were among the last to arrive on board, which won them a knowing wink from Janc and smiles from the rest of the squad. *Morgan*'s crew were assembled in the main auditorium. Dellian was still getting used to the relatively fast gravity spin of the toroid, so he had to hold the back of the seats as he made his way down the row to his squad. Captain Kenelm walked onto the stage just as Dellian sat down. Sie was tall, though not as tall as Yirella, wearing a smart grey and blue uniform that had a single star on hir epaulette. Dellian gave the uniform a curious look as part of his brain categorized it as a sad and silly historical throwback. It wasn't that the crew hadn't worn their uniforms before, but seeing the Captain standing there in the flesh ready to give hir departure speech was a hard reality strike. He'd been operating within a hierarchy for his whole life, but this – being on a warship about to launch into the galaxy – this made it suddenly very tangible. They were going out to fight, and there was a good chance they might actually die.

His hand fumbled for Yirella's. Even the melancholic humour she'd shown a few minutes ago in the garden had now vanished. He knew she was just as nervous as he was.

The screen at the rear of the stage came on with a live feed showing a battleship accelerating slowly away from its skyfort berth. Dellian's databud identified it as the *Asher*. Three advance seedships accompanied it.

'I wish Alexandre was here,' Yirella whispered. 'I miss hir.'

'Me too. But sie did see you reunited with the rest of us before hir traveller generation ship left. I think that made hir happy at the end.'

Yirella nodded, a glint of moisture in her eyes. 'I wanted hir to come with us.'

'Sie couldn't. Sie was too old. Sie knew that right from the start, when sie left her own family behind to raise us.'

'I know. I'm being selfish.'

He squeezed her hand. 'Me too.'

Up on the screen, the *Asher* and its escorts were closing on the clump of coiling fronds, barely a hundred metres across, that was an interstellar portal. The loops began to glow a dark blue. Then they were blossoming, expanding out as if a circle of the planet's midnight-blue sky was spilling across space. The cerulean haze faded to black, and the portal was indistinguishable from the rest of the starfield above Juloss. The *Asher* slipped through the hole first, quickly followed by the seedships. As soon as they were all through, the portal closed up behind them, its constituent fronds shrinking back to a seething clutch of insubstantial energy folds.

The auditorium burst into a round of applause, but Dellian carried on watching the screen. He knew people on the *Asher*. Now they were gone, lost to him forever in both space and time. The other side of that portal had been travelling at point nine-eight lightspeed away from Juloss for over five hundred years, ever since the traveller generation ship had arrived – one of thousands of identical portals that had been sent out along random courses, providing an escape route should the enemy detect Juloss was home to a human civilization.

Now another portal was expanding, glowing a hellish orange against the stars as it opened to its twin deep in Cathar's atmosphere. The skyfort began to twist and buckle as it was captured by the pull of abnormally strong gravity. Chunks broke off, twirling away into the blaze, streaming ahead of the skyfort itself that was now moving with increasing speed into the smouldering abyss.

There was no applause this time, just a wise, sober acknowledgement of the skyfort's fall into the heart of the gas giant, where the hypervelocity storms and terrible gravity gradient would pull the detritus down and down until it became nothing but a smear of heavy atoms slithering atop the planet's metallic hydrogen core. All of Juloss's orbital defences were scheduled to follow it, then the portals themselves would surrender and collapse. The Juloss system would be naked among the myriad stars once more, with teeming terrestrial life and crumbling ruins the only legacy that humans used to live here.

'I would like us to take a moment,' Captain Kenelm said in a level voice. 'We should thank this star and its planets for being a peerless haven to so many of our ancestors. Humans have lived a good life here. And now it is our turn to honour and repay that gift. We venture out into the galaxy to join the very Saints themselves. Somewhere out there, they are waiting for us. When they call – and they will – we will join them, no matter how far away they are in time and in space. Know this, Saints: we will not let you down.'

'We will not let you down,' Dellian intoned, along with the rest of the audience. He'd said it a thousand times in his life, but this time it finally meant something. *We're on our way!*

Kenelm gestured with hir palms, and everybody stood. 'The *Morgan* is about to launch,' sie said. Behind hir, the screen was showing a view from the front of the *Morgan*. Up ahead, a twisting grey knot was churning amid the stars.

'We thank you, Saint Yuri Alster, for your fortitude,' Kenelm said respectfully.

'We thank you, Saint Yuri,' the auditorium responded.

The portal turned deepest blue and began to swell out, its physical components undulating in a fast rhythm.

'We thank you, Saint Callum Hepburn, for your compassion.'

'We thank you, Saint Callum.'

Morgan started to accelerate smoothly as the hole across interstellar space stabilized.

'We thank you, Saint Kandara Martinez, for your strength.'

'We thank you, Saint Kandara.'

Beautiful new stars were glimmering through the darkness at the centre of the portal.

'We thank you, Saint Alik Monday, for your resolution.'

'We thank you, Saint Alik.'

Dellian smiled and held his breath as they travelled over five hundred lightyears in a single heartbeat.

'And lastly we thank Saint Jessika Mye, for travelling out of darkness to guide us.'

'We thank you, Saint Jessika.'

Unknown constellations shone bright around the *Morgan* and

its accompanying seedships. Behind it, the portal closed. Then the entanglement ended and the mechanism died.

Dellian stared at the wondrous sweep of fresh stars outside. 'The Olyix are out there, somewhere.' He said it loudly, as a raw challenge to the universe into which he was venturing. 'Hiding like we used to. But we're not hiding any more now. We're coming for *you*, fuckers!'

The Assessment Team

Nkya, 26th June 2204

Everyone in the lounge was perfectly still. Three targeting lasers produced small red dots on Jessika's forehead. The only sound was the steady *drip drip drip* of blood from Feriton's ruined skull.

Jessika kept hold of the fire axe handle, her gaze moving across the room, from Alik, to Kandara, to Callum, and finally to Yuri. In an astonishingly level voice she said: 'Look at the brain.'

'What the FUCK?' Callum bellowed.

Eldlund began a high keening sound of distress, slapping hir hand across hir mouth. Loi turned his head away and threw up.

'What?' Yuri demanded. '*What?*'

'I said, Look at the brain.'

'The . . .'

'Can I take my hands off the axe?'

'You move like a glacier is fast,' Alik growled at her. 'You let go, and put your arms high, then link your fingers over your head. Take one step back. Understand?'

'I understand. Letting go now.' Very carefully, she released her grip on the handle. The axe sagged down as the blade pivoted round inside the skull, ripping more brain tissue. Feriton's body began to slouch forwards, only just staying in the chair.

Kandara's face produced an expression of extreme distaste. 'Mother Mary!'

Her arms in the air, fingers locked, Jessika took a step back. 'Look at the brain.'

Alik and Kandara glanced at each other.

'You cover her,' Alik said.

Kandara nodded sharply, keeping her gaze on Jessika. 'Got it.' Her left arm was held perfectly level, a slit of flesh along the forearm open to expose a small silver cylinder that never wavered from its lock on Jessika's head. 'Go see what the sweet fuck she's talking about.'

The target laser shining from Alik's upper wrist switched off. He took a cautious step forwards. Even his forehead crinkled up as he peered at the slumped figure. He held his breath and reluctantly pulled the axe free. It made a horrible squelching sound as the blade came out. Alik leant forwards a fraction. Everyone heard him suck down a breath. He gave Jessika a confused stare. 'What the fuck?'

'What is it?' Yuri asked.

'I . . .' Alik flinched. 'I don't know.'

Yuri took an impatient step over and examined the massive wound in Feriton's skull. 'Shit.' He gave Jessika an astonished look.

'What the bloody hell's in there, man?' Callum demanded.

'It's an Olyix brain,' Jessika told him.

'Bollocks!'

'See for yourself,' she said. 'That's not human grey matter. The Olyix scooped out Feriton's brain and replaced it with one from a quint. Does that procedure sound familiar?'

Yuri scowled at her.

Callum walked over, grimacing against the carnage, forcing himself to look into the gore. He knew what a human brain looked like, and whatever the mass of tissue was inside Feriton's skull, it wasn't human. The structure was all wrong, long strands arranged neatly rather than the usual jumble of lobes, and beneath the thick splatter of blood, the surface was fish-belly-white.

'No fucking way!'

'It is a brain of a quint unit,' Jessika said. 'Which means the other four bodies in the union have seen and heard everything that Feriton heard and saw – including their damaged ship. They will also know every aspect of your Olyix Monitoring Office.'

'Fucking hell!' Yuri grunted in dismay.

'What do you mean, *their* damaged ship?' Kandara asked.

'That ship outside? It's an Olyix mid-level transport. It was travelling back to their enclave when my colleague crashed it out of the wormhole.'

'The Olyix have a wormhole?' Callum asked numbly. 'But . . .' He turned to Yuri. 'Did you know all this?'

Yuri shook his head, his gaze never leaving Jessika.

'That's how I knew Feriton was part of an Olyix quint,' Jessika said. 'The fourth chamber in the *Salvation of Life* is not full of precious artefacts. It contains a wormhole terminus, which leads back to the enclave. They all do.'

'All?' Callum implored.

'The Olyix always arrive in vessels like the *Salvation of Life*. It is a subterfuge which allows them to observe the species they've discovered before they elevate them.'

'Elevate?' Eldlund asked weakly.

'Take them on their pilgrimage to the God at the End of Time. And, trust me, joining them isn't voluntary. They seize every sentient race they find. They already have thousands imprisoned back in their enclave, maybe more.'

'I don't believe a fucking word of this,' Alik snapped. 'I mean, just how the fuck could you know all this shit?'

Jessika's expression turned sorrowful. 'Because I am Neána.'

'What the fuck is *that*?'

'Alien, but not Olyix. We're very different.'

'Oh Je-zus wept!'

'Do you recall the Fermi Paradox?' Jessika asked. 'Fermi asked: *Where are they?* You always assumed life in the galaxy is rare, that because of its size you would never coexist with another species. That is only partly true. When sentience arises and begins to make itself known with radio emissions, the Olyix arrive – with their

520

false friendship, and their religious greed. So, in truth, the answer to Fermi is: we have been hiding. And now you must join us, out in the silent darkness between the stars. That is where you will be safe.'

'Your colleague is Soćko, right?' Yuri said.

'Yes. He allowed himself to be captured by Baptiste Devroy's people during the firefight on Althaea. We have been searching for an Olyix snatch operation since our arrival. Horatio Seymore was a stroke of good fortune. The Olyix proxies like Devroy would be instructed to snatch low-visibility humans, and that's what Horatio was – apart from Gwendoline. She was a rogue factor that would elude even the most talented matcher.'

'Holy shit,' an ashen Loi muttered, looking as if he might be sick again.

'So Soćko is the one who crashed that ship out of the wormhole,' Yuri said. 'He flew it here. He switched on the beacon before he went back into hibernation.'

'Correct. Our bodies have the ability to resist contamination by Olyix biotechnology. They would have been unable to elevate him, though that would not have been apparent to them at first. It gave him time to infiltrate their operation. I have been waiting for a disabled Olyix ship to be detected ever since the firefight at the warehouse.'

'Son of a bitch,' Alik spat. 'Then the others in the ship, they've been . . . elevated?'

'The Olyix truly believe the God at the End of Time to be real. It will coalesce out of the thoughts of every species left as the universe collapses. Because life is so rare, and so many civilizations are destined to fall long before the end of time, the Olyix see it as their duty to carry every sentient species to the apex of evolution. But the God only needs your thoughts, your personality, not your body. The Olyix have been stealing humans right from the start to experiment on. We were the ones who started the rumour about Kcells making brain transplants possible, because we knew that's what they'd do – allowing a captured, cored-out body to move among you unseen. But their main focus, the reason they snatched so many people, was to research the best way to sustain a human brain on the pilgrimage. Their technology is far more advanced than they have revealed to you.'

'That's insane!' Callum protested. 'Even if the universe was cyclical, and due to collapse, that won't happen for billions of years. I don't care how bloody good your technology is – you can't keep a brain alive for that long.'

'The Olyix's journey will not take them billions of years,' Jessika said wearily. 'Their enclave is an extremely sophisticated manipulation of spacetime; minutes pass inside it, while the millennia flow by outside. It is what makes them so difficult to fight.'

'Is that why you're here?' Kandara asked. 'To get us to join you in some kind of galactic war? A counter-crusade?'

'No, you are on your own. I do not know where the Neána are, or even if they still exist. My people fled the Olyix aeons ago; there is no knowing how far they have gone now. I know some part of them remain in this galaxy, for that is where I came from. But we were never given any knowledge of them, in case we were captured. My colleagues and I have discussed this many times. We assumed the logical thing for the Neána would be to leave this galaxy altogether. It may be that they just left automated stations behind, alert for new species so they can send guides like me.'

Kandara looked over at Yuri. 'Do you believe her?'

He glanced down at the pale alien flesh inside Feriton's skull. 'I believe they caught Feriton when he was on his spy mission. That means Ainsley was right all along. I don't know what they'll do, if they'll elevate us like Jessika claims, or just nuke us back to the stone age. But I accept the Olyix are not our friends.'

Kandara nodded. 'I agree – until anything better comes along.' Her targeting laser switched off, and she lowered her arm as the flesh resealed over the weapon. 'I'm watching you,' she told Jessika.

If it bothered Jessika, she didn't show it. 'If any of you have received Kcell implants, I would advise you to have them surgically removed immediately,' she said. 'They can alter and multiply faster than any tumour; that's why they were given to you. And the *Salvation of Life* now has confirmation that humans have been warned by the Neána. I'm sorry, but that isn't good. They will begin your elevation.'

'Yeah? How?' Alik demanded. 'I'd like to see them try. The *Salvation*'s a big-ass ship, for sure, but it's only one, all by itself. And Alpha Defence has a shitload of real evil weapons.'

'I told you,' Jessika said, 'the *Salvation of Life* contains the entrance to a wormhole that leads back to the Olyix enclave. They will send an armada of their deliverance-class ships through to elevate you. In simple terms, that's a planetary invasion force.'

'Je-zus fucking wept!' Alik snarled. He turned to confront Yuri. 'We have to go. Now! We have to get back to the portal and warn Alpha Defence.'

'We certainly do,' Yuri said.

'How the fuck are you so calm about this?'

Smiling, Yuri took a dark ten-centimetre disc from his pocket and placed it on the floor. 'Thread it,' he said loudly.

Callum peered at the disc's eerily black surface and grinned. 'I taught you well.'

Yuri gave him the finger as a slim rectangular portal slid up from the disc.

'You son of a bitch,' Alik grunted.

A wider rectangle was threading out. Callum and Loi deployed the short legs on its back, readying it to thread a full-sized portal door. 'Old times,' Callum said.

'No,' Jessika told him. 'They are over. Forever.'

'Ainsley and Emilja are going to love talking to you,' he told her.

'Good. I have a lot to tell them.'

Jio-Feriton Quint

Salvation of Life 26th June 2204

The Olyix do not have pain. We eradicated it from our new bodies when we elevated to them at the beginning of our pilgrimage to the end of the universe.

But our human body, Jio-Feriton, experienced a ferocious spike of pain impulses as the female alien's axe blade smashed into our skull. We were attuned to human thought routines, enabling our responses and reactions to emulate original Feriton Kayne without arousing suspicion.

The nerve signals from the blade cutting into our strange Jio-Feriton flesh and bone was interpreted correctly. It was *agony*.

Our remaining four Olyix bodies temporarily lost control of their limb function. We wanted to cry, but we had no tear ducts. We wanted to scream, but we had no vocal cords. We wanted – we *yearned* – for the pain to end. That was swiftly granted.

Our Jio-Feriton body died. Its mindfunction vanished from our entangled essence. We had experienced single mindfunction loss hundreds of times before as we replaced an old body within the quint, but never like this. The rest of our bodies were almost paralysed from the shock. We have no coping mechanism for such an experience. We have no endorphin override. Feriton's legacy was an immediate craving for both these very human things.

Slowly, we regained equilibrium. Our thoughts first turned to replacing our Jio-Feriton body, to become full quint again. This was accompanied by *regret* at the loss we had just suffered. Regret is alien. Therefore we learned that absorbing alien thoughts to perform a subterfuge is dangerous; it detracts from our purity. We will not undertake such a task again.

We have no need to.

The *Salvation of Life*'s onemind queried us, its serene essence curious at our eccentric outburst of chaotic thoughts. 'Explain the occurrence,' it asked.

'We are now four Jio. Our Jio-Feriton body was killed.'

'How?'

'The suspect human, Jessika Mye, inserted an axe into Jio-Feriton's head, causing immediate fatal damage.'

'Why?'

'We must have said something to betray Feriton was Olyix. We determine this would be our statement that the fourth chamber was a biochamber containing holy relics. If Jessika Mye knew this to be incorrect, she would know Feriton Kayne had been compromised. In order to know that, she would have to be Neána.'

'They are here,' the *Salvation of Life* said in disapproval. 'Therefore Soćko is also Neána.'

'Yes. He ruined the transport ship's onemind and crashed it out of the wormhole.'

'The humans now know our purpose.'

'They do.'

'We cannot lose the humans to the sedition of the Neána. Humans are vibrant and beautiful. The God at the End of Time will love them. It will love us for carrying them with us.'

'Yes,' we agreed.

The *Salvation of Life*'s onemind opened itself to all its Olyix. 'We will now begin the human elevation.'

*

The end of SALVATION

**The story will continue in volume two
of the Salvation Sequence,**

SALVATION LOST

Salvation timeline

1901   Guglielmo Marconi transmits a radio message across Atlantic Ocean.

1945   First nuclear explosion (above ground).

1963   Limited Test Ban Treaty signed, prohibiting atmospheric nuclear bomb tests.

2002   Neána cluster near 31 Aquilae detects electromagnetic pulse(s) from atomic bomb explosions on Earth.

2005   Neána launch sublight mission to Earth.

2041   First commercial laser fusion plant opens in Texas.

2045   First commercial food printers introduced.

2047   The US Defense Advanced Research Projects Agency reveals artificial atomic bonding generator – so-called force field.

2049   US Congress passes Act to create Homeland Shield Department, charged with building force fields around every city.

2050   China forms Red Army's City Protection Regiment, begins construction of Beijing shield.

2050   Saudi kingdom installs mass food-print factories. Twenty per cent of the kingdom's remaining crude oil allocated for food printing.

2050 Russia starts National People's Defence Force, its shield generator project starts with Moscow.

2052 European Federation creates UDA (Urban Defence Agency) – builds force fields over major European cities.

2062 **November** Kellan Rindstrom demonstrates quantum spacial entanglement (QSE) at CERN.

2063 **January** Ainsley Baldunio Zangari founds Connexion.

2063 **April** Connexion twins portal doors between Los Angeles and New York, charges $10 to go between cities.

2063 Global stock market crash, car companies lose up to ninety per cent of their share value. Shipping, rail and airline stocks fall. Aerospace stocks rally as space entrepreneur companies announce ambitious asteroid development plans.

2063 **November** Space-X flies a QSE portal into Low Earth Orbit on a Falcon-10, providing open orbit access. Commencement of large-scale commercial space development.

2066 Astro-X Corporation's mission to Vesta. Establishment of Vesta colony.

2066–2073 Thirty-nine national and commercial colony/development missions to asteroids (the Second California Rush –so called because of the number of American tech company CEOs involved). Large number of World Court injunctions filed by developing nations and left-wing groups against exploitation of exo-resources by for-profit companies.

2066 Connexion Corp merges with emergent European, Japanese and Australian public transit portal companies to form conglomerate. Major cities now portal networked. Non-commercial vehicle use declining rapidly.

2067 Globally, thirty cities now protected by shields, two hundred more under construction. Start of decline of conventional military forces. Phased Air Force and Navy Reduction Treaty signed at UN by majority of governments. Armies reconfigured as counter-insurgency paramilitary regiments – numbers cut substantially.

2068   Seven corporations established at Vesta. Astro-X completes its Libertyville habitat colony, housing three thousand people.

2069   First solar powerwell portal dropped into sun by China National Sunpower Corporation. Five-kilometre-long magnetohydrodynamic chambers built at Vesta, positioned on large asteroids, outside Neptune orbit.

2070   Armstrong resort dome assembled on Moon. Similar resorts under construction on Mars, Ganymede and Titan.

2071   All major cities on Earth linked by Connexion stations – except North Korea.

2071   UN treaty forbidding non-equitable exo-resource exploitation. Any asteroid or planetary minerals mined for use by commercial companies must be equally distributed among all nations on Earth. US, China and Russia refuse to sign. European Federation awards treaty Principal Acknowledgement status; starts to draw up its own non-exploitation regulations, where 'excess profits' of asteroid development companies will be channelled into Federation foreign aid agencies. Commercial asteroid development companies re-register in non-signatory countries.

2075   Seventeen self-sustaining habitats built in asteroid belt. Construction of Newholm starts at Vesta (by Libertyville) – fifty kilometres long, fifteen kilometres in diameter. Takes three years to form, two years to complete biosphere.

2075   Fifty-five per cent of Earth's energy now comes from solar powerwells. Decommissioning of nuclear power stations begins, radioactive material flung into trans-Neptune space via portals.

2076   Increasing number of asteroid developments become self-sustaining and Earth-exclusionary. Start of habitat independence movement.

2077   Interstellar-X launches first starship, *Orion*, propelled by QSE portal solar plasma rocket. Destination Alpha Centauri. Achieves point seven-two lightspeed.

2078   **March**   Global tax agreement signed by all governments on Earth, abolishing tax havens.

2078   **August**   Nine space habitats declare themselves low-tax societies.

2078   **November**   First Progressive Conclave gathers at Nuzima habitat; fifteen billionaires sign Utopial pact to bring about post-scarcity civilization to humanity. Each launches asteroid colony expansion, with an economy based on AI-managed self-replication industrial base.

2079   China National Interstellar Administration launches starship *Yang Liwei*. Destination, Trappist 1. Achieves point eight-two lightspeed.

2081   All Earth's energy supplied by solar powerwells. Connexion largest energy customer.

2082   Major national currencies now backed by kilowatt hours. Global de facto currency is wattdollar.

2082   Interstellar-X-led General Starflight Accord signed between all starfaring organizations (capable of building starships) and governments, ensuring open access to new stars, and no duplicated star missions.

2082–2100   Twenty-five portal-rocket starships launched from Sol to nearby stars.

2083   *Orion* arrives at Alpha Centauri. Psychroplanet discovered two point eight AU from star, named: Zagreus. Too expensive/difficult to terraform. Eleven government missions transfer into Centauri system and establish asteroid manufacturing bases, along with eight independent asteroid companies. Construction of multiple portal starships at Centauri system begins.

2084–2085 Twenty-three starships launched from Centauri.

2084 Last car factory on Earth (in China) shuts down. Connexion hub network serves ninety-two per cent of human population, including space habitats.

2085 Utopials launch starship *Elysium*.

2086 Alpha Centauri asteroid manufacturing stations abandoned. Small joint-venture solar rocket plasma monitoring station maintained in orbit around the star, providing drive plasma for the starships.

2096 Chinese starship *Tranage* arrives Tau Ceti, exoplanet discovered.

2099 Chinese begin terraforming of Tau Ceti exoplanet, named Mao.

2107 US starship *Discovery* arrives Eta Cassiopeiae. Exoplanet discovered.

2110 US begins terraforming Eta Cassiopeiae exoplanet, named New Washington.

2111 European Federation agrees to terraform exoplanet at 82 Eridani, named Liberty.

2112 *Elysium* arrives at Delta Pavonis. Terraform-potential planet discovered, named Akitha. Construction of habitat Nebesa and extensive orbital industrial facilities. Terraforming of Akitha begins.

2127 *Yang Liwei* arrives at Trappist 1. China begins terraforming two Trappist exoplanets T-1e and T-1f, Tianjin and Hangzhou.

2134 New Washington terraforming stage two complete, open to American-only settlers.

2144 Olyix arkship, *Salvation of Life*, detected point one lightyear from Earth as its antimatter drive is switched on for deceleration. Communication opened. Four-year deceleration to Earth/Sun Lagrange-3 point opposite side of sun from Earth.

2150 Earth population twenty-three billion. Nearly seven and a half thousand space habitats completed, population one hundred million.

2150 Olyix begin to trade their biotech with humans in exchange for electricity to generate antimatter, allowing them to continue their voyage to the end of the universe.

2153 Mao declared habitable. Farm settlers transfer from China, begin stage two planting – trees, grass, crops. Fish introduced into ocean.

2162 Neána mission reaches Earth.

2200 Eleven exoplanets now in stage two habitation. Large-scale migration from Earth. Twenty-seven further exoplanets undergoing stage one terraforming. No more being developed; fifty-three marked as having terraform potential. Portal starship missions ongoing, but reduced.

2204 Portal starship *Kavli* arrives in Beta Eridani system, eighty-nine lightyears from Earth. Detects beacon signal from alien spaceship.